The Narrowboat Girl
and
Water Gypsies

ANNIE MURRAY is the author of
nine successful novels, including *Miss Purdy's Class,*
Water Gypsies, Chocolate Girls, Where Earth Meets Sky
and *The Bells of Bourneville Green*. She studied English
at St John's College, Oxford and has four children.
She lives in Reading.

ALSO BY ANNIE MURRAY

The Bells of Bourneville Green
Chocolate Girls
Where Earth Meets Sky
Family of Women
Miss Purdy's Class
Poppy Day
Orphan on Angel Street
Birmingham Blitz
Birmingham Friends
Birmingham Rose

ANNIE MURRAY

The Narrowboat Girl
and
Water Gypsies

PAN BOOKS

The Narrowboat Girl first published 2001 by Macmillan
First published in paperback 2001 by Pan Books
Water Gypsies first published 2004 by Macmillan
and simultaneously in paperback by Pan Books

This omnibus first published 2008 by Pan Books
an imprint of Pan Macmillan, a division of Macmillan Publishers Limited
Pan Macmillan, 20 New Wharf Road, London N1 9RR
Basingstoke and Oxford
Associated companies throughout the world
www.panmacmillan.com

ISBN 978-0-330-50798-1

3 5 7 9 8 6 4

A CIP catalogue record for this book is available from
the British Library.

Typeset by SetSystems Ltd, Saffron Walden, Essex
Printed and bound by CPI Group (UK) Ltd, Croydon, CR0 4YY

The Narrowboat Girl

For my daughter, Katie

Acknowledgements

Thanks are due in large measure to David Hearmon, owner of *Raven* for so generously sharing his time and expertise, and for his e-mail friendship; to my sister and brother-in-law Julia and Timothy Woodall for their hospitality and help, to Stoke Bruerne Canal Museum and to the staff of Banbury Museum.

I also owe a debt to canal enthusiasts Ray Shill, Wendy Freer and the Birmingham Canal Navigations Society for their publications. Above all, thank you to Sheila Stewart for her wonderful book about life on the cut – *Ramlin Rose*.

PART ONE

One

'Oi, Maryann – pack that in or your shoes'll be all scuffs. You'll 'ave our mom after yer!'

Sally Nelson sat primly on the step of the Garrett Arms, skirt pulled well down over her knees, thick blonde hair fastened back with a rag ribbon, and her baby brother clasped tight on her lap. There was a frown on her round, pretty face as her younger sister skipped impatiently up and down, aiming kicks at the grime-encrusted wall.

Maryann turned, sticking her tongue out as she sprang back and forth, an ice cream in one hand and ample signs of it in evidence round her top lip. She stopped for a moment and stared down the length of her skinny, scab-kneed legs to her feet, pushed into an old pair of cast-off shoes, their buckles dulled with wear.

'They're all scuffs any'ow, so what yer on about?' She licked urgently at the ice cream before beginning again on her hopping and twirling, her bobbed, black hair flying wildly round her face. 'Oh – where's our dad got to? 'E should be 'ere by now!'

Sally's big-sister bossiness couldn't rile her today. Maryann was as full of fizz as a bottle of Nanny Firkin's dandelion and burdock and just as close to exploding with excitement. It was 17 September, her twelfth birthday, the sun was still shining even though

3

the summer was over and they were back to school, and today was the day their dad had promised they'd go and fetch the kitten home from Nanny Firkin's. Even though she'd have to share it with Sal and Tony and babby Billy, really it was going to be *hers*.

After school that day she'd come dashing home well ahead of Sal, her excitement even overcoming her wariness of her mother. 'Mom! Mom! You there?' She tore up the entry, to find Flo Nelson in the yard still toiling away on the mangle outside the brewhouse. It was Monday, washday. Billy, with just a vest on, was stamping to and fro in a scummy puddle of washwater with his little peter out on show, the lot. Wet clothes strung on lines along the yard, flapped against Mary-ann's face.

'Course I'm 'ere. Where else would I be, sunning meself in the South of France?' Flo Nelson snapped, wiping her wet hands in an irritable gesture over her blonde hair to keep it out of her face. She was a broad-hipped, rather stately woman, once as beautiful as Sal would one day be, but sagging now. Her manner was petulant and long-suffering. 'And keep yer grubby 'ands off of there. I ain't been slaving away all day for you to come and bugger it all up. 'Ere—' She reached down the front of her blouse for a twist of cloth from which she took a sixpence.

Maryann's eyes widened with glee. Mom was never going to give 'er a whole tanner! Blimey, she knew it was her birthday, but Mom never handed out even a farthing without being *asked*! Flo Nelson bent and hoiked her youngest son to his feet.

'You and Sal go and find yerselves an ice cream – and get some drawers on 'im and take 'im with yer – 'e's running me ragged.'

4

A beam spread across Maryann's freckly face.

'Ice cream, oh *ta*, Mom. Come on, Billy – eh Mom, what about Tony?'

Her five-year-old brother would be whining round her if he saw her with an ice.

''E's round with Alec.' Flo jerked her head towards the wall adjoining the next-door yard. 'What 'e won't know won't hurt 'im. Make sure yer finish 'em before yer get back 'ere!' Her face surrendered to a rare moment of softness at the sight of her scallywag of a daughter. 'Go on with yer, birthday girl. This time twelve year ago I weren't enjoying meself any too much I can tell yer.'

Sal was just coming along the road.

''Ere Sal! Our Mom's being nice today – I've got a tanner!'

The girls found an Eldorado ice-cream cycle on the corner of Garrett Street and went back and settled by the door of the pub. Dad wouldn't be back yet, however much Maryann willed him to be. They'd long finished the ice creams, wiped Billy's face and were trying to stop him crawling in to play on the beery, sawdust strewn floor of the Garrett Arms when the men started coming out of the factories.

'Awright, Sal?' some of them said, coming into the Garrett for a pint or two after work. 'Waiting for yer dad, are yer? 'E'll be 'ere in a tick, Walpole's is out.'

Maryann noticed that when some of the men spoke to Sal, their voices altered, as if they were telling her a joke that Maryann didn't understand. And one or two of them would give her a wink. Sal favoured her mother's fair looks: the pale skin, gold hair, the white, rounded body. Quite the young lady she was and they treated her almost as if she was a grown-up woman.

5

They didn't do that to Maryann, a skinny whippet of a kid, with her black hair hacked off straight round her jaw and her face all freckles. She didn't care: she was a tearaway, a tomboy, besotted with animals and hungry for adventures.

She carried on skipping about. Walpole's were out! Walpole's, a firm making aluminium ware, was where her dad worked, the only man she cared about. After all these years he had a proper job and was earning a good wage and everything was getting better and better. Next year Sal would turn fourteen and there'd be two wages coming in. Then Mom'd never have to take in washing again.

Sally turned from bending over Billy to find Maryann shinning up the lamp-post on the corner by the pub.

'Oh get down before yer kill yerself,' she snapped. ''Ere, look – it's our dad. Yer that busy fooling about you've missed 'im coming.'

Maryann slithered down the pole and tore along the road, all sharp knees and skirt flying.

'Dad!'

Harry Nelson, a tall man with a lean, tired look, watched his daughter's wild progress along the street, followed more sedately by her older sister and baby brother. Harry stopped, throwing his coat over his shoulder, a grin spreading across his face. He held his arms out as Maryann catapulted herself at him.

''Eh – you're getting too big for that!' He laughed, fending her off.

'Dad, Dad – can we get the kitten now?'

'Well—' He eyed her, teasing. 'I had in mind a couple of pints with the lads first.'

'Oh *Dad*!'

He laughed. Harry Nelson had big, tombstone teeth

and needed only to part his lips to look as if he was smiling. 'There'll be no peace till we do, will there?'

'She's been keeping on and on,' Sal said, trying to sound superior, although in truth she was almost as thrilled about the kitten as Maryann.

Maryann dragged him by the hand. 'Come *on* then!'

Nanny Firkin lived in a back house on a yard off Ledsam Street, along from the Borax factory. It was a short way across Ladywood, the other side of the railway shunting yard and the cut in which lay the sluggish, scum-ridden water of the Birmingham Main-line Canal to Wolverhampton. The house where Maryann and the rest of the Nelsons lived was also a back house, with two tiny bedrooms on the first floor and an attic, but Nanny Firkin's house at the far end of the yard was more by way of a cottage: two up, two down, with a little patch of garden at the front, and Maryann loved going there. Nanny Firkin, a widow of some years, loved animals too and told Maryann she was a 'chip off the old block'.

When they reached Ledsam Street, Maryann ran on ahead, heart pounding with excitement, up the entry to Nan's and across the greyish-blue bricks of the yard. The door was open, as it nearly always was, and one of Nanny Firkin's cats, an exceptionally hairy ginger tabby, was curled, asleep on the front step. Maryann peered into the dark kitchen, which smelled of coal and onions and the sour odour of the parrot's cage.

'Nan? It's me, Maryann! Dad's brought us up for the kitten.'

'I didn't think it'd be long before you made an appearance.'

7

Nanny Firkin limped over to the door, a twinkle in her eye. She was a tiny lady, thin as a wisp, who lived on next to nothing and was always dressed stiffly in black, but with a little wizened face from which looked two eyes, watery and blue, and brimming with warmth and vivacity. She was full of affection for her granddaughters and son-in-law. It was her own daughter Flo she found it less easy to rub along with, forever mithering and carrying on, although Nanny Firkin had done everything in her power to help Flo while Harry was away fighting – and the pair of them once he came back from France. Flo was a houseproud chit but lazy and self-pitying with it. Always hankering for a spick and span house but thinking it ought to get done by magic instead of knuckling down and doing the work herself. Flo Nelson called her own mother's house a 'bloody flea-ridden menagerie – yer go there alone and you come back with company.'

But Maryann had hardly ever caught a flea at her nan's. She'd be more likely to pick up company of that sort at her friend Nancy's house in another yard across Garrett Street, if the truth be told.

Nanny Firkin's kitchen was a cosy place. Her grandmother had been chopping an onion at the table and the kettle was hissing on the hob over the black range. Beside it was squeezed the old chair with its horsehair stuffing bulging out through holes in each of the arms. In one corner, balanced on a crate, was the cage where Walt her parrot lived, named after her late husband.

'Talks to me a darn sight more than Walter the flesh and blood man ever did,' Nanny Firkin often said.

''Ello, Walt!' Maryann called to him.

''Ello,' Walt said. ''Ello.' And added a metallic

8

sounding shriek for good measure, closely resembling the noise that came from one of the factories behind the yard.

When Harry Nelson appeared at the door with Sal and little Billy, Maryann was already bent over the black cat who was lying under the big chair with her litter. Out of the mass of warm, hairy bodies, Maryann saw a tiny face, tiger-striped grey and black, with shiny brown eyes gazing up at her.

'Oh look, Nan! Look at this one – the little tabby!'

She took the creature on her lap and it settled there, seeming quite content.

'Ain't they grown, Nan!' Sal exclaimed. 'No, Billy – yer must be gentle with 'em.' She restrained Billy's strong, pinching fingers.

'Oh Nan, can I 'ave this one!' Maryann looked into the animal's eyes and knew he wanted to be hers. 'Look at the way 'e's looking at me.' The kitten twisted playfully on to its back and pawed at her fingers.

'Don't I get a say then?' Sal stood over her, but she was smiling in spite of herself at the kitten's antics.

'It *is* madam's birthday,' Nanny Firkin said, brewing tea for Harry. She was always mothering him, trying to feed him up. 'Anyroad, I reckon 'er's picked the best of the bunch.'

While her dad gratefully drank his tea and ate Nanny Firkin's sticky ginger cake, and Sal and Billy played with the other kittens, Maryann sat with her new pal in her lap, laughing as his fur tickled her bare knees. She could scarcely believe it: a living creature, so tiny and perfect and beautiful, and he was all hers ... She stopped, looking carefully at him and turned to her grandmother who was sitting, as she always did, perched at the very edge of her chair as if in her long

9

life she had never learned to take her rest and be comfortable.

'Is this one a boy or a girl, Nan?'

'Oh that's a lad, that one. Tigerface I call 'im.'

'Tigerface—' Maryann cocked her head at him. 'I think I'll just call 'im Tiger.' She nuzzled her cheek against him, brimful with delight. 'Thanks, Nan. 'E's the best ever.'

Maryann lay cuddled up close to Sal that night on the bed they shared in the attic. There was a strong whiff of damp, but they barely noticed, being used to it. They had an army blanket and a couple of old coats, and apart from that they had to keep each other warm. The nights were still quite mild now but it was perishing cold in the winter. Now she was older, Sal refused to have a 'bucket of wee' by the bed and, however cold the night, if she needed to go, she took the key and went off down the yard to the freezing toilets. Maryann wasn't so fussed and would go down and relieve herself in the bucket in Tony and Billy's room if needs be. Sal was getting far too particular, she thought.

'Move over,' Sal moaned. 'I'm half hanging off the edge of the bed over 'ere.'

'Sorry.' Maryann shuffled along the lumpy mattress. There was a pause. A mouse scuttled across the floor. 'Tiger's so lovely, ain't 'e?'

'Oh Gawd, not again. Yes, Maryann, 'e's lovely. 'E's the most perfect cat in the whole blinking world. Now will yer shurrup?'

There was silence for a moment, then Maryann poked her in the ribs and Sal rolled over, giggling. 'Oi, pack that in!' But she was only pretending to be cross.

The two of them snuggled up together. Despite being so different they were close. They'd had to be, the way their mom was.

There'd been great excitement when they carried Tiger home. Nancy Black and three of her brothers had invaded to look him over until Flo Nelson unceremoniously shooed them out again. Maryann had spent the whole evening holding him and playing with him and even Flo admitted he was 'awright, I s'pose'. Now he was asleep, exhausted, on a strip of rag by the range.

Maryann lay looking up at the dim rectangle of sky through the uncurtained attic window. The nights were drawing in now. 'I don't want to leave Tiger when I go to school,' she whispered. 'I wish 'e could come too.'

'Don't talk so daft,' Sal murmured. They lay together talking fondly about the kitten's antics until the downstairs door opened and they heard their father's tread on the stairs. Flo Nelson was always harassed and irritable in the evenings and hustled them straight from playing in the yard up to bed out of her way. She had Billy to settle down and didn't want any added trouble from them. But their dad always came up to say goodnight. Maryann squirmed with delight. It felt so cosy in bed, with Dad coming up to give them a kiss.

He had been a stranger to them when he came home from the war in 1919. Sal had been eight then, and Maryann five and it had taken them some time to get used to one another. Flo, exhausted after years of coping with two young daughters alone, of scrimping and queuing and struggling, had expected a man to come home who she could lean on, who would take over. Instead, for those first years, she had an unpredictable, helpless wreck on her hands. Often she exclaimed angrily that the men who came home may

11

have survived, but they were 'no bloody good to anyone, the state they were in'. The girls didn't understand what it was all about. They didn't understand the war, or the suffering of the soldiers, or that the man who had come home was one who had changed and couldn't fit in, wouldn't, for a long time, be able to hold down a job. But they did know they were loved. Harry Nelson was a man who felt incomplete away from his family. He adored his children, and that separation, added to the horror and degradation of the war, had increased his trauma further.

'How's the birthday girl?' he said, stooping his long body and sitting down on the bed.

Maryann giggled.

'That little Tiger of yours is asleep. Worn out.' Maryann felt him rub her back with his warm hand and he gave Sal a pat. 'Night night.' He leaned down and kissed them both. Maryann felt his lips press her cheek, the prickle of stubble on his top lip.

'Eh – 'ow about you sing to me, eh – our special song? Just the first bit. How'ds it go?'

The song was one Sal had sung at school while the war was on, a prayer for the soldiers and sailors. She had told her father about it when he came home and they had sung it many times. Now they both piped up:

> God bless our soldiers
> Guard them each day
> Make them victorious
> All the way.
> In the great conflict
> May they endure,
> And God bless our soldiers
> And make victory sure.

In the early months after he came home, he would ask for the song, and when they sang it he would sit on their bed, his shoulders beginning to shake until he was weeping uncontrollably. It had frightened them at first, but he was such a kind, gentle man that they used to sit beside him and put their arms around him. Flo had become resigned to his suffering and fractionally more understanding. They had had the two boys, who filled Harry with joy. It had taken years, but now, with the passing of time and the help of his family, in particular his children, Harry Nelson knew that the emotional wounds of the war were slowly healing.

Now he no longer wept when they sang to him. He sat quietly listening, then stood up as they finished.

'Nice voices, you wenches. Sleep tight.'

Maryann listened to him going slowly down the stairs to see the boys, the familiar creaks of each tread. She closed her eyes. She felt safe and warm and loved. Later, looking back at those cosy nights, she would wonder how she could have taken them for granted, when they were all too soon snatched away.

Two

It happened two months later, quickly, horribly, all in an afternoon.

Maryann was with her friend Nance. Nancy Black had been Maryann's best pal ever since they'd started school together. Maryann loved going to the Blacks' because there was always something going on. Even when Nance's dad came home tanked up he never took any notice of her – he and Mrs Black had a right lot of shouting matches, but he'd never done her any harm. As often as not when he arrived, Maryann and Nance'd shoot across the road to Maryann's house to keep out of the way until the trouble died down.

The Black family consisted almost entirely of boys: Nancy was sandwiched between three older and four younger brothers. Her dad, Joe Black, known as Blackie in the district, scratched what might have been a reasonable living as a cooper, going round the yards mending the maiding tubs, if he hadn't parked his barrow and drunk his earnings away most afternoons. Nancy's mom, Cathleen Black, had a head of salt and pepper curls, one crossed eye and a moany voice. Maryann's mom said Cathleen Black was a Catholic and 'not up to much' and having one eye crossed like that 'served her right'. Nancy said her mom was born like that so Maryann never understood how it could serve her right. Did God do things like that? Didn't

14

he like Catholics? And was that why she had to take in washing and cart other people's bundles off down the pawn shop on a Monday morning to make ends meet?

'Well, it's no good relying on that drunken bastard,' Cathleen said, placidly, of her husband. 'Or we'd all've starved to death by now.' But then, with a distant look in her eyes, she'd add, ''E was never like that before the war.'

Cathleen Black seemed to overlook the fact that Nancy was a girl most of the time and except for school, Nance wore her brothers' cast-off shorts and shoes, and her hair, black and curly as her mom's, was cropped short. Nance strutted about with her elbows stuck out and you didn't cross her. She was tough. Flo Nelson said it was a shame, her never looking like a proper girl, but she was damned if she was passing down her girls' clothes to people like that.

It was chilly that November afternoon, threatening rain, the air damp and rank with factory smells from all around and the stink of the yard privies. Both Maryann and Nancy had been ordered to keep an eye on their baby brothers, and Billy Nelson and Horace Black were at one end of the long, narrow yard, playing with a collection of marbles.

'Don't you go putting 'em in yer mouth, Horace,' Nancy shouted to him. 'They ain't rocks for sucking.'

Billy's fair head and Horace's dark one were close together and they kept picking up the marbles, throwing them at the wall, watching them bounce off and roaring with laughter.

'They're awright,' Nancy said, long-sufferingly. 'Let's leave 'em be.'

She strode over in her patched, baggy shorts to

where two of her older brothers, Jim, thirteen and Percy, ten, were trying to cobble together their own cart out of a wooden meat-crate they'd bought for tuppence – the proceeds of selling empty jam jars – and some old pram wheels.

'Get lost!' Perce scowled at her as he did something important with a piece of wire. 'You'll only muck it up.'

'Let's play hopscotch,' Maryann suggested. 'I gotta bit of chalk.'

For all her boyish ways, Nancy loved having another girl to play with. Blowing on their cold hands, they ran up the yard and started marking out a hopscotch grid. Nance started the game, throwing a pebble along the ground and jump-hopping back and forth. Mrs Black came out of the house with a scarf over her head and a cigarette jammed in one corner of her mouth and started hanging out a line of washing. She took the fag out and turned to them. 'Yer'd better not muck this lot up or I'll belt the pair of yer.'

The girls ignored her. One or other of their moms said this to them several times a week every week and had done ever since they could remember. It had the same effect as 'Don't get dirty', which also went straight in one ear and out the other.

'Is yer dad in yet?' Maryann whispered to Nancy as she took her turn on the hopscotch.

Nancy pulled her mouth down and shook her head. Not many minutes later though, they heard his voice in the entry, mumbling furiously to himself as he staggered along. He was a red-eyed, barrel-chested man, with such skinny legs to support his rotund girth that they looked as if they'd been pinched off someone

16

else's body. He came lurching into the yard, cap in hand and swearing fit to blister paint.

'Oh, 'ere we go,' Cathleen Black said, vanishing inside her house to clear away the breakables.

Blackie stormed into the middle of the yard and bawled, 'Someone's nicked me fuckin' barrer!'

Nancy and Maryann looked at each other. Nancy's big brown eyes rolled expressively skywards.

Jim and Percy straightened up at the end of the yard. Other neighbours round the yard barely turned to look, this was such a usual occurrence. Blackie's favourite watering hole was the Beehive Inn in the next street. He'd bring his barrow, loaded with iron strips for mending the maiding tubs in which everyone did their washing, and leave it out at the front of the pub. By the time he came out it had almost invariably gone – moved for a lark by local lads who then watched Blackie's alcohol-befuddled indignation at its disappearance. Week after week he never seemed to remember that if he left the barrow outside the pub, the same thing would happen. That, Flo Nelson said, was because he was 'so bloody thick yer could stand a spoon up in 'im'.

'You sure, Dad?' Jim said, cautiously.

Blackie attempted to stride masterfully towards them, but ended up struggling to keep his balance.

''Course I'm bleedin' shewer! What d'yer take me ...'

'It'll turn up, Dad,' Percy said. 'It always does, don't it?'

He and Jim weren't going to volunteer to go and get it and face the jeering ridicule of the lads in the next street.

'Someone's nicked my . . .' Blackie was just beginning all over again, when Sal came rushing up the entry, her face white as a china doll's.

'Maryann – oh Maryann!' she cried, then burst into hysterical sobbing. At the sight of her sister's emotion, a sick, cold feeling came over Maryann. For a moment they all stood numbly, waiting.

'Our dad's been in an accident,' Sal blurted out at last. 'A terrible accident.'

Cathleen Black left her sozzled husband to his own devices, picked up grime-streaked little Horace and marshalled all the children across the road to the Nelsons' house. Maryann immediately caught hold of Tiger and hugged him to her. Her chest felt tight, as if it was going to tear open. Nancy watched her with wide, concerned eyes.

'Our mom's up the h-hospital.' Sal sat down, still crying, at the table. 'This copper come and said our dad'd been hit by a c-car and 'e couldn't come home and Mom had to go with him. M-Mom told me to come over and get Maryann and stay 'ere with Tony and Billy till 'er gets 'ome.'

'Did the copper say 'ow yer dad is?' Cathleen stood over her. She couldn't stand Flo Nelson, always looking down her nose as if from a great height, but she was fond of the Nelson children, and she couldn't just leave the kids in a state like this.

Sal shook her head. Maryann started crying then. They'd taken her dad away and she'd never been inside a hospital and didn't know what it was like, only they looked big, frightening places, and he was hurt and she just wanted him home and everything to be back to

18

normal. Her tears started Tony and Billy off crying too, and Horace looked at them all and began bawling as well.

The evening passed like a terrible, blurred dream. They tried to eat the mash and mushy cabbage Mrs Black cooked for them, but Maryann felt as if her throat had closed up and she could hardly swallow. The older ones went out into the yard after tea, but all Maryann wanted to do was play with Tiger and hold him tight.

Nancy tried to get her involved in a game, but Maryann just shook her head. Her dad, was all she could think of. She ached for him to come home, to pick up Tiger in his big hands and say, 'How's our little moggy then?' But the evening dragged on and still he didn't come, and neither did their mother. Everything felt strange and horrible.

It was after eleven when Flo Nelson finally walked in. Cathleen had got Tony and Billy to bed. Tony had cried and screamed and Maryann went up and sat with him, stroking his head until his eyes closed, his distraught little face relaxing finally into sleep. Sal and Maryann had been adamant that they would not go up until their mom came back. They sat silently at the table, Nancy with them, draped wearily over its surface, too tired to do anything and too worried to sleep. The younger Black boys had dozed off on the floor and Horace was fast asleep on his mother's lap with his thumb in his mouth. His nose was bunged up and his breathing was the loudest sound in the room.

Despite the fact that Cathleen Black barely ever set foot in her house normally, Flo Nelson showed no surprise at them all being there. As she came in through the door, Maryann knew immediately that everything was different. Her mother's eyes wore the glazed, exhausted look they had had in the days after she had given birth to Billy, only then she had been cheerful, had carried him proudly about. Now her pained, defeated body looked as if she had been punched so hard she would never stand straight again. She closed the door and turned, seeming unable to raise her head and look at them all.

'How is 'e?' Cathleen said, softly. She struggled to her feet, still holding her sleeping son.

Flo Nelson shook her head. She couldn't speak. After a moment she put her hands over her face.

''E's not . . .?' Cathleen was deeply shocked. She hadn't thought it would be the very worst. Not this. 'Flo, 'e's not . . .?'

Flo nodded, hands still over her face. Slowly she pulled them away, staring at the table, not looking directly at anyone. 'Ten o'clock. 'E never came round – never knew what happened. 'E was in Icknield Port Road – it was a motor car knocked 'im down – his head . . .' She put a hand to her own head. At last she looked directly at her neighbour, eyes wide with shock and bewilderment.

'He was on the Somme, Cathleen. He came all through the Somme.'

Maryann and Sal lay clinging to one another in the cold darkness.

'We'll never see 'im again,' Sal sobbed.

The word 'never' stabbed through Maryann like a sharp sword. Never. Ever. No – it couldn't be true. Wasn't real. Tomorrow he would come back, she'd wait for him outside the pub, take Tiger for him to stroke with his long, rough fingers. Sundays they'd go down the cut or go over to Edgbaston reservoir with a fishing line and a jam jar. She'd hear him slowly, wearily climb the stairs to say goodnight, the same rhythm of his tread night after night . . . Never. Never again. She pressed her face against Sal and felt sobs jerk out from the very depths of her body. Everything felt frightening, and cold and utterly lonely.

Three

During the time between Harry's death and the funeral, his children stayed away from school. Flo couldn't cope with any of it and the girls had to take over their brothers completely. Sal minded Billy, while Maryann looked after Tony, helping him get dressed, trying to keep him occupied and out of Flo's way. For two days their mom scarcely moved from her bed, lying there with her pale hair matted round her head, face swollen with crying, and it was Nanny Firkin who came to take charge. She was not one for kisses or cuddles but she kept them fed and her busy presence in her rustling black dress was a great source of comfort. As she had all through the war, Flo leaned on her mother for help. Nanny Firkin came and cooked for them and stayed with the children while Flo hauled herself out of bed to go to the undertaker's on Monument Road, to make arrangements.

'Where's my dad?' Tony kept asking. He was five, and he didn't understand death. His dark-eyed little face was so solemn, so hurt, that Maryann could hardly stand looking at him.

''E's not coming 'ome again, Tony,' she said, gently at first.

'Why? Where's our dad gone?'

''E's – 'e's had an accident, Tony, and 'e ain't coming back.' She sat him on her lap, cuddling him, stroking his soft, squashy legs.

Night-time was the hardest, when he didn't come back from work. They couldn't hear his voice through the floorboards from downstairs, his loud yawn as he came up to see them. The house felt so quiet and empty. Their mom's sobbing was the only thing they heard, sometimes with Nanny Firkin's voice trying to comfort her.

'What 'm I going to do?' she kept saying over and over again. Every time she said it Maryann froze inside. Her mom was afraid they'd all starve! 'Four children and no 'usband! 'Ow're we going to get by? It were bad enough in the war, but then you 'ad to put your own troubles aside when they were over there fighting. But now there's four instead of two, and there'll be no end to it all . . .'

'You'll 'ave yer widow's pension,' Nanny Firkin said.

'But that's next to nowt! 'Ow'm I going to keep 'em fed and clothed?' She was tearful again. 'Life's cruel – so cruel. After all these years, these bloody 'ard, struggling years, Harry gets 'imself a decent job and then this 'as to go and 'appen!' She sank into a chair by the table and broke down. 'We'll not 'ave a stick of furniture – I'll 'ave to sell it all. Oh, I can't go through all that again – I want a bit of rest and comfort in my life, not scratching and scraping for every farthing till the end of my days!'

Nanny Firkin pursed her lips. It grieved her more than she could ever express that Harry had been killed. She'd loved the man like a son and her own heart was leaden with it and even more at the sight of her grandchildren's faces, especially little Maryann, so like him in looks and his favourite. The child was heart-broken, clinging to that kitten. They should have had a better life, Harry and Flo. Married at eighteen, then Sally had come along. Harry had an apprenticeship then and they looked set for a fair passage. He was going to work his way up to being a skilled worker, then emigrate with his family. There'd been big advertisements before the war, asking for people to go to Australia. That was Harry's dream, to start a fine new life away from the stink of Birmingham factories and the shabby, vermin-ridden houses of old Ladywood.

'I've got the energy of two men,' he used to say. 'You'll see, Mother Firkin. This family's going up in the world, up and out of 'ere and right the other side of the world. Flo and me'll live like kings – and we'll see to it you do as well. You can come and join us when we're all set up.'

And then the war came, and instead they faced the shadow of a man whom the fighting had spat out and sent home to them: used, then discarded, abandoned to eke out a future on ruined health and confidence, on shattered nerves. Whatever rays had broken through from that bright, possible future had faded and gone out and now all was darkness for Flo.

But Nanny Firkin had never been one to get carried away by dreams. You could dream, oh yes, dreams were what kept you going, kept you living one day after another. But stepping right into them and thinking life would pull itself round just to suit you – that was something else. Moonshine, that was. She watched her daughter's grief, day after day, and she saw things very clearly as they were.

'Well, Flo,' she said in her cracked little voice. 'You know I'll give yer all the help I can. It's no hardship to me spending time with my grandchildren – when I'm allowed,' she added rather tartly. Flo looked up at her, her tear-stained face desperate. 'But as for you, you're gunna have to get yerself a job, one that pays enough to keep this family together. I can't do that for yer, Flo, I'm past all that. If I 'ad anything to give yer, yer could 'ave the teeth out of my head, but I ain't even got them now. You'd best get yerself into a factory on the best wages yer can find.'

In Loving Memory of
Harold Nelson
Who entered into rest 16th Nov 1926
Aged 33 years
Interred at Lodge Hill Cemetery

Funeral furnished by N. Griffin & Son,
Monument Road

Harry's funeral was held at St Mark's Church, next to St Mark's School, where Maryann and the others attended. Maryann sat next to Tony in the immense gloom of the church while grand words from the Book of Common Prayer whirled round her head. Her dad's coffin was draped with a Union Jack, the reward of respect given to a serviceman of the war.

At the cemetery they stood round in watery sunshine and a cold wind. Flo was distraught. She seemed to have no comfort to give to her family. She stood across the grave from them, being consoled by her younger brother Danny and his wife Margie. It was Nanny Firkin who stayed close to the children, arms stretched out, trying to spread her tiny frame behind them like a fan. Tony clung to Maryann. As they lowered the coffin into the grave, Tony turned and buried his face against her.

The undertaker, Norman Griffin, was a tall, respectable-looking, middle-aged gentleman, his broad shoulders encased in a smart black coat with a white wool muffler at the neck, black gloves and shoes gleaming with polish and elbow grease. She could see, from under his bowler hat, that his hair was a faded ginger, and his complexion also had the faded freckliness of the redheaded. His manner was tactful and deferential. When they had driven back to the house from Lodge Hill and Mr Griffin had dispatched the carriages, he lingered in the street with them for so long that eventually Flo felt obliged to say, 'Can we offer yer a cup of tea or summat for your trouble, Mr Griffin?'

'Well, I must say,' Mr Griffin said, rubbing his hands together, giving a practised, moderate, undertaker's smile, 'it's a right cold day – I won't stop for long, of course, but I'd be very grateful, I truly would.'

Flustered moments followed of building the fire and Nanny Firkin fetching water for the kettle while Mr Griffin sat by the hearth, looking round the room and lighting up a cigarette. Maryann watched him. He had sat himself, without a by your leave, in the chair that had been Harry's when he came home from work. Maryann gritted her teeth. She didn't like the smell of Mr Griffin's cigarette smoke (her dad had never taken to smoking), and even more she didn't like him parking his backside in her dad's chair, however much of a gentleman he was. Besides which, it was the most comfortable seat, so Nanny Firkin was left perched on a hard chair by the table.

Flo laid out their handful of best cups and saucers and poured the tea after the eternity it seemed to take to get ready, while none of them had anything to say. She spooned condensed milk into the cups, her fingers trembling.

'I'm afraid it's a bit on the weak side,' she apologized miserably, as if the tea was representative of their desolate state. 'Get Mr Griffin some sugar, Maryann,' she ordered, adding in a hissed whisper, 'and don't bring it in the packet.'

Maryann tipped the large grains of sugar on to a saucer, found a spoon and dutifully offered it to Norman Griffin, coughing as his blue smoke wafted up into her nostrils.

'Ah—' Mr Griffin turned to her and she felt herself turn red under his close examination. 'Thank you . . . er, my dear.' Close up to him, as well as the smoke, Maryann could smell sweat and some other funny chemical smell. Without meaning to she wrinkled her nose. Now he had taken his hat off she could see his hair was thinning on top and was smoothed back with soap or Brylcreem. He sat very straight, with an almost military bearing. As well as his smell, Maryann disliked his affected way of talking as if he was really posh, and the way he had ousted Tiger from by the fire with a rough shove of his shiny shoes, their soles muddy from the cemetery.

But they had to be polite and thankful to Mr Griffin. He had handled Harry's funeral at a discount: the hearse pulled by gleaming black horses, the wreath, the cards announcing the death. In the circumstances, Flo Nelson had genuine cause for gratitude.

'We couldn't 've managed it – not proper like – without yer being so kind,' she was saying, from a wooden chair opposite him, a tremor in her hands as she held her cup and saucer.

The children sat round, dumb with misery; Maryann squeezed on to a stool next to Tony, each of them with one leg on, one off. Sal was sitting holding Billy, asleep in the dim gaslight. Cathleen Black had looked after him for the day and he'd worn himself out playing with Horace. Mr Griffin seemed to take for ever to drink his cup of tea. Maryann could see the strain in her mother's face, her need to be left alone, not to have to be polite, to weep.

'Of course, I understand your feelings at this inauspicious time,' Mr Griffin was saying, clinking his half empty cup down on the saucer. His fingers were pale and stubby, the backs of his hands freckly and still red from the cold. 'My own dear wife passed away not two year ago.'

'Oh,' Flo Nelson said, with an effort. 'I'm sorry to 'ear that, Mr Griffin. I didn't know.'

''Course I've only the one son – worked for me in the business for a bit, till 'e decided to go his own way. I tried to persuade him to stay – 'e made a beautiful coffin when 'e put his mind to it . . .' As he spoke he looked round the room again. Sizing it up, Maryann thought.

'You've got yer 'ouse looking nice, Mrs Nelson. Daresay you'd move to a bigger place given the chance though, eh? Very cramped these yard 'ouses – with all the family you've got.'

''Er's always managed,' Nanny Firkin put in, sharply.

'We ain't got much chance of moving now,' Flo said. 'To tell yer the honest truth, Mr Griffin, I don't know 'ow we're going to manage with my Harry gone . . .'

Unable to hold back her emotion any longer, she burst into tears and Sal began sobbing as well. Maryann felt her own emotions swell inside her as if she might explode, but she wasn't going to cry with *him* here! She folded her arms tight across her bony ribcage, pressing herself in.

Mr Griffin leaned forwards, breathing loudly through his nose. 'Oh dear, oh dear, now, now. I am sorry for your trouble, my dear. I do know what a terrible time this is for you ... You know, I feel very sorry for you, a woman left to fend for 'erself with family. Now if you need any help – if there's anything I can do for you ...'

Maryann squeezed her eyes tightly shut. *Go away, you horrible smelly old man!* her mind screamed. *Get out of our dad's chair, and out of our house!*

At last he stood up, seeming to take up half the room, and put his hat and coat on. Suddenly he turned and enacted a little bow towards Sal and Maryann.

'Goodbye then, girls. You'll help look after yer mother, now won't yer?' They sat, mute, not even meeting his eyes.

'Thank you again, Mr Griffin,' Flo said meekly. 'I don't know what to say, yer've been that good to us.' She saw him to the door.

'Goodbye, m'dear.' Mr Griffin lingered for a moment. 'Now don't you go forgetting what I've said, will you?'

Flo stood on the step, staring thoughtfully after him as he disappeared into the smoky gloom.

Four

December 1927

'And where d'yer think you're going?'

Flo's question was flung furiously across the room, through the paper streamers which hung in sagging loops from yesterday's Christmas festivities, at Maryann, who was by the door, forcing her arms into the sleeves of her coat.

'Out.'

Flo advanced on her, hands still black from shovelling coal.

'Oh no you ain't, yer little madam. You get back 'ere and find a civil tongue for Norm – for Mr Griffin for once in yer life. 'E'll be 'ere any minute and yer can sit there and be polite. There's summat 'e wants to say to you all.'

But Maryann was already out and across the yard, still pulling the coat round her, the door rattling shut in Flo's face. It opened again.

'You get back 'ere, yer uppity little cow!'

Maryann disappeared at a run, down the entry to the street. She felt the cold come down on her like a weight, the raw air biting into her cheeks on this day of deep, silent midwinter. The cobbles were icy and the slates glazed with it: the sun hadn't broken through all day. She pushed her hands deep into her pockets, thrusting her chin down. She had on a pair of Sal's old stockings, held up with garters. Everything she had handed down from Sal was on the big side. She could feel the stockings wrinkling down her legs.

Flo's angry words seemed to propel Maryann along the road. 'I'm not staying in there – not to see *'im*,' she said out loud, her breath swirling away from her, thick and white.

She turned down towards Nanny Firkin's. In her left pocket she found a halfpenny, and gripped her hand round it, squeezing hard. She and her mom had never been what you'd call close, but nowadays all she ever seemed to be was on the wrong side of her. All year it had been like this, getting worse and worse. Since her dad had died and since Mr Griffin kept on coming round week after week bringing presents: joints of meat, cakes, thrusting bags of sweets under their noses, sitting himself by their fire on Sunday afternoons. He had even begun to take off his shoes and park them up against the fender as his socks steamed in the heat.

Maryann knew exactly what Mr Griffin wanted to say that afternoon. She was sick at the thought, because it had been coming all year. He was going to sit there in the chair, her *dad's* chair, with them waiting on him hand and foot. There'd be her mom's, 'Oh yes, Mr Griffin, no, Mr Griffin,' which had gradually turned into, 'Oh yes, *Norman*, no, Norman,' as Flo recognized a chance if ever she saw one. Mr Griffin was going to sit holding a cup of tea in those pudgy, freckled hands and tell them he was going to marry their mom. And he would say it in that wheedling, smarmy voice which made Maryann want to be sick all over his shiny shoes.

She knew this as clearly as anything, because as his visits had become more frequent, Norman Griffin had come making hints and promises.

'You're a good woman, Mrs Nelson, showing such

31

kindness to a poor old widower like me. You shouldn't 'ave to spend the rest of your days slaving away on yer own . . .' 'Nice little family you've got 'ere, Mrs Nelson – you need someone to take care of yer . . .' And gradually, 'You want to get yourself wed again, Flo – the factory's no place for a fine woman like you . . .'

Late in the summer, when a reasonable period of mourning was seen to have passed, and Flo had wept and worried and worked so hard in the brassware factory she had turned scrawny, she started going out for the odd walk with Mr Griffin on a Sunday afternoon, returning with flushed cheeks and a hard, determined look in her eyes.

When he came to the house Maryann tried to avoid even looking at him. She hated him being there and refused to speak to him unless forced to. Sal was more biddable. She missed her father but brushed out her long, pale hair on a Sunday, made tea and was polite. Maryann pulled hideous faces behind his back and dropped dust and dead ants in his tea, reduced to being childish by her powerlessness over the situation. She missed her dad with a terrible ache in her that never seemed to get any less.

She kicked at a rotten piece of wood on the pavement and it skittered into the gutter. She bent over and spat on it. 'Norman! Bloody sodding *Norman!*' She stamped and spat until tears ran down her cheeks.

Walking on, wiping her eyes, she crossed over the railway and went along to the spot where there was a hole in the fence and she could get down to the cut, scrambling down through scrubby bushes and alongside the wall of a warehouse on to the path. Down here it felt even more cold and utterly still. Fog hung thickly over the canal so that she could see only a few yards ahead: the factories, chimneys and warehouses were all shrouded in the saturated air. The place felt completely deserted. It was Christmas of course, and she saw the water of the canal was frozen over. Near where she was standing a stick poked up, frozen in at an angle, black against the grey ice. She walked along the path in the eerie whiteness, in towards the middle of Birmingham, over a little humpbacked bridge and past the Borax Works towards the wharves at Gas Street. Ahead of her she could just see the ghostly shapes of the wharf buildings and in front of them two rows of joeys, the boats which mainly did journeys of a day there and back. They were tethered shoulder to shoulder along the Worcester Bar. As she moved closer, she became aware of a sound coming to her intermittently through the fog. She wasn't alone down here then. Someone was coughing, a laboured sound which went on and on.

Then she saw him, on the path in front of her, close to a boat which was tied by the bank. He was bent over, coughing from drenched-sounding lungs and struggling for breath. At first she assumed he was an old man, but as she approached, intimidated, yet somehow fascinated as well, she saw this was not so. He was quite unaware that she was there because he had to submit completely to the process of coughing and this made him seem somehow vulnerable. Maryann was also drawn by the look of him. He had a thick head of curls and a beard, all deep auburn, which appeared to glow in the greyness of the fog like a sanctuary lamp in a church, and he was clad in thick, brown corduroy trousers and heavy boots, and a thick jumper with a worn, black worsted jacket over the top and a muffler at the neck. As he stooped, hands pressing on his thighs, one hand also held a black cap.

She saw that the boat by which he was standing was a horse-drawn family boat, and she noticed too that the man's hands, clasped so tightly on his thighs, were black with coal dust. Near him, on the ground, was a galvanized bucket.

At last the fit passed and he stayed in the same position for a moment, seeming exhausted by it, let out a low groan and shook his head quickly from side to side as if to shake the fit off. Then, still bent over, he raised his head and looked up along the path. Maryann felt her heart beat with panic, and she stayed quite still. For a moment the two of them looked at each other in silence. The man had a round face, though his cheek-bones jutted a little, adding a chiselled look to it. His eyes, from the distance at which Maryann stood, looked dark and his gaze was strong and unflinching. He stared at her without hostility. Just looked, taking her in. Then slowly, he straightened up and replaced the cap on his head.

''Ow long've you been stood there?' His voice was soft and quite gentle.

Maryann swallowed. She had been ready to run if he was angry or strange, but didn't feel the need now. The man didn't talk like Birmingham people, she noticed.

'Only a minute.'

'What're you doing out? It's Christmas, ent it?'

Maryann shifted her weight from one foot to the other. She felt conscious of her stockings, wrinkled round her ankles. 'Well, you're 'ere.'

'Well – yes, that's true.' She thought she heard him give a wheezy chuckle.

'Why?'

He indicated the boat. 'I live 'ere. We ent s'posed to be 'ere – brought a load of coal from Cannock to the

Borax Works – before Christmas that was. And got blooming iced in, dint we? They ent 'ad the icebreaker out to free us up. I've been smashing it up at the edge 'ere to give 'er a wash out.' He indicated the bucket. 'Got to get the coal washed out, see, before we can put a new load in.'

Maryann nodded and moved closer. The long hold of the boat was black with coal dust and the rope fenders were grubby with it too, but apart from that she looked in good trim. She was painted red and yellow, with castles painted in the panels of the cabin doors, roses round the edge, and on the side of the cabin was painted her name, *Esther Jane*. Maryann looked at her with great curiosity, at the painted water can on the roof, the brass trimmings on her chimney, from which drifted dense yellow smoke. She looked round.

'Where's yer horse?'

'Old Bessie? Stabled up. Having a rest.'

'Can I see inside?'

The man smiled. She saw he had big, square teeth. The smile creased up his face and gave him a comical, cheeky look. 'You'll get dirty.'

Maryann shrugged. 'Don't matter.'

'Come on then – just for a minute but mind where you put your 'ands.'

She thought he seemed pleased. He climbed aboard ahead of her and when she stumbled climbing down into the boat, he gripped her arm. He felt very big and burly and strong.

'Go easy!' Another low chuckle came from him. For some reason he seemed to find her rather amusing. 'You don't want to hurt yourself. Look – that's the tiller – what we steer the boat with. Now, come on in.'

He opened the cabin doors and Maryann found herself stepping down into a miniature house. The man, who was too tall to stand upright in the cabin, sat down on a bench along the side, and gestured for her to sit beside him.

'There you go – this is our 'ome in 'ere.'

She gazed round, astonished. It was like being in a magic story where everything had shrunk. In front of her was a little black-leaded range, which made the cabin so stifling hot that Maryann unbuttoned her coat and took it off. There was a brown and white teapot and a big brass kettle, well polished, on the hob, which gave off a lovely warm glow. To her right was what looked like a cupboard, which jutted out into the cabin, and further back, a little area where there was another bench, divided off by red and white check curtains, tied back at each side. On the near side of the cupboard and on shelves on the wall by the stove were pretty china plates, some with lattice edges with velvet ribbons threaded through and tied in a bow. The man watched her taking it all in with some amusement.

'We pull this down 'ere—' He opened a small cupboard in front of him and the flap folded outwards. 'That's our table. That cupboard you can see' – he pointed towards the back – 'folds down for a bed.'

'But it's so . . . *small*!'

'It's small all right.'

'Don't you 'ave a house to live in an' all?'

'Nope. I was brung up on 'ere – lived 'ere all me life. Only time I been on the bank was in the war.'

She gaped at him. 'I've never seen in one of these before.'

'I can see that!'

'Who lives on 'ere with you then?'

'My dad, my little sister, Ada – she'd be a bit younger 'un you I'd think – and Jep, that's our dog. They've gone off to get us some food and see about who's going to get the ice broke up. We can't stick around long, you see – 'ave to get moving. We was s'posed to be at Napton by Christmas but we got stuck 'ere. We ent starving yet though. 'Ere—' He reached to a little shelf at the side of the cabin. 'Want a bit of this?'

'Ooh yes!'

She took the two thick squares of Cadbury's chocolate, nibbled and sucked slowly, making them last. The man bit some off too, smiling at her enjoyment. He had such a kind face, she thought, somehow old and boyish at once.

'How old're you?' Maryann said.

'Me? Old as the hills.'

She frowned. ''Ow old's that?'

'I'm going on twenty-nine. What about you, since we're asking?'

'Thirteen. What's yer name?'

'Joel Bartholomew. And what's yours?' He was making a game of it. Maryann found the corners of her mouth turning up.

'Maryann Nelson. I'll *always* be Maryann Nelson.'

'Will you? Why?'

''Cause no one's going to make me be called anything else.'

'Well – that's settled then.' Joel watched her carefully, rubbing his huge hands on the legs of his trousers. Then he stirred himself. 'Best get on – the others'll be back soon and they won't take to me idling.'

They stepped back out on to the bank. It felt very cold outside after the snug little cabin. Joel showed no sign of being cold, but he saw her shivering.

37

'D'you live far, Maryann?'

'Garrett Street.'

This meant nothing to him. 'Shouldn't yer be at home?'

Maryann shrugged, miserable again at the thought of home. 'I wish I could come with yer.'

Joel smiled. 'Not this time o'year you don't.'

They stood by the bank and she felt shy again, as if she'd stayed too long. She put her coat back on.

'Better go then.'

Joel suddenly held out his hand in a teasing way and she took it. His was big and very rough.

'Nice to meet you, Maryann Nelson.'

'Can I come and see yer again?'

''Course you can – if you can ever find us. T'ent easy that, on the cut!'

She turned and left him, pulling her too-big coat in closer round her, face and hands aching with cold. Reaching the bridge she turned back and saw Joel watching her. She waved, and for a moment he raised an arm.

She went to Nanny Firkin's house next, although she didn't say a word to her grandmother about Mr Griffin and why she wasn't at home and her nan didn't ask. She could see the girl's unhappiness in every line of her. She'd had words with her daughter and would have more, but she wasn't going to inflict more on her granddaughter.

'Yer just making up to 'im for a meal ticket!' she'd accused Flo, and Flo whirled round, livid.

'Yes – I am! 'E's said 'e'll move us into a bigger 'ouse and I'll not need to stand in that stinking factory

38

turning out kettles all day long. I'll be able to live without being worried to death about where every meal's coming from. Harry's gone – 'e ain't coming back and a meal ticket's what I need, without any sodding lectures on the subject. I don't want to end up like you, living on nothing and surrounded by mangy flaming cats for company!'

Maryann stayed with Nanny Firkin, warming herself again by the fire and drinking a cup of tea. She sat stroking the cats and talking to Walt the parrot, in the musty familiarity of her grandmother's house and she waited long enough so that Mr Griffin would have gone through his usual rigmarole of wiping his mouth, putting on his jacket and shoes and standing, holding his hat in front of his stomach and thanking her mother, with a little bow, for the afternoon tea which, he always said, brightened his lonely life. She thought about Joel and the boat and hugged this to herself as a lovely, warming secret.

When she got home she pushed the door open cautiously, making absolutely sure she was not going to see Norman Griffin's head, with the pasty, balding patch at the back, still in place in the chair.

Sal was putting away cups and saucers on the shelf. She turned and raised her eyes to the ceiling, implying that Flo was upstairs, then shrugged, with an expression of sorrowful resignation. Tony ran to Maryann.

'Where've yer bin, Maryann? Our mom's ever so cross with yer and she's going to get wed to Mr Griffin. Don't say anyfing and make a row, will yer?'

They heard their mother's tread on the stairs. She had almost reached the bottom and stopped, staring across towards the door. Maryann waited for her temper to erupt, but she just stood there and they all gazed back at her. Maryann looked at Sal, then back to her mother.

''Ow can yer, Mom?' Maryann said quietly. ''Ow can yer do it?'

'I'll tell yer how I can do it.' Flo came down the last of the stairs and across to fix her younger daughter with the steely, determined expression that had become hers since her husband's death. 'By thinking about what life'll be like if I don't. Norman Griffin's got a business. 'E's got enough money to keep us, we're going to a new 'ouse and 'e's got a job lined up for Sal.'

'Do I 'ave to work with 'im, Mom?' Sal asked timidly. 'I like where I'm working now.' Sal's first job after school was with a local bakery.

'*Yes.* You do. We'll be all right now. We shan't 'ave to worry. I know 'e's not yer dad, but from now on 'e'll be the head of this family and you'll treat him with respect and a bit of gratitude. D'you 'ear?'

Five

1928

'There's someone at the door, Maryann!' Flo Nelson shouted.

Maryann went to the front door and found Nancy grinning in at her. 'So this is yer new 'ouse then!'

Maryann's solemn expression broke into a smile as well. 'Come on – I'll show yer.' Nancy went to St Peter's, the Catholic school, so the girls didn't see one another in the daytime.

Flo and Mr Griffin were married in the new year, and soon after he announced that there was a house waiting for them two roads away in Anderson Street and they were to move in immediately. He had it all planned. It was a little bit nearer his premises, where Sal had started work straight after Christmas, and was a two up, two down, with a tiny yard out at the back behind the kitchen and definitely a step up from a back-to-back.

You stepped straight in off the street into the front room. By the hearth was a peg rug, which Flo and Sal had botched together, and Harry Nelson's chair. Apart from that, the only piece of furniture which came from the Nelsons' old house was a small cupboard. The other two chairs and a low table were provided by Mr Griffin. He had a little china cabinet, a table and chairs and another comfortable chair (although he still preferred Harry's) and a heavy brass oil lamp which he liked to keep well polished and light in the evenings. It had been his father's, and his 'beloved mother' who lived in Handsworth, had passed it on to him.

Nance's eyes were wide, looking round.

'Ooh, it's nice, Maryann—' After the cramped squalor of her family's back house this seemed almost palatial.

Flo was in the kitchen cooking and there was a smell of ham knuckles boiling.

'Oh – 'ello, Nancy,' Flo said, rather snootily. Cathleen Black may have helped her out in her time of need, but that didn't make them equals in Flo's eyes. They had only moved two streets away, but it felt far enough to represent a new start. Flo was managing to pull herself up in the world and she was going to do it, no matter what the cost. There always was a price: that was just how it was. She hadn't anything in the way of feelings for Norman Griffin, except for gratitude that he'd come along and been prepared to take on her and her family. That was no small thing. But he was gentlemanly in his ways, and he'd shown her the gateway out of absolute poverty: she never, ever wanted to be faced with that again. She'd have to live with his mauling her about in bed of a night – she shuddered slightly at the thought of Norman's white, flaccid body, his thick lips and tongue. But that wasn't too high a price to pay, she thought: he wasn't one of these oversexed men, thank heaven. And he showed great consideration – never went all the way, so to speak. They'd agreed that there weren't to be any more children. Her own four were enough of a handful.

'Go on and show Nancy upstairs,' she said, irritated by the girls watching her.

'You ain't been round our 'ouse for ages,' Nancy complained as the two of them clattered up the stairs.

'I know. We've been busy. Moving and that.'

Upstairs were two rooms, one shared by the new Mr and Mrs Griffin, with Billy on a little bed on the floor, and the girls and Tony in the other. Maryann wrinkled her nose as they went in. She could smell urine from where Tony had wet the bed again that morning. He was forever asking if he could get in with her and Sal, but they said they weren't having him wetting them too. Tiger was curled up asleep in the middle of the bigger bed that Maryann shared with Sal. She and Nance sat down on it and Maryann reached for Tiger and stroked him. He arched his back, purring.

'D'yer wanna come and play out then?' Nancy said. She wasn't one for sitting still for long.

Maryann kissed the stripy top of her cat's head, between the ears. He was such a comfort, amid all the changes.

'Maybe – in a bit,' she said. She felt edgy, almost tearful, sitting there with Nance. Nance was her best pal, but there was a distance between them suddenly that Maryann didn't know how to overcome. Her emotions were all tangled up and confused and she couldn't find the words to tell Nance how she was feeling. She cuddled Tiger tightly. The day they moved their few possessions out of Garrett Street, Norman Griffin had stood in the living room and prodded Tiger with the toe of his boot.

'We don't need to take *that* with us, do we?' he said.

Flo looked at him, not understanding for a moment. 'You mean the cat?' Even she could hardly believe what he was suggesting.

'We don't want a cat in the new house, do we? Dirty animal, under yer feet all the time. I nearly tripped down the stairs over the thing the other day. Be a good time to get shot of it.'

Maryann stood behind him, so tensed with shock at what he'd said that for those moments she couldn't react. She saw her mother look across at her. Flo ran her hands over her pale hair, as if preparing herself, and stepped closer to her new husband.

'Norman – I really don't think we can leave the cat behind. The children ... I mean, it's Maryann's. It'd break 'er heart.'

Norman turned and saw Maryann's piercing expression. For a moment he hesitated, then decided to smile. 'Oh, awright then. If we must, we'll take the thing. It'll most likely follow us over there anyhow.'

So Tiger had come. At least her mom had stood up for her over him. That was something.

''Ow's Sal getting on?' Nancy asked. 'What's she doing at Griffin's? Eh—' She dug Maryann in the ribs. 'She ain't building coffins?'

'No!' Maryann elbowed her back. 'Don't be daft. I dunno. She's in the office. Bits and bobs. Messages, taking down details for cards and that. She ain't really said a lot.' Sal never seemed to say a lot about anything nowadays.

'Sounds awright,' Nancy said. 'Soft job that.' With a giggle she added, 'If yer go for that sort of thing.'

Maryann managed a laugh, feeling Nance dragging her up out of her gloomy mood.

'Yer dad home yet?' she asked Nancy.

Nancy rolled her eyes. 'Sleeping it off. But we could go over the yard, take Billy – Tony as well, if you like?'

'Awright then.' Maryann stood up without much enthusiasm.

'We're going over Nance's!' Maryann called out, downstairs.

'Take Billy with yer then!' Flo predictably shouted back.

It was cold, but bright outside. The girls set off with Billy between them holding their hands, and Tony dragging his feet behind so they kept having to turn round and call, 'Come on, Tony – get a move on, will yer!'

Maryann took a deep breath of the freezing, acrid air and managed to grin at Nance. This is better, she thought. Away from that house, *his* house, she felt lighter, free again.

'I'm glad yer came over,' she said to Nance.

Norman Griffin had habits of almost clockwork precision. On certain nights of the week he locked up his premises, went down to his favourite pub, the Duke of Wellington, for a pint, then came home. Every evening he expected them all to polish their shoes and line them up against the fender ready for the next day. He inspected them every night, turning each one over, frowning if there was obvious wear in the sole. On Sundays they all had to go to church with him, and afterwards he spent the rest of the morning in Handsworth with his mother. But for once tonight he was late, and Flo was especially exasperated as it meant Sal was late too, and she had the dinner all ready.

Maryann was pleased. The later he came back the better so far as she was concerned. The place felt much more like home, their real family, when he wasn't there. It was quite cosy with the gas mantle popping away and the warmth from the range. Flo was dishing up stew and potatoes when they heard the door open out of the dark winter evening.

''Bout time,' Flo muttered, relieved. Norman didn't take too kindly to them starting without him.

'Summat smells good!' they heard him say. Sal, her face paler than ever in the gaslight, slid into the room and sat down quietly at the table.

Norman came through, smoking the butt end of a cigarette. Maryann didn't like it when he stood over them. He was so big it felt intimidating. She saw Tony shrink down in his seat.

'What's happened, Norman?' Flo asked, serving his food. 'You seem pleased with yerself.'

'Oh no, no – nothing much. Just glad to be 'ome with you, my dear,' he said, sitting himself at the table. As he did so, Tiger stirred from where he had been sitting under the table and brushed against his legs.

'Get that thing out while we're 'aving our tea!' Norman said, scraping back his chair. He stood up and kicked Tiger out through the door. The cat let out a screech of pain and Norman slammed the door. Maryann burst into tears.

'Never mind.' Flo, startled by this sudden outburst, tried to appease her. She watched Norman anxiously. He was breathing heavily. 'Shoosh now,' Flo snapped at her. 'T'ain't summat to blart about.'

But Maryann couldn't stop. The tears just kept on coming out of her eyes, though she tried as hard as she could not to make any noise. Norman kept eating, steadily. Tony and Billy were wide-eyed, but they ate up obediently. Sal kept her eyes on her plate. Eventually Maryann let out a loud sniff and Norman leapt to his feet.

'Go on – get out of 'ere! I'll not 'ave yer snivelling and blarting at my table. If you can't eat quietly you'll not eat at all.'

Maryann, keeping her head down, left the room and ran upstairs. She lay curled up, crying, the clogging taste of the stew still in her mouth. When she was calmer she lay looking up into the darkness. She thought about her father, about the dreams Nanny Firkin had told her about. That he'd said he was going to take them to Australia.

That's what I'm going to do, Maryann thought. The resolve burned through her. I'm going to get out of here, as soon as I can. She didn't know where to: her young life had given her experience of nothing further away than these few Ladywood Streets and an occasional rare trip to the Bull Ring. But there was more out there, there had to be, beyond these smoke-blackened houses and stinking streets.

Comforted by this, she was already almost asleep when Sal came in to put Tony to bed and get ready herself. She brought a candle with her, and Maryann watched as she bent over and roughly undressed her younger brother. Her expression was tight, wooden.

'Sal?' Maryann wondered if she was cross because it was usually her job, not Sal's, to look after Tony.

'What?' She didn't look round.

'D'yer want me to do our Tony?'

'I've done 'im now. And don't you go wetting the bed again!' She pushed his shoulder. 'D'you 'ear me?'

When Tony was settled she turned away and undressed. Maryann frowned, looking at Sal's curving shape in the candlelight. She was clearly in a mood over something, turning her back like that, when normally she just pulled off her clothes casually and flung on her nightdress. Tonight her movements were abrupt. She put her nightdress over her head and her arms through the sleeves. Suddenly she sat down on the edge of the bed and put her hands over her face.

''Ow's it with the job, Sal?' Maryann asked.

There was no reply.

Maryann sat up and moved nearer, laying a hand on her sister's shoulder. 'What's up?'

'Nothing!' Sal flung her off and stood up. She threw her clothes savagely into the corner of the room, then climbed into bed. She turned her back on Maryann, blew out the candle and wouldn't say another word.

The next day, when she came home from playing with the Black children, Maryann ran up to the bedroom looking for Tiger. He was always her first thought when she came home, and very often she found him curled up in the dip of hers and Sal's bed. But he wasn't there. She peeped into her mom's and Norman's room. No sign there, either, nor was he in any of the warm spots downstairs, by the range or the chimney breast.

''E must be out,' Maryann said, disappointed.

Not long after, Flo got in, tired and irritable from an extra afternoon of chores. Nanny Firkin was feeling poorly and Flo had felt obliged to go and help.

'You seen Tiger?' Maryann asked her.

Flo stoked the range. 'Course I bloody ain't – I ain't been 'ere all afternoon, 'ave I?'

'Is Nanna better?' Tony asked.

'Not as yer'd notice,' Flo said. ''Er's in bed and that ain't usual. But she said to leave 'er, she'd be awright.

I've rubbed 'er chest with goose grease and left 'er 'er tea.'

When their own meal was over, Norman stood up behind Sal, hands on his waist, looking round at them all with a satisfied expression on his face.

'We'll all 'ave a game of cards, eh?'

He did this, every so often. Decided they were all going to sit together, 'be a family' and play whatever he was in the mood for.

'After I've got our Billy to bed then,' Flo said, sounding pleased. 'That's nice of Norman, ain't it?'

'I don't want to play cards,' Maryann murmured. 'I want to go and look for Tiger.'

'Look for Tiger!' Norman snorted with laughter. 'Yer don't want to bother with that! Cats can look after themselves, that they can.'

'I'm tired,' Sal said quietly. 'I think I'll just go to bed, 'stead of playing.'

Norman laid his hand on the back of her chair. 'Oh, I don't think a game of cards'll hurt before yer turn in, Sal.' His voice was soft, but Maryann heard a firm edge to it which always meant Norman wasn't going to be crossed. 'Young girl your age shouldn't be tired this early. Come on – help yer mother clear up then we can get to it the sooner.'

They had no choice but to do as they were told, as was the case with all his 'treats'. His taking them to church every Sunday, visits to the pictures, walking down the street all together, usually to see something that was too old for Tony and Billy, who would sleep or fret through it all. Maryann did like the pictures, but she loathed sitting anywhere near Norman.

Before going in for the dreaded card game she opened the back door into the little yard.

'Tiger! Come on, puss – where've yer got to?'

Nothing. No sign of him. She was filled with unease. He'd never done this before. What if he'd got under a train – or a car like her dad. Or what if he'd fallen in the cut?

Sal stuck her head through the door from the front. 'Come on – 'urry up. Let's get it over.'

'Coming,' Maryann said reluctantly.

Norman had pulled out the little table and was sitting shuffling his dog-eared packs of cards.

'Come on, our Maryann,' he said in a jolly voice as she slipped into the room.

Maryann sat down next to Tony.

'We'll 'ave a game of rummy,' Norman said, licking his thumb and dealing the cards. He paused to light a cigarette.

'You play with me,' Maryann whispered to Tony. Flo sat yawning. She wasn't the least keen on card games, but if Norman said they were going to do something there was no arguing.

'I'm not used to being a family man,' he'd said to her. 'I'm out of practice, Flo. But I'm doing my best . . .'

He jollied them along through a couple of games, laughing loudly at the least thing except at one moment when Tony picked a card to play and he frowned and said, 'Stupid boy . . .' and Tony turned his dark eyes on Maryann, looking worried about what he'd done. He lived in constant nervousness of Norman and his exacting ways. His lisping voice and tense face only seemed to aggravate Norman further.

'S'awright,' she told him, loud enough to be heard. 'You ain't stupid, Tony.' She put her arm round his shoulders, avoiding looking at Norman. Apart from that, and Norman's efforts at thawing them out, they barely said a word, all waiting for the moment when they could go.

Finally, Norman sat back at the end of a game and said, 'Well – that's enough for one night, I'd say.'

Maryann jumped up. 'Come on, Tony!' she said, and they ran upstairs, anything to get away from him.

By the time they went to bed, Tiger had still not come back, although Maryann had been to the door several times to check if he was waiting out there.

'What if 'e comes back in the night and wants to come in, Mom?' she said. 'Can we leave the back door open for 'im?'

'You mad?' Flo said. 'It's perishing cold. 'E's a cat, Maryann – 'e knows 'ow to fend for hisself without you coddling 'im!'

But Maryann lay in bed that night, miserable without Tiger's warm shape at her feet.

Six

Sally Nelson sat behind the desk in the austere office of 'N. Griffin's, Undertaker's'. In front of her lay two open ledgers and a small pile of newly printed death cards, almost identical to the ones they had had for her father. On another pad on the desk were Norman's various tottings up of the prices of coffin, hearse and cards. It was Tuesday evening.

Sal's demeanour was anything but relaxed. She sat chewing hard on the end of her thumb. Every so often she got up and tip-toed over towards the staircase leading down to the double cellar which ran under the building, and stood, head cocked, listening. After waiting at the top of the staircase for a long time on one occasion, she crept halfway down and stopped. She could hear Norman Griffin's voice, talking to Fred, the lad who worked down there building coffins. The last boy had left not long back and Norman was training Fred up. On Tuesdays he sent Fred home early.

'Shall I put all these away now?' Sal heard Fred say.

Then Norman's voice. 'No – leave that to me. I keep that cupboard locked, with the chemicals and that about. You can get off now.' She heard the clink of a key. Fred was about to leave. Her heart beat even faster. She opened her mouth to speak but her throat had dried out and she had to swallow before she could get any words out.

'Mr Griffin?' she called downstairs. She knew it was futile, but she had to try it. She felt she was going to explode inside. 'I'll be off 'ome now – our Mom'll be needing some help.'

Norman Griffin's face appeared round the cellar door, pale and moonlike in the gloom as he looked up at her.

'No, Sal – yer not to go yet. There's a few things want finishing.' He spoke in the low, respectful tone Sal and Maryann called his 'Undertaker' voice.

'But—' She tried to protest.

He closed the cellar door behind him, and then came another of his voices. 'No, Sal.' Now the voice was soft, wheedling. 'Yer to stay a bit longer. Don't want yer going home yet – or you know what'll happen, don't yer?'

Sal returned to her chair upstairs, trembling from head to foot. She was in such as a state she felt as if her throat had closed up, that she couldn't swallow. Oh God! She could run out and down the road now. But she daren't. Couldn't. Sooner or later she'd have to go home. And when she got home he'd be there. And she couldn't tell anyone and she'd have to come back to work with him and then he'd ... he'd ... She dug her nails into the palms of her hands.

They were coming up the stairs, Fred clumping along in his boots. He was none too with it, Fred wasn't. Gangly, greasy brown hair, big feet, yes, Mr Griffin, no, Mr Griffin, everything Norman wanted.

'G'night then—' He nodded at Sal, and Norman Griffin stood at the door as he went out.

Norman pulled his watch up from his weskit and squinted at it.

'Ah yes – time to close up.' He locked the door,

pulled the blind down over the door and windows and turned to look at her.

'Don't do that again, will you?' He spoke casually, but she could hear the threat underneath.

'What?' She could only manage a whisper. The tension in her was like a crushing sensation in her chest.

'Don't talk back to me in front of my employees like that,' he said, as if he had a whole empire of workers, not just herself and Fred.

'I'm sorry.' She kept her gaze on the desk in front of her, hands clasped tightly together in her lap. Her heart was beating so hard it hurt.

Then the wheedling voice was back. 'Come on then, Sal. You know what *will* please me, don't yer?'

She didn't answer, just kept her head lowered, and she heard him moving towards her. Sal squeezed her eyes tight shut. When he reached down and took hold of her hands she cried out, startled.

'Oh, don't get in such a state,' he said impatiently. His voice became clipped and cold. 'You know what yer 'ave to do – and then it's over and yer can go home. Simple. It ain't asking much.'

Much, she thought, as he pulled her towards the stairs. Ever since that first time, the start of it, when he had come up behind her and pressed his hands over her breasts, hurting her, it had been much. Far too much.

The cellar was a double one, extending under the premises behind. At the back end, through a white door, was the chapel of rest. The walls in there were plastered and distempered and it was kept very neat and clean. It contained a long trestle table and a small side table on which were a Bible, a candle and an arrangement of dusty silk flowers. There was access to it from the street behind, and any visiting bereaved were escorted in through there and all hammering silenced while they were there. Tonight, on the long table in the Chapel of Rest, a Mr Alfred Johnson lay in his coffin. His family hadn't wanted him at home taking up the room. The front end, under the shop, was much more workmanlike: unplastered brick walls, cobwebs trailing under the grating through which only shreds of light filtered from the street so that it had to be lit by gas lamps all day long. At one end, abutting the wall of the Chapel of Rest, was Mr Griffin's cupboard, but most of the space was taken up by a workbench and a long table. On the workbench tonight sat the almost completed coffin which Fred was due to finish the next day.

Mr Griffin was breathing rather fast. He reached up and made some adjustment to the light so that it burned less brightly. 'Now then, Sal, my dear.'

'No,' she begged, starting to cry. 'No – please. Not today. I'll do it tomorrow, but not today – I feel a bit bad today and I can't . . .'

'Sal—' He was speaking in his soft, fluid voice. 'You're just not used to it, my dear. You're young – you have to learn to enjoy it.'

She was shaking her head, wretchedly, unable to stop the tears from pouring down her cheeks.

His mouth was right close to her, his hot breath wafting the words into her ear. 'And if you don't, you know what'll happen, don't you?' He pointed to the far end of the cellar. 'There's my cupboard.' He patted his pocket. 'And here is the key. And you know what's in my cupboard, don't you?'

Sal nodded, gasping.

'Right then.' There was nothing wheedling about his speech now. It was icy, clipped. It made Sal wither

55

inside. He pulled at the buckle of his belt with one hand, reaching out with his other to grasp her by her long hair, yanking her close to him.

His other hand was under her skirt, tugging, tearing.

'Let's get on with it.'

When Maryann got home from school that day she ran straight in shouting, 'Mom – Mom! Is Tiger back? Has 'e come home?'

Flo Nelson shook her head. She hadn't given a thought to the flaming cat. 'No – I ain't seen 'im all day.' She saw the hope drain out of Maryann's face. Maryann had been so sure he'd gone wandering and would be back by now. Her lips quivered and her eyes filled with tears.

'Tell yer what.' Flo saw an opportunity for a few more minutes peace. 'Yer could go and ask up and down the road if anyone's seen 'im – the neighbours and that. Someone might of done. 'E might be asleep by the fire in someone's 'ouse just along the street, yer never know. Or maybe 'e's sloped back off to Garrett Street. And take our Tony with yer, eh?'

A little cheered by being able to do something, Maryann called Tony. They went to Garrett Street and called at the Blacks' house. Blackie came to the door and the usual stink of urine and soiled baby's napkins assailed their nostrils as it opened. He stood blearily in the doorway, not seeming to know who they were. His shirt was unbuttoned halfway down and she could see black, springy hairs on his chest.

''Allo, Mr Black,' Maryann said. 'It's me – Maryann Nelson.'

'Oh ar,' Blackie said. For a second Maryann felt

sorry for him. He looked such a wreck. But she had more urgent things on her mind.

''Ave yer seen my cat? 'E's a little tabby with a face like a tiger . . .'

'Cat? No – I ain't seen no cat . . .' He stood looking at them, as if thinking what to say next.

'Maryann, is that you?' Nance came running down-stairs. 'What's up?'

'It's Tiger – 'e's gone missing.' Maryann felt a lump come up in her throat again. ''E never came in last night and I dunno where 'e is. Our Mom said to come looking over 'ere.'

'I'll 'elp yer,' Nance said. She'd changed out of her school clothes and put on a grubby pair of boy's trousers.

Maryann was pleased to have some more company for the search besides Tony who kept saying 'Where d'yer fink 'e's gone, Maryann?' until she wanted to scream at him. They asked round some of the back-yards in Garrett Street, Maryann saying hello to some of their old neighbours who asked a bit sniffily how they were getting on. Flo hadn't been back to visit a single one of them. Then they went back to Anderson Street. As the afternoon wore on, Maryann grew more and more dispirited. No one had seen Tiger.

'Ow can 'e just've disappeared into thin air?' she said to Nance. 'Someone must've seen him.'

'Yer never know with cats, do yer?' Nance said. She grinned, showing her wonky teeth, trying to cheer Maryann up. 'Knowing 'im 'e'll be back large as life. P'raps 'e's gone and got 'imself a lady friend!'

Maryann tried to smile. 'I 'ope so. It's lonely at home without 'im. Come on, Tony – we'd best go back. D'yer wanna come round ours for a bit?'

'Will yer dad be there?'

'*'E ain't my dad.*'

'No, I know. Sorry, Maryann. I daint mean anything by it.'

They went back to the house where Flo put out a plate of broken biscuits for them. 'Ooh!' Nance cried, her face lighting up. This was sheer luxury by her standards. She tucked in as hard as she could and sat at the table chatting away happily to Maryann and Tony. Then Tony went to the back door, trying to open it, clutching himself urgently at the front with his other hand.

'D'yer need a wee?' Maryann opened the door as Tony nodded emphatically and ran out to the privy in the yard and pulled the door squeaking shut.

A few moments passed, the back door swinging open into the darkening afternoon, then they heard Tony shouting, 'Maryann, Maryann! Come 'ere – 's a nasty fing!'

He was standing at the end of the yard, his eyes wide, fascinated, beckoning urgently.

'What's up, Tony?'

Maryann and Nance both went out and looked along to see what he was staring at. Between the privy and the low wall at the back was a gap of almost a yard, which had a load of rubbish chucked into it by the last occupants. It was smelly down there, the corner of the yard best avoided. But Tony's gaze was fixed on the pile of refuse. What had caught his eye was a little patch of white, the white of a small, furry throat.

It was Nance who went down the gap and very carefully picked up the cat's cold, rigid body. She kept her head down as she came back, and only when she was standing right in front of her did she look at Maryann.

'Tiger?' Maryann whispered. 'No – not Tiger!' She just stood and looked, dumb with horror. Then she shouted, 'What's happened to 'im? Oh, Tiger!'

Beside herself, sobbing, she took him from Nance, who also had tears in her eyes, and hugged him to her.

'Oh, Tiger – my poor little Tiger!'

She held him away from her, looking for signs of blood, of injury. There was nothing to see, but as she did so, his head flopped back all at the wrong angle.

'Oh my God – look! His head's all – oh look, Nance!'

Tony was crying as well then and Flo Nelson came out of the back door to see what the matter was with them all. As she did so, Nance said, 'Someone's broke 'is neck. They must've throttled 'im and broke 'is neck.'

Maryann started running then, still hugging the cat's body to her, through the house and out of the front door .

'Maryann – where're yer going? Wait for me!' By the time Nance reached the front step Maryann was off down the road, disappearing into the dusk.

Her eyes were blurry with tears so that she could barely see, but she knew the way well enough. Every so often she slowed and looked down at the precious friend she was carrying in her arms. For a second each time there was a flicker of hope. It was all a mistake. Tiger wasn't dead. He'd look into her face and purr at her and close his eyes as she stroked the side of his head, then he'd wriggle around because he wanted to be let down to play. But Tiger didn't raise his head. His fur was bunched into damp points from lying out in the wet. In the half-light, just for a second it seemed his eyes opened and she gasped. But of course it was a trick of the light and her own wishes. His eyes were two tight, pained lines and his face didn't look like him any more. All the cheeky, fiery life that was in him had gone. Maryann could hardly stand to look at him, with his poor, floppy neck. She ran along the street sobbing her heart out.

'Oh, Tiger, my little Tiger!' She didn't care who saw her. And mixed with her grief she could hear Nance's words in her head, 'someone's broke 'is neck ... throttled 'im and broke 'is neck' and the terrible knowledge, as she ran along, that she knew who that someone was. Someone who kicked Tiger out of the way with his shiny boot every time the cat crossed his path, the someone who liked to have clean hands and clean nails, who had sat making them play cards with him when all the time he knew where Tiger was because *he* must have put him there. She thought she might burst with her rage and hatred of Norman Griffin.

She ran down Ledsam Street and tore across the yard to her Nan's cottage, pushing in urgently through the door.

'Nan, oh Nanny – look what that bastard's done to Tiger!'

But Nanny Firkin was not in the kitchen and the place was as cold as ice, no fire in the range. Maryann had been in such a state she hadn't noticed the unusual darkness of the windows. There was a rank smell of cat urine and as Maryann burst in the three cats all rushed at her, tails up, miaowing for food, their fur appearing to be standing on end in the gloom. Walt the parrot shifted silently on his perch. There was a dish on the table containing the dried-up remains of porridge.

'Nan?' Maryann wiped her eyes with the back of one hand, the eerie feel of the place breaking through her grief over Tiger. The other cats were rubbing against her legs. 'Nanny, where are yer?' It was unheard of for her Nan not to be in her kitchen. Then she remembered Nanny Firkin was ill, that she'd had a cough and her chest was bad. Hadn't her mother been in that day? The cats were acting as if they hadn't eaten for a week.

Maryann went to the stairs. 'Nanny? It's Maryann.'

But there was no reply. She laid Tiger on the floor and climbed up, somehow feeling she needed to tip-toe. Maybe Nanny Firkin was asleep.

The old lady was lying in her bed. Maryann saw the little bump where her little feet were sticking up under the cover. The room smelt stale. When Maryann went over to her she saw in the dimming light from the window that her grandmother's hair was down out of the pins and straggly round her face and her cheeks looked hollowed out. She was on her back with her eyes and mouth half open and she looked like a wizened doll. There was no movement from her, not a flicker.

'Nan?' Maryann whispered. She knew there would be no reply, that whatever it was that really made Nanny Firkin her Nan, was gone, but she couldn't take it in. Nanny Firkin was always there like the sky, she was supposed to live for ever. This wasn't really her any more, this body lying here. Maryann suddenly felt a prickle of terror pass through her, her whole body shuddered and she backed away, and ran back down the stairs. She left Tiger and ran all the way home again.

'Mom! Mom!'

Seven

The lamplighters were round lighting up as they all ran back to Ledsam Street, Flo still in her apron, with Maryann, Tony and Billy. Flo told the boys to stay out and play in 'Nanny's yard' and snapped at Tony when he tried to come into the house. A Mrs Price, one of Nanny Firkin's neighbours, on hearing what had happened, asked if the boys would like to come into her house. She said she was sorry she hadn't been in to see old Mrs Firkin, hadn't had any idea how ill she was.

At that, Flo poured out her own guilt.

'I never realized myself,' she said to the woman. 'She weren't so bad yesterday – just a bit of a cough like. I'd've come earlier, only with it being washday and that I've 'ardly 'ad a moment to spare.' Maryann watched her mom as she spoke. She was full of grim, pounding emotion. Was it true what her mom was saying? How could Nanny Firkin have not seemed ill if she was poorly enough to die?

She followed Flo back into the dark house. Flo lit a candle, her fingers trembling so much that she had difficulties handling the match, then, carrying the flickering light in front of them, they went up to Nanny Firkin's bedroom.

'Oh—' Flo's hand went up close to her mouth as she looked down at her mother. 'Oh my word – fancy 'er going like that. 'Er heart must've given out. I'd never've thought . . .' She looked across into Maryann's reproachful eyes. 'I ain't stopped all day! I can't be everywhere at once, yer know. I never knew she were this bad – anything like. She just 'ad a bit of a chest on 'er. I was only 'ere yesterday afternoon. You can't say I neglected her – my own mother!'

'I ain't said a word,' Maryann said stonily. 'Did yer feed the cats yesterday, when yer come over?'

She saw her mother's brows pucker in the candle-light. 'No – I never thought. I mean, she were in bed, but I thought she'd been up and about . . .'

Clearly Nanny Firkin had been putting a brave face on things when Flo was there.

'Anyroad – I've got more to worry about than sodding cats. Maryann – go and get the range lit and ask Mrs Price who's nearest to lay 'er out . . . And Norman'll 'ave to come . . .'

Maryann found another candle downstairs. There was a small amount of coal and slack in the coal bucket and she stoked the range, as she had seen her mom and dad do on so many occasions, standing over it to check it was burning. Then she went across to Mrs Price's house. She felt numb and strange, suddenly, as if she were moving through a dream.

'Oh, it's Eve Leadbetter you need,' Mrs Price told her. She gave Maryann the address, directing her to another house further along Ledsam Street.

Mrs Leadbetter was a strong, jolly-looking woman.

'A death in the family, is it? Well, 'er won't be going nowhere – give me an 'alf-hour and I'll be over. Ask yer mom to 'ave some water ready.' She looked down into Maryann's solemn little face. 'Yer nan is it, bab? I'm sorry for yer, that I am. Tell yer mom I'll be over.'

As Maryann walked back across the old, familiar

yard, she saw the shape of the house she'd known as her nan's all her life. Maryann stopped, the biting cold and smokiness of the air hurting inside her nose. The moon was rising, half full, casting a white sheen on the slates. There was still a candle burning in the upstairs window, and another where she had left it on the table downstairs. It looked as if Nanny Firkin was in, going about her normal evening's jobs. But she wasn't in. Nanny wasn't there, despite the frail old body lying stiffly in the bed upstairs. She would never be there any more to go to for comfort, to tell her about school, about Tiger and his antics as he was growing up . . . With a terrible jolt she remembered the earlier events of the day. Tiger was lying there in Nanny's house, at the bottom of the stairs! And soon Mrs Leadbetter would come, and Norman would come – she would be sent to fetch him. No – she couldn't stand any more.

The front door was ajar as she went quietly into the house. There was no sign of the cats, but the fusty, urine-soaked atmosphere in there persisted. Maryann picked up Tiger's body, cradling him in her arms once more.

'Mom,' she called up to Flo. 'There's a Mrs Leadbetter coming. She said she'd be about 'alf an hour.'

'Oh thank God yer back,' Flo called down the stairs. Maryann heard her coming closer and she shrank back. 'Now listen to me, wench – there's a few jobs I need yer to do.'

'What's them, Mom?' Maryann was creeping back through the downstairs room. As her mom descended the stairs, her feet loud on the boards, Maryann pushed the door open and slipped out. She was away and across the yard in seconds.

*

She was running as if her life depended on it, as if by doing so she could escape the terrible events of that day. She still had the feeling of being in a dream.

It's not true, she thought. None of it. Please let it not be true.

Clutching Tiger against her chest was making it hard to breathe and she stopped for a moment when she'd turned out of Ledsam Street and stood panting under a lamp. For the first time she tried to think where she might go. If she went home Norman would be there. Before, she'd have run to Sal to pour out everything that had happened, but Sal was so odd and shut off from her nowadays. And she could go to Nance's. They'd be kind to her, but she couldn't face being there tonight. The house was always so smelly and chaotic and you never knew what state Blackie might be in.

Running on, she climbed through the gap in the fence and down into the cut, near to the bridge where the road passed over the canal. Down on the path, she was suddenly forced to stop. It was so dark! It felt as if a blanket had been thrown over her head and she couldn't see where to take her next step on the muddy path. From under the bridge she could hear, magnified, the drip of water and behind her, in the distance, the clink of a horse's harness. Thank God, someone was coming along – she wasn't alone down here!

She waited a few moments as it came closer, seeing the dim light from the oil lamp on the boat growing stronger, and the shadowy movement of the horse along the bank. She pressed back to let it pass, not wanting to attract attention to herself, then followed on behind. The boat was a joey, a long open cargo boat with a tiny cabin at the back, and a man was standing up at the back, steering it in towards the bank. The carrying area was filled with a dark, gleaming cargo of coal on its way to fuel a factory boiler-house in Birmingham. The horse was walking slowly, wearily, but at a steady pace. As the prow of the boat slid alongside the bank, another man, who Maryann hadn't even noticed, jumped across on to the bank in front of her and reached for the horse's harness.

'Awright!' he called out. 'Come on,' he said to the animal. 'Let's just get 'ome now.'

Maryann was extremely glad of their presence. She knew that sooner or later something would have come along on this busy stretch of water, but the idea of walking along the path, edged by dark warehouses and wharves was very frightening. She soon realized, as the joey continued its journey in front of her, that another boat was following not far behind. She waited for it to pass and saw it was a horse-drawn family boat, also laden down with coal. She couldn't read what it said on the cabin in the darkness, but it looked the same sort of boat as the *Esther Jane* and she followed behind, holding Tiger, comforted by the leathery creak of the horse's harness. They passed under bridges and between such a density of high buildings that even in the daytime the canal at that point was forever in shadow, and the only thing visible was the tiny light from the oil lamps on the boats. The joey had vanished ahead, and she followed the boat to the basin where the cargo was to be unloaded. There were other boats underway with the task, the sounds of shovels digging into the coal or scraping at the boards of an emptier vessel to gather up the last pieces into the waiting barrows to be trundled into the boiler storehouses. Maryann could hear voices and the hard breathing of men exerting themselves, men who had already worked for sixteen or so hours that day. The horse stopped and they found a place to tie up. There were gas lamps here, and she saw the breath unfurling from the animal's nostrils. The lights of the basin jittered brokenly in the black water.

Maryann stood on the edge of this activity, looking along the row of boats, her eyes searching in the dim light. Could it be – please God could it be that the *Esther Jane* was here, and Joel? She crept along peering into the gloom. Many of the boats were joeys, with a few family boats among them. Looking down into one she saw it was nearly empty and the man shovelling up into the barrow on the bank was having to lift each shovelful almost five feet in the air to get it into the barrow. Every time he lifted one he gave a loud grunt at the effort required. Small pieces of coal rattled back into the boat. Noticing her watching, he straightened up, expelling air loudly from his mouth and pressing a hand to the small of his back. He rested on the shovel, wiping the back of his arm over his forehead.

'What're yer after?'

'I want to see a man called Joel Bartholomew,' Maryann said. She was still holding tight on to Tiger and felt small and silly. She wondered if the man could see what it was she was carrying.

'What 'd 'er say?' The figure who had just approached behind the barrow, waiting to empty it, spoke up and to her shock, Maryann realized it was a woman.

''Er's after some bloke, Joel what was it?'

'Bartholomew.'

The two of them were silent for a moment.

'I dunno 'im,' the man said. ''E work on the day boats, does 'e?'

'No – 'e's on a boat like that one—' She pointed. 'Called the *Esther Jane*.'

'Oh well—' The man bent over to start work again. 'Sounds like one of the Number Ones. 'E could be anywhere, bab, if 'e's a long distance ... Needle in a bleeding 'aystack.'

The woman stood braced by the barrow as the man started shovelling again.

'Tell yer what,' she shouted over the racket. 'We'll keep a look out for 'im, like. The *Esther Jane* did yer say?' She called over to another man who was passing. 'D'yer know the *Esther Jane*? One of the Number Ones I should think.'

The man shrugged, seeming almost too exhausted to speak. 'No. Can't say I do.'

'We'll ask around for yer,' the woman yelled across. 'And who shall we say was asking for 'im?'

'Maryann Nelson,' she said, without hope. She wasn't going to find him tonight and that was what mattered.

'Awright then. Cheer up. Word gets about fast.'

Maryann thanked her and turned back along the towpath. There were more joey boats, pulled by plodding horses and mules towards the city's canal loops and basins from the Black Country coalfields, so it was not completely dark, the edges of things picked out by the glow from their lamps. The disappointment that Joel had not been there was an ache in her that cut through her numbness. She hardly knew the man, but he was kindness and warmth; she knew instinctively that he was someone who could help her bear all the feelings that were welling up in her. Of course Joel wasn't just going to be there, like he had been the time before when she came down here by chance! How could she have been so stupid, as if she could just will him to appear? The horror of that afternoon came flooding back to her. First Tiger, then Nanny Firkin. And Sal had gone all funny and wouldn't speak to her any more . . . If only there was someone she could run to . . .

'Oh Tiger!' She held him to her and brushed her cheek against his fur but it was wet and nasty and pent-up sobs began to shake her. She felt her way to the side of the path and laid Tiger in the undergrowth, covering his body as well as she could with grass and cold leaves, then she wiped her hands down the front of her coat.

'Goodbye, Tiger,' she sobbed. 'I loved yer, that I did.'

She walked back, still crying, beside the black water, towards home. Where else could she go? The cold sliced through her now, and under the bottomless winter sky she felt more alone and lost than ever in her life before.

Eight

May 1928

'Where're yer going? Oi come on – wait for me!' Nance trotted imploringly along beside Maryann.

'Down the cut.'

'Can I come with yer?'

'No.'

'Well, *sod* yer.' Nance stopped, hands clasped to her waist as Maryann strode off between the rows of terraced houses without even a glance back in her direction. Bloody charmed, I'm sure, Nance thought. What a pal she'd turned out to be. There was no getting near Maryann these days. Nance turned back towards home. She'd come out specially to see her friend after school. Now she'd be stuck playing with all her brothers again, if they'd have her.

'Still – better than that mardy little cow any'ow.' But she was hurt. She missed Maryann and the days when they'd been able to tell each other anything. Best pals they'd been, ever since they were knee high. But nowadays Maryann was just closed in on herself and they saw rather more of Sal at the house, hanging about, making eyes at Charlie. She'd never much taken to Sal though. She was older than Nance and she'd never been such a laugh as Maryann.

Nance stopped for a moment, almost changing her mind and following Maryann down to the cut. She'd had a few things to tell her about Charlie and Sal and what they were getting up to. But her pride got the better of her again. She'd keep it to herself. She wasn't going where she wasn't wanted. Maryann could stew if that was the mood she was in.

Kicking an old Woodbine packet irritably into the gutter, Nancy slouched back towards Garrett Street.

Maryann climbed through the fence and down through the scrubby trees at the edge of the cut. The leaves were bright green, crumpled and newborn-looking and even with all the various pongs in the air from the factories – metallic, chemical, getting in your throat – down here just in this scrubby little patch you saw some green and got a whiff of spring, which lifted her spirits. She spent all the time she could down here now, drawn to the back-to-front magic of the canal, the way it felt like another world when you were down there, closed in from the rest of the city, somewhere where, for her, the normal troubles of life no longer existed. You saw everything from the other way round down here: the rear ends of buildings, the low level of the path making you look up at things, the watery veins of the canals flowing round and through and under the heart of Birmingham like its secret circulation. It smelled of the murky, bitter water and of the trees, it smelled of a root to the country and of freedom.

'Did you know, children,' Maryann's teacher once told them, 'that Birmingham has more canals running through it than Venice? By length that is, I assume.' She had smiled. 'That's quite something, isn't it, when you consider that Venice is built only on canals instead of roads.'

'What's Venice, miss?' one of them asked.

'Well, I was hoping you'd ask . . .' She had grainy pictures of black and white poles edging canals in front of grey and black houses, gondolas tilting across expanses of dark water towards churches.

'Venice,' she said. '*Venezia.*'

'Bet our canals are a darn sight muckier,' one of the boys said and the others laughed.

'Well, perhaps. But they're very dirty in Venice too, when you consider that *everything* gets tipped into them.'

Everyone sniggered and made revolted noises. Venice didn't really sound like a real place. Real life was contained in these streets of Ladywood, collecting pails of horse muck and jam jars to sell for pennies. Maryann found herself smiling as she reached the path. Only two years ago that had been. Happy days. At school, and her dad and Nanny and Tiger all still alive. The smile fell from her lips and her face took on the scowl it wore habitually now. People had commented for a while: teachers, Cathleen Black – 'well, *she* don't look any too 'appy nowadays' – even her own mom. Now they'd just got used to it.

'I don't know what's come over you two girls,' Flo complained to them. 'There's Sal with a face like a wet Sunday and now you're even worse. And your behaviour to Norman, Maryann – I didn't know where to put myself.'

She'd come back from the canal that night, leaving Tiger's body with the cold companionship of the undergrowth and canal rats. They were all back by the time she got in. She had no idea how long she'd wandered in the cold but it must have been longer than she realized. She expected Flo to scream at her – the usual 'where've *you* been?' – but they barely seemed to

72

notice when she walked in. They seemed only just to have got in themselves: Flo cooking, Norman Griffin sitting by the fire, feet up on the fender, his presence seeming to fill the room. Maryann slipped past and upstairs, where Sal was settling Tony and Billy. Tony was crying and without a word to each other the two sisters sat and tried to comfort him.

'It's awright, Tony,' Maryann told him, starting to cry again herself. 'Nanna's going to heaven to see God and Jesus and all the angels – and our dad an' all.'

'Bu-b-b- . . . I wanna . . . I wanna see 'er!' He was so bewildered, upset and tired.

'I'll see to 'im,' Maryann whispered, and Sal nodded and got up, sniffing. Maryann could see from her expression that she'd been crying too. The children had all been very fond of their Nanny Firkin. She'd always been good to them. Maryann expected Sal to go downstairs, but instead she went across and lay on their bed, the springs creaking as she sank down on it and put her hands over her face.

'And 'e took all Nanna's cats away, and Walt, and I dunno where 'e took 'em!'

'What're you saying?' Maryann turned to Sal.

Sal raised her stricken face. 'Norman took them outside and . . .' She made a wringing movement with her hands. Maryann went cold.

'Not Walt? Not *all* of them?'

Sal nodded, glancing anxiously at Tony.

Choking back her feelings, Maryann managed to sing a lullaby through her tears, stroking Tony's head until his breathing changed and she could tell he was drifting off to sleep. Sal lay on the bed, buried her head in her arms and shook with sobs. The smells of cooking floated upstairs: liver, potatoes, cabbage. The boys had

had slops and if it had just been the family there they'd have had the same, but Norman Griffin had to have his meat and two veg whatever the time of night. Maryann got up and went over to Sal, tapping her gently on the shoulder. It was like after their dad died when they'd cried together up here and Maryann expected her to sit up so they could put their arms round each other. But instead Sal seemed to shrink from her.

'Get off me!' Her voice came out muffled but the venom in it was unmistakable. 'Just don't bloody well touch me.'

'Please yerself,' Maryann said, feeling more tears well in her eyes. Why was Sal being like this? And today, of all days, when they'd lost their nan? The two of them had always been different and they'd always fallen out a lot, but in the end they had been close. But these last few months Sal seemed to have changed so much Maryann couldn't get near her, and tonight those changes felt unbearable. She was going to move away, but she looked back at Sal. She was curled on her side now, her hands over her face as if she couldn't bear to see anything. Now she was looking carefully at her sister she noticed the boniness of her fingers – Sal, bony! She'd always been the plump one. Maryann felt a sudden physical shock go through her. She knew her sister had been strange, moody lately. You couldn't miss the fact. But people said that was wenches for you when they began to get a bit older: she was just going through it, growing up. But now Maryann saw it was more than that.

In a soft, hesitant voice, she said, 'You don't look well. What's up with yer?'

Sal sat up with an abrupt movement and Maryann flinched, thinking for a second Sal was going to slap her. Her blonde hair was wild round her face and she spoke through clenched teeth. 'Why should there be anything up with me – eh? Just bloody well leave me be, stupid!'

Maryann stood up and backed away, leaving Sal glaring at her in the candlelight.

'I dunno what's 'appened to yer' – a sob caught in Maryann's throat – 'but you ain't like my sister any more. Yer 'orrible, I 'ate yer . . .'

'Oh who cares.' Sal lay down, indifferent. 'Just sod off, will yer?'

Maryann got halfway down the stairs and then sank on to one of the steps in the dark, hugging her knees, utterly miserable. She sat rocking for a moment, everything flashing through her mind, all the horrible things that had happened. Norman had done away not just with Tiger but all Nanny Firkin's animals! The swelling, explosive feeling built and built inside her until she could hardly breathe, she was so full of hatred and grief. At last she got up, not giving herself more time to think, and ran down to the front room where Norman Griffin was reading the *Mail*. She snatched the paper out of his hands, screwed it up and threw it into the grate before he had even taken in what was happening. The fire leapt into a great yellow blaze.

''Ere! What the . . .?'

Maryann saw his slitty eyes widen with astonishment and he sat forward as if to get up.

'You killed Tiger, didn't yer?' she shrieked at him. 'Who d'you think you are, killing my little cat and my nan's pets and throwing them out like bits of rubbish! I *hate* yer, you 'orrible man, coming 'ere thinking yer can take over from our dad. Well, yer can't because 'e

75

was a good man and you're just a . . . a fat, murdering pig, that's what you are and I 'ope someone cuts yer bloody throat for yer!'

There were a few seconds of stunned quiet while the clock ticked and the fire crackled, then Flo's voice, 'Maryann!' at the door, her expression more appalled than Maryann could ever remember seeing it before. But she was past caring now, she was in a storm of crying, kneeling on the hearth rug, beside herself with grief and exhaustion.

'How could you've let him, Mom? 'E's a nasty, cruel man. 'E put his hands round Tiger's throat and squeezed the life out of 'im and that's the man you're married to, Mom . . . What'd Tiger ever done to 'im, poor little thing?'

The slapping Flo Griffin administered at that point almost floored Maryann, an almighty swipe across the side of the head.

'What d'you think you're on about, yer little bitch! Shut your mouth before I knock the living daylights out of yer!'

'Flo . . . Flo . . .' Norman Griffin's voice was calm, measured. 'That's enough now – calm down.'

The heat from the fire was intense on Maryann's back and her cheek was raw and burning. She looked out from behind her hands, keeping her gaze lowered, to see them both standing over her. Her eyes were at the level of their thighs. She knew without looking that her mother's face was contorted with rage. Next to her, Maryann looked down at Norman's stockinged feet planted wide apart. His shoes, well shined, were tilted up against the fender beside her. Slowly, she raised her eyes towards him. He seemed immense, looming over her, his face a great doughy ball on the end of his neck. She looked for the fury in his face, the eyes narrowed with loathing. But instead she saw something more puzzling. Norman Griffin looked relaxed, not smiling but as if a smile was waiting under the surface of his face. He seemed in some way triumphant. Maryann stared uncertainly at him, waiting, but then Flo started up.

'I'm so sorry, Norman, for Maryann carrying on like this. The girl's a disgrace, but what with losing my mother today and all . . .'

'Feed the girl and get her to bed,' Norman said. The expression on his face didn't alter and he spoke evenly, betraying no emotion. 'Today's not an ordinary day, is it? We don't want her going hungry.'

'Oh Norman.' Flo sounded quite awestruck. 'D'yer hear that, Maryann, after all the terrible things yer've said? Norman did the only thing that could be done with all yer nan's animals – we couldn't bring them 'ere, the filthy things. Now you get on yer feet and say yer sorry or you'll feel my hand across yer again, wench. Yer've got far better from Mr Griffin than yer deserve, that you have.'

Maryann stood up, her eyes fixed on the coloured splashes in the rug. She was astonished herself, but she couldn't say sorry. The word bulged like an egg stuck in her throat but it wouldn't come out. Sorry! She wasn't bloody well sorry. She wished she'd said far more. She wanted to get a red-hot poker and burn and burn him till he screamed.

'Maryann – say yer sorry!' Flo was almost shouting at her.

Maryann shook her head.

'Let it go,' Norman Griffin said quietly. 'We'll let it go. For now.'

Maryann lay in bed next to Sal. Sal hadn't come down, despite Flo calling her repeatedly. By the time they ate it was eleven o'clock and Maryann almost collapsed into bed and, exhausted and overwrought, fell asleep.

But she was wakened in the dead of night by Sal, moving restlessly at first, whimpering, then thrashing about more and more violently. Her arm came over and whacked Maryann across the chest.

'Eh – Sal!' Maryann pushed herself up on one elbow. 'Sal? You dreaming?'

Sal sat up suddenly and started gagging. Maryann's heart was going like a drum.

'Sal, Sal!' She tried to put her arm round Sal's shoulders, shaking her to wake her. Sal's whole body was heaving as if she was choking on something, her breath coming in sharp, desperate gasps.

'Sal, for God's sake stop it – say summat to me. What's the matter with yer?'

She gabbled on and on at her sister until Sal suddenly took a huge gasp as if something had come unblocked and her breath calmed a fraction. Maryann held her tight.

'Maryann?'

'Oh Sal. You frightened the living daylights out of me! I thought you was choking.'

For a moment Sal seemed to snuggle into her sister's skinny arms as if glad of the comfort. 'Help me, Maryann,' she said sleepily.

''Ow can I help yer?'

'Help me – I've got to get out.'

'Sal—' She wondered if her sister was asleep or awake. It was so dark she couldn't see if her eyes were open. She stroked Sal's shoulder and kissed her. 'I wish yer'd talk to me. Tell me what's up. Yer never talk to me these days, Sal. I want us to get on.'

There was silence then Sal said, 'Don't ever let 'er make you work for Mr Griffin.'

'I won't.' Whatever was she going on about? 'I wouldn't any'ow. Don't think 'e'd want me.'

Sal gripped her arm. 'Just don't. Promise me.'

'I promise.'

Nine

All that spring Maryann stayed away from home as much as she could and haunted the canal bank. The paths were not readily accessible – they were kept well walled and fenced off to stop thieving from the wharves – but she had her place where she could squeeze through. It was her secret escape route through which she could climb into this other world, different and hopeful. She was keeping out of everyone's way and it suited Flo Griffin to keep the cheeky little bint well out of her hair, except that she'd have liked her out of the way with her brothers in tow as well and Maryann had other ideas. Sometimes she took Tony with her, out down to play in the street or to the rezzer, but she never took him to the cut. That was her place. She tried to sneak out as quickly as she could every day, before Flo could tell her to mind her brothers, sometimes even slipping out the back, over the wall and away.

No one had got round to cutting her hair in months, and it hung in black trails each side of her thin face. When school was over she untied the strip of rag which held it back all day, put on her cotton frock in faded checks of dark and lighter blue and old rubber-soled pumps with no socks and she was off, the air on her bare arms, the sun pricking out freckles on her nose.

Ever since the morning a few weeks ago when Sal had sat up to find an ooze of blood between her legs, and Maryann learned that Sal had 'got her first monthly and become a woman' Maryann had decided she didn't want to be a woman very much herself. If it meant putting rags in your knickers and sitting about looking weighed down, groaning that your stomach hurt, they could keep it. And to have to marry horrible men like Mr Griffin so she could live in a half decent house and have meat every day of the week. She wanted to stay as she was for ever, light as wisp, to slip through the fence and run and run along the canal bank until there were fewer factories and more trees and she could lie looking up into leaves arched over her like a great green cathedral.

But she did have a companion to take on her wanderings. That week, after Mr Griffin murdered Tiger, Sal came home from work and, when they were alone, slipped something into Maryann's hand.

''Ere – saw this in the pawn shop. S'for you.'

To her delight, Maryann saw a little china cat, painted quite crudely in grey and black. It was lying down looking up with an alert expression. It didn't have a white throat, but in every other way it could have been Tiger.

'Oh Sal – ta!'

'S'awright,' Sal said.

It didn't make up for Tiger of course, and Sal soon sunk back into herself, but it meant such a lot that she'd thought to buy it. That Sal had reached out to her. Maryann loved the china cat. She called it 'Little Tiger' and carried it everywhere with her in the pocket of her frock.

At the weekends she went down to the cut and walked miles, closing her mind tight against her family, her life at home. She'd been down on the path out through Selly Oak, round the back of Bournville, her mouth watering with the smell of chocolate from the Cadbury factory as trains rumbled past close by, purple lupins amid the grass. Up Winson Green way, on a cold day, water outlets from factories making steam hiss up out of the icy canal, the routes winding and looping round the back of firms and out again, the path darkening under dripping bridges. And when she looked up and took notice she began to realize that Sal was sloping out every weekend too. Nance told her Sal was turning up round their place and she and Charlie were going off together. The park, they said. Never spelled out where. When Nance said it, Maryann shrugged.

'Good for them.'

'I don't know what's got into yer,' Nance said, offended. Before, they'd have gossiped and giggled about this development. Sal and Charlie – ooh, what was going on there!

'There ain't nothing wrong with me,' Maryann said. Nance got on her nerves nowadays. She seemed young and daft, wanting to play games all the time. Maryann just wanted to be away from it all, on her own.

But all the time, even though the canal had become a place of refuge in itself, she was on the lookout for that man, with his big smile and glowing red beard. Joel, who occupied her mind like a great burnished rock. The canals were busy with traffic day in, day out, mostly the joeys, day tripping, doing local deliveries round the factories, but among them were the family boats, the kings of the cut. Maryann narrowed her eyes when she saw one coming, looking for the right colours, the *Esther Jane*'s reds, yellows and greens, the scrolls, roses and castles painted on her doors. One day she thought she saw her, moving slowly along, a mile or so further out from where she had first met Joel. She ran towards the boat, full of excitement. But when she got closer she saw that it was wrong, everything was in a different place from what she remembered. The horse turned out to be a mule, not Bessie, and the boat was called the *Mariella*. A woman stood at the back holding a baby. Walking beside the mule, there was also a boy, about the same age as herself.

'D'yer know a boat called the *Esther Jane*?' Maryann asked him.

The boy hitched up the sleeves of a huge shirt.

'I dunno. *Mom!*' he bawled across towards the boat. At the same full volume he repeated Maryann's question, still plodding along as the mule towed the boat.

A man appeared. '*Esther Jane*? That'll be Darius Bartholomew's,' he called across.

'And Joel Bartholomew?' Maryann shouted.

'Ar – that's 'is son. You looking out for 'um?'

The boy's father gave the same promise as the coal-shovelling man had, those months ago, that he would pass word round. And why didn't she leave a message with the toll clerks?

So she had, a little note saying:

Dear Mr Bartholomew,
    When you pass this way again I'd like to see you, please keep an eye out for me. I'm on the path most afternoons.
    Yours,
        Maryann Nelson.

And one day she was suddenly there, a hazy afternoon when the cut seemed clogged with factory smoke and no breeze to blow it away. She'd walked out almost as far as Smethwick Junction. The horse was skewbald, a solid little mare, and behind her Maryann saw the red, yellow and green of the boat and once more her pulse speeded as she ran closer. Before she could read the name she saw a man in a black hat standing holding the tiller, a huge white beard curling across his chest and, standing behind the small fore-cabin, staring out, a dark-haired girl of about ten years old. On the roof a brown mongrel dog was standing by the water carriers, wagging a long tail. Maryann's excitement drained away. No sign of Joel. It was the wrong boat again.

But as it drew alongside she saw the writing on the side of the cabin. *Esther Jane*. It was her! But where was Joel? Was the old man steering the boat his father?

She was too shy at first to call out to him. He looked rather grand standing there, face shaded by his hat, his back straight, beard billowing in the slight breeze, looking straight ahead of him along the canal. Maryann followed behind the horse towing the *Esther Jane*, and she kept glancing across to see if there was any sign of Joel. After a while, she saw the old man had noticed her and he raised his hand and saluted her. He reminded Maryann of a king in a fairy story, or what she'd been told God was supposed to look like. She waved back, uncertainly. She heard him say something into the cabin of the boat and in a moment she saw Joel's head appear out of the cabin. He waved as well and Maryann felt her cheeks turn pink with pleasure.

'Maryann Nelson!' he called across to her, and she giggled. She heard old Mr Bartholomew call to the girl at the bow of the *Esther Jane*. His voice was deep and growly and Maryann liked the sound of it. The girl began pulling on the tow rope, guiding the boat into the side. The old man moved the rudder and the *Esther Jane* glided up beside her. The girl leapt across the gap once she was able, and caught hold of the horse's bridle.

'Keep her moving, Ada,' Mr Bartholomew ordered. Maryann stood waiting nervously as the boat slid slowly along the bank. Now he was close to her, she could see that Darius Bartholomew had piercing grey eyes under the bushy white brows, and a forehead criss-crossed with lines like a railway junction. When he spoke he had several missing teeth. But best of all, she saw Joel smiling and reaching out his hand to her.

'Come on then, Maryann Nelson, hop in quick.'

She took Joel's hand with no hesitation and her own felt tiny, gripped in his palm, which was caloused and rough as a brick wall. She jumped across into the *Esther Jane* as it glided along, on to the tiny platform from where the boat was steered, and they pushed off again, Darius holding the long tiller while the girl stayed on the path guiding the horse.

''Ere,' Darius said to Joel. 'Tek over.' He stooped and disappeared into the cabin.

'Ent no locks to stop us along 'ere, see,' Joel said.

Maryann nodded. She was rather pleased with their little feat of getting her on board. And she liked the way he treated her as if it was quite natural that she should be there. The dog, who Joel said was called Jep, jumped down beside them, tail wagging frantically.

''Ello!' Maryann cried, patting him.

She stood with Jep beside Joel, looking round. The city began to close in on them more and more, factory walls blocking out the sky and from behind which she could hear clanging and shouting and the roar of machines. The boat moved smoothly along, her paint-work vivid against the blackened walls and leaden water. In places there was a pall of smoke across the cut. She had never felt so excited. There were plenty of other boats coming the other way; some empty, others filled with different cargoes: metal products from the foundries, boxes or barrels of provisions, heaps of refuse. As they passed other boats, Joel touched his cap and called 'How do!' and usually got a reply. Maryann was standing inches away from his elbow. His sleeves were rolled and she could see the red down of hair on his brawny left arm. She could hear his breathing, rather fast, his lungs seeming to make a rustling sound at each breath.

'So – you've been on the lookout for us?' he said eventually. She had been comfortable with his silence and was quite startled when he spoke.

'I wanted to see you again.'

'Bloke in the toll office said. Just tell 'im next time – 'e'll pass it on. Letters ain't no good to us.'

'Oh.' Maryann looked up at him. ''E don't like to be left letters to look after then?'

''E don't mind, but we don't read, us. Never 'ad much schooling. D'you want a go at this?' Joel indicated the tiller. Maryann nodded and Joel showed her where to put her hand, then laid his over the top of hers. 'It's busy down 'ere. Once we get round there we turn in and we can get unloaded.'

He guided her, tweaking the rudder, feeling his way.

'Is that your sister?' she asked, nodding over to the girl leading the horse, who kept looking round at her, curiously.

Joel nodded. 'That's our Ada.' Maryann was wondering how old the girl was, when Joel said, 'Ten years of age she is now. She could pretty well run the boat 'erself if she had to.'

She heard the pride in his voice. How she'd love that! To know how to look after a boat, steer it all herself, live in one of these cabins, away from the streets, from everything about home! Although Ada was younger than her she found herself looking at her with awe. She'd grown up on a boat and knew everything! She was a skinny girl, with dark brown hair and a pinched face, but in Maryann's eyes she looked very capable and grown up walking along at the side of the horse.

After a time of winding through the network of the city's canals they turned into one of the shadowy loops of water branching off it, where they brought the *Esther Jane* to a halt for unloading behind one of the factories. Joel told her they were carrying firebricks from 'up Staffor'shire'.

'Yer can get off of 'er for a bit now,' Joel said. Darius had emerged and was standing out on the side. Ada was strapping a painted can of feed under the horse's nose.

'I don't want to get off,' Maryann said and she heard Joel give his chuckle, like a wheeze in his chest.

'Awright – well, yer can stay on if yer want. But it'll take a good while.'

A little round man with glasses came bustling over, smiling.

'Yer early, ain't yer, pal – what're yer feeding that pony o' yours?'

It was more than two hours before all the firebricks were unloaded. After a time, as Joel, Darius and two other men shifted the cargo, hand over hand, working as a team, Maryann jumped out and went to see Ada and the horse. She was standing watching Bessie finish off her fodder, patting her brown and white neck. Jep was near by, sniffing round.

'She's called Bessie, ain't she?' Maryann asked.

Ada nodded.

'She yours?'

'Oh ar – she's our 'orse. She's a good'un, Bessie is.'

'Never seen an 'orse eat out of a bucket before.'

'That ent a bucket – that's a nostern!' Ada laughed. Maryann liked her cheeky face. 'I got to fill up wi' water. You coming?'

'Awright.'

They each took one of the colourful metal water cans, both covered in painted flowers, and went to a tap round the side of the factory. The ground was a crunched up morass of broken brick, dust and mud.

'So you're Maryann Nelson,' Ada said, holding her can under the tap. 'You met our Joel.'

Maryann nodded.

'You writ a letter.'

'I wanted to see Joel again.' She looked over at him. Joel had stopped, was coughing.

'Why?'

''E was nice to me. And I like the boat.'

'She's called the *Esther Jane* . . .'

'I know,' Maryann said, rather impatiently. It was her turn to fill her can. She heard the water rising in it and supported it with both arms.

'That was our mom's name.'

'Where is she then?'

'She passed on when I was born. Our dad called 'er the *Esther Jane*. Joel says before that she were called *Elizabeth Ann*.'

They carried the water back to the boat. Once more, Maryann was able to go inside the cosy little cabin and she watched as Ada stoked up the range, stood a big pot on the heat and made cups of tea, handing them out to the men. She gave one to Maryann, with lots of sugar in, and the two of them sat out, balanced on the edge, each side of the stern. Ada told her that she and Joel had an older brother called Darius who worked what she called 'fly' on a Fellows, Morton and Clayton boat. This was the city's biggest carrying company, Ada explained seriously, and Maryann nodded: she had seen boats with their name on many times. Working fly meant having a shift of five or six men working day and night to cover the long distances.

''E goes down London,' Ada said. 'Works the Gran' Union.'

Ada asked a little bit about her family, but Maryann could tell as she talked that Ada didn't really understand what her life was like, just as Maryann didn't hers. Ada had never lived in a house that stayed still in one place, the same every day. She was a boat girl, born and bred. Maryann could feel the difference between them. The weather-beaten look of Ada's face, the confident way she dealt with the boat, the horse. Her strength, thin and small as she was, the way she thought and spoke differently.

When the butty was finally empty, Joel came over to them. He looked exhausted.

'Got the stew on, Ada?' he asked. 'And you'd better get yerself home, hadn't yer, little Maryann?'

'But I don't want to go 'ome!' Maryann protested. 'I don't ever want to go home!'

Ten

The light was fading now and the two Bartholomew men's faces were hollowed out with shadows as they stood looking at her. Jep was between them, looking up at their faces questioningly. Maryann presented them suddenly with a strange puzzle, an obstacle to be overcome. Darius, as if at a loss, moved stiffly away and the dog followed him.

'Well, you can't just stay 'ere, can you?' Joel suggested gently.

'Why not?' Her voice was fierce. 'I don't want to go 'ome. I'd rather stay with you.' She looked imploringly at Joel, who was standing with his arms folded. '*Please* – just for a bit.'

'Look – come up 'ere—' He reached his hand out and pulled her up on to the bank, going down on one knee in front of her. 'What's all this, Maryann? You've got a mom and a dad . . .'

'I ain't got a dad!'

'What about your mom?' Ada said. 'You can't just stay out, can yer?'

'She most likely won't even notice,' Maryann said mutinously. She gripped her hand round the little china cat in her pocket, felt her lip begin to tremble. More than anything she'd wanted ever, more even, she thought, than wanting Tiger, she longed not to have to go home that evening. Home meant Sal's terrible silences and Mr Griffin being horribly oily and nice to her. There was something wrong with that after the way she'd shouted and raved at him and she felt as if she was living on borrowed time, that he was cooking up some punishment for her, made all the worse because she didn't know what it was. And there'd be Tony with his big eyes, imploring someone, anyone, to take some notice of him.

'I'll run back in the morning,' she pleaded. 'I'll go to school. And I could sleep anywhere – outside if I 'ave to!' But saying this, she hugged herself, running her hands down her bare arms. It was chilly now the sun had gone down and all she had on was her cotton frock. She put her head on one side, looking with the full force of appeal into Joel's face. He was watching her with a mixture of amusement and concern.

'Sleep outside . . .' He shook his head and she heard him laugh, his chest making a rustling noise. 'Look, Maryann – this ent right. We'll be loading up at dawn and then we're off out of Birnigum again . . . You can come on the boat again – leave a message with the toll clerks. Let me walk you back to your house tonight and see you safe, eh?'

She looked down at her shoes and wanted to cry because it felt as if Joel was babying her, as if she was younger than Ada. She swallowed hard and looked him in the eyes, annoyed at the fact her own were swimming with tears.

'Please, Joel,' she whispered. 'Just once. I won't get in your way.'

'Go on, Joel – let 'er,' Ada said. She seemed excited by the idea. 'She can bunk up on the bench. I'll go on the floor.'

Joel sighed and pushed himself upright so he was

standing over her, hands on his waist and she stood looking up at him like one might at a mountain. She could see his beard silhouetted round his face. She knew he was exhausted, that they'd had a long, hard day's work and why would he relish the thought of having to walk her back home through unfamiliar streets, houses pressing in, to be greeted by her angry family?

Eventually he said, 'Best 'ave summat to eat, then.'

Maryann turned to Ada and saw her grin, her teeth gleaming, and she smiled back, hugging herself even tighter with excitement.

Joel lifted the lid off the stew pot and stirred the contents. Maryann went with Ada to stable Bessie for the night. On the way back Ada explained cheerfully that they had a bowl in the cabin and if she wanted to wee she'd have to go off and find somewhere. Maryann blushed.

'I'd best go now,' she said.

Ada handed her the bowl and Maryann slipped off in the dark and squatted down near the edge of the canal. She decided she liked weeing in the open even if it was a bit nerve-racking – anyone might come along. She saw that the moon had come out.

When she climbed down into the cabin of the *Esther Jane* over the coal box which was used as a step, she found a big smile spreading over her face. She was enchanted every time she stepped inside. However did they manage to live in a space this small? The house she'd grown up in in Garrett Street had been cramped enough, but here the whole living space was nine feet by seven.

'You sit 'ere—' Ada indicated the side bench, next to Joel. Maryann sat shyly beside him, smelling the delicious frying potatoes he was cooking. Jep came up and sniffed at her and she stroked his head until Joel said, 'G'won – out with you,' and he squeezed out past Ada on the step of the cabin.

Darius Bartholomew who was already sitting on the bench at the far end, dressing a wound on one of his fingers with a strip of rag, had given her a grunt of acknowledgement. She was shy of Darius, but sensed that he was gentle, even if he was not sure about her being there. Now he had taken off his hat Maryann saw he had a fine head of grizzled hair. An oil lamp fixed to the cupboard beside the range cast a cosy light round the small space, though she could see Darius was squinting to see properly. She looked round at the grainy ceiling, the pretty paintings of roses and castles on the cupboards, the strips of crochet work edging some of the shelves. It was warm in the cabin from the heat of the stove and the steam gushing out from the kettle. Maryann enjoyed every moment of it.

'You hungry?' Joel said.

Maryann nodded. Joel suddenly grinned at her. 'Nearly ready now. Table down.'

Joel swivelled the lamp round on its bracket so they could see better. Her eyes felt stretched very wide, taking everything in. Joel chuckled again at her amazement and she saw Darius smile as well, his bushy moustache making the smile appear even broader. They were enjoying seeing their own life through her eyes, this quaint little wench from off the bank, who saw things that they had always known and taken for granted as new and surprising.

They ate what tasted to Maryann like the best meal she had ever had. Mutton stew with big chunks of carrot, fried potatoes, bread, from pretty plates and a cup of sweet tea. No one said much and that suited her. Jep was peeping in through the door, nostrils working. She could feel the weariness of the men, although Joel said it had been not too hard a day for them. He was squeezed in on the bench next to her, her skinny legs dwarfed by his solid thighs. She could hear his jaws working as he chewed on huge bites of bread, and in the confined space, the wheezing sound of his lungs. During the meal he started coughing and had to go outside. She heard the coughing go on and on and he came back wiping his eyes.

'Where's she going to sleep, then?' Darius asked. Maryann saw that though he was the older man, the father, it was Joel who was in charge of the *Esther Jane*.

''Er can 'ave the bench,' Ada said again. 'I'll go down under for tonight.'

Joel nodded, patting the bench they were sitting on with his hand. 'This is your bed then, Maryann. How d'yer like that?'

'Ooh yes,' she said. 'Ta, Ada.'

Ada laughed. She seemed to find a lot of things Maryann said funny.

She watched, after they had cleared away the meal and folded back the table, as Darius pulled out the door of the bed cupboard and inside was a thin mattress and a couple of blankets. She thought for a moment he was going straight to bed, but it seemed the men were off to the pub.

'Back a bit later,' Joel said. 'You'll be all right with Ada 'ere.'

Ada grinned, shuffled herself down under the bed with another blanket, rested her head on her coat arm and, to Maryann's surprise, fell asleep straight away. Jep was allowed to come and curl up next to her.

'You can have this,' Joel said, handing her what felt like an army blanket. He indicated that Maryann should lie on the bench. Maryann settled herself down. The bench was hard, but she didn't care. The cabin felt so snug and warm. Joel took off his jacket and folded it roughly. 'Put this under yer head.'

The jacket was worn and the material scratchy, and it smelled of Joel.

'Ta,' she whispered.

Maryann dozed for a while in the light from the lamp, and was woken by the two men coming back in. Darius manoeuvred his way across the cabin and was very soon just as fast asleep as Ada.

'You awright, little 'un?' Joel asked. She caught a whiff of beer on his breath.

'Yes – ta,' she whispered.

'Oh – you won't wake them two – not once they've gone off.' But he still spoke in a soft voice. She watched as his huge shadow moved round the walls of the cabin.

'Joel?'

'What's that then?' He came and sat beside her, his feet up on the step.

''Ve yer always lived on 'ere?'

''Cept for the two year – nigh on – I were in France.'

'Our dad was in France. 'E was a soldier. Were you a soldier an' all?'

Joel nodded. There was silence before he spoke. His talk came in brief bursts, as though he had to get himself ready for it.

'Was 'e killed in the war?'

'No, by a motor car.'

Joel watched her face. 'You got to go back in the morning, little 'un. You shouldn't be 'ere, should you?'

'I know. I will. I just wanted . . . I just like it 'ere.'

For a second she felt his huge hand laid on her head. 'Sleep, that's a girl.'

''Night, Joel.'

He put the lamp out and the cabin was in complete darkness while she heard him move carefully across and settle himself on the bed beside his father.

She did not sleep well that night. The bench was very uncomfortable and she kept feeling she was going to fall off it. It was quite stuffy, and she could smell Jep's doggy smell and it was all strange being there, with no Sal beside her and no Tony across the room. She lay listening to the silence, thinking of the water under them, wondering if she was sleeping above any fish or frogs. After a time she realized it had started to rain, the drops drumming steadily on the roof, which made the cabin feel even more of a cosy refuge when the sky was only a thin shell away. Lulled by its rhythm she dozed, but later was woken by Darius Bartholomew snoring. Some time after that Joel was moving about, coughing, and once he got up and left the cabin. She listened to him straining for breath outside. The sound made her feel sorry for him; a big man's cough so loud, such a wrenching, painful noise.

When she heard him come back in, she said, 'Don't your cough ever get any better?'

He felt his way across, hands moving over her feet, and sat down on the edge of the bench. She heard him say 'Lie down!' to Jep.

'So you're still on the go, are you? Was it me woke you?'

'No.'

'Have yer heard of gas?'

''Course.'

'The sort they used in the war?'

'Did you get gassed?'

'Could've been a lot worse. But my chest's always bad. Worse in the winter.'

'Don't you 'ave a missis?' Maryann asked.

She heard another small seizure of laughter from Joel. 'No.'

'Don't yer want one?'

'Me?' There was a pause. 'Well – yes, course. But it ent happened yet. You don't meet up with people for long, working the cut. Here today, gone tomorrow. Don't s'pose I'm very easy to live with, neither.'

'I wouldn't mind living with yer,' Maryann said.

She heard Joel's laugh again. She liked the way he laughed when she said things, as if he found her surprising and funny.

'Don't know what yer mom'd say about that. She won't be very pleased with you in the morning, will she?'

'No. I s'pose not. But can I come and see yer again?'

'I told you you could. We work up and down this route. We can send word when the *Esther Jane*'s coming through.'

'Oh, *will* yer?'

Joel stood up. Once more she felt him pat her, this time her shoulder. 'You don't give up, do yer? Go on – off to sleep.'

They were up at dawn, the sky grey and rain still falling, the men with many hours of work ahead of them. Maryann said her goodbyes and thanked them.

'Look out for us!' Ada called to her.

'Oh – I'll be back!' She was shivering in her thin frock in the wet, but so happy she didn't care.

She watched as the *Esther Jane* began to slide along the wharf, off to collect her next load to be moved north, Jep standing on the cabin roof, Bessie plodding along, the white blotches of her coat standing out in the overcast morning. Joel waved at her.

'Go on now – I want to see you on your way!' he called, then coughed.

'Come back soon!' she shouted, watching until they were out of sight before she tore back round on to the towpath towards home. She had to get changed into her school clothes!

It was fully light when she got home, the lamps were out, people were setting off for work. When she opened the front door she could hear the sound of her mom shovelling coal. The cellar had flooded so they were keeping it out the back under a tarpaulin. She stood in the front for a breathless moment, hearing footsteps on the stairs, which came down into the corner of the front room. The stairs door opened and Sal appeared, face white as a sheet.

'Maryann! Oh my God, Maryann. Where were yer? I thought summat 'ad happened to yer! Our mom's going to 'ave yer for this!' To Maryann's astonishment, Sal flung her arms round her, sounding tearful.

Flo came and stood in the doorway, hair still plaited from bed.

'Well—' she began menacingly. 'Where in God's name 've you been?'

Maryann shrugged. She wasn't telling *them*. 'Out.'

'Out!' Flo was about to get herself worked up but then the effort seemed too great. She badly wanted a cup of tea and there was obviously no harm done. 'Well – you're back now, ain't yer? We'll 'ave to see what yer father 'as to say.'

Eleven

That evening Maryann was settled in the kitchen after tea, about to start on her bit of homework. She was still wondering with astonishment why no one had said anything. They'd all sat through the meal together and there'd been not a word. Had she got away with it? Then she heard Norman Griffin's voice from the front.

'Maryann – come through 'ere.'

Her heart started racing then, stomach tightening in dread but she kept her expression blank as she went through to the front room, clutching one of her books to her chest. Sal had stood up and was hovering behind Flo's chair. Maryann didn't look at her stepfather. She fixed her gaze on the grate: the poker with its brass handle was lying across the fender. The room stank of his cigarettes.

'I've not heard anything in the way of an explanation about you disappearing off for the night, Maryann, worrying yer mother half to death.'

Maryann hung her head.

'So where were yer?'

She said nothing. Nothing on God's earth was going to make her tell him, even if he took a stick to her. She'd slept on the *Esther Jane*! That was something they couldn't take away from her and she'd never forget it.

'Are yer going to tell me, or what?'

'What.'

Norman propelled his rotund bulk up out of the chair. 'Why, yer impudent little bugger!'

'Maryann!' Flo sat forward on the edge of her chair, eyeing her husband. 'I'll not 'ave yer speaking to Norman like that. Now come on – spit it out. Was you at Nance's, or what?'

'I ain't telling yer.' She looked up into Norman's face. Her legs had gone weak and trembly. Sal had a desperate expression in her eyes, her hand over her mouth.

Norman seemed at a loss for words. 'Go up to bed,' he said, his voice tightly controlled. 'But you needn't think I've finished with yer.'

'Don't do that, Maryann,' Sal said when they were upstairs, undressing in their candlelit room. 'Just tell 'im where yer went for God's sake, we was all worried. Where were yer?'

'I'm not telling you neither!' Maryann flung her cardigan on the chair. Her voice was a fierce hiss. 'And I bloody ain't telling 'im, Mr Smelly Pig!'

'Keep yer voice down – you'll wake Tony. You're a silly little cow, Maryann. You're just making trouble for everyone.'

'Not for everyone – just me. You ain't in no trouble, are yer?'

'That's what you think – you don't know what 'e's like, none of yer – you ain't got no idea . . .' Sal's voice started to crack. She put her hands over her face. 'Oh God, Maryann . . .'

'What the 'ell's the matter now?' Maryann managed a rough transition from being furious to sounding sympathetic. At least Sal was talking to her for once and not just telling her to shove off. She was really crying her heart out as well, shaking with it. 'Come on, Sal – I'm on your side, you know I am.'

'I can't . . .' Sal was shaking all over, could hardly speak, teeth chattering. 'You don't know what 'e might do!'

'Don't talk daft – what's 'e going to do? 'E can't do nothing!'

But the emotion she could feel coming from Sal was so strong that she hugged her tightly with one arm, taking her hand with the other, trying to steady her. 'God, Sal, you're freezing! What's happened – you can tell me. I won't breathe a word, you know I won't. Cross my heart.'

'It's . . . it's . . . I can't . . . It's too dirty . . . I'm dirty . . .'

'Sal!'

But they both froze then, eyes meeting each other's, as they heard the door open at the bottom of the stairs.

'Don't you worry, Flo love, I'll deal with it my way. You stay 'ere – it'll all be sorted out in a few minutes.'

Moving as one body the girls blew the candle out and flung themselves into the bed, half undressed as they were, the springs on the bed giving them away as they pulled the covers up over them, lying down and squeezing their eyes tight shut. Maryann could feel her heart thumping as if it might burst.

The heavy steps came closer. He was in the room, standing looking down at them. They could hear his breathing. Maryann felt Sal grip her arm, squeezing until her nails dug in.

'I know you're not asleep. I don't need a candle to know that.'

There was a long silence, so long that Maryann had an odd floating sensation as if she was dreaming, that he was not really there, but she couldn't open her eyes because it felt as if Norman Griffin could see everything, each flick of an eyelid, as if the room, for him, was full of light. It wasn't completely dark outside and you could just see the outlines of things in the room. She felt Sal give a gasping little breath. What was he waiting for? Why didn't he say anything? Then at last he moved closer along Maryann's side of the bed.

'So – secrets, eh?' Speaking more softly this time, almost singsong.

Another pause.

'Maryann?'

She said nothing, stopped breathing, remembering to do so again with a gasp.

Norman cleared his throat. 'We all have our little secrets, don't we, Sal? See, Maryann, Sal and I've come to a sort of agreement, haven't we, Sal? And I don't see why you shouldn't be part of that now as well. Sal's getting older and there are certain things older girls ain't no good for.'

Maryann felt him sitting himself down on her side of the bed and she squirmed further across towards Sal. What was he talking about? She didn't understand at all. It was no use carrying on pretending to be asleep. She forced her eyes open and, though fully aware that he was there, she jumped when she saw him leaning close, looking at her. Her heart was racing frantically. With an abrupt movement he pulled back the cover and laid his hand on her chest, fumbling round her tiny breasts. His hand felt hot and heavy, pinching and hurting her, and Maryann whimpered.

'Don't touch my sister!' Sal sat up, trying to find a thread of courage, then her own voice trailed pathetic-ally. 'Please Mr Griffin. Not 'er as well. 'Er's only a child. It ain't right.'

'Oh – jealous now, are we!' He laughed. Maryann had the same feeling she had the night she found Nanny Firkin dead, that this couldn't really be happening. It was a horrible dream.

'D'yer want it an' all, Sal?' He reached across and Maryann heard Sal cry out.

'Stop it – I'll call our mom, yer dirty man.'

'Call yer mom!' he mimicked her. 'D'yer think she'd believe a word you say, little Sally Griffin. She ain't gunna believe any of this in a month of Sundays. And you ain't so brave, are yer, not normally.' The voice was hard now, cold as steel, talking on and on, and they had no choice but to hear it.

'Just remember, Sal, what I'll do if I 'ave any trouble from you. Do I 'ave to remind you again, eh? You ain't no good to me now, and I need someone who is. And this one' – Maryann felt him prod her – 'she's still clean and she's got a bit of spirit to 'er an' all. You can leave school in a couple of months, can't you, Maryann? And then we'll see about a job for yer.' He ran his hand down the length of her body, hovering at the top of her thighs. 'Secrets, Maryann. Yer a good wench if yer can keep a secret. Because if you say a word . . .'

He left the threat hanging over them, unfinished, as he got up and went off downstairs.

Sal turned away, crying, curling herself up as tight as she could.

'Sal – oh Sal, don't! Talk to me!' Maryann felt horrible, having him touching her, but she didn't understand what it was all about, she just knew it was all wrong. 'Why was 'e doing that? Sal, tell me what 'e's been doing!'

'I can't.'

'Why not?'

'I just can't tell yer – couldn't say the words. Just, Maryann—' She rolled over, peering down intensely into Maryann's face. ''E's bad and dirty and I don't want 'im going anywhere near you. 'E does things 'e shouldn't.'

'What d'you mean?' Maryann asked in a small voice.

'Things you shouldn't even 'ave to know about. Look, Maryann – you're better at standing up to 'im than me – do anything yer can, even if you get into trouble. But don't let 'im make yer work in that place. Get yerself another job after you've finished school.'

'I will,' Maryann said. 'But why don't you leave an' all? You don't 'ave to stay there, do yer? Just walk out – 'e couldn't do nothing about it.'

'I can't,' was all Sal would say.

Maryann couldn't understand her. It was as if their stepfather had cast a spell over her and she couldn't resist anything he did, wouldn't stand up to him. She just couldn't get Sal to tell her more. She lay awake, full of disturbed feelings at the thought of Norman Griffin's hand moving over her. At the end of this school term she would reach the end of her education, of being a child. She was nearly fourteen. What had he meant when he said Sal wasn't clean any more? Was that to do with the bleeding? None of it made any sense. All she knew was that nothing at home felt safe any more. She thought with sudden longing of Nance. Nance had always been a good pal and she'd treated her badly. If only she could patch things up with her. She needed Nance now more than she'd ever needed her.

Twelve

''Ello there, stranger!'

Cathleen Black appeared when Maryann knocked on the half-open door.

'Well – we ain't seen you in a while, even though Sal seems to think she lives 'ere nowadays! Awright are yer, Maryann?'

'Oh yes, ta,' Maryann said, distracted from everything else by the sight of Cathleen Black's enormously swollen belly. It would have been impossible not to notice that she was expecting another child, she was so big she looked as if it might decide to pop out any moment.

'Look who's 'ere, Nance.' Cathleen waddled over to the range and picked up her cup of tea.

Nancy was doling out spud at the table to the four youngest, and a grubby lot they were, all grime and snot but cheerful. Perce was eleven now, William and George, nine and six, and Horace who was two and a half and kept sliding off his chair and running about. Nance tutted and banged the pan down.

''E won't keep still, Mom!' She picked Horace up and slammed him down on the chair again. 'Just park yerself and for God's sake stay there!'

'Ain't yer going to say 'ello to Maryann?' Cathleen said.

Nance's eyes were unmistakably hostile under her curly black fringe.

'So yer've turned up all of a sudden then. Don't I stink after all?'

Maryann blushed. Nance was in the right. She had been vile to her for ages. 'I know I've been a bit mean to you, like, Nance. Only I wanted to see you.'

'Go on with yer, Nance.' Cathleen put her cup down. 'Get yerself a plateful and yer can go and eat it on the step and cant with Maryann – I'll see to this shower in 'ere.'

'S'awright, Mom,' Nance said stiffly. 'I'll 'elp yer first.'

'Don't talk daft.' Cathleen waved a hand at her. 'You've been carrying on about 'ow yer ain't seen Maryann, so get off with yer. You'll 'ave plenty of 'elping to do when this babby comes, so yer might as well enjoy yerself while yer've got the chance.'

Nance doled the unappetizing food out on to a plate. Maryann watched with a pang of guilt. Her family had much better food than the Blacks – meat every day! 'What won't fatten will fill,' were words often on Cathleen Black's lips, and most of the Blacks' meals were in this vein. Then they both sat squeezed in side by side on the step. The yard was full of metal smells from the foundry at the back.

'Sorry I ain't been over,' Maryann said. 'Only things at 'ome 've been a bit . . . well, you know . . .'

'Is it yer old man?' Nance asked through a mouthful of tater.

Maryann hesitated, then nodded.

''E killed that cat, daint 'e?'

'Who else?' She wanted to pour everything out to Nance. Coming back here again felt nice. Mrs Black chatted to her children, asked them the odd question about school, was always on about one or the other of

106

them's First Communion. She took an interest, unlike her mom. Being here was a taste of the old times and it made her long for everything to be as it was before, back on the old footing, without all the horrible things going on at home. But she didn't have words for all of it. How could she say what had happened last night, Norman Griffin pawing at her through her nightshirt? She couldn't tell Nance or anyone that, but she did want to joke and laugh like they used to, before her dad died and everything went bad.

'It's my birthday next week,' Nance said. 'I can walk out of that school and never go back – get myself a job of work. You can an' all soon, eh?'

Maryann shrugged. 'S'pose so. Where're you gunna go?'

Nance grinned. 'Kunzle's'd be nice. Eat cakes all day! I'll go round the firms, see who'll 'ave me. Eh—' She nudged Maryann. 'If you're looking too, why don't we go round together?'

'I've got a bit of time to go yet.' Maryann felt cheered. Nance was so warm-hearted and she already felt forgiven.

'Oh ah, that's a thought. Anyroad, I'll let yer know what it's like, wherever I end up.'

They chattered on a while while Nance scraped up the last of her food, and they had a bit of a giggle.

''Ere—' Nance grinned and budged up a bit closer. 'I saw your Sal and our Charlie at it kissing the other night. They was in the brew'us and they never knew I was 'aving a look in!'

'They never!' Maryann didn't know whether to feel glad or not. Sal had turned fifteen. She was growing up. But she'd never said a word about it. There were too many things about Sal she didn't know nowadays.

'She was all over 'im,' Nance went on with relish. 'She ain't backward, your Sal, and that's a fact!'

The two of them were tittering over it, but while Maryann was intrigued – Charlie Black was a handsome devil, there was no denying – she felt hurt and left out.

'She never breathes a word to me about it,' she complained to Nance.

'Well, what d'yer expect! – O-oh,' Nance said as they heard loud muttering and blaspheming approaching along the entry.

Blackie appeared in the yard, walking with a gorilla-like gait, arms swinging, cap on askew, his jacket hanging open.

'Dad,' Nance said. 'Over 'ere.' She and Maryann got up out of the way and Blackie looked and looked.

'The door!' He pointed a wavering finger. 'Shome-one moved . . . the fuckin' door.'

'Oh come on in, yer silly sod,' Cathleen shouted from inside.

Blackie stumbled in through the door and they heard a grunt as he fell into his chair, followed by a loud, grating belch.

'Well,' Nance said with a wry look. 'That's 'im finished for the day.'

Friday night was bath night. Maryann got home feeling much more light-hearted after her visit to Nancy's and found Flo filling up the tin bath which usually hung on a rusty hook on the wall of the privy outside.

'Glad you're back at last,' she said resentfully. 'Yer can come and bath the boys for me.'

Maryann agreed gladly. She enjoyed soaping the

boys in the warm water, the feel of Billy's soft little body. He was nearly five now, still small, with shoulder blades like little angels' wings.

While she was pouring in a last kettle of water, Norman arrived home, bustling through the front door. Maryann felt herself tense as if there were pins pricking her skin. He was not a man who could move quietly. He was always a noisy, disturbing presence about the place. She hated the way he came and looked in when they were bathing, especially after last night. Sal refused ever to have a bath in the house now: she went down to the public bathhouse.

He came and stood at the kitchen door, hat in hand. 'Oh-ho, bath night, eh?'

Well, it's not as if we only do it every hundred years, Maryann thought. She didn't look up at him or answer, but she could feel him staring at her.

'Your tea's nearly done, Norman,' Flo said. 'Yer might as well come and sit down.'

'I'll just wash my hands.' He came and leaned over the bath opposite Maryann, took the bar of soap and rubbed his stubby white hands, using the nails of one hand to dig out the grime from under the nails of the other. She watched, repulsed. For a moment he looked into her face and she could feel his breath on her cheek. Maryann got up abruptly and moved away to call Tony and Billy.

She bathed the two of them while Norman sat at the table eating his mutton stew, Flo sitting opposite him. He ate up quickly, then sat back and lit a cigarette, watching them lazily, his eyes narrowed a little.

'I can do myself,' Tony said, so Maryann concentrated on Billy, splashing about to make as much noise as she could and drown out the sounds Norman made when he was eating. Billy laughed, pouring water energetically over his fair hair.

'Go easy,' Flo snapped. 'You'll soak the whole floor else. Where's Sal got to, Norman?'

'She said she 'ad to go to the shop for yer.'

'For me? I never asked 'er.'

Maryann rubbed Billy dry on a strip of cloth and he put his clothes on again.

'You go in next,' Flo said. 'Use the water 'fore it gets cold.'

Maryann felt her body go stiff. Not with him sitting there, she thought. 'When tea's finished,' she said.

'Oh, that's awright – you can carry on,' Norman said.

Maryann looked at her mom mutinously. 'I'll wait till you've finished.' And she walked off upstairs, knowing Flo was too idle to follow. When she was certain Norman was ensconced in the front room with his paper, she crept down, closing the kitchen door. Flo was in there, tutting about how long Sal was going to be. Maryann could hear the boys playing out with some other lads at the back.

She slipped her brown skirt off and her cream blouse, wishing she had the room to herself, without even her mom there. She felt suddenly curious about her body and would have liked to be alone to have a good look. Lately she had sensed it changing, little swellings on her chest when it used to be quite flat. But there never seemed to be a place where you could be on your own without a brother or sister or *someone* gawping at you.

She dipped one foot in the water.

'Can I 'ave one more kettle, Mom?'

Flo sighed. 'Oh, go on then. As it's boiled.'

She topped up the bath with hot water and it felt lovely as she sank down into it, even though it was scummy from Tony and Billy going in it before. She couldn't quite lie down full stretch any more, she had to keep her legs a bit bent up and in the winter you could feel the cold nibbling round whichever bit of you was sticking out of the water. But today it was warm and she relaxed, then sat up and began soaping herself. She was just rubbing suds over her shoulders and arms when the door opened and Norman came in. Maryann instinctively crossed her arms over her chest and tucked her head down.

Get out! she felt her whole being scream. *Just get out of here and don't look at me.*

He had his hands pushed down in his trouser pockets. Maryann turned away, trying to block him out.

'That looks nice in there,' he said. ''Ere – let me put some of that soap on your back for you.'

'No!' she almost shouted. 'I can do it myself.'

'Oh, don't talk so silly, Maryann,' Flo said irritably. 'Norman won't bite yer – 'e's just trying to give yer a hand. You can't reach yer back, can you?'

He was kneeling down, rolling up his sleeves and grinning at her. She cringed away from him.

'There you go—' Round and round he rubbed the soap in his hands until they were frothy with it. Her back was rigid. She wanted to jump out of the bath and run away from him, but she couldn't move.

Flo went to the back door. 'Billy? Billy! Get in 'ere now. It's time you was getting to bed.'

He was kneeling on her left, she could smell him. Death, he smelled of. He began to soap her back, his right hand circling round and round, caressingly.

'There,' he said. 'Nowt wrong with that, is there?' The soap slid from his left hand into the bath with a plop. 'Oops. Now where's that gone then?'

He was pretending to look for the soap, but she saw his eyes were on her breasts, his hand still circling on her back.

'That's the trouble with soap . . .' His breathing was louder. 'Slippery blooming stuff . . .'

'Billy!' Flo was shouting, furiously.

Maryann couldn't believe at first what she was feeling: a hard poking between her legs which for a second she couldn't connect with anything but then knew it was Norman's finger or thumb, jabbing, forcing up into her.

'Youch!' she cried, pulling away with a splash. 'What the 'ell 're yer doing?'

'Ah – 'ere it is!' A quick sweep of the bath and he brought up his hand, triumphantly holding the soap. They looked into each other's eyes and his were as icy as pebbles. Maryann turned cold all over.

'Sorry – did I catch yer by mistake?'

Flo, oblivious to all this, was bringing Billy crossly in through the back door. 'Look at the state of yer – you'll need to go back in the bleedin' bath!'

'Language, love!' Norman stood up. 'There we go – another one all fresh as a daisy.'

'Out you get then, Maryann,' Flo said. 'Billy's dipping back in.'

Maryann sat quite still. She couldn't look at Norman, at any of them. Shame seemed to burn up from her chest to the top of her head. Was this what Sal meant, this, and more, things Maryann could not even imagine? After a moment, Norman went out again, closing the door.

'It's nice the way 'e tries to be a dad to yer,' Flo commented.

Two days later, when she went up to their room, Maryann found Sal sitting on the bed. Her left arm was held out, underside upwards in front of her. In her other fist was a kitchen knife with which she was stabbing at her outstretched arm, making jerky little digs into her flesh, some not breaking the skin, others harder. There was a thin trail of blood running down over her fingers.

For a second, Maryann couldn't believe the sight in front of her.

'Sal! What 're yer doing!' She seized the knife, stopped its jabbing motions which seemed to be happening almost independently of Sal's will. She opened her sister's fingers and prised the knife away from her. Sal looked round mildly as if woken from a dream.

'Blimey, Sal – what've yer done to yerself? Look, I'll go and get summat to wipe yer.'

She bound her sister's arm with a rag then sat beside her, half afraid to touch her. Sal looked so beautiful sitting there, pale and still, the evening light catching her hair.

'Is it *him*, Sal? What's 'e done to yer, eh?'

Sal just shook her head, seeming unable to speak.

'Is 'e . . . is 'e . . .' Maryann could barely say it, like when she had wanted to talk to Nance and no words would come, not for something like that, that couldn't really be going on, not in real life. She sensed that whatever had happened to Sal was much worse than anything he had done to her, but she didn't know about anything, couldn't imagine what it could be. 'Is Norman *dirty* with yer?'

To her enormous vexation Sal suddenly started laughing, head back, until the tears ran down her cheeks.

'Well, *what*?' Maryann said furiously. She was trying to help and this was what she got. 'What's so bloody funny then, eh?'

'Dirty! Oh, Maryann!' Still laughing away.

'Well, I meant like the other night – touching yer and stuff.' She couldn't go on.

Sal turned to her, solemn again. 'Don't let 'im near yer, Maryann, that's all.'

Thirteen

Cathleen Black had her new baby. Nance had been allowed to help out with the birth and there was great celebration when it turned out to be a girl.

'I tell yer, Maryann,' Nance said after, 'I never want to go through that in my life. Our mom says it's like passing a pig's bladder. She was on the go till right the last minute an' all. I kept telling 'er, "Mom, just go and 'ave yerself a lie down," but she says, "No, Nance – I've got to see the lads 'ave 'ad their tea. Any'ow, the longer I'm on my feet, the quicker the babby'll come."'

Maryann had her first peek at baby Lizzie when she was only one day old, with her mop of black hair, scrumpled up face, closed eyes and tight little fists. She was allowed to go up into Cathleen and Blackie's room where Cathleen lay in a motley mess of bedding consisting of what looked like rags and coats. The room was bare except for the metal bedstead and a chamber pot, and though the window was open there was a sickening miasma of sweat and blood. Cathleen looked hollow-cheeked but she raised a smile when Maryann said, 'Oh, ain't she lovely!'

'Makes a change from all them lads, don't she?' Cathleen said. ''Bout time we 'ad a wench to finish off with, 'cos I'm buggered if I want to go through all that again.'

Billy was also captivated by Lizzie, by her sheer

smallness. He stood for ages stroking her waxy hands, trying to get her to straighten her fingers.

'Why don't our mom 'ave any babbies?' he asked.

'Well, you was a babby not so long ago,' Cathleen said, adding as an aside, 'She's got more bloody sense, that's why.'

Outside, when the boys had gone off, Maryann asked Nance, 'What's yer dad been like over 'er?'

'Oh, 'e's soft as anything with 'er. 'E's always wanted another girl. Said she were 'is life's work or summat – and that were before 'e'd been down the pub!'

'Nance—'

'What?'

'How do – I mean, how does the babby get in there – d'yer know?'

'All I know is it's got summat to do with a man's – yer know – thing. 'Is willy.'

'Oh.' Maryann's brow puckered. 'Has it? You sure?'

''Course,' Nance said, all worldly-wise, though she wasn't really sure at all.

Maryann had never seen a man naked, except for her brothers. When she was younger she'd wondered whether their little willies grew with them when they got bigger, or did they stay the same size?

But she knew the answer to that now, for certain. On Sunday afternoon, Sal had gone out, and Flo was with her brother Danny and her sister-in-law Margie who had come on with her babby and she'd promised to help if she could. Norman was in the front room. Maryann was just about to call the boys to go up to the Blacks'.

'Maryann—' She heard his voice calling softly through to the kitchen where she was clearing up.

'What?' She stuck her head round the door.

'Come 'ere a minute, pet.' His voice was wheedling. It didn't quite sound like him.

She went and stood beside the chair. He was lolling back, feet up on a stool, and his face was flushed even though there was no fire in the grate.

'Fancy going to the pictures?'

'What, now? All of us?' She had had other plans, but she did love the pictures. There were the talkies now, too, people really speaking instead of just the piano banging away while you tried to read the words off the screen.

'I'll give yer a shilling and you and that Nance can go with the lads. Treat yerselves.'

'Oh – ta,' Maryann said awkwardly. Was this him 'trying to act like a dad' again? Anyway, if he was in a good mood she might as well make the most of it.

'C'm'ere first.' He beckoned her closer. 'Part of the treat for yer. There's a couple of tanners in 'ere – you come and get 'em.'

He held his pocket open, shifting in his seat.

'Go on, Maryann, I won't bite!' He was grinning, showing his yellow teeth, sweat on his forehead.

She slid her hand into the open pocket, expecting her fingers to find the two sixpences tucked in the soft material. But as soon as her hand was in there Norman slapped his own hand over it and pulled hers over, pressing it down on to his hard willy, waiting down there. She yanked away, managing to pull free and run to the door.

'Tony! Billy! Come on, quick – I'm going now.'

He was laughing. 'Don't you want your shilling then, eh?'

He wouldn't leave her alone these days. Watching

her all the time, so the feel of his eyes on her made her feel dirty. Once or twice, when he got the chance, he'd rub against her, or feel her round her chest. She could never relax when he was about and she stayed out all the time she could. Outside, at school or with Nance it was all right. She could shrug it off because these disgusting things weren't happening away from the house. It wasn't real out there, and she could forget. She dreaded being at home. Sometimes Maryann thought about trying to tell her mom. But any little thing she criticized about Norman and Flo was down on her like a ton of bricks. She'd never believe Maryann. She was always on his side. He seem to infect everything. Even when he wasn't in there were reminders of his presence: the oily dent in the chair where his head went, the paper thrown on the floor where he left it, the smell of his fags hanging about the place. Always there. Always.

It was well into June and the weather was warm now. Thin shafts of evening sunlight had found their way in through the back windows, dust motes swirling in them. Maryann smiled, remembering how Tiger used to jump up and biff at them when he was a kitten.

Sal had come in with Norman from work, had eaten her tea and the last Maryann had heard from her was the slam of the front door as she took off out again. Huh, Maryann thought, covering Tony up in bed. But she couldn't really blame Sal. She really seemed to be sweet on Charlie Black and if Maryann could have thought of a place to go she'd have gone out as well. She was beginning to get the hang of when the *Esther Jane* might be likely to be in town from the run to

Stoke. She left messages at the toll offices and ran down to ask. But she didn't hang around the cut any more, waiting. She'd seen Joel, Darius and Ada once since her night on the boat, but they'd been held up along the cut and were pressed for time, so Maryann just walked along a bit of the way with Ada and Bessie and Jep, and left them to get on. They all seemed pleased to see her though, and Joel waved.

'See yer next time!' she yelled as they headed into the gloomiest part of the cut.

She'd sung Billy a lullaby and was coming downstairs again when she heard a knock at the front door, then Flo's voice, 'Danny – what're you doing 'ere? Oh my God, what's up?' Danny's wife Margie had also given birth to a little girl, Cissie, who was now four days old.

Maryann heard her uncle panting. He must have run all the way over.

'It's the babby, Flo, 'er's bad and Margie's in a right state over 'er. Can yer come over and 'elp us, right quick? 'Er breathing's terrible.'

'Well, I don't know as there's much I can do,' Flo was saying. 'You'd be better fetching the doctor out.'

'We 'ave, but she wants you there – please, Flo—' Maryann came down into the front room and saw her Uncle Danny looking as if he was going to burst into tears. 'We'd feel better if you was there. You know what to do with babbies – we don't know 'ow to go on!'

'You go, Flo,' Norman said. 'Yer brother needs yer – there'll be summat you can do, with all your know-'ow, I'm sure.'

'Awright,' Flo agreed reluctantly.

Maryann watched her mother disappearing out

through the front door, and it was only then it dawned on her. If Flo went out she'd be all alone in the house with Norman, except for the boys sleeping upstairs. She tore out behind her mom as if she was on springs.

'I'm coming with yer! I might be able to 'elp.'

'Oh, don't be daft, Maryann!' Flo was all flustered. 'Go on in with yer. Danny and Margie've got enough on their plate without you getting under all our feet.'

'Please, Mom, let me come!'

'Maryann, go back inside.' Danny spoke roughly in his anxiety. 'Do as yer mom says. We need 'er for now.'

Maryann knew she couldn't argue. She stood on the step watching them disappear along Anderson Street. The sun was sinking now. Martins' huckster's shop was still open of course, along the way. She felt like going and standing in there, amid all the mixed smells of rubber and soap and sweets until her mom got back, but she had no money and whatever could she say to Mrs Martin?

'Come in and shut that door, Maryann,' Norman Griffin ordered her.

Her heart was thudding. The idea of being left alone with Norman Griffin now alarmed her so much that the hairs on the back of her neck were standing up and her hands shook as she closed the door. But how could she refuse?

There he was, sat in his chair as normal, she told herself, clasping her hands together so that he should not see the tremor in them. What was there to worry about? He was just sitting, looking across at her. And she knew better than ever to put her hand in his pocket again.

'So, then,' he said.

'I think—' Maryann swallowed. She was straining to keep her voice casual. 'I'll go up to bed now.'

'Oh, it's too early for that, ain't it? Why don't yer come over 'ere and sit with me for a bit?'

'No, I, er . . .' In her awkwardness she rubbed one shoe against the back of her other leg like a much younger child. 'No, thanks.'

Mr Griffin leaned forward with a grunt and eased himself up out of the chair. Blood started to pound in her ears. But Norman went over and drew the curtains, even though it was still light outside, so that the room turned dim and green. He lit the gas mantle and the pop-pop sound started up. Then he stood with his hands straight down by his sides, looking at her. Maryann ran her tongue over her lips and looked down at the floor. Slowly, knowing in her heart that he was not going to let her go, that there was something he wanted badly from her, she began to edge across the room towards the door to the stairs.

'No, don't go!' His voice had a hard edge. 'I said stay 'ere with me.'

He walked over to her.

'I like you better than your sister, I must say.' He picked at a lock of her dark hair and stroked it. She drew her head back. 'D'you know why, Maryann?'

Still not looking at him, she shook her head.

'You ain't like her. You've got more fire about yer and I like that in a woman.'

Woman? Maryann thought. *But I'm a girl, not a woman. I'm still at school.*

'Sal were good to me for a bit. Helped me out and did what I told 'er. See, we men are different from you women.' He spoke in a very reasonable voice. 'We need – satisfying – now and then. That's what comes natural

121

to us, see, that's all. And you girls have a way of getting me ... excited.' He was taking his jacket off. She heard him throw it on to the chair.

His hands came down on her shoulders and she cried out.

'No need for that. I'll show yer what to do. This is what wenches're made for. I'm just teaching yer, that's all. Now – you just do as I say and we'll 'ave a nice time.'

His arms came round her and she felt herself lifted off the ground and carried to the peg rug by the hearth. When he pushed her down she banged her head on the floor and gave a moan of pain, which seemed to arouse him. She heard his hard, ragged breathing.

'What're you doing?' Her voice had gone squeaky. 'You shouldn't be doing this.'

'Who says so?' His voice had lost its wheedling tone and was as cold as the frozen east wind. 'Who's gunna stop me now? You, yer little bitch, eh?'

His hands forced up her skirt and she felt him tearing her underclothes down.

'No!' She lashed out, trying to kick him. 'Stop it ... stop it! Get off me.'

'Shut yer mouth.'

Everything went darker as he leaned over her, blocking out the light and his weight came down on her so she was struggling then only to be able to breathe, gasping. Her legs were being forced apart and that hard prodding started like in the bath until she was sobbing it hurt so much, with him pushing and jabbing, burning his way up inside her, panting in her face, filthy words dropping from his lips.

When he climbed off her she was like a rag doll, dizzy, her back sore and smarting. She went very cold, starting to shiver until her teeth chattered, wet stuff oozing out down her legs as she stood up.

Mr Griffin went out to the kitchen and she heard the splash of water. He came back, buttoning his fly.

'Now. That's it then. Sal could keep a secret and I know you can. Anyhow – your mother wouldn't believe a word if you started on about this – you know that, don't you? You can go to bed now.' He turned away. 'I've finished with yer.'

She could barely remember getting to bed, struggling to wash first, shaking so much she could scarcely attend to herself. All the water in the sea could not wash Norman Griffin off her. She lay alone in the bed, hugging herself tightly with her arms, sobbing and shaking. She felt frightened and sick and bereaved, as if there was something enormous that she had lost, and she wept for all the losses she could think of: her lovely dad, her nan, her little cat. All those she had loved and would never again be able to hold in her arms.

Fourteen

She slept for a time in fits and starts, crying at first, dozing, dreaming dark, broken dreams, and still feeling, even in sleep, the ache between her legs. Then she jolted awake as she heard Norman Griffin coming up to bed. The light of his candle and his shadow moved past the crack in the door, and for those moments she stopped breathing. Was he coming to her room . . .? Not with Tony here, surely? She gripped the cover close to her throat.

But she heard him go to his and her mother's room across the tiny landing. She knew from the solitariness of his sounds that Flo was not here, had not come home. There must be something dreadfully wrong with baby Cissie that she'd had to stay out at Uncle Danny's house so long. But even more worrying was that Sal was not lying beside her, and that had never happened before. Where in heaven could she have got to? She lay there, hearing him moving, fear and anxiety growing in her until she could hardly breathe.

She wasn't going to be able to sleep. She got out of bed, tiptoed over to pull the door open and listen. She could hear Norman's loud, stertorous breathing from the front bedroom. Pig, she thought. She pulled on layers of clothes and crept downstairs to the front. The fire was dead in the grate so, as quietly as she could manage, she scraped the ash out, leaving it in a metal pail by the back door, then built up a new fire. She'd always liked putting a fire in the grate, even though it was dirty work. It made the room cosy, and she was a little comforted by the sight of her twists of newspaper as they jumped, flaming into life at the touch of her spill. The flames filled the room with warm, twitching light. She sat on the rug with her knees close to her chest, pulling her baggy cardigan down over them, and watched the fire, sometimes leaning down to blow on it, or adding a few more bits of coal to keep it going properly. Behind her the room was very dark, but the fire in front of her felt like her warm protector.

She tried to shut out any thoughts of Norman Griffin, even though this was the very spot where he'd forced her down on the floor. If she hadn't been so sore still it wouldn't seem real now. But she wouldn't let her mind dwell on it.

Where are you, Sal? she wondered again and again. With each half-hour she grew more worried. The fire was glowing a deeper orange now. After some time there was a tiny rattle of the mechanism from the clock on the mantle before it struck its gentle bong-bong-bong, then it went quiet again and there was only the sound of the fire.

She woke to the sound of Norman Griffin's feet on the stairs and found herself lying cold and cramped by the grey ash of a dead fire. Her heart pumped violently at the sound of him approaching and she sat up. The clock said half past seven. When Norman appeared he was already dressed.

'Where is everybody?'

125

'Mom must still be at Uncle Danny's.' Maryann sat hugging her legs again, shivering.

'Sal still abed?'

Slowly Maryann shook her head, though with a sense of unreality. Perhaps Sal *was* in bed after all? Maybe she'd been there all the time, or slipped in after Maryann had fallen asleep?

'Well, where is she?'

He turned impatiently and went back upstairs, looked in girls' room, then was back down. 'Where's 'er gone?'

'She never come in,' Maryann said, looking down at her knees, the loose-knit mesh of her blue cardi stretched over them. She knew then for certain that something had happened.

'No bloody breakfast on the go neither, I s'pose.' There was a coarseness to Norman this morning, usually hidden under his oily smoothness when Flo was about. 'Get the kettle going, wench – at least yer can make a cuppa tea.'

Maryann did as she was ordered, then went up to wake Tony and Billy. She sorted out breakfast for Norman and the boys, blanking out all other thoughts.

'Tony, you'll 'ave to go to school with Alec,' she told him. 'I'll have to stop here till our mom gets home.'

'Oh Maryann!' Tony complained.

'Do as your sister tells yer!' Norman said, with such savagery that Tony cowered.

'You'll be awright,' Maryann said to him. 'Only I've got to stay – who's going to mind Billy, else?'

Tony nodded, dumbly.

'Tell that Sal to get 'erself down the shop when 'er turns up,' Norman said, putting his hat on by the front door. 'I'll 'ave a few things to say to 'er, that I shall.'

'Come on, Billy – we've gotta go out.' Maryann impatiently shoved her little brother's shoes on. 'Push yer feet in, will you!'

'Where we going, our Maryann?'

'You'll see when we get there.' She dragged him out and along Anderson Street, then softened. 'You can come and play with Horace.'

'Oh!' Billy moaned. 'Horace is a babby, I don't wanna play with 'im!'

'Well, 'ard luck 'cos yer gonna 'ave to.'

Pulling Billy along so he had to run, Maryann went as fast as she could to Garrett Street. They were about to run down the entry but found it blocked by Blackie Black and his barrow coming the other way, loaded with his tools and metal hoops. He wasn't looking any too good but he managed a wan smile.

'Awright, Mr Black?' Maryann said.

'Awright,' he murmured amiably. Maryann turned to watch him, saw how his walk had become a shambling, dragging gait. But he didn't seem to have noticed anything was amiss, anyroad.

Everyone was out except Cathleen and Horace and the baby Lizzie. The room was in a right state, spilt tea and crumbs all over the table, and on the floor, dirty clothes, a pile of nappies, the lot.

Cathleen was at the table, Lizzie tucked in on her lap, feeding. She pulled her blouse together a little, but not before Maryann had seen the white, mottled skin of her breast. 'What're yer doing 'ere, Maryann? No school?'

'Mom's at Uncle Danny's – the babby's took bad,' Maryann said. She felt tears come into her eyes. All the fear and worry of the night welled up. 'And our Sal's disappeared. She daint come home last night so I come to see if she was 'ere last night, sleeping over?'

Cathleen gave a laugh which dislodged the baby from her breast. 'Sleeping over – 'ere? Where d'yer think 'er'd sleep – in the coal scuttle? Sorry, Lizzie – 'ere yer go.' She pushed her nipple back between the baby's gums.

'But she was with Charlie last night, wasn't she?' Maryann was frustrated by Cathleen's lack of concern.

'They went off together in the evening. I never saw 'em – Charlie must've come in late last night. I were that tired what with this one up and down, I got me 'ead down when I could, and Blackie were too kalied to notice, or 'e'd've been giving out to 'im.'

'So Charlie was here this morning?' Maryann struggled to be patient.

'Well, I s'pose 'e was – I never saw 'im though, come to think of it. 'E must've come down and gone off to work, like.'

Clearly Cathleen had no real idea whether either of them had ever come back the night before.

'They'll turn up,' Cathleen said serenely. 'I s'pect they're both at work by now. Don't get mithered.'

Loath as she was to go anywhere near Norman Griffin, Maryann called in at Griffin's Undertakers. There was no sign of Sal.

'I'll tan 'er bloody hide when I find 'er,' Norman ranted. 'We've got a lot on today.'

*

Maryann spent the rest of the morning worrying and trying to occupy Billy. She could see why he drove her mom mad with his non-stop chattering.

At last, just as Maryann was thinking she ought to get something for his dinner, she heard the front door open and she rushed through from the back, leaving Billy in the yard. Flo came in, exhaustion showing in every line of her. When she turned from closing the door, Maryann saw that her eyes were red and her face was different, somehow, tighter.

'How's little Cissie, Mom?' she whispered.

Flo shook her head, taking off her hat. 'She daint make it, Maryann. The doctor came, but she breathed 'er last this morning, poor little mite. I stayed for a bit to be with Margie.'

'Oh Mom!' Maryann was so tired and worried that she was not far from tears as it was, and the thought of babby Cissie dying brought them on fast. Poor little thing, what had she ever done to anyone!

Flo sat down, filling up herself. 'Oh, it's a terrible thing to see a babby die, Maryann. Thank God I never had any more of yer to worry about.' Unguardedly she added, 'I've been lucky marrying a man who's not that way inclined, that I have!'

'Mom—' Maryann wiped her eyes, though the tears just wouldn't seem to stop coming. 'It's – I know yer've got enough to worry about, but – it's Sal . . .'

'What?' Flo's tone was sharp. 'What about 'er?'

'She never came 'ome last night, she ain't at work and Mrs Black don't know where she is neither.'

'Mrs Black? Why the hell should she know where our Sal is?'

'Because—' Maryann stopped. Sal didn't want

anyone to know, that was obvious, or she'd have told them herself.

'Because what? Come on, get on with it.'

'Well, Sal's been knocking about with Charlie Black – and Mrs Black ain't quite sure 'e came home last night neither.'

Flo stared at her as if none of the sense of this was getting through to her brain. 'You mean they might've took off together?'

'I dunno,' Maryann said miserably.

Flo sank down on the chair behind her. 'They can't've done. What would Sal want to do that for? She's comfortable enough 'ere. Got no worries. Anyone checked where Charlie works?'

Maryann shook her head.

'Go on. See if 'e's there.'

It was quite a walk to the place where Charlie had his current employment, a dark workshop in a side street where they turned out copper rods and wire. Charlie Black? No, he hadn't been in. And if he missed another day there were plenty of others who could do his job.

By the time Maryann got home Flo was asleep and she slept for the rest of the afternoon. The evening wore on and there was no sign of Sal. Norman came home in a bad humour because he had been without his general dogsbody all day. After tea, Flo ordered Maryann upstairs, took her into their room at the back and closed the door.

'Now look – what's going on?'

'I told yer – Sal's gone. Charlie Black weren't at work today. I think Sal's sweet on 'im. They must've gone off together. And she . . .'

'She what?' Flo hissed.

'She – I'm ever so worried about 'er. She ain't right in 'erself and . . . and . . .'

'Ain't right – what're you on about?'

''E touches us. Mr Griffin. Where 'e oughtn't – and 'e – 'e's a dirty man, Mom . . .'

Flo had been soft and emotional over babby Cissie: they'd almost felt close in those few moments. Surely her mom would take her word on this? Maryann started sobbing all over again.

'What *are* you saying to me, yer foul-mouthed little bitch?' Flo sprang at her and slapped her face so hard that Maryann cried out at the pain. 'How dare you say such a filthy thing! I've a good mind to put carbolic on your tongue for that. Where d'you get such disgusting ideas from?'

'From 'im!' Maryann sobbed. 'Where else would I know 'em from?'

She received a matching slap, this time on the other cheek. Flo swelled with self-righteous fury. 'How *dare* you? Norman's a good, clean-living man. Almost a gentleman, that 'e is, and I ain't having that talk in my house from my own daughter!'

Holding her burning cheek, Maryann went up close to her mother, speaking right into her face.

'You don't see what's in front of your nose, Mom, do yer? You think more of that disgusting man than you ever do of yer children 'cause 'e buys you dresses and keeps you comfortable. But 'e ain't what you think. 'E's evil, but it don't suit yer to see it, does it?'

Flo stood before her, speechless, and Maryann fell sobbing, distraught, on to her bed.

Fifteen

Days passed, and still Sal didn't come home. Charlie
Black didn't make an appearance either, and it was
obvious they really had done a bunk together. Maryann
couldn't stop thinking about them: where had they
gone, and was Sal all right? Sometimes she was angry
with Sal for leaving her alone. Mostly though, she was
just worried.

Norman was all concern.

'I just don't know what can've come over the girl,
Flo,' he said, shaking his head. 'I'm only sorry she's
causing yer all this worry. That's young 'uns for you –
selfish, never give a thought for anyone else. Don't you
get upset, my dear – the pair of 'em'll be back with
their tails between their legs sooner or later.'

'You 'adn't 'ad words with 'er had you, Norman?'
Flo asked cautiously. 'Not done anything to upset 'er?'

'Oh no!' He laughed. 'Not our Sal. That Maryann's
the minx I'm most likely to 'ave words with, as yer
know. But not Sal – a good girl that one. I've been very
pleased with 'er.'

Flo was appeased by the fatherly tone in which he
spoke. He was right – Maryann *was* a minx, running
off here, there and everywhere, making up terrible
stories, like about Norman killing that kitten – and
now, all that filthy language she'd come out with. She
needed watching, taking in hand, that she did.

132

Flo went reluctantly to Cathleen Black, picking her way grandly across the yard and smoothing her hair as if she was too superior ever to have set foot in such a place before. Cathleen, who was holding the baby, looked very worried.

'Sal's been coming 'ere ever such a lot of course,' she said, laying Lizzie down on a blanket on the chair. She felt her own poor drabness beside Flo's relative glamour. The woman was wearing lipstick and powder. 'Look – won't yer 'ave a seat and a cuppa with me now yer 'ere?'

'No ta,' Flo said, wrinkling her nose at the frowstiness of the house. 'I'll not be stopping long.' Heaven only knew what you might sit on if you accepted a chair in this house, and as for drinking from one of their cracked, grimy cups, oh dear no! She wanted to be angry with Cathleen, to lay blame on her and her son, but she felt at a great disadvantage as a mother who had known nothing of her daughter's whereabouts for what had apparently been quite a long time. It made her look very bad.

'So,' she probed, 'Sal and Charlie've been knocking about for quite a time?'

'Ooh yes – din't yer know, Flo?'

'Well, of course I *knew*.' She could hardly let Cathleen Black realize she'd had no idea Sal could prefer spending her evenings in this slovenly household. 'What I daint know was she was hanging round with some idle good-for-nothing who'd make off with 'er to Christ only knows where!'

Cathleen rounded on her. 'Don't you come 'ere carrying on about my son like that! Your Sal wouldn't've gone off with 'im if she weren't a little trollop – you obviously ain't seen the way 'er's been carrying on lately or yer wouldn't be as surprised as you are. You want to pay a bit of attention instead of preening yerself, Flo Griffin, with yer frocks and yer warpaint. Looking down yer nose at my family – we may be rough and ready but we rub along. You want to look at what's going on under yer nose, 'cause one thing's for certain – your Sal never wanted to go back 'ome when she were 'ere, and that's a fact.'

'Don't you talk to me like that, yer filthy slut!' Flo yelled back. 'Yer the lowest of the low you are – look at this place! I'm surprised that babby of yours 'as survived in this filth. You ain't any place to carry on at me with yer drunken husband and yer bloody idle sons. I just 'ope our Sal comes to her senses before long and gets 'erself back 'ere because what sort of life's she gunna 'ave with one of your lot, eh?'

Flo stormed out of the Blacks' house and across the yard, all too aware that her old neighbours had probably heard all that loud and clear.

Life for Maryann at home had become one of constant fear and dread. Every time she stepped into the house she began to feel sick. The very walls were tainted with Norman Griffin. Once she heard him come home she could never relax for a moment. His eyes seemed to be on her so much of the time, watching, waiting. Her mom showed no sign of having believed what she'd told her. There was no one she could trust or rely on. She missed Sal dreadfully. School was the one thing that got her out of the house: it was somewhere to go.

One morning, though, as they were all having break-

fast, Norman said to Flo, 'Our Maryann's almost finished with school now. When can she leave?'

'She's got to see out till the end of term,' Flo said.
'She ain't fourteen till September.'

'Well—' Norman sat back at the table. Maryann
watched him link his hands over his belly. 'No need to
see out the last stretch, is there? Dragging it out, that's
all, when 'er's fit and ready for work. Let's 'ave 'er take
over where Sal left off – I'm short-handed and I could
do with it. Start 'er straight away.'

Even Flo was not oblivious to the pleading look of
horror on Maryann's face, and Cathleen Black's
remarks hadn't entirely passed her by.

'But, Norman – if Maryann leaves early she won't
get her bit of paper from the school and that – for
getting work.'

'Well, she won't need it if she's coming to work with
me, will she? I'd see 'er awright, Flo, you know that.
I say start 'er today – soon as possible.'

'No, Mom.' Maryann's tone was desperate. 'I 'ave to
stay – Miss Bentley said. I *do* 'ave to!'

'It's only another couple of weeks, Norman,' Flo
reasoned. 'Then she'll be ready for yer.'

Norman pushed his chair back and leaned over to
kiss the top of Flo's head. Maryann looked away.

'Awright then, my sweet. Whatever you say. You
can twist me round yer little finger, can't you?'

Maryann looked back in time to see Flo glancing at
her. She experienced a rare moment of gratitude
towards her mother.

'I do think it's for the best, Norman. I'm thinking of
Maryann's future.'

*

After school every day she haunted the cut. She left message after message at the toll houses and was becoming a familiar figure to the workers there.

'Look,' one of them said to her that week. 'I think they'll be through in the next couple of days if they're on the normal run. I'll make sure they get yer message.'

The next couple of days! Maryann could think of nothing else. But suppose she missed them? What if they came through when she was at school? She *had* to see them, to see Joel above all, hear his lovely country accent. The very thought of him was comforting. She didn't know what she could say to him, she couldn't tell him what was happening to her, that she would not, could not work for Norman Griffin, not for anything ever. But she did know he was the one person with whom she felt safe and happy. And she liked Ada, with her raucous voice and cheeky face as well. She longed to see the *Esther Jane* come gliding along the cut with Bessie plodding alongside.

The next day she was so keyed up with nerves she could hardly stand it. She set off to school with Tony and his pal Alec. She waved them off at the boys' entrance.

'See yer later, Tony!' But he hardly took any notice, he was so thick with Alec. Maryann smiled with relief. She was glad Tony had such a good pal. She didn't feel able to give him any attention herself.

She looked round, making sure none of her own classmates was in sight, and darted off again down the road, looping round the back and along to where she knew she could get down to the cut. In each of her pockets was tucked a piece of bread she had sneaked from the kitchen. That'd keep her going. This could be the day they came and she couldn't miss it – just couldn't!

They came in the late afternoon, when the sun was sinking behind strips of candyfloss cloud. She saw them as they drew into view near Soho Loop. Peering into the smoky gloom she wasn't sure at first. There was the horse, all her white splotches standing out, no one walking with her on the bank. Maryann ran forward to meet her. A train clattered over the iron bridge across the loop, but Bessie barely even twitched her ears. It *was* her, and there was Joel, she could see now, standing majestically at the tiller. The boat was clothed up, tarpaulins tied over to cover the cargo, so she couldn't see what was in there. They must've come through rain.

'Joel! Joel!' Maryann bounced up and down, waving, saw him turn his head, then the slow arc of his wave back to her. Could she see his smile, or did she imagine that? After a moment she saw Darius's head appear out of the cabin and he waved as well.

'Shall I walk along with Bessie?' Maryann shouted.

Joel nodded. 'We'll need yer!'

'Where's Ada?'

His voice floated over to her. 'Gone.'

Gone? It was too far to talk properly. She'd have to ask when they stopped. Where could Ada have 'gone'? And where was Jep? She patted Bessie's neck, feeling the dried sweat on it.

'Have you had a hard day, Bessie? Poor old girl – you'll soon be there and have yer nostern.'

She felt proud, knowing a word of the canal dialect. It was different, the way they spoke. Birmingham was

Birnigum. She'd heard Darius call Rugby 'Ruckby', and Ada had run together the names 'Fellows, Morton and Clayton' as if she had no idea where each began and ended. Reading and writing was a mystery to her. She had no pictures of words in her head to know the edges of them.

The city closed in on them and every so often there was a horse bridge where Bessie had to be led over. It grew darker and darker, the blackened walls and filthy overhead enclosure of roads, railways, mills and foundries. The canal had been so built over that in parts it was so dark the gas lamps burned day and night. The water was horrible here, choked with scum and oil and refuse. No wonder Joel said Birmingham was always the grimmest part of their journey. Once she saw a man's sleeping body slumped by the wall at the side, which she mistook at first for a pile of rags. She shuddered. The place felt gloomy and hostile and she was glad Joel was not far away.

Eventually he shouted to her that they were to turn into the private wharf to unload. As the *Esther Jane* pulled in, Joel stepped across on to the bank, ruffled Maryann's hair in greeting and handed her the nostern containing Bessie's feed just as if she was Ada. Maryann grinned and tried not to show she was struggling as she fastened it on.

She knew the next couple of hours would be spent unloading. She left Bessie for a moment and went timidly up to Joel.

'Shall I make you and Mr Bartholomew a cuppa tea?'

'That'd be grand.' Joel's brow wrinkled. 'Think you can manage it?'

Maryann grinned. 'Just 'cos I'm off the bank don't mean I don't know 'ow to do nothing.'

'Go on with you then.'

He walked off, smiling. He seemed well and cheerful.

She was dying to ask where Ada was, and Jep, but she knew they were preoccupied. In the meantime she stoked the little range in the cabin, filled the kettle from the water can, which was always in place on the cabin roof, and put it on the heat. When it was ready she took the tea out to them, Joel winking at her in thanks. She made herself busy then, looking for a spot where the water didn't look too mired up to pull bucketfuls out to do some cleaning. However did Joel and Mr Bartholomew manage to keep things clean without Ada?

She found they weren't managing all that perfectly and the cabin was well in need of a scrub. To the grunts and shouts of the men unloading the firebricks outside, she wiped down the shelves and surfaces in the cabin, moving things off carefully and replacing them. She eyed the crochet pieces along the shelves, the precious work of the real Esther Jane. It was grimy grey in colour.

'I'd give *you* a wash given the chance,' Maryann said, stroking a hand over it. 'But there ain't no time for that now.'

She swept and scrubbed and kept the range going and eventually all the unloading was done and she stood up on the steering platform, watching as Joel and his father finished off with the factory men and finally turned back to the boat.

Joel climbed aboard, followed by Darius, who gave her a nod.

'I'm going for water, Joel,' he said, and went off with the can.

Joel and Maryann went into the cabin and he sat on the bench, looking at her with amusement in his eyes.

'So, little Maryann Nelson. Can't keep away from the cut then?'

She beamed. 'No, I can't. D'yer like what I've done?'

Joel looked vaguely round the cabin.

'I've been cleaning for yer.'

'Ta. She could do with it.'

'Where's Ada gone?'

'Oh, working another boat, the *Lucy* – another of the Number Ones. Their little 'uns're all grown now and they needed some 'elp.'

'But to send 'er off without you!'

'It's done on the cut. Times are hard, Maryann – more boats than cargoes these days and we're all chasing the work. You don't keep moving, you don't eat. Ada's a good little crew – she'll earn 'er keep on there. They let her take Jep with her.'

'But don't you need her?'

'We could do with 'er, but needs must. Good job you came today to find us. We're starting a new route tomorrow. Going south, Oxford way, back to where us came from. Any'ow—' He rubbed his hand wearily over his face. 'I'd best start on cooking.' He pulled a paper bag with some bacon in it off the shelf and put a pan on the stove.

'How's our Maryann then?'

The question was asked lightly but it brought tears flooding to her eyes. Oh Joel, she wanted to cry out, help me! Please help me!

'I'm awright.'

Joel turned to look at her. 'Don't sound too happy to me.'

Maryann didn't say anything. She shrugged and sat

140

watching Joel as he went back to work. He cut thick chunks of bread. She wanted to touch him, feel close to someone. Most of all she wanted to curl up in his arms for comfort, like a child.

'Joel—' she burst out at last. She wanted to speak to him before Darius got back because she was more shy of talking in front of him.

'What's that?'

'Please let me come with yer! I could help – do all the things Ada ain't 'ere to do, like cleaning and stabling Bessie and . . . and everything. And I wouldn't get in yer way and I don't eat much, honest I don't!'

'No, I shouldn't think yer do, the look of yer.' Joel sat back and gently put his arm round her. She leaned against him, feeling the great warmth he gave off. 'Maryann – what's wrong with being at 'ome with yer own folk, eh?'

'I just – nothing. Only I know they won't miss me, not at all. There's nowt happening now – it's the summer holiday and it'd be awright, I promise.'

She knew Joel would have no idea when school terms began and ended. 'I ain't fourteen until the autumn and then I'll 'ave to start work, but I could come with yer till then – my mom'll be glad to get me out of the way!'

She felt Joel looking at her, his face close to hers.

'Well – I dunno,' he said eventually, sitting back. 'It's one thing having an extra from another boat, but one off the bank is different.'

'I'll learn. I'll do anything!' Maryann begged excitedly. She touched Joel's hand. '*Please.* I don't know how else to tell yer 'ow much I want to come with yer!'

'Oh, yer not doing too badly,' Joel said wryly. 'But

I don't want it causing no trouble, them turning up saying we've taken yer off or anything.'

'No – I'll go 'ome and tell them. I'll get some things. Oh Joel!' She was jigging up and down with longing to hear the word 'yes' come out from Joel's lips.

'Well—' he said again, ruminatively. Then looked round at her. 'Go 'ome and see. If it's awright, meet us back here with your things tomorrow – not too much mind. We'll be gone before daybreak so make it early.'

'Oh!' Maryann's face was alight. 'Oh Joel, you're the best!'

Sixteen

She was back at the wharf by five in the morning in a light mizzling rain, her coat pulled round her and a bundle of belongings in her arms.

On her bed she had left a note:

Dear Mom,
  I am going away for a bit. Don't worry I'll be safe, no need to look for me.
  Maryann.

She had crept downstairs, weak-kneed with anxiety, and once she reached the street she tore along until she'd turned a corner, convinced she was going to hear a shout or running feet behind her and equally anxious in case the *Esther Jane* had already left without her.

The men were up and having breakfast when she arrived, frantic and panting, and she climbed on to the steering platform helped by Joel's outstretched hand.

'Morning, nipper.' He gave his slow smile. His cap was shiny with minute droplets of rain.

Maryann grinned, overjoyed. She was here – at last!

Joel sat her down inside and handed her a cup of tea and a thick, man-size wedge of bread.

'I don't know as I can eat all that,' she said.

'I should get it down you. You'll need it.'

Darius Bartholomew had not said a word in greeting,

so Maryann turned to him. 'Morning, Mr Bartholo-mew.'

In reply she received a reluctant-sounding grunt from behind the magnificent white beard, but Darius didn't meet her eye. After a few moments, chewing on the last of the bread, he got up, bending over as usual in the low cabin, stuck his hat on and ducked out through the door.

The joy had faded on Maryann's face. ''E don't want me 'ere, does 'e, Joel?'

Joel finished his mouthful, ruminatively. You couldn't hurry these men into speech.

''E's glad of an extra pair of hands. It's only that, well, living on a boat's quite a close life, intimate like. It'll take a bit of getting used to, someone about who ent family. But we'll manage. Plenty of others do.'

'I'll do whatever you want,' Maryann said desperately. 'I'll do yer washing, cooking – anything, only let me come. Don't send me back 'ome!'

Joel ruffled her hair again. 'I know yer will. We'll manage for a round trip. Don't you fret.'

When Darius came back, Joel went out and spoke to him, the two of them standing over by the stack of firebricks, and when they came back in, Darius nodded at Maryann.

'Mornin'.'

'Morning, Mr Bartholomew. I shan't be any trouble, I promise.'

Darius nodded. 'Let's get on then.'

Warmed by her breakfast and by Darius at least acknowledging her, Maryann went with Joel to fetch Bessie from the stable and watched with great attention as he harnessed her up.

They moved round to a new wharf to load up. Maryann stood watching with Bessie munching beside her as a crane lowered the cargo of iron pipes, load by load, down into the *Esther Jane* with much clanking and banging in the morning air. As she waited there it stopped raining and grew lighter though the rising sun was obscured by cloud and the smoke and smuts in the air. Joel went off to pay the toll and Darius went to fill up with water once more. Maryann offered to go, but he seemed not to hear her. She watched his slightly stooped back moving away from her.

At last they set off: Bessie straining hard against the harness to get the *Esther Jane* on the move, her hooves sliding and scraping, easing the boat forwards until it would begin to drift off and gather its own momentum. Joel led the horse, telling Maryann to stay on board with Darius.

She felt her eyes stretching wide to take everything in, thrilled at the boat beginning to start off slowly under her, and so caught up in the sight of the wharves and chimneys and canal cottages sliding past that she forgot to feel anxious standing beside Darius Bartholomew. She felt bubbly with excitement. They were really going, and she could leave it all behind her: home and school and Sal's disappearance and most of all, Norman Griffin. He'd be livid that she'd given him the slip – there he was commanding her to go and work for him without even giving her a say, and she wouldn't be there in two weeks after school ended, she'd make sure of that. Miss Bentley was a kind teacher and she'd persuade her somehow to give her her school leaving certificate. She'd cross that bridge when she came to it. But for now, in this one precious week, she was going to learn to work the cut and see something of outside Birmingham for the first time in her life. Up until now she'd hardly set foot outside Ladywood!

She held on to the cabin of the *Esther Jane*, a smile on her lips as she watched Joel stepping along the bank. She took in a great lungful of air. Stinking and smoky as it was, just then it felt like the breath of freedom.

The days that followed she would always remember as the closest heaven ever came to earth. It was the newness of it all, how right it felt – her being on the boat and life opening out in front of her like a picture in a storybook. For the first time in such a long while, she felt safe.

That morning, as they moved south, Maryann watched carefully, drinking in every detail as Joel and Darius manoeuvred the boat through Camp Hill Locks. Gradually the dark city began to fall away, the sun burned through the clouds. They left Birmingham with a cap of cloud over it, but outside the haze cleared and at last the sky was a rich summer blue.

'Is this the Oxford Canal then?' Maryann asked, excited.

'Oh no – we don't get on the h'Oxford till after Wigram's Turn – down at Napton. This is the Warwick and Birnigum. We're headed for a cleaner part of the cut now, you'll see,' Joel told her. They referred to 'Birnigum – that stinking 'ole' and as they progressed out into the Warwickshire countryside, Maryann could see why. She kept gazing round her, enchanted by the space, the wide, rolling country with its green pastures, black and white cows, its cornfields and snug-looking cottages, amazed at being able to see so *far*, further than she'd ever been able to see in her life before.

She could have sat and stared around quite happily all day, but she was anxious that Darius shouldn't regard her as a 'good-for-nothing' while she was aboard. Also the place felt rather lonely without Ada and Jep and she wanted to keep busy. She asked Joel what she should do.

'Well, you could give the brightwork a polish,' he said, pointing to the brass fittings on the chimney, kettle, horse brasses and handles inside the cabin. Since Ada left they hadn't had the time for 'prettifying' the place and the brasses were tarnished. Gladly Maryann set to work until they were smooth and gleaming and she could see a distorted version of her face looking back at her in them. Then she cleaned the cabin, wiping out all the smuts and dust and sweeping the floor. She was small and agile, kneeling to poke right into the corners in a way she could see was hard for big, muscular men. The cabin was so small, yet so prettily decorated inside with its scumbled paintwork, its roses and castles and scrolls, and its shelves of china, that Maryann felt as if she was playing houses. She had to remind herself that this really was their house and that Joel, and certainly Darius, had never known any other home.

In the middle of the afternoon, with Joel's help, she pulled a bucket of water out of the cut, and with a chunk of soap set to and washed the cabin's crochet work until she had it looking, not gleaming white, for it was already yellowed with age, but at least a good deal better.

'Can I hang them out to dry?' she asked Joel. She

always went to him instead of his father, although the two of them were both there in the stern. Bessie knew the routine and plodded along for a lot of the journey without being led.

'Oh – can't rig up a line any too easy with a load on,' Joel said, dismissively. 'We do that when the boat's empty, see.' But he caught the crestfallen look on Maryann's face. She had so wanted to do something to help!

'Awright then – I'll see what I can do. Those little bits don't need to hang down far, do they?'

Maryann felt Darius's eyes on her and wondered what he was thinking. She watched nervously as Joel climbed forward over the cabin and made his way along the planks which were laid over the cargo. He was holding a line attached to the cabin and unravelling it. He stretched it across to the low mast at the front and tied it, creating a washing line.

'There y'are!' he called to her, scrambling back across the planks.

It was obviously her turn to climb over. Joel handed her some pegs which she put in the bucket. She was glad it was a calm day without wind, and that the boat didn't have its tarpaulin sheeting on – the planks would be positioned higher, over the top of it, if they had to cover the load. The only time she felt really wobbly was when she straightened up after bending over to pick one of the cloths out of the bucket, almost losing her balance and falling off the planks. It wasn't far to fall but she was determined not to lose her dignity. Soon, not far above the cargo, the line of crochet work was fluttering like bunting. How pretty it was! Fancy being able to make things like that, Maryann thought. She saw Darius exchange a quiet smile with Joel as she came back to them. Suddenly Darius said, 'Why don't you 'ave a sit up there and look round. You've bin working enough I reckon.'

She realized he meant she should sit up on the cabin. He said he could see past her.

'Ooh,' she said, climbing up. 'It's hot up 'ere again!' The roof of the cabin was baking to the touch in the sunshine. Joel handed her the soaking mop. Periodically, in the heat, they swabbed down the roof of the cabin to stop the heat shrinking the timbers and cracking the paint. Maryann laid her coat on the damp roof and sat feeling the sun blazing down on her skin, screwing her eyes up against the bright sunlight on the water. Life on the cut was so quiet and peaceful compared with home, where there were always factory sounds, the whirring, whining, clanging of machinery, trams and buses and people shouting over all the other racket. Out here there were just the gentle noises of Bessie's hooves, mostly muffled by mud now they were out in the fields; the boat passing through the rippling water; the creak of the tiller and the men's occasional speech. Maryann began to attune herself to new sounds: birdsong from across the fields and in the trees, the occasional lowing of a cow, waterbirds quacking away from the boat and the breeze in the grass. There was nothing to look at that was grimy or ugly, just fields, trees and sky, farm cottages and church spires, and the bright paintwork of the boat winding along the ribbon of water. As they glided along, she thought the cut was the most beautiful place on earth.

Every so often another boat would appear, coming from the opposite direction, and the boats would pass one another a few inches apart in the middle of the channel, the boatmen exchanging a 'How do!' or more if they were better acquainted, as they often seemed to be. A couple greeted Darius and Joel with, 'We ent seen you for a bit!'

She was still sitting dreamily on the cabin roof that afternoon when there came another, incongruous sound advancing towards them, a ceaseless 'phut-phut' getting louder and louder, until round a bend in the cut they saw a vessel coming along with smoke streaming out from it.

'See that?' Joel shouted up to her. 'That's one of they moty boats!'

As it drew closer Maryann saw it was towing a butty, both of them clothed up with tarpaulins over the cargo so she couldn't see what it was. The noise it made seemed extraordinarily loud after all the quiet. The family aboard all waved and shouted greetings, trying to make themselves heard over the engine. Maryann turned to watch it disappear behind them and saw that Joel and Darius were doing the same. Darius was shaking his head as if in disapproval at this noisy 'moty boat'.

Joel leaned over to her. 'You don't get many of them down the h'Oxford,' he said. 'The locks're wider down 'ere to London.' On there, he explained, the boat could tow a butty through all in one go, whereas on here they had to pull them through the narrower locks one by one and it all took time. Maryann was learning that the one overwhelming command on the cut was 'keep moving!'

That night they tied up near a pub called the Cape outside Warwick, a little distance after the long flight of locks at Hatton which Joel told her were called the 'Steps to Heaven'. There were three other boats tied up there too. Once Bessie was fed and stabled, Joel, Darius and the other men caught up with the gossip in the pub. Maryann sat out on the bank and played with two little children from the other boat and their mother seemed grateful to have them occupied while she got on. Joel and Darius came back with groceries they'd bought from the pub.

Maryann bedded down on the side bench again that night, as she had before when she slept on the *Esther Jane*, and watched Joel ready himself for bed. She was lulled by the reassurance of his presence, his huge shadow moving round the cabin. Neither of the men undressed much for bed. They left their boots by the door and took off their jackets, undid their belts which they fastened at the back to keep the buckles from digging in when they bent over, and unfastened a few buttons. Both of them lay to sleep in shirts and their thick, corduroy trousers.

Before he lay down, Joel stepped over to her. 'You tired after your first day, Maryann?'

'Ummm.' She smiled sleepily up at him. His face was in shadow. 'It's been *bostin* – the best day ever.'

He patted her shoulder and she could hear the smile in his voice.

'Night – young nipper.'

The bed creaked as he lay down beside his father.

Maryann wanted to lie awake, to hear the sounds of the countryside at night, but she could scarcely manage it, she was so exhausted after all the new sights and a day in the fresh air. Everything smelled different. There was always the smell of the canal all round them. The sounds of family life from the boat moored behind them were dying out. Her mind passed over the day they'd had, what she'd seen, how she'd learned the way a boat manoeuvred through a lock. Something screeched outside. She imagined the *Esther Jane* from the outside, under the stars, resting on the black water. And then she was asleep.

Seventeen

Soon after the *Esther Jane* set off again the next morning, they passed through Warwick and later that morning, the stately, calm town of Leamington Spa. As they approached each town, buildings and roads grew up along the cut, shutting out the view, and with more people about there was a sudden sense of bustle.

When they reached the lock at Radford Semele, Joel said, ''Ere – you give me a hand this time.'

The day before he had told her to stay on the boat at most of the locks, but today he took her with him and showed her how to attach the windlass and turn it to open and close the gates. Maryann watched with intense attention, all her senses alert to learning to do everything as quickly and as well as possible.

He brought her round in front of him and she took the handle of the windlass which was warm from his grip on it. Each of the men had a favourite one or two of these implements for turning the locks, and the handle of Joel's was smoothed with use. His rough hand tightened over hers, concealing it completely and together they turned on the windlass, opening the gate to let the *Esther Jane* through now that the water was level. Maryann felt the immense strength of Joel's arm.

Just before they reached Wigram's Turn where Joel had told her they would join the Oxford Canal, Maryann was in the cabin and heard Joel and Darius suddenly start shouting and calling outside. She was astonished to hear them so voluble and excited and she poked her head out to see them both waving like mad at a boat approaching from the other direction.

The man at the other tiller was waving back.

'Who's that?' she asked.

'That's our Darius,' Joel said.

As they drew nearer, Maryann saw a large, muscular man with black hair curling out from under his cap, dark eyes and strong, chiselled features. He wore a rather solemn, austere expression. He reminded her of Ada except he didn't have her cheeky grin. She wondered if old Mr Bartholomew had looked like that as a young man. The younger Darius was one of the crew on a Fellows, Morton and Clayton boat which was lying low in the water, its hold heaped high with packing cases.

There was a lot of 'how do'ing and exchanges of greeting as the boats passed.

'You're low in the water,' Joel called out. 'You'll 'ave sparrows drinking from yer gunwhales!'

The young Darius grinned back and what had looked rather a forbidding face lit up suddenly and Maryann decided he looked nice after all. Joel called out that he should keep an eye out for Ada with Josiah Morley and there were shouts of 'see yer at Christmas time if not before!' and then they were past. That was the nearest they were going to get to a family reunion. The boats had to keep moving. Maryann wanted to ask Joel more about his family but she was shy in front of the elder Darius.

She helped Joel as they went up the flight of locks south of Napton, carefully doing everything she was told. The day became blisteringly hot as they set off down the Oxford Canal, so much so that Maryann found that at times she could barely touch anything on the outside of the cabin without scorching herself. She busied herself with the mop. The sun glared off the water, blinding to the eyes, and she felt her nose and cheeks turning red and sore. There were trees in a few places close to the canal, but mostly it ran through remote, open fields, and the need to keep the towpaths clear meant discouraging anything inclined to hang down over the cut. So there was little shade either for the boat or for Bessie.

For a time, Maryann walked beside Bessie along the path, enjoying the feel of stretching her legs, the smells of the fields and the hot horse beside her. Bessie wore little crocheted sleeves on her ears to keep the flies off and she seemed to plod more slowly in the intense heat. The route wound and twisted along, nestling against the contours of hills. Sometimes there were villages and little wharves tucked right beside the canal but much of the time there were just the fields stretching into the distance, trees outlined against the skyline, and it felt as if they might not see anyone else ever again. The only sounds were the rustling reeds and the twittering of invisible birds. Once she saw a huge bird lift from the bank ahead of her, its legs trailing, flying off with a heavy, cumbersome flapping of its wings.

Later, back on board, Joel told her it was a heron. She went into the cabin. It was stifling hot in there and a heavy bluebottle was batting against the windows. Maryann felt like lying down and going to sleep, but she knew she mustn't. The last thing she wanted was to be seen being lazy.

Joel's head appeared at the door. ''Ent you got a bonnet with you?'

She shook her head. 'I ran off in such a hurry – I forgot it.'

He hesitated for a moment, then seemed to decide something. He came into the cabin, squatted down and rummaged right at the back of the cupboard he called the 'monkey 'ole'. He brought out a large, squashed paper bag and from it he drew an old-fashioned boat-woman's bonnet with a peak at the front and layers of black frills which went right over the top of the head and ended up hanging down at the back.

Maryann stared at it. It looked old and dusty, like a dead raven.

'It were my mother's,' Joel told her gruffly. 'She 'ad it made special in black when the old Queen died. These 'ere bits' – he pulled at the long material at the back – 'them's your curtains – 'll keep the sun off yer neck.'

Was he expecting her to wear it? The hat looked so worn and old-fashioned. It was a heavy, *ugly* thing and she wished she had her little straw bonnet with her.

'I can't put that on. Not if it was your mom's.' This was a rather awesome thought.

'I'd like to see yer in it.' Joel held it out to her. 'It's ten year since it were worn. She passed on before I came home.'

'Why daint Ada wear it?'

'Oh – she had her own bonnet.'

Seeing she didn't take it, he put it on her head himself. Maryann felt strange, seeing the fond look in his eyes. The bonnet felt much too loose.

'Bit big on you, ent it? But it'll do just for a bit while it's so hot. We don't want you getting caught by the sun.'

Joel was the last person Maryann would ever want

to offend so she smiled uncertainly at him. She felt like a granny in the bonnet. She had seen a few older women wearing them along the cut.

She followed him up out of the cabin. As she straightened up she saw Darius's eyes fasten on her. He actually started at the sight of her and a look of utter outrage came over his face.

'What's 'er doing in that?' he demanded.

'I thought she could wear it for a bit,' Joel said. 'She ent brought a bonnet with 'er. And it's nice to see it wore again.'

Joel had made a terrible mistake. Maryann could see just how terrible by the look in Darius Bartholomew's eyes.

'That's my Esther's bonnet – moy best mate. Not one else ever wears that bonnet. Get it off yer, lass!'

Maryann was already tearing the hat from her head, her hands trembling at the emotion in the old man's voice. Joel took it from her.

'Sorry, Dad – only I thought yer'd like to see it on again, the way I did.'

Darius was breathing heavily. 'Put it away.'

Joel ducked back into the cabin with the bonnet. Maryann couldn't look up. Her cheeks were burning and she had a horrible feeling inside as if she'd committed a crime. She had offended Mr Bartholomew so badly when what she wanted more than anything was for him to accept her. It was unbearable that he would think her uppity enough to take his dead wife's bonnet and wear it.

'I'm ever so sorry, Mr Bartholomew,' she managed to say, her voice quavering.

'It weren't your idea I don't s'pose,' Darius said abruptly.

Though she knew this was true, his rough words scarcely made her feel any better. Joel came back out and laid a hand on her shoulder for a moment.

'My mistake, not yours,' he said.

But it was not until much later that day that the feeling of discomfort this incident had brought Mary-ann began to ease off and she could feel a little more comfortable with Darius Bartholomew again. After that she doubled her efforts to show him she could work hard and try to please him.

That night, after fourteen hours on the go, they tied up at Fenny Compton, where there was a small wharf and a pub. A couple of other boats were tied up there and the men went out to the pub as usual after they'd eaten. Maryann didn't mind being left behind. She rather liked the novelty of having the cabin to herself.

As it was so warm, she didn't feel like slaving away cleaning the cabin. She was hot and tired and she went out and sat on the bank in the evening air. She could smell smoke and food cooking and she breathed in deeply, a great feeling of well-being coming over her.

Glancing towards the pub, she suddenly noticed that Joel was on the bridge and there was a young woman with him. Maryann screwed up her eyes to see better. She was short and rounded looking, with a wide, healthy face and curly brown hair. She and Joel were standing quite close together, relaxed, each leaning on the bridge, and now and then their laughter floated over to her. Maryann was immediately curious. Was she someone Joel was very close to? She found herself full of mixed feelings. Joel had told her he had been courting a girl before the war changed everything. Of course he'd want to get married like other men, but she had had in her mind a future stretching ahead in which she could live on the *Esther Jane* and everything would stay the same.

After a time, the two of them left the bridge and walked round the wall of the pub, out of sight. Maryann sat on, feeling suddenly desolate. She wasn't really part of all this, however much she wanted to be.

When Joel came back in she was already lying down. 'Who was that lady you was talking to?'

He frowned for a second.

'On the bridge.'

'Oh – that's Rose.' He laughed, then coughed to clear his chest. 'Ent seen 'er in a good long while. We've been catching up.'

'She's pretty,' Maryann said. She knew she sounded sulky.

'S'pose she is. Known 'er all my life.'

'Are you going to marry her?'

To her surprise, both men started laughing.

'Marry Rose? Bit late for that – she's got a chap and three kiddies, Rose 'as!'

Maryann went off to sleep feeling much happier. However much she told herself she was stupid to think she could have Joel all to herself, the thought of him being in love with that pretty Rose had made her feel jealous and left out.

The next day was just as long, and in the evening they pulled into Thrupp where the canal was edged by little terraces of canal workers' cottages. Joel told her they were now only about three hours away from Oxford.

She helped to get the range going and cook the food.

159

Joel had also made her responsible for unharnessing Bessie, feeding and stabling her. On these scorching days she also had to wipe out Bessie's eyes with a rag dipped in paraffin, to keep them free from flies and parasites. Mostly, as they went about their evening chores, even Maryann was too tired to speak. Darius went off and kept himself separate, collecting water, or coal if they needed it, and at Thrupp he asked around for return loads to take back north after they had delivered the pipes in Oxford. She and Joel did their chores, often in silence, but always at ease. Sometimes he looked at her and smiled and she'd grin back.

She was more than ready for bed every night after all the physical activity and fresh air of the daytime. As they drew further south away from Birmingham, home seemed more and more unreal, like a bad dream. In the daytime she was so caught up in all the details needed to keep the *Esther Jane* on the move that she barely had time to think, and that suited her very well. She wanted to forget all of it: Sal, Norman Griffin. When she did allow herself time to think, she was filled with anxiety. Where had Sal gone? Was she with Charlie Black and were they both all right? And what about Tony and Billy, left at home? Most of all she felt badly for Tony, about her going off and leaving him. But nothing would have made her give up these days on the cut. Nothing.

By ten the next morning they were pulling into Juxon Street wharf in Oxford amid a collection of boats waiting to unload. The wharf was very busy. Maryann stabled Bessie, gave her a feed and cleaned her harness. She wound her way back to the *Esther Jane* through the stacks of cargo standing on the wharf waiting to be collected: coal and stone, barrels, packing cases, sacks. The hard work of loading and unloading was going on all round and she could have stood all morning watching, but instead she hurried back and got the stove going to make cups of tea. The *Esther Jane* was due a big clean-out while they were tied up. In the meantime she heated more water, got the tin tub and dolly from off the roof and did some washing, scrubbing at the men's thick corduroy trousers, struggling to lift them when they were saturated with water.

'They're *filthy*,' she said to Joel, pummelling them wearily with the dolly. Her shoulders were aching like mad.

'You should see 'em after a hold full of coal.' Joel grinned. '*That's* filthy!'

The afternoon passed loading the *Esther Jane*, the long iron pipes swinging high in the air above her head before being deposited with a loud clanking on the bank. Joel and Darius were preoccupied with securing a return load to take north again. The country wharves sometimes wanted loads of grain taken up for grinding in the Birmingham mills, but it was close to a new harvest now and the stores were low. They needed to find something in Oxford. Joel went off to some of the other wharves, and by late afternoon he had secured a load of timber to be taken to Birmingham. In the meantime, Maryann strung the washing along the boat and helped Darius to swill her out with water. She was ill at ease being left to work with him, but she did everything he said to the letter and by the end of the afternoon she felt that even if she did not have his approval in great measure, at least he had accepted the help she was offering and she had not let herself down.

Eighteen

That evening though, for the first time, she felt lonely. With the work done and the cargo to be loaded in the morning, Joel and his father went to see Joel's auntie, Darius's sister, and then for a few pints at the pubs round Jericho, the area near the wharf. Maryann, as ever, was left alone.

She cleared up the tea things, put everything away. The men brought food in daily if they could, as nothing would keep in the heat, so there was only a bit of bread and bacon on board for next morning. The place was tidy, and as she had been washing and cleaning most of the day she could think of nothing she needed to busy herself with. Now they had achieved the journey down to Oxford the urgency had gone out of things. Before, she hadn't minded being left here, had rather relished having the cabin to herself, but tonight, with nothing to do, she felt suddenly bereft. She sat by the table for a time, biting her nails, and unwelcome thoughts of home and Norman Griffin began to crowd into her mind. She knew if she started on that it would just keep on going round in her head. No – she must think about anything but him.

She got up and folded back the table so she could make up her bed on the side bench with the little flock mattress and the blanket she slept under. She lay down and concentrated on the rosy light of the lamp reflected in the brass fittings. It was such a snug place and it felt like home now. Maryann found herself smiling, snuggling down cosily and growing more sleepy. Every so often she heard the sound of the water lapping gently against the wharf. She was coming to love the sounds of the cut at night. If only she could stay here! There were a few lonely moments, but nothing like the isolation she felt at home where there was no one she could turn to. There was no threat here, not with these big, quiet men. She felt safe with Joel, safe and reassured, as if he was a strong, fairytale brother who'd come to rescue her.

The thought of home filled her with dread. She would have to go back – for Tony if no one else. But why did she have to stay at home? Why could she not just live on the cut with the Bartholomews? Joel had said it was hard enough working the *Esther Jane* three-handed, let alone two, and Darius wasn't a young man any more. But what would Joel say if she asked him? And Darius? Had she proved her worth enough during these last few days?

By the time the men came in she was dozing. She woke again as the cabin door squeaked open, letting in the night air. Darius, walking unsteadily, immediately went and let down the bed at the back, gave out a loud, beery belch, then readied himself for the night. Joel, however, seemed restless. Seeing Maryann looking sleepily up at him he came and sat on the end of the bench. She slid her legs out of the way for him. For a time he just sat there holding his cap while she watched him. His wiry beard and wavy hair were a lovely bronze colour in the pink, subdued light. She looked at his gentle face and huge, worn hands and felt she couldn't imagine a time when she had not known him.

Why was he just sitting there instead of going to bed, she wondered. But she liked it, didn't want him to move, wanting instead to ask him if she could stay with them, but Darius was there and she didn't have the courage.

He looked across at his father now and then, and when Darius was obviously asleep he turned to her and said, half whispering, 'Well – it's been a soft day for us today. I don't know about you, but I ent ready to settle yet. I fancy a walk. How about you, young nipper?'

'Ooh, yes!' She sat up, immediately cheerful. Anything Joel suggested seemed good. An adventure!

She put her shoes back on and her cardigan and they climbed back out into the starry night. The moon was almost full and the wharf buildings were sharp edged, the colour of pewter under its light.

They set out along Juxon Street. Maryann found it strange to be back on a road, with buildings hemming you in on either side, after the cut. She tried to imagine how it would feel never to have lived on the bank.

'D'yer think you'll ever live in a house?' she asked, looking up at Joel.

'Oh – you can never tell, can you? There are folks moving off the cut all the time. It ent easy, with the moty boats and lorries taking over the cargoes. We'll hang on as long as we can though. It's what we know.'

'But you wouldn't give up the *Esther Jane*, would yer?'

Joel shrugged. 'I hope not. But we had to sell the butty – we had a pair before, but we had to part with one of 'em. That's how it goes these days.'

Maryann felt sobered by this. The thought of the Bartholomews living like other people was inconceivable. They turned into another street, then another, in silence, except for the sound of their feet on the road. Silence was easy with Joel. It never felt uncomfortable.

'But—' she said eventually. 'You were born on the cut, weren't you?'

'I was s'posed to be born 'ere at h'Oxford. My mother was coming to town to 'ave me and I was in too much of a hurry – arrived just south of Banbury!'

'On the *Esther Jane*?'

'She weren't called the *Esther Jane* then.'

'No, I know. Joel – will you tell me about your brothers and sisters?'

They turned on to a wider road where there were a few more people about, coming out of the pubs.

'You're a proper chatterchops, ent you?'

'I ain't!'

She liked Joel calling her a chatterchops, but in fact it was hardly justified. There'd been very little time to talk much on the way down. They were always busy, or the men were in the pub or too tired.

'When'll you see Ada again?'

'Well, if we don't run into 'er on the cut, it'll be Christmas. We all try and 'ave a rally at Christmas time, tie up at Braunston or Hawkesbury for a couple of days. See young Darius and Ada.'

'Won't she miss you?'

'She will. But a lot of young 'uns work away from their families. It's the only way to do it – someone always needs a pair o' hands.'

'What about the others?'

'Darius is the oldest. There was Daniel who fell sick and passed on as a little 'un. I never knew 'im. Then there was Esther – she drownded when she was not more than fifteen. Then Ezra – 'e died in the war, and so did Sam, then there was me, then Sarah and we lost 'er to the h'influenza and our mother lost a pair of babies in between – she was very poorly after them – and then there was Ada and through her we lost our mother.'

'Oh Joel, your poor mom!'

'Yep—' he said gruffly. 'She were a good'un, our mother.'

'Did Darius go away to the war?'

'No. Someone 'ad to stay. We younger ones went and I was the one come back. Anyhow – that's how it went. How many's in your family?'

She told Joel all about Tony and Billy, and Sal running off and her dad dying and Mom marrying Mr Griffin, but she didn't want to say much about him. She could feel Joel listening beside her.

'Is your stepfather good to you?'

'No,' she said abruptly. 'Well – I mean, we eat enough and that. But . . . I don't want to talk about 'im, Joel. Don't let's spoil it – it's lovely out 'ere.'

As she began to take an interest in the town unfolding round her, she saw that it was indeed beautiful. There were a few lamps, but mainly the buildings were lit by the moon. Maryann looked up at the spires and towers, the grand, dark fronts of the colleges all around them.

'This is h'Oxford University,' Joel told her. 'They do a lot of book learning 'ere, that's what.'

To Maryann it seemed like fairy land, like nowhere else she'd ever been before.

'I'll show you summat lovely,' Joel said. 'Come along 'ere.'

He led her down a side street, then another, and into a square. All along the sides were castellated buildings, no factories or houses at all. There was a huge, rounded building in the middle. It was covered in little stone arches and columns and stone balustrades, and its roof was domed. Its windows reflected back the moonlight.

'Oh!' She looked round in wonder. 'What is it?'

'They say it's full of books,' Joel said, with a slight air of disbelief. 'Let's go down by the river, shall we?'

Maryann could tell that, while awed, he was not comfortable between all these walls. He led her out the other side of the square and across another road hemmed in by buildings that seemed like palaces to Maryann.

'D'you wish you could read?' she asked him. 'If you wanted to learn I could 'elp yer.'

She heard Joel's wheezy laugh come to her through the darkness. 'Reckon I've got this far without. There ent much call for it on the cut.'

She walked with him, down to where the river flowed past the backs of the colleges. For a moment they stood looking back. It was a beautiful sight, the old stone lit by soft moonlight.

'S'funny how many different ways there are for folk to live, ent it?' Joel said. She felt him reach down and take her hand in his, and she nuzzled against his arm, happy. 'Bet you've never seen nothing like this before.'

Maryann shook her head. 'Joel?' Her heart began thumping fast.

'What's that?'

'I don't want to go home. I want to stay with you and your dad and work the cut.'

There was silence as Joel stared down into the water, that flowed past quite briskly, not like the still, sluggish canal water.

'I don't know about that. You've been a good'un,

learning how to work the boat, no doubt about it. And I can't says I won't miss you, specially with Ada gone. But you can't just stay on without your family giving their by-your-leave. That ent right.'

'Oh *please*, Joel. I can't go home. It's not . . . I can't say why. But it's horrible at home and they won't care if I'm there or not . . .'

'Now, now—' He turned to face her. 'That can't be true now, can it? You got family – people who need you.'

'But Ada just went off to live with someone else, daint she? Why shouldn't I do it too?' She knew she sounded desperate, almost tearful.

'That's what life is on the cut. We boat people do that. But it ent the same where you come from, is it? I ent saying we don't need you – a pair of hands is like gold to us. But you should go back and make things right with your family first. I can't feel right about you just running off and them not knowing where you are, Maryann. You can see that, can't you?'

'I know.' Her voice sounded high and young. 'But I just want to stay with you, Joel.'

'Oh – now—' He pulled her towards his big, burly body and she felt herself pressed against his scratchy weskit, her little budding breasts tender against him, his strong arms tight round her. She put her arms as far round him as she could reach, laughing. She hadn't felt so warmed or happy since she was a little girl, held in her dad's arms after he came home and she nestled against him, loving the feel and smell of him. Joel could save her, he could take her away from that life at home that she so dreaded, she knew he could. He could do anything.

'Don't you get all upset,' Joel was saying, tenderly

stroking her hair. His hand felt enormous on her head. 'We'll see what can be done.'

She looked up into his face and saw his eyes twinkling down at her affectionately in the moonlight.

Nineteen

During the small hours of the next morning, the weather broke. Maryann woke in the night to hear thunder and, soon after, the sound of rain drumming on the cabin roof. The next morning it was still raining. She went out with her coat on and the water was soon running off her hair and down her cheeks.

They moved the *Esther Jane* down to Isis Lock – Joel and Darius called it 'Louse Lock'. To load up, Joel explained, they had to move from the narrow Oxford Canal on to the wider Thames, the adjacent 'Mill Stream', to where the imported timber was brought from London on lighters, towed by tugs, which were too wide for the Oxford Cut.

'When they come up 'ere' – Joel pointed after they had come through Isis Lock – 'they got to get past the railway, see? There's a bridge there, cranks up by 'and, lets 'em through.'

'But what if there's a train coming?' she said.

Joel laughed at her foolishness. 'You don't do it when there's a train coming!'

Maryann did not see any of the lighters coming through, but on the wharf waiting for them was a stack of timber sawed into all sorts of different lengths and thicknesses.

'It's one of the awkwardest bloomin' loads we ever carry,' Joel said, taking off his wet jacket. 'We've to load each bit by hand, or it won't fit in. You can help.'

Maryann soon found out what he meant. Darius, with his lifetime's experience of settling a load into a boat just the right way, stood in the hull as Joel, another worker and Maryann passed him down each plank, piece by piece. Darius said which bit he wanted next and laid them all in, fitting them like a patchwork quilt. The wood was very rough and splintery, not planed smooth. Some of the pieces were so heavy that Maryann couldn't lift them, but she worked hard taking over whatever she could. She wore a thick, hessian apron over her dress. Sometimes she squatted, resting a plank across her knees for Darius to take it from her. The rough wood burned her hands, splinters jabbing into her like needles, and she was soaking wet. The men never seemed to stop and rest: the boat and load always came first. By mid-morning, when the load was almost on board and the rain was still falling, she was close to tears she was so wet and tired, and her hands were bleeding and swollen. But she was determined not to show Darius how close she was to getting up and running off. She gritted her teeth and passed him another plank, wishing he'd at least notice how difficult she was finding it. But after they had secured the last pieces and the *Esther Jane* was now riding low in the water, Darius patted her shoulder briefly as he passed her.

'That were a good job,' he said.

Maryann beamed back at him, elated yet with a lump in her throat. She had truly done something right and won his approval! She skipped along to help Joel harness Bessie, who was quite frisky after her extra half-day's rest. Once she was harnessed up, tolls paid, coal and water aboard, they were off.

Maryann was thrilled to be on the move again. The cut stretched out ahead of them as they slid slowly out of Oxford, the spires and towers receded into the distance and they were in the country again.

'This is the proper life,' she said.

Joel grinned at her. 'If you say so, missy.'

They only travelled as far as Thrupp that day and the sun never broke through. The second morning, they woke to rain and the wind was getting up. Their clothes from the day before were still not dry even though they'd hung them in the warm cabin while they were in bed, but it was obvious that if they put their spare set on they would soon be soaked through as well. Once Joel and Darius had gone out she pulled her damp dress over her head with a shudder. It was slightly warm from being close to the stove, but it soon cooled on her and she was shivering before she had even gone outside. For the first time she started to have misgivings about this life. If this was what it could be like in the middle of summer, what must it be like living here in the freezing winter wind and rain?

They warmed themselves with a cup of tea as they went along. But the day started out as a hard, maddening one. The wind was the real enemy on the cut, pushing even a well-loaded boat about like a plywood toy from side to side. Joel stood at the tiller working it with all his strength to keep it from being blown into the bank, and the shallows where often there were reeds, and other plants with big leaves that looked like rhubarb. Maryann annoyed him by asking, before she realized, 'Will you teach me to steer today, Joel?' and he snapped back, 'Not today – can't yer see what it's like?'

As the wind got up further, Darius took to the bank

to help keep Bessie steady. Every so often the boat was caught by a gust and blown into the side. The water was the colour of milky cocoa. Joel abruptly ordered Maryann off to help pull them off. The first time, the stern of the boat was forced right into the side. Joel yelled at her, telling her how he wanted her to pull. She hauled on the rope with all her strength, the rope yanking away and burning through her agonized hands until she couldn't help crying with the pain. They'd no sooner get straightened up again than another gust would send the *Esther Jane* off at some other angle. As well as keeping the boat on course, round Banbury there were all the lift bridges over the cut to be raised and lowered again as they passed. The morning seemed endless; cold and hard and wet. Maryann was already near to exhaustion and everyone was tense and bad-tempered. Darius kept yelling at her to pull harder, Joel was cursing on board the boat. Maryann almost wished she was at home. She had a sudden longing to see Tony and Billy – someone younger who looked up to her and loved her and didn't order her about.

But the worst was to come on the afternoon. Worse than Maryann could ever have imagined. They'd passed Banbury and reached Slat Mill Lock. As they struggled into the lower pound – Joel striving to keep the boat straight, another boat following close behind, which added to the pressure on them – he shouted to Mary-ann, 'D'you think you can do it?'

'Yes!' she called back proudly. ' 'Course.'

Darius was already out on the bank too. 'You take the 'orse,' he said.

'No, please,' she said. 'I can do it. I know how.'

With obvious reluctance he handed her his windlass, which he carried tucked in his belt, and stayed holding

Bessie. Maryann fitted the windlass on to the lock mechanism and started turning. One of the men from the boat behind pushed on the gate beam to swing it open and Maryann stood out of the way, feeling pleased with herself. Joel had spelled out many times the danger of standing in the wrong place and getting swept into the cut. None of them could swim and even if they had been able to, the men especially would have been weighed down by their heavy trousers, boots and over-coats. Maryann stood with her hands behind her back, the windlass clutched between them as the two boats moved into the lock chamber and the men closed the lower gates, trying to look as if she had lived on the cut all her life and knew just what she was doing. But she noticed that on the boat behind there was a boy with only one leg, and it was a sobering sight. People with missing limbs were not uncommon on the cut. What accident had befallen him in this dangerous life?

When the lower gates were closed and the boats were secured, waiting for the water to rise, she struggled along, leaning into the wind, to the upper gates, hearing Joel shout something to her as she went. The wind whisked his words away.

'S'awright!' she called back. 'I can do it!'

She started turning. Though she'd done it a number of times with Joel, it was hard by herself but she was determined to manage. The muscles on her arms strained and eventually it was so difficult that she was leaning her whole weight on the windlass to turn it and haul it back round at the bottom. The paddles were opening and the water started to gush in with a great roar.

And then it all went wrong. She was leaning back, bringing it round, when she lost her balance. Her hands

174

slipped off the windlass and it snapped back the other way, flying round and round, and Maryann fell over backwards. Frantic and mortified, she scrambled to her feet just as the windlass flew off the spindle. There was a metallic clink, then a splosh. She stood there, paralysed. No – it couldn't have done! Darius's precious, favourite windlass, the one Esther Jane had given to him, his wife, his best mate, had disappeared down into the cut.

Everyone was shouting: Joel, Darius, the other men in the boat. Tears welled up in her eyes. She didn't know what to do.

Darius was suddenly beside her. 'Take care of th 'orse,' he shouted at her.

She saw him go to the shaft where the windlass should have been. He looked round on the ground, then down into the water. He went to Joel, shouting to him for his spare windlass. Maryann slunk back to Bessie with the most leaden heart she had ever had. She was sick with shame. She wanted to hide her face in the horse's hot, wet neck and give in to crying, but she knew this would put her in even more disgrace.

'Your windlass taken a look in the cut, eh?' one of the men on the wharf called out to her. 'Oh dear, oh dear!'

The teasing was not unkind, but it made her feel even worse; young and stupid and incompetent. Worst of all, it made her feel an outsider again, just as she thought she was beginning to get the hang of it. Waiting to finish getting through that lock felt the longest few minutes she could ever remember. When they were through, she went to Darius, looking down at her muddy shoes, unable to face him.

'I'm ever so sorry, Mr Bartholomew.' The tears ran

down her burning cheeks. 'I never meant to lose your windlass. I wish I could go down and get it. I feel ever so bad.'

Darius Bartholomew could not seem to speak. Maryann looked up to see him trying to gather himself. He was breathing deeply and she could see he was furious, but seemingly unable to find the words to yell at her as she knew she deserved. He looked at her for a moment, then strode past. Once they were through the lock Maryann climbed back into the boat, wishing she could just disappear.

'The windlass – I lost Mr Bartholomew's favourite windlass. I don't know what to do, Joel – he's so angry with me.'

'Well, of course 'e is!' She had never heard Joel raise his voice to her in anger before. 'I told you to wait for 'im. You have to do what you're told, not just mess about! What d'you expect him to do? He'd had that windlass more'n half his life.'

'I daint hear you. I promise I daint, Joel!' Maryann was really sobbing now. It was no good thinking she could come here and be one of them and start a new life. She was hopeless, even at the first test and now Joel was fed up with her as well. She wanted to get off the boat, get away from them and from feeling so small and ashamed.

'Oh, there's no need for all that,' Joel said crossly.

Maryann stood looking out, wiping her eyes as Joel wrestled with the tiller, struggling to keep the boat moving straight. He took some time to gain control again. After what seemed a cold, miserable age, he turned to her.

'Eh – cheer up. You weren't the first and you won't

be the last.' He patted her shoulder. 'We'll make a boatwoman of you – don't you worry.'

But to her it still seemed a huge and awful thing she had done and she didn't know how she was going to face the rest of the journey with Joel's father.

Later she apologized again to Darius Bartholomew and he said gruffly, 'These things happen. It taught you, I hope.'

Maryann felt almost forgiven by the men, but she was finding it very hard indeed to forgive herself.

For the rest of the journey she was quiet and subdued. She listened with great care to what she was asked to do and did it with all her concentration, trying as hard as she could to make amends. Darius treated her much as he had before, but he did not reach out to her with any words of reassurance and she couldn't feel forgiven, even though Joel tried to jolly her along.

The last night, when the men were asleep, she gave into her feelings and lay sobbing, trying to be as quiet as she could. After a time, though, she heard the cross bed creaking as Joel sat up, then came over to her.

'What's up, chatterchops? You ent been yourself these last days. Eh – come on now, you don't want to worry so much. There ent nothing wrong.'

He sat down beside her and took her hand in his.

'Oh Joel!' She pressed his hand against her cheek. 'I feel so bad about eveything – I can't stay 'ere 'cause I'm no good to yer, but I don't want to go 'ome. I just can't go back there!'

'Now, now—' She became aware that he was stroking her hair with his other hand and it gave her such a warm, reassuring feeling. 'Don't go saying you're no good to us. You've been a good little boatwoman.

Everyone loses a windlass some time – that's life on the cut.'

'But Mr Bartholomew's best mate's windlass!'

'Well, that were a pity, but what's done's done. In the past now. You want to forget about it.'

But Maryann's heart was so heavy she couldn't feel consoled yet. She couldn't stop crying.

'What is it, eh?'

'Can I stay with yer, Joel? Just come and live 'ere?' she pleaded again.

'We said all this already.' His voice was gentle but firm. 'You must go back and tell 'em where you've bin. It's no good. If they're happy about it . . .' His voice trailed off.

'What? Tell me, Joel!'

'Truth is, I can't say I won't miss you. I've got used to you, sort of thing.'

'Oh please—' Maryann sat up eagerly. 'Say I can stay!'

He took her in his arms and rocked her, and she clung to him. In wonder, she felt him kiss the top of her head.

'You go 'ome and sort things out. Then we'll see. 'Ow about that, eh?'

Birmingham grew up around them, dark and rank with factory smells and the grim stenches of slum living. Buildings blocked out the light.

'I never knew 'ow much it stank 'ere till I got out of it,' Maryann said, standing on the steering platform. Darius was on the bank with Bessie. 'It's so dirty and dismal, ain't it?'

Joel laughed. 'Don't say that about your 'ome!'

As they moved further into the town, the noise increased: the cut busy with laden joey boats, the boatmen in a rush and shouting and swearing at each other to get ahead, trains clattering overhead dropping smuts, the air laden with factory smoke. Maryann's spirits dropped again. She had to get out of here. The narrow streets, the meanness of everything – and worse, much worse than that, Mr Griffin ... Winter on the cut, however cold and hard, could not be worse than this.

When they pulled into the wharf under the labyrinths of factories to offload the wood, Joel said to her, 'You'd best get off now, 'adn't yer – be getting back to your own people.'

'I'll be back,' she said. 'I will, Joel – I'll leave word for yer!'

She saw his slow smile. 'Well – we'll see, won't we. We'll try and stay on the h'Oxford. I know my dad's happier going down that way.' He leaned over and rumpled her hair. 'Cheerio for now, young nipper.'

She politely said goodbye to Darius Batholomew. He said, 'G'bye, lass,' in a kindly way and his leathery face creased into a smile, even though they were in a rush to get unloaded, and that made her feel better. Waving at Joel, she left with her little bundle of clothes and set off towards Ladywood.

Twenty

'Well.' Flo's face was distorted with anger and her arms tightly folded across her chest. 'What've yer got to say for yerself then?'

Maryann had made sure she didn't arrive until after Norman Griffin had left, and when she got in only Flo was at home with Billy, who ran through from the kitchen calling, 'Maryann!'

''Allo, Billy love.' She put down her bundle and squatted down to cuddle him.

'Norman's been going mad!'

Maryann's expression darkened. She scowled at Flo over Billy's blond head. 'Ain't that typical, eh? I go away for a week and all yer can say is "Norman's been going mad!"' She mimicked her mother's tone. 'That's all you cowing well care about, ain't it?'

Flo stood glaring at her, then suddenly kneeled down so her face was level with Maryann's.

'That's always the way with you, ain't it? Never a thought for no one else. Do you know why I married Norman? Do yer?'

''Cause yer wanted his money.'

'Yes – 'cause I wanted his money! And d'yer know why I wanted 'is money? So I could feed my family and keep it together. So you could 'ave the clothes you're wearing on yer back, Maryann. So's I daint 'ave to hand over Tony and Billy to Barnado's when I couldn't afford to keep them!'

'No, Mom, that's the excuse you've always had but I don't believe yer. We wouldn't've starved the way you'd like us to believe. You 'ad a job – in a couple of years Sal was out at work – then I'd've been. Other people do it – look at Mrs Winters.' Mrs Winters was a widow with five children who they'd known in the Garrett Street days.

'Huh,' Flo said contemptuously. 'Yer needn't think taking in washing was the only way *that* one was making ends meet! She had men in and out of there like rats in a nest. And look at the state of 'er – 'er looks sixty if 'er looks a day and she ain't no older than I am. I weren't living like that – I struggled and scrimped all through the war, and then with yer dad coming home in the state 'e was—' She leaned closer, spitting the words into Maryann's face. 'You was too young to know what it was like. You don't feel it all when yer a babby, all the worrying and going without – you just 'ave the bread put in your mouth and that's all you know. It's the mother feels it. I'd 'ad enough, Maryann. Norman ain't yer dad – course I know that. I loved my Harry, that I did, even when 'e come home half the man 'e'd been. But when 'e'd gone I couldn't face no more. You needn't think it's easy for me. You don't know what it's like to lie every night next to a man yer've no feeling for.'

An expression of revulsion came over Maryann's face. 'Don't I? And Sal – don't she?'

'Don't start on them lies again.' Flo turned away in disgust. 'I don't want to hear 'em.'

'No – you don't, do yer?' There was great bitterness in Maryann's voice. 'That's the one way I can rely on you – not to want to hear the things that don't suit yer.'

'Norman's given us a good home and a good life – and you girls just can't see it. We could get on awright but you go running off – you're nothing but trouble. First Sal, and then you . . .'

To Maryann's vexation, her mother put her hands over her face and burst into tears.

'That's it – go on and cry then.' She walked away across the room. 'Twist everything round so everyone has to feel sorry for you. That's always your way, Mom, ain't it? You never want to hear what anyone else's got to say.'

She stamped her way upstairs, full of bitterness. The bedroom felt damp, and very cold and empty. After a moment she heard her mom following her up. Flo came and stood at the door with Billy who was watching them both, wide-eyed with alarm.

''Ve yer heard from Sal?' Maryann asked, her back to Flo.

'Not a word.' Flo wiped her eyes on her apron. 'I've been worried to death. And then you take off as well – fancy leaving a note on your bed like that. You can be a cruel, selfish little bint, can't yer? And I can smell you from 'ere. Yer stink as if yer've been living in a ditch. Where've you been?'

'I ain't telling yer.' Maryann turned, hands clasping her upper arms and her jaw thrust out. 'You can ask me till you're blue in the face. I've been somewhere where I can 'ave a better life than I ever do around 'ere with you and that dirty husband of yours. But of course you don't want to hear about that, do yer?'

Flo was breathing hard. She narrowed her eyes. 'Tell me the truth, Maryann, or I swear to God I'll take my hand to yer. You've been with Sal, ain't yer? You know where she is!' She was shouting, moving closer. 'And I bet that Cathleen Black knows an' all!'

'I am telling you the truth. I ain't seen Sal. I wish I had but I don't know where she is, on my life.' She backed away from her mother. 'But I ain't telling you where I've been. One thing is – I'm going again, soon as I can. I ain't staying round 'ere for a second longer than I 'ave to!'

'So – you're back.'

Flo was in the kitchen with the boys when he came in. For the few moments Maryann was alone with him in the front room, Norman Griffin looked older and flabbier than she remembered, such a contrast to the muscular strength of the Bartholomews. He was looking at her with undisguised lasciviousness, as if his eyes were fingering her through her clothes, and her skin prickled with revulsion.

He moved closer, speaking very softly to prevent her mother hearing, in his low, wheedling tone. 'I'm not going to ask where yer've been, so long as you're back now.' His hand reached out and stroked her left breast. 'To stay.'

Maryann's lip curled with disgust and she stepped backwards, folding her arms tightly across herself. She stared past him, at his brass lamp on the table by the wall.

'I do believe you're growing up.' He was smirking at her, undeterred. 'Quite a young lady all of a sudden.'

'Norman?'

He turned as Flo came in. She looked at them both for a moment, as if puzzled, then continued. 'Oh –

you've seen she's home?' She kept her voice light and persuasive, as if Maryann was forever just disappearing for a week at a time.

'Yes. And ready to start work.'

Maryann stared hard at Flo, willing her to speak. When things had calmed down a bit earlier in the day, Flo had said to Maryann, 'The wag man was round earlier in the week. I told 'im you was ill and lucky for you 'e didn't come in to make sure. But yer'd better get back to school next week.'

Maryann agreed readily. She could collect her leaving certificate, even if she might never need it, and it would keep her away from Norman for a week. By the time she was supposed to start work for him, it would be about the time Joel and his dad would be back from another run if they worked the Oxford Cut again. And she'd be off and away for good ... She felt calmer facing them all because she knew that. There was nothing for her here.

'So I've told Maryann she'd best get back to school next week,' Flo was saying.

Norman put on his most amenable tone. 'All right, m'dear. Whatever you think. So long as she's ready to start a week on Monday.'

It felt odd to be home. Maryann felt as if she'd been away far longer than a week. As if in those few days she had grown up and changed so much that she just didn't fit. But the changes were not just in her. She was most anxious about her brothers, how they had been while she was away. Billy seemed much as usual. Tony, though, didn't come home until it was almost time for tea and when he did he didn't seem at all pleased to see her. He slouched to the tea table and sat down without looking at any of them.

'You been out with yer pals, Tony?' she asked him.

She received barely a grunt in reply. She watched him, hurt. Tony was eight now, tall for his age and thinning out. He had a tight, closed expression on his face and was shovelling his stew down as if he wanted to get away from them all as soon as possible. Maryann looked at Flo, who shrugged.

Upstairs, when Tony was in bed, Maryann went and sat on his mattress and tried to get him to speak to her. He lay on his side facing the wall with his back to her, tucked down under the bedclothes so that she could only see dark tufts of his hair.

'Tony – turn over and look at me.'

He didn't move.

'Tony – please. I'm sorry I went away without saying goodbye and that, but . . .' She couldn't tell him where she'd been or that she was going back. A pang went through her. He felt abandoned, she knew, but it was her and Sal who were the ones at the mercy of Norman's disgusting habits. She couldn't tell Tony that, couldn't tell him why . . .

'Look, I'm back now, Tony. Can't you speak to me? Let me make it up to yer?'

But there was still no reply. She wondered if he was asleep and not just pretending, but she sensed that he wasn't. With a sigh she got up. 'All right then – let's 'ave a talk another time.'

Lying in bed, she heard Flo come up and settle herself down. She waited for Norman to come up too: the terrible, familiar sounds of him breathing heavily on the landing from climbing the stairs, his cough, all of which made her lie so tensely that she was scarcely breathing, then his murmured words to her mother as he bedded down beside her. But there was nothing. He had not come to bed. She waited for what seemed hours and she was so tired. Eventually, thinking about Joel and missing him, wondering where the *Esther Jane* was tonight, and were they missing her, she fell asleep.

It wasn't the squeak of the door which woke her. She was conscious a second before that, perhaps from his furtive tread on the stairs, or some second sense which alerted her. Before she had come to properly, his hand was over her mouth and nose and she was fighting for breath, panicking and struggling out of the bed-clothes, tearing at his arm.

'Ssssh.' He moved his hand so that it was only over her mouth and she took fierce, gasping breaths, feeling her nostrils flaring in the darkness. He was sitting on her bed, his face close to hers.

'Don't you dare make a sound, yer little bitch, or I'll do to you what I did to that cat.'

He was manoeuvring himself in the darkness, with difficulty, she could tell, hearing his loud breathing, his hand still over her mouth, though less tightly. She was paralysed with fear and horror at the thought of what he was going to do, unable to move. She heard a small whimpering sound escape from her and felt his fingers claw at her face.

'I said not a sound . . .' His voice was tight, strained. 'I've been waiting for you – I don't like waiting. I'm going to 'ave you. I've waited long enough.'

It did not take him long. When he had gone she crept downstairs and out into the yard in the thin moonlight. Dizzily she leaned over the low wall, resting her head wretchedly in her hands. After a few moments her body revolted against what had happened. She bent over and was violently sick.

186

Twenty-One

Maryann's teacher, Miss Bentley, didn't seem perturbed by her absence and asked if she was feeling better.

'Yes thanks.' Maryann couldn't manage a smile. She quite liked Miss Bentley, and in some ways it was nice to be back at school and see all her pals. But she felt cut off from them now. She couldn't ever tell them what went on at home. But she also felt rather superior to them all. After all, she'd been working the cut all last week, learning all that she'd learned about real life while they were still all sitting here in rows! But now she had joined them again and was back in her school frock looking round at the tiled walls with pictures hanging on them, and at all the other girls round her, there was a poignancy about those few days. Many of the children had been at school together since they were infants and by the end of this week quite a number of them would be signed off from education for ever, into the adult world of work. Some of them were talking about what jobs they were going to.

But I, Maryann thought, will be off: gone for good. She wanted to tell them, but thought they'd laugh. Children off the cut were the butt of jokes because they couldn't read or write and were regarded as dirty and ignorant. So she wasn't going to say anything. This was her secret. Only a few days now and she'd be away . . .

But on the last Thursday something happened which

she could not have foreseen. They were at home after school when someone hammered on the front door.

'Go and see who's making that racket, Maryann!' Flo shouted from upstairs.

Nancy was on the doorstep, still in her school dress. She looked astonished to see Maryann.

'Well, where've you been?' she demanded, panting. 'Your mom said you'd gone off!'

'Never mind that,' Maryann interrupted. She wasn't going to say anything, not even to Nance. 'I just went away for a bit, that's all. What's up with you, nearly banging the door down?'

'It's Charlie . . .'

'What's all this?' Flo appeared downstairs.

'Mom sent me. Our Charlie – 'e's come 'ome – just now.'

Maryann and Flo both started talking at once. 'Where's Sal then? Where's 'e been?'

Nancy was shaking her head. ''E won't say.'

'Won't say! Well, bugger that. Billy – get in 'ere! We're going out.' Flo was already heading for the door. 'I'll soon get it out of 'im!'

Hoiking Billy by the arm, she marched off down Anderson Street like the wrath of God, with Maryann and Nancy following. When they reached the old yard in Garrett Street it was full of the Black youngsters who'd obviously been sent out of the house. When Flo marched in without a by-your-leave, only Charlie was in, with Cathleen and Lizzie.

'So – where is she then?'

Charlie was in the chair by the grate, hunched forwards, arms resting on his thighs. He clearly hadn't had a haircut during the weeks he'd been away and he looked haggard and very tired. Seeing Flo, he seemed to shrink further into himself.

'I said where is she? Where's our Sal?' Flo stood by the table, grasping the back of a chair so tightly her knuckles whitened. Maryann and Nancy stayed watching by the door. Maryann couldn't take her eyes off Charlie. In just a month he seemed different. Older, and dulled. Cathleen, standing with Lizzie on one arm, looked agitated.

''E won't say,' she told Flo. 'I can't get out of 'im where they've been or what's been going on.' She advanced on her son. 'You'd better tell Flo where Sal is, Charlie my lad. You've caused nothing but trouble and worry – there's her on my back and we'll 'ave Father Maguire round again and you just sitting there – you're a disgrace, Charlie.' She was shrieking. 'You tell us where she is – now!'

''Er doesn't want yer to know,' Charlie said to the floor.

Cathleen and Flo exchanged looks of utter exasperation. Flo went to Charlie and poked at his shoulder with her finger. 'Well, why don't she? Eh? What's up with 'er? Why ain't she come with yer?'

Charlie shrugged. 'I wanted to come back 'ome and she daint, that's all.'

'Yer needn't think I ain't asked him all this before you come in,' Cathleen said. 'It's like talking to a block of wood. Will I get Father Maguire round 'ere now, eh? Will that get yer to open yer mouth?'

Flo's expression darkened further and she leaned even closer to Charlie. 'What's to hide, eh? What's ailing 'er? Have you got 'er in the family way and now she can't come back and face us? Is that it? You'd better start talking, Charlie, 'cause I ain't going away till yer do. Why d'yer just take off and leave 'er, eh?'

Charlie stood up with a fierce movement and slammed his hands flat on the table. 'Because 'er ain't right in the head, that's why.' He lifted a finger to his temple and swivelled it round. 'I don't know what's up with 'er – 'er never used to be like it. It got so's I never knew what was going to happen next with 'er, and I weren't sticking around no more to find out!'

'What d'yer mean, Sal ain't right in the head? What's 'e done to 'er?' Flo yelled at Cathleen Black. 'There weren't nothing wrong with 'er when she left.'

'You sure about that?' Cathleen said.

'What do you mean?' Flo snarled at her.

'Sal ain't been 'erself for a good long while. You only 'ad to look at the girl.'

Flo drew herself up, ablaze with defensive indignation. 'There ain't nothing wrong with my wench – or there weren't till she got in with that lout of a son of yours. What's 'e done to 'er?'

Maryann and Nancy jumped out of the way as Charlie seemed set to slam out of the house. But Flo was too quick for him. She nipped round and barred his way.

'Where d'yer think you're going, you no good little bastard? You needn't think yer can just run off. You're not leaving and neither am I. You're gunna tell me if I 'ave to beat it out of yer!'

He pushed his way to the door. 'Oh awright. Yer welcome to 'er, the silly cow.' He gave them an address in the Jewellery Quarter.

*

190

Maryann sat nervously on the tram over to Hockley, beside Flo, who had Billy on her lap. She was desperate to see Sal. Now she knew they would see her she realized just how much she'd missed her sister and was full of worry on her behalf after what Charlie said about her. *She*'d known Sal wasn't herself, and now she knew exactly why. She would have given anything to put the clock back, to feel young and innocent herself, not living in terror of what her stepfather would do next. And to have Sal back as she was – her bossy big sister, who had been full of herself and her budding young womanhood. She felt like crying at the thought of it.

'Mom – don't be too angry with 'er, will yer?' she begged.

Flo seemed thoughtful. She looked round at her. 'We might be able to talk some sense into her between the pair of us. Not that you've got much yourself. I don't know what's come over this family, that I don't. Where *did* you take off to last week?'

She kept asking this every so often. This time, though, she didn't sound angry. Her voice was soft, persuasive. 'I ain't going to keep on at yer, Maryann. I want to get this sorted out. First Sal, then you. I want to know where a girl your age goes off to if she ain't with 'er pals or 'er sister.'

Maryann almost yielded to the concerned tone in her mother's voice. What a relief it would be to be able to talk about all the confused and turbulent feelings inside her. To tell her properly about Norman without it turning into a shouting match, for her to make it stop, and about Joel and how he was like family to her, like a big, loving brother, and about working the cut.

To be able to stop having these burdensome secrets. She looked into her mother's pale eyes. She came so very close to pouring it all out. But then she remembered the last time she had tried.

'I *am* your mom,' Flo was saying. 'I was worried about yer. And Norman was. I said to him, there's summat wrong with both my daughters taking off at once. Is there summat the matter, Maryann?'

I've told you! a voice seemed to scream in Maryann's head. *I've told you and you wouldn't listen. You wouldn't believe me.*

'No, Mom.' She turned away. What was the point in trying? 'I was just . . . with some pals.'

'But who?'

'Just pals, that's all.'

'Well, next time yer decide to go gallivanting off,' she sounded indignant now, 'don't go bloody doing it without telling us. Anyway' – she shifted Billy on her lap – 'you'll be working for Norman soon, so we won't be having any of that. D'you 'ear?'

Maryann didn't reply. She stared out of the window at the streets outside.

They found Sal's lodgings in a street off Constitution Hill: a terrace with an attic. The landlady, a sharp-faced individual, looked at them suspiciously.

'I've come to see my daughter,' Flo said, pushing Billy in front of her as if he was a certificate proving her motherhood.

''Er ain't 'ere,' the woman said. ''Er's at work.'

'Well, we'll wait then,' Flo said haughtily. 'We've come a distance and I ain't stopping out on the street.'

The woman hesitated, then shrugged as if she

couldn't be bothered to argue. 'You'll 'ave to wait up in 'er room,' she said in a snooty voice. 'I'm expecting company down 'ere.'

They all climbed up to Sal's room. The first flight of stairs was covered by a threadbare runner of grubby carpet, its original colour impossible to tell. The attic stairs were bare and their feet made a racket as they went up. The room at the top was a good size, but the boards were rough and stained and the distemper on the walls was in a terrible state, flaking off and discoloured. Cobwebs hung in the corners, and the ceiling near the front end of the house was bulging with damp, right over the head of the bed. The bed was three-quarter size, and against the opposite wall stood a rickety table and chair. There was a small grate, full of dust, with no sign of a fire in it. One of Sal's dresses was hanging on a hook behind the door, her nightdress was on the pillow, and there were a few of her belongings in the room: a pair of shoes, a cup and a bar of soap on the table, a candle stuck on a grubby white saucer and, beside it, hair pins and two little pots. Maryann opened them and looked inside. One contained rouge, the other face powder.

'Well, this is a cheerless bleeding 'ole,' Flo said, peering out through the filthy, curtainless window at the houses opposite. She seemed sobered by the sight of it. 'What the 'ell does she want to stop 'ere for?'

Maryann sat on the bed in the chilly room and made Billy sit beside her. There was one threadbare blanket folded on the mattress. The idea of Sal here on her own made her want to cry. She tried to imagine Sal coming here with Charlie. They must've told the landlady they were married though, heaven knew, they looked too young.

It wasn't long before they heard voices down below, then feet on the stairs. Maryann braced herself for seeing Sal. Flo turned, standing with her back to the window, silhouetted in its meagre light, and sharply shushing Billy who'd got up and started clattering about on the bare boards.

The landlady had told her they were waiting there so Sal was prepared. She flung the door open and stood looking brazenly across at her mother. Maryann gasped. She might have walked past Sal in the street and not recognized her! She'd put her hair up like a grown-up lady's, all piled and pinned round her head, and she was all made up lipstick, the lot. There was something else queer about her face. Maryann saw that Sal had plucked out all her fair eyebrows and painted them in instead, with dark, thin lines. She looked ten years older than she really was.

Flo fixed her with a stare which took in all of Sal's altered appearance, and her mouth twisted with distaste. At last, in a bitter voice, she said, 'Well – I hope yer proud of yourself. You look like a proper tart in all that warpaint.'

Sal stayed in the doorway, as if ready to run. 'I ain't coming back if that's what yer 'ere for.'

'Look, Sal—' Flo moved towards her, realizing she'd started off on the wrong foot. 'I only wanted to see yer – see 'ow you are. After all, yer just took off, never a word or a thought for the rest of us. We've all been ever so worried about you. Look – if there's any trouble we'll get it sorted out, but you can't just stay 'ere on your own. You're only young, running off with that no-good Charlie Black . . .'

' 'E's a darn sight better than some I could mention,' Sal spat at her. 'Don't you come 'ere lecturing me, mother. I ain't coming home whatever you say. I've got a job and I can look after myself.'

'But Charlie's left you!' Flo had been trying to be appeasing, to control her temper, but it all came spilling out again. ''E 'ad more sense than to stick around 'ere in this dump. What the 'ell's got into yer, taking off and going about looking like a trollop! You'll be in trouble soon, my girl, that you will, if you go about looking like that.'

'Charlie Black ain't the only fish in the sea,' Sal retorted smugly. 'I don't notice no shortage around 'ere. And you're a fine one to lecture me – you're no more than a slut yourself, taking up with Norman for 'is money.'

Flo whipped her hand out to slap Sal's face, but she stepped back out of the way.

'Don't, Mom!' Maryann cried. There were tears running down her face. 'Don't hurt her! 'Er'll never come 'ome if yer treat 'er like that.'

'That's awright with me!' Flo blazed back. 'You can stay 'ere and rot, you ungrateful little bitch. If you can keep yerself then all the better for the rest of us. But don't come whining round me when yer in the family way and thrown out on the streets! I've warned yer, and I wash my hands of you. Come on, Maryann, Billy – leave 'er. She don't want 'er family.'

'No—' Maryann sobbed. 'I want to stay. You go on home.'

Flo stopped by the door. 'If that's what you want.' She looked hard at Sal. 'You used to be a good girl – you were the easy one. I don't know what's got into yer, that I don't. I've done my best – whatever 'appens now, you can't blame me for it.'

They heard her clomp noisily away down the stairs with Billy, leaving the sisters alone.

195

'Oh Sal,' Maryann cried. 'Are you awright? I know why yer don't want to come 'ome, but . . .'

'What do you know?' Sal snapped.

'About . . . about . . . you know, *him*, what 'e done to yer.'

'Don't talk about him!' Sal came over and got her by the shoulders. 'I don't want to talk about him. I've got away from him and I'm making my own life now – and you've got to do the same, Maryann. Don't work for 'im – don't let 'im near yer. Don't let 'im get you in that cellar down there . . .' She sank down suddenly and Maryann thought for a second that she was choking, her chest heaving, but she was crying, gasping. Maryann was about to embrace her when she stood up and began banging her head against the wall, hard, sobbing and crying.

'Sal! Sal, don't!'

Maryann pulled her away, trying to take her in her arms. Sal tore away. 'Don't touch me!'

'Sal – what's the matter with yer? I know what's 'e's done, what e's like, but why're yer doing that to yourself?'

Sal stepped back and collapsed limply on to the bed. She stared ahead of her so strangely that Maryann was even more frightened. At last she whispered, 'Maryann – don't leave me. I don't know what else to do.'

Sal broke down and cried and cried, at last allowing Maryann to put her arms round her and hold her tight.

'I'm losing my mind,' she sobbed. 'Oh Maryann, I don't know what's happening to me – I keep thinking such terrible things I'm frightened to be 'ere alone. It's not so bad when I'm out at work, but when I get back 'ere . . .'

'Can't yer come home?' Maryann pleaded. 'You don't 'ave to work for Norman no more . . .'

'No!' Sal clutched at Maryann's wrist so hard her fingers were digging in. 'I'm never going back there. Never! I'm never going anywhere near 'im again – you don't know what 'e can be like, Maryann. You've got to get out too . . .'

'I will, Sal – I was going to. But I can't leave you – not like this!' She could hardly bear to look at Sal. She used to be so pretty and now, with that paint on her eyebrows, she looked cheap and horrible. 'Why did yer go and do that to yourself?' she asked.

Sal shrugged, not replying.

'Oh Sal!' She put her arms round her sister again and held her close. She wanted to say, let's go somewhere together, just you and me. Somewhere where they can't find us and we can start again. But she didn't want to live in some slum with Sal. She wanted to be out on the cut with Joel, with Bessie plodding alongside. It wrung her heart to see Sal in this state, but it also frightened her. Sal was supposed to be her big sister, but now she was different, not the same Sal. How could she live with her in this state?

'Look, Sal – I'll 'ave to get 'ome. But I'll come and see you tomorrow – and every day I can now I know where you are, awright? And Tony and Billy can come an' all. And Mom – I'll talk 'er round . . .'

Sal's eyes widened. 'Not him! Oh God, Maryann – what if she tells 'im where I am! What if 'e comes 'ere? What if 'e starts following me about?'

''E won't,' Maryann tried to assure her. 'Course 'e won't. You can tell the landlady not to let 'im in. Anyhow – he thinks he's got me now.'

Maryann stayed on until it was almost dark and then

she made her way home in a turmoil of emotions. This was the afternoon she had been going to leave a message for the *Esther Jane* when she came back through some time in the next few days. But how could she leave now with Sal like this? She'd felt badly enough about leaving because of Tony and Billy when she thought at least Sal was happy with Charlie. But now she was the oldest one at home: she couldn't just desert them all.

Twenty-Two

On Sunday she left a written message for Joel, hoping one of the toll workers would read it for him. 'I can't come yet because I've got to look after my sister but I'll be back again soon. Love Maryann Nelson.'

She started work for Norman on the Monday, promising herself that if it was too bad she'd go somewhere else. She didn't want to cause a family row. Flo was in a good mood, and she watched with approval as the two of them set out together.

Maryann walked beside him along Monument Road. He wore his hat and top coat although it was high summer. He had a rolling, stately walk, said good morning to people with a gentlemanly lifting of his hat and was always greeted with respect: a pillar of the community walking out with one of his stepdaughters. The shops were opening up, awnings rattling open over the pavement, cars, carts and bicycles weaving along the busy street at the heart of Ladywood. They passed all the shops with their smells: cooked meat from the butcher's, strawberries outside the green-grocer's, bread from the bakery, then the Palais de Danse on the corner. At last they reached Griffin's, with its shrouded frontage and sober gold lettering, and Norman pulled out his bunch of keys and opened up.

Inside, he pulled up the little blind that covered the

glass in the door, turned the sign round, and Griffin's was open for business.

'Right then,' Norman said, hanging up his coat. 'You sit down at the desk. You're a quick-witted young thing – you'll soon pick it up.'

Maryann did as she was told, looking at the ledgers, cards, pens and blotter. She kept eyeing the door of the shop. If only Fred, the lad who made the coffins, would come in so that she wasn't alone with Norman.

'I'll come and show you what you need to know.' Norman walked round behind the desk and her skin felt suddenly as if it had been scrubbed with sandpaper. He leaned over at one side of her and his smell of sweat and smoke seemed to envelope her. She found herself breathing through her mouth so as not to smell him.

'This is a quiet time of year compared with the winter, but then of course you're going to have people coming to their natural end any time of year,' he said whimsically. 'When someone comes in, the golden rule is you treat 'em with courtesy and respect. Our job is to be invisible. If you do it well they don't remember much about you, but set a foot wrong and you're out of business. No laughing or joking in the presence of the bereaved, *ever* . . .'

Maryann nodded, listening as Norman outlined procedures concerning dates for interments, churches, death cards, hearses and coffins. All the while she was on edge because she thought he might touch her like he did when they were alone at home, pawing at her breasts or trying to pull her against him. But he made no attempt at this. This was work. Gradually she began to relax. And after a few minutes Fred arrived, crashing in through the front and saying 'Mornin', Mr Griffin!'

in his clogged, adenoidal voice. At last, she wasn't alone!

Later, Norman went out and Maryann was left sitting expectantly in the chair which Sal had occupied all those months. Norman had told her she was responsible for keeping the shop clean but it already looked immaculate and the desk was tidy. She was soon bored. She could hear Fred sawing away at some wood in the cellar.

'Don't let 'im get yer down in that cellar . . .' Sal's words came to her. What had she meant? Was that where Norman had always forced his vileness on her? Or was it more than that?

Maryann tiptoed to the top of the stairs and looked down. She could scarcely see the bottom of the staircase, it was so gloomy down there and the sight of the place brought her up in goose pimples. That was where they took the dead bodies. Surely he hadn't been down there with Sal when there were dead bodies . . . It was too horrible to imagine. Looking down there, she thought, *I can't stand being here*. She'd have to bring Flo's and Norman's anger down on her head and say she wouldn't work for him . . .

She climbed down, jumping as the treads creaked, but Fred was making such a noise he couldn't have heard her, and she wasn't bothered about him. Maybe, she thought suddenly, if she could make friends with Fred, it wouldn't be so bad working here. She could get him to stay on until she went home each day, so she wasn't left alone with Norman . . . Sal had described Fred as being 'as thick as horse shite' but Maryann was hoping she'd been exaggerating.

Peering round the door, she saw into the poorly lit

cellar. The door to the chapel of rest was closed. In the far corner she saw the cupboard, almost like a smaller room built into the cellar, with brick walls, about six foot by four, extending halfway along the far wall. The long bench on which Fred was working was at the front end under the grating.

Fred was a pale boy of eighteen, with a gaunt face and prominent lips, his eyes set far apart, and thin brown hair.

'Hello!' Maryann called out.

He looked up, bewildered, and stopped sawing so abruptly that the quiet was startling.

'I'm Maryann. Sal's sister.'

'Oh . . . ar – I saw yer. Upstairs.'

He stared at her. Maryann, with a sinking heart, began to see that Sal's assessment of Fred might have erred on the side of generosity. He stood watching her as she explored the cellar, walking over first to see what he was doing. He had sawdust all over his boots. She liked the smell of the bruised wood. She went to the cupboard and tried the door, which was locked.

'What's in 'ere?'

'That's Mr Griffin's cupboard.' He didn't leave the workbench, just turned to watch her.

'Yes. So what's inside?'

He shrugged. 'I dunno. Chemicals and suchlike for that em . . . emb . . .'

'Embalming?'

'Ar – that's it. 'E don't let anyone go in.'

''Ve you been in there?' Maryann grinned conspiratorially.

'No!' Fred looked alarmed. 'I don't want the sack – I'd never go in there! No call to.'

'It's awright, don't get all worked up. I was only asking.'

She tried the door once more. Sal knew what was in there. There was something down here that had frightened her badly. Something that had seemed to make her lose her will.

'I'll leave at half past five when Fred goes, shall I?'

Maryann was watching the clock, both out of boredom and anxiety. Norman had come back at dinner time and Maryann told him she'd had one woman in who needed to bury her mother. Maryann had felt sorry for her, had taken down her details and thought she'd handled it all right. The woman had been calm and unemotional. Norman had been in all afternoon as various people came and went, and all the time he had on his sombre, upright citizen face. But when she asked him about leaving he turned, scowling. 'You'll leave when I tell you and not before. Now get this floor swept – there's dust and bits all over it.'

Maryann obeyed, sweeping the brown linoleum of the dirt Norman seemed to imagine he could see there. She worked slowly, still glancing continually at the clock. Whatever happened she was going as soon as she could. She had to get over and see Sal. And she could sense a change in Norman as time wore on. He was at the desk, thumbing through the ledgers, not looking up at her, but all the time she could hear his breathing. As she swept beneath the chair the pace of his breaths increased a fraction. She had heard it before, when he made her put her hand in his pocket, and when he touched her. It was the barometer of his excitement.

Her own heart beat faster with dread and she was all nerves. Any second she expected him to reach out and grab her. She couldn't do this. Not stay and work here. Until now she had held on to herself, kept her mind aloof from it: although he'd done things to her that sickened and disgusted her, she still had her spirit. But she could not endure more of it. It wasn't going to work. She knew that much more of it and she would lose herself, like Sal, and wither away inside. As she turned, pushing the few bits of dust and fluff away with her broom, Norman's hand fastened on her thigh, pushing her skirt between her legs and she jumped, letting out a little scream and moving quickly away.

He stood up, cleared his throat and crossed the room to the stairs.

'Time Fred was off.' She saw his wide shoulders disappear through the door, heard him going down-stairs.

Oh Lord, Maryann thought, *why did I come here?* Why hadn't she just stood up to them and said she wouldn't work for him? She looked wildly round the room. It was five and twenty minutes past five. She left the broom against the wall, grabbed her hat and cardi-gan and ran to the door, cursing the loud, tinkling bell, and fled out on to the street.

He arrived home soon after her, not taking the trouble to conceal his fury.

'What d'yer think yer doing running off before I tell yer to go? Eh?'

He became aware that Flo was watching from the kitchen door. She could see a sheen of sweat on his pale, freckly face. 'Don't you *ever* do that again,' he snarled. 'D'you hear?'

Maryann kept her gaze turned down to the floor so he should not see the defiance in her eyes.

'No, Mr Griffin. I certainly won't.'

She hurried over to Hockley that evening, but the landlady said Sal wasn't in.

'Can I wait for a bit?' Maryann asked. 'I don't s'pose she'll be much longer.'

'I shouldn't bet on it.' The woman was even less friendly than last time and sounded very disapproving. 'To tell yer the truth I'm thinking of looking for a new lodger. That feller who came with 'er weren't 'er 'usband at all, was 'e?'

Maryann didn't answer. She felt an ugly blush creep up her cheeks.

'Thought not,' the landlady said, sounding self-satisfied. She stood back, folding her arms. 'Go on up then.'

Maryann sat in Sal's dismal room, picking at the loose threads in her frock and reduced to twiddling her thumbs, until it was almost dark outside. She got up from time to time and stood on tiptoes to look out of the window, though she could not see the street properly from up here. Gradually the night came on, lamps were lit outside, and still her sister didn't come. Maryann grew more and more anxious. Where had Sal got to? Her landlady would never put up with her if she carried on like this.

Eventually she had to give up and go home, and by the time she got there Flo had already gone to bed.

Maryann realized her mistake as soon as she walked in through the front door and found herself looking into Norman's eyes as he sat waiting by the fire.

'I'm going to bed,' she said, hurrying across the room.

'Oh no – not yet.'

He sprang out of his chair and grabbed her just as she reached the door to the stairs. He clamped his hand over her mouth.

'Thought you'd avoid me today, then, did yer? I'm not 'aving that.' He ran his hands over her chest. His eyes were terrible; cold, full of hatred. 'You're turning into quite a young lady nowadays, aren't yer, eh? And I'm going to make the most of it while yer still a child. Yer no good to me once yer've got yer monthly . . .'

Maryann tried to speak, shaking her head and making a strangled noise.

'What's that?'

'I 'ave – come on. Just last week,' she babbled as he released her. She yanked herself away from him. 'You touch me again and I'll scream. I'll get my mom down 'ere and then she might believe what an evil, filthy bastard you are.' She had her hand on the door to the stairs. 'You're never touching me again.'

Norman lunged at her and Maryann opened her mouth and managed to force out a scream.

'Shut it!' He was ablaze with fury and frustrated lust. 'Shut up that racket, yer little bitch.'

He went to put his hand back over her mouth but she yanked the door open and screamed again. There came the sound of a door opening upstairs.

'Norman?' Flo Griffin's voice was full of sleep. 'What's the noise? What's going on?'

Maryann fled up the stairs, not meeting her mother's eye.

'Nothing, love – just Maryann being silly. Now she's gone and woken yer.'

'I'm not working for you no more.'

He was eating breakfast. She stood by the table, in front of all the family.

'What're you talking about?' Flo turned on her at once. 'You've only been there one day!'

'I ain't staying.' She screwed up every ounce of self-possession and courage and looked into Norman's eyes. *I'm not scared of you*, her expression said. She was, she was terrified, her hands were shaking, but she pressed them together. She wasn't going to let him see. 'I'm going to look for another job today.'

'How *dare* you talk like that!' Flo erupted. But Norman raised a hand to silence her.

'I can't say I'm not disappointed in yer, Maryann. It'll cause me a lot of trouble 'aving to get someone else. But if yer not happy – I know some people don't take to working with the dead. I don't want anyone saying I'm not a reasonable man. And if you go in one of the factories you should get a decent wage.'

'But, Norman!' Flo protested. 'You're surely not just going to let 'er get away with this, the little minx?'

'It's awright, Flo. 'Er's more hot-headed than our Sal. Let 'er go 'er own way. As long as you work out the rest of the week, Maryann, that's all I ask.'

'There,' Flo cried. 'See 'ow nice yer father's being after all the trouble you've caused!'

There was a long silence. Maryann felt Tony's eyes

on her face. She looked away across at the range where the kettle was starting to boil.

She spoke quietly. 'I'm finishing today.'

'You'll work the week out.' She couldn't look at him any more, couldn't face the cold hatred in his eyes. She knew that beneath the calm exterior, Norman Griffin was seething with rage at being thwarted.

'No,' she said. 'Today.'

She found a job at a jam factory, where she had to be in as the hooter went at ten to eight. Another went off at eight and work began. The girls all wore clogs, which were hard and blistered her feet. Fruit and sugar were brought on carts and the jam stirred in huge vats, its smell sweet and cloying. Maryann was in the labelling department, not an arduous job, but even if it had been, anything would have been better than working with Norman Griffin. She had some laughs with the other girls, biding her time. This wasn't where she was going to be for ever. As soon as Sal got herself sorted out a bit she'd be off. She spent as little time as she could at home and at night she took to ramming her bed close up against the door so it couldn't open. She wasn't going to let him get at her, never again. When she heard him come up to bed the first time, and push at her door, she lay seething with hatred of him and fierce satisfaction.

That's stopped your game, she thought.

As the summer passed and turned into autumn, she knew Norman, too, was biding his time. But she was at work all day, and she managed carefully to avoid being alone with him at any time. Her main worry was Sal. She couldn't keep going over every day, especially as Sal often wasn't there. She did try and go at least once a week. But after that time of closeness when Sal had cried in her arms and admitted how wretched she felt, she never let Maryann see her true state of mind again.

Twice when Maryann went in August, Sal came home late and clearly the worse for drink.

'What the hell's kept yer?' Maryann raged at her the first time, as Sal came staggering in after dark. She'd been waiting ages, cursing Sal, worrying about her. She felt as if things had reversed and she was the older sister now, having to keep an eye on Sal all the time. 'You're in a disgusting state. You're going to have to pull yourself together or you'll get thrown out – she's already said she don't like the way you carry on.'

Sal lurched over to the bed. Her cheeks were grimy with sweat and face powder, she was dishevelled, hair all in a mess and she stank of drink.

'I'm in a disgusting state!' she repeated. She rocked back and forth as if thinking about this, then started laughing, a drunken, foolish laugh that made Maryann feel like slapping her. Instead she stood over her and shook her by the shoulders.

'Who've yer been with? Who is it's buying yer all this booze?'

'Oh, mind your own bloody business,' Sal sneered. Her face was grotesque in the candlelight, with its pencilled-in eyebrows. 'I've got my own pals now, ta very much. I've got my big strong friend Bill, looks after me. Oh yes 'e does – 'e's a big'un now, 'e is . . .'

'You're horrible—' Maryann pushed her away. 'You're nearly as bad as Norman. Look at yourself, Sal. What's going to become of you?' She went to the door.

'I'm not staying with you like this. There ain't no point in talking to you.'

'If you don't want Norman on you,' Sal called after her, 'just tell 'im you've come on.'

'I did,' Maryann snapped back at her. 'I ain't stupid and nor's he. He daint believe me. Don't you worry about me – not that you were. I've got my own way of dealing with him.'

A week later Sal was caught trying to smuggle a man up to her room and the landlady threw her out. She moved to another grim attic in a nearby street.

Maryann felt desperate about her. She tried to talk to Flo about Sal again, but all Flo said was, 'What can I do about 'er? 'Er's the one walked out on us. If 'er's going to the bad there ain't nothing I can do about it. I washed my hands of 'er. Sal can go to hell 'er own way, that's my way of looking at it.'

Sal was the only thing keeping Maryann at home now. And she was dangerously close to giving up on Sal herself.

Twenty-Three

Another month had passed. It was October, the nights drawing in, leaves in the gutters and foggy mornings. Maryann had been loyally visiting Sal so far as she could manage it. Sometimes Sal was in when she got there; more often she wasn't, and Maryann was fed up with waiting, anxious and hungry, in those dismal lodgings for her to come back. She kept thinking one day Sal would walk in and be the sister she had been before, bossy and hoity-toity, but kind and good for a laugh. But when she did come back, Sal was often rude and offhand.

Maryann had confided about it to Nancy only the previous weekend, she had felt so heavy-hearted. The two of them sat at the table in the Blacks' downstairs room, sipping lemon pop out of jam jars. Her mom and her dad were out and Nance was holding Lizzie on her lap and minding some of the younger ones who were running in and out. Nance hadn't got her dream job at Kunzle's and was working in a laundry, but she seemed cheerful enough about it.

'Last time I went to see 'er,' Maryann complained, 'she come in – in the end – and says to me, "What're *you* doing 'ere?" As if I was vermin or summat. She's drinking ever such a lot, Nance. And the other night I was sat there and I 'eard 'er come in. There was giggling and shushing on the stairs – I could tell there was someone else with 'er. In they come – 'er and this bloke.

Oh Nance, I swear to God 'e was the 'orriblest looking man I've ever seen, broken nose, the lot, and 'e was ever so much older than 'er.

'"Who's this then?" 'e says, swaggering about like one of them cowboys. Sal 'ad to shut 'im up talking so loud 'cause 'e weren't meant to be there. "That's just my baby sister," she says. "And 'er's just leaving, ain't yer, Maryann?" She was all nasty and superior – didn't care about me at all and that I'd been there waiting for 'er.'

'Ooh,' Nance said. She was biting at the nails of her right hand, which already looked red and work-worn. 'Fancy your Sal carrying on like that. I mean our Charlie would've married 'er, you know, when they was old enough, if things'd've been different. He was ever so sweet on 'er. And when yer think what 'er used to be like!'

'I was that upset – well, I was furious with 'er! But I could see they'd 'ad a few and I wasn't going to start a shouting match or I'd've got 'er thrown out again. But, oh Nance, it made me feel so bad seeing 'er with that great *ape* of a bloke . . .'

'So what did yer do?'

'I went 'ome and left 'em to it.'

Nance shook her head in a way that reminded Maryann of Cathleen. 'What's up with 'er then? I mean there's you and 'er – had everything the same and there's 'er going right off the rails.'

Maryann quickly looked down. She couldn't tell Nance. Blackie Black may have been a broken man and a drunk but he didn't do those things, did he? Not like Norman Griffin, who had shut them off from everyone, alone with their sense of disgust.

*

She'd delayed going back to Sal's place in Hockley, putting it off after the way Sal had treated her. Why should I keep running after her if that's how she goes on? Maryann thought, I'd be on the *Esther Jane* with Joel if it wasn't for her. She dreaded going, wondering who she might find Sal with. She knew deep down that this wasn't the real Sal, that her sister was broken and desperate inside, and it wrung her heart to see her behaving the way she was and not know what to do about it.

That day, after work, she forced herself to go. When she got off the tram her heart started pounding and her legs turned shaky with misgiving.

Don't be so daft, she told herself. Sal won't even be in yet – not this time of day.

When she reached the house, the front door was half open. The usual fusty smells greeted her. She walked straight in and tiptoed up the stairs, holding her breath. When she reached the top, Maryann stood uncertainly outside. Should she knock? Just supposing Sal was in there with some man, she'd be livid with her and the last thing she wanted was to witness such a scene. Sal had never told her anything, not directly, but Maryann knew what Sal let those men do to her. She could see it in her sister's eyes, she had seen the lust on the ape bloke's face when he looked at Sal, drunken and lecherous.

But surely it was too early for that. She leaned close to the door. Not a sound. The door opened with a squeak. She could tell immediately that the room wasn't deserted after all. It had the feel of a person in it. It smelled stale. The bedclothes, such as they were, were pulled up over the hunched shape of a body lying face to the wall.

'Sal?' Maryann cried, alarmed. 'What's up? Are you bad?' She yanked the blanket down. Sal seemed to be in a very deep sleep. Maryann nudged at her, pulled her so that she flopped over on to her back and at last Sal managed to prise her eyes open.

'Sal! 'Ve you been lying there all day like this? What's up?'

Sal winced, laying an arm over her eyes to shut out the light.

'Ooh,' she groaned. 'My *head*! What time is it?'

''Bout half past five, or later. Ain't you been to work today?'

'Nah.' There was a silence, then, 'They let me go – Monday. Said I weren't no good to 'em.'

'They didn't! How're you going to get by? You bin out to find summat else?'

Sal pulled her arm away and attempted a smile, which emerged as a sly grimace. 'There's easier ways to earn money.'

'Sal . . .' Maryann stared at her. 'Yer don't mean . . .?'

'Oh, pack in carrying on at me, will yer? My 'ead's fit to split. Go down and see if yer can get a cuppa tea out of that skinflinty old cow down there, will yer? I gotta 'ave summat to ease it.'

'Awright,' Maryann agreed reluctantly. 'But I can't see 'er handing over a cuppa tea.'

She went down the dim kitchen at the back of the house where a hairy Scots terrier, as corpulent as its mistress, was lying by the range. Without bothering to shift itself, it started up a shrill barking as soon as Maryann appeared. The lady of the house was slumped in a greasy old armchair close by, everything about her seeming to be drawn inexorably down towards the floor: her sludge-coloured hair, cheeks, chins, sagging breasts. She was drinking out of a cup and there was a jug on the table. Maryann could tell from the smell that it was ale.

'Stop that yapping, will yer!' the woman bawled at the dog. Looking round she spotted Maryann. 'What're you doing barging in 'ere, eh? Made me bloody jump.'

'Can my sister 'ave a cuppa tea?' Maryann asked as politely as she could. 'Only she ain't feeling well today.'

The woman took a mouthful from her cup, which left froth on her top lip. 'Kettle ain't on,' she said, turning away indifferently. 'And it won't be neither.'

In the end, Maryann ran down the street to find a coffee house where she bought Sal a glass of tea and paid an extra penny to retrieve when she took the glass back. Sal was still lying staring at the ceiling. The light was going and the sight of her made Maryann feel so sad she almost started crying. Her emotion made her speak sharply.

'Come on – get this down yer, sis, and pull yerself together.'

Sal hauled herself, wincing, up to a sitting position and leaned forward, cradling her head in her hands. She still had her black dress on from the night before, rucked up round her waist.

'Oh God, Maryann, I feel that bad, I do.'

'Drink up,' Maryann said, more gently. 'It's getting cold. I got it down the road – there's plenty of sugar in it.'

'Ta.' But Sal still couldn't seem to move. Her blonde hair was loose and hanging lank round her face. Maryann pulled it back over her shoulders and held the cup to Sal's lips.

''Ere—' Her voice was tender now. ''Ave a sip, Sal.'

Sal leaned towards the glass and sipped. The sisters

215

sat quietly together as Sal managed to get almost half the tall glass of tea down her. Maryann stroked her back.

'You can't go on with all this boozing,' she said.

But Sal stopped drinking and began to whimper. 'I'm going to be sick, Maryann!'

Maryann rushed across the room, ducked under the table for an old yellowed newspaper that was lying there and opened it in Sal's lap just in time. A gush of tea and bile pooled in the newspaper. Sal retched miserably, and when she'd finished, Maryann folded the ends of the dripping paper into a bundle and dumped it by the door. Sal panted and then her gulping from being sick turned into gulping from her tears.

'You don't want to keep on like this, do yer?' Maryann said, wrapping her arms round her. 'Oh, sis, I hate to see you like this.'

Sal cried even more, shaking her head. 'I'm scared, Maryann. I'm so scared.'

'What're you scared of? You're just feeling poorly, that's all.' But Maryann was scared too. 'You need to get some food inside you and you'll feel better. Shall I go out and see if I can get yer a couple of cobs from somewhere?'

'No!' Sal shook her head, then groaned and pressed her hands to each side of it to still the pain. 'It ain't only that, Maryann. It's . . . I think I'm expecting.'

'Expecting?'

'A babby.'

Maryann drew back, gaping at her. The thought had never crossed her mind. 'Oh no – oh Sal! Whose babby?'

Sal wouldn't look at her. 'I don't know. God 'elp me, I don't even know.'

She just couldn't tell her mom when she got home, not out with it, cold like that. It didn't seem real to her. She only had the vaguest knowledge of the connection between what men and women did together and how babies came out of it. She knew her mom'd be livid and most likely go over there and give Sal a beating.

'Well, what's ailing 'er?' Flo was demanding, standing over Maryann as she tried to force down some of a mutton chop and congealed gravy.

Maryann looked up at her. 'I've never seen 'er so bad, Mom. She ain't 'erself, and she's poorly. Will yer go and see 'er? Be a bit nice to 'er, like?'

Flo put her hands to her waist in a defensive posture. 'I don't know why Sal can't get 'erself over 'ere to see us. I mean, I've got quite enough going on, what with Billy and the house . . .' She saw Maryann's face. 'Awright – I'll try and get over to see 'er some time. She don't deserve it though, everyone running at 'er beck and call, that she don't!'

Maryann knew she had to go over and see Sal the next day. Poor Sal would have been there all day on her own, with only her thoughts for company and hardly the strength or will to get herself any food to eat.

She changed into her shoes and left the factory at the end of her shift, absent-mindedly calling goodbyes to her workmates as they all streamed out to the street, eager to get home. The light was fading and the air, foggy and full of smoke, stung her nostrils.

The lamps were lit by the time she got to Sal's lodgings and the pubs were already doing a brisk trade. This time she had to knock and it seemed ages before she heard the woman shuffling along the hall to open the door. The landlady peered out, suspiciously.

'Ow, it's you. I ain't 'eard nothing out of 'er today.'

Well, that ain't any surprise, Maryann thought. When you've got your nose in a jug of ale all day long. She didn't say anything, just went on up the stairs.

'Sal?' She tapped the door and went in. To her surprise the room was dark, and she felt a sudden rush of hope. Maybe Sal had been mistaken, had just had a fancy that there was a babby on the way because she was poorly. Maybe today she was feeling better and had gone out. Even Sal's old habits seemed better at the moment than the plight of being in the family way.

Cautiously Maryann stepped across the dark room.

'Blimey, it's cold in 'ere today!' she muttered. It was bad enough normally, but this was worse than ever. She stepped closer to the dormer window and heard glass crunch under her feet. From the faint light from the street she saw that one of the panes was broken. 'No wonder Sal's gone out. I wonder 'ow that 'appened? P'raps a bird hit the window.'

She decided to wait, at least for a time. If Sal was all that long she'd go out and treat herself to some faggots and peas instead of buying them for Sal. She felt more cheerful. Maybe soon she'd be off on the *Esther Jane* after all! She felt her way to the table where Sal kept a candle and a box of matches. There was only a stub of candle left. Never mind, she thought, generous in her sense of relief. She'd go out and get her some, and other things she needed. Maryann lit the candle, which was stuck on the lid of a treacle tin, and took it closer to the window again to look, but the flame began to gutter in the draft so she turned away, treading carefully over the sharp slivers of glass.

And then she jumped so hard she almost dropped the candle. The light of the flame was caught, reflected in Sal's open eyes.

'Oh my God, Sal—' She could make out Sal's shape lying along the bed. 'Why didn't you say you was in?' Maryann pressed her hand over her heart. 'Flamin' 'ell. You nearly frightened the life out of me! Sal?'

She leaned closer and smelled it, the heavy, sickening stench of blood.

'Oh Sal . . . oh Christ no, Sal. What've yer done?'

It was everywhere. Holding the candle high, Maryann saw that most of the middle part of the mattress was dyed with it and it was dripping from Sal's left arm, which hung over the edge of the bed, to a black pool on the floor. Maryann seized her arm, memories rushing back to her of Sal, that day, sitting jabbing, cutting at her arm.

Maryann heard herself whimpering, making strange, unbidden sounds. She knew now what had happened to the glass in the window, knew it all. Howling, she threw herself down on her knees beside her sister's bed, regardless of the pool of blood, kissing her poor cold face, stroking her hair again and again, beside herself.

'Oh Sal, my Sal – why did yer do it? I'd've taken care of you – I would. Oh Sal, don't die, you're my sis. We can look after each other!'

But she knew it was over, that there was no point in running to any doctor for help. Sal must have lain for hours like this. Maryann knelt with her arms round her sister, holding and rocking her, rage and sorrow possessing her like no emotions she had ever felt before. Sal was released from her agony now. Her heart was not beating. But she had not killed herself: she had been murdered slowly, brutally, over these long months, and the person who had killed her was Norman Griffin.

Twenty-Four

The day they buried Sal was wet and cold. The carriages followed the hearse to Lodge Hill Cemetery, and the horses' hooves sounded louder in the damp weather, their warm breath swirling round them in the damp. They were decked out in black feathers and smartly polished harnesses.

It was an extravagant funeral, beyond anything they could normally have afforded.

'We'll make sure she has the best,' Norman had told Flo. 'We can't bring her back – Lord knows what possessed her – but we can give her a good send-off.'

'It's more than 'er deserves really,' Flo had sobbed. 'Taking 'er own life like that – it ain't right. But it's all we can do for her now.'

They stood at the graveside as rain fell all round them, pattering on the leaves banked up at the sides of gravestones, dripping off the brims of their hats and gathering in little pools on the lid of the coffin. The priest looked thinly clad and unwell, and the only sound apart from the rain and his voice nasally intoning the burial rite was that of Flo's weeping.

As the first handfuls of earth were thrown down on to the coffin, she burst into uncontrollable sobbing.

'My little girl,' she moaned into her handkerchief. 'My baby – oh my little baby . . .' Maryann saw Norman lay his hand on her shoulder for a moment to quiet her.

Tony was crying silently, his hand in Maryann's, and she squeezed it and kept Billy close to her. There were no tears in her eyes. She watched Norman across the yawning slit in the ground into which Sal had been lowered, fixing him with an unwavering, icy stare. As she stood watching him across the grave she knew she would not weep here, at the funeral he had provided. Never, in front of him. Not after what he'd done.

'... blessed are the dead which die in the Lord,' the vicar was saying, '... for they rest from their labours.'

Maryann raised her eyes past Norman at the skeletal trees behind him. The wind was blowing rain sideways across the graves. In a few moments it would be over, the final prayer was being said and then they would leave the gravediggers to finish shovelling in the earth. She looked back at the coffin once more in a final farewell.

I won't let him get away with it, Sal. I'll make him pay, that I will. But you rest now, sis. You rest.

Holding the boys' hands, she followed the others back across the cemetery to where the horses were waiting. She looked at Norman's back, long and tall in his black coat, and she knew with sudden certainty what she was going to do.

She lay beside Tony that night, waiting for him and the rest of the household to settle for the night.

Flo came up first, followed by Norman, and Maryann relaxed a little, breathing more easily. He wasn't waiting up the way he did when he was going to try and come to her room. Gradually it all settled down, the padding of feet, the wrench of bedsprings, then quiet at last. The rain seemed to have stopped now but it was still windy.

She had thought she was far too pent up to sleep, but some time later she found had been dozing and woke very suddenly and sat up, her heart hammering. It came flooding back to her: Sal was dead. She had to do it, to go tonight. Now. Getting out of bed with enormous care, she lit the candle and looked anxiously across at Tony – at his thin face, his straight, dark eyebrows, so relaxed as he slept – and for a moment all her resolve withered.

How can I just go away and leave him and Billy? she thought. But then she thought of Sal, of Joel and, fortified, put the candle down on the floor and crept round the bed to gather up her few things: her shoes, bits of clothes, and the little china cat which she laid lovingly on the pile.

When it was all ready she tiptoed round to Tony's side of the bed and kneeled down by him. I mustn't touch him, she thought, or I'll wake him and mess it all up.

'I've got to go away, Tony,' she whispered. 'I'm sorry to leave yer, that I am. I know I'm not much of a sister to you, but you've still got our mom and Billy and your pals. You look after our Billy now, eh?' Tears came into her eyes at the thought of the two of them, little blond Billy and dark-eyed Tony, hand in hand as if alone in the world without her.

'Only – I've got to go tonight, 'cause if I don't, I'm gunna be in trouble, Tony. I don't *want* to leave you, Tony, honest I don't. 'Ere—' She got up again and went over to her little pile of things, took out the china cat and brought it to him, laying it on his pillow, close

223

to his sleeping face. 'You 'ave little Tiger so yer know I'll be thinking of yer.' She couldn't quite bear to go without touching him, and she reached out and stroked her hand over his head. 'T'ra, Tony.' He didn't stir.

Taking deep breaths to calm herself, she lifted the chair away from the door and blew out the candle. Every sound she made seemed deafening. The door opened almost soundlessly, but when she went to cross the small landing, one of the boards gave a loud, unexpected crack. Maryann froze, panic-stricken. The house was full of boards like that, which might suddenly betray her!

All you've got to do, she told herself, is get into that room. He sleeps nearest the door, so you can just reach across . . .

Clenching her teeth over her bottom lip, she pushed the door of her mother and stepfather's room. To her amazement it swung open without a sound. She could hear Norman's breathing, a rasping sound which helped her get her bearings as she stepped through the door. She could tell where the head of the bed was all right, with him making that racket. She stepped behind the door and, holding on to the wall, slid along the gap between it and the bed until she got to the chair. As she reached out for it her mother sighed and shifted in the bed, and she froze again, waiting. But all was well. Her hand met the scratchy tweed of Norman's jacket which was flung over the back of the chair and she felt along it, searching for that pocket he pushed his hand into when he was walking along . . . The cold weight of the keys seemed to fall into her palm as if they had been waiting for her and she clenched her fingers tight to stop them jangling together.

'Got yer,' she mouthed in the darkness.

Moments later, shoes on and holding her belongings, keys in the pocket of her coat, she slid out through the front door.

The street was deserted but it was warmer than she expected, the sky busy with puffy clouds moving across a thin crescent moon. There was still lamplight to guide her, reflected in the puddles along the pavement.

She couldn't believe she'd managed it, that he wasn't behind, following her as she walked along to Monument Road. Even though hers were the only steps she could hear on the street, she kept turning to glance behind, expecting to see him. Pulling up her collar, she shrank down into her coat.

When she reached the door of the shop a cold feeling overcame her, a creeping sense of horror. She should forget this thing she had come for, the obligation she felt towards Sal, and just go, get right away from here for good. What was it Norman had said to Sal, or shown her, that afterwards, together with those dirty things he had made her do, had meant she was never free of him? She had steeled herself to do this and she couldn't just walk away.

'Don't let 'im get yer in that cellar . . .' Sal's warning rang in her mind. She took out the keys and as she did so, she noticed in the faint light that one of them seemed to be a darker colour than the others. As she examined them, a sound came from along the street. Quickly she unlocked the door and shut herself inside. She waited, but heard nothing further.

Norman kept matches for the lamps in one of the

desk drawers. Groping her way over to the desk she talked to herself in her mind, trying to fight her irrational terror of darkness.

Once she'd lit the lamp she started to feel a little better. The blinds were all down so no one could see in. The office looked exactly as she remembered: a small, bare, workaday place, much as it would have looked had she been left alone there on a winter's evening. Now she just had to go downstairs, she told herself. That was all. Just have a look. Pretend Fred was down there, hammering away . . .

She lit a candle to take with her and, keys in the other hand, climbed quickly down the yawning darkness of the stairs, knowing that if she hesitated she might seize up with panic and run back out into the road. She had to unlock the cellar door – she had not known Norman kept it locked at night – and, with a huge effort of will, she went inside. She knew she must check inside the chapel of rest to see if there was anyone laid out in there. If so, she would have to rethink what she was planning to do. It took her a few minutes to find the courage. First of all she lit the gas lamps in the cellar and though the light was reassuring, she was trembling so much she could scarcely manage to insert the key in the lock and open the door of the chapel of rest. Every fibre of her was poised ready to run away should there be the slightest sound or movement.

Gritting her teeth, she swung the door open suddenly and held the candle high in the doorway. The long table was empty, with just a sheet folded on it. She let out a long, relieved breath. Thank goodness!

The place suddenly felt much more normal and unthreatening. She noticed then, though, that it was unusually messy: the floor covered in rings of wood shaving, which gave off a sweet smell, sawdust and offcuts of wood all over the place, hammer, chisels and other tools left out on the bench. Norman was so obsessed with tidiness and precision and chivvied Fred to leave the cellar looking tidy. Getting ready for Sal's funeral had evidently been a rush.

She turned then to Norman's cupboard. 'Right, mister – let's see what yer got in 'ere . . .'

Holding up the bunch of keys, she eyed the keyhole of the metal door and saw instantly the one which must fit. The keyhole had been smeared with black paint. Her heart beating painfully hard, she inserted the black key into the lock.

''Ere goes . . .'

Peering inside, holding the candle out, she could see nothing very much to start with. Her eyes grew more used to the deeper darkness in there and she saw that running along each wall were two shelves, one above the other, neatly arranged with an assortment of objects. There was a sense of order and fussiness characteristic of Norman. On one side seemed to be stored old ledgers, and a musty odour of aged paper mingled with the chemical smells. On a low shelf lay what looked like old tools – hammer, chisel, fretsaw, awl – each rather rusty, laid out straight, one by one. On the higher shelf to the left were arranged dark glass bottles and jars and beside them, an assortment of books. Stepping inside she pulled one down. It had a soft leather cover and worn gold letters on the spine. *Whiteacres' Manual for the Practice of Embalming the Human Body.* Quickly she put it back, not wanting to look inside. Her toe kicked against something and she looked down to see a can of paraffin for the stove they used in the cellar on the coldest winter days. Maryann smiled grimly. *Good.*

Turning to look at the back of the cupboard, she saw to her surprise that in the small space at the back, right in the middle, was a chair. It looked like an ordinary kitchen chair. Maryann moved closer, frowning, holding the candle higher. It took a moment for her to make out any details, but when she did the very blood seemed to freeze throughout her body. Her free hand went to her mouth.

Details jumped out at her one after another in the flickering light. The chair was straight-backed, with two struts across the back and a flat wooden seat. Fastened round the uprights of the chair back were two iron brackets which were screwed into the wall. Resting on the seat was a carefully coiled length of chain, curled round itself like a Swiss roll and glinting in the candle-light. With it was a pair of manacles – another pair was positioned on the floor by the chair legs – and a second length of chain dangled from the back in a snakelike loop to the floor. Over the back of the chair, folded very neatly, was a square of white cloth, perhaps a scarf. Maryann took in the sight, unable to move, the implications of it sinking into her mind. Had he threat-ened to tie it round and round Sal's mouth? Had he actually done it? Left Sal chained and gagged here – for how long? What else had he done? Was this the threat that he had held over Sal, month after month, until he had invaded her with fear, emptying her of her very self?

The restraining cords with which Maryann had held back her emotions that week burst open. She strode out of the cupboard and put the candle on the workbench. Moving with increasing frenzy, she began to gather up the mess that was strewn on the floor: the sawdust and wood shavings, the ends of wood, the sheet from the chapel of rest. Anyone who had seen her just then might have said she'd lost her mind. Going to the cupboard, she pulled out the armful of ledgers, tearing at their pages and throwing them down, their remaining pages splayed, then the books on embalming the dead. She tore into the cupboard and yanked with all her strength at the chair, trying to wrench it apart, levering it against the hold of the iron brackets, but it was strong and she couldn't release it. In the end she brought the other chair from the cellar and added it to the pyre. Going back into the cupboard, she picked up the tin of paraffin and poured it over the mess. Finally she rested the candle, with almost reverential care, on its side in the middle of it all. She stood the tin carefully by the door.

Flames immediately began to work on the dry curls of wood with a tiny crackle. Maryann stood for a moment, arms tightly folded, watching it all begin to burn.

'Burn, burn!' she hissed, her eyes gleaming. 'You evil, murdering bastard, burn!'

She seemed to do everything automatically, laughing, crying, as she did so, looking round for more things to stoke the fire. There was too much brick down here, too many hard surfaces. But she hadn't started on upstairs yet . . .

The smoke was beginning to build up, the flames reaching up towards the chair. She'd have to get out of here, but she needed to drag the trestle table out from the chapel of rest to make sure it carried on burning, or on the stone floor it might go out. She was coughing now, the cellar filling with smoke.

'Burn, go on, burn!' she urged, laying the trestles on their side amid the flames.

She heard a sound that penetrated her concentration. A bang from upstairs.

Norman. She was paralysed. It must be – he was here. Had followed her!

She stood listening, trying not to cough, but it was impossible. The smoke was getting too much. But he mustn't get her down here! If she was to encounter Norman it must be upstairs, where she stood a chance.

Halfway up the stairs, she stopped and listened, taking in deep breaths. Nothing. Was he waiting, in that spot just by the door? She could see no shadow. The smoke was winding up the stairs with her and the coughing was impossible to control. Suddenly, unable to bear it, she tore up the stairs into the office, just as there came another *bang*! The front door slammed shut. The office was empty, but the door was not properly closed, had gusted open. Maryann found she was so unsteady with shaking that she had to sit down at the desk. For a few moments she put her hands over her face and wept, distraught.

'I've got to try and forget this.' She knew even then, without time to reflect. 'Or I'll lose my mind thinking of it. Sal's gone – I'll be gone. No more girls for 'im.' She stood up, fiercely wiping her eyes. 'And this place'll be gone. I'm gunna make sure of that.'

Trying to hold her breath for as long as she could, she felt her way down the dark cellar steps once more. At the bottom she could feel the heat through the door and she picked up the paraffin can and ran up again, gasping frantically for breath as she reached the top. She splashed some paraffin over everything she could manage: ledgers, the padded seats of the chairs, the blinds over the windows, the contents of the desk drawers which she unlocked and took out. On opening the bottom one she paused, looking inside. In this, the deepest drawer, Norman kept his petty cash box. She quickly searched the bunch of keys for the little one which unlocked it. There it was. She tipped all the money into her pockets.

Striking match after match, she went round the room. The blinds were already ablaze as, picking up her things, she ran out into the street and tore away along Monument Road.

Twenty-Five

Running along the cobbles which gleamed wet in the gaslight, she headed instinctively towards Garrett Street and the old yard where she'd grown up, past all those childhood places, the Garrett Arms, dark entries into the back yards, the huckster's shop on the corner near her house: all so familiar, and yet tonight everything felt changed. Because she was changed. Nothing now could ever be the same again. She had to go now, to run away. She had no choice.

In the entry she slowed, treading softly. Though it was pitch dark she could remember every lump and bump in the bricks, the big hole three-quarters of the way down on the left where you could turn your ankle and break it. In a moment she was standing under the lamp in the yard, panting, but feeling suddenly much safer.

There was no hint of dawn, the houses black against the dark sky. She had no idea what the time was. She wondered whether she should wait out the rest of the night in the brewhouse along the yard where they kept the copper for washing clothes, but there was no telling who might come in and find her there first thing in the morning and there might be chickens and all sorts in there. No, she'd have to knock up the Blacks and get them to take her in until she could find Joel.

She knocked cautiously on their door. When she'd

paused and tried a second time the door opened and a tousled head and indignant face appeared. It was Alf Black, holding a candle. He and Charlie, now seventeen and eighteen, slept downstairs.

'It's me, Maryann,' she whispered, going up close to him. 'Don't make a racket, Alf, will you? I don't want no one to know I'm 'ere.'

'What's going on?' Alf demanded.

'*Sssh* – for 'eaven's sakes. Can I come in?'

'Yer do know what time it is, don't yer?'

'No.'

'The middle of the fucking night, that's what.' All the same he stood back. 'Lucky I got up for a piss or I'd never've 'eard yer – and 'e'd never've neither.' Charlie was snoring on the old lumpy sofa. Maryann looked down at him with very mixed emotions. He must have lain beside Sal like that, handsome, his dark hair curling at the nape of his neck, long dark lashes. He had loved Sal, Charlie had, or so Nance said. If he hadn't gone off and left her, maybe she'd be alive . . . Alf stood at a loss for a minute. 'I'll get Nance, shall I?'

Nancy appeared a few minutes later with a candle.

'Maryann? What's going on? Flamin' 'ell, you stink like Smoky Joe. What've yer been doing?'

'Can I stop 'ere for a bit?' Maryann heard her voice turning tearful. 'I don't want them to know where I am. I've done summat terrible, Nance.'

Nance eyed her brother. 'Come up and yer can bunk down with me. You go back to bed, Alf, and keep yer trap shut about this, awright?'

Nance shared one of the two upstairs rooms with Percy, William, George and Horace. Maryann snuggled down with Nance on her single mattress on the floor.

'Come on then,' Nance whispered. 'Out with it.'

233

'Cross yer heart and hope to die yer won't tell no one?'

'Cross my heart.' Maryann felt Nance going through the motions of crossing herself in the dark.

'I set fire to Norman's offices – I 'ope I've burned the 'ole bloody lot down!'

'You *what*? What did yer do that for?'

'Because 'e . . .'e . . .' Maryann felt a sudden lurching inside her, as if she might be sick and she sat up, gulping. She was still shaking.

'You awright?' Nance sprang up again as well.

Maryann fought back the feeling. She felt so strange. All the time since she'd found Sal she'd felt peculiar, as if disconnected from everything around her, from her own feelings. She didn't know she was in shock. She just felt as if she was living behind a glass wall which she couldn't reach through.

'I can't tell you, Nance. I just can't. But Norman Griffin's not like what 'e seems at all, you know, kind and a gentleman. It's all lies. 'E killed our Sal, Nance – 'e did . . .'

'Maryann! What're you saying? You've 'ad a terrible time with Sal . . . dying and that. But that can't be right, can it? Yer stepdad daint *kill* 'er – she . . .' Nance paused. 'She ended 'er own life, Maryann.'

Maryann was shaking her head. 'I 'ad to do it. I 'ad to get 'im somehow. 'E killed our Sal . . .' She was gulping again. Nance's arms came round her, warm and comforting.

'Oh now, Maryann, there, there. I know yer in a state – and yer can stop 'ere with us for a bit if it'll make you feel better. Our mom won't mind . . .'

'I'm going away—'

'Are yer?' She could tell Nance was humouring her

and didn't really believe her. She was stroking her arm. 'Where're yer going then?'

'I can't tell yer.'

'Awright then, Maryann. Look – you lie down 'ere with me, eh? We'll get some kip and see 'ow things look in the morning.'

'They mustn't know I'm 'ere!' Maryann was still rigid, resisting lying down. 'The coppers'll be after me.'

'Awright, awright . . .'

'I *mean* it! I need 'elp, Nance. This ain't pretend, you know. If them lot see me' – she jerked her head towards the sleeping boys – 'they'll be gabbing away to everyone.'

'No they won't – we'll just say yer've come to stay for a bit. They ain't interested. Come on – lie down.'

Maryann tried to sleep, but felt by the morning that she hadn't had a wink. The bed was cramped, there were mice scuttling round the room and she was too churned up with emotion. She got up to face the mayhem that was the Blacks' household.

Nance told the boys Maryann had just come round to 'stop for a day or two' after which they lost interest. Maryann met Blackie on the stairs, clad in a greyish singlet and trousers, who said vaguely, 'Awright? What're yer doing 'ere then?' but he didn't stop long enough to wait for an answer.

Cathleen noticed she was there sure enough. In the midst of all her sons guzzling down bits of bread, she sat feeding Lizzie who was kicking her legs enthusiastically as she suckled. Cathleen had a cold and a hacking cough and kept wiping her red nose on an old rag. When Maryann and Nance came down she squinted with her lopsided eyes, the rag halfway to her nose, then let out a huge sneeze.

'Oh – oh . . . atchoo! Jesus, Mary and Joseph – where did you spring from in the night?'

'Maryann just wanted to stop 'ere for a bit,' Nance said, making faces that indicated she'd tell more when her brothers were out of the way.

She sat Maryann down and gave her a jam jar of weak tea and a slice of dry bread, which made Maryann feel a bit better. She had scarcely eaten all week.

Cathleen stirred herself from her chair to chase her husband and children out to work and school. As soon as she moved she began coughing again, doubled up with it.

'Oh—' she groaned. 'I got through four pair of bloomers coughing last night – I'll be washing all morning . . .'

'Is it awright if I stay for a night or two?' Maryann said, hesitantly. 'I can give yer some money . . .'

'Don't be daft, course yer can,' Cathleen said, shoo-ing the youngest ones out of the door. 'So long as your mother don't mind.'

'They mustn't know I'm 'ere.'

Cathleen turned, Lizzie under one arm. 'Ah now – I'm not so sure about that. Why's that then?'

'Please,' Maryann begged. She searched round for a reason. 'Mom and me 'ad a bit of a ding-dong. It's only for a while.'

Cathleen gave a wan smile. 'Ah well. Can't say I ever liked yer mother, she's a stuck-up bit o' stuff if ever I saw one. So she won't get nothing out of me.'

Nance grinned. 'Thanks, Mom.'

'Thanks, Mrs Black,' Maryann said. 'I'd best get off to work now.'

*

The light was fading as Maryann waited at Camp Hill Locks, later that week, her bundle of possessions in her arms. She was waiting close to the cut, as she had waited now for most of the time since she had run away. The Blacks thought she was at work. Each morning she left the house after breakfast and went to the cut. That first day she said goodbye to Nance when she turned off to go to the laundry and hurried to the toll house where she thought the *Esther Jane* was most likely to come through.

'You back again, are yer?' the man said. 'Darius Bartholomew? S'far as I know they're still working down the Oxford, tekking what comes. I'd say they'd be through 'ere soon if they'm coming. I ain't seen 'em in a while.'

She spent the days walking to keep warm. She had enough money to buy food and cups of tea to keep a bit warmer. The coins in Norman's cash box had added up to four pounds, eleven and sixpence and she felt great satisfaction in spending it on her own comfort. She was afraid of missing the *Esther Jane* but knew she could ask at the toll house. Most of the day she walked along the bank, sometimes sitting down for a while or leaning against a bridge to watch the activity on the cut, but it was too cold to rest for long. These were cold, brittle days. You could see your breath on the air all day long. Under her coat she had on a warm dress and woolly jumper and stockings, though her heels were through them like potatoes and her shoes were too small and pinched her feet. On the second day she went up into Small Heath and looked round the pawn shops for another pair, but she could find nothing but battered old shoes that were all too big. In the end she decided to spend fifteen shillings of

Norman's money on a new pair of brown boots with sturdy soles.

These'll be good for on the cut, she thought, walking along, breaking them in. She kept looking proudly down at her feet. She felt no guilt whatever at having stolen Norman's money. The boots were like the sign of a new life. But she was very, very lonely. The ache in her to see Joel was almost overwhelming. Joel, who was the only person left who felt like family, who had shown her real affection and tenderness. If only they'd come and she could climb on board with them and feel safe and warm at last!

That evening, as the sun was setting, the night growing even colder, she was standing at Camp Hill Locks, where a conglomeration of bridges crossed over the cut as the road, railway and canal all met. She was hungry, her hands and feet were frozen and she felt low and desperate. The sun was setting and the cold becoming more intense, the air sharp and smoky. A line of joey boats was queueing to get through the locks and into basins for the night, all in a hurry to get tied up, and Maryann watched as a fight broke out between two men when one tried to barge in ahead. The loud, cursing voices and snarling expressions jarred right through her, making her feel all the more lonely and desolate as if they were attacking her. It seemed to stand for all the anger and meanness in the world and she turned and walked away, her arms folded across her chest, her head down and despair in her heart.

She longed to go back to the warm, fuggy atmosphere of the Blacks' house, but it was only about six o'clock. If the Bartholomews were putting in a long hard day it could be ten o'clock before they came into

Birmingham. She walked on, past the dark backs of warehouses.

She had walked up and down for another half-hour when a family boat came out of the darkness, its dim headlight moving steadily towards her. Her heart began to race. Surely she could make out the faint glow of white patches on the horse! She tried to keep her hope at bay – she couldn't bear the disappointment if it wasn't them.

'Bessie!' she whispered, peering through the gloom. Cautiously she started to run. Surely that was Bessie, couldn't that be the light of the *Esther Jane*?

As she came close she saw someone was leading the horse, someone big, solid. The one person in the world she longed and longed to see . . .

'Joel! Joel – it's me, Maryann!'

She heard the low rumble of his laughter out of the darkness, then its lapse into coughing for a moment. Then his arm came round her and she was safe.

'How do, our young nipper! Where've you bin then?'

Twenty-Six

She was woken very early the next morning by the delicious smell of bacon frying. Someone was sitting pressed up to her feet. Opening her eyes she saw Joel, bent forward towards the range, outlined against the light from the open cabin door. He was pouring dark, steaming tea from the brown and white teapot.

'Why didn't you wake me?' She sat up. Usually the faintest sound disturbed her. The men must have got up and moved in and out doing morning chores and she hadn't heard a thing. It was the first really sound night's sleep she'd had since Sal died.

Joel turned and grinned at her. His gingery beard glowed in the white dawn light. 'You was sleeping like a baby. Seemed a pity to wake you.'

Maryann smiled back, drinking in the sight of him. Now she had seen Joel and was back on the *Esther Jane* everything felt so much better and full of promise. Even Darius had seemed quite pleased to see her last night. 'I feel as if I've come 'ome, Joel.'

He nodded. 'Reckon so. We're finding it hard two-'anded – 'arder than it's ever been. My father ain't getting any younger and we're chasing loads wherever we go. Another pair o' hands'll be a godsend. All right with your folks now, is it?'

'Oh yes.' She spoke lightly. 'S'awright with them.'

'Good. Well, that's that then.' Maryann felt his blue

eyes on her, as if really examining her for a moment, and she hugged her knees. It was a special sort of look he was giving her and she didn't know what was he was thinking, but it felt nice, him looking at her like that.

He handed her a plate on which there was a thick wodge of bread topped with crispy bacon.

''Ere you go. Get that down you.'

They loaded up that morning, their cargo sacks of bolts and screws bound for Banbury, and by midday they were well underway. Maryann worked as hard as she could, pulling on ropes with all her strength, turning lock gates with the windlass. Both men knew they didn't need to tell her to be careful. She had learned that lesson back in the summer. But she still felt nervous in front of old Darius.

'I'll try not to do anything wrong,' she told him. 'And I'll work ever so 'ard for yer.'

'That's all right, lass,' he said. 'Everyone makes a mistake now and then. I can see you're stroving 'ard as you can.'

His leathery face stretched briefly into a smile. Maryann thought he seemed tired through and through. She had seen that both his hands and Joel's were rough and cracked, the tips of their fingers split from the wet and cold, and Joel was wheezing and coughing badly.

'Your fingers look sore,' she said to him. Joel held out his enormous hands, turning them this way and that.

'Not very pretty, are they?' he said.

Maryann was proud to think she might be of help, but she knew she was about to find out about the

241

harshness of life on the cut in winter. The day was another bright, frosty one and she was very glad she'd bought the new boots. But she was ready for it all.

For that first morning she was filled with an almost insane sense of relief and excitement. She'd got away, she'd found the *Esther Jane*, she was safe, and no one would ever come and find her here! She ran along the bank, a ball of energy, taking the windlass and running at the locks until Joel said, 'Eh, steady on there. There's a long way to go yet!'

But she couldn't seem to help it. As the day wore on, though, her energy began to flag and the cold, strange feeling that had possessed her came back. They had left Birmingham behind, and she shrank into herself and quietened. For a time she climbed up and sat, huddled in her coat, on the roof of the cabin as she had in the summer, and she looked out at the beauty of winter on the cut in Warwickshire. The fields spread out around her, grass hard and sparkling with frost in the low sunshine, the reflection of which rippled along the water. Where there were hedgerows close enough she could see blood-red berries, and the grating cry of crows echoed across from the hoary trees in the distance. The sights were magical, but the further they went, the more the awful numbness seemed to possess her. She was back behind the glass screen where nothing around her felt quite real. She looked down at her hand with its bitten nails, stroking it along the *Esther Jane*'s wooden roof. Even her own hand seemed distant and unreal. She was frightened by it.

''Er's steadied down a bit,' she heard Darius say to Joel. They were at the tiller and didn't seem to expect her to hear although she was not far away. 'Like a barrowload of monkeys she was, this morning.'

Joel must've nodded or made some other sign because she didn't hear him reply. Maryann sat listening, head lowered so that her long hair fell forward. She heard Darius say, 'That child's grown up into a proper lass since we last see'd 'er. She's a proper 'and to us now, Joel, and that's a godsend.'

Maryann felt a blush rise up through her cheeks, filled with a contradictory mix of pride and self-consciousness. It was true, she had grown, suddenly, her body filling out, but it felt odd to hear them talking about her like that. Darius was pleased with her and wanted her on board! She really had found a new life where she was wanted, away from all the disgust and fear and sorrow of her life in Ladywood. Tears blurred her eyes as she looked along the cut. If only she could start to feel back to her normal self, everything would be truly fine.

They were back in the rhythm of the cut, working hard, not speaking much throughout the jouney. Maryann fell exhausted into bed the first night while the men were still in the pub. She was too tired to feel lonely. The second evening they reached Fenny Compton. It was the first of November and very cold, though not quite severe enough to freeze over the cut. By the time Bessie was stabled and Maryann had prepared the evening meal, the frost was setting in. The sun set over the fields in a glow of orange fire and the spare shapes of the trees were silhouetted against the eggshell-blue sky higher up. She saw Joel looking at her as she wiped unexpected tears from her eyes. She never seemed to know what her mood was going to be from one moment to the next.

They ate the stew round the tiny table without saying much, but she felt Joel's eyes turning to her often, his face anxious, and to her frustration her own eyes kept filling with tears which she had to wipe away. All that afternoon, however hard she had tried to force them away, memories of Sal kept pushing into her mind, not as she had last seen her, in despair and death, but as she had been when they were young, so lively and pretty with her long blonde hair, running and laughing in the park or leading Tony by the hand. Sal had loved having a baby brother. Maryann could hardly swallow down any of the food, however much she tried not to think of it. After a while she gave up. She went out and climbed on to the bank, trying to calm herself, looking out across the stern of the *Esther Jane* along the darkening water, her vision blurred by tears.

''Ere – you'll need this.'

Joel was holding out her coat and she put it on, glad of it.

'Come on with me, this way. We'll 'ave a bit of a walk.'

He led her away from the cut and the pub, along a footpath into the fields. There wasn't much light and she had to concentrate on walking on the frozen mud track. For a while Joel led her in silence, along the edge of the field until they came to a gateway, which opened out into another field where black and white cows were just visible in the dying light, standing huddled together not far away.

Joel leaned over the gate for a moment. Maryann looked up at him. He seemed so familiar standing there, his face, the shape of him, his big, work-roughened hands on the gate – it was as if she had known him all her life. He turned to her, one elbow still leaning on the gate.

'You ent yourself since you've come back with us, Maryann.'

'I'm ... I'm awright.' Once more the rush of tears. She wanted to stamp: stop it, stop it, I'm all right! Don't make me talk or remember. I'm where I want to be, just leave me alone!

He stepped away from the gate and put his hands on her shoulders, turning her towards him. She had grown a little, she realized. Her head now came up to his chest.

'Look, little 'un—' Despite his affectionate names for her, she sensed he was treating her differently, like someone older. There was vulnerablilty as well as kindness in his expression. 'I can see there's summat amiss. I don't know what's driven you away from your family, but I do know what a sunny face you 'ad before, Maryann, and I don't see it now. The Maryann that left us is 'ardly the same 'un that's come back.'

Maryann kept her eyes on the ground, shoulders heaving as the great swell of her grief struggled to the surface.

'Speak to me, girl,' Joel said gently. 'It can't do no harm.'

'M-my sister ...' she managed to say, eventually. 'She ki ... ki ... took 'er own life. We only buried 'er in the week.'

'Oh no – oh—' she heard Joel say. 'My poor little bird.'

He took her in his arms and she felt herself held tight against his chest as his deep, growling voice made ceaseless, comforting noises. Over and over again he stroked her hair as she wept, beginning to let out some of the reservoir of horror and pain inside her.

He held her, murmuring his comfort to her for as long as she needed it, not asking questions, just letting her weep until she began to grow quieter. She went limp, leaning against him, gulping and sighing.

'Oh Joel,' she said eventually in tired despair.

'Poor little thing.' There was great tenderness in his voice.

'I thought I'd be awright back with you, and look 'ow I'm carrying on.'

'You will be awright. In a while.' There was a pause, then he said gruffly, 'We didn't half miss you. *I* missed you.' He squeezed her shoulders. 'You ent 'alf growing up, Maryann. I can't help seeing you a bit different. I've not 'ad soft feelings for many lasses, but you – you're coming to be special to me. Silly old fool, ent I?'

Maryann felt the affection and warmth of his words go through her. She gave a tiny laugh. 'No you're not, Joel. You're just you and I want to be with yer.'

He leaned down and carefully planted kisses, first on one cheek, then the other, and she giggled as his whiskers tickled her. His face was still close to hers and he was looking into her eyes.

'You're so sweet,' he said longingly. 'Just so sweet, lass.'

His holding her, the desire in his voice, aroused a flicker of excitement in her. He brought his lips close to hers and gave her a soft peck of a kiss. When she didn't pull away, he embraced her properly, closed his eyes and kissed her more passionately, hungrily. For those first seconds as he had looked at her, kissed her, she had been deeply touched by his gentleness, his desire for her. Then she felt his tongue between her lips, his hands pressing her now more ardently, and in her hurt state, her confusion, something hard and cold slammed down in her like a shutter. What was he doing? He was supposed to be her friend, her brother! And he was starting on this dirty stuff, *invading* her like Norman Griffin had done! But this was Joel. Joel didn't do things like that . . .

'No! Stop it!' She pulled away with such vehemence that he released her immediately, confused. 'Get off me! Don't you ever touch me. I hate anyone touching me!' She was crying again, distraught, starting to run from him, but she had only gone a few paces before her ankle turned on a hummock in the frozen ground and she fell over.

Joel reached down to help her up but she slapped his hand away. 'Don't you ever touch me, yer dirty bastard. I hate yer!' She scrambled up.

'Maryann, don't – what've I done to you?' He seized her arm and made her stop. 'I'm sorry. I just thought you'd . . . You seem so grown up and I've such feelings for you, but I wouldn't hurt you for the world. Please – don't be like this. I'd never do a thing to harm you . . .'

'Take me back to the boat,' she snapped, yanking her arm away. 'Don't touch me. Just take me back.'

Joel stood, hands on hips, staring at her, completely bewildered. 'We'll get back then.' He sounded confused, irritated even.

They walked back in silence. Maryann's mind was in turmoil. How could he have done something like that? He was a grown-up man and she was just a girl! This was supposed to be her safe place, the refuge she had run to for help. But it wasn't safe. He was just like

Norman, he'd made her feel foul and loathsome, and nothing on the *Esther Jane* would ever feel right again.

She refused to speak to Joel again that night, despite him trying to make up with her. She lay down on the side bench and turned away from him. She barely slept at all, listening to the sound of the men a short distance from her, repelled by both of them, wanting now to be anywhere else but here.

The next day they docked at Banbury and work began on unloading the cargo. Darius was busy overseeing that, and Joel had gone in search of another load to take on south or back up to Birmingham. Maryann would have expected to use the time to clean up the cabin, do some washing and put a sparkle on the brasses. Instead, once the men were out of the way, she wrapped up her few things again, pocketed the last of the money she had taken from Norman and climbed ashore, looking round her to make certain both the Bartholomews were out of sight. She walked briskly through the busy wharf area and slipped away, unnoticed, into the bustling town of Banbury.

PART TWO

Twenty-Seven

1934

Maryann carried the tray along the gold carpet of the landing, at pains not to slop tea from the large cup into the saucer. Beside the cup, arranged on delicate china plates, were two boiled eggs, one in the cup, one tucked beside it in a cosy, three slices of buttered toast, a pot of Chivers marmalade and a starched linen napkin in a silver ring. When she reached the last door along the landing, she set the tray down on the floor and knocked.

'Come!'

Each day she carried his breakfast to him, after she had already been up for four hours and had had her own meal in the servants' hall. Roland Musson liked to lie late in bed and eat his breakfast late, and it had been long agreed by the rest of the family that he should because this was what was good and right for him.

'On the table as usual please, Nelson.' He was sitting, tousle-haired, on the edge of his bed, his sturdy frame wrapped in a tartan wool dressing gown although it was May and quite warm. As usual, the room was fuggy with cigarette smoke.

'How do you come to look so hot and rosy-cheeked,' he complained petulantly, arms folded tightly across his chest. 'I feel quite shivery this morning.'

251

Maryann smiled. 'I keep warm working – it's non-stop this time of day.'

Roland Musson didn't reply, but sat looking sunk in gloom. He had the solid Musson looks, large blue eyes and a shock of thick fair hair, but his complexion was growing ruddy from too much drink. When she first arrived at Charnwood House Maryann had found him bad-tempered, demanding and unlikeable. She asked the other housemaids why this young man, a robust twenty-seven-year-old, as he had been then, spent his life confined in the parental home, and much of the time lounged about without purpose in his room.

'It were the war,' Letty, the first housemaid, told her. 'Shot 'is nerves to bits. 'E's better now, Mrs Letcombe says.' The housekeeper could remember the five Musson children as babies. ''E were ever so bad when 'e came 'ome. Crying, nightmares and everything. Wouldn't 'ardly go out of 'is room for months on end.'

'Why doesn't 'e go and get a job?' Maryann asked, thinking this a rum way to go on.

Letty laughed. ''E don't really need to, living 'ere, does 'e? 'E's comfortable enough, and to tell you the truth—' She lowered her voice to a whisper, as the two of them were polishing the dining-room floor and anyone might be within earshot, 'I don't think *she* wants 'im out of 'er sight, what with John being gone and that.'

John, the eldest Musson, an officer in an Oxfordshire Regiment, had been killed in 1917 and Mrs Lydia Musson, an elegant, though rather vague woman with a wreath of thick, wavy hair coiled round her head, seemed to encourage her second son's invalidity. She referred to him as 'poor, dear Roland' and he remained, at once petulant and pitiable, neither challenged to leave, nor seeming to have the will or incentive to do so.

It was getting on for six years since Maryann had come to Charnwood House, four miles out of Banbury, and in that time Roland Musson did seem to get out more. He worked in the grounds in the afternoon with Sid and Wally, the two gardeners, and he had a motorcycle on which he roared dangerously along country roads and across the fields. He had a few friends locally and they sat for hours at a time in village pubs. Maryann, though, couldn't help but compare his plight with that of her father, also scarred by the war, trying to adjust back to family and civilian life and having somehow to struggle on and get jobs, keep afloat, without the cushion of wealth that Roland Musson had beneath him. And Nance's father, Blackie Black, too, and Joel ... But no – she wasn't going to think of Joel. Whenever her mind strayed down any path which would lead her to think about home she blocked out such thoughts. She had found a life that was free of pain and trouble and she wanted to keep it that way. And over the years her dislike for Roland Musson had faded as she grew to understand him better, turning instead to a mixture of tenderness and pity.

Sometimes when she carried Roland's breakfast tray in he was quite jovial and chatty; other times down and sunken into himself. That morning, Maryann stirred two lumps of sugar into his tea and handed it to him, thinking today was one of his depressed days, but he suddenly looked up at her.

'How old are you, Nelson?'

'Nineteen, sir. Twenty come September.'

'You look *different*,' he said taking the cup. 'What is it about you?'

'I really don't know.' She hadn't changed her hair, her morning dress was as usual. She wasn't aware that

Roland ever *saw* her anyway. She was a servant, and they had to stand to one side in the corridors when a family member passed, trying to make themselves invisible.

'You look *yourself* – as if that's how you're meant to look. Chap in my unit – that's what it makes me think of.' Roland spoke musingly into his teacup. 'Went out on a night patrol – one of those bloody woods on the Somme. Can't think what it was all for now but anyhow, they were successful. We'd heard the shots – didn't know who was getting it at the time. But they came back, all of them, full of it.' Roland spoke in his odd, clipped way. 'Anyway, this fellow was one of them. When I saw him the next morning, he looked, well, *altered*. That's it. That's what you made me think of. As if he'd grown into himself overnight.' He took a long drink of the cooling tea and Maryann, puzzled, thought he'd finished and began to turn away. But he carried on.

'Day after that the chap stood up for a few seconds and bang – killed by a sniper. So what was that all about? Man grows up, becomes himself overnight, then –' He snapped his fingers. 'Like a bloody butterfly.'

A moment later he looked up at her again. 'All right. I don't expect you to have an *answer*. Off you go.'

She went back down the stairs, pausing on the landing to look out over the garden, where Wally, the elder of the two gardeners, was bent weeding the long border which edged the drive. It was at its most beautiful at this time of year, the lawn wide and green, the beds bright with flowers, trellises of climbing roses up the outbuildings and the mock orange and laburnum in blossom. The mingled scents drifted in through the open window. From close to the house, out of sight, she could hear the Mussons' two dogs barking: Freddie, a wild young fox terrier with his insistent yap, and the deeper bark of their spaniel, Lily Langtree, who was beginning to run to fat. Freddie suddenly launched himself, a black and white flash across the lawn, with Lily lumbering after him.

Different? What had Roland Musson been on about? Maryann looked down at herself. She may be different, but it certainly hadn't happened overnight. She had grown, of course, and filled out on the plentiful and stodgy servants' food at Charnwood House. When she first arrived she had had no appetite and even Mrs Letcombe cajoled her to eat.

'Come on, girl – you'll have no energy for the work if you eat like a sparrer.'

Gradually, she settled into the rhythm of the house. As she got to know the characters of the other servants and appreciated that she had a good employer and a comfortable life, she felt secure and happy. She liked the predictable routine, the steady days and years. She was under-housemaid to Letty and Alice, and once she'd got used to the place, resolved that she would try hard and work her way up through the pecking order of servants. Two years later, Letty, who was then twenty-one, had married and moved on and Maryann became second housemaid. That was a start, but the job she had her eye on was not to be a housemaid at all. The job she wanted was Ruth's. Ruth, who was in her mid-twenties when Maryann arrived, was lady's maid to Mrs Musson, and to the Misses Diana and Pamela Musson when they were at home, which Pamela still was. Ruth was a quiet, dark-haired, neat young woman, whose job seemed to be regarded in realms high above that of housemaid. As she looked dreamily out at the spring garden that morning,

Maryann was speculating excitedly about the fact that Ruth was now courting with a young baker from the nearest village. If they were to marry, surely Ruth would leave and then perhaps . . .? But would they give the post to Alice, the first housemaid? Surely not! Alice was a good, hard worker, but she was a rough diamond. Was she, Maryann, neat and respectable enough for the job? She had done her darndest to make herself so. Every morning she brushed out her long, black hair and pinned it immaculately in a bun behind her head. She kept her nails short and her uniform mended. Smoothing her hand over her apron and trying to walk with Ruth's cool serenity, she went on down the stairs. Could that have been what Master Roland meant, she thought hopefully, that she looked like someone who wasn't meant to be a housemaid? Was she really destined to be a *lady's* maid?

''Urry *up*!' Alice snapped when Maryann appeared down in the kitchen. 'You should be half done with the bedrooms by now!'

Evan, who worked under the butler, Mr Thomas, winked at her over Alice's shoulder as he passed with a tray of steaming cutlery ready for drying. Maryann ignored him. Suddenly, after a few months of banter with Evan, he was becoming too friendly. He had started creeping up on her in the pantry and putting his arm round her. 'Gerroff!' she'd say to him. 'What're yer playing at?' It made her feel horrible and prickly.

'Master Roland was talking to me,' she retorted to Alice. 'I couldn't just walk out, could I?'

'Well, you'd better get on with it double quick now's all I can say,' Alice ordered.

Maryann made a face behind Alice's back. Since she'd been first housemaid Alice had gone power mad.

She began on Pamela Musson's room. Pamela,

voluptuous, blonde and loud, was only two years older than Maryann and was the youngest of the Musson children. The room was pretty, decorated in pale blue and white, with a soft, silky bedspread, curtains the colour of bluebells and a thick blue carpet. As usual, Pamela had left her nightclothes strewn across the floor and the bedding tipped off right over the side. Her dressing table was a litter of powder puffs and perfume, there was face powder spilt on the floor, stockings dangling languidly over the edge of one drawer and coat-hangers and underslips dropped on the floor by the cupboard. Maryann sighed. When she had arrived she found it almost impossible to take in that Pamela was the same age Sal had been. She was both a child and a young woman, both so much more sophisticated and knowing than Sal, yet so much more sheltered and childlike in other ways. She and Diana had gone about in their 'flapper' outfits, or their fashionable lounging clothes in bright colours with wide flowery bandeaux round their hair and hanging jauntily down at the back. Maryann had been astonished by their energy, their colourful freedom and confidence as they danced and giggled their way through life. Diana was married now and had stopped giggling some time soon after the ceremony. Pamela, who had done secretarial training, did her 'bit of work, to show willing' and otherwise existed in a round of social visits and Young Farmers' dos and 'hops' in Banbury and kept talking about 'getting a little job in London'. Pamela was rather hoping someone would marry her quite soon too and she sometimes told Maryann about her beaux.

Maryann gathered up and folded Pamela's fine stockings. If she was a lady's maid she would deal with their pretty clothes all the time and help them do their hair instead of cleaning out grates before the sun had risen of a morning and polishing floors with beeswax and turps! She pictured herself. Maryann Nelson: lady's maid. And then her hope withered. They most likely wouldn't even think of her for the post. They'd stopped wincing now every time she opened her mouth, but she'd never forgotten Diana Musson's mirth the first time she heard Maryann speak.

'Where on earth,' she screamed, between red-lipstick lips, 'did she get that *terrible* accent?'

'Birmingham, my dear – I gather,' Mrs Musson told her, and Diana looked closely at Maryann as if she was a rather exotic wild animal.

'How perfectly extraordinary! Is the child quite well? She looks so dreadfully *thin*.'

Maryann shook out the crumpled underslips and put them out for Ruth to iron. Then she stood and looked at herself for a moment in Pamela's long mirror. A dark-eyed, serious face stared back at her. She was no longer 'dreadfully *thin*', that was one thing for certain. Slender, but curving, and rounder in the face than she had ever been.

I'm a woman now, she thought, looking herself up and down in surprise. Women were supposed to marry and have babies. Maryann had spent so much time not thinking of herself, of her body, of her past, it came as a shock to her to notice she had grown up so much.

Will I ever be able to be normal? she thought. Questions, feelings, which she had closed off in herself, were beginning to nudge their way to the surface.

She pushed the cupboard door shut, closing off her view of herself. She didn't want to look. It was too frightening.

Twenty-Eight

Charnwood House had been a haven to her, a place where she had enjoyed a long period of calm, like an animal in hibernation. Her fondest memory of arriving to work at Charnwood, after the nerve-racking interview with Mrs Letcombe (for which she prepared herself in the local baths with a good wash and change of clothes), was that first Christmas. By then she had been in the Mussons' employ just a few weeks, having arrived at Banbury in early November, and she was still thin and withdrawn, closed in on herself. Looking back on it now, she could see that she had been really beside herself, in shock at Sal's death, at her own cruel treatment by their stepfather, and by her feelings that Joel had betrayed her.

That Christmas she began to close the door on the past. By the time the celebrations began she was already getting used to the day-to-day work of Charnwood House. She liked Letty and Alice wasn't too bad, if rather petty. Letty was fair-minded and made sure everyone did their share, and life in the servants' quarters was orderly and amiable. Mrs Letcombe was a motherly person – indeed she was a widow and mother of four grown-up children. Cook was blunt and strange and there were rumours that she had been crossed in love. Her dearest pleasure was to moan and mither, but most of it was just talk, and the butler Mr Thomas was touchy and pompous, but a kind man at heart. All of them assured her she had landed on her feet, and she soon found it to be so.

The week before Christmas, Sid and Wally, overseen by Mr Thomas, dragged a huge Christmas tree in through the front door and it was set up in a gleaming brass pot in the front drawing room where there was a fire blazing for the holiday season. Maryann and some of the others were allowed to watch Mrs Musson dressing the tree, accompanied by Diana and Pamela; Hugh, the third boy, whose age fell between that of the two girls, was not yet home from boarding school. Maryann stood warming herself in the lovely room, with its comfortable chintz-covered chairs and long, sweeping curtains and watched, rapt, as the girls trimmed the tree with baubles and red and gold ribbons and a beautiful angel with gauzy wings which was pinned to the very top by Diana, on tiptoe on a chair.

'There—' She stood back afterwards and admired their work. 'How do you like that?'

She turned to Maryann, who mumbled back nervously, 'It's very nice.'

Diana burst out laughing, looked at her sister and said, 'Noice – oh isn't she a scream!'

Maryann blushed, but they laughed so much and without malice that she joined in in the end.

'Don't mind us,' Pamela said sweetly. 'It's just we've never met anyone from Birmingham before.'

Diana suddenly peered closely at her. 'You're very young, aren't you? Why have you come down here?'

Maryann's throat went dry. 'Erm – I was looking for work.'

'But however did you *get* here?' Pamela asked.

'Down the cut.'

The two girls found this hugely funny.

'Down the *what*?'

'She means the canal, I believe,' Mrs Musson said, selecting sprigs from a pile of holly and laurel leaves from the garden. 'Did you now, dear – that *is* an unconventional way to travel, I must say.'

Maryann was very relieved when they left her alone. But she couldn't stop looking at the tree, which was the biggest and most beautiful she had ever seen, and the fire beside it, stacked with apple wood which made a delicious smell as it burned.

They had had a very busy time preparing the house. Maryann drew pleasure from simply moving about in such a lovely home, with its shining wood floors smelling of beeswax, the wide staircase with its red carpet and smooth wooden banister, the long windows and beautiful curtains. So much space, such sumptuous furniture. Compared with this, the houses in Ladywood seemed so dwarfed and mean.

On Christmas Eve, the Mussons' relatives started to arrive and the house was full of cries of greeting, doors opening and shutting, luggage being carted up to the rooms and the frantic barking of the two dogs. Mrs Musson's sister came with her daughters, and Pamela and Diana ensconced themselves in their rooms in the evening with their cousins – giggling, exchanging clothes and making themselves up for dinner.

In the days before Christmas, Diana had called the three housemaids together in the hall, lined them up with an indulgent grin on her face, and said, 'Now – we always give our people a little gift for Christmas. I'd like you to think of something you'd like. Nelson – what about you?'

Maryann, standing to attention with her arms by her

sides, felt her hands begin to sweat and her heart was thumping hard. Whatever was she supposed to say?

'I ... er ... I dunno, miss,' she gasped. She looked desperately at Alice and Letty but they were both staring straight ahead of them.

'There must be some little thing you could do with, surely?' Diana Musson quizzed her.

'Well – I could do with a comb,' Maryann dared to say.

Diana gave her loud laugh. 'A comb? Oh my dear, how sweet! I think we can manage a comb, don't you worry.'

Maryann was relieved to find that Alice and Letty's requirements were barely less modest than her own. Alice asked for a roll of ribbon and Letty wanted some needles and sewing thread. Diana went away, laughing cheerfully.

On Christmas morning the family walked out along the frosty lane to the village church and came back gusting in on the cold air and still singing scraps of carols. Mr Musson had evidently been asked to read from the Old Testament. His loud, declamatory voice boomed up to her as she passed along the landing upstairs.

'The Lord has forsaken me; my God has forgotten me! Can a woman forget the infant at her breast—' There was a pause as he seemed to be struggling, with a grunt, out of his coat and there was laughter downstairs. '—or a loving mother the child of her womb?'

Maryann had slowed, listening. The words brought back the smell of St Mark's Church in Ladywood, the dark, hushed space inside. And they pierced her heart. 'A loving mother...' A great pang of homesickness passed through her. She could picture the house in Anderson Street, Christmas Day: Tony and Billy waking to find one of Mom's old stockings on the foot of the bed with a penny and and orange, maybe a knob of sugar and a little notebook and pencil or toy inside. Her mom'd never been bad at that sort of thing. It was the thing to do and she'd always been all right at 'the thing to do'. It was anything requiring more emotional effort she couldn't seem to manage. Maryann's eyes filled at the thought of Tony and Billy. Half the family gone, no sisters to give them any love.

She wrote notes home to Tony and Nance every now and then, wanting them to know she was still thinking of them. She couldn't bear to think of Tony believing she had completely deserted him without a thought. In all this time though, she had never had letters back, as she had not disclosed her address to them. She didn't want anyone knowing where she was. But sometimes she felt so desolate, never hearing from any of them. Had Tony still got the china cat she'd given him that looked like Tiger? Did he ever think of her, she wondered. He and Billy must be quite grown up by now. Her throat ached with tears. She was just on the point of breaking down and crying when she heard footsteps coming towards her. It was Letty.

'Maryann – you all right? Mrs M wants us all down in the games room.'

When they went to the games room at the back of the house, Maryann found the servants all beginning to line up, and on the billiard table, a row of little wrapped parcels. Mrs Musson was there, and her daughters and their female cousins. Mrs Musson's greying hair was pulled back into a more elegantly styled bun than usual, and she wore a dress of rich red velvet trimmed with gold brocade, which Maryann thought the loveliest she had ever seen.

As she and Letty joined the end of the line, Mrs Musson was already calling the names of the servants one by one. Each parcel had a label in the shape of a leaf. Maryann saw Mrs Musson shaking hands with Mr Thomas and wishing him 'the good health and joy of the season'. Then Mrs Letcombe, followed by Cook. When Mrs Letcombe opened her parcel, which was rather larger than most of the others, the layers of flimsy paper revealed a batch of balls of soft, lilac-coloured wool. Mrs Letcombe did a great deal of knitting and she gasped with pleasure.

'Oh Mrs Musson, Miss Diana, *thank you*.' She laughed. 'Oh that's beautiful, that really is.'

'Now you make sure you knit something for yourself and not just all those grandchildren of yours!' Diana teased her. 'It's for *you* to have something nice.'

When Maryann's turn came, she felt her hand taken into Mrs Musson's cool, smooth palm and she glanced up at her shyly before lowering her eyes in confusion to the floor.

'A happy Christmas to you, my dear,' Mrs Musson said. 'I do hope you're settling in well with us. Mrs Letcombe says you're a credit.'

'Thank you,' Maryann mumbled, unsure where to put herself. 'It's very nice 'ere – thank you, Mrs Musson.' She glanced up again at Diana, whose red-lipped grin was bearing down on her as usual.

'Here's a gift for you, Nelson.'

'Thank you, miss.' She gave an awkward sort of curtsy as she accepted the parcel excitedly. Whatever it was, it wasn't just a little comb!

Tearing the paper off carefully, she found a brush and comb set, with a mirror included. The comb was tortoiseshell and the brush had a smooth wooden handle. She felt a big smile spreading over her face. 'Oh these're lovely, oh they are!'

Letty had been given a beautiful little embroidered sewing pouch with needles and coloured threads, a silver thimble and a tiny pair of scissors, and Alice had three rolls of satiny ribbon in green, purple and royal blue. They were all delighted.

'Back to work now,' Letty said. 'No rest for the wicked.'

The day was indeed hard work, feeding the Mussons and their visitors, clearing up and tending to all the rooms, but Maryann loved the atmosphere of the house, the comings and goings, the laughter and loud air of festivity. Christmas was her favourite time at Charnwood, even though every year since she had been there she had to fight back poignant thoughts of home.

The years gradually took on a routine. In the summer the Mussons went to the sea for several weeks, living in a cliff house they owned that looked out over the Salcombe estuary in Devon. Roland never went with them, however much Mrs Musson entreated him, saying the change and sea air would do him good. It was as if any such change to his habits had become impossible for him. But Maryann was allowed to go some years and every time plans were being made she hoped and prayed she'd be taken along. That first time, in 1929, was the first time she had ever seen the sea. They arrived, snaking slowly down the coast road on a dazzling July day, seeing the blue spread out until it faded into a blur at the horizon, and Maryann thought she had never felt so happy and excited. The month she passed there with Letty and the family was not arduously hard work and the two girls were allowed to go paddling in the sea, walk on the cliffs smelling the yellow gorse and sit on the beach licking ice creams. Maryann thought she was in heaven.

'I don't ever want to go 'ome!' she said to Letty. 'I never knew there was places like this in all the world!'

Letty laughed, wiggling her back into a comfortable position on the sand. 'Well, if you play your cards right you'll come back next year.'

And so the seasons went, and so she grew up: Christmas, spring cleaning, summer holidays, autumn coming round again; living through the events of the family: Miss Diana's wedding, Pamela's ups and downs with 'chaps', Hugh leaving school and joining Mr Musson at the bank, and Roland, who was always, disquietingly, at home. The three girls followed the lives of their employers like characters in a storybook or a play. The Mussons' events were often their events. And this suited Maryann more than she even realized. Living through their lives saved her from having to live her own.

And then Evan came and began to prise her feelings open again.

Twenty-Nine

Maryann stood in the kitchen, waiting as the toast for Roland Musson's breakfast tray browned on the griddle. The back door was open as it was a warm morning of blue sky and puffy clouds, and a breeze blew into the kitchen, dispersing the smells of egg, soap and disinfectant that lingered there. Cook was at the table laying chump chops in a row ready for lunch and murmuring about needing to 'get on and steam that pudding'.

Maryann snatched the toast from the griddle and on to a plate before it could burn and went to the pantry to fetch the butter. Out of the corner of her eye she saw Evan come into the kitchen and did her best to ignore him. She removed the eggs from the pan with a spoon and arranged them as usual on the tray. But as she was buttering the toast she sensed Evan sliding round beside her. For a second his hand rested on her buttocks.

She twisted away from him furiously, hoping Cook would notice and tick him off, but it was her turn to disappear into the pantry.

'*Don't*, Evan!'

His dark eyes looked laughingly into hers. 'You're a proper tease you are, aren't you, girl? Never mind – there'll be time for us to have some fun later on.'

Maryann looked into his round face with its habitual jaunty expression, his plump little neck squeezed into the collar of his uniform. He winked at her, as usual, and she turned her back on him again. Whatever she said to Evan, however many times she asked him to leave her alone, it seemed to make no difference.

'I dunno why you're so nasty to 'im,' Alice said to her sometimes, jealous that no one was fixing their attention on her. ''E's handsome and 'e'll get on – 'e's a good worker.' Maryann and Evan were the same age, and in the months Evan had been there he had pursued Maryann with increasing determination. She realized she represented a challenge, even if he didn't like her very much.

Maryann would shrug. How could she explain what she felt to Alice, how much the sight of Evan filled her with panic. He revolted her and she was enraged by his assumption that she didn't know her own mind, that if he kept on and on at her she'd fall willingly into his arms.

'Go on – come for a walk with me this afternoon, eh? You and I could 'ave a lot of fun. Spring fever and that, eh?' He nudged her with his elbow and gave a wink. It was her afternoon off every Wednesday and by hideous coincidence it was also Evan's.

'No,' she said abruptly. 'I don't want to walk out with yer, Evan. I don't know how else to get it through your thick head. I ain't coming with you and I never will. Now get out of my way – I've got to take up Master Roland's breakfast and you're holding me up.'

'Evan,' Cook commanded. 'Get on with your work or you won't be going anywhere this afternoon.'

Evan backed away, making gestures behind Cook's back and grinning in a way that made Maryann want to punch him. She put the teapot on the tray and set off upstairs. She felt horribly unsettled. Evan had only been in the house a matter of months, but gradually he had begun to transform it from her haven of safety and certainty to a place where she was always on her guard if he was about. She would creep softly to the door of the kitchen to check that she was not likely to be alone with him in there. She very seldom was, as Cook was almost always at her post. She checked round corners now, to see if he was coming. When he came near her the feeling of panic that rose in her set her pulse racing uncomfortably. He was so single-minded, so cunning and yet so stupid, and the combination was completely unnerving.

As she put the tray down and knocked on Roland Musson's door, the thought came to her that not once, in all the time she had been at Charnwood House, had Roland ever felt dangerous to her in this way.

'Come!'

The door swung open. He had actually got up off the bed and opened it for her. Maryann stood in the doorway, astonished.

'Thank you.' She bent for the tray but he said, 'Allow me,' and swooped down beside her, looking like a tousled-haired little boy.

'Another delicious breakfast,' he said, sniffing at the toast. 'I'm well ready for it today.'

'You won't be needing me then.'

'Oh yes, do come in. Come and do some of your tidying up or something.'

'But—' Usually she worked on his room later, once he'd gone out.

'Don't argue. I don't mind you doing your work with me in the room.' He closed the door behind them. 'In fact, you're one of the few things that breaks the monotony round here.'

He sat on the bed, pulling the small table close to

put the tray on, and began to eat. Uncertain for a moment, Maryann looked round the room, then began to pick up Roland Musson's clothes which were thrown on the floor all round the chair. As she was folding his shirt, trying not to watch him eating as it seemed rude, he said, 'How long have you been here now, Nelson?'

'Five years last November, sir.'

'Extraordinary. Is it really that long? God, what an appalling thought.'

'What's that?'

'Well, here're you, five years later, grown-up, opening up like a bud and a lovely one at that. Moving on, you know. And here am I, thirty-three years old, stuck here like an old fossil in a lump of rock.'

Maryann hesitated and looked across into his eyes. She felt she had to be very careful what she said. 'You had to go through the war, sir.'

'So did plenty of others. I'm not the only chap in England who's terrified of sleep, you know. Did you lose anyone in the war?'

'Yes, sir. My father. At least – no, well he didn't die in the war . . .'

Roland paused, a spoonful of egg in mid-air. 'What d'you mean?'

'He didn't die in the war. It just felt as if 'e did – in a way.'

'Yes.' He pointed the spoon at her. 'Yes, that's it exactly. You're a sharp girl, Nelson.'

After a moment he said, 'I suppose you find me a useless piece of goods. The way I've never picked up.'

'No, sir.' Not useless. What was more puzzling to her was that there was no *necessity* for him to work. It went against everything she had grown up used to.

'Don't pretend to me, Nelson, please. I have buried

myself alive here. Buried in the safety of mother love and a full belly. But d'you know what?'

He waited for her to speak.

'What – sir?'

'I almost think that one day I shall leave here. I shall do it. Resurrect myself. Live.'

Maryann said nothing, not knowing what to say. She picked up his shoes and laid them straight on the gold carpet. They were very big, moulded touchingly into the shape of his feet.

'D'you think I could manage it? I shall go to . . . to, let's say, Algeciras. Yes. What about that?'

'I – I don't know where that is.'

'It's somewhere Johnny always wanted to go, you know. Don't know why now. Its name seemed to have a magic for him. Algeciras . . .' He drifted off into silence. Often he couldn't finish a conversation, lost the thread of it somewhere.

'Yes,' he said eventually. 'It's all a great pity.'

That afternoon when Maryann had finished her lunch-time duties she went up to change. Hers was a small attic room, with a rug on the bare floorboards, but with a high window facing over the drive and she had grown very fond of it. She had few possessions, but over the years had accumulated things to decorate the walls; pictures from magazines of soft-faced, smiling ladies with silken clothes. She loved to look at them and imagine dressing up like that herself. And now spring was here she had gathered a little posy of flowers from the garden. Last time she had been out, as she some-times did in the evening, she had come across Roland, walking up from the lower end pushing a wheelbarrow.

Usually if she wanted flowers she asked Sid or Wally. This time though, she had not even had to ask. Roland had lowered the handles of the barrow, stepped over and picked several sprigs of orange flower which he presented to her with a shy gallantry.

'There you are. I expect you'd like those. All women like flowers, don't they?'

She'd thanked him, startled. The flowers were still sitting in the jar in her room and the scent of them came to her powerfully every time she went in. Poor Master Roland, she thought, smiling at them. His awkwardness had touched her. What would become of him?

She changed out of the grey dress and white cap and apron which made up her morning uniform and put on her one summer frock, a cotton dress in a pretty blue floral print which Pamela Musson had handed on to her, and put some money in her purse. She now earned ten shillings a week at Charnwood House, but apart from a few small necessities found little to spend her money on, and she had savings of almost thirty pounds which she kept in her room, wrapped in an old handkerchief. She had long grown out of her boots bought for working on the cut, so she kept her black work shoes on, picked up her cardigan and set off downstairs. She planned to walk into Banbury and post another note she had written to Tony. Of course, the family could have moved house by now for all she knew, but every couple of months she dropped him a few lines, and included messages for Billy. It was hard to believe that Billy must be nearly ten by now – and Tony was old enough to start work. Billy had most likely forgotten who she was, but even if that was true, she wanted her brothers to know she still thought of them and cared for them.

Carrying the letter she crept down the attic stairs, then the back stairs to the kitchen, where she found Cook dozing on an upright chair by the window, her head sagging on to her chest. Sensing someone standing close to her she woke with a start and looked, for a few seconds, quite demented.

'Oh! Maryann you didn' 'alf make me jump. Ooh my word!' she grumbled, clutching her chest. 'What're you creeping about like that for? I thought you was off out.'

'Where's Evan?' Maryann whispered.

'Oh 'e's gorn – 'alf 'n hour back I should think.'

'Oh good. That's awright.' She felt she was breathing more easily. 'I'll be off myself then.'

She walked down the drive of Charnwood House, along the scented border of flowers, between the tall elms, all pushing out fresh green leaves, and on to the side lane that, after about half a mile, joined the main road to Banbury. At the road she stopped for a moment, emerging from the shade of the trees, put her head back and closed her eyes, enjoying the feel of the sun on her face and arms. It was a warm, calm afternoon and she breathed in deeply, luxuriating in a few hours of freedom.

She walked quite briskly along the road, bordered on each side by hedges, hawthorn and blackthorn and buttercups, bindweed and blue field madder in the grass beside them. Young blackbirds and thrushes twittered from the hedges. After a few moments she stopped, moved close to the hedge and looked across to the field beyond. It was a rough pasture and a short distance away she could see the white tails of rabbits as they bucked nervously around a warren, so far oblivious to her presence. Maryann smiled, watching them. A gentle breeze ruffled the grass, but otherwise it was very quiet, not a sound except for the birds. Somewhere over there must be the cut, winding through the fields. She looked down, suddenly aware of herself, standing here alone, with time to think. It seemed very *odd* suddenly that she was here in this life so divorced from her childhood.

How did I get here? she thought. Here am I, nearly twenty – I could be here doing this for the rest of my life. She turned the envelope in her hands and looked at her brother's name. 'Master Tony Nelson'. He was supposed to be Tony Griffin, but she would never, never call him that. This was her family now: two boys who she might never see again. She didn't count her mom. A great feeling of loneliness came over her. Would she never have anyone to call her own? Would her whole life be spent here? She might become a lady's maid, but then wouldn't she just be a dried-up, middle-aged woman, living through all the events of the Mussons' life instead of having any real happiness of her own? The bleakness of this outlook brought tears to her eyes. Until now, Charnwood had offered the haven she needed. It had brought her a sense of calm. But now it suddenly didn't seem to be nearly enough.

She walked on, wiping her eyes, deep in thought, no longer noticing the beauty around her, and turned on to the main road. For the first time in a very long while, she allowed herself to think about the events that had driven her to this place. Sal's death, the fire, Joel ... Joel's betrayal of her, the disgust she had felt. She relived that journey down to Banbury on the cut, the night he had taken her out to the fields, trying to see his face in her mind. The lust in it, the disgusting, frightening emotions that drove men ... Joel's face swam into her mind, lit by the silver light of that winter night.

'I've such feelings for you . . .' He'd said that. She hadn't heard, she'd only panicked and fought him off. That face had been full of Joel's tenderness and shame and bewilderment.

I was only a child, she thought, clinging bitterly to her anger. He shouldn't've done that to me.

But now the memories came to her of the feeling of being held by him, the comfort and power of him, the sense of safety he had always given her. Had she made a mistake? Had she got it all wrong and twisted because she was young and in a terrible state? She stopped, looking up the road. Joel was long gone now, of course – she couldn't say any of this to him. But she needed to admit it to herself. There was a gateway up ahead and she decided to go and rest on it, to let herself think for a little while, however much it hurt.

On her usual visits to Banbury what Maryann normally liked to do was to spend a couple of hours strolling round the town, along the Horsefair, past the famous Banbury Cross, looking in the windows of shops, perhaps buying a few small things, sometimes more notepaper to write to Tony. She would often treat herself to a cup of tea and a Banbury cake in one of the teashops. Today she bought a stamp and posted Tony's letter, first kissing the envelope.

'Hope yer get this, Tony,' she murmered, slipping it into the posting box. Her hand was shaking as she held it out. 'I hope yer awright, you and Billy. God bless yer both.'

She began her usual wandering, peering in the window of a china shop at the beautiful Wedgwood cups and saucers, the pretty ornaments, little vases and painted animals. Further along was a dressmaker's and haberdashery store. Should she buy a length of poplin to make a skirt? But her heart wasn't in it. She wasn't very good at sewing, even with all the help and guidance Mrs Letcombe had given her, and today she couldn't seem to keep her mind on anything. She found herself wandering purposelessly among the Banbury streets, across the Market Place amid the clamour of the busy vendors and shoppers and smells of food.

Before she realized it she found warehouses growing up around her, the scents of bread and fruit fading to be replaced by more grimy smells of coal and dust, wharf buildings growing up around her and the sudden sight and smell of the cut. She had only once been back to the cut before, further along, when she wandered there by mistake a few years earlier. Since then she had kept away deliberately.

The sight of it flooded in on her. A pair of narrow-boats were gliding towards her, towed by a stringy mule, his reflection shimmering in the grey, murky water. A great rush of memories flooded into her mind. The cabin of the *Esther Jane*, the beauty of the Oxford Canal when she had seen it in glorious summertime and with the white frost of winter. And the steady, tranquil glide of the boat, with Joel at the tiller, his great strong arm guiding her. In her mind she heard his laugh, the way she had heard it that first time she met him, then later, when she ran to him in the dark by the lock. She found tears welling in her eyes again at the thought of him, at the love she had for him that she had rejected, that she had run from and turned her back on.

'Oh Joel,' she whispered. 'Wherever you are – I shouldn't have run away from you like that!'

Thirty

She went back to Charnwood House to start work that evening. When she walked into the kitchen Evan was there, leaning nonchalantly against the table talking to Alice.

"Ello, Maryann,' Alice said. 'D'you 'ave a nice afternoon?'

'Yes, ta,' Maryann said abruptly, walking past them both. 'I'll take the water upstairs,' she added.

One of her tasks in the evening was to carry up the heavy brass cans of hot water which the family used for their evening wash before dinner, draping them with a towel to keep the heat in before the water was poured into the porcelain basins. Polishing the cans was also one of her daily duties. Once they were down having their dinner, she and Janet, the third housemaid, had to scurry round tidying rooms, picking up dropped clothes, plumping cushions and, in winter, brushing round the grate and refuelling the fire. In the summer the workload was lighter.

She took Pamela Musson's water to her room and found her lolling on her bed. 'Oh my – is it that time already?' she said languorously. Next, Maryann went down and fetched Roland's water. Once the cans were full they were quite arduous to carry. She felt herself starting to sweat. She hoped Roland wouldn't be in his room as he always seemed to want to delay her these days. But when she knocked he called, 'Come!'

'Your water, sir.'

'Ah – it's the lovely Nelson again.' He'd clearly just come in from the garden and was still dressed in his working clothes. There was a glass of whiskey on the table and she could smell it in the air. 'Very civil of you, Nelson,' Roland said. 'Pour it in – usual place.' He held out his arm expansively.

Maryann obeyed, thinking, someone's been pouring something stronger down him by the look of him.

'I don't know why – I feel in a damn good mood today,' Roland said, flinging himself down on the bed.

'That'll be a bit of sunshine, sir.'

'Yes, perhaps you're right.'

She went to the door.

'Nelson?'

'Yes, sir?'

'I—' He opened his mouth, then closed it again, brow wrinkling. 'I was on the verge of saying something tremendously important just then, but I'm damned if I can think what it is. God – d'you think I'm really past it, Nelson? Is this the first sign?'

'I think it may be the whiskey,' Maryann suggested.

Roland Musson lay back and roared with laughter. ''Course it is! Course it is! Why didn't I think of that?'

She slid out of the door and downstairs. As she reached the bottom, Evan came out of the kitchen on his way to the dining room.

'Aha!' he hissed. ''Ere she is then. 'Ello, beautiful!' He came up close to her so that she had to press herself against the wall with Evan's face close to hers. She was immediately filled with panic. Every encounter like this brought back Norman Griffin, him forcing her against

278

her will. Head back against the wall, trying to get as far away from Evan as possible, she managed to look into his eyes, praying her own would not betray her fear. He was smirking at her. This was just a game to him. He breathed into her face.

'I'm still waiting for that kiss.'

It went on and on. She avoided Evan at all possible times, but it got so that everywhere she went she seemed to see his round, leering face, even if he was nowhere near. She even dreamed about him, thinking he had come into her room at night and she woke sweating with fear. All her old ghosts came out to haunt her. The horror of being pursued, trapped by a man for his own dirty purposes, rose in her until she was beginning to live on her nerves and couldn't sleep at night.

Both of them were busy most of the time. Evan was under Mr Thomas's wing and Maryann had plenty of work. But eating meals together in the servants' dining room next to the kitchen became a torment. His eyes scarcely seemed to leave her face. Every time she looked up, there he was, ogling at her until she was put right off her food. Once she found herself on the point of bursting into tears and had to hurry out to compose herself. He was always looking for opportunities to get her on her own. Usually she could dodge him, but the time that was most difficult was Wednesday afternoon: the time they both had off together.

'Alice,' Maryann asked one day. 'D'you think we could change – you 'ave Wednesday off and I'd 'ave the Thursday instead?'

Alice frowned. 'Ooh no – I don't think so.' She had

no good reason for wanting Thursday as her day off. She just wasn't one to oblige other people. 'No – I'll keep my Thursday.'

Maryann got so she was too scared to walk into Banbury in case Evan followed her. Even staying round the house she felt very uneasy. In the summer months she liked to go into the garden. To one side, near the bottom end, was a walled rose garden, bright with blooms at this time of year, sheltered to sit in and deliciously scented by the rose petals. The servants were allowed to sit there during their leisure time, provided none of the family wished to use it.

So, one Wednesday in July, a baking hot afternoon, Maryann went out of the house, looking round her as she seemed to do all the time at present. The garden was warm and peaceful. She could see no sign even of Sid or Wally, and Roland only worked when it suited him. Taking her cardigan to sit on she walked down under the trees – a mature old oak, a young monkey-puzzle tree, maples with beautiful coloured leaves – and into the rose garden. Peering through the gap in the wall she saw no one was there, and immediately she was within the walls she relaxed.

The rose garden was square and immaculately maintained, with beds all round the edge, a path running round inside them, and two large beds of roses in the middle. Between them was a long lozenge-shaped patch of grass. Though the two benches along the side received the most sun, Maryann spread her cardigan on the grass and lay down. She was tired and longed to lie in the sun, have a snooze and relax after all the hard work of the week.

It was very hot. Lying back with her eyes closed she felt immediately drowsy. Somewhere in the far distance she could hear a tapping noise, a mallet on a wooden post, which seemed to echo on the air, and closer by there were the sounds of birds and buzzing insects. The sun's rays beat down on her face and she began to fall asleep straight away.

It took her a few moments to notice that the sun had gone in and a shadow had fallen across her. She put a hand up to shield her face and open one eye, then sat up with a horrible start. Evan was standing, straddling the place where her feet had been, hands on his waist, staring down at her.

Maryann wrapped her arms tight round herself in protection.

'What're yer doing creeping up on me?' She tried to sound angry and commanding but her voice had gone squeaky.

Evan lolled down on the grass beside her, shuffling up close so that Maryann had to lean away from him.

'I saw you come down here. Don't seem to be able to find you on your own these days, Maryann.'

'What d'yer want?' As if she didn't know. She edged away from him.

'You're a funny one you, aren't you?' He sat back, leaning on his hands and looking at her. He sounded reasonable.

'Am I?'

He leaned towards her again and she felt his hot breath on her cheek. 'Look, there's not much time around 'ere, is there? Why can't you stop being so prim and proper and enjoy yourself while it's on offer?'

Maryann was all knotted up inside and her limbs had gone weak. She pulled her chin down on to her knees. 'I don't want it, Evan.'

'Come on—' He budged closer and started to play with her hair. 'You just need to get started.'

A moment later his other hand slid in behind her knees, feeling for her breast, and she felt his lips on her ear.

'Come on, girl – I've got something for you in 'ere—' He pressed his body hard against her, pinching her breast as he did so. 'Why don't we go up to your room and I'll show you? No one'll see.'

'Oh, get *off*!' Maryann launched herself to her feet, catching Evan off balance and leaving him sprawled on his side. 'Get yer dirty 'ands off of me. I don't want yer touching me.'

She saw a really ugly look come over Evan's face that chilled her. 'You're not normal, you, you know that? Not a proper girl at all.' His top lip curled in a snarl of disgust.

'Leave me alone—' She was growing distraught. 'Whatever I am, just leave me alone. I don't want yer anywhere near me. Go and make up to Alice – she'll 'ave yer like a shot. But if you come near me again I'll go to Mrs Letcombe and I'll get you sent away from 'ere.'

'She won't listen to you!'

It was Maryann's turn to stand over him. 'Oh, you're wrong there, Evan. I've been 'ere a hell of a sight longer than you have and Mrs Letcombe's been good to me. So you keep yer filthy hands to yourself from now on.'

She snatched up her cardigan, determined not to let Evan see that her legs and hands were trembling, and strode back to the house.

As the summer passed in the usual way, events in the wider world seemed very distant from Charnwood

House and its inhabitants. Mrs Lydia Musson sat every afternoon with a shawl round her shoulders and her feet up on a stool reading a newspaper, so the hunger marches from the north of England and the rise of Fascist groups constituted some of the drawing-room conversation. But they were not a highly political family. And Maryann was barely aware of the world outside Charnwood and its small domestic dramas.

Evan continued to smirk at her and make snide remarks, but he had not made any more attempts to touch her or kiss her and gradually Maryann could relax again a little. But the inner calm that she had possessed for the last years had deserted her. She felt restless and lonely. Ruth was to be married in a few weeks, but no one had said a word about who was to replace her as lady's maid. A year ago Maryann would have been on pins with anxiety about this, she had wanted the post so badly for so long. But now she began to find Charnwood confining. She loved her afternoon off and made sure every week now that she went out, into the town to the shops and for a wander along the cut to see the boats being loaded and unloaded. She liked the bustle, the smells and sounds, and the way the canal made her feel connected to things again, instead of buried alive at Charnwood. For that was how it was coming to feel.

The turmoil inside her that she had avoided for so long was returning to her like an old family chest being opened. Norman, Sal, Joel and her brothers. Round and round in her head. And her own future. Was there happiness waiting for her somewhere else? Would she be capable, after all, of love?

*

Ruth was married on a Saturday at the church in the nearest village and the staff were allowed leave to attend the service before coming back to Charnwood for a celebratory meal. Ruth, as ever, looked calm and serene; her long, dark hair was knotted beautifully and she wore a simple cream dress. Her husband, tall and blond, kept looking at her as if he couldn't believe his luck. The two of them left for Banbury in a horse and trap decorated with garlands of flowers, to begin their married life. Both the servants and those of the family who were at home came to wave them off. Maryann saw Roland shake hands rather awkwardly with Ruth. Pamela flung her arms round her tearfully and Mrs Musson slipped a little package into her hand. Maryann kissed her and wished her every happiness.

'I hope some of you'll come and see us,' Ruth said, kissing and hugging everyone. 'We're not far away, but I'll miss you.'

It had been announced that Ruth was to be replaced by a young woman called Eve. As Mrs Letcombe told them, Maryann experienced a pang of envy and disappointment, closely followed by relief and a surprising sense of freedom. If she'd been given the job, somehow in her mind it would have tied her to Charnwood, when in her heart she could feel the stirrings of change.

Thirty-One

That week, when Maryann walked into Banbury, she didn't even get as far as the shops. Slipping along the side streets, she found herself heading for the cut. More and more now, she found herself thinking about the past.

She went past the Strugglers Arms and down to the cut, walking on the towpath for a time. There were horse boats and motor boats on the go. She stood aside every now and then to let a horse go past pulling one of the boats. The smells of the water, the hot horse scent, the water splashing on the sides of the cut and the sunlight glaring on the ripples all filled her with a great sense of nostalgia and excitement. When she'd walked a way along, tied up on her side of the cut she saw a family boat called *Miss Dolly,* a rather scruffy vessel with chipped red and yellow paint. From the back on the steering platform peered three young children and Maryann heard a woman's voice shouting crossly to them from inside the cabin. Several others were playing along the bank and there was a string of threadbare clothes, stained grey with coal dust, strung on a washing line along the boat.

Maryann smiled at the children in the boat and said, ''Ello there, awright?'

''Ow do!' one of then chirruped back. The older ones were throwing stones into the cut with little plopping noises. She saw they were aiming at something floating in the middle of the channel. It was sodden and feathery: a dead pigeon turning gently in the water. She stood watching for a moment, then turned back, still smiling.

It was hard living on the cut, she remembered that very well. She knew how they rushed and competed for the loads, how the Number Ones were up against the company-owned boats, how it was work work work for long hours every day. Yet there was a freedom in it too. She stood looking north along the long, thin strand of water, following its course in her mind. On it went, out through those remote fields where you scarcely saw anyone about, only trees and birds and the sky overhead and the sun glinting in the brasses. What a life that was!

After a time she came towards the dry dock called Tooley's Yard where boats were taken in for repairs. She remembered Joel telling her about the place. Every so often the boats had to be taken there for recaulking. 'So they don't go letting no water in,' Joel had said. 'They seal up the seams and blacken 'er bottom to keep 'er watertight.'

She'd never been in the place and she thought she'd slip in and have a look. Just as she was about to go into the yard, two men came out, talking earnestly. One was a portly, middle-aged man with a red face looking out from under his trilby hat. The other, in contrast, was much taller, dark and strong-featured, with black curly hair and a large, slightly beaked nose. The tall dark man's face looked furrowed with some strong emotion, worry or anger. They passed her, talking earnestly together, and turned off away from the cut.

It was only as Maryann turned into the yard that she

realized she recognized the tall, dark man. She stopped for a moment. Where had she seen him before? If she could only think! She looked across Tooley's Yard and could just see the hull of a boat in the dry dock. Those lovely yellows and greens. And then it came to her, where she knew him from. A boat passing, Joel calling out as they slid beside each other, smiling, happy to see each other . . . the man with dark curly hair was Darius Bartholomew the younger: she was certain of it! Heart racing, she turned and ran in the direction they had gone, but they had disappeared. In any case, what could she say to Darius? He didn't know who she was, did he?

But she couldn't resist a look round the yard. It wasn't a large place – there was a brick shed and the dry dock, which would take one boat at a time, was a long, rather ramshackle building by the cut. She saw a couple of the Tooley's workers eyeing her up admiringly. She felt as if her skin was prickling. She knew she looked pretty in her blue dress, slim and shapely, black hair tucked under a little navy straw hat with a down turned brim. But she so disliked the feeling of being stared at, sized up in that way.

'Was you looking for someone?' One of the men approached her, looming over her.

'I – I just wanted to see—' She spoke timidly, but then found the courage to say, 'That man who just went out, was that Darius Bartholomew?'

The man took his cap off and rubbed sweat from his forehead with his arm. 'That 'un? Darius the younger. That's 'is boat, the *Esther Jane* down there. We'll be working on 'er next.'

'That's the *Esther Jane* – over there?' She couldn't keep the excitement out of her voice. Along from the dry dock she could just see the prow of another boat. 'Oh – can I go and see?'

The man shrugged. 'Don't see why not. Ain't no one aboard 'er though.'

He left her to walk over by herself, picking her way over the muddy ground. The boat was tied up by the bank, waiting for her turn in the dry dock, where she'd be strapped up while the water was drained out of the dock so that the men could work underneath her. It was with a feeling almost of disbelief that Maryann approached her. There she was, the *Esther Jane*! And on the roof, curled asleep, a little brown and white dog.

'Jep?' She could hardly believe it! He looked up on hearing his name and, jumping down on to the bank, came and licked her hand. 'Oh Jep – it *is* you!' He was a little grey round his sandy muzzle, but still full of life. 'Oh – is Ada back on board with you now then?' She was full of happiness and excitement. How could she have left them? How could she have stayed away so long? Still squatting, petting Jep, who was all awriggle with pleasure, she looked over the boat.

'Hello there,' she found herself saying softly. 'So 'ow're you then, old girl?'

While the boat made no reply, the state of her seemed to speak for itself. The last time Maryann had seen her she was in good repair, freshly painted and spick and span, brasses polished, her hold washed out as often as they could manage between loads. But now what she saw filled her with dismay. She looked a sad, worn-out old lady. The paint was cracking off her, it looked a long time since her brasses had had a rag anywhere near them and she was covered in grime all over. Chances were she was in the same state inside – dirty and heaving with bugs if they hadn't had time to stove her. In her dismay Maryann immediately felt like jumping aboard and setting to work but she knew she mustn't. It was clear the *Esther Jane* had fallen on hard times. Her mind was jumping with questions. What had happened? Why was Darius back running the boat? Where was his father and, above all, where was Joel?

With Jep following her she went back to look for the man who she found in the dry dock, working on another boat called the *Venus*.

'D'you know if Mr Bartholomew's coming back soon?'

The man looked at her over his shoulder. 'Oh, I should think so. That was one of Essy Barlow's men 'e went off with. Don't s'pose 'e'll stay with 'im long.'

'Samuel Barlow?' S.E. Barlow owned one of the carrying companies and she'd often seen his pairs of boats on the cut. ''E ain't selling the *Esther Jane*?'

'Seems like 'e might be,' the man said. 'E could do worse. Times're tough, everyone chasing about for not enough loads. If 'e sold out to Barlow 'e wouldn't 'ave to chase the loads 'imself, would 'e?'

Maryann was appalled. She knew how hard old Darius and Joel had always worked to stay independent, to be Number Ones like they'd always been, not tied to a boss, a company. How would Joel feel about this?

'Can I wait till Mr Bartholomew gets back? I'd like to speak to 'im.'

'Stay as long as you like.' The man winked at her. 'Don't see anyone complaining, do you? So long as you don't get under anyone's feet.'

She went over to the side of the yard. From somewhere near by she could hear the sounds of a forge: a horse being shod. She hoped Darius Bartholomew wasn't going to be too long. In a couple of hours she would need to set off for Charnwood House, but the way she felt just then she would have waited for ever and damn everything else. Having seen the *Esther Jane* it was almost as if the past six years had not existed. She was back on the cut with the boat and the people she loved and she was desperate to know what had befallen them. Suddenly it was all that seemed to matter.

Almost an hour later Darius Bartholomew came back. She saw him the second he strode, grim-faced, into the yard. He was a large, striking presence. He looked puzzled and not especially pleased to see someone standing by his boat.

'Mr Bartholomew?' she said, even before he reached her.

She found him rather forbidding, in the same way she had often found his father. Those strong, chiselled features seemed to scowl down at her.

'My name's Maryann Nelson. I—' How did she explain? 'A few years back I lived on your boat – with yer dad and Joel – and Jep here – until Ada went off. . . .'

For a moment he stared blankly at her, then his face softened a fraction. 'Did you? I remember they 'ad a lass on board for a bit.'

He seemed about to turn away, sinking back into his own thoughts again, so Maryann asked quickly, 'Only – I wanted to ask after everyone. Your father and Ada – and Joel.'

Darius Bartholomew climbed over into the *Esther Jane* and stood on the steering platform looking back at her. He shook his head. 'You won't be seeing our Ada no more. She were drownded four year ago, God rest 'er.'

'Ada?' Maryann gaped at him. 'Oh no . . . No!' Not cheeky, vivacious Ada.

'They was working the Grand Union – right down to the Thames. It's all wider and faster there, with currents and that. Our Ada was knocked overboard – got swept away. Took 'em days before they found 'er.' Seeing the tears in Maryann's eyes he looked down with a sigh. 'She were a good'un.'

Maryann swallowed, wiping her eyes. 'And your father?' She could hardly bear to ask about Joel.

'I left 'im down at h'Oxford with 'is sister what lives on the bank. What with Joel and the boat in this state I said I'd bring 'er up 'ere one 'anded. He ent a young man. He's finding the life harder and harder and 'e's been poorly.'

'And Joel?' she breathed.

Darius started shaking his head in that grim fashion again and Maryann felt as if a great pressure was bearing down on her chest. Not him as well. He couldn't be drownded as well, oh please God, no!

'Bad,' Darius said. He seemed almost glad to have someone to whom he could pour out all his troubles. 'He's took real sick. He's been heading for it since the winter, what with 'is chest, but this time it went from bad to worse. I had to get him took away to the 'orspital at Birnigum even though 'e begged me not to leave 'im on the bank. But he was that burning up with fever I couldn't look after 'im and see to the boat and the loads . . . And with fighting for regler loads and back loads—' He wiped one of his huge, dark hands over his face. 'It looks as if we're giving in – going to Essy Barlow. S'the only way now.'

'Oh dear.' Maryann wiped her eyes again. 'I'm ever so sorry you've had such troubles, Mr Bartholomew.

I truly am. I know how Joel and your father felt about selling up.'

'Times move on – what with the roads taking over ... Some of 'em're acting like they've never heard of the cut these days. I don't know what can be done, that I don't.' He pushed open the cabin door. 'I'm going to get the stove going and brew up. You stopping for some tea?'

'Yes please.' She was desperate to know more about Joel. She had to know how he was, where he was ...

'Come aboard – that's if you don't mind?' He eyed her pretty frock. 'It ain't spick and span like it oughta be.'

Stepping into the *Esther Jane* again after all this time was a wonderful feeling and despite her anxiety, Maryann found herself smiling as the memories poured back. She sat by the tiny table, looking round, itching to get to work and clean the place up: the plates and copper kettle and Esther's brown and white teapot. The crochet work was filthy, the whole cabin dull and dirty compared with how it had been before when either she or Ada had kept it nice. She watched Darius stoking the range and suddenly found herself aching for it to be Joel here beside her so that she could see him again. She remembered her younger self, confused and frightened, lying alone at night in this cosy cabin, this place of refuge as it had been.

'Where have they taken Joel?' she asked as the kettle was heating.

'I told you – to the 'orspital up Birnigum.'

'Yes, but which one? D'you know?'

Darius looked round at her, stooped over, scraping old leaves out of the teapot. 'I never 'ad the chance to see 'im. Our father weren't well neither and what with chasing the loads I don't know 'ow Joel is even. 'E'll not like being on the bank for long. That's if 'e even . . .' He trailed off, but she knew he was going to say 'lives'. 'Never been right really, 'e ent – not since that war.'

Every moment she sat there, she was filling more and more with an urgent determination. Joel was sick, maybe dying, and she had to see him. He'd been so good to her and she'd repaid him unkindly. Now it was her chance to do something for him. She didn't need to ask if there was anyone else in Joel's life. No one had been mentioned and Joel would only have married someone who could live on the cut, who would be his 'mate' aboard the *Esther Jane*. If there was any such woman in his life, where was she?

'Is 'e all alone there?' she asked. 'No one who can visit?'

Darius shook his head, ashamed. 'There ain't no one.'

'Can't you think which 'ospital it *might* be? Daint they say when they took him?'

Darius's brow wrinkled. 'I think it might be the one near the chocolate fact'ry.'

'The chocolate factory? Bournville. Would it be the Infirmary at Selly Oak?'

'Might be,' he said hopelessly. 'Ain't no good me knowing when I can't 'ope to get there, is there?'

'But I could go.'

Darius stopped in the middle of handing her her cup of tea. 'You?'

She reached out and took the cup and the absolute resolve in her face was plain to see. 'Yes. Me.'

Thirty-Two

'I'm sorry, Mrs Letcombe, but I really do 'ave to go – it's someone in my family.' How else could she describe Joel? 'He's very ill, maybe dying.'

'But when will you be coming back?'

'I don't know. I'm ever so sorry.'

And she was sorry. Almost heartbroken. Throughout the train journey to Birmingham the tears kept rising up in her eyes. She could go back, Mrs Letcombe said. They'd give her a week or two. But she knew that she wouldn't be returning, that everything had changed and that she could only look forward. Deep in her heart she had known that one day she would have to go back to Birmingham and face her family and now that day had arrived. And it was Joel who had brought her there. He seemed closer to her now than he had in all the years she had been away. The thought of him, and her worry about him and his weak lungs, was with her all the time. Now she knew she had to see him she was in a desperate hurry to get there. Darius had said he would try and get to Birmingham when the *Esther Jane* was ready. But she had to get there more quickly. Throughout the journey she wanted to command the train to go faster, faster!

She looked out as it chugged slowly into Birmingham. It was a hot but overcast day and a grey pall hung over the city: all the smoke from the factory chimneys and no breeze to blow it away. A blackness lay over everything and along the tracks the buildings seemed to be closing in, the workshops and warehouses, with what windows they had poky and filthy, their walls covered in soot and grime. The sight of it shocked her. What a grim, stifling place it looked! She had been away so long, had become used to the space and clean air of the country, the warm-coloured stone of the houses, and felt almost panic-stricken at the thought of being enclosed behind these dark, cramping walls again. But down there, under it all, she told herself, was the cut, slipping through and between and under. Another world, sealed off from the rest of the city, and the thought gave her hope and a way out, a sense of freedom.

When the train lurched to a standstill her pulse began to race even harder. This was really it now. She was back. People were jostling to get out of the train and she pulled her little case down from the luggage rack.

'Time to face the music,' she thought. 'But not before I've seen Joel.'

Changing platforms, she waited for a local train to Selly Oak, and it wasn't long before she was stepping out of the station. It was dinner time, a bit early to go and visit, so she went along the Bristol Road to find a place to sit and have a cup of tea and a sandwich and try to steady her nerves. She found a workmen's café and sat listening to the voices round her, remembering how much Diana Musson had laughed when she had first heard her talk at Charnwood. That place which had at first felt so strange and foreign had become a second home to her. It felt very odd to be back in this big, clanging, rackety city. Once again the thought of Charnwood brought tears to her eyes.

She had said her goodbyes the evening before. It was no hardship to part with Evan, but even the crustier characters like Sid and Wally and Cook had shown surprising affection for her. Cook had flung her arms round her and gone all dewy round the eyes. Parting with Mrs Letcombe had been very emotional even though the housekeeper herself was rather unconcerned, because she was sure Maryann would soon come running back, and kept saying, 'There there, m'dear, I don't know what you're crying about.' Even saying goodbye to Alice had brought tears to her eyes: though she'd never had very warm feelings towards her, they had spent a lot of time working together.

To her surprise, though, it had been Roland Musson who had aroused the most emotion in her. When she went up last night to prepare his room during dinner he had come in as she was turning down the bed for him.

'Oh—' he said, taken aback. 'I forgot you'd er, be ... Just popped up to er ...' She saw him go to his decanter of whiskey, pour himself a generous couple of fingers and gulp them down. He turned to her, shamefaced, still holding the glass. 'Ah – that's better. Mother doesn't like to see me – you know. Says I drink too much.'

'Er—' Maryann delayed him, nervously. 'As you're 'ere, sir, I'd just like to say, I'll be leaving the 'ouse first thing in the morning. I don't know if I'll be coming back.'

Roland just stood staring at her.

Maryann blushed. 'I'm sorry, sir ... I know it don't matter to you one way or another who makes your bed and that, but I just thought it'd be polite to say goodbye.'

'But, Nelson – you're not really *going*, are you? You don't mean it?'

'I 'ave to, sir.'

'This is appalling news. I mean, you can't! You're just *always* here – in fact you're the one really cheering person about the place. I rely on you, Nelson!'

She looked at the carpet, not knowing what to say.

'Well – damn it. I can't just shake your hand, not after all you've done for me over the years. Come here, girl.'

And he wrapped his arms round her in a rather clumsy but, she could tell, heartfelt embrace, and for a moment she allowed her arms to rest round him as well. She felt him kiss the top of her head.

'You're a damn fine girl, Nelson,' he said thickly. 'Damned fine.'

'Thank you, sir. And good luck to yer.'

When he'd left the room she kneeled down for a few minutes by the bed and wept silently with her hands over her face. Sitting thinking of it now, a lump rose in her throat.

Pulling her thoughts back to the present, she wiped her eyes and stood up to pay for her tea. The café proprietor stared at her curiously but she was too preoccupied to notice. Pressing her hat down she went out into the street. It was threatening to rain and she walked on quickly, carrying her case, towards the hospital.

When she enquired inside, she was told she was too early and would have to wait another half-hour. So she went out and strolled up and down Raddlebarn Road feeling more and more nervous.

What was Joel going to think of her turning up all of a sudden? Would he even remember who she was?

She felt ashamed when she thought of him, and worried. How ill was he? Was Darius exaggerating when he said he didn't know if Joel would come through? He must be seriously ill if they'd got him to move away from the cut and his beloved boat, especially at such a worrying time. Maryann's thoughts spun round and round. She turned at the bottom of the road again. It must be nearly time for them to let her in. Oh God, her heart was beating so hard! She pressed her hand over it. It felt as if all her future depended on the next half-hour. All her feelings, wounded and battered as they had been, were now reaching out to Joel with great longing. How would she find him, and what would his reaction be to seeing her again?

She approached the door of the ward with great timidity, her stomach clenching uneasily. Hospitals frightened her. They had ever since her dad had been taken away to one and never come home. The nurses in their stiff uniforms, their starchy white veils and starchy manner also intimidated her and there were those smells: bodily stenches, disinfectant.

An older nurse, with a cross face and muscly arms and legs, walked briskly up to her. 'Yes? Who is it you've come to see?'

Maryann cleared her throat. 'A Mr Joel Bartholomew . . . please.'

'Bartholomew? Chest case. Oh no – I don't think so.'

'P-Pardon?'

'No visitors. Too ill to see anyone. And you're not a relative, I assume?'

'I'm . . . no, a friend, but . . .'

'Relatives only, I'm afraid.' The woman started to turn away.

'But they can't come – any of them!' Maryann burst into tears in vexation. 'They all work on the cut and they can't leave the boat. His dad's poorly too and his brother's stuck in Banbury and there ain't anyone else and I *know* he'd want to see someone. *Please* let me – just for a few minutes. I've come all the way from Banbury myself today!'

The woman stood, considering. Maryann was afraid she'd be snooty and spiteful because she knew Joel was off the cut. But she said, reluctantly, 'Very well. A couple of minutes. But he is very ill. And don't go cluttering up the ward with *that*. Leave it with me.' She took Maryann's case and walked off with it, saying over her shoulder, 'He's just down on the right.'

She found him halfway down, a physical jolt of shock going through her when she first saw him and took in that it was him. If it had not been for his blaze of hair against the pillow she would not have recognized him. For the big, burly Joel she had known was now much thinner, his cheekbones pushing out the flesh of his face, and they had shaved off his beard. His frame, as he lay prone under the sheet, was shrunken and weak and his eyes were closed. She could see that each breath he took was a painful struggle to him.

Her instinct was to stand there for a long time staring at him, trying to take in his changed state, but she was afraid the bossy nurse would come back, and she slipped alongside the bed and sat on the chair, trying to shrink down and make herself as invisible as possible. She could feel the man in the bed opposite staring at her.

Close up, she could see a film of perspiration on Joel's face and hear the rasp of his lungs. His face wore a frown, as if of pain and concentration. Watching him she felt as if the years since she had last seen him were very short, like a dream which takes only moments yet in which you can experience half a lifetime. She felt as if her heart would melt with sorrow and tenderness. She sat torn between fear of disturbing him and the unbearable thought that she might be ordered to leave before he knew she was there. Slowly, trembling, she reached out her hand and laid it over his.

'Joel?'

For a moment she thought he had not heard, but then his head moved a fraction and she saw him struggle to open his eyes, as if even the effort to prise his lids apart was enormous. He looked round, eyes unfocused for a moment, then slowly rolled his head, sensing someone next to him. She felt his eyes on her.

'Joel,' she whispered, leaning towards him, finding there were tears streaming down her face. 'It's me – Maryann. I saw Darius and he told me you was here and how poorly you are.'

There was a moment while he took her in, staring at her as if he couldn't make sense of her presence and she watched his reaction fearfully. He swallowed, frowned slightly. His hand lifted, then laid over hers.

'You came . . . My little . . . nipper . . .'

This made her all the more emotional. 'Oh Joel,' she sobbed. 'It's so lovely to see you. I'm so sorry, Joel – I've wanted to say to you for ever so long that I'm sorry for running off the way I did when yer'd been so good to me. I was in a state. So many terrible things'd happened and I daint know what I was doing and I know you daint mean anything bad. You were the one person I could always go to and I can't stand to see yer looking so poorly like this.' She took his hand and kissed it again and again. She could hear his breathing becoming more agitated and she looked anxiously into his face. There were tears running down into his hair and she wiped them gently away with her fingers, knowing how unmanly it must seem to him to weep. He was trying to speak and she leaned close, barely able to hear his whisper.

'I did wrong—' He had to rest between the words to gather enough breath. 'You was ... only a young 'un ...' He closed his eyes as if condemning himself. 'My fault.' The final words cost him a huge effort. 'You seemed older ... I felt for you. It weren't ... just lust ... Truly ...'

'You were lovely, Joel – you were. I know that now and I'm sorry. Only I *was* young and I was in a mess ... I've grown up a bit since then. I've thought about you – when I let myself. And I missed you ever such a lot.'

He gave a nod which seemed to encompass and elaborate everything she'd said, and he clutched her hand.

'I'll be here now – till you get better.'

Joel laid his spare hand over his chest, gasping for breath. 'I knew they'd get ... me ... in the end ...'

She knew he meant his damaged lungs and a chill went through her.

'Don't say that, Joel! You're in your thirties – that's not old! You just feel it because yer sick at the moment. You can get better – you can! I'm going to come and see yer every day. Please don't give up – say you won't give up, you'll try for me, won't you!'

Slowly he brought his other hand across and cradled her hand in both of his.

'Oh Joel—' She leaned forward and kissed his cheek, barely knowing what she was saying. 'I love you *so* much.' She was laughing and crying together, but quietened herself to hear the words he whispered, still clasping her hand.

'My little . . . love, you . . . came back.'

Thirty-Three

When the tram reached Ladywood, Maryann stepped down a couple of stops early so that she could walk along Monument Road and try to get used to being back. Glancing down Waterworks Road she looked for Perrott's Folly, the old brick tower which loomed over the houses, and she passed some of the old familiar shops, St John's Church, the Dispensary, all looking the same as when she left and it gave her a strange feeling. She prepared herself for the fact that while buildings change little in six years, people do, and that she might even walk past one of her own brothers without recognizing him.

Turning down Anderson Street she was filled with a dread so strong it forced her to stop and stand nervously near the corner, trying to find the courage to go on. Again, the place looked much the same. School was out and there were kids playing on the pavement, skimming marbles along the blue bricks as they always had. She might have run along the road with Norman Griffin's keys in her hand only weeks ago. For a moment she could smell the choking smoke from the fire in her nostrils. She was going to have to see *him* again. However much she knew she was now a grown woman, that she could leave at any time, that he had no power to do anything to her, she could only feel herself as a child in relation to him. A powerless child who he could use for his own cruel, disgusting appetites as he had used her sister and then destroyed her. The old anger in her rose up again until she was trembling with it.

Oh I can't, she thought. I can't go back there. I ain't got the strength. She put her case down and stood facing the wall of a house, composing herself, clenching her teeth, trying to get her shaking under control. I will not, she told herself, let him do this to me. I *won't*. Furiously she snatched up the case and marched along the road. But she still couldn't go straight to the house and walk in. She had to know how things stood.

The Martins' huckster's shop still looked just the same, the windows plastered in labels: Oxo, Cadbury's, Woodbines, the same little 'ting' of the bell as she pushed the door open. The smells hit her: soap, camphor, rubber, cough candy. For a second she saw Tony in her mind's eye as she remembered him, standing on tiptoe to peer over the counter.

'Penn'orth of rocks yer got there, bab?' Mrs Martin would say.

Maryann imagined Tony's wide-eyed nod.

Mrs Martin, her hair now white instead of metal grey, came through from the back, wiping her hands on her apron.

'Can I 'elp yer?'

''Er – Mrs Martin, it's me – Maryann Nelson.'

The woman stared at her, bewildered. 'Who?'

'Maryann – Flo Griffin's daughter. Tony and Billy's sister.'

Mrs Martin's mouth sagged open. '*No!*' she exclaimed eventually. 'Little Maryann? Ooh – I can see now, them blue eyes. Ooh my word!'

'I've been working down south and I've come back

for a visit, only I just wondered – you know, 'ow things are . . .' She jerked her head over in the direction of the house.

'Oh no – you won't find 'em over there. Daint yer know?' Her brow furrowed at Maryann's extraordinary ignorance of her own family. 'Your mother went to live back over in Sheepcote Lane when 'e left 'er. Couldn't pay the rent no more, could 'er? In a right state 'er was. But that were a good while back – five year or more. We don't see 'er round 'ere no more. Daint you know, bab?'

Maryann shook her head, her pulse racing. 'You mean Mr Griffin ain't living with them no more?'

'Ooh no – 'e took off after 'is premises went up. There was a fire, like. Gutted the 'ole damn place. You must remember that, daint yer? They've only just got it put back up now and Steven's the drapers're setting up. But your mother, Flo – well 'er version of events was 'e was never the same again after it and 'e took off and left 'er. Oh, Flo was in a right state I can tell yer.'

Maryann could tell from the way Mrs Martin was squinting at her with her head a bit to one side that any moment she was going to start interrogating her. She backed away towards the door, almost falling over a pile of galvanized buckets.

'So you say Mom's gone to Sheepcote Lane?'

'Sheepcote. Ar, that's it, bab.'

Maryann pulled the door open again. *Ting!*

'You're a right grown-up wench now, ain't yer?'

Maryann smiled. 'Ta very much, Mrs Martin.'

She passed the old house, peering closely at it. There were pale lilac curtains inside the lower window, and a black dog was lying asleep beside the step. She could sense it had all changed, would look very different inside from how she remembered, yet the thought of walking in through the front door made her flesh creep. Too many memories. Too many ghosts of the tormented little girls she and Sal had been in that house. She held on to the thought of Joel, to the love she had seen in his eyes which made her strong. Knowing she had Joel again she could face anything. Much better to keep walking and see what the present held than to linger here dwelling on the past.

The only way she could think of finding her mom in Sheepcote Lane was to ask, yard by yard, even house by house down the poor end. Poverty would have driven her to a smaller house – what fierce resentment that must've bred in her! But maybe, when Norman left her, she had been able to see him as he really was: a conman who had married her for his own vile motives: for the fact that she had two young daughters and would look after him in comfort in exchange for his money. God knows, she thought, he wasn't *rich* – not really. It was just that Mom was desperate. Maybe at last she'd be able to face the truth.

She did not need to look far. In the second back court she went into she was confronted by the sight of a woman, her back to Maryann. Her legs were thin and stringy, and her hair which had once been thick and blonde was now faded to grey, twisted and pinned up savagely behind her head. She was reaching up to unpeg a sheet from a crowded line of washing which billowed in the damp air. Maryann knew her immediately. She felt a surge of pity. Flo's bitterness and exhaustion was clear in every movement she made. Even during the war she had been quite a voluptuous woman, but now she was very thin. She kept reaching up to the line, unpegging and yanking sheets, bloomers, an apron down from it, shaking them angrily when the breeze tried to force them the wrong way. Maryann hadn't the courage to go to her in the yard. She hovered in the entry until Flo had picked up her enormous basket of washing and struggled into the end house.

It was about five o'clock. Her mom'd be cooking soon. Best go over there and get it over with. She was just stepping out across the narrow yard when two boys ran out laughing from another house. They were both about ten years old, one dark, one blond. Seeing the fairer of the two, Maryann stopped. Something about him, the way he moved, his colouring told her immediately that this was Billy. He and the other boy were tearing up and down the yard chasing one another and laughing. They saw her looking and took no notice. Both of them were in shorts cut down from longer trousers and grubby shirts hanging loose at the back. As they came closer, Maryann called, 'Billy?'

He slowed, peering at her, and came closer. His face was grubby and red from running and she saw he had a trail of freckles across his nose. From the big blue eyes, the way he held his head, she knew that he was her brother.

'Billy – it's me, Maryann. I'm your big sister.' Tears came as she said it. All those years of his life she'd missed. A little, soft thing he'd been when she left, who'd sit on her lap for a love and let her bath him. Now he was a long, skinny lad, almost grown up!

'Are yer?' She could see him searching his memory. Surely he'd been old enough when she left for him to remember her? But then she'd changed too. A sad look came over his face for a second, and she thought he was going to say something else. But then he seemed to remember the other boy with him and he wasn't going to go all soft in front of him. 'Our mom's indoors,' he said with a toss of his head. 'See yer.' And the two of them careered off again.

Gripping the handle of her case, Maryann walked along the yard. If it had been a house she'd ever lived in herself, she'd have just walked in but here she felt she must knock. She saw one of the front panes was broken and covered with cardboard, and the green paint on the door was flaking and dirty. She rapped it with her knuckles.

'Oo is it?' Even her mother's voice sounded different, thinner, somehow cracked.

Maryann pushed the door open. It was gloomy inside and it took a few seconds for her eyes to adjust. She immediately recognized the table and chairs which stood to one side of the little room as the ones they had had in the last house, bought by Norman Griffin after they left Garrett Street. Her mother was standing between the table and the range, gutting herrings which were stinking the place out. She had looked up without stopping what she was doing until she saw Maryann. Flo straightened up, holding out blood-smeared hands in front of her.

''Ello, Mom.'

The expression on Flo's face, already harsh and unsmiling, grew more taut. Maryann was shocked by just how much she had changed, as if in six years she had fallen into old age. Her face was pallid, almost yellow, the skin had lost its elasticity so that it sagged over her cheekbones. She looked hard and shrewish.

'Is that you, Maryann?'

Maryann nodded. 'I've been in service. Not in Brum.' Even now she couldn't bring herself to give away where she'd been.

Flo became suddenly aware of the mess her hands were in and picked up a damp rag from the table to wipe them. There was an ominous silence as she did it and Maryann could tell she was gathering her thoughts.

'Where's Mr Griffin?'

Flo slapped the rag back down on the table before walking round and advancing on Maryann, staring at her with her eyes full of loathing.

'Where's Mr Griffin?' she mimicked. For a few seconds she couldn't seem to find any more words. Maryann shrank back as her mother came right up close.

'Mom! What're yer doing!'

'You did it, daint yer? You set that fire at Griffin's before yer buggered off. Norman knew it was you, you evil little bitch. You destroyed my life, d'yer know that? D'you even care what yer did? You ought to be banged up in Winson Green, that's where. You ruined everything we 'ad. He walked out and left and I 'ad nowt and two boys to bring up. I've been slaving in factories ever since, thanks to you. And d'you know why 'e left? 'Cause 'e said 'e weren't staying in a family of bloody lunatics who'd taken away his livelihood. And it was all your fault, Maryann.' The words rained down, sharp and hateful. 'You ruined your own family – so 'ow d'you feel about that, eh?'

Maryann thought Flo was going to go for her throat with her fishy hands and she twisted away from her and backed across the room. She had such strong emotion rising in her she felt she might burst. The injustice of everything her mother thought and felt, the way she'd never listen or see the truth – never had. She'd never taken their side, hers and Sal's. She was beyond tears: her feelings were too raw and harsh.

'You're a sad, blind woman, ain't yer, Mother?' She stood clutching the back of one of the chairs as if to contain the violence that raged inside her. Her voice was low and trembling with emotion. 'Yes – I set fire to Norman Griffin's offices and I 'oped they'd burn to the ground so there was nothing left for him. But that ain't why he left you and you know it. 'E left because *we*'d gone, me and Sal, and there was nothing left for him that he wanted. 'Cause 'e didn't like grown-up women, did he? He liked little girls he could bully and do his dirty business with and turn them into ... rag dolls, with no feelings or life left of their own.' She in turn advanced on her mother. 'D'yer know what it was he did to our Sal so she lost 'er mind and he'd've done to me too if 'e'd 'ad the chance? D'yer want to know what I found in the cellar of those offices the night I went down there? Do yer?' She was shouting at the top of her voice, distraught.

'No, *no*, shut up, you lying, wicked girl ...' Flo laid her arm across her face as if to protect herself.

'No – you don't want to hear that anything might be *your* fault, *your* greed, putting money and dresses and your comfort over and above your children.' Now she'd begun to open the floodgates she couldn't stop. She was growing hysterical. 'You don't want to hear about Norman, the oh-so respectable Mr Griffin chaining our Sal to a chair and doing God knows what to 'er and most likely promising to leave her down there with a corpse for company all night. Because that's something that wouldn't be my fault or Sal's, would it? You'd have to face that you didn't see and you wouldn't see because all you could think of was saving your own skin. You daint see her stabbing at her own arms with a knife because she couldn't live with

310

herself. And it weren't you that found her with her wrists slit open, was it? You never even went to look at her after ... Was the mess too much for you, Mother? Too real for you that, was it?'

She couldn't go on. She bent over the chair with her hands over her face as sobs choked her, the long-buried grief welling up from deep inside her. After a few moments she glanced up to see her mother looking at her with a terrible, twisted expression on her face.

'Get out of my 'ouse.' Her voice lashed across the room. 'You've done enough damage to us. We've lived without yer all these years. We don't need you back 'ere now. Tek yerself and yer poison away from 'ere. I don't want yer coming 'ere again.'

Maryann wiped her eyes, chilled by the hateful finality of her mother's words. 'I want to see my brothers.'

'You ain't seeing no one. Get out!' Flo shouted. 'Get out now and don't ever come back. Never!'

Thirty-Four

Maryann walked back out of the yard in Sheepcote Lane so blinded by tears that she could barely see where she was going. Her mother's rejection of her was so total, so final it had cut her to the bone. They had never been close as mother and daughter but she had hoped that somehow, after all that had happened and with Norman Griffin gone, there could have been a reconcilation. Now she had lost that hope for ever.

If only Nanny Firkin was still 'ere, Maryann thought. I could've gone to her – she was proper family. She'd've been glad to see me and it would've felt like home. The thought of this made her cry even more.

As it was, the only person she could hope to turn to now was Nance. She found her feet turning almost automatically to the familiar territory of Garrett Street. Somehow she didn't doubt that the Blacks would be living in the same place. Before she went into the yard she tried to compose herself and dried her eyes. She was pleased at the thought of seeing them and even smiled slightly as a familiar sight met her eyes in the old yard: Blackie Black's 'fuckin' barrer' leaning as drunkenly as she had frequently seen its owner do, against the wall of the brewhouse.

The Blacks' door was open and Maryann peeped her head round. The family was at the table having tea.

Cathleen's squiffy eyes, Blackie's bloodshot ones and those of the six children round the table all peered at her.

'Oo're yer looking for, wench?' Cathleen said. – 'Eh, 'ang on a minute, I know you, don't I? It's . . . It can't be Maryann?' She pushed back her chair and stood up.

'It is,' Maryann said shyly.

''Eh, Blackie, it's little Maryann, our Nance's pal!' Blackie squinted at her but there was a vacant look in his eyes. He made a sound between a grunt and a whine.

'Come on in, bab!' Cathleen came and stood gazing at her. 'Don't mind Blackie – 'e ain't none too well these days. Well – look at you! Our Nance'll be ever so pleased to see yer. You ain't been round to see 'er, 'ave you?'

'No – I've only just got 'ere.' Maryann put her case down gratefully, trying to keep the tears from welling up yet again. It meant so much to be greeted kindly by people who were pleased to see her.

''Ere – 'ave a cuppa tea – it's just brewed. You seen yer mom?'

Maryann nodded.

'Well – what'd 'er say?' Cathleen was stirring the teapot vigorously.

'She daint offer me a cuppa tea, I'll tell yer that much.'

'Ooh dear – like that, was it?'

Maryann nodded, conscious that the family were all staring at her. Good heavens, – that oldest one was Perce – he was eighteen now! And young Horace who'd still been sucking his thumb and peeing his pants was a lad of nine now! There was Lizzie who'd only been a babby. And who was that? There was another

313

little girl sitting at the table between William and George, who were now also a good deal more grown up.

'You 'ad another daughter then?' Maryann smiled at the child.

'Ar – that's our Mary,' Cathleen said. 'She were the last. Four year ago that were. I 'ad to 'ave all my – you know – taken away after. It were a blessing really, God forgive me, but I've 'ad my ten and that were enough for anyone.' She watched anxiously as Blackie pulled himself up from the table and lurched over to his old chair with the fag burns and settled into it with a loud groan. She leaned forward shaking her head and whispered, ''E ain't 'imself.'

'What's up?' Maryann whispered back.

'Oh, they don't really know. They think 'e might 'ave 'ad a bit of a turn. 'E can 'ardly speak. Not that 'e was a great talker before. I dunno.' She sighed, looking across at him worriedly. Maryann felt sorry for her, poor, worn-out woman. Cathleen and Blackie had both aged considerably.

'Any'ow, enough of our problems – where've yer been, Maryann?'

She told them a bit about Charnwood, then asked after the rest of the family.

'Where's Nance – and Charlie?'

'Oh, our Charlie's been wed a good while now – three kiddies they've got. All girls, would yer believe it! Alf and Jimmy've got one apiece. Alf was wed two year ago and Jimmy last year. They're all good wenches they've found themselves, all Catholics 'cept Jimmy's wife Lena, but she ain't no trouble.

'And our Nance married Mick just a few months

back – in the spring. She 'ad 'er nuptial mass in April. It were lovely, weren't it?'

'Me and Mary was bridesmaids,' Lizzie chipped in.

She reminded Maryann a little bit of Nancy when she was younger, with her head of black curls, although she had a softer, more feminine look about her.

'Nance'd've asked yer to the wedding only she daint know where yer were,' Cathleen said. 'Er missed yer, yer know, after yer went.'

'I know,' Maryann said. 'I missed 'er too. But I 'ad to get away.'

Cathleen nodded sympathetically.

'Where's Nance living? And what's 'er name now she's married?'

'Oh, Mrs Mallone. Mick Mallone's 'er 'usband. They only live over the back in Alexander Street. Yer can pop round and see 'er when yer've 'ad yer tea.'

'Any babbies on the way yet?' Maryann said smiling.

Cathleen shook her head. 'No – but they've only been wed a few month. It'll give 'er time to settle.' But Maryann thought she seemed rather lacking in warmth on the subject of Nance's marriage, however nice the wedding had been. She glanced at Blackie and saw that he appeared to have fallen asleep, his head lolling down on his chest.

''Ere – if you're going round to see our Nance, take the girls with yer and get 'em out of my hair for a bit, will yer? They like going round there.'

Nance was living in a front house which opened on to the street. The door was open and the two girls ran straight in.

'We've got Maryann!' she heard Lizzie shouting excitedly.

Immediately, as Maryann reached the house, Nance's face appeared at the open door, looking out with a combination of wariness and disbelief. For a second Maryann was shocked by Nance's thinness and the dull sullenness of her expression under her mop of black curls, until she registered that it really was Maryann and burst into delighted laughter.

'Oh my God – well I never! It really is – Maryann!'

Laughing and tearful at the same time, the two of them flung their arms round each other.

'Why didn't yer tell me where you was living?' Nance reproached her. 'I wouldn't've let on to anyone and I couldn't drop yer a line back or invite yer to the wedding or nothing! 'Ere – come in. It ain't much but we've got it to ourselves.' She drew Maryann inside and shut the door. 'Let me get that kettle on – or d'yer want a nip of summat stronger, eh?'

'No – tea'd be nice, Nance.'

The two little girls seemed to have disappeared upstairs. 'I've got a couple of old dollies and a few bit of clothes up there for when they come round,' Nance said. She rested the kettle on the hob, then stood back to look at Maryann.

'You ain't changed – not really. You look ever so well.'

Maryann smiled. Hadn't changed? How could Nance say that? She felt like a different person. And Nance looked different, too, in a middle-aged woman's dress and her apron. She was beginning to look just like her mom!

'I'm awright,' she said. 'Got lots to tell yer. But what about you, Nance. Look at you – a married woman!

What's your 'usband like?' She had noticed uneasily the cut healing on Nance's left cheekbone, a yellowed bruise round it. Nance seemed to feel her looking and put her hand to her cheek.

'I could tell yer everything's perfect, Maryann. Wedded bliss and that. But I've never lied to yer. 'E's a boozer like me dad only not so soft-hearted. 'E's down the pub now. 'E ain't too bad when 'e's sober but with a skinful inside 'im 'e gets all maudlin and sorry for 'isself.'

'Why's 'e sorry for 'imself?' Maryann asked.

'Oh Christ alone knows,' Nance said impatiently. ''E's one of them 'as a few and 'e 'as to wallow. 'E ain't got me expecting yet – 'e 'as a wallow about that.'

'But yer've only been wed, what a few months?'

'Three months – nearly four.'

'Well then.'

Nance shrugged. 'To tell yer the truth I'm bloody glad of it. I only married 'im to get out of 'ome. There's kids and mess and noise everywhere and now our dad's bad 'e's sat there like a dummy even when 'e ain't been on the bottle. I thought, I've got to get out of 'ere or I'm going straight round the bend. And Mick came along and 'e was willing and a Catholic so I married 'im and we kept our mom 'appy doing it proper like. And I got me own 'ouse. That's worth 'aving to put up with Mick, I can tell yer. If 'e stays down the boozer, good riddance.'

It sounded to Maryann as if there was a fair bit of bravado in what Nance was saying, making the most of a bad situation, but at least her spirit was far from being broken.

'If I don't get a bun in the oven for a year or two it'd suit me, I tell yer,' she said rattling cups. 'It's not all on one side, yer know – I give 'im one back sometimes, the mardy bugger.'

While Nance finished making the tea Maryann sat down at the table in the sparsely furnished little room. There was nothing but the range, a couple of shelves for keeping their few crocks on and the table and three chairs. On the table in a jam jar was a bunch of buttercups. Maryann smiled at the sight of Nance's homemaking. She thought of the luxuriant vases of flowers at Charnwood.

'Right then—' Nance sat down with a grunt. 'You tell me all about it. For a start, where the 'ell've yer been all this time?'

With the luxury of knowing that there was little of her past Nance was ignorant of, Maryann told her: Joel, the *Esther Jane*, Charnwood, Evan and Roland Musson. And finally meeting Darius and Joel again, and what had happened when she went to see her mom – only Nance kept chipping in.

'You were never on the cut all that time, were yer? They're a rough lot, them canal workers – they're like gypos!'

She oohed and aahed when Maryann told her about Joel and Roland Musson and listened spellbound when she got to the bit about seeing Flo again. Maryann poured out everything, how she felt about Joel and how sick he was and how Darius was going to be forced to sell the *Esther Jane*.

When there was a gap in the flow, Nance put her head on one side and said, 'You're in love with 'im – really in love, ain't yer?'

Maryann smiled bashfully. 'Am I?' she said in wonder. 'Yes – I do love 'im. I *do*. I'm going to spend every minute I can with 'im and try and 'elp 'im get better.

I've missed spending so much time with him – all those years, and 'e could've married someone else but 'e daint.'

'In love . . .' Nance said wistfully. 'Well, yer one up on me there, Maryann.'

'Nance – I know this is a cheek with me coming breezing back in after all this time – but could I stop 'ere with you a while? Only I ain't got nowhere else to go and I've got to be near Joel. I've got money saved – I can pay my way and that.'

Nance looked hesitant for a moment. Then her face cleared. ''Course yer can. I'd love to 'ave the company with ole misery guts coming 'ome kalied every night. Don't take no notice of Mick if 'e says anything. You can stay and that's that.'

'Ta, Nance – oh, it is good to see you!'

Nance grinned. 'Seems like yer never left.'

Maryann couldn't help feeling it didn't seem quite like that to her. 'Did you 'ear anything about where 'e went – Mr Griffin?'

Nance shook her head. 'No, but by all accounts 'e left only a week or two after the fire. Our mom went to see yours but she wouldn't even open the door to 'er. It weren't long before she 'ad to move back over Sheepcote Lane but she still 'ad a smell under 'er nose – sorry to say it, Maryann, but Flo always thought she was above us. We ain't 'ardly seen 'er: she don't want nothing to do with my family.'

'I know,' Maryann said apologetically. She was frowning. 'Norman Griffin can't've gone that far, yer know. I wonder if 'is mom's still alive – he was all over 'er.'

Nance shrugged. 'Good riddance to 'im I'd've said. Any'ow, you don't want to go asking questions about

319

where 'e is, do yer? What about what you did to 'is business?'

'No, I s'pose ... But, Nance – what about Tony? I've got to see 'im. I've written to 'im and Billy ever since I left. How is 'e? D'you ever see 'im?'

'Oh – Tony's awright. 'E's got a job carrying hods for Paddy Murphy. Going to be a brickie. 'E's a strong lad and 'e's doing awright. I've seen him about now and then.'

'Does 'e ever say anything about me?'

'Said 'e'd heard from yer – nowt else.'

Maryann sighed, holding out her cup as Nance offered more tea. 'I saw Billy. 'E barely knew who I was.'

'Well, yer been gone a good while. You can't expect them to be all over yer from the word go.'

'No, I s'pose not ...' Maryann was saying, when the door burst open, kicked by a heavy workman's boot which set the latch rattling.

'Oh, 'ere we go,' Nance said. 'Oh my God, Maryann!' She gasped, panic-stricken. 'I've forgotten all about making tea! Oh Jesus, I'll be for it now!'

She stood up as a stocky, dark-haired man stumped into the room. He had ruddy skin and a weatherbeaten complexion with lines under his eyes that were almost creases. Maryann's first thought was, but he's so *old*! She realized then that he was no older than Joel, but she had expected Nance's husband to be much closer to her own age. Mick Mallone must have been nearer to forty than thirty and looked rough with it. He was swaying from the drink and stood looking at the pair of them. Maryann stood up as well.

''Oo the 'ell's this?' Mick demanded.

'No, Mick – don't start,' Nance said. 'This is my pal

Maryann – I told you about 'er. I've said 'er can stop 'ere with us for a bit, 'cause 'er ain't got nowhere else to go.'

He gave Maryann a mere glance. 'Where's my dinner?'

'I'm going out to get us fish and chips,' Maryann said quickly. 'And I'll take Lizzie and Mary home. Give us a few minutes and I'll be back.'

As she went to the door, Nance shot her a powerful look of gratitude.

Thirty-Five

Carrying the fish and chips back down the road, warm and delicious smelling in their newspaper, Maryann realized how hungry she was. What a long, long day it had been! But she felt relieved after pouring her heart out to Nance. She tried to keep the thought of her mother out of her mind and instead recalled the look in Joel's eyes when she had told him she loved him. This made her so happy that she grinned at a group of children out playing, remembering how she used to play out just round the corner, waiting for her dad to come home.

Back at Nance's she found Mick slumped asleep over the table. She could hear Nance moving about upstairs and, leaving the bundles beside Mick's head, she crept up the creaky stairs to find her.

'That you, Maryann?'

'Yes – I've got the fish and chips. Mick's asleep I think.'

Nance rolled her eyes. 'Best thing. We'll wake 'im up for 'is tea. I was just making up the bed for yer.'

Once again Maryann was struck by how middle-aged Nance seemed. 'Ta, Nance – I dunno what I'd do without yer.'

'Well – pals, eh?' Nance said quite bashfully. Suddenly for a moment they were little girls again. 'Never found another pal quite like you.'

Maryann grinned. 'No – nor me.'

They woke Mick up and he sat blearily with them as they all ate out of the newspaper. The fish and chips tasted to Maryann like some of the best food she'd ever had.

'D'you get work from Marron again?' Nance asked Mick cautiously. He nodded, mouth full of chips. 'What about tomorrer?'

'Maybe.'

Maryann watched him out of the corner of her eye. Nance had told her he could only find work as a casual labourer, bits here, bits there, hanging about early morning with groups of men all looking to be taken on. Long, gruelling days in builder's yards or toiling on roads, and no security. She thought of Evan with his soft cheeks and his soft job at Charnwood, his certainty of 'getting on', and she pitied Mick Mallone. He took no notice of her at all and behaved as if she wasn't there, but she didn't really mind.

Later, when they'd all gone up to bed, Mick and Nance were arguing next door. Every word of it floated through to her as she lay on the lumpy mattress in the back bedroom.

'Yer've never got a word to say to me when yer get in – they get more out of yer down the pub than I ever do. You just expect me to be 'ere like a skivvy – tea on the table the minute you set foot in the door . . .'

'Yes – I do!' Mick yelled, his Kerry accent thickened by drink. 'And I don't think that's too much to expect you to manage when you're here all day. You've got no one else but yourself to think about, now have you?'

'Well, if I ain't got a babby coming whose fault's that then, eh?'

'Shut your blathering mouth, woman!' There was a sound of struggling.

'Stop it, Mick! Yer cowing filthy navvy, don't yer touch me!' Then a cry of pain. ''Ow – you bastard!'

'Fuckin' barren bitch!'

On and on they went, the shouting getting louder. Maryann sat up, all tensed up. Was this what always happened at night? Or did Nance need her help? There was another sharp yell of pain from Nancy and Maryann pushed back the bedclothes, her heart pounding, ready to rush in next door. Maybe her visit had provoked Mick beyond what was normal.

Suddenly all went quiet. She sat on the edge of the bed listening. Gradually another sound rose from the next-door room. Listening in disbelief she realized it was weeping she could hear. Mick Mallone's weeping.

Drunken bastard! she thought. He's knocked Nance about and now 'e's gone all maudlin and sorry for 'imself!

But she heard Nance's voice, soft now but with an edge of impatience, saying 'there there' and 'it's awright' until Maryann heard them climbing into bed, and at last there was quiet until Mick started snoring.

'I'm sorry about the row last night,' Nance said next morning. She was downstairs before Maryann. Mick had already gone. Her lip was cut and very swollen. She handed Maryann a cup of tea.

'Oh Nance – you shouldn't 'ave to put up with that! Have you bathed your lip? That looks ever so sore.'

'I'm awright.'

'Does that happen often?'

Nance gave a bitter laugh. 'Not every night, if that's

what yer mean. Look—' She turned, holding her teacup cradled next to her chest. 'You 'ave to understand – about me and Mick. I married 'im to get out of 'ome. 'E married me 'cause 'e wanted someone – *anyone*. 'E 'ad a wife before me – Theresa O'Sullivan she was before she married 'im. Mick doted on 'er. She was nice so far as I remember – sweet natured, gentle like. Died three year ago. They never 'ad any kids. Broke Mick's heart. 'E thought they never caught for a babby 'cause of 'er. Thought she weren't the type. Too weak and frail. But it ain't 'appening with me neither and 'e's starting to think it's 'im – probably is 'im I reckon and that ain't easy for a man to come to terms with. 'E don't love me – not really and I don't love 'im. But I feel for 'im. 'E used to be a fine man.'

'But 'e knocks you about, Nance!'

'I can stand up for myself,' she said with a sigh. 'You don't really know what the last few years've been like shut away out in the country, do yer? There've been that many out of work and the Means Test. It's been bitter 'ard for the men.' She put her cup down. 'I took what I could, Maryann. Couldn't see much else on offer . . .' Her hands went over her face suddenly.

'Oh Nance—' Maryann went to comfort her as her shoulders began to shake.

'And now I don't think 'e'll even give me a babby either. I try not to mind, but I don't know 'ow I'm going to face being married to Mick if it's just 'im and me and no one else for the rest of our lives!'

Maryann spent the morning with Nance, helping her out round the house and listening to her pour her heart out. Whatever brave face Nance was putting on about her marriage, however much she tried to laugh it off, Maryann could see how unhappy she was. She was thinking about Nance as she travelled to the hospital that afternoon to see Joel.

I'll slip Nance a bit of extra money to treat herself, Maryann thought. She had her savings and she wasn't going to go scrounging off Nance and Mick – she'd pay her board. But she could try and cheer Nance up a bit too.

She stepped off the tram and walked along Oak Tree Lane, hurrying anxiously to get to Joel. How would she find him today? She hoped he'd be just a bit better – better for seeing her perhaps?

But when she said, 'I've come to see Mr Joel Bartholomew,' to the plump, red-headed sister, the woman's expression turned very grave.

Maryann's blood seemed to freeze with dread. 'What's the matter?'

'I'm afraid Mr Bartholomew took a turn for the worse in the night.'

'Oh no ... Is 'e—? 'E's still ...'ere?' She looked wildly down the long Nightingale ward to see if she could see him.

'He's here,' the woman said stiffly. 'But perhaps not for much longer without a miracle. Are you the girl who came to see him yesterday?'

Maryann nodded, her eyes full of tears. Oh this couldn't be true, Joel couldn't die, not when they'd found each other again and they had so much between them! How could she face the future again without Joel? She wanted to give so much love to him, to make up for all their lost, lonely years.

'I really don't think ...' the woman began, but seeing Maryann begin to weep in front of her she hesitated.

'Please,' Maryann sobbed. 'I told the nurse yesterday – 'e ain't got no one else.'

The sister relented. 'You better calm down before you go to him.'

Maryann nodded, unable to speak. She wiped her face, pulled her shoulders back and walked along the ward, feeling the eyes of the other male patients on her.

Joel looked very bad. For a moment as she approached the bed she thought he wasn't breathing and his face was sunken and pale, head turned to one side like someone trying to catch the sunlight. Her tears started to fall again in spite of herself as she looked at him. He seemed so weak and defeated.

Kneeling in the narrow gap by the bed, she took his hand and brought it to her cheek.

'Oh Joel,' she whispered. 'Stay with me. Please don't go – don't die. Can you 'ear me? Joel, please open your eyes – please still be 'ere.'

Watching his face, she saw, rather than heard, his shallow breathing and waited, staring intensely at him, for a flicker of movement, some sign that he was not leaving her. For a second his lashes flickered and she thought he was going to open his eyes.

'Joel?'

But the movement stopped and left her feeling more desolate than before. He couldn't hear her. He was slipping away. She talked to him frantically in a low voice, begging him, talking about all the things they'd do when he was better, saying over and over again how she loved him, clinging to his hot hand. But there was nothing. Eventually the sister came and approached the bed.

'I think it's time to leave him now, dear.' Her

kindness terrified Maryann more than brusqueness would have done. It seemed to indicate that she was sure Joel was going to die.

'If only I could stay with 'im—' She found it unbearable to tear herself away from his hand. 'D'yer think – will 'e last the night?'

Her gaze not meeting Maryann's, the sister said, 'I'm afraid I couldn't tell you that.'

She stepped out of the ward as if into another world. It was late afternoon and sultry, the air full of acidic smells from the battery factory near by. She turned away from the city and walked numbly towards Lodge Hill Cemetery, stepping in through its gates to the tranquillity of flowerbeds and trees and gravestones. She made her way to the two graves which belonged to her, not side by side but not far apart, each with a modest headstone.

'HAROLD NELSON – 1892–1926' she read, and then, 'SALLY ANNE GRIFFIN – 1913–1928'.

The sight of Sal's gravestone brought all her rage and hurt to boiling point. Griffin! Her mom had buried Sal under that bastard's name – the one who'd all but killed her himself.

'How could she have done it?' She found herself kicking at the stone, screaming out her pain and fury. 'How could she, how *could* she?'

Not even looking to see if anyone was about, past caring, she sank to her knees and rested her head on Sal's grave, sobbing. 'Oh Sal ... oh God ... sis ... sis ...' The memory of that night she had found Sal filled her mind, of the day her dad died, and then Joel, lying there, hardly seeming to be alive even now.

Would she be visting him here too, having no one to talk to but the graves of all the people she loved? She curled up tight by Sal's grave, smelling the earth close to her face, and cried until she could cry no more.

Thirty-Six

Nance only had to look at Maryann's face when she got back.

'Oh Maryann – 'e's not . . .?'

She came to greet her, anxiously wringing a cloth in her hands. The bruising had spread round Nance's lip but the sight of her friend pulled her mind right away from her own troubles. Maryann sank down at the table.

'No. But I don't think—' She looked up at Nance, her eyes filling again even though she thought she'd cried all the tears she was capable of. 'They don't think 'e'll last the week – maybe not even the night. 'E hardly seems to be breathing. I can't bear it, Nance . . .'

'Oh Maryann, no!'

Nance pulled the other chair round and perched on it beside her, clasping Maryann's hands in her rough ones as her friend poured out her feelings.

'I was hoping 'e'd be better today, but he couldn't even open his eyes and look at me. It almost seemed he was dead already. Oh and 'e's got no one with 'im – I wish they'd've let me stay with 'im!'

'What about 'is family? Ain't there anyone round about for 'im?'

'No – there's only Darius, his brother and 'e's—' She got abruptly to her feet. 'Darius! I must let 'im know 'ow bad things are. I don't know if 'e can make it but I'll 'ave to give 'im the chance to try. Have you got a bit of paper I could write 'im a note on?'

Nancy managed to find a scrap of paper and left Maryann with it at the table while she went out to see if she could beg an envelope off one of the neighbours. She soon came back with one and Maryann addressed it to Tooley's Yard in Banbury and ran out to post it. Someone would have to read it to Darius – if he was still there. She told him in the note that she'd leave her address for him at the toll office at Farmer's Bridge. She slipped it into the box, praying Joel would hang on. The thought made her cry all over again.

She went to the hospital the next day, sick with dread. But she found Joel in much the same state as he had been in the day before. She sat beside him, willing him with all her strength and love to hold on to life.

'I'll be here, Joel, waiting for you, praying for you. Just don't leave me – I love you.'

She could hardly bear to let go of his hand and go away, she was so afraid that she might not see him alive again. She was living from moment to moment. Thinking about the future was impossible. She couldn't face it now without Joel.

That evening she went to find Tony, waiting at the end of Sheepcote Lane, hoping she could intercept him before he reached home. She stood watching both ends of the street, afraid she would not be able to recognize him and full of misgiving that if she did see him he would reject her just as angrily as her mother had.

At last when he appeared she knew immediately who he was. He turned into the road, walking briskly, whistling, a small canvas bag slung over one shoulder, his jacket slung back over the other. His boots and clothes were pale with dust and smears of cement, his cap was pushed far back on his head, showing a dark-eyed face which was also covered in muck. He was much bigger, just about her own height, quite grown up into a wiry, muscular lad. When he drew nearer and caught sight of her, he stopped in mid-whistle.

''Ello, Tony.'

He came nearer. She couldn't read his expression, except that it didn't hold surprise. Her mom must have told him she'd been back. 'Maryann?'

She was full of emotion, remembering the little boy she had left sleeping the night she ran away. 'I s'pose you thought I was never coming back.'

'Well – I dunno. I mean it's been—' He shrugged, looking down at the ground, awkward, and embarrassed by her emotion. 'Mom said you'd been to see 'er.'

'It's a wonder she could bring 'erself to mention my name,' Maryann said bitterly. 'What did 'er say?'

'Not much. Said yer wouldn't be coming again.'

Maryann wiped her eyes and looked into his face. 'What about you, Tony? You angry with me too?'

She saw a flicker of hostility, then sorrow in his dark eyes. She could sense his confused loyalties. 'Dunno. No. Not really.'

'And *he* left then? Norman?'

Tony nodded, raising his head. 'Mom said it were your fault.' He sounded angry, despite his denial. 'We had to come back down 'ere—' He jerked his head to indicate the lane. 'Why did yer do it, Maryann? I know 'e weren't our dad but 'e weren't all that bad. What did yer 'ave to go and ruin everyfing for?'

It was Maryann's turn to look away, shame rising in

her, the blood rushing to her cheeks. Her tears started to fall. How could she tell Tony what Norman Griffin had done to her and Sal – above all to Sal? How could she speak like that to her little brother? Little Tony who spoke in a gruff man-boy voice, who still couldn't say his 'th's properly?

'I'm sorry, Tony . . .' She couldn't help crying however hard she tried, and she stood in front of him weeping there in the street. 'I'm sorry – I had to go. *I had to do it* . . . I can't explain it to yer.'

'Why not? Don't yer think I'm grown up enough to be told what's going on, eh? I feel like a right bloody mug I do. I'm old enough to keep food on the table but I ain't old enough to be told anyfing. 'Ow about letting me in on a few fings, eh?'

'Ssh – oh Tony, please be quiet!' Maryann seized his arm. 'Don't – not in the street. I don't want people staring and gossiping. Look – come for a walk with me, away from 'ere.'

'I'll come,' Tony said, on his dignity. 'But you'd better be straight with me, Maryann. So far as Mom's concerned you were the ruin of the family. It ain't how I remember yer or think of you, but you'd better 'ave summat to say to me.' Suddenly he seemed near tears himself. She wanted to put her arms round him as she had done when he was little, but knew she mustn't.

'Oh Tony – I will tell you. Only you have to promise me you'll believe what I say. Mom never would – that's why I had to go in the end. I couldn't stand telling you if you start saying I'm a liar.'

She led him, as if automatically, to the place where they could squeeze through down to the cut, and they walked side by side away from town, breathing in the murky smell of the canal, reflections shifting on the water's surface. She found it very difficult to talk. What had happened in the past had been buried in her for so long that at first she skirted round and round what she needed to say and at last she blurted it out clumsily, knowing she owed Tony the truth.

'You daint know – you were too little. I know Mr Griffin took us to the pictures and we always had enough and didn't go short, but there was another side to him, Tony. A filthy, wicked side. And it was Sal had the worst of it. He was ... he was ...' Oh God, how could she say it?

She forced herself to glance round at her brother. He was watching his feet, a slight frown on his face. Maryann took in a huge, ragged breath and forced herself to go on, telling him, explaining, indirectly at first, then, uncertain if he knew what she meant, in more detail. The memories came back, raw and sickening. She stopped walking and sobbed out to him how she'd found Sal that day.

'He destroyed her. Week by week. He killed her from inside, Tony. That's what happened to your sister. She took her own life because she couldn't stand living no more after him and what it did to her. She thought she was expecting a babby as well, Tony – you won't've known that. And I ... d'you know, that night I went down there I daint 'ave a plan. I knew I was going to do summat, I was so full of grief and anger for Sal but I daint know what. And then when I saw what I saw down there – I went mad. I was ready to do him in – destroy him and everything that was his. That was when I started the fire, and then I had to go—' Tears on her cheeks, she begged her brother, 'Don't say you don't believe me, Tony. Please don't. It's the truth – I swear to you on my life!'

She could see just how much she'd got through to him. Tony's thin face looked stunned. Eventually he said, 'Did Mom know?'

'I told 'er. I kept trying to say, but she daint want to 'ear it. All she wanted to see was the respectable side of him. I s'pose she shut it out of her mind. She was scared to frighten him off. In the end I did it for 'er.'

They stood in the dusk on the canal bank. Maryann found she could not look into his eyes. She felt dreadful after what she had had to tell him. Tony was silent for a time and she ached to know what he was thinking. At least he hadn't rejected her story straight away and told her she was a filthy liar. She sensed he was thinking hard.

'I fink I remember,' he said eventually. 'Yes – I do.'

'What?'

'Him – Griffin – coming in – of a night. When you and Sal was in the bed. It feels like a dream – but I know 'e was in there sometimes – on your bed. I remember the creaking and his voice in there.'

'Oh Tony! D'you really – you remember that?'

'I remember the bed squeaking – and 'im breathing and saying fings to yer.'

'Oh thank God!' Maryann cried. It was then, at last, she went and put her arms round him. 'Someone who knows I'm not making it up – oh Tony ... I'm so happy to see you again. I've missed you so much – you and Billy, but especially you. I've been so lonely without you.'

He was awkward in her embrace at first. But then he dropped his jacket and bag on to the dry ground and his arms came round her as she cried.

'Did you get my letters?'

'Yes.'

'And the little cat I left on yer pillow?'

'Yes—' He sounded embarrassed. He was crying too.

''Ve you still got it somewhere?'

She pulled back and looked at him. Tony nodded, quickly wiping his eyes on the back of his hands.

'See – I was always thinking of you. Tony?'

'What?'

'What d'you call yourself – Nelson or Griffin?'

'Griffin.' He looked at her, ashamed, then said quietly, 'But not any more, Maryann. Never. Not after what you've told me.'

They walked on through the half-light, talking much more easily now. Maryann told Tony about Charnwood House, about the *Esther Jane* and Darius, and that he was so desperate he might have to sell her, and about Joel and how worried she was. And Tony told her something of how it had been after she left.

'When 'e saw what'd happened – with the fire, he came 'ome and knocked our mom across the kitchen. I copped 'old of Billy and took 'im outside, out the way of mean old man Griffin – 'e was like someone else that day. Frightened us.'

'He *is* someone else,' Maryann said grimly. 'That's who is really is underneath. Cruel and scheming. I wonder where 'e went to after.'

'Oh – we know where 'e is,' Tony told her, almost casually.

'*Do* you? What – somewhere near by? In Birmingham?'

'Oh yes – course. Near 'is mom.'

'Oh my God – she ain't still alive?'

336

'I dunno – she was a while back. 'Er must've been nearly ninety then. 'E's set 'imself up again, over on the Soho Road. The other place was insured, yer know – 'e ain't no fool.'

'No,' Maryann agreed. 'So our mom knows where 'e is?'

'Oh ar – I mean when it first happened 'e went and lived with old Mrs Griffin. Mom went over to 'ers a number of times begging 'im to come back but 'e weren't 'aving it. Said 'e'd had enough and that was that.'

Nothing there for him, Maryann thought grimly. Not without me and Sal. 'What, so Mom just gave up?'

'Had to. She wanted money off of 'im but 'e said the family'd already caused him quite enough trouble and she weren't 'aving a farthing. She come back ever so upset every time but there was nothing 'er could do. She 'ad to come to terms with it – 'e'd gone and that was that. She 'ad to make the best of it and fend for 'erself. So we moved up the old end and got on with it.'

'But she ain't going to forgive me, is she?'

'Not in a hurry, no.'

By now they'd reached the part of the bank in Ladywood where they had to scramble up and climb through the broken fence.

'It's him should be paying for all the grief he's caused – not Mom. Not us either,' Maryann said, once they were up on the road again. 'If I could just see 'im, I'd . . .' But her voice trailed off, hopelessly. What could she do? What did it matter now? The only things that mattered were that Joel was lying in hospital fighting to stay alive, and that she had seen her brother and he forgave her.

'Meet me again, will yer?' she said to him. 'And bring Billy with yer.'

Tony nodded, his eyes very dark in his pale face.

'You'd best get 'ome. You must be hungry.'

'I could go and 'ave a look – over round 'is place,' Tony said suddenly.

'Well – if you can stand the sight of 'im.' Maryann touched his arm, smiling. 'T'ra, Tony. See yer soon.'

When she got back to Nance and Mick's, Nance started up from the table as she walked in, trying to pretend she hadn't been sitting crying, and quickly wiped her eyes.

'Oh Nance – what's wrong?' Maryann wasn't fooled for a moment. 'I do wish you was happier, that I do.'

'I'm awright—' Nance hurried over to put the kettle on. 'It's just I wish Mick'd stay in a night or two sometimes. 'E never seems to be 'ere lately. But never mind, eh? How's Joel?'

'No better.' Maryann sank down at the table. ''E just seemed the same as yesterday. Oh Nance – I wish there was something I could do.'

Thirty-Seven

Maryann spent the following days in an agony of waiting. Though she was pleased to have had such a good meeting with Tony, and enjoyed Nance's company, her mind was never far from Joel. She was sick with worry. Her appetite had disappeared almost completely and she had trouble sleeping, thinking of him lying there as she saw him every day, hanging between life and death, not quite belonging to either. She often cried out her desperation in bed at night, trying to keep quiet so Nance and Mick wouldn't hear her next door.

On the other hand, they often weren't quiet themselves and Maryann realized her own presence was making things worse.

'How much longer've we got *her* hanging about for?' she heard Mick demanding one night.

Another time he made some comment about her living off them.

'She ain't 'ad a penny off of us,' Nance snapped back at him. 'So yer needn't start on like that. Maryann's got money of 'er own and she ain't mean with it neither.'

But this only seemed to increase Mick's resentment, and the added conflict she was causing between Nance and her husband made Maryann feel even more desperate. If only she could leave them in peace, but where else did she have to go?

On the third day after she had seen Tony she woke

after a broken, wretched night and lay in bed, unable to sleep but too limp and tired to get out of bed. She heard the door bang as Mick went off to work, and closed her eyes. She always felt relieved knowing he was out of the house.

She was still dozing when there came more banging. Nance was downstairs and Maryann heard voices, then Nance calling up the stairs, 'Maryann – someone to see yer!'

Bewildered, she hastily pulled her dress on and ran down without combing her hair, her mind full of irrational questions. Was it news about Joel? Had he passed away in the night? But no, of course not – no one came out to tell you. And it still felt very early.

Downstairs, she found a man with dark curly hair, looking enormous in the little room, his head almost touching the ceiling. He looked exhausted and was twisting his cap between his hands, obviously most uneasy to be in this strange place. It took her a moment to realize who he was.

'Darius – you got my letter then!' She felt so pleased to see him, as if he was a member of her own family. 'How did you get 'ere?'

'I come almost non-stop,' he said. 'After I 'eard from you. Bessie's all in. Pulled into Birnigum as it was getting light. So—' He stepped closer, urgently. 'What about Joel – have I got 'ere in time?'

'Oh Darius . . .' Tears came so readily to her eyes at the moment. 'You have if 'e's the same as yesterday. I've been waiting and watching every day and 'e's been lain there, not knowing what's going on around him and his breathing's that bad. Every day when I go I don't know . . .'

'Well 'ow about us go now – where is it? Is it far?'

Maryann managed a wan smile through her tears. 'We 'ave to go in the afternoon – they won't let us in now.'

''Ere—' Nance gestured shyly at the table. ''Ave a seat, Mr Bartholomew, and I'll make us some breakfast. I've even got some eggs today, thanks to Maryann.' Maryann noticed that Nance seemed quite over-whelmed by his presence.

Darius sat down rather reluctantly, as he had been all primed to spring into action straight away. Maryann sat with him and they drank tea as Nancy cooked, quietly listening and turning often from the range to look curiously at Maryann and this great, rugged visitor.

'So you came in the *Esther Jane*?' Maryann quizzed him.

''Course. What else? You got to me just in time. They'd just finished 'er up at Tooley's Yard and I was off to load up when your letter came.'

'So, you ain't sold 'er yet – to Mr Barlow?'

Darius shook his head slowly, swallowing a mouth-ful of tea. Maryann saw the muscles move in his thick neck. She waited for him to speak. The Bartholomews never hurried anything they wanted to say.

'Not yet. I couldn't sell 'er out from under the nose of my father without 'im being there. Nor Joel. Mr Barlow said 'e could wait.'

'So ... you didn't come the whole way single-handed?'

'No. There's a nipper come up with me this time. The Higgins family loaned me young Ernie. I left 'im asleep—' For the first time something like a smile came

341

to Darius's weathered face. Maryann saw Nance watching him, intrigued. 'That's a trip 'e won't forget in a hurry!'

'How's old Mr Bartholomew?' Maryann asked.

Darius shook his head. 'Mending – slow though. Oh, ta – very good of you.' He nodded appreciatively at Nance as she set before him a plate piled with bread and butter and *three* fried eggs. Maryann's plate held one and Nance appeared to be having only bread. Maryann raised an eyebrow at her.

''E's 'ad a long night,' Nance said, blushing. ''E deserves a good feed.'

They ate in silence for a time. Darius seemed ravenous and emptied his plate quickly, wiping up every last drop of yolk with the bread. Nance's knife and fork looked like toys in his big hands. She nibbled at her bread, seeming fascinated by Darius. Maryann also found her eyes drawn to his face as she ate. Having him here was wonderful to her, like having part of Joel. Though they looked different, there was something about the way they both moved and in the tone of their voices that was similar. She felt proud that he had appeared. But she was longing to ask him, keep on at him – you can't really sell the *Esther Jane*? You're not really going to? And her heart ached. She knew how much this would mean to Joel, how much he would struggle with every ounce of strength he had to stop it happening if he were able. But now perhaps Darius would be left alone for ever. Perhaps Joel would never . . .

Feeling tears welling in her eyes again she tore her thoughts away and looked up at Darius. He'd drunk his tea and his eyes were drooping, his whole body sagging with weariness.

'You need a sleep,' she told him. 'Would it be awright if 'e went up on my bed for a bit, Nance?'

For a second Nance looked put out, and Maryann knew she was calculating what Mick would have to say about this. But Darius would be gone long before Mick appeared.

''Course 'e can.' She smiled warmly. 'You show 'im up there, Maryann.'

Darius was dead to the world all morning. Maryann helped Nance around the house, glad to have plenty to do to while away the morning. She scrubbed the front step and helped with a load of washing, mangling it and pegging it out in the hazy sunshine, a shaft of which penetrated into the yard round the back where they were working.

'On the cut they hang the washing out along the boats,' she told Nance, shaking out a dress of her own before she pegged it on the line. It smelled rather harshly of soap.

Nance looked up, bent over the mangle. 'Do they? Fancy—' She frowned. 'I always thought them people on the cut were just a bunch of gypos. But that Darius seems a nice man.'

'They ain't gypos,' Maryann said hotly. 'And they ain't *all* rough. They just live a bit different, that's all.'

Nance looked doubtful. '*Very* different, going by what I've 'eard. Still – some of 'em are awright I s'pose.'

'Yes.' Maryann still sounded cross. ''Course they are. You want to see for yerself before you start canting on about things you don't know.'

''Eh – there's no need to bite my 'ead off—' Nance

began mangling again furiously. 'Bet you'd've said the same if yer didn't know.'

Maryann took Mick's spare trousers as they rolled through the mangle. 'S'pose so,' she conceded. 'Sorry, Nance.'

'That's awright. I know you're on edge.'

After a few moments, without looking up from the mangle, Nance said, ''E's got a wife, I s'pose?'

'No.' Maryann was stretching up to the line.

Nance looked over at her. ''E ain't married? Your Joel ain't married. I mean they're getting on, the pair of 'em. What's the matter with 'em?'

'There's nothing the matter with them!' Maryann snapped again, irritated by the way Nance said it. 'Joel 'ad a sweetheart when 'e was young and she married someone else by the end of the War. I don't know about Darius – they're working almost every hour of the day and it ain't that easy to meet up with anyone on the cut. You just don't know what it's like, Nance.'

'No. So yer keep saying. I'm just surprised a man with 'is looks ain't wed by now, that's all. 'E looks a bit of awright to me.'

'Does 'e now?' Maryann teased. 'Well – you'd better watch yerself then. Old married woman like you.'

She didn't fail to notice the blush that rushed through Nance's cheeks.

They had to wake Darius after midday. He emerged from sleep utterly bewildered as he looked round, then seeing Maryann, he sat up in a panic.

'Is it time – are we too late?'

'No – yer awright. Nance's done us a bit of dinner, and then we'll go.' She gave her hair a hasty going over

344

with her treasured brush she had had that Christmas at Charnwood. 'Don't worry – we'll be in good time.'

Don't worry! she thought later as she sat beside Darius on the tram along the Bristol Road. Well, there was a daft thing to say. The whole of her life was consumed with worry. She looked round at Darius. He didn't look any too happy on the tram. It was quite full and she could sense how uneasy and out of place he felt.

Inside the hospital was even worse. He walked along the corridor beside her, tense and silent, looking about him. Maryann felt the usual sense of panic and dread engulf her as they approached the ward but she fought against it, determined not to show Darius how bad she was feeling.

At the door she forced herself to look along, her gaze racing to the spot where Joel had been lying all that week. For a moment she couldn't take it in, could not make sense of anything, and then she saw properly as the room came into focus.

'Oh—' she gulped. 'Oh, it's awright, Darius – 'e's still there! Come on.' She found herself taking his arm, leading him down to Joel's bed.

She had grown used to the sight of how Joel had become through illness and that his beard had gone, and she had not thought to warn Darius. The shock registered in his face. Plainly Joel looked a lot worse than when Darius had last seen him.

They went to the side of the bed and Maryann searched hungrily for any sign of change. Joel still lay with his eyes closed, his breathing shallow and laboured. Each time she saw him his body seemed more slight and the sight of him filled her with pain. He was disappearing. Slowly, inexorably, day by day, the man she loved was slipping away. Darius sat on the chair, cap in hand, staring at his brother in appalled silence.

Maryann kneeled down and took Joel's hand, kissing it as she always did.

'Joel? It's me again – Maryann. And Darius – your brother – he's here with me. He's come all the way up from Banbury to see you – brought the *Esther Jane* out of Tooley's Yard and she's 'ere—' On her own she often broke down talking to him, receiving as much reply as she would from a stone, but today she wanted to be strong for Darius's sake. She looked round at him. 'D'yer want to say anything to him?'

Darius leaned forward. 'Joel. It's Darius—' He looked round the room distractedly, as if searching for the right words. 'I 'ope you're going to get better, Joel – on your feet soon, eh?' He sat back, clearly at a loss, but his gaze never left Joel's face.

'D'you 'ear that, Joel? What Darius says? Please get better and come back to us. We all need yer – Darius and me and your dad and the *Esther Jane* . . . .' More softly, she added, 'And I love you, Joel – I do love you so much.'

It was then she felt it. Just for a second. She turned with a gasp to Darius. 'He moved his hand! I felt it. 'E sort of squeezed mine – there, 'e did it again!'

'Don't 'e do that normally?'

'No – no! I've not had anything out of him. Oh Joel – can you hear us?'

Again, a pressure round her hand. Then a faint fluttering of his eyelashes. She and Darius stood waiting, absolutely still. There was nothing more, though they waited on and on.

'Nurse!' Maryann was too emotional to be frightened of the nurse. The woman came over to her, her face grave, obviously steeling herself.

'What is it?' Her voice was sharp.

''E just squeezed my hand – a few times. He squeezed my hand!'

The woman's face relaxed, looking relieved, then pleased. 'Did he, now?'

Maryann left the hospital with Darius feeling like a different person. It had been a small thing, that tiny movement that told her Joel knew he was still with them, but it changed everything. They had hope, hope which lit the day brighter than the brightest summer sun.

'I'm so glad it happened with you 'ere,' she told Darius, who seemed to be grasping just how much this meant. 'Oh – I feel so happy!' She felt like shouting and singing. 'Are you coming back to Nance's?'

'No – reckon I'll get back to the boat.'

'I tell you what, let's take Nance to see 'er. We've got to go back that way any'ow and it's not far. How about that?'

'Awright. If that's what you want.' He smiled. 'Reckon young Ernie'll just be awake by now and starving 'ungry!'

Nance was all of a tizz when they got back and asked her to come out with them. 'But I can't – I mean I've got to do the dinner, and . . .'

'Oh come on, Nance!' Maryann chivvied her, untying her apron. 'No arguments – you're coming.'

'Maryann!' Nance laughed. She could see the change in Maryann immediately.

'We'll get some liver or summat on the way back – that's nice and quick. It's a lovely day today – you don't want to spend it stuck in 'ere, do you?'

'Well – if Mr – if Darius don't mind?'

Darius shrugged. 'I can stay 'ere a bit longer. If you want to come that's all right with me.'

They walked out into the bright, hot afternoon. Darius told them he had tied up not far from Farmer's Bridge and Maryann led the way through the streets of buses and trams and hurrying people, which seemed to be as foreign as a jungle to Darius.

'Did you bring her up empty?' Maryann asked him.

'Oh no – I got a load on grain into 'er – unloaded that this morning.'

'There she is!' Maryann cried as they reached the spot. The boat sat high in the water. 'Ooh, she's looking nice, Darius – much better than when I saw 'er before.'

'She's 'ad a good going over,' he agreed. 'And a lick of paint. She was in a bad state before. Only we 'ad to keep getting ahead – there was never time.'

Young Ernie Higgins was sitting out on the bank beside the boat chewing on an apple. Darius helped Nance on board and Maryann followed.

'Oh my – it's tiny in 'ere!' Nance said, peering into the cabin. Astonished, she turned to Darius and Maryann. 'D'you live in 'ere – all year round?'

'Got nowhere else,' Darius said. 'That's it – home to us.' He smiled, obviously enjoying her amazement.

'And you lived on 'ere an' all?' she said to Maryann. 'Where on earth did yer sleep?'

Maryann took great pride in showing her the cabin, where they slept and cooked and old Mrs Bartholomew's crochet work, almost as if she'd been born to the life and wasn't a newcomer 'off the bank' herself. Nance sat at the tiny table.

'It's like playing doll's 'ouses!' She laughed. She was more light-hearted than Maryann had yet seen her. 'I've never seen anything so tiny. And it's ever so clean – not like them dirty old joey boats. Ooh – ain't it nice?'

'There's nothing like it,' Maryann said, taking a seat beside her. She looked round contentedly. Darius had had time to polish the brasses while he was at Tooley's Yard, and the cabin was fairly clean too. Her eye still picked out a lot of things that needed doing. It felt like *her* home.

'Oh Nance—' She squeezed her friend's hand. 'Joel's going to get better. I know 'e is! This feels like the happiest day of my life!'

'I'm glad for yer,' Nance said sincerely.

Darius poked his head through the door of the cabin and smiled. 'I'll brew up a cuppa tea, shall I?'

He seemed to enjoy their company and was far more relaxed now he was back on the cut, having come through the ordeal of going to the hospital. They sat drinking tea – Darius and Nance perched at the stern, Maryann sat half twisted round on the cabin step. Darius told Nance about the life and how they worked. Maryann could see she admired Darius and he was at ease with her, seemed to like her. She made him laugh. And Nance basked in the sun, her pale, thin body seeming to relax and become more youthful away from home. Maryann saw Darius looking at her often. If only things were different, she thought, I do believe these two might've had something. But it was no good thinking of that. She thought bitterly about Mick. Shame you could never see what was just round the corner.

'Now I've seen Joel,' Darius was saying, 'I'll go looking for a load tonight – get off in the morning. I'd thought I might 'ave to be here longer, if . . . but I'll get ahead for a bit. Keep 'er going. There's nothing I can do 'ere for now.'

'Oh – I wish I was coming with you,' Maryann said.

'I almost wish I was from what you've told me.' Nance laughed. Maryann hadn't heard her laugh like that in ages.

'Ah well.' Darius smiled. 'God knows, you'd both be welcome. I could do with more hands on board. I s'pose we'll manage though.' He nodded his head towards Ernie. 'For now.'

Thirty-Eight

'Don't tell 'im where we've been, for God's sake,' Nance implored later as they got the tea ready fast and furiously. They'd stayed too long down on the cut and had had to run back, via the butcher's. The prospect of Mick's fury if everything wasn't ready when he got home set the pair of them off and the cooking became a joke. Maryann was chopping onions frantically at the table. Nance was so dithery she dropped the liver on the floor so it had to be washed and then she got the giggles.

'Oh, look at that! What'd Mick say if 'e saw me throwing 'is tea on the floor!' Her laughter almost got the better of her as she mimicked her husband's indignation, swaggering and waving a piece of liver around in her hand like a weapon. ' "Sure I don't see my dinner ready. What sort of a wife is it who can't even put a meal on the table when a man walks through the door!" Oh my Lord!' she spluttered. 'I don't know what's got into me!'

Maryann was laughing just as much, her eyes also streaming from the onions. She was bubbly with relief and hope over Joel, and really happy to see what difference a little break had made to Nance, who looked younger again suddenly, face pink from the sun and full of mirth under her mop of black curls. They were both laughing so much that for a few minutes they were incapable of cooking anything at all and the liver and onions lay untouched on the table.

A rattle at the door sobered them instantly.

Nance gasped, horrified. ''E can't be back already!'

But the door didn't open.

'Must be someone else,' Nance hissed and crept over to open it. 'Oh – 'ello, Tony love.' She started giggling again with relief. ''Ow're you? Come on in. Don't mind me.'

'S'Maryann there?'

Maryann experienced a flutter of pleasure that he had come to find her. *My brother.* He had clearly just got off work again and was as grubby as the last time she saw him.

'Awright, Tony – ain't yer coming in?'

He looked awkward and anxious at the same time. 'Can yer come out – just for a bit?'

Maryann looked doubtful. 'Can you manage, Nance?'

'Yes, go on – I'll get on quicker without you setting me off.'

She walked with Tony down to the end of the street, passing men on their way home from work, a few kids playing out. Smells of cooking drifted from the houses as they walked along.

'I thought you were going to bring Billy to see me,' she reproached him.

'Not this time.' Tony seemed tense.

'What's up?'

'I know where 'e's living.'

Maryann didn't need to ask who. 'You went to see him?'

'*No.* Course not. I followed 'im home. 'E does just what 'e did when 'e was with Mom. Leaves and locks

352

up just the same time, quick pint and 'ome. 'E lives up behind the park in Handsworth.'

'And has a shop on the Soho Road? An under-taker's?'

'It's an undertaker's, but it ain't under the name of Griffin. 'E set 'imself up under a new name: Arthur Lambert. 'E's made 'isself a new life awright.'

'The slimy . . .' Maryann began, but Tony inter-rupted.

'T'ain't the main fing though. After I followed 'im home I waited for a bit to see if I could see anyfing. I daint see much, but when it was getting dark this woman come and shut the curtains at the front.'

'Woman – what, you mean . . .? Could be a landlady, couldn't it?'

'Could be. I dunno. But then, when I was getting fed up, nuffing to see – I s'pose they'd been 'aving some tea – the door come open and two girls came out and went off down the road.'

'Girls?' Maryann stopped, full of foreboding. 'How old?'

'Couldn't see for sure. Younger'un me.'

Maryann felt herself swell inside with suspicion and fury. 'Oh no – oh Tony, d'yer think . . .?'

Tony shrugged. 'Dunno – couldn't make out anyfing else.'

'No. Course yer couldn't.' She felt sorry he was involved. He was still only a kid, even if he was tall and muscular and doing a man's work. He shouldn't even have to know any of this. 'Look – thanks, Tony. For doing that.'

'What're yer going to do, sis?'

It warmed her heart to hear him call her that – already, when she'd been away so long. Made her feel she belonged. This search for Norman Griffin was bringing them together. Once again she thanked God that Tony believed her, was on her side. She couldn't have faced this alone.

'I don't know, Tony. I really don't. What *can* I do? It makes me feel bad just thinking about it.' She wouldn't say more to him, didn't want to fill his head with disturbing details.

''E wants a good 'iding, 'e does,' Tony said fiercely.

Maryann almost smiled. A 'good hiding' sounded so innocent, like something a child might be threatened with. It was the least of what she had in mind. ''E does that, Tony. And I'm going to think about how he's going to get it an' all.'

When she got back, Mick was home, eating in silence. Nance winked at her over his head but Maryann could tell the atmosphere between them was very sour. Nance was back to the cowed, weary-looking woman she had been before and Maryann felt Mick's resentment of her as soon as she walked in. She ate up her own tea quickly and said she was going to bed.

Soon after she'd gone up she heard them start downstairs, arguing, voices getting louder, savage in tone. She undressed, full of tension. It was horrible to hear.

'Don't you start carrying on like that!' she heard Nance shout. 'I 'ate it when you show yer face through the door these days, yer miserable sod. I don't know why yer bother coming 'ome the way yer keep on when you're 'ere!'

'This is my house and you'll not talk to me like that.

If I'd known what sort of a wife you'd make I'd never've married you, so I wouldn't . . .'

'Not like the blessed Saint Theresa yer mean!' Nance shrieked harshly. 'Well, 'er was never so bloody perfect as yer make out – and you never managed to get 'er a bun in the oven neither, did yer?'

It always came back to that. Maryann screwed up her eyes, hearing Nance's howl of pain and then a crash as something fell and smashed on the floor. There was more shouting, followed by a roar which almost made Maryann's heart stop.

'You bitch! You evil fecking bitch – look what you've done!'

She ran down and stopped at the bottom of the stairs, appalled. Suddenly everything was quiet. Mick was standing clutching his left forearm, blood oozing out round his fingers. Nance, mouth open in horror, was still holding the knife she'd used to slice up the pig's liver.

'Oh . . . Mick!' Nance gasped. 'What've I done?' She seized a cloth and went to him to staunch the wound but he snatched it and backed away from her.

'Don't you come near me, you mad bitch!' he snarled. 'Look what you've done to me! You're not right up top – you're not fit to be a wife to anyone.' Clutching the cloth to his arm he backed out of the door, kicked it shut so the house shook and then they heard his feet going down the path.

Nance looked stunned. Maryann went and took the bloodstained knife from her quivering hand and laid it on the table.

'He punched me.' Nance's mouth was trembling, the tears starting to come. 'It 'urt so much . . . I daint know what I was doing.' She laid her hand over her right breast. 'Punched me just 'ere.' She sat down and started to cry. Maryann poured her a nip of whiskey and put it down beside her. ''E should've never punched me there – it 'urt too much. Oh Maryann – what've I done?'

''E'll be awright. It's only a cut.'

But she knew Nance didn't just mean Mick's arm. She meant everything.

Maryann scarcely slept that night. She lay awake, awaiting the sound of Mick coming home again. Her thoughts swirled round. She was so upset for Nance, and in the night's darkness she felt full of doubt about everything and very afraid. She had felt Joel squeeze her hand and had been so hopeful, but he was still so ill. It didn't mean he was going to get better, did it? Perhaps even now he was slipping away and she'd never see him again ... She pushed this thought away but it was replaced by all the things Tony had told her about Norman Griffin.

I'm free of him, she thought. I need never have anything else to do with him. I should just give all my strength to Joel and go away and never think about any of it again. He probably has a landlady with children – or they were just visiting ... She tried as hard as she could to persuade herself that this was what was right. It was nothing to do with her. But she could not stop thinking about Sal and herself when Norman was living with them, of the trap of fear and disgust he had built round them. What if he was doing it all again and those two girls were having to live through the same hell that he had put Sal through?

She twisted back and forth in the bed, then lay on her back, hands behind her head looking at the window. There was a full moon and its light was shining through the gap between Nance's thin curtains.

'Tell me what to do,' she whispered. 'I don't want anything to do with this. Let it all just go away.' She ached for the morning to come.

She had left the hospital full of happiness yesterday, but going back today she approached it with terrible misgiving. She was weighed down by the grim thoughts brought on by lack of sleep and what had happened the night before. Mick had not come home all night.

'Oh – 'e'll've gone to 'is mom's to get fussed over,' Nance said. She was trying to take it lightly but she was pale and drawn and Maryann could tell she had not slept either.

This didn't feel like a day for anything good to happen. Her head aching, eyes watering in the sunlight from sleeplessness, she walked to the hospital.

She arrived to find Joel with his eyes open. All her dread drained away, seeing his gaze follow her hungrily towards his bed as if she was the one thing he had been waiting for. There was a little cup on the chair so she sank down on her knees by the bed and for a moment they just gazed at one another in silence. Joel tried to squeeze her hand and she could tell how weak he was.

'You're back,' she said. And burst into tears.

Joel tried to speak but the attempt produced instead a fit of coughing. He reached out for the cup and she passed it to him. He coughed painfully into it, then covered it with his hand. A nurse came and whisked it away and returned it empty a few moments later. Maryann wiped her eyes and got up to perch on the edge of the seat. Joel lay back, panting from the exertion.

'You poor thing,' she said.

Joel patted his chest. Maryann leaned over to hear him whisper, 'I think I've got half the cut in there from what's coming out.'

'But you're going to get better. I know you are. Oh Joel – I've been that worried about you. You've no idea.'

He looked very tenderly at her and she smiled tearfully and buried her head for a moment in the bedding beside him, still holding his hand and drinking in the feeling of being close to him. Then she sat up and examined him again.

'D'you feel better in yourself?'

He nodded. 'Seeing you.'

'I've been in here every day. Did you know? Did you know Darius came?'

Joel looked confused. 'Darius – in here?'

'No – I don't s'pose you remember. He stopped off to see you and then 'e went back to chase another load . . .' She remembered with a pang that perhaps Darius had seen Samuel Barlow again – perhaps had sold the *Esther Jane* already. She didn't know if Joel knew anything about it and she didn't want to have to tell him – not now especially. 'Anyway – your dad's on the mend. 'E's still down at your auntie's in Oxford but Darius said 'e should be back aboard soon. Darius had a young lad with 'im – Ernie Higgins I think 'is name was.'

She saw Joel nod faintly, and she could tell he was drinking in everything she was telling him. The boat was his life and she could see the hunger for it in his eyes. She leaned forward to catch his words.

'Want to get back aboard . . . soon.'

'Oh Joel – I don't think you'll be ready for a while yet.'

'Soon as I can . . .'

'All right—' She appeased him. How long would it be before he could even walk, let alone work the cut! But she didn't want to upset him.

'Maryann—' He pulled her closer.

'What, love?'

He gazed, very seriously, into her eyes. 'When I get back to 'er – will you be there this time – with me?'

He was coughing again and once more she had to wait for the seizure to pass. It exhausted him, but still he pulled her to him, full of urgency.

'Please . . . will you and me get wed?'

'Oh Joel, love—' She laid her hand against his cheek, stroking it, gently cradling his head. 'You're everything to me. Of course we will.'

He closed his eyes for a moment, quite spent, but with a smile of great joy on his face.

Thirty-Nine

The summer was slipping past. The schools closed and the streets, back yards and parks were full of the sounds of children playing.

Maryann had settled into being Nance and Mick's lodger and for the time being things were better. Mick had stayed away for three days and nights and came home with his arm bandaged and the look of a man who has been severely lectured by his mother. Mrs Mallone the elder, a staunch Catholic, wouldn't countenance the shame of a broken marriage in her family and had told him so in no uncertain terms. He arrived home at the end of a day's work and Maryann got out of the way to let him and Nance sort things out. They arrived at a truce.

'We've decided to stop arguing about us 'aving a babby,' Nance said bravely. 'We'll just 'ave to see what 'appens. And 'e said 'e should never've hit me the way 'e did and 'e don't really mind you being 'ere.'

Maryann thought that remained to be seen, but she was relieved as well. She just hoped Mick could put up with her until Joel was better.

Each day Maryann saw an improvement in Joel. He became a little stronger, bit by bit. Although he was still terribly thin his skin started to lose its deathly yellow colour, and he was able to talk more without being crippled by the agonizing cough. They talked a great deal on every visit, catching up with some of the time they had missed over the intervening years.

Sometimes Joel looked longingly at her. 'I wish we weren't sat here on full view of everyone – then I could give you a proper kiss.'

Just for a moment Maryann experienced her old surge of dread at the thought of any man touching her, and she had to reason with herself. Not every man was Norman Griffin. And this was Joel – her beloved Joel. She laughed happily. 'You *are* getting better, ain't yer?'

'Every day. I'll soon be strong enough to pick you up and carry you out of 'ere.'

She knew he'd give anything to be away from the alien place which the hospital was to him. 'Not long now,' she told him. 'Your chest'll be clear as a bell soon.'

'Oh – I don't think it'll ever be that!'

But she thought with misgiving about Joel going back to the cut. Was he going to find that his home of a lifetime no longer belonged to him? It didn't matter so much to her. It would still be the same boat, even if it did have Samuel Barlow's name painted on the side. And Darius had said there were a lot of advantages to working for someone else. They chased the loads and you got regular pay and insurance. But she still knew Joel would want to fight it.

She hadn't seen Darius since he'd visited Joel in hospital, although she left messages for him regularly. She wondered what was going on. She was almost as impatient as Joel for this time of waiting to be over so she could get away from Nancy and Mick's house and she and Joel could be together and plan their wedding.

Wedding! She was overcome with excitement and disbelief every time she thought about it. It felt so right, as if from the first time she had met Joel they had been picked out for each other and he had been just waiting for her to grow up. The two of them could go away. She imagined herself gliding off along the golden water of the cut at sunset, into a new life.

It was early one morning when she went to Hands-worth and walked past Norman Griffin's new premises, reading the sign, 'Arthur Lambert'. She saw her own reflection, her tight-lipped expression, in the shop's dark window. The place wasn't open yet. She knew Norman Griffin horribly well and recalled the time of his methodical comings and goings. Oh, he was always organized, all right. You had to give him that. She waited in a shade-filled doorway on the other side of the road from his house so that he would not have to pass her. It wasn't that she didn't believe or trust Tony, only that she had to see him for herself.

He came, as she knew he would, a few minutes before nine o'clock: a black, square-shouldered figure, topped by a Homburg hat and moving at a stately pace along the street towards her. She could barely make out his face and didn't dare move closer. She clenched her fingers, digging in with her nails. He looked like any other respectable, middle-aged man who was running to fat a little. How could he look so ordinary, so harmless?

He took the keys from his pocket and unlocked the shop, then stepped inside out of sight. Maryann found she was sweating, her pulse racing. Six years had passed. She was a woman now, but the effect he had on her was just the same. She wanted to run away and never set eyes on him again.

But those little girls ... She had to know, somehow, whether they were suffering as she and Sal had suffered. If they weren't, then she could feel free to leave, never to go anywhere near Norman Griffin ever again. With slow, reluctant steps she set off towards the address Tony had given her, feeling very nervous and foolish. What on earth did she think she was going to do? A strange woman turning up, trying to talk to two girls who'd never seen her before, who'd be bound to tell their mom and then she'd tell Norman ... They wouldn't know who she was, but he almost certainly would.

I've got to find a way, she thought grimly. I just have to. When she reached the street of small terraced houses, she discovered with relief that almost opposite the address Tony had given her, number twenty-two Beechwood Road, was a side road leading into the next street and it was deep in shadow this morning, while the sun was shining brightly on the opposite side. At least she could walk less conspicuously up and down.

A half-hour passed. Some people moved up and down the pavement. A couple of women looked curiously at her as they passed. Another half-hour. A clock struck ten in the distance. Maryann was beginning to feel very bored and worried that people were watching her.

I'll come back tomorrow, she was thinking, when she saw the door open and someone coming out! She stood in the shade and watched. First she saw one girl appear with long auburn hair and carrying a shopping basket. Maryann guessed her age to be about twelve. She was followed by another, smaller girl, very similar looking though her hair was curlier and not as long as her older sister's. They were dressed in buttery yellow frocks, like a pair of pretty dolls. They obviously weren't living in the depths of poverty. But then they wouldn't be, would they? Maryann thought bitterly.

Then she saw their mother appear on the step, her own auburn hair coiled up at the back and a pleasant, though tense-looking face. She was leaning forwards, supporting herself on two sticks, and it was clear she had great difficulty in negotiating her way down. She handed one stick to the younger child and was helped down the front step by her older daughter. Taking up with both sticks again she waited while the older girl shut the front door, and then they began to make their way along the road. Maryann realized that there was going to be no danger of losing them. In fact, it was going to be hard to follow and not be seen because she was having to walk so slowly. The woman was apparently able-bodied in every other respect than in her right leg, which left her body at the hip at such an awkward angle that her walking on it was greatly hampered and twisted her from side to side as she did so.

She followed the grindingly slow progress of this family as they made their way round the shops fetching their groceries. Maryann saw that the girls were quite used to this routine and helped carry everything, or sometimes went into shops for their mother who called instructions to them if the entrance was particularly awkward for her. They seemed close and amiable together. She learned that the older girl was called Amy.

When they finally reached home, Maryann waited, and at last saw the two of them emerge from the house alone and set off towards Handsworth Park. Amy was carrying a hoop and they were skipping along quite fast. With a pang she saw herself and Sal, before, when their real dad was alive and they'd gone off to play like that with Tony in tow, scurrying off to the rezzer on hot summer afternoons. Maryann had to hurry now to keep up with them.

Once they reached the park they started throwing the hoop. There were other children playing in the park and Maryann relaxed, feeling she could stroll round them, keeping an eye on them. They kept busy with their hoop amid the yells and laughter of the other children. Maryann watched them carefully and in a very short time noticed something that made them stand out from the other children around them. They played with great intensity and never once did she see them laugh or even smile. They seemed only to notice each other, as if they were sealed in, away from everyone outside. Maryann knew that feeling. She saw the younger one surreptitiously touch herself, just for a second, between her legs, wincing. It was a gesture that probably no one else would have noticed. But Maryann began to know then, really know. She had to be absolutely sure though.

Moving round, she positioned herself in the path of the hoop that the older one was holding behind her head ready to lob overarm. It bounced and skittered across the grass. The younger girl ran but Maryann got there first, catching it as it spun past her.

'Oh – caught it for yer!' She smiled as the girl ran urgently towards her. 'Here you are, love.' She held it out but when the girl took it, Maryann held on so she couldn't just run off.

The girl tugged at it, frowning furiously when Maryann didn't immediately let go.

'It's awright – I'm not taking it away. It was just coming at me so fast I caught it.' Out of the corner of her eye she saw the older girl running towards them. 'It's a nice one, ain't it? Who bought you that then?'

There was no reply.

The older sister arrived, looking very wary.

'I just caught your hoop – you threw it so hard,' Maryann said.

'Sorry,' she said, dully.

'No – it's awright.' Maryann gently released the hoop, asking as she did so, 'You must have a mom who's good at sewing – did she make your lovely dresses?'

Amy nodded. She seemed to see that Maryann was being friendly. While she still looked solemn, the hostility drained out of her expression. She stood holding the hoop against her legs, with her weight on one foot, the other leg bent back, the toe of her black rubber pump resting on the ground.

'Well, she's better at sewing than I am.' She fought desperately for a reason to keep them with her and fumbled in her pocket. 'Look – I've got some toffees. D'yer fancy one?'

The girls looked at each other, then nodded in unison.

'Here y'are.' Maryann sat down hoping they would do the same, but they stood above her, the toffees bulging in their cheeks. They each had freckles, the older one just across the bridge of her nose, while the younger one had them scattered, golden, all over her face.

Maryann wanted to be gentle with them, befriend them, but she was also worried they'd run off before she could ask them anything, so she came straight to her questions. 'So – your mom or dad not out with you?'

Amy shook her head.

'Your dad's at work I expect?'

The two girls seemed to draw physically close, together as their eyes lost contact with hers and looked down at the ground. The fierce tone of the older girl's voice as she half spoke, half whispered, brought Maryann's flesh up in goose pimples.

''E ain't our dad.'

The emotions were there for anyone who knew how to read them the fear, the disgust and loathing. And for Maryann it was like listening to herself speak, as if her own soul had addressed her from out of the young girl's mouth.

She kept them with her for as long as she could. They accepted another toffee but still wouldn't sit down.

'What's your name?' she asked the older one. Of the two she had the longer face, was rather pretty with her autumn looks. But her gaze slid distractedly away when Maryann spoke to her. She might meet her eyes for a fraction of a second, then she would stare away across the park towards the trees or look down at her feet.

'I'm Amy. This is Margaret.'

Margaret's gaze didn't leave the ground. She was standing with her weight on the outside of her feet, concentratedly chewing her toffee. Hers was the rounder face, hair more carroty, expression closed tight as a trap.

'How old're you then, Margaret?'

'She's nine,' Amy said. 'I'm twelve.'

Maryann longed to ply them with questions but she did not want to frighten them. Margaret had still not said a word to her. 'You'd better get back to your game then,' she said. 'D'you come to the park every day?'

Amy nodded in her vague way, eyes sweeping the park. Margaret put her head on one side and looked sulky.

'Might see you again then.' Maryann got up. 'T'ra for now. Have a nice game.'

They returned immediately to their hoop as if she had never existed.

She found them the next day sitting on the grass not far from the park entrance, the hoop lying on the ground beside them, each wearing turquoise dresses and a white bow in their hair. They were turned slightly towards each other, their heads bowed, and Maryann thought that from the way they were sitting they must be busy playing or making daisy chains. As she came closer, though, she saw they were not doing anything.

'Amy? Margaret? Hello there – thought I might see you again.'

Margaret, as ever, kept her head down, but Amy glanced up and her mouth almost twitched into a smile. Maryann sat down on the grass beside them. What she said next had taken some careful thought.

'I never said what my name was when I saw yer yesterday. I'm Esther. Esther Bartholomew.' She didn't want to tell them fibs. But nor did she want to ask them to keep her meeting them a secret from their mother. If she told them her real name though, and they mentioned it in front of Norman ... She went cold at the very thought. ''Ere – I brought some bull's-eyes today – d'yer fancy one? I never go anywhere without a bag of rocks.'

When the girls were both sucking their sweets, she

took the plunge. 'So you live with your mom and stepdad, do you?'

She got no reaction from little Margaret, but Amy nodded, tugging furiously with her thumb and forefinger at the short, dry grass.

'What happened to your real father?'

'He went away.' Amy spoke so quietly Maryann could barely hear.

'Oh dear, did he? How old were you when he went away?'

'Nine.'

'And has your stepdad been with you a long time?'

Amy nodded. A long time could mean anything, Maryann realized. Most likely it seemed like an eternity to them.

'I had a stepdad when I was your age,' she told them. 'My own father died in an accident and our mom got married again.' She took a deep breath. 'I daint like 'im. In fact I hated 'im.'

Amy looked at her, her expression betraying nothing more than mild curiosity. She was tapping her foot up and down on the grass.

'Is your stepfather nice to yer?'

''E's awright. Takes us to the pictures, and that, sometimes.'

'D'you like going to the pictures, Margaret?'

The girl's head seemed to sink further down, her hair hanging over her face. There was a long silence.

'You're a quiet one,' Maryann said gently.

'She don't speak,' Amy said.

'Not to anyone?'

'Only me. Sometimes.'

'I s'pose you'll be back at school soon.'

369

Amy nodded. 'Next week.'

'D'yer like school?'

'S'awright.'

She could think of nothing to say which might lift their apparent dull acceptance of life. It was as if there was a wall round the two of them. How could she, a stranger, break through it? She didn't want to frighten the girls. Mostly she wanted to put her arms round them and comfort them.

She left them that day, feeling desperate, as if she had let both them and herself down.

That afternoon when she went to see Joel again, she didn't mention Amy and Margaret. She hadn't told Nancy either. She couldn't bring herself to speak of it. And if it was hard for her, she knew that it was well nigh impossible for those little girls to put into words what was happening to them. She couldn't go barging into their family and confront Norman. After all, who would believe her? Her own mother hadn't. It seemed hopeless, the seal of privacy around respectable family life behind which a man's tormenting habits could hide and grow monstrous. Whatever could she really do to help them and stop Norman Griffin's vileness – for good?

Forty

'What're yer wearing that long face for?' Nance asked the next morning. She was clearing away the remains of Mick's breakfast – a bloater and bread and butter – screwing up her nose at the fishy smell. Maryann leaned over to wipe the table, glad that her hair swung forward to hide her face.

'*Have* I got a long face on?'

'Yes, you 'ave. I thought everything was awright – you said Joel was looking much better yesterday.'

'Oh – 'e is – I was just thinking, that's all.' Maryann quickly rearranged her expression along less perplexed lines and stood straight, shaking back her hair. The strain of the past weeks showed in her face, even though she tried to look calm.

She couldn't tell Nance just how much those two little girls were possessing her. She lay awake at night thinking of them. One minute she was telling herself she was imagining it all. They were well dressed and cared for, they played in the park like any other children. She should stop thinking she had any place in their lives. But it was the tiny signs which she understood so intimately that gave them away. Margaret's silence, the shame that made Amy's eyes slide away from anyone's gaze, the very way they held their bodies, never quite at ease. They were suffering and only she could imagine how. What could she do? She felt furious at her helplessness. That night she had resolved before she went to sleep that she would go and see the girls' mother and speak to her. At least tell her what she suspected, alert her to what might be going on in her home. Now, this morning, this seemed preposterous. Maryann ran the cloth over the table, mopping up rings of tea and crumbs. She must talk to Amy and Margaret again first, see if she could get them to trust her, open up to her.

'How long d'yer think it's going to be before Joel can go out of the hospital?' Nance was saying, scraping off Mick's plate into a piece of newspaper.

'Wish I knew, Nance. 'E's so weak it's hard to watch 'im sometimes. 'E can barely stand out of bed. Sometimes I want to just pick him up and carry him he looks that thin.' She went and rinsed out the cloth in the pail of water Nance kept out the back. 'I just want 'im out, Nance. All this time I've been away and now 'e's stuck in there. It feels as if we'll never be able to be together.'

'Oh – you will.' Nance turned and looked through the door at her, wistfully. 'You're ever so lucky. You know – starting out right with someone.'

Maryann came back in from the scullery. 'But you and Mick're getting on better. I mean you ain't been fighting and carrying on like you did before . . .'

'No – I know.' Nance pushed her hands down behind the belt of her apron. She looked miserable. 'But there's no *feeling* between us. Never was really – we both sort of went along with it. I'd never 'ad those feelings, see. So I daint know I was missing anything. But I know there's summat more and you've got it – you and Joel. It's made me see . . . And now I'm stuck with 'im for ever . . .' She stopped, looking down miserably. 'I've always tried to be good, you know, Maryann. Listened to what the priests said and done what I was told. But I don't 'alf 'ave some bad thoughts lately. I don't even dare go to confession and say what's been going through my mind.'

'Oh Nance . . .' Maryann, who'd never had to go to confession in her life, struggled to find the right words, but failed and just stood looking at her, full of pity.

Nance put her hands over her face for a moment, then drew them away and turned round. 'Well – this won't get nowt done. I'd better get cleared away and off up the shops.'

'I'll finish clearing up,' Maryann said. 'You go on out. It'll make you feel better.'

When Nance had gone she washed and dried the breakfast things as usual, swept the room and got ready to go out, feeling nervous and unsettled. Should she talk more to the girls today? Tell them the truth: that their stepfather had also been hers? Would that be the best thing? But her heart was heavy. What did she think she was trying to do – break up a family? Thrust them out of one kind of suffering into another – the insecurity and poverty into which she had condemned her own mother?

It was raining gently outside, through a heavy, late summer warmth. She took her coat and started off down the road. But before she had got very far she saw a tall figure turn in at the end of the street, walking towards her through the drizzle with an unmistakable gait. Her pulse quickened.

'Darius!' Overjoyed, cheeks flushing a healthier pink, she ran down the road to meet him. He smiled, seeing her dashing along the street, impatiently pushing strands of her black hair out of her face. 'When did yer get in? I daint know when we'd see yer again!'

'I'm glad to see *you*,' he said. 'I wasn't sure I'd find the right place again.'

'You just caught me – I was off out. Come on down to the 'ouse. Nance is out shopping but she'll be back soon. Oh Darius, you should see Joel – 'e's looking so much better than last time you was 'ere.'

'Oh—' Darius seemed to sag with relief. 'Thank 'eavens for that. I've been thinking, round and round, what we're gunna do. My father's still not right and I've 'ad to keep Ernie on. I couldn't think 'ow I could manage – even selling out. Joel looked that bad – I thought 'e might not come through after all. Is 'e going to be in there much longer?'

'I don't know – he's ever so keen to get going. You know Joel. He'd be out of there by now if he had the strength to move hisself.'

Darius chuckled. Once more he seemed very tired, but more relaxed now he had heard the good news. He sat at the table in Nance's house and Maryann stoked the fire and put the kettle on again.

'You'd like some breakfast, wouldn't yer?'

'Wouldn't mind – if you've enough. Been going most of the night again.'

'We ain't got much in till Nance gets back, but 'er won't be long.'

'Oh – a cuppa'd do me.'

'You can 'ave that for a start – our Nance'll feed you up like a turkey cock.'

She made tea for them both, scraping out the last of the condensed milk, and sat down, beaming at him. 'I've got summat to tell you.' She couldn't wait any longer. It already felt as if he was her brother. 'Me and Joel, we . . . well, 'e asked me if we'd get wed.'

Darius stared at her, swallowing a mouthful of tea.

A smile spread slowly across his face. 'What – and yer'd come and . . .?'

'Live on the *Esther Jane* – course we would. Where else d'yer think Joel'd ever live?' She was full of excitement. 'I'm so glad you've come now because I was afraid you'd already've sold her and you don't need to – we can all work her together and stay as Number Ones . . .'

Darius held up one of his huge, callused hands. 'Now – 'old your 'orses a minute. You don't know the life, Maryann – not 'ow things've got now. For a start, we could all keep the *Esther Jane* going, but you and Joel ain't gunna want me about for long if you're wed, with a family coming along. That's one thing. Now I'd go back and work a Fellows' boat down London like I done before and leave you to it once Joel's got 'is strength back if that were just it. But it's all changing. We just ain't keeping ahead and getting the loads we need. Now – I've thought long and hard about this, and tomorrow Essy Barlow's gunna be 'ere and 'e's taking on the *Esther Jane* – and what's more—' He held his hand up again to prevent Maryann from interrupting. 'There're going to be changes. 'E's promised to put a motor in 'er and we'll work a pair again. When you and Joel are ready to work 'er together you can 'ave 'er for your home with my blessing, but that's 'ow it'll 'ave to be. I don't like it neither, but we're going to 'ave to 'just to it. That's the only way we're gunna keep up.'

'A motor? You mean – no more Bessie?'

'No more Bessie, and a lot of noise and stink besides. But it's the only way forward. There's more and more moty boats now and they shift the loads. We ent keeping up – simple as that.'

Maryann was digesting this when the door opened and Nancy appeared, panting with two heavy bags of shopping, her coat shiny with rain.

'Oh—' She had expected the house to be empty and was really taken aback. ''Ello ... Darius.' She seemed very flustered and turned away to put the bags down, but not before Maryann saw how much she was blushing.

'Can I get Darius a bit of breakfast? 'E's been on the go a long while again.'

'No – let me get it,' Nance said at once.

'Very good of you, Nancy,' Darius said gruffly.

'No – it's – I'm glad to. I wish I'd've known you was coming – I'd've got a bit of bacon in ...'

While Nance fussed about cooking eggs and sawing doorsteps off a loaf of bread, Maryann reported to her what Darius had said. Nance presented him with a moutainous breakfast of eggs and fried bread and bread and butter, then sat down with some satisfaction to watch him eat it.

'You come to visit yer brother again then, 'ave yer?' she asked.

Darius nodded, his strong jaws working away. 'Thought I'd see Joel. And deal with Mr Barlow tomorrow ...' He paused, then added, 'I just wondered. Today's the last day she'll be our boat, proper. D'you want to come out on 'er for a bit – see 'ow she really goes before they stick a moty on 'er?'

Maryann was just about to answer when she realized his question had been addressed to Nance. After all, she was no stranger to the *Esther Jane*!

'Ooh, well ... today? What, now like?' Nance seemed to swell with excitement.

'The day'll be over, else. See, a bloke at Gas Street

said if we go down the Worcester and Birnigum Cut it goes past the back of the chocolate fact'ry and we can turn down by Selly Oak Wharf – and you said that's near Joel's 'ospital.'

'Yes, it is,' Maryann said. 'We could go and see him from there. We'll 'ave to stop 'im breaking out of the 'ospital to come and see 'er! Oh go on, Nance – it'll be lovely, look – the rain's going off already.'

Nance was all smiles. 'Oh – go on then. I'd like that, Darius – I really would.'

Maryann could tell from her expression that this was something of an understatement.

'Poor old Bessie – she's tired,' Maryann said as they slid out away from Gas Street amid a busy to-ing and fro-ing of joeys, some empty and riding high, others laden and low in the water. The sky was hazy with cloud and smoke, but the rain had gone off and it was clearing up.

'Well – we'll go gently. Tomorrow she can 'ave a long rest,' Darius said.

Young Ernie, who'd worked his way up with Darius, was quite happy to spend a day away on the bank. Nance had stepped aboard saying, 'Just think, Maryann – this'll be your home soon. How on earth are you going to manage?'

Maryann laughed, patting Jep, who had greeted them wagging not just his tail but the whole of his body. She felt she could manage anything so long as Joel was going to get better and be beside her. 'I'll 'ave to get good strong arms, that's all! It's a killer on yer shoulders working on 'ere.'

'Bet I could manage,' Nance said, prodding her

muscles. Nancy had always had a robust frame and now she was thinner she looked wiry and strong, like a greyhound.

Maryann saw Darius watching Nance appraisingly. 'Reckon you could,' he said.

They wound along between the smoking factories, the wharves and warehouses, down the Worcester Canal, moving south. As they glided out through the Edgbaston tunnel to Bournbrook then Selly Oak, the route became greener. Trains chugged past to their right and occasionally the sun broke through the cloud and transformed the dull, scummy ripples to silver. After a short time Maryann had taken up her favourite position on the cabin roof, her hand stroking Jep who sat panting beside her. Coots and moorhens scooted away from the bow of the boat. Butterflies shimmered round flowers in the grass. She took deep, contented breaths. However hard this life, whatever the struggle, this was what she wanted: this was her place and these were her people. Somehow it seemed to have chosen her.

Nance stayed with Darius at the stern and Maryann could hear him instructing her how to work the tiller. Often she heard Nancy's laughter and smiled. It was so good to hear Nancy enjoying herself. She felt herself swelling with happiness, everything else forgotten except that she was here and Joel was getting better. She throbbed with love and longing for him. If only he could be here today, it would be perfect!

They tied up at Selly Oak. Jep pottered off to explore the towpath while they ate bread and cheese that Nancy had brought. Darius had some plums on board, the skins a beautiful reddish orange that seemed to contain the very sunshine that had ripened them. They were sweet and delicious, and they spat the stones overboard.

'So're we gunna turn round 'ere then?' Nance asked.

Darius laughed. 'You can't just turn 'er anywhere. The cut's narrower than the boat – look.'

'Oh yes—' Nance chuckled. 'So it is. I never thought about that before!'

'You 'ave to find a winding 'ole where you can turn – it's just keep going otherwise.'

All morning he had been explaining things to her. Maryann had never heard him speak anything like as much before. She watched them as they perched together at the stern, eating their lunch. It was only then it truly dawned on her. It was so clear in their eyes, the way Darius looked at Nance, her radiance in his presence. However much they tried to hide it, to behave normally, she could see the two of them were falling deeply in love, and she was filled with dread and sorrow.

Maryann turned away from them. What Nance had said this morning, *But now I know there's summat more* . . . Had she just been talking about what Maryann and Joel had? She hadn't, had she? She had been saying so much more. She could hear their voices behind her, and it only increased her sense of disquiet. She thought of Mick and pitied him. But she pitied Nance just as much, and Darius for his lonely, hard-working existence.

There came another peal of laughter from Nance; a youthful, carefree sound.

God, Nance, Maryann thought, just keep yourself under control.

Whatever happened, if they gave rein to their feelings, someone was going to end up broken-hearted.

*

'Look who I've brought!'

Joel was just waking as they arrived and Maryann leaned down and kissed him tenderly. He returned the kiss, clasping her hand, then caught sight of his brother.

'Darius!' He made a couple of attempts and finally managed to haul himself up. 'Damn it – I keep forgetting I'm weak as a kitten!'

'This is my friend Nance – she's putting me up for the time being.'

'Putting up with 'er more like.' Nance laughed. 'Nice to meet yer at last.'

'We'll go out for now,' Maryann said, taking Nance's arm firmly. She had words to say to her. 'Let you two 'ave a chat.' She knew Darius was going to have to tell Joel about Mr Barlow.

'What's going on, Nance?' she demanded in a fierce whisper, once they were out in the corridor. There was a constant flow of people up and down, nurses and visitors, so no one took much notice of them.

'What're you on about?'

'You – making up to Darius, that's what.' Maryann found she was furious and boiling over with frustration. Of course Darius and Nance were right together! It stood out a mile. When she was with him, Nance was the happy, laughing person she had been before her marriage. She should be able to be with him and spend her life with him. But it couldn't be like that because Nance was Mrs Mallone and Mrs Mallone she would have to stay.

Nance looked crestfallen. 'Oh Lor', Maryann – does it show that much? I never meant it – I know 'ow wrong it is. Only whenever I'm near 'im I just can't help myself. I know 'e likes me – you can tell, can't yer? I just feel so *right* when 'e's here. Oh, I'd give anything. . . .' She looked appealingly at Maryann. 'Look – I know why yer going on at me. But Darius'll be gone soon and once you're away I'll never see 'im again. I'll just 'ave to swallow the fact. Let me enjoy today, that's all.' With tears in her voice she finished, 'Then I'll 'ave to get back to my proper life.'

They pulled back into the Gas Street wharves in the cool late afternoon.

Maryann had been leading Bessie for the last part of the journey, patting her and talking to her to encourage her. Despite the horse's obvious weariness she seemed happy enough to plod along. There were few flies to bother her and it wasn't too hot.

'I'm going to miss you, Bessie,' she murmured, kissing her hot, smooth neck. 'What's going to become of you, eh?'

When she had gone back in to see Joel, Maryann looked anxiously to see how he was taking the news about the *Esther Jane*, but he looked calm enough.

'You've told 'im then?' she asked Darius.

'We'll still have our home.' Joel looked at her and she swelled inside with happiness. 'After all this I'm happy knowing I'm going to be alive. Everything else comes after that.'

As the afternoon wore on, she felt increasingly that she should leave Darius and Nance alone together and give them a chance to say anything that needed to be said.

She was walking ahead of the *Esther Jane* with Bessie, but once when she looked back she saw that Darius had an arm round Nance's shoulders, their faces were close as they talked with obvious intensity. The shortage of time together had speeded up events. Mary-ann looked away, full of sorrow.

When they had tied up and stabled Bessie and it was time to say goodbye, Nance could contain herself no longer. Maryann had come back from the stables, tear-ful at parting with Bessie, to find her and Darius in each other's arms. Seeing it was time to go home, Nance also burst into tears.

'Oh, I can't leave yer, Darius. I can't – it ain't right. Today's been the best day of my life – I just want to stay with you!'

'I know,' he said, gently trying to loose her from him, though Maryann could see how little he really wanted to. 'But you can't just come with me, Nancy. You're married – it'd be wrong.'

'Why's it wrong when I don't love 'im? I love *you*. Oh, I've said it now—' She stood sobbing, distraught, beside the *Esther Jane*. 'But that's how it is. I've never loved 'im and now I'm stuck with 'im and it ain't right!'

'Oh Nancy . . .' Darius put his hand on her shoulder, casting a desperate look at Maryann. 'You don't know what I'd give for things to be different . . . I'd like you as my wife, and that's the truth of it . . .'

Still weeping, Nance thrashed her hands back and forth through the air in furious frustration. 'It ain't fair. Why do things 'ave to be as they are – eh? Why did I go and say I'd marry Mick? It was so stupid – *stupid* . . . as if 'e was the only man who was ever going to come along!'

'Come on, Nance—' Maryann said gently. 'We're going to 'ave to get home . . .'

'Go on—' Darius said, his voice cracking. 'Please – go now.'

They held each other one last time before Darius pulled away and stepped down into the *Esther Jane*. He ducked into the cabin as if he could not bear to watch them both walk away.

Forty-One

On Monday morning Maryann set off to find Amy and Margaret again. It was a cool, overcast morning with a definite nip of autumn and she was worried that the girls might not come to the park. If they didn't come out she would be forced to go to the house. She knew she had to see them.

It had been a difficult weekend. Nance was as low as Maryann had ever seen her and she had spent as much time with her as possible, trying to console her and keep her mind away from Darius. Maryann had gone to Mass with her and Mick, and Nance kept filling up with tears all the way through.

'What the hell's the matter with you?' Mick demanded when they stepped outside the church.

'Nothing *you*'d ever understand,' Nance snarled at him which sent Mick swearing off into the distance in a temper.

'I feel as if my life's over,' Nance sobbed to Maryann.

All weekend she had been casting hateful looks at Mick. Maryann felt terrible for her, but they both knew Nance was going to have to settle down and forget Darius.

On Sunday when Maryann went to see Joel he was sitting up waiting for her.

'They've said another week or so and I can be off

out of here!' He beamed. 'Oh – I've almost forgotten what it's like to breathe in fresh air. Just the idea of being able to go out and walk round outside seems – well, I can hardly take it in!'

'Oh Joel – I can't wait until we can be together,' Maryann said. She was desperate to leave Nance's house with all its unhappiness. Although she felt guilty about leaving Nance there was nothing she could do about her situation. She longed to get on with her life with Joel after all the waiting.

'We'll 'ave to start fixing up a wedding day.' Joel looked into her eyes with a sense of wonder. 'Little Maryann – and you're going to be my wife.'

She smiled back, face alight with happiness. 'Soon as we can manage,' she said.

He stroked a finger gently down her cheek. 'We can share everything that comes – best mates, eh?'

She thought about this as she walked to Handsworth. Joel had said they could get married in Oxford, near to where his auntie lived and where old Darius Bartholomew was recuperating.

'But if you want to get wed here – so your family can come,' he said. 'We could think of that instead?'

'No,' she said firmly. 'My mom won't come wherever my wedding is. I might be able to get our Tony down for it, but your family's my family now, Joel. Oxford's lovely and it'll suit me fine.'

She felt strong and joyful inside, as if nothing could ever harm her again, Joel's love warming and strengthening her. Her only anxiety was his leaving hospital so soon. Where were they going to go if Darius didn't get back? But even this didn't seem insurmountable. She still had some money left. If necessary they'd have to rent somewhere until the *Esther Jane* was ready. She wouldn't stay with Nance any longer than she had to. She felt she'd already brought enough trouble into her life.

Turning into the park she looked round for the girls. It was much quieter today, an end of summer quiet. School was due to begin the next day. With a sinking feeling of dread she thought for a moment that they weren't there. It was almost midday – this was when she had found them before.

After a moment strolling round she spotted them over by the pond, both kneeling, peering down into the water. Her heart went out to them.

'Hello, girls,' she said softly.

Still kneeling side by side, they swivelled round together so that the tops of their heads were almost touching. Their eyes held the usual closed blankness, though she thought she saw a flicker of welcome in the older girl's expression. Amy stood up slowly.

'Hello.'

Margaret turned away.

'I thought I'd come and see you – school tomorrow, ain't it?'

Amy nodded.

'I've er . . . I've got some nice peanut toffee – d'yer want some?' She felt like a wicked witch in a fairy story, luring them with sweets, but she had to get them to come and sit with her somehow. Margaret just shook her head and carried on facing the other way.

'I'll 'ave a bit,' Amy said. 'Please,' she added.

''Ere – I'll sit down next to yer,' Maryann said, tucking the skirt under her on the grass, sitting quite close to Margaret. Even if she couldn't get her to come and sit with them she wanted to be sure she heard what

386

she was going to say. Amy sat on her left, chewing the toffee, her legs bent, leaning sideways on one arm.

There was no point in dilly-dallying. She had to say something.

'Look, Amy – you must've thought it was a bit strange me coming and seeing yer in the park. I mean it's been nice for me getting to know you a bit – but there's another reason why I've been coming.'

Amy's hair was hanging half across her face and she didn't look up but Maryann could tell she was listening.

'I've seen your stepfather – going to his shop and that. I know he calls himself Arthur Lambert, but the truth is, that ain't his name. Or at least that ain't always been his name.' Her heart was beating terribly hard. Was she wrong to do this, was she? She forced herself on. 'The thing is – I used to know 'im under another name. He was called Norman Griffin and he was my stepfather an' all – when my sister and me were not much older than you are now. And . . .'

She swallowed, almost unable to go on. Amy cast her a quick glance, then looked down again. Margaret was sitting by the water, absolutely still.

'The thing is – when 'e was living with us, he daint treat us like . . . like a dad ought've done. He was . . . bad. 'E . . .' She took a deep, shuddering breath. 'Oh God help me for saying this to yer!' She spoke with her gaze fixed on Amy's face, watching for her reaction to her words. She didn't want to leave them in any doubt as to what she was admitting to them, but she was trembling as she spoke.

'He was wicked, the way he was with us. At night he came to our rooms and . . . and made us do things –

things children ain't s'posed to do – and he made us feel dirty and different to everyone else . . .'

She couldn't go on. Her voice was choked with tears. Looking at Amy she saw that the girl had turned her head and it was tilted so that her hair completely hid her face. She had brought her hand up and pressed it tightly over her lips. The gesture spoke more loudly than any words.

Maryann wiped her eyes, trying to control herself. Very slowly and gently she reached out her hand and pushed the girl's hair aside.

'Amy? I was so frightened of speaking out of turn and getting it wrong. Is it . . . is he still the same?'

She released Amy's hair and watched her. There was a long pause during which Maryann almost despaired of an answer. But then the coppery hair began to quiver and she saw the girl was nodding. A quick, frightened nod.

'Oh God,' Maryann gasped. 'You're saying yes, ain't you, Amy?'

This time the nod was more definite.

'You poor things . . .' She wanted to reach out and take the child in her arms, but she restrained herself. Half whispering she said, 'What about . . . Margaret?'

Again the nod, more vigorously this time.

'Your mom – does she know anything about it?'

This time a shake of the head.

They all sat in silence for a minute. Margaret had still not turned round.

Maryann sat thinking furiously. Her own mother had not believed her. Why should theirs be any different? She had her life to protect, her security. And Norman was so smooth and respectable. Why would the woman listen to a complete stranger?

'There's one more thing I want to tell you, Amy. My name's not Esther Bartholomew like I told you. I daint want to tell you my real name in case you mentioned it at home in front of him. I'm Maryann Nelson – you can call me Maryann. Look, I can't promise you anything, Amy. I don't know if I can make it stop – if I was to see your mom. She won't want to hear it. But d'you want me to try?'

Amy's head swung round and for the first time she looked into Maryann's eyes. Her own were full of tears. Never had Maryann seen a more desperate, yearning face.

'Please,' she whispered. 'Make it stop.'

'Come on then.' Maryann stood up and Amy did the same. 'It's now or never, Amy.'

She looked warily at the younger girl. Amy went to her.

'Margaret – come on. We're going 'ome. This lady's coming with us.'

Margaret slowly, almost mechanically it seemed, got to her feet and turned to come with them. As she did so the blank expression in her young eyes chilled Maryann to the bone.

Maryann brought her hand up to knock at the door. Amy had been about to open it but she said, 'No – wait. I can't just go walking into your mom's house. I'll knock first.'

She was terrified, her knees like jelly, yet somewhere in her she was also triumphant. No longer did she have to feel wicked, to be told she was imagining things. She was not alone. She and these girls could stand together.

'She'll be cross,' Amy said uncomfortably as Mary-ann knocked. 'Takes 'er a while to get to the door.'

They heard her moving painfully along the hall. When the door opened Maryann suddenly found herself looking into the face of the auburn-haired woman. There were lines across her forehead and at the corners of her mouth which indicated that she suffered pain. She had pale skin, lightly freckled, wide eyes of a deep blue and a gentle, patient expression. Maryann was reassured. Her face was not the tight, bitter mask her mother had taken on through her hardships.

'Oh—' the woman said, eyeing her daughters. 'Is summat the matter? I hope they haven't done anything wrong?'

'No—' Maryann smiled nervously. 'Nothing like that. Only – I've met your daughters over in the park a few times recently and we've got a bit friendly like. There's a reason why I was looking out for them . . . D'you think I could come in and talk to you for a minute or two? There's summat I'd like to say to you.' She glanced at Amy and Margaret but their faces were blank once more.

'Well – awright then,' the woman said doubtfully. 'I 'ope it won't take long though. I've got the dinner on.'

She led them into the nearest room, which was the front parlour. Maryann was not in a state to take in much detail except that the room was very clean and neatly arrayed, with polished brasses by the grate and moss green curtains.

'Sit down, won't you?' the woman said, easing herself into a chair. They were positioned either side of the fire and there was a rag rug between them in bright colours. Maryann could smell lavender. Nervously she took off her straw hat and sat holding it on her lap.

'Why don't you run along, girls?' Janet Richards said.

'Oh – no, please,' Maryann said quickly. 'They need to stay.'

'But I thought you said – I mean they're not in trouble . . .?' She frowned anxiously.

'No – at least, not the way you mean. Oh dear, this is so . . .' She clasped her hands under her hat to try and stop them shaking. 'I don't know where to start.'

Janet was beginning to look as if she doubted her own wisdom in letting this stranger into the house, so Maryann plunged in and began talking quickly, explaining, trying not to put things too harshly nor to skirt round the truth. The girls stood close by.

'See – as soon as I saw him again I knew it was him,' she explained. ''E weren't called Arthur Lambert when 'e lived with our mom – Norman Griffin was his name. But it was him, and when I saw your daughters, the way they were, I just knew. It's hard to explain unless you've suffered it yourself. No one'd believe me when I was their age. My mother turned against me – she still won't see me. And today I asked Amy whether 'e was . . . well, doing the same to her and Margaret and when she said 'e was I just couldn't let it rest. I know this'll be a shock to you and you must think I'm terrible to interfere, but I had to come and say something rather than let them go through the same . . .' She ran out of steam at last.

The woman's expression was frozen. Shock, fear, disbelief all competed and for a time she couldn't speak.

'Amy—' she gasped eventually. 'Amy? What's she saying – who is she? And what've you been telling her?'

'Oh, don't be angry with them!' Maryann implored

391

her. She all but got down on her knees in front of the woman to plead with her. The girls stood listening, hanging their heads. She wanted them to speak up and plead with their mother, but she knew they couldn't do it. 'They shouldn't get in any trouble for telling me. They've been through enough – it's him you want to ask questions of. He's the one who takes over people's families, wrecks their lives. I know 'e looks like a gentleman and 'e's polite and well dressed and everything but underneath 'e's summat else – there's a side to 'im only a few of us have seen.'

The woman's eyes narrowed into slits, the look of sweetness quite gone from her face. She struggled to her feet, raising her walking stick as if she was going to hit Maryann, who hastily stood up as well.

'Who *are* you?' she hissed. 'What d'you think you're about, coming into my house and coming out with this *filth* in front of my two young girls? What've you been saying to them – poisoning their minds and filling them with these dirty lies. What do you want? You must be wrong in the head. Why didn't you say this woman'd been hanging around yer, Amy? What's she been saying to yer? Did she tell yer to come and make up stories about your father?'

Maryann's hand went to her throat as she watched Amy. For a second, which seemed eternal, the girl stood motionless. Then she raised her head a little and her face was burning red. Eyes still looking at the floor, she said, 'She daint make me, Mom. It's true. It's what 'e does – to Margaret and me. 'E does . . .' Her mother was shaking her head in horror. ''E *does*, Mom – upstairs, at bedtime.'

They all froze then, because there came the sound of the front door opening and a man's heavy tread entering the house. The front door was closed, loudly, and his footsteps moved through to the back.

'Janet!' They heard a moment later, 'Janet?'

She looked round at her daughters and at Maryann with utter contempt. Maryann, feeling her legs give way, sank down on to the chair.

'He's come home for his dinner.' Janet's mouth twisted bitterly. 'Now we'll see, won't we? Arthur!' she called. 'We're in the front.'

The door opened and Maryann found herself face to face with Norman Griffin.

Forty-Two

He looked so wide, filling the doorframe, standing there in his black coat. There was a long silence. In a corner of her mind, Maryann could hear the clock ticking and a horse's hooves passing in the street. His glance swept round the room, rested on her for a fleeting moment during which her pulse seemed to stop, then passed over to his family.

He had shown not a flicker of recognition. Have I changed that much? Maryann thought. Looking at him she was stunned once more by his familiarity, as if even now when he was fatter and his hair thinned she could remember every pore of the skin on his face, every quiver of expression. Her body, seeming in his presence to remember even more, his loathsome touch, felt turned to water. If she had not already been sitting down she would have collapsed.

'My dear? What's going on?'

Janet Lambert was standing, leaning on her stick, the girls near to her. 'Oh Arthur,' she said and then burst into tears. He was beside her immediately.

'Whatever's the matter, love? What's been going on? Who's your visitor?' His words dripped concern like syrup.

'She came in with the girls – she's been saying the most terrible things, Arthur . . . And now Amy's saying them too – the same lies . . . I can't even bring myself to tell you . . .'

He turned, looked at Amy and Margaret, then Maryann felt his eyes boring into her.

'What's going on in my 'ouse? Who're you?'

She thought her anger might choke her. She managed to stand up, clutching folds of her skirt in her hands to steady herself. 'You know perfectly well who I am, Mr Griffin,' she spat at him. 'I'm Maryann Nelson. Remember – your stepdaughter? And under the law you're still married to my mother, Mrs Florence Griffin.'

She heard Janet Lambert gasp. 'Arthur no! She must have the wrong person. What's she saying?'

Norman Griffin gave a bewildered shrug that could have won him a part in a troop of actors. 'I've no idea, my dear – where on earth did you pick 'er up from? Has she got loose from the asylum or summat?' He even managed a chuckle. 'Never heard anything like it. Why did you let her in?'

'You know who I am!' Maryann shouted at him. She could feel herself becoming hysterical. There was such a pressure rising inside her that she felt as if she might explode.

'D'you think I'd ever forget the man who did things to me that shouldn't be done to an animal, you vile, filthy pig?' She faced Janet Lambert. 'He's the one who came to our room night after night and interfered with us so's we prayed every day that night would never come. D'you think anyone'd ever forget that? And now' – she turned on Janet Lambert – 'you've got two daughters praying the same thing. Because from the day you let that *animal* into the house they lost their childhood. They were never safe again. Tell her Amy—' She stepped over to the girl and held her shoulder.

Speaking softly she said, 'You know what you told me – say it to your mom. Tell her the truth or he'll just go on and on and you'll never get away from it.'

Amy's shoulders were shaking. She put her hands over her face. Her mother watched, appalled, her eyes stretched wide. Maryann squeezed her shoulder.

'Come on then, Amy.' Norman's voice was soft, mocking. 'Let's hear it then. All the terrible things I do to yer – buying you nice frocks and taking you both to the pictures. Tell us all about that. Oh – and we're going to the zoo next weekend, aren't we – better get that off yer chest as well.'

'Amy?' her mom said quietly. 'Have you got anything to say or was it just this woman talked you into it – got you to make up a story?'

As Amy sobbed, Margaret remained in stony silence. Her gaze never left the floor.

Norman turned to the girls' mother. 'I don't know who this woman is or what she wants, but the last thing I'd ever want is for you to think badly of me or have any suspicions about me. Is there anything else you want to ask her before I put her out of our house?'

Janet looked round desperately at all four of them: her daughters, silent except for Amy's weeping, at Norman who was looking at her in wide-eyed appeal, and at Maryann who was staring pleadingly at Amy, her own face wet with tears. She stepped towards Maryann, a hateful expression in her eyes.

'How could you come and say such terrible things to us. What's wrong with you?'

'But they're true – every one of them! Look at your daughters! They're too frightened of him to speak. When did Margaret last speak at all? And that's what he's done to them – you've got to believe me. Why else would I come to you – you're strangers to me. But I saw your daughters and I saw myself in them . . .' Her weeping took her over then. 'Oh why doesn't anyone ever believe us?'

'That's quite enough of that.' Norman suddenly laid both his hands on Maryann's shoulders and began to propel her fowards. 'Get out of my house, away from my wife and daughters with your filthy lies . . .'

'If she's your wife then you're a bigamist!' Maryann shrieked helplessly. She twisted round. 'Amy – Amy, I wanted to 'elp you. I did – I wanted to be there with you.'

Amy looked across at her, her face blotchy with tears. Suddenly they heard her voice raised in a howl. 'But you *won't* be here, will you?'

That was Maryann's last sight of her as Norman propelled her to the front door. In the few seconds before Janet managed to limp out into the hall he spun Maryann round and forced her up against the front door, one hand against her throat. This time there was no doubt as to whether he recognized her. His eyes were malicious slits.

'Don't you *ever* come near me again, or you'll regret it. You know I mean what I say, don't you, Maryann?' He pulled her back and opening the door, handed her out into the street.

'I know you!' she yelled, spinning round. 'I know who you are even if they don't!'

The door slammed, sealing the family in behind its solid green exterior.

For a moment she stared at it, stunned, then took off along the road.

*

She slid down into a deep black hole that afternoon, wandering the streets with no thought as to where she was going. Seeing Norman Griffin again at such close quarters, his physical presence, his denial of her had stripped her in just a few moments of the calmness and sense of identity she had painfully erected for herself over the years. She had come crashing back down into her childhood emotions. The child who had lain in her bed looking up into the empty darkness, helpless against the progress of Norman's feet up the stairs. Never again, she had said, never again will I let him have power over me – yet just a few minutes with him and she felt close to disintegration. She walked and walked, in such a state she saw nothing of the people, houses, factories, parks around her.

At some point in the afternoon she found herself walking along the boundary of a cemetery and when she reached the gate she went in and sat down in a quiet spot on the damp grass, looking out across the graves, scattered and tilted like old men's teeth. The sky was hazy and it was still warm. She gave no thought to whether she was warm or cold, hungry or tired. She tried to think clearly but only terrible, negative things came to her.

I can't stand up to this. Sal couldn't and I can't. Sal's dead and I'd be better off dead, peaceful like these people in here. I can't face anyone again. I can't marry Joel. Can't do anything . . . There's nothing left . . . And she had let those girls down so badly. She had utterly betrayed them. She kept hearing Amy's last despairing cry, 'But you *won't* be there . . .' What would Norman do to them now?

She lay on her side on the grass, wishing there was something that could cover her: a blanket, a mantle of leaves or a thick fall of snow, or that she could burrow into the earth like an animal, anything so that she could hide her grief and self-disgust away. Curled up tightly, she could smell the grass, the earth. Birds chirruped in the trees. Eventually, overwrought and exhausted, she fell asleep.

It was dusk by the time she turned into Nance's road, the light going and the air full of smoke, trapped in the breezeless space between the houses. She was trembling with weariness and lack of food and couldn't put on a brave face to hide her leaden despair.

Nance was sitting at the table darning a sock with sharp, angry movements but she got to her feet immediately. 'What's 'appened? You look terrible!'

Maryann sank down at the table and began to weep wretchedly. 'Oh Nance . . .'

'What is it? It's not Joel, is it?'

Maryann shook her head. 'I ain't seen Joel today. It's *him* . . . I've seen him, his family. . . .' Nance sat back down again as it all came pouring out. Norman Griffin, Amy and Margaret, everything.

'I wanted to save Amy and Margaret and all I've done is let them down and make everything much worse for them and I can't do a thing now. I can't marry Joel – I can't even face seeing him. I feel like I did that time I ran away from him before – I thought it was all better, but it ain't. I ain't normal, Nance. I'd be better off finishing myself off, that I would.'

'What *are* you going on about?' Nance blazed at her. 'You love Joel and 'e loves you! What the 'ell's got into yer? You can't let that bastard wreck yer life for you the way 'e did Sal's! You and Joel are made for each other. How can yer even think about saying that? If I had even a tiny bit of a chance to

399

marry Darius I'd be off like a shot and there's nothing standing in your way, Maryann. You're lucky – just you remember that!'

Maryann put her face in her hands, shaking her head. Through her fingers she said, 'I don't feel lucky. I feel dirty and disgusting. You can't be happy, Nance – so why do I deserve to be?' Face wet with tears, she looked up at her friend.

'Oh Maryann,' Nance said sadly, her anger gone. 'I know I don't know 'ow it feels to 've 'ad all that going on with him and Sal and that. Only – there must be a way of making things right. If you let 'im wreck yer chances with Joel he'll've spoiled all yer life . . . Look – you ain't in a state to think about anything. Let me get you a bite to eat and a cuppa tea and then you can 'ave a sleep. You'll see everything straighter in the morning. I saved yer a helping of stew – soon get it heated up. And there's apple and custard.'

'Ta, Nance,' Maryann said dully, wiping her eyes on her sleeves, grateful for Nance's mothering. 'Don't know what I'd do without you.'

Nance gave a crooked smile. 'You don't 'alf look a sight, you do.'

Maryann looked down at herself. She knew her hair was all hanging down. Her hands were grubby and there was mud on her grey skirt and shoes. She got up to wash her hands in the scullery.

'Where's Mick?'

She saw Nance's expression tighten. 'Not been 'ome yet.'

'What – not for 'is tea? That ain't like him.'

'Nope.' Nance stirred the stew fiercely.

Maryann went to her. 'You don't think summat's happened to him – an accident?'

Nance shrugged. 'If it 'as, no one's been to tell me about it.'

Maryann sat to eat her tea and did feel a little less wretched after it. She and Nance sat drinking tea together and still there was no sign of Mick. The hands of the clock moved past ten o'clock and Maryann found she could no longer keep awake.

'I'll have to go up,' she said. 'I'll doze off down 'ere else.'

'I was just thinking,' Nance said. 'Them little girls – you could at least tell them where you live – you know, just in case like.'

Maryann got to her feet. 'But this is your address.'

'Well – if it'd make yer feel any better, I don't mind them knowing that. For the time being.'

'Awright, thanks, Nance.' Maryann was grateful but felt suddenly hopeless again. How could she even get it to them?

'You go on up,' Nance said. 'A good sleep'll sort you out.'

But a good sleep was not what she was destined to have that night.

Forty-Three

Before Nance had come up to bed the front door opened with a bang that shook the house. Within moments the shouting and screaming had begun and Maryann was jerked out of a deep sleep. She soon realized that Mick and Nancy were fighting with a ferocity beyond anything that had gone before, and she climbed out of bed, disorientated from being woken so suddenly. She hated interfering between them, but it sounded as if someone would have to. As she put on her shoes and slipped a cardigan over her nightdress, she heard crashing and the splintering sound of china breaking and she ran downstairs.

Mick was so drunk he couldn't stand without swaying perilously. He still had his work jacket on, covered in muck, his face was puffy and florid and he was standing by the humble little shelf they had in the living room to keep their few crocks on, picking them up one by one and hurling them across towards the far end of the room.

'Stop it!' Nance shouted, pushing at him. 'You'll break the whole lot, yer kalied bastard!' He swung round and smacked her in the mouth and Nance groaned, reeling back away from him, too stunned to have a go at him. He reached round for another cup, lurched to one side and seized hold of the shelf to save himself. It came off the wall with a crunch and everything crashed down, plates, cups, saucers, Mick falling with it, ending up in a pile of broken china. He hit his head on the wall and there was a split second's quiet.

'Look what yer've done, yer drunken Irish navvy!' Nance had recovered enough to run at him, so beside herself with fury that she kneeled down, oblivious to the shards of white china all over the place, and began raining blows down on her insensible husband. There was blood trickling from the left side of her mouth and another shiny mark on her cheek.

'I hate you!' she yelled, hitting and slapping. 'Hate you, hate you, yer fucking useless bastard. Yer not even a proper man, are yer? Yer useless to anyone ... I bloody hate yer ...' She was sobbing hysterically.

'Nance!' Maryann could barely get near her. 'Nance – stop hitting 'im – I think 'e's knocked himself out – look!'

'Good! I 'ope 'e bloody kills hisself!'

'*Nance!*' She succeeded in grabbing both of Nance's arms at once and held on, gritting her teeth while Nance fought like a rabbit in a sack before suddenly going limp. Maryann let go of her and gingerly went over to Mick, afraid for a moment that the bang on the head had really done him in.

'Is 'e awright?' Nance suddenly sounded frightened.

Maryann prodded Mick and he stirred, groaning.

'Oh, 'e's awright,' Nancy said, disgusted. 'Can't even knock 'isself out properly, the silly bugger.'

'What the hell was all that about?'

Nance's face crumpled. 'His brother Paddy – 'e's gone and got Marie in the family way *again*. That'll be their fifth, popping them out like peas every year and God can't spare us even one – just one little babby—'

Her voice cracked and she let out a howl of distress. 'Oh Maryann – if we could at least 'ave a babby I could think of staying with 'im without wanting to cut my own throat.'

'Oh Nance . . .' Maryann kneeled down with her amid the wreckage and held her tight. 'Poor old Nance . . .'

'What 'm I going to do, Maryann? I'm going to go round the bend living like this.'

Maryann rocked her, feeling desperately sorry. There was nothing she felt she could say.

'I feel as if there must be summat I did when I was younger to deserve punishing like this.'

'Oh, yer didn't do anything. Course yer didn't.'

'I'd better go and see Father Maguire and make a clean breast of everything that's been going through me 'ead,' she said. 'I might be able to stand it better then.'

There came another moan from beside them and suddenly Mick sat slowly up, rubbing his head. 'Christ Almighty.'

'Don't blaspheme, yer bleedin' navvy,' Nance snarled at him.

He stared blearily at the chaos of breakage round him, saw Nance and Maryann staring at him in disgust and groaned, 'Oh God save us.' Slowly, like a great ox, he lumbered to his feet and disappeared up the stairs.

'Well,' Nance said dully. 'Now yer can go back to sleep.'

'Not before we've cleared up.'

'Maryann—' Nance took hold of her wrist as she squatted, about to get up.

'What?'

'Go and see Joel tomorrow.'

Maryann hung her head, not meeting Nance's eyes.

She barely slept at all after that, hearing Nancy crying next door, Mick snoring, and all their troubles churning round in her head. She couldn't stop thinking about Amy and Margaret as well, full of frustration, anger and pity. In the morning she woke early from an uneasy doze, her head aching. But she got up, dressed silently and slipped out of the house. There was at least one small thing she could do.

There was a mist and the streets looked ghostly but she was glad of its grey obscurity in which to hide herself. When she got to Handsworth she waited in the side street where she had stood before. As time passed the streets took on a purposeful atmosphere. Children started coming out of the houses in their school clothes and scurrying down the road. Soon, the door of the Lamberts' house opened and she saw Amy and Margaret come out. Maryann shrank back. Janet stood for a few moments with her arms folded, her hair a bright flame in the pale morning, face turned to watch her girls. Then at last she stepped back and the door closed. Maryann slipped round quickly after them.

They were almost at the school gates when she caught up with them. She watched them tenderly from behind. They stood out amid the rag-taggle bunch of children as among the best dressed and neatest. Amy's hair had been plaited immaculately and each plait tied with a blue ribbon and Margaret's was put up in bunches, big bows tied with the same ribbon. As ever she was walking with her head jutting forwards, eyes fixed on the ground.

'Amy—' Maryann spoke softly, but her urgency was clear. Amy turned and gasped, seeing her. They stopped for a moment, letting the other children stream past them.

'What d'*you* want? Mom'll kill us if she sees yer!'

'Don't worry – I won't get you into trouble. You awright?'

Amy's gaze slid away. She swallowed. Nodded.

'I'm sorry, Amy. I'm so sorry,' Maryann said help-lessly. She felt a huge lump rise in her throat. 'I was hoping yer mom'd listen – but then she daint know me from Adam, does she? I don't know what else to – 'cept I brought you this—' She slipped a scrap of paper into Amy's hand with Nancy's address on. 'That's where I live just now. It's my friend's house. I won't always be there but if you need help, go to her. She's kind, and she can get in touch with me . . .'

'Where'll you be then?' Amy asked.

'I don't know where I'll be—' It was her turn to look away. 'Look – yer'd better go now. I can't do any more for yer, not the way things are. But remember – if you want to get away, go to Nancy. I know she'll 'elp yer. Don't let yer mom see that though.'

She saw Amy look down at the piece of paper and nod.

'Tara then—'

And they were gone, two little figures amid the tide of other children.

*

Nance looked terrible. Her face was all in a mess, she was exhausted and in a foul temper. Mick had woken with a splitting head, said he wasn't effing well going to work and rolled over back to sleep. When he woke later in the morning he was contrite and gave Nance the money to buy some more crockery as they scarcely had enough left for a cup of tea between them. Maryann had wondered about buying some on the way home but resisted the thought. It wouldn't do Mick's pride any good having her chipping in again. Nance went out and came back with a few cheap willow-pattern crocks and an even more raging temper.

'If 'e ain't pouring 'is wages down 'is throat 'e's up to these sort of tricks,' she said, slamming the parcel down on the table so hard Maryann wondered if anything inside was left intact. 'Moan, moan, moan about not 'aving enough and now we 'ave to go and spend it on summat we 'ad already. 'E can 'ave bread and lard for 'is dinner and like it 'cause we ain't got enough for anything else.'

'Well, Nance – I could give yer . . .' Maryann began.

'No! Yer bloody couldn't! You've done quite enough. Let 'im put up with it. That'll teach 'im where 'is boozing and carrying on gets us!'

Whatever Maryann did to try and help, she got her head snapped off. She'd have to leave this house soon, she knew, however much Nance kept begging her to stay. She was only making everything worse.

After they'd had their bit of dinner and Mick had slouched off out somewhere, Nance turned on her. 'Now – you get yerself down to that 'ospital.'

Maryann was washing up the new plates. She didn't answer.

'Maryann?'

She hung her head over the sink. 'I can't, Nance. Not today. I'm not myself today. I just can't tell yer 'ow bad I feel . . . I can't face 'im.'

'Well, what're yer going to do?'

'I'm going to bed. 'Ave a sleep. I can't do it, Nance – not today . . .' She felt her voice crack with tears.

'Right—' Nance pulled her apron off and flicked it so hard down on a chair that the cloth made a snapping noise in the air. 'I've 'ad enough. If you're too bloody stubborn to go, I'll go meself.'

'Nance!'

But she was already out of the front door and off down the road.

'Nance – what the 'ell're yer playing at?' She was already a good way down the street, striding furiously along. She turned for a second, gave Maryann a look of complete exasperation, then carried on at the same breakneck pace.

'Oh Nance . . .' Maryann stood biting her nails, helplessly watching her friend disappear. She wasn't sure which she felt most, anxiety or gratitude.

'Maryann . . .'

There was a persistent tapping on her arm. Nance was standing over her and the light in the room had changed. She must have slept for hours.

'Nance – what time is it?' She sat up at once. 'Did yer see him? What did you say to him?'

'Plenty,' Nance said non-committally. The bruising on her face looked worse in the shadowy light. 'Come down – I've got the kettle on.'

Maryann scrambled guiltily off the bed. 'I never thought I'd sleep that long . . .'

'Come on,' Nance said grimly. 'Get yerself downstairs.'

Maryann frowned at her tone. Whatever had happened? Full of misgiving she followed Nance down the stairs, clothes all rumpled. Nance reached the bottom and stood back to watch her. Maryann got halfway down, then gasped.

'Oh my . . . what're *you* doing here? How did . . .?' She looked back and forth between them.

'Couldn't stop 'im,' Nance said, beginning to smile. 'Any'ow – I'm popping round to spend a penny – back in a few minutes.'

He was sitting in the chair by the fire. His cropped hair had grown a little, he had not been shaved for a few days and he was just beginning to look more like the old Joel. He looked across at her, a gentle, loving smile of anticipation on his face and started trying to get up.

'No—' She was across to him immediately. 'You mustn't . . . You must be worn out! How did you get here?'

'Trams.' He reached out and took her hand, holding it between his two enormous ones. 'She said you was in trouble . . . family troubles like and you was upset. So I came – wasn't staying in there a moment longer than I 'ad to. You awright, little 'un?'

She was overcome by tears at the sight of him, at his loving tone. 'Yes . . . no. Oh Joel, I don't know – I'm sorry . . .'

He pulled her closer. ''Cause I know you when you get all in a state – running off like a rabbit. Couldn't

409

'ave that, could I? Come 'ere, my lovely – come and sit with me.'

Her resistance broke like a dam as he pulled her on to his lap and she sat crying, her head tucked close to his neck as his hand smoothed her hair. Her worry poured out of her, her shame that she could have doubted her feelings for him.

''Eh now – there's no need for all this, is there?'

'Oh Joel,' she sobbed. 'I'm sorry.'

'Sorry – what for? There's nothing to be sorry about – you got me out of there, dint you?'

'Are you all right? Aren't you too weak?' She wiped her eyes and sat back to look at him.

'It was hard going – still wheezing like anything, but it's getting better. Bit by bit, every day.' He smiled at her joyfully, and reached up to wipe a tear off her cheek. She tried to smile back.

'Now what's up?'

'I'll tell you,' she said wearily. 'But not now. I saw my stepfather . . .'

His face darkened. 'Oh. I see.'

'It'll keep. Now I've seen you.'

He pulled her closer again. 'Your Nance'll be back in a minute. You got a kiss for me before she does?'

'Oh Joel, course I 'ave.'

They held each other close and she kissed him, full of love and gratitude, and felt the strength of his passion for her in the kiss he gave her back.

'We'll start again away from 'ere,' he told her. 'You need never see 'im again.'

Maryann looked into his face. 'I do love you such a lot.'

Nance came in to find her still sitting on Joel's knee

410

with a watery smile on her face and steam gushing in great clouds out of the kettle.

'God in heaven,' Nance said, rushing to lift it off the heat. 'Don't crush the life out of 'im, will yer?'

Forty-Four

They had waited in dread that night for Mick to come home. But he was back in good time, sober and contrite.

'This is Joel Bartholomew, Mick,' Nancy said nervously as he walked in. 'Maryann's intended.' Joel stood up with an effort which made him cough and held out his hand.

'How do, Mick. Your wife said I could stop 'ere for a few days until our boat's ready.' Seeing Mick frown, he explained, 'I'm a boatman – on the cut.'

'Oh – right then.' Mick nodded.

'If you don't like it, we'll move on somewhere else. It's your home . . .'

'Joel's just come out of the 'ospital,' Nance explained.

Mick nodded again. 'Ah – right. Well – sit down.' Nance immediately laid Mick's plate of tea in front of him and winked at Maryann as if to say, 'So far so good.'

They ate in silence but the atmosphere was not hostile, and when Maryann got up to clear the dishes away she heard Joel say, 'D'you fancy a pint then, Mick?'

'Joel!' Maryann said. 'You've 'ardly got the strength to stand up let alone get to the pub!'

'It ain't far!' Joel grinned. 'Anyway – 'ow'm I going

to get my strength back without a few pints inside me? I can tell you, Mick, it's been a good long while since I've 'ad anything but tea and slops.'

Mick looked warily at Nancy.

'Just don't let 'im overdo it,' she said to Joel. 'And you look after 'im, Mick. The poor feller's only out of 'is sickbed.'

'I'll do that,' Mick said. He looked relieved. 'You don't look too well,' he said to Joel. 'We'll take it easy now.'

Nance raised her eyebrows at Maryann. When the men had gone the two of them looked at each other and laughed.

'Jesus,' Nance said. 'They'd be dragging themselves off their deathbeds if it meant getting a drink inside them.'

But she looked pleased too. It was the most harmonious evening they'd had in ages.

The week passed quite peacefully, though it was a time of mixed feelings for Maryann. She was so happy Joel was out of hospital and they spent hours talking. She unburdened herself to him about Amy and Margaret and he agreed there was not much else she could do. But it was unsettling being here. They both wanted now to be off, to start their new life. Every day one of them – usually Maryann – went to see if there was any message from Darius, but so far they'd heard nothing. The weekend came and went. Tony and Billy came to see them. Billy was a young bruiser of a lad, and though they got on all right, Maryann knew it was going to be hard to see much of her brothers once she and Joel were working the cut, and this was a cause of sadness. All she could do was do her best to keep in touch.

Nancy had gone to confession on Saturday night and came back looking stern after a lecture from Father Maguire.

''E said I've got to put anything else out of my mind and sort out my marriage. And 'e told me God sometimes doesn't give people children for a reason.' She looked bleakly at Maryann. 'I mean I know 'e's right really, about my marriage and that. And Mick's really trying hard at the moment. But if God's got 'is reasons for not giving me a babby I wish 'e'd bloody well let me know what they are! – Ooh, Lord forgive me . . .'

She went to Mass with Mick on the Sunday, leaving Maryann and Joel a blissful couple of hours alone. Joel was asleep at first. Maryann had insisted he have her bed upstairs and wouldn't listen to any argument.

'You're the one that needs to get better and the sooner you do, the sooner we can go.'

He slept a huge amount. 'This is the first time I've had any peace at night,' he said. 'In there there was always someone coughing or summat going on. I haven't slept so well in months.'

He slept late that Sunday. At last, before Nance and Mick came back, Maryann took a cup of tea up for him and for a few moments watched him sleeping. His hair was longer, he was gradually letting his beard grow back and, slowly, her Joel was reappearing. He looked so pale and thin, though, and his coughing was still terrible at times. She sat by him thinking what a fool she'd been. He was so steadfast in his love for her. Through all the bad things that had gone on – were still going on – he had always been there, strong and gentle. He had been the one really good thing in her life.

She leaned over and tenderly kissed his face, pressing little kisses on his eyelids, cheeks, forehead until he stirred and woke to look at her. A smile spread across his face. 'Well – that's a nice way to wake up.'

'I brought you some tea. Nance and Mick've gone to Mass. I should've let you sleep but I wanted to see you before they get back.'

Joel pushed himself up. 'You should've woke me earlier.'

'No – I want you better.' She handed him the tea and he downed it in several big gulps, then put the cup down. He shuffled over in the bed, patting the space beside him.

'Come on in and sit with me. You'll 'ave to get used to a narrow bed on the *Esther Jane*.'

Maryann hesitated, blushing.

'It's all right, little bird – I just mean sit with me.' He held his arm out to embrace her. 'Come on – I won't bite. Promise.'

She slipped her shoes off and climbed in beside him, resting back against his warm arm. Blushing even more, without looking round at him, she said, 'I do ... I mean ... Oh dear, I don't know how to say this.' How could she tell him she wanted him, that she wanted to be held and touched, that when they were married she wanted to be his the way married people were supposed to – only she was afraid of herself, of finding she couldn't bear to do it when her only experiences of it had meant pain and fear?

'I do want – you know – to be properly married, Joel.'

He squeezed her gently. 'I know, love. And I'm not him, you know. I'm not your stepfather. I wouldn't want to hurt you, ever – you know that now, don't you?'

She rested her head against him. 'Yes,' she whispered. 'Course I do.' She leaned round and her lips reached for his, wanting to show him, to give all her love to him and he kissed her back, his arms pulling her close.

They stayed there snuggled close together, looking round at the bare room with its whitewashed walls and the little window behind them.

'I've scarcely ever been in a house before,' Joel said. 'I mean it's all right – a lot more space, of course. But I couldn't live like this. Not in one place all the time. Don't think I could breathe proper. D'you think you can live on the move all the time?'

'Think so. That feels the right way to live to me. So long as you're there.'

'It's a tough life, Maryann.'

She nodded. 'It's what I want though. That life – with you. I wish Darius'd get here, don't you?'

'Well – we've waited this long – a few more days don't make a lot of difference.'

'Poor Darius.' Maryann sighed. She'd told Joel about Nance and his brother. 'There's so much unhappiness we're leaving behind and nothing I can do. I just wish we could go now.'

'I know—' Longingly, he pulled her closer into his arms. 'I don't 'alf feel like the lucky one.'

'Joel! He's coming! There's a message from Darius – he should be up 'ere some time on Thursday!' Maryann

416

came panting into the house two days later to find Joel sitting talking to Nancy as she worked.

Even in her excitement she noticed Nancy taking special care to control her expression. Maryann bit her lip. It seemed awful even to mention Darius's name if it upset her, but he was Joel's brother – what else could she do?

''E's got the moty in then,' Joel said. 'I wonder how 'e's managing?'

''E said it'd be easier,' Nancy said, attempting to join in the conversation brightly.

'Should be in the long run,' Joel said. 'But it'll all take getting used to.'

From then on, while they were waiting for Darius, everything changed. Joel and Maryann were full of expectation. Nancy, though, however hard she tried, became more and more glum as the time passed. By Wednesday afternoon, she was finding it impossible to remain cheerful at all. Maryann felt terribly awkward. It had been a peaceful week with Joel and Mick hitting it off well enough and Nance having company, and Maryann knew the parting was going to be hard.

On the Wednesday night Joel and Mick went out for a farewell drink while Maryann and Nance stayed in. Maryann tried to keep her talking, but Nance stared desolately into the fire. For a time they sat in silence. The clock struck ten with its mellow chime and roused Maryann from her thoughts.

'It'll be better when we've gone.' She sat forward in her chair, leaning closer to her friend. 'It's only making everything worse, us being here and talking about Darius – it's rubbing salt in the wound.'

Nance's face in the firelight looked hard in her

unhappiness. Maryann thought about her prettiness when she was with Darius on the cut.

'You and Mick,' Maryann persisted gently. 'I mean – things seem a bit better . . .'

Nance's lips began to tremble as she spoke. 'I s'pose they are. I think it's 'aving Joel 'ere – just knowing 'e can come 'ome and . . .' She lost control of her voice and the tears broke through. '. . . and not just find me 'ere . . . Oh God, Maryann, I know I married 'im in the sight of God and I know what the right thing to do is, but it's breaking my heart, it's so hard! I want to see Darius again more than anything else in the world, but I don't know as I can manage to see him. I don't think I could bear it.' She kept wiping her eyes furiously as if it was disloyal even to weep.

Maryann was just about to suggest that she try and keep Darius away from the house when she met him the next day, when they heard a knocking sound.

Nance frowned. 'Was that ours?' She looked round at the door.

The noise came again, and another sound of someone crying outside. Both of them got up and went cautiously to the door.

'Anyone in there?'

Nance opened the door, and in the dim light they saw a young, rather startled-looking policeman, and beside him a mane of red hair and a terrified, tear-stained face looking up at them. At the sight of Maryann she began sobbing uncontrollably.

'Amy?' Maryann went to her immediately and put her arm round her. She took in that the child was wearing a coat over her nightdress, her bare legs pushed into her boots. 'Are you awright? What's happened?'

The policeman was parking his bike up against the

wall. 'I found 'er, wandering about – over Winson Green way. In a right state she was – all she'd say was she 'ad to get over 'ere. You know 'er then?'

'Yes—' Maryann guided Amy into the room as she gulped and trembled. 'This is one of them,' she said to Nance over her shoulder. 'I wonder what in God's name's happened?'

'Oh my word,' Nance said, full of pity.

'Wouldn't say nowt to me,' the constable complained from the doorway. 'Thought the best thing to do was bring 'er here on my bike.'

Maryann put her hands firmly on the young girl's shoulders, trying to calm her. 'Amy – it's awright. You're safe here, love. You can talk to us – no one can hurt you here . . .' Seeing the distraught state of the girl brought Maryann close to tears herself. What had he done? What terrible harm had that cruel, self-obsessed man inflicted now?

Amy could scarcely get the words out. 'Sh-sh-sh . . .'

'It's awright—' Maryann caressed her shoulders. 'Slowly now.'

Amy took a great gulp of air and burst out, 'It's Margaret – I think sh-she's killed him.'

Forty-Five

That evening had, outwardly, begun like any other. Amy and Margaret came home from school, spent their few blissful hours alone at home with their mother before their stepfather arrived home. Janet had cooked mince for tea with potatoes and gravy and they had all sat to eat together. Margaret said nothing, as usual. Their stepfather asked polite, jovial questions about how school had been and about their mother's day. The conversation was strained. Afterwards, as it grew dark, they had put on the gas lamps in the front room, and Norman lit the wick in his brass oil lamp and placed it with its glowing light on the little table in the corner. He'd sat down to read the *Mail*, for the duration of that dreadful pause between tea and his stretching in the chair and saying, 'It's time you wenches were up in bed.'

To anyone watching it would have seemed a normal evening.

Yet the girls were living in constant fear and dread. Since Maryann's visit, nothing had been the same. Before, he had used them, abused them, convinced them of their subservience. But now it had become something much worse.

The night after Maryann had been, he had come up for the usual 'bedtime story'. Amy and Margaret got ready for bed, as ever, with feverish haste because if he was upstairs when they were still changing his hands were everywhere, pinching, poking. He stood in the doorway for a moment, smoking a cigarette, leaning on the frame with a nonchalant air, taking his time.

'So,' he said softly. 'You thought you could get away with squealing on me, did yer?' He gave a low laugh, then took a drag on the cigarette. Its tip flared orange for a second. 'Did you really?' Smoke curled from his nostrils. 'Poor little things – that was silly. Wasn't it? Very silly. I don't like that. I think I need to show you how much I don't like it.'

He yanked the thin pillow out from under Margaret's head and with both hands pushed it down over her face. Amy heard herself whimper and saw Margaret's hand clawing at him, her young body fighting against suffocation. He forced it down over her for what seemed an age, his expression a cruel grimace. Amy felt she was going to burst. She could bear it no longer.

'Get off her!'

She sprang off her bed and flung herself at him. He was perched at an angle on the edge and her weight threw him aside. Amy dragged the pillow away from Margaret's face and Margaret sat up, panting, frantic.

'You could've killed her!'

He was half sprawled across Margaret's bed and the look he gave her chilled her to her very core. Inside him, where most people had a heart and soul, was a place of hard, emotionless cruelty. She backed away from him.

'So – you're getting uppity now an' all, are yer?'

He advanced on her slowly.

'No!' Amy moaned. She curled herself at the top of her bed, her knees brought up to her chest. 'No – don't touch me ... don't, please ... I'll do anything, but don't ...'

But it was no use. It made no difference. Whatever she said or did would never make any difference, she could see that now.

This evening he had come up, his plume of loathsome blue smoke trailing after him. Once again he stood, as he liked to do, in the doorway, like a man looking down a menu, choosing, relishing. He strolled over to Margaret and sat down. With the cigarette jutting at the corner of his mouth he whipped back her bedclothes. Amy jumped violently. She saw him yank Margaret over on to her back and pull up her nightdress. Then, clamping his left hand over her mouth, he took the cigarette out of his mouth and stubbed it hard into her stomach. Amy's hands went over her own mouth. Margaret's body lifted off the bed, writhing. A thin, terrible noise was coming from her. He held his hand there until Margaret quietened, then removed it.

'Now—' He wagged his finger at her. 'Don't do it again.'

Do what? Amy thought wildly, biting on her fist to stop herself shouting out. What had she done?

'I've put my mark on you, wench. You show anyone and there'll be worse. I can do much worse than that.'

Margaret was gasping, crying in agony. Amy slid down the bed and blocked her ears. She knew he wouldn't have finished, that cruelty always led to something else, it excited him. She closed her eyes, pressed her hands over her ears while he raped her sister. Then he buttoned himself up tidily and went downstairs. Margaret lay, absolutely silent.

Amy went over to her. 'D'you want me to put summat on it for you?'

She stroked her sister's shoulder but Margaret was quite still, eyes closed, like a dead person. She must've have been in great pain but she made not a sound. Not knowing what else to do, Amy waited for a long time until she thought Margaret must really be asleep. At last, she crept back to bed.

It was almost an hour later when she heard Margaret moving about. She got up and just stood for a moment as if she was in a trance.

Amy turned over. 'Margaret?'

She waited a moment longer, like a little ghost in her bare feet, then went out of the room. Amy sat up, wondering if Margaret was sleepwalking. She heard her going down the stairs and through the open door, the faint sound of her mother clinking cups in the kitchen. Uneasily, Amy got out of bed and stood shivering at the top of the stairs, waiting to hear her mother's voice ordering Margaret back to bed. Was she going to show her the burn? It must hurt so badly. Amy trembled at the thought. He'd said she mustn't! What if she did – what would he do then?

She heard nothing and crept further downstairs. Her mother was still in the kitchen. Where had Margaret gone? Amy stood on the bottom step. And it was then she heard the crash, the sound of glass breaking from the front room, a shout from her stepfather, 'What've yer done, yer little vixen?' then high, agonized screaming which grew louder and more panic-stricken. Amy knew it was not Margaret who was screaming.

'Arthur?' Janet hobbled from the kitchen. 'Amy, whatever's going on?'

Amy reached the front room first. For a split second she thought the room was on fire but saw an instant later that the blaze was confined to her stepfather. Flames were leaping all over the top half of him, shooting out from his hair, his clothing, and he was leaping a wild jig around the room, shrieking in agony as the fire took hold of his hair and clothes. As she came to the room he flung himself down on the floor, rolling back and forth trying to douse the flames but they refused to be put out and leaped back into life in the places where his body left the floor and met the air again. Not far away, Margaret stood with her arms folded, her expression blank. Near him on the floor lay his brass lamp, its glass shattered. His head must have been doused with paraffin.

'Oh—' Janet Lambert gasped. 'Margaret – oh Margaret, what've you done? Help him, one of you – get the rug round him!' She pulled herself frantically across the room on her sticks. 'Help him I said!' she cried. 'Don't just stand there.'

But her daughters offered no help at all. Margaret stood quite still as if she hadn't heard. Amy slipped upstairs, running as if possessed, and fetched her boots. Throwing her coat over her nightdress she slid past the front parlour, past the sobbing screams, past her mother beating helplessly at the flames and out into the night, running, running to the one person who she knew would help and understand.

The story she managed, in her distress, to sob out to Maryann and the policeman was a brief, disjointed summary of this.

'What'll happen to her? She must've smashed the lamp right over 'is head. What if Margaret's killed him? Will she go to prison? They mustn't put her in prison, it ain't right – it was him, he drove her to it! He burned her with his cigarette.'

The young policeman appeared rather out of his depth. 'Look – I don't s'pose it's as bad as you think,' he said.

'Of course it's as bad as she thinks,' Maryann stormed at him. 'Ain't you heard what she just said? The man's an evil bloody maniac!'

'I see,' the policeman said uneasily. 'Look – you keep 'er here for tonight and look after her. I'll get over there now and see what's happening and tell her mother where she is. The address is . . .?'

'Blimey – that's a good distance away, that is . . .' He was just writing it down laboriously in his notebook when Joel and Mick rolled in from the pub.

'What's all this then?' Mick started aggressively. Joel looked at Maryann, her arm round Amy's shoulders and guessed who the girl was.

'Now, Mick—' Nance stepped in. 'Don't you go getting on yer 'igh 'orse. The wench is in trouble and 'er'll be stopping 'ere tonight. You just keep quiet.'

Amy looked fearfully at Mick's red, rough-looking face.

'It's awright,' Maryann whispered to her. 'He won't hurt you. This is Joel – the man I'm going to marry—'

''Ow do.' Joel smiled kindly at her. 'You'll be all right here. We'll look after you.'

They saw the policeman out.

'You can sleep down here with me,' Maryann reassured Amy.

'Oh no you don't,' Joel said. 'You're having the bed, you two, and no arguments.'

It took Amy a long time to calm down enough to fall asleep. Even after she had gone off, her body twitched in a disturbed way. Maryann lay with her arm wrapped round the child, making soothing noises, trying to comfort her. But her own mind was spinning round. She would have to take her back the next day to her mother. What sort of reaction was she going to get? And what would happen to Margaret? Was Norman really dead as Amy feared? It was a long time before she got any sleep herself.

The next morning Maryann, Nance and Amy went straight to Handsworth.

'I'm glad you're with me,' Maryann said to Nance on the tram. She felt horribly nervous at the thought of facing Amy's mother.

The house had a very quiet feel about it when they got there and Maryann wondered if anyone was in. But after she knocked on the door, they heard Janet Lambert pulling herself along the hall to open it. Maryann gripped Amy's hand as the door swung open.

All her remorse and worry was evident in Janet Lambert's sleepless, tear-stained face. 'Oh – Amy!' she cried and Amy, also crying, ran into her arms. 'Oh love – are you awright?' Janet sobbed. 'I'm sorry – I'm so, so sorry, Amy ... Oh my God, as long as you're awright ...'

Maryann and Nance watched as the two of them cried in each other's arms.

'Oh my girls – how could he've done it – all this time?'

Maryann felt her own overwrought emotions surfacing and it was all she could do to stop herself crying as well. To see Amy was at last believed by her mother and accepted back tore at her heart.

Janet looked over Amy's head at her, her eyes full of shame. 'Come in,' she said.

Once more they sat in the little parlour room, Amy on the arm of her mother's chair, leaning close to her.

'This is Nancy – my friend,' Maryann said. 'I'm living with her at the moment so it's her house Amy stayed at last night.'

'Good of yer,' Janet said absent-mindedly. Nance nodded, sympathetically.

'Where's Margaret?' Amy asked.

'They took her away.' The woman was distraught, tears running down her face as she spoke. 'The ambulance came for him. He was burnt terrible. They took her as well. I don't know what I'm going to do . . .'

'Did she show you?' Amy whispered.

They all knew she meant the burn that Norman Griffin had inflicted on her, the bruises.

Janet lowered her head, nodding. 'They want to make that better – only they think there's other things the matter with 'er – her mind. Oh . . . my little girl. What've I done? Why couldn't I see it? He was always so kind, such a gentleman with me! I just couldn't believe he could ever . . . I mean he was never even demanding that way, you know, with me . . .'

'He was just the same with us,' Maryann told her. Now she saw how sorry the woman was, how she wanted to do right by her daughters, she felt great sympathy for her. 'My sister took her own life because of him.'

Janet's head jerked up. She looked deeply shocked. 'Did she? You never said . . .'

'You wouldn't've believed me.'

'No.' She shook her head. 'I wouldn't. It's like having two whole different lives, different *worlds* going on in your house at the same time. You look at him, the way he is, and you can't believe ... I mean you can't believe *anyone* could do things like that, can you? I still can't ...' She shook her head as if to reassemble her thoughts. 'Still can't ...'

'I know,' Maryann said gently. 'He's the one with summat wrong in his mind. He's like a devil. He's going to live then?'

'They think so.'

There was silence for a moment. Janet pulled Amy on to her lap and held her.

'Whatever happens, we'll be together now – we'll manage somehow. I'll never let him near you.'

Forty-Six

Maryann cried all the way home, as if releasing years of pent-up sadness and however much Nance tried to comfort her she was unable to stop. And Nance was feeling so miserable that she was tearful herself.

'If only my mom'd been like that.' Maryann sobbed. She knew people were having a good look at her but she was past caring. 'I mean I know Janet daint believe them to begin with – but seeing 'em like that, her cuddling Amy ... She wants the best for her girls at heart. But that poor Margaret – what ever's going to happen to her?'

'I s'pect 'er'll be awright,' Nance said doubtfully, adding, 'the poor little mites.'

Maryann was even less hopeful. Nance hadn't seen what Margaret was like. 'I feel terrible leaving with all this going on. But we'll come and see them – and you, as often as we can.'

Nance nodded, staring bleakly ahead of her.

When they got back home, Joel saw what state she was in and came and took her in his arms. Nance began bustling about to hide her own emotion. There was no one to embrace her.

'She believes them now,' Maryann said into Joel's chest. 'Whatever else happens, she's on their side.'

'Thank 'eavens,' Joel said. 'That poor little nipper. What about him?'

'Oh – he'll live, they say.' Her voice was savage. 'I'm glad for Margaret's sake anyway.'

When they'd told him what had happened Maryann whispered to Joel, 'No sign of Darius yet then?' They were almost certain he was due in that day.

'Thought 'e might've got 'ere by now,' Joel said, shaking his head. 'Still . . .'

'We could go down there and wait for him,' Maryann suggested.

'What's all the whispering about?' Nance demanded sharply.

Maryann looked into the dregs of her teacup. 'We was just saying – maybe it'd be better – for you, like – if we was to go and wait down by the cut for when Darius gets in.'

Nance came and stood by the table, hands on hips. 'No need for that – I think me and Darius both know how to behave,' she said tartly. 'And Joel don't look as if he could walk another step at the moment. He wants to save 'is strength for later, that 'e does. I don't know how 'e's going to manage on that boat.'

'Darius'll be there – and me. We can make sure he takes it easy.'

Maryann was tensed with anticipation. After the events of last night and now this waiting she felt very churned up and unsettled. And she was dreading having to say goodbye to Nance. If only they could just go, be there on the *Esther Jane* without all this to-do!

The afternoon crawled by. Nance declared she wasn't going to lift a finger that day to do anything in the house. There'd be plenty of time for that when they'd all gone. Maryann thought of Nance's days stretching ahead, full of work, just her and Mick, and she pitied her terribly. Nance had a home and a husband all right, but her life seemed so empty.

They sat reminiscing that afternoon, each trying to take each other's mind off the coming departure, laughing about their antics and Blackie Black with his barrow.

'Poor old Dad,' Nance said. 'Never managed much with 'is life neither, did 'e? 'E was always on about how 'e was going to get us out of Ladywood to somewhere better – soon as 'e had a shilling on him 'e was off down the pub.' She shook her head. 'The old sod. I can 'ardly stand to go and see 'im. 'E ain't going anywhere now.' Blackie's health was failing week by week. 'It's a good job our mom's got all the boys to bring in some money.' She looked across at Maryann. 'You not going to go and see yer mom again before yer go?'

Maryann bit her lip. 'I can't, Nance. Mom's made it clear what her attitude is to me. Tony said she's never said a word about seeing me and I ain't crawling to her again if she don't want me.'

'But what about Amy and Margaret – if you told 'er what's happened to Mr Griffin?'

'It makes no difference now. It's too late, Nance. She daint believe anything I said when it really mattered. Joel's my family now – 'e was always the one who was good to me in any case. Me and Mom were never close.'

Nance stared at her, smiling gently, her old friend with her wayward black hair and face that was still rather impish even now, in her twenties.

'You – a bargee – I can't believe it.'

'We ain't bargees.' Maryann sat up straighter. 'We're

Number Ones. Well – we were. I'll miss yer, Nance – but I'll be back. We always were best pals, eh?'

Late in the afternoon, when the waiting was becoming almost unbearable, at last there came a tap at the door. Maryann saw Nance's face tense up as Joel opened the door and they all saw Darius's stern features lifted into a rather flustered smile.

'At last!' Joel cried. 'I thought them moty boats was s'posed to be quicker.'

Darius stepped in, acknowledging everyone with a nod. 'The trouble I've 'ad with the bloody thing – there's been many a time today I'd've said we'd be better off going back to 'aving a horse any day. Once she got going though, she did put on a bit of speed. Takes getting used to I can tell you – she vibrates fit to shake your teeth out! Anyway – I've got a load on so we're all set. You ready then, are you?'

'Can I get you a cup of tea, Darius?' Nance asked softly.

'Nancy.' He nodded again, not meeting her eyes. 'Er – no ta. I think we'll be getting on.'

Nance nodded. Maryann could tell how much it hurt her that Darius was being so distant with her, but what choice did he have?

'Come on—' she said briskly. The less drawn-out the farewells the better, she thought. 'Let's get moving. You got everything, Joel?'

She had her case with her things in and Joel had a small bundle. They had few possessions and even if they had had more, there was little space for anything on the *Esther Jane*.

When they had gathered themselves together, Nance

432

suddenly untied her apron and said, 'Look – I don't want to say goodbye 'ere. I'll come down with yer—'

'You sure that's a good idea?' Maryann asked anxiously. It just seemed like prolonging the agony.

'It's awright,' Nance said staunchly. 'I just want to see yer off properly.'

Darius said he'd brought the boat through to Gas Street as it was nearer, and he'd already picked up a load of brass fittings to take south the next day. There was only about half a mile to walk. They took it slowly for Joel's sake. Maryann was concerned about how very easily he tired. She walked ahead with him, and Nancy and Darius followed at a distance which increased gradually as they went along. Maryann could just hear their voices, lowered, talking urgently. By the time they reached the cut, Nance was in tears. Maryann saw that while Darius was talking earnestly to her, trying to comfort her, he refrained from putting his arm round her shoulders.

The sun was beginning to set, glinting on windows, casting gold on the dark water and turning the chimney stacks and warehouses round them into black silhouettes. They had to step across a couple of other boats to reach the *Esther Jane*, turning their faces away, as was the custom, from the private living quarters of their occupants. When Joel stepped down into the *Esther Jane* his legs almost gave way. Maryann caught him.

'No work for you,' she said. 'You've got a lot of resting to do.'

But he sat beside the tiller, panting a little, and looked round in sheer delight. The boat was sitting quite low in the water, filled with sacks of brassware.

'Home – at last. It's felt like an eternity – 'specially in that 'ospital.'

'Saved your life though,' Darius said.

Joel nodded. 'They did. But I reckon it was someone else 'ere coming back to me really did it.' He laid his arm round Maryann's shoulder. She nestled into his embrace, though painfully aware of Nance's presence. They were all squeezed in at the back together. 'You'll 'ave to show me what they done to 'er.' Joel eyed the new chimney of the Bolinder motor jutting out of the *Esther Jane*'s cabin roof. 'When I've got my breath back.'

There was an awkward silence. A sliver of cloud crossed the setting sun and for a moment a chill darkness passed over everything, the gold leeching out of the ripples.

'Well,' Nance said, with a huge effort at cheerfulness. 'I'd best be getting back then. Get Mick's tea or there'll be trouble.'

'You've been very good to us,' Joel said. 'I'm ever so grateful to you, Nance.'

'Oh – that's awright,' she said, struggling not to cry.

She and Maryann flung their arms round one another.

'Thanks, Nance – for everything. We'll be back to see yer – often as we can.'

'You'd better—' Her voice was choked. 'Hark at me – I must go.' Hastily she held out her hand. 'Goodbye – Darius.'

'Tara.' He spoke very quietly, painfully reluctant to let go of her hand.

She turned and climbed back over on to the bank. 'Don't go falling in, any of yer!' she called, and Maryann could hear her tearfulness. She watched Darius as Nance gave a final wave and slipped away into the dusk

434

which lay in thick folds along the wharves. His eyes didn't leave her until she was out of sight.

Though they spent the evening busily, somehow Nance was still with them. Darius and Joel spent some time peering into the engine as Darius explained how it worked and how they had to maintain it, while Maryann fried up their evening meal and then they sat in the tiny cabin together: Darius on the step, his plate held in his enormous hands; Maryann and Joel at the table under the little lamp bracket. It was as cosy as she remembered and she felt herself glowing with happiness. Here she was, on the *Esther Jane* with her two favourite people in all the world.

'Soon as Joel's up to scratch,' Darius announced, 'I'll go back and work for Fellows, Morton and Clayton. That way we'll 'ave another wage coming in. I don't think our dad's going to be up to coming back on the cut. You two can make this your 'ome. Essy Barlow'll give us another butty to tow so you can get a decent load.' Putting the motor in had taken up some of the space previously occupied by cargo.

Joel nodded. He knew how sore Darius was about Nance, but they would not put this into words. And on the cut necessity meant getting work and keeping moving at all costs. 'Thanks,' he said. 'You've held everything together, Darius. I 'ope it won't be long now – this blessed chest of mine.'

'Keep her in the family any'ow,' Darius went on. 'You'll 'ave another family growing up on 'ere.'

As soon as they'd eaten, Joel said he had to lie down and Darius pulled down the cross bench for him. Blushing, Maryann wondered where she was going to sleep. She'd have the bench, she decided – until she was married. The two brothers could sleep together.

As soon as Joel was settled, Darius said, 'I'll be off out for a couple of pints,' and out he went.

Maryann finished the washing-up. Joel was quiet, sleeping, she thought. She tried to put the plates away quietly, not clatter them and wake him. She eyed the cabin. She'd get the place spick and span again. She wasn't having any of the other boatwomen saying she couldn't keep it nice. The crochet work was looking worn and grey. She was going to learn how to do it and make her own, all fresh! When they were tied up somewhere she'd get one of the women to teach her.

Turning, she saw Joel was watching her.

'Ooh – you made me jump!' She laughed. 'I thought you was asleep!'

'Come and get in 'ere with me.'

'Joel! We ain't married!'

'We will be soon enough. Go on. Just a cuddle.'

She went and sat beside him. 'I thought you were tired?'

'Not that tired.'

'What if Darius comes back?'

'He won't. Why d'you think 'e went out?'

She unfastened her frock and lay down beside him in her slip. They lay very close together on the narrow bed, looking at one another in the rosy light of the cabin. She saw the speckled colour of his lashes and his loving expression.

'Back home.' He smiled. 'Maryann – my lovely Maryann.'

She stroked his face. After a week at Nance's his cheeks were covered by a down of gingery hair. 'Your beard's coming back. You're starting to look right again.'

He laughed. 'That's nice to know.' His arm pulled

her even closer and they kissed. Their bodies were pressed together and in panic she realized how aroused he was. 'That's not the only thing that's coming back,' he murmured.

She stiffened and he sensed it immediately.

'It's all right.' He kissed her flushed cheek, drawing back a little, and stroked her hair. 'It's awright, little 'un. I ent going to force myself on you without your say so. It just shows how much I love you, that's all.' He kissed her face in between talking to her. 'You're my little bird and I don't want you flying away. Just let me love you a bit tonight – bit by bit. I want you to love me too – not to find me horrible.'

She felt herself relax at his assurances. This was Joel – she had always been able to trust him.

'Oh Joel – I could never find you horrible. And I know how long you've waited. It's just – we ain't married and I'm – I'm a bit frightened of it . . .'

'I know . . . I know. But don't be frightened, lovely one . . . You're meant to like it.'

Gently, slowly, he began to love her body into life. She was moved by his desire for her as he stroked her.

'Your hands are softer these days,' she said.

'Oh – that won't last long on 'ere!'

She began to relax as he ran his hands under her slip and touched her breasts. Gradually he pulled the slip down and kissed her and the sensation made her gasp. Excitement rose in her, sudden and strange. For a moment her mind rebelled – no, no, it was wrong to feel this, it was horrible! And she tensed, but when he continued to touch her and she saw the pent-up pleasure and need in his face she tried to relax. No, it wasn't wrong. It had to be right. She and Joel could make it right.

She clung to him, stroking him. 'Oh Joel . . . oh . . .'

'It's all right—' He moved his hand between her legs and she flinched, then forced herself to relax. All the vile poking and prodding that Norman Griffin had done flashed back to her for those moments and she moaned, forcing her eyes open.

'It's all right, my love,' he kept saying. 'I don't want to hurt you – just to love you . . . love you, little bird . . .'

After a time he leaned close, his breathing very quick. 'Can I – please?'

She knew she couldn't refuse him. She loved him too much to refuse him anything and she gave a tiny nod. She must do it for him.

That first moment, feeling the weight of him and his moving inside her she almost screamed, but she watched him, seeing the love in his face, the way he didn't abandon her for his own pleasure but stayed with her, looking into her eyes. 'My love . . . my love,' he gasped. 'Oh my little love . . .' When he had reached his climax he kissed her again and again, and they lay holding one another tenderly.

Maryann was full of wonder, of relief. They'd done it! She knew it was something every married woman had to get over with. And it was going to be all right. With Joel it could be. She could be married in every sense, and not have to dread any part of it.

She woke next morning before dawn, cramped and stiff, and lay looking round, for a few moments, beside Joel's warm back. There was very little to see, but she could just make out the dark shape of the range and hear Darius breathing loudly on the other bench. She was here, on the *Esther Jane*! It was really going to be her

438

home. How long would it be before she could stop pinching herself and really believe it?

And last night – Oh Lor', she thought. Did I really . . .? The thought that they'd fallen asleep and Darius must have come back and found them both side by side and dead to the world was mortifying. But this was outweighed by her happiness. She smiled, sleepily. It'll be all right, I can love him – I can be a normal woman! It was really too late to worry about Darius now. The next night she'd suggest sleeping on the other bed. But she found herself hoping Darius would refuse to let her.

She kissed Joel's warm back, then eased herself off the bed, pulled her clothes on in the dark and crept out, taking the bowl to relieve herself, thankful that there was little sound from anywhere around. Then she went back in and lit the lamp and got the range going to put a kettle on and by the time she'd done that, Darius was up and she heard others around them beginning to stir.

'We need to be on our way,' Darius said. 'I'm going to get her going.'

Maryann got a huge shock when Darius started the engine. It felt all wrong without old Bessie hauling away on the bank. He had said the boat vibrated, but when all the china in the cabin started rattling and she felt as if she was being shaken up inside a salt cellar, she realized life was going to be very different from when the *Esther Jane* had Bessie pulling them serenely through the water. Soon she could also smell the acrid fumes from the funnel as well as the constant phut-phutting sound of the engine. It woke Joel.

'It's *horrible*,' she said, dismayed. 'How on earth're we s'posed to get used to this?'

Joel didn't look too happy either. 'Darius says you

do get used to it after a bit. Thing is, Maryann – it's this or selling her altogether. At least we've got our home, eh?'

'I s'pose so,' she conceded, handing him a cup of tea. She smiled shyly, kissing him. 'Our home. That sounds nice, don't it?'

Darius swung in through the door. 'We'll untie and be off now—'

The boat seemed to make a lot of noise starting off, but when they were moving, she settled down to a more regular sound. They eased away from the other moored boats. Joel stood at the stern, watching in amazement in the pale dawn light.

They were just straightening up to move off when they all heard a cry from on the bank, a voice shouting with all its strength, '*Maryann! Darius!*'

'My God—' Maryann peered through the door out into the dim light. 'That sounds like Nancy!'

'*Wait! Don't go – wait, wait!*'

Darius instantly steered the *Esther Jane* towards the bank where Nancy was frantically shouting and running to keep up with them. He brought her in rather awkwardly and they bumped the side, almost causing Maryann to fall over.

Nance was panting so hard she could scarcely speak. Darius held out his hand and she jumped in.

'Nance – what the hell're yer playing at?' Maryann was quite annoyed. She'd said her goodbyes – that was that. Why spin it out even longer? She saw, though, that Nance had a fresh shiner on her left eye, which was only half open.

In any case, it was not Maryann Nance wanted to speak to. All her attention was fixed on Darius. 'I 'aven't slept a wink!' she panted. 'It's no good – I'm coming with yer! 'E gave me this as a present last night—' She pointed at her eye. 'I ain't never going back, Darius – it's you I want to be with – for ever!'

Darius's face took on a look of wonder and disbelief. 'But . . .' he stuttered. 'Nance – you, I mean . . .'

'Nance – what're you saying?' Maryann asked her. 'What about Mick – I mean, you said you'd never . . .?'

'I know what I said. I married 'im, I took vows in church and I can't divorce 'im and I'm most likely damned into the bargain. But it's you I love, Darius. I've never felt the way I feel when I'm with you – *ever* before. I've only got one life and I can't spend it with 'im when I can hardly stand the sight of 'im and 'e knocks me about and there'll be no babbies neither. It ain't a marriage, it's a prison sentence. If you'd not come along, Darius, I might never've known I could fall in love. I know we can't make it legal and regular but out 'ere it don't seem to matter. It's you I want to spend my life with – if you'll 'ave me.'

'If I'll have *you*?' Darius said. He could scarcely believe what he was hearing. He handed the tiller to Joel and pulled Nance into his arms. 'How can you even ask, girl?' He was laughing with sheer joy.

'Flamin 'ell, Nance!' Maryann was only just beginning to take in what had happened. 'Joel – this family's getting bigger every minute.'

Nance, laughing and crying at once, hugged each of them in turn. 'I can't believe I'm doing this! I'm going to wake up any moment!'

'Well,' Darius took command of the *Esther Jane* once more, 'let's get going before you do.'

With the water churning behind them, they weaved their way through the shadowy Birmingham Cut and out towards the fresher country air.

441

Forty-Seven

December 1934

The day of their wedding, Maryann woke in the little house where she and Joel were staying with old Darius's sister in Oxford. Joel's father was still in poor health and was staying on the bank for the forseeable future.

Maryann had been given a bed upstairs and Joel was sleeping on an old sofa down in the tiny back room. She could see that the sun was shining brightly behind the curtains and she climbed out of bed, shivering as she pulled her woolly on and then going to draw back the curtain. The sight that met her eyes made her laugh with pleasure. It was a diamond-hard, cold day, creaking with ice and from the roof hung huge icicles glinting in the bright sunlight. The rooftops were white and the tree she could see a little way along the street looked as if it had been dipped in icing sugar. She couldn't have asked for better than this sparkling white perfection.

Old Mrs Simons, Joel's aunt, had married away from the cut and spent her wedded life in Oxford, where her late husband had a grocer's shop. She was a diminutive lady with scrubbed pink cheeks, little spectacles and she wore black, old-fashioned bombazine dresses with white lace collars. She was delighted that Joel and Maryann had decided to be married at St Barnabas Church, just a couple of streets away, and where she attended regularly.

'Now, moy dear,' she said to Maryann later in the morning when they were ensconced together upstairs away from the men and she was helping Maryann dress. 'Just you stand still so's I don't nick you with this.' She bent over with a needle and thread in one hand, finishing a seam in the woollen dress Maryann had chosen. It was second-hand but in good condition and a lovely violet-blue colour. 'Looks very nice with your pretty hair.' Maryann's hair was fastened back in a shiny, raven twist behind her head, and with her rosy cheeks and bright, happy eyes she looked very beautiful.

Mrs Simons stood back and clasped her hands in front of her breast, her china thimble still on one finger, beaming with excitement. 'We haven't had a wedding in this family for such a time – what with all poor Esther's boys . . . the War, you know. I began to think Joel and Darius'd never settle. . . .' She drifted off sadly, then regained her state of glee. 'But it always makes me feel young again, a wedding! Now just you remember, moy dear – they're good men in this family, good sound men. But sometimes you do have to take a firm hand with them.'

'Do you?' Maryann asked, surprised.

'Oh yes.' Mrs Simons neatly packed away her needles and thread. 'Give 'em half the chance and they treat you like a man – like a *packhorse*, moy dear, to tell the truth – have you toiling day and night. Just remember to get Joel to treat you proper, however much strovin' there is to be done. You 'ave to pull your weight of course, on the cut, but don't let 'im forget you're a woman for a moment, that's my advice – specially when you're carrying a child. Nothing worse for child-bearing than toiling like an animal day in day out. Saw my mother's life come to an end through it, so I should know.'

'I'll try.' Maryann smiled.

She had a smart, royal blue hat with a white feather in it to top off her outfit, and blue shoes with an elegant heel.

'I suppose this is the last time I'll feel this smart in many a year.' She laughed.

'Well, you're realistic, I'll give you that,' Mrs Simons said. She squeezed Maryann's hand and stood on tiptoe to kiss her. 'Joel's a good boy – always has been. I hope you'll be very happy, moy dear, and have a big, healthy family.

It was unconventional, she knew, but as she had no one there in the way of family, Maryann asked old Mr Bartholomew to walk up the aisle with her and present her to his son. She did feel rather wistful that morning. Even Tony wasn't going to travel all the way down from Birmingham, although he had written her a letter. She knew there was no question of her mother coming. But Nancy and Darius were there, Nancy acting as her 'assistant'.

'I don't know whether I'm a bridesmaid or a matron of honour!' Nance joked.

She and Darius were working another of Samuel Barlow's boats and had managed to reach Oxford that morning by the skin of their teeth in time for the wedding.

And old Darius Bartholomew seemed delighted that Maryann was marrying Joel. 'I'd 'ardly've known you,' he said, looking her up and down when he first saw her. 'You was only a child when last I saw you.'

She would have known him anywhere. He was certainly shrunken and more stooped in stature compared with how she had first seen him, but his beard and bushy white eyebrows and his tanned, leathery features were unmistakable. He was rather splendidly dressed in an ancient suit which shone with wear, a red cravat in the neck of his shirt. She remembered how intimidating she had found him in the past. Now she felt only respect and fondness. It felt absolutely right when he took her arm and led her along the aisle while the organ was playing the wedding march, and she saw Joel dressed up – for the first time ever probably – in a black suit, his beard trimmed, waiting for her before the altar. Mr Bartholomew gallantly handed her to his waiting son with an expression of great solemnity. Maryann was surprised to find that her legs were trembling so much she could barely stand.

When they came out, their few well-wishers sprinkled them with rice and Joel kissed her in the doorway of the church as the others watched and cheered. A man took their photograph.

Nance kissed her enthusiastically, almost knocking both their hats off in the process. Nance's was perched precariously on her curls.

'I'm ever so 'appy for yer, Maryann! You look really lovely.'

'Ta, Nance – you do an' all.' Maryann linked arms with Joel on one side and Nancy on the other as they all walked along to the pub where they went afterwards to celebrate. It was lovely outside but so cold that they were anxious to get into the warmth and they walked briskly, watched by a few curious passers-by in the little Oxford back street with its rows of neat terraces.

Nance looked a picture of health. In the three

months since she'd been with Darius she seemed to have filled out and her eyes were alive with happiness.

'I've got muscles on me like bed-knobs!' She laughed. 'Eh Darius – bring the bride a drink, will yer!'

They were a small wedding party, but they settled down very happily together. Old Mrs Simons became quite merry drinking glasses of ginger wine. Maryann sat between Nancy and Joel.

'Well – there's not many of us, but we wish you well,' Mrs Simons said, raising her glass. 'You're a lovely girl and I know you'll make our Joel very happy.'

They all drank to Joel and Maryann's health. Nance nudged Maryann.

'My wedding to Mick was quite a big do and look where that got me,' she said quietly. 'You be happy, my girl.'

'I'll do my best,' Maryann said. She thought to herself that if she'd had the finest wedding in the land she couldn't be happier. She laid her hand over Joel's under the table and he smiled and leaned close to kiss her.

Maryann and Nance had a good old chinwag about adjusting to life on the cut, catching up on the past couple of months. After a month apart, when Darius had gone off to earn some money with Fellows, Morton and Clayton and Nance had stayed on the *Esther Jane*, the two of them had got their own Barlow boat and Joel had said he felt strong enough to cope – especially now the boat had an engine.

'I tell yer, Maryann,' Nance said. 'Some nights I'm so tired I'm near falling asleep standing up and I'm dreaming the engine's still going at night even when it ain't.' Maryann nodded her agreement. 'I never knew what work was till I went off with Darius. 'E's 'ad a right go at me a few times when I get things wrong. Still, I learned a lot off Joel when I was still with you so it could be worse. And I tell yer summat, I wouldn't swap it for the world – when yer get up in the morning and look out on the fields all white with frost and the sun coming up – never seen anything like that in my life before.'

'You don't miss the old life then?' Maryann asked.

'Sometimes, when I'm trying to do a wash and get it hung out and moving about in that cabin I curse it and wish I 'ad a house to live in. But then when I think back – when I did 'ave, I've never felt so miserable in all my life.' She looked sober for a moment. 'No. I couldn't go back. I mean I'll 'ave to go back *some time* soon – I've writ me mom, trying to explain. I know I've done Mick wrong and sometimes it weighs heavy on me. But we love each other, me and Darius. I 'ope Mick finds some way of getting on without me – but I wanted a life, Maryann . . .'

Her brown eyes earnestly sought Maryann's, needing reassurance. Maryann patted her hand. ''Course you did.'

'You been back to Brum?'

'I was there only last week. Went to see if Tony and Billy could come down for the wedding but Tony daint seem to think 'e could. And I went to see Amy and her mom.'

'Oh – how are they? What's 'appened to *him*?'

'*He*,' Maryann said, 'is still in hospital. Janet said his face and the top of him's burnt so bad you can scarcely recognize him. She was sort of shuddering as she told me. Said 'e's a terrible sight – it all got infected and it's taking time to heal.'

447

'Serves the bastard right.'

'She said she daint think he'll find any more young widows with families to charm his way into. Said they'd run away at the sight of him.'

'What about those poor girls of 'ers?'

'She and Amy are just living quietly together. She's taking in some sewing – it's very hard for 'er to get by but they're managing. She says she don't care what she has to do just so long as she can keep Amy safe. Amy seems awright – much more cheerful, though heaven knows – the scars run deep, Nance . . .'

'Poor child. What about Margaret though?'

'Well—' Maryann's face clouded. 'They've still got 'er in the asylum. She ain't right. God alone knows what he did to her. Her mom's worried to death and she visits, but she's that busy trying to make ends meet. She says they can still barely get the kid to say a word.'

Nance made a hissing sound through her teeth and was interrupted before she could say anything by Joel leaning over.

'My dad wants to say summat.'

They all looked at old Darius Bartholomew. Slowly he got to his feet and his stooped figure loomed above them.

'It's a very happy day for us all today,' he began ponderously, then stopped and cleared his throat. 'Turns out I've known the lass what's marrying our Joel since she were a nipper, and a fine young woman she's turned out to be.' He paused and Maryann smiled, blushing with surprise. 'It's a pity today couldn't be the wedding of both my living sons. My Esther Jane, God rest 'er, would've taken both daughters-in-law to 'er heart, even if they was off the bank.' It was Nancy's turn to go red. Darius said no more about her situation. It was a difficult one, but they could all see how she and Darius were together and Nancy, who was sturdy and a good worker on the boat, had been accepted.

'I don't have no finery to give you both on your wedding day, 'cept my blessing. But there is things I'd like to give to you. My working days on the cut're over now and it's no use in thinking they ain't. So...' He indicated to his sister to pass up a cloth bag from beside the chair and dipped his hand into it. 'This 'un's for you, Joel.' It was his second windlass, the one he'd had to use all the time after Maryann so shamefully lost the first.

Joel soberly nodded his thanks. Both of them knew what it meant: old Darius was handing over the *Esther Jane* after a lifetime's work.

'And there's summat for you too, missy.' From the bag he drew something black and crumpled, and as he opened it out with his twisted hands, Maryann gasped, seeing the honour that was being conferred on her. It was Esther Jane's black bonnet.

'Oh—' She hesitated then, seeing Joel smiling, took it gingerly from the old man's outstretched hand. 'I – I don't think I deserve this...'

'Well—' Darius sank into his seat and picked up his glass. 'Time'll tell. But you're a boatwoman now. A Bartholomew. My Esther was my best mate on the cut through good days and bad. Now it's your turn and Joel's. You look after each other, eh – and you two an' all—' He nodded at Darius and Nance who had tears in her eyes.

They all raised their glasses and Joel turned to Maryann, his face full of love.

'Best mates.'

She clinked her glass against his and kissed him. 'Best mates.'

Joel and Maryann had said their farewells for the moment to the family. Darius and Nance were going straight back to pick up a load and get ahead. Darius said they'd be likely to work the Grand Union next.

'Might not see yer for a bit,' Nance said as she and Maryann hugged each other goodbye. 'We'll get back on the Oxford soon as we can.'

'Try and get to Napton for Christmas!' Joel said.

That evening they moved the *Esther Jane* out away from the town and tied up in a beautiful, isolated spot where fields stretched out all around them and the only thing filling the middle distance were the sharp outlines of winter trees against a white half-moon. They left old Jep snoozing in the cabin and stepped out on to the bank in the moonlight. The cold was so intense it seemed to come down on them like a weight, but the sky was full of stars and they wanted to enjoy the sight of it. Joel put his arm round Maryann and they stood close together in silence for a few moments, looking across the silver fields, hearing the gentle slap of the water against the bank. A bird screeched somewhere in the distance, a high, lonely sound. Maryann shivered and snuggled closer to Joel.

'It's so beautiful,' she said. 'Feels as if there's no one around for miles.'

'Probably ain't.'

She looked up at him, the pale sheen of moonlight on his face. He was filling out gradually and beginning to look like his strong, burly self. She could hear, though, the loud wheezing of his lungs, an utterly comforting sound because it had always been one which accompanied him, but also a worrying sign of his vulnerability. She knew how close to death he had been, the risk that any illnesses meant to him in the damp atmosphere of the cut. She stood on tiptoe and kissed his face, overflowing with love and gratitude. She would treasure every day with him.

He took her in his arms. 'So – what happened to the girl who said she would always be called Maryann Nelson?'

She laughed. 'Fancy you remembering that!'

'You were very strong on it at the time. Funny, scrawny little thing you were.'

'I know – well, thanks for changing my mind. Maryann Bartholomew'll do me well. 'S a funny thing – being married does feel different. Even though we've been living on here – I just feel properly married now, 'stead of "living in sin"!'

'Can't 'ave you living in sin, can we?'

'Even if Nance is.'

'Ah well – what else can they do, eh?'

'And they're happy,' she said.

'And you?'

She hesitated. 'Happier than you know . . . Joel?'

'Umm?'

'I think, in fact I'm sure – I'm expecting.'

'A baby – a little 'un?'

She could hear his excitement and she nodded solemnly.

'Oh,' he said, awed. 'My Maryann. That's lovely, that is.' Suddenly, laughing, he lifted her off the ground. 'Oh love – a little 'un!'

They held each other close.

'Come the summer,' Joel said, kissing her nose, 'we could lie out in the fields of a night . . . no one about.'

'By summer,' she laughed, 'I'll have a belly on me like a barrel!'

'Well – tonight . . .'

'Not tonight, no,' Maryann said firmly, pulling on his hand. 'I'm turning rigid with cold already. Come on – let's go in.'

They took one last look at the star-flecked sky, the friendly land spreading out around them, then, still holding hands, they stepped back into the cosy little cabin.

Epilogue

August 1936

'If it's a girl,' Maryann was saying, 'let's call her Ada.'

'Or Sally,' Joel said. 'After your sister.'

'We'd better have two girls then.' Maryann laughed.

She and Joel were walking out along the road away from Banbury towards Charnwood House, on a boiling August afternoon, ripe wheat stretching away on either side of them, swaying and rustling in the languorous breeze. On Joel's shoulders, his legs jutting forward each side of his father's face was their little son Joel, who had had his first birthday the month before. Maryann, who was four months into another pregnancy, was still looking trim.

'Margaret's a nice name,' she mused. 'Only it feels unlucky – poor little Margaret.'

'And Margaret's – well, she's not dead like our Ada and your Sally, is she?' Joel said carefully.

'Might just as well be, where she is.' Her voice was so hard and bitter, Joel reached out and touched her shoulder and little Joel gave a squeak of panic as his father loosed one of his legs.

Margaret, like Sal, was someone Maryann tried hard never to think about. Such thoughts had great power to make her feel sick with rage and sorrow and as there was nothing she could do, she pushed them away.

There had been plenty else to think about over the past couple of years. Most of her first year on the cut had been spent pregnant and she found it completely exhausting, with the added worry that if she was able to do less Joel would be forced to work even harder and could fall sick again, so however tired or heavy she was feeling she pushed herself on. Little Joel was born slightly early, on the *Esther Jane* with a nurse present, and Maryann had then been faced with the challenge of bringing up a child in the confined space of the boat. It was all right when he was a tiny baby, but as he grew and began to move about she worried constantly for his safety. More and more she heard stories about infants losing their lives on the cut through accidents or sickness and she became acutely protective of him. But he was a steady, sensible little fellow, even as a young toddler, and he had come well through his first year. She longed now for a daughter who would be a companion for him as he grew up.

Every so often they saw Nancy and Darius. Blackie Black had died of a seizure back in the winter of 1935 and Nance had gone home to visit. While she was there she was afraid she'd have to face Mick. Cathleen told her that a few months after Nancy went, Mick had left too, taken off and no one knew where. Cathleen, in her usual placid way, had not made an issue of her daughter's actions and was more concerned that they remain on good terms.

Nance and Darius had had a baby son, who in the family tradition they had called Darius and who must, Maryann calculated, have been conceived on about the first night the two of them were together, a fact which gave Nance enormous satisfaction after the agonies of living with Mick.

Every time they passed through Banbury, Maryann had thought fondly of Charnwood and she said to Joel she'd like to go back and visit. She often remembered them all, especially Mrs Letcombe, and she wondered whether Roland Musson had found the courage to leave and make a life for himself, and whether Miss Pamela was married now. She even wondered about Evan. Up until now though, they'd always been passing through or too busy or tired to make the effort. Today, however, it was the *Esther Jane*'s turn to revisit Tooley's Yard, and the beautiful, sultry day seemed to be calling them out across the fields.

When they turned in at the gate of Charnwood she said, 'Oh – this does feel peculiar. It all looks just the same as it did – only the trees've come on a bit more.'

As they neared the house Joel said, 'My goodness – this is a smart place. Can't think why you ever wanted to leave!'

'I daint, for a long time. But I met Darius, remember? And he told me that *someone* was very poorly in hospital . . .'

'Ah yes.' Joel laughed.

'We'll have to go in the servants' entrance,' Maryann said. They went round the back of the house, with the wistaria sprawling across the back. As she glanced across the garden, Maryann's eye was caught by a figure sitting in a sunny spot near the wall of the rose garden. There was a new bench that had not been there before, and on it sat a figure dressed completely in black.

'That looks like Mrs Musson,' Maryann whispered, frowning. 'The lady of the house. She looks to be in mourning, wouldn't you say? That hat's got net on and everything. I wonder – it could be the anniversary of John's death. That was her oldest son, killed in the war. Or I wonder if Mr Musson . . .'

Someone must have opened the front door as she

spoke because there was a sudden frenzied barking and Freddie the fox terrier tore round towards them, followed at a waddling pace by Lily Langtree, the spaniel who had been quite fat when Maryann was working there and had now expanded into a dog of truly corpulent proportions. Little Joel laughed and pointed at them, but other than sniffing at the visitors' legs and barking loudly the dogs did nothing else except run back round the end of the house.

'Well, they ain't changed.'

Inside, they found that not a huge amount had changed among the servants either. She found Mrs Letcombe, looking exactly the same, seated in her little room, dozing over her knitting in the warm afternoon.

'My dear, it's very nice to see you,' she said, kissing Maryann and greeting both Joels warmly. She loved small children, and took little Joel on to her lap immediately. 'Oh – and this little fellow must have a piece of Cook's best seed cake. Come on now – we'll all have a nice cup of tea. Oh, I am glad things have turned out well for you, Maryann. You left in such a hurry, I was rather afraid that Evan drove you away – he was always more forward than he ought to be.'

They filled in the news of the past two years. Evan and Alice had got married, but were still living and working at Charnwood. Sid the gardener had died unexpectedly – 'His heart, they think,' Mrs Letcombe said as they all sat at the kitchen table with the tea and cake and little Joel tottering around practising his new walking skills. 'Otherwise down here, things are really much the same. It's a settled sort of house. But upstairs—' She rolled her eyes. 'Oh dear me.'

'What's happened?' Maryann said. 'I saw Mrs Musson – all in black.'

'Terrible. Only last month. It was Master Roland. Went off to that war in Spain. Upped and went. Said war was the only thing he knew and if he couldn't make a life here he might as well go back to that. So he went and fought for Franco. He lasted just three weeks.' She shook her head sorrowfully. 'That poor, poor boy.'

'No!' Maryann let the news sink in. She wanted to weep. The image of him roaring through the quiet countryside on his motorcycle came to her, as if nothing of stillness or quietness could satisfy his troubled mind. 'How terrible,' she said. 'Poor Mrs Musson.'

'Nothing'll console her. Two sons gone – there's only Master Hugh left and somehow she doesn't seem to have the same affinity with him. Miss Pamela's married now of course. To a farmer chappie, over near Thame and she seems happy enough.' She turned to Joel. 'And what is it you do for a living?'

When he told her, Mrs Letcombe seemed quite taken aback at first, then she laughed. 'I thought you were looking very brown and sturdy,' she said to Maryann. 'Well – I'd never've put you down as doing that but you look as if it's suiting you.'

'Oh – it is.' She laughed. 'Most days, any'ow!'

They spent a very friendly hour in the kitchen and she kissed Maryann again when they left. 'Come and see us again, won't you? With all your lovely children as they arrive.' She chucked little Joel's cheek as Maryann held him. 'Sorry you didn't see anyone else.'

But Maryann was glad. She hadn't wanted to see Evan or the others especially. As they left she looked down the garden and saw that the bench where Mrs Musson had been sitting was empty, and she was filled with a great sense of poignancy. Handing Joel their son to lift back on to his shoulders she slipped her arm through his. Among so many sad things, so much pain and unhappiness, her own joy seemed miraculous: a hard-won, precariously existing miracle.

'I'm glad I came to see them,' she said as they set off along the road. 'But I don't think I'll want to come again.' She felt oddly lost now, out in the country, without that sinuous line of water to guide her, to show her where she belonged.

'Today is today,' she said to Joel suddenly. He looked down at her, not quite sure what she meant. 'No one can take today away, whatever else happens.'

He did understand. 'No. Let's try and make a good tomorrow too.'

'Come on.' She squeezed his arm affectionately. 'Let's get back to the cut. Let's go home.'

Water Gypsies

Part One

1942–3

One

August 1942

'There we are, my dear.' The midwife leaned over to receive the baby from the doctor after the cord was cut. 'And it's another little lady!'

In a moment the screams of the second twin joined those of her sister, who was already lying, wrapped in a scrap of sheet, in an apple box on the side bed of the cabin.

The young mother's groans of pain had ceased and she lay back, drained of strength, without even the energy to raise her head and look at her babies. Her eyes were glazed with exhaustion, the dark hair slicked to her head. She seemed barely conscious as the doctor stitched her up. The second babe had been awkwardly positioned and he had resorted to forceps.

Miss Lyons, the midwife, stepped outside onto the counter at the back of the boat while he finished off, pleased to be out of the blasted man's way. She was running with sweat, her hair damp round her temples and the nape of her neck, but it was blazing hot outside, the breeze so sluggish that it was barely more than a ripple against her clammy skin. She perched on the gunwale, wiped her face with her hanky and let out a long sigh. Thank heavens that was over! She could scarcely remember a labour that she had so dearly wanted finished, such was the distress and fragility of the mother. And birthing women in these cabins was a challenge all of its own, with it being dark and no more room than a shoebox, and the stove lit – in this weather! – to boil water. It was like a furnace in there. Even so, the doctor had done more than his fair share of complaining, she thought.

When she'd realized it was twins and sent to him for assistance, only one of them could attend to Mrs Bartholomew at a time and neither could stand up fully without hitting their head on the ceiling. The doctor, who was new to delivering boaters' babies, had cursed disbelievingly at the lack of space.

At last he emerged from the cabin with his bag, clothes crumpled and puce in the face.

'All yours,' he said curtly. 'Everything's as it should be.'

The air in the cabin smelt rank with sweat and blood.

'Let's get you all cleaned up now, shall we?' Miss Lyons said kindly, pouring water from the kettle. Poor lamb, she thought, watching the silent figure lying limply on the stained bedding. Many of the boatwomen she saw were hardened and robust, born to the life, but this one was finding it all a struggle, though she certainly tried hard. She occasionally saw Mrs Bartholomew standing at the helm of the *Theodore* in her long, dark skirts with a colourful scarf round her hair, a slim, wiry figure, chin jutting out at a determined angle. There were usually one or two of the kiddies up on the cabin roof. Course, she'd had a bad time losing that last little one, and now she looked so beaten down. The cabin floor was covered in filth and the crochet work along the shelves, which the most houseproud boatwomen kept scrubbed white, had turned a jaundiced grey. As she washed the young woman's body, talking soothingly to her, she couldn't help but see the bug-bites on her skin. The bed was

4

obviously alive: she'd have a little word once things were sorted out.

Maryann could barely even manage to open her eyes, even though the babies were crying for attention. Miss Lyons gave each of them a quick dunking, which made them roar even more, then wrapped them securely in the old bits of sheet and blanket Maryann had put ready.

'Come on now, lovey – these little ones need you,' she said gently. 'Let's get you sat up a bit. We'll get a nice cup of tea down you and I'll show you how to feed them both at once, shall I?'

She helped Maryann position the infants to suckle, and the cabin suddenly went quiet, except for one of the babies making tiny squeaks as she fed. Miss Lyons perched beside her as the tea brewed.

'Well, you've done it. And these two look fit as fiddles. How d'you feel?'

Maryann looked up at her, lank hair falling down each side of her thin cheeks. She tried to smile.

'As if I've been under a tram!' But her eyes filled and her mouth wobbled. 'Oh, Lord above – twins! Whatever'm I going to do?' Tears rolled down her face. 'I can hardly manage the other three as it is – what with everything else.'

'It's a shock, I know.' The midwife touched her hand comfortingly. She was about thirty, not much older than Maryann herself, though she seemed far more mature, a motherly person, with a round, pink face and blonde hair. She had delivered Maryann's last son, Harry, and had wept with her when eleven months later Harry, sick with pneumonia, gasped out his last breath on a November day as grey and hard as the steel billets they were carrying in the boats. When she came this time to attend to Maryann in early labour, she put her instrument to

Maryann's ripe belly and kept moving it about, frowning.

Eventually she said, 'I'm sure I can hear two heart-beats.' She looked into Maryann's eyes. 'Did you know you were carrying twins?'

Maryann stared down at them now, each suckling a breast. She was very sore underneath from the stitches, and the babies' feeding made her belly contract so that she winced with pain. The midwife had shown her how to hold them facing her and latch them on with their legs back under her arms, supported by a pillow just behind her on each side. The girls sucked greedily. The larger of the two was dark haired, but the other had ginger colouring like their father. The combination of the pain and her confused emotions of wonder at her new babies and dread of what their arrival would mean made her cry all the more.

'Here –' Miss Lyons helped her sip the sweet tea – 'let's get some energy into you. Husband off with a load today, is he?'

Maryann nodded, managing to free a hand to wipe her eyes. 'Only to the Light. He'll be back soon.'

'They're a good size, anyway, the two of them,' the midwife comforted her. 'Both over five pounds – that makes things easier. You've done ever so well. There's just one thing – you know you've got a little problem with vermin in the bed, don't you?'

'I know.' Maryann blushed miserably. 'Only we've been so pushed on this last trip and I was so heavy and tired and there was all that rain on the way up . . .'

'Of course, of course – I just thought I'd mention it. You can stove the place as soon as you're on your feet again. And you *will* cope, dear, I'm quite sure. I know you boatwomen – you're marvellous.'

6

With further words of comfort and advice she left, saying she'd come back later and urging Maryann to 'have a nap while you can, lovey'.

Stepping out onto the path in the sultry afternoon, she looked back at the tiny cabin and shook her head. *Good luck to her*, she thought, *because, my goodness, she's going to need it.*

Though she was exhausted, Maryann found it impossible to sleep. Childbirth sent her into a high, jangled state from which it took time to come down, and she was conscious of the two snuffling bundles on the bed beside her. Carefully, wincing at the pain from her stitches, she leaned up on her elbow and looked into their tiny, squashed faces. So sweet, they were, so beautiful! And healthy by the look of them, thank heavens.

'Hello, our girls,' she whispered tenderly. Tears filled her eyes again. 'I just hope you're not going to be the death of me.' She felt so worn down, so alone. She'd had no idea how hard this life would be, and harder all the time as they had more children. Other boatwomen – *real* boatwomen – always seemed so tough and capable. Some boats were more rough and ready than others, of course, but they had grown up seeing their mothers cope with all their offspring in these cramped cabins, which were only nine feet long by seven wide. They'd grown up used to the life, whereas Maryann was increasingly coming to feel she couldn't cope any more. Joel, bless him, was such a loving husband, but he often seemed to forget than she was not a narrowboatwoman born and bred. Even after eight years on the cut, she still felt she was having to prove herself, and lately all she had felt was that she was making a miserable job of it.

She lay back, feeling as weak as a baby herself and about to give in to a good weep, when she heard distant voices on the path, and a moment later someone leapt onto the counter of the butty and knocked on the open hatch.

'Coo-ee! Anyone home?'

Maryann's heart beat faster with pleasure. 'Nance?' She pulled aside the red gingham curtains which screened the bed. 'Oh, Nance, am I glad to see you! Get yourself in here, quick!'

A pair of worn, brown boots appeared on the coalbox, and then a long black skirt fastened at the waist by a belt with a brass buckle and a dark blouse scattered with huge, scarlet flowers. A second later, Nance's face followed on, weatherbeaten and brown as a berry, topped by her unruly black curls. In her ears were large, gold hoops. Following her was her daughter Rose, a two-year-old, robust, curly-haired copy of her mother.

'We've only just got in. They said you was here. You've had it then?' Her brown eyes were full of delight and anticipation. 'Thought I'd come along and find you screaming blue murder!'

Maryann pulled back the shawl covering the two infants and Nance's mouth gaped open.

'Two? Oh my word – twins? Look, our Rose, two babbies! Oh, Maryann!' She sat down on the edge of the bed, staring at them in astonishment, then leaned back and let out her loud, deep laugh. 'Oh my God! Ooh, they're beautiful, Maryann, that they are –' She wiped her eyes. 'But you're going to have your work cut out for you, aren't you? – No, don't poke them Rose, gentle now! – What are they? Wenches?'

Maryann nodded. Seeing Nance had made her feel better already. They'd been friends since childhood in

Birmingham; their men, Joel and Darius, were brothers from the Bartholomew family, from generations of boaters. The two women knew each other back to front and they were both from 'off the bank', not born on the cut. In Nance's company, Maryann was completely at home. With the life on the cut of long journeys and chance meetings, they sometimes didn't see each other for weeks on end and she was always overjoyed to see Nance, and never more so than now.

'Twins – fancy. And you never knew?'

'Not till the midwife said. Got a hell of a shock – I still can't take it in. Though, thinking back, carrying them was like having a flaming great octopus squirming about inside, so I should've guessed.'

'What you going to call them?'

'I've hardly thought yet.' Maryann eased herself up, grimacing.

'Bit sore are we?' Nance said sympathetically, but then pulled a mocking face.

'Stop making me laugh!' Maryann groaned, laughing anyway and trying to find a way of sitting comfortably.

'So where's your old man – he taken a load up?'

'Mr Veater's sent him to the 'Lectric Light.'

Maryann was lying in her usual sleeping quarters on the butty boat, *Theodore*, one of a pair which she and Joel worked for the carrier S. E. Barlow. They were moored up at Sutton Stop, the boaters' name for Hawkesbury Junction at the meeting of the Oxford and Coventry Canals, where they usually received their carrying orders from Mr Veater, the traffic control officer. Many a child came into the world at the 'back of Mr Veater's shed', and Samuel Barlow and Mr Veater would kindly send the expectant father on short-haul trips while his wife and 'mate' was indisposed. Joel and Bobby, the lad who worked with them, had taken the motor boat, the *Esther Jane*, on a local trip to Baddesly colliery to bring coal back for the Coventry's Light – the voracious power station at Longford. With them they'd taken Maryann's other three children – Joley, who was seven, Sally, five, and Ezra, three.

'We've just come up from the jam hole,' Nance said, referring to the jam factory at Southall, which was always hungry for coal. 'And we brought a load of cement up for some airstrip they're putting in, worse luck – filthy lot that was. I'll have to get back and clean up. Here – let's have another cuppa first, though.' She reached up to the cabin roof for the painted water carrier – to the annoyment of Spots, one of the family's two cats, who had been snoozing in its small patch of shade – filled the kettle and set it to boil again on the tiny range just inside the door. 'I'll go and fill your cans for you and get your groceries in – and I'll bring a bite to eat round later for you and Joel. The kids can come and eat with us tonight. Save you moving.'

'Thanks,' Maryann whispered, tears welling in her eyes. 'You're golden you are.'

'Nah,' Nance said easily. 'It's not every day you have twins, is it?'

Maryann was ashamed of the state of the stove, all grease and rust spots. She hadn't got round to cleaning or blacking it. She watched Nance move about so capably. Nancy had taken to the life and never looked back, especially as she'd had to risk so much to be with Darius, leaving her violent husband, Mick, to whom she was still officially married. Except during the unhappiest time of her marriage, Nance had always been full of wiry energy, a tomboy as a child, who now managed the all-weathers, ever-demanding work of the cut with vigour and enthusiasm. She even looked the part, with her dark hair and earrings glinting in the light from outside. But just as Maryann was about to pour out her woes, her fear of how she was going to manage, Nance turned, the teapot in her hands.

'I've got news for you an' all – I'm expecting again!'

Maryann swallowed the lump in her throat and tried to smile. She knew how much this meant to Nance. Her marriage to Mick had been childless and she'd ached for babies of her own. Now she already had Darry, Sean and Rose, but at the turn of the year she'd miscarried and Maryann knew how upset she'd been.

'Oh, Nance – that's lovely!' Maryann hoped Nance couldn't hear the tears in her voice. 'I'm ever so pleased for you both!'

They spent half an hour, snatched away from Nance's chores, drinking tea, and Nancy handed her a good hunk of bread with more butter than the scraping of wartime frugality allowed.

'You should have triple ration today!' she said, as Maryann ate ravenously. The twins slept and for the moment Maryann felt quite lifted out of herself and less desperate as she reminisced with Nance. She even managed to doze for a little after Nance left, and the twins, exhausted from the process of coming into the world, slept on.

Joel got back in late that night when Joley, Sally and Ezra were already asleep on the *Esther Jane*.

'Two little 'uns, then?' he said in wonder. His thick beard glowed bronze in the lamplight and he sat, his burly form perched on the edge of the bed, staring at the two little girls. In the light from the oil lamp, the look on his tired, gentle face at the sight of his new daughters filled Maryann with a deep, poignant joy. There was

11

such pride, such tenderness, in his eyes. She told herself how ungrateful she was being to feel so burdened by the arrival of these little ones. She'd made Joel so happy! He was always cock-a-hoop at the births of their children. And she couldn't help remembering the last one, when he first saw their little Harry with his pale hair, now in his grave in a Banbury churchyard. Joel had been heart-broken when they lost him. It was the only time she had seen him cry like a child himself.

'I think that one looks like an Esther,' Maryann said, pointing at the dark-haired infant who was lying dozily beside her. 'And madam here – ' the ginger-headed one was at her breast, a tiny fist flailing in the air – the fidgety one – well, she seems more of an Ada to me.'

Joel's eyes met hers and he reached over to stroke her head, drawing her closer to kiss her lips.

'Thanks, my little nipper. Thanks, my lovely.'

Maryann smiled back at him, her feelings twisting inside. He was so loving, his children meant so much to him after his years of struggling on alone with his father. How could she ever deny him this joy and satisfaction? But couldn't he see it was wearing her down, all of it, week by week, until she wondered if one day she would just drop with exhaustion and sink under the waters for good?

Two

'Hello, my sweet little bird.'

Joel's warm hand moved over her in the darkness. They were in their bed in the *Theodore*, the babies Esther and Ada deep in a snuffling sleep together in a nest of bedding on the floor. The other children were with Bobby on the *Esther Jane* to keep them from being disturbed by the twins' nightly squalling when they woke to be fed.

Maryann lay facing the back wall, the bulwark between cabin and cargo, eyes squeezed closed. Joel's hand brushed her hair back and kissed the nape of her neck. This whiskery tickling used to make her giggle so she couldn't keep up any pretence of being asleep. And the girls were nearly six weeks old now; her stitches had healed. Her husband wanted her. What reason could she find for depriving him any longer? Yet the thought filled her with dread.

Opening her eyes, she turned slightly towards him. There was nothing to see. The lights were out in the cabin, checked curtains drawn across the bedspace.

'My girl . . . My lovely . . .' He was easing up her shift, kissing her breasts, and she stiffened against him. She was alarmed at herself. Hadn't she always loved his caresses? Loved being held and cuddled close? Making love with Joel was such a solid, reassuring thing. She loved lying with him in the cosy light from the lamp,

13

taking time to look into his face, stroking the strong hairs of his beard, seeing the love in his eyes. She would run her hand across the firey hair on his chest, down over his belly, its comforting softness into which she could burrow, teasing, nuzzling, yet tight like a drum when he tensed. She had been so afraid at first, at the thought of lovemaking, after her stepfather. But she had pushed those memories away, buried them deep and learned how to love Joel.

And yes, she did love him, with all her heart, and would have turned to him happily, tired as she was, if it was not for the thought of another child. She lay beside him stiffly, frightened to respond. She couldn't face all that again. Not the sickness, the feeling so done in that sometimes she nearly fell asleep at the helm of the butty, the gruelling agony of birthing them . . . and all that even before the constant worry of their little lives. Of them toppling off the boats, catching in the locks, or falling sick like their poor Harry, who never got better.

'Joel?' she whispered. 'I can't. Not another babby. Not yet.'

He nuzzled her, stroking her belly. It was stretched now, used. A place for people to stop in for a while, she thought, like a cabin. She felt like a battered old boat, trying to keep moving on.

'You won't, will you? Not so quick after the last?'

'I don't know,' she pleaded. She knew nothing about how her body worked, what she could do to keep things under control.

Joel lay back with a long sigh which cut right through her. Her ghosts, her insecurities, crowded in. She hated to hurt him, to refuse him anything. She knew how kind he was, how loving. He didn't complain about any of her shortcomings. But what he called his 'bit of loving' was so important to him. He never tired of her: she was his wife and he needed it from her. What if she couldn't give it to him? What then? He had taken her in, saved her, and her greatest fear was that of being without him.

'Joel?' She reached over and kissed him and Joel took this as a sign that he should continue. They clung together in the darkness and soon she heard his quick gasps of need and pleasure as he moved on top of her, and she felt the bite of him entering her, that pain of the first time after a birth. But the sharpness did not last and she held him close as he rested in her afterwards. He laughed softly, close to her ear.

'Back to normal,' he whispered. 'My dear one. With our lovely family. We'll make Number Ones out of them again – you'll see. We will.'

His arm round her waist, he fell into a deep, satisfied sleep.

The next day they set out to take coal to Birmingham. Bobby Jenks, a twenty-year-old lad from another boating family, had been working with them for a couple of years. Working a motor and butty two-handed with children had soon proved too much for Maryann. 'Bow-hauling' the butty, having to haul it by hand with ropes into locks, was almost too much for her small frame, and she worried constantly about the children's safety. They needed a third hand. They'd had a succession of helpers, but now Bobby had stuck – he was a good worker who'd been steering boats solo by the age of seven or eight. He was a strong, cheerful lad, with a head of wild hair and a sudden, cheeky smile. His family, the Jenks, were a much respected family of Number Ones who had been working boats for generations, but had now also sold out to Samuel Barlow. Bobby had been schooled in the true boatman's qualities of agility and hard work, as well as a quiet courtesy, and Maryann had never had any problems with him joining them. Though she was only a few years older, she had developed a motherly fondness for him.

Joel had worked short trips with the monkey, or motor boat, during those weeks. Maryann stayed tied up at Sutton Stop to get to grips with looking after two extra children and to go and be churched in the parish of Longford. One day, when Nancy and Darius tied up there again, she was able to leave the twins with Nance and go into Coventry to collect new ration books and indulge in a beautiful long soak in the public baths. She knew she'd had more rest than most boatwomen had after their births.

The twins took it out of her good and proper and she often felt weak and tired, but Nance had been a marvellous support. Darius had left her with them for a couple of days, working his boats two-handed with a lad on board, and she helped Maryann stove the cabins and scrub and clean them. She'd washed the curtains and crochet work, hanging them in a flapping line along the *Theodore* to dry in the August sunshine, then polished the brass strips on the chimneys and knobs on the doors.

Maryann sat feeding the babies, watching helplessly, but with relief and gratitude as Nance whisked about, while Joley, Sally and Ezra played with Darry, Sean and Rose on the bank. Darius had tied a rope to the branch of a tree and knotted a stick onto the bottom to serve as a seat. The older ones were having a fine time, swinging and whooping as they did so.

'You can start off nice and fresh now, can't you?' Nance said, blacking the stove.

'It looks lovely,' Maryann said, gloomily wondering to herself how long it would last. *What's the matter with me?* she asked herself. She never seemed to feel she could get on top of things somehow. She'd wanted to keep such high standards on the boats, like some of the boatwomen whose curtains and pinners were immaculate, their brasses winking in the sun against the bright colours of the boats. She dreaded their scorn. They seem to accept her because she had married Joel, who was so respected, one of the old families of Number Ones who owned their own boats, even though the declining trade had forced them to sell out to Essy Barlow before the war.

'You'll soon pick up,' Nance said. 'Eh – ' she turned to look at Maryann, cloth in hand – 'I hope Darius's going to get us a load up to Brum one of these days. I want to go and see our mom.'

Maryann nodded. She couldn't say she felt the same about seeing her own mother.

'Still gives me a shock when I go there – the mess! Great holes and that all over the place. I'm glad we were out of it, really.'

They had been aware of the Blitz, of course. Who couldn't be? And there were a few hairy nights round Birmingham, Coventry and the London docks when the bombing had come frighteningly close. But in many ways life went on much the same on the cut, war or no war, except for identity cards and ration books. The sides of the locks and the bridge-holes were painted white, and they'd had to keep the hatches closed at night and paint over the lamps on the boats for the blackout regulations, but in the countryside and along the cut things went on much as usual, except that now there was an increase in traffic. More loads to fuel the war effort:

17

to make munitions and vehicles, to build air strips and shadow factories.

They travelled into Birmingham from the north side, along the Bottom Road or Birmingham–Fazeley Canal. Maryann knew this was most people's least favourite trip. They came in from the collieries, their boats loaded up and low in the water. Once they'd got past Minworth, coming into Brum, the cut became more and more filthy, walled in by factories and warehouses and built over so heavily that it seemed steeped in muck and gloom. On top of that the locks were all single, so instead of being able to breast up the motor and butty side by side and put them through, the butty had to be bow-hauled in with a rope, which was exhausting. Thank heavens they had Bobby with them!

It was here you could see a few more signs of the war. She caught glimpses of fat, fish-shaped barrage balloons in the sky. As the city closed in, she was filled with an increasing sense of unease. Her mother still lived here and her two brothers, and it was where she came from, yet Birmingham could always arouse the painful memories buried inside her, which she tried strenuously never to think about. Above all, she dreaded ever seeing *him*. What was he calling himself these days? she wondered. To her he had been Norman Griffin, undertaker, wrecker of her family, thief of her childhood, and the man responsible for her sister's death. He had disappeared afterwards, and none of them knew where he was. But he must be somewhere, could easily still be in Birmingham.

Once, just once after all this time, she thought she saw him. It was a few months ago when they were tied up at Tyseley, one smoky, drizzling winter night. A figure walking along the wharf caught her eye, making her freeze inside. Moving along the row of warehouses ahead of the boats was a dark figure, burly, hat pulled down so that she could see nothing of his face except the glowing tip of a cigarette. There was something in the build, the gait ... Maryann stepped down onto the coalbox and peered out.

'Mom – what're you doing?' Joley asked, puzzled at his mother bobbing in the hatches.

'Nothing – just eat your piece,' she snapped.

Narrowing her eyes, she watched, heart thumping, as the figure moved further along then out of sight. Joley had squeezed in front of her.

'Who was that?' he said, following her gaze.

'No one, Joley. Come on – let's see if we can find a scrape of jam to go with that, eh?'

It was ridiculous, she knew. He was long gone with his foul, cunning ways. With his disfigurement he wouldn't be able to con his way into another family to trap its daughters in fear and shame. Margaret had seen to that. Little Margaret, whose widowed mother had innocently taken on the 'respectable Mr Lambert' as he was calling himself then, after he left Maryann's mother. Margaret, whom he had pushed past the bounds of sanity. Margaret, who was in the asylum now ... The feelings began to rise in her, swelling until her very veins seemed ready to burst with rage, with shame. She was breathing as if she had been running. No, she must push this away! All the memories he brought with him of her past, of her dead sister Sal. That wasn't the man she saw – it was a mistake. Norman Griffin belonged to the past and there he must stay. Ever since that day she had frozen out those thoughts. She was never going to think about the past again.

When they tied up that afternoon at Tyseley Wharf,

19

she left the babies and Ezra with Joel and took Joley and Sally with her to pick up groceries, the ration books pushed into her pocket. As they crossed the wharf, she caught sight of a gangling young man in dark clothes which appeared too large for him passing in through the gates. Tucked under his arm was a thick, black book.

Sally tugged on her arm. 'Who's that?'

Maryann barely glanced at him. 'Dunno. Some holy Joe I s'pose. Come on – let's get going.'

They shopped as fast as the queues and length of young children's legs would allow. Sally solemnly carried the bread. Joley staggered along, insisting he could manage the vegetables. At seven years old, he was already very strong.

'Now then,' Maryann said, 'shall we go and see Mr Osborne?'

Joley and Sally perked up.

'Will he have summat for us?' Joley asked.

'You'll have to wait and see, won't you?' She grinned at them. 'I think Mr Osborne must have filled his cellar with sweeties before the war like a squirrel, don't you?'

Mr Osborne owned a butcher's shop in one of the streets near the wharf. Maryann had switched to buying her meat from him over the past few months as she found him so cheerful and kind that she always looked forward to seeing him. He made a point of remembering their names, invariably had a treat to offer the children and tried to stretch the ration for her as far as possible, unlike some other shopkeepers, who would scrimp on it. He seemed to have taken a shine to her, so that now Joel teased her whenever they reached Tyseley. 'Off to see your fancy man then?' and she'd protest, 'He's old enough to be my father, you daft thing!'

Osborne's shop had an entry along one side and Joley

and Sally always liked to run up and down it. Houses, with their warrens of entries and back yards, were an exciting novelty for them, coming off the cut.

'Come on,' Maryann scolded. 'I want to get home today!'

The shop window was bare, denuded of its peacetime array of joints and chops. It was hard to get hold of anything but essentials these days. As the door opened with a 'ping', they walked into the smell of meat and sawdust and saw that Mr Osborne still had a decorative pig's head on the counter with an apple in its mouth, something that always fascinated the children.

'Ah, hello there!' Mr Osborne cried. He was a short, comforting looking man in his white overall, balding crown lapped by soft white hair. Despite his friendliness he had a hesitant, shy way with him, barely meeting Maryann's eyes, but he was always very attentive towards the children.

'Down at the wharf again then? Seems a long time since you were last here. Now, you youngsters, before your mother and I get down to business, how about a chocolate lime each?'

Joley and Sally nodded with delighted smiles.

'Thought you must be sold out as there's no queue,' Maryann said as he handed out the pale green sweets.

'Oh – never you fear.' Mr Osborne went briskly back behind the counter, while Joley and Sally drew patterns in sawdust with their feet across the black and white tiles.

'There, just a bit extra,' he said, eyeing the scales as he weighed her mince and began parcelling it up. 'Everyone well on board?'

'Yes – thanks.' She told him about the twins and Mr Osborne went quite soppy, marvelling at the thought.

'No wonder you look tired. I thought there was something – dark rings under the eyes. Well, well. Bring them in and let me see them next time, won't you? Nothing like new, young life.'

Maryann asked after Mrs Osborne. The couple lived a few streets away rather than over the shop.

'It's the smell, you see,' Mr Osborne had explained once. 'It's a silly thing, really, but the wife's almost a vegetables-only sort of eater. We're a bit like Jack Sprat and his wife! She can't tolerate the smell, you see, not living here . . . So I rent out the upstairs, off and on.'

'Anyway.' He smiled now. 'I'm glad all's well. What're the names of your boats again?'

'The *Esther Jane* and the *Theodore*,' Joley and Sally piped up.

'Of course, of course,' he laughed. 'Now –' he held up one finger like a magician about to perform his most demanding act – 'I've got something special for you. A little treat – no charge.'

Disappearing out the back for a moment he returned with a male pheasant, fully feathered.

'Here we go – no questions asked. Have that to be going on with.'

It was the season, of course. Out in the country they kept hearing the sharp squawk of the birds across the fields. If they'd had a dog they could have nipped one in the bag more often, but they only had cats now. Jep the old dog had died years back. And all food was welcome.

'Thanks ever so much,' she said, taking the dead weight of the bird from him across the counter. 'Are you sure you don't want anything for it?'

'No, no. Growing family you've got . . .' He seemed almost bashful. 'Will you be coming up this way again soon?'

'Oh – you never know.' She gave the children a look that indicated it was time to go. 'Pick up your bags,' she told them. 'We can never be sure where we'll be off to next.'

'See you again, then,' he said.

They pinged their way out, Maryann saying, 'Ta for the bird,' once more.

'I think he must like us,' she said to the children as they headed back to the wharf. 'Not sure why, though.'

'I think he likes *us*, not you,' Sally said smugly. 'He gives us sweets, not you.'

'Huh!' Maryann said indignantly. 'He gave me a pheasant, didn't he?'

'He says there was a bloke round looking for you!'

The lad ran out of the toll office the next morning, urgent with a message which he had remembered at the last minute. He pursued the butty, shouting to Maryann.

'Me?' Maryann squinted across at him, with Esther held in one arm and the tiller under the other. 'Oh – ta. That'll be my brother. If he comes again, tell him I've had twin girls. I'll drop him a line when I get a minute!'

The boat slid away faster, her words unfurling behind it. She attempted a weary smile, as Bobby, who had been checking the snubber, climbed back towards her over the sheeted-up planks and took the tiller. Her younger brother Tony was the one person in her family she had any contact with now. She didn't know if the message would get through, but it was nice to think of him coming to look. It gave her a feeling of ties, however slim. Joel's family, the surviving members of the Bartholomews who had not been taken by war or sickness or the dangers of the cut, shared strong bonds. Being with them made her feel safe and protected.

Maryann stood in the hatches for a few moments cradling Esther, while Bobby steered the butty. Joel, as normal nowadays, had their sons aboard the *Esther Jane* with him. Sally was on the roof of the *Theodore* next to the chimney, smudging her fingers in the dust and murmuring to herself. The cut was busy with joeys and other working pairs, and the sounds of traffic clattering over bridges, a train, a screech of metal from a nearby works, filled the air. It was a beautiful, early autumn morning, and even the weary, soot-choked walls, the glamourless industrial buildings cramped shoulder to shoulder, took on a pleasing mellowness in the rich light. A feeling of sudden, swelling contentment rose in her and after the past weeks of feeling so drained and tired she felt more optimistic. The night had not been so bad – she had only been up once with the girls – and with more sleep and in the freshness of morning she looked at her old home with fondness and a touch of regret.

It'll be all right, she thought. *At least today. I can manage today . . .* She didn't want to count her chickens too soon, but it was a moment of lightness after so many exhausting weeks. She saw Joel ahead of her and watched him tenderly, doing so expertly what he had always done. What he was born for. *Nothing like this life*, she thought, suddenly full of optimism. *Maybe I can manage. I can get by, so long as . . .*

The worry was there, always, the deep pang of dread. So long as she didn't fall with another child. Not yet. Preferably not ever. But please God – she repeated the prayer she'd made in the church at Longford – no more babbies for a long time yet.

Three

The trip down to Oxford was always Maryann's favourite. The cut followed a beautiful, winding route along the toes of hillsides, past Braunston and round the curves south of Napton, where the sails of the ruined mill on the hill appeared then disappeared with each bend, only to appear again unexpectedly a few wiggles later. They were blessed with glowing autumn days, early morning mists over the water, berries clustered red in the hedgerows and early frosts.

This route was the first Maryann had ever travelled with Joel and his father, many years ago now, it seemed to her, when as a desperately unhappy child she'd run away from home and asked to stay on the boat with him. There were always ghosts of her former self along the way. There were also, along the route at Claydon, Cropredy, Fenny Compton, the familiar faces of lock-keepers and lengthsmen and their families, other boat families and smiles and hellos from behind the counters of pubs, tiny grocer's shops, and bakeries, greetings of 'Nice to see you down this way again!' and exclamations at the sight of the twins. Sometimes the cut and its people felt like an extended family, one in which Maryann had always done her utmost to try and belong and be accepted.

Joel knew this section of the cut so intimately that a newly felled tree, a section of the path more or less overgrown than usual or a silted bend in need of dredging where the propeller struggled and threatened to go aground – all these details he noticed at once. And it was this cut, the Oxford, which Maryann knew gave him the most poignant reminders of what had been lost. Though he seldom spoke of it, she knew it cut Joel to the heart that the old ways were slipping into the past: that he was no longer a Number One like his father had been, with his own boat, a king of the cut, gliding along silently, accompanied not by the relentless grinding of the engine, but pulled by a horse, its hooves and the chink of the harness or flick of a rope the only sounds, except for those of animals and birds and the swish of water. There were certainly compensations for working for an agent like Samuel Barlow, one of which was not having to chase loads. Essy sorted those out, as well as maintaining the boats and paying tolls and insurance. For Maryann these seemed adequate compensation. They still had the *Esther Jane*, after all. But for Joel being *owned*, having S. E. Barlow painted across the panel of the *Esther Jane* amid her roses and castles instead of the name Bartholomew and No. 1 – no, she knew there wasn't a day that passed without him still thinking of this painfully.

It wasn't just ownership. The demise of horse-pulled boats meant that a way of life which had previously supported all sorts of other tradesmen – stable hands, saddlers, blacksmiths – was also disappearing. A number of them had gone off to war. Even some of the lock-keepers were now in the ARP. Though the cut was now busier than it had been for years, friendly faces were gone. And Joel had plenty of time to brood on the fact as he steered the monkey boat up front, still with the proud, upright stance of a Number One, but feeling aggrieved, diminished inside.

When the boats were empty they travelled with the butty tied up close behind the motor, which meant that the butty needed little steering. This was usually not for long, between dropping off one load and collecting another, and Maryann made the most of her hands being free to get ahead with cleaning or cooking and feeding the twins. The *Theodore* was their family butty now since, not having a motor on board, the cabin was a little bigger. So when she wasn't steering she could duck inside and put the kettle on or see to the babies' napkins.

Once there was a load on, however, the butty was towed further behind, the snubber or towing rope extended seventy feet between the two, and it was necessary to steer almost all the time to prevent the butty veering from side to side, out of control. On a long pound with no locks Bobby came back and steered, jumping off the *Esther Jane* under a bridge-hole where the cut narrowed right down, then leaping easily onto the *Theodore* as it came past.

Without Bobby life would have been impossible. Even before Ada and Esther were born, Maryann found the days a long succession of strains and stresses. There never seemed to be a moment when she could relax. As well as keeping the boats moving and steering, there were constant thoughts of *Oh, I must make a cup of tea* or *I must get the dinner on*, or *the stove and floor need cleaning*, or *Sally and Ezra are bored and roaring on the cabin roof*. Not to mention all the washing, mending and shopping she had to to catch up with when they stopped to unload. She had forced herself to develop the other boatwomen's ability to perform several tasks all at once. Everyone did it – there was no choice. You'd tuck the helm, or 'elum' as the boaters called it, under one arm, and with the dipper full of water and potatoes on the roof, stand and peel them as you went along. Or you'd sew or splice ropes – whatever was needed. There was one woman she saw sometimes with a sewing machine in action on the cabin roof while she steered her butty boat.

This particular trip they had a 'good road'. There were so many possible calamities and delays on the cut – clogged propellers, other boats stuck in locks or bridge-holes when the water was low, locks all set against you, not to mention foul weather – that they had developed a patient fatalism which overlay the general need to get a load on and keep moving.

They reached Juxon Street Wharf in Oxford a bit later than hoped, after a delay on the second day with a snarled propeller south of Duke's cut. As the men began unloading, Maryann set off, a twin under each arm and Sally and Joley beside her, to go and 'find Granddad'. The chores could wait a few minutes while she went to the little terraced house in Adelaide Street nearby to tell old Darius Bartholomew that they'd tied up at the wharf. The old man never missed possible moment on his old home, the *Esther Jane*.

The door was opened by his sister, Mrs Simons, a rosy-cheeked, sweet-natured woman, who still had a look of the boatwoman she once was, her stout body dressed in a dark blue skirt, topped by a rusty red woolly. Her feet were pushed into baggy old slippers to ease her bunions.

'Oh, *hello*, moy dear! Oh, my goodness me, look what we have here?' She gazed, astonished at the sight of Maryann's face smiling out between those of the two babies. 'Come in, come in! Hello, Joley, Sally, Ezzy – how're you, moy dears? Darius – look who's here!

You'll be wanting to see! – Come on through – he's having a snooze by the fire,' she added.

Though Mrs Simons had not lived on the cut for many years now, her backroom looked like a home from home, a larger version of a narrowboat cabin, with its gleaming range and colourful peg rug, and plates, their filigreed edges threaded with ribbons, and photographs and brasses displayed all over the walls. Maryann's father-in-law was getting out of his chair by the fire. Darius was in his shirt sleeves and adjusted his braces as he smiled shyly. Maryann was always delighted to see him. He looked just the same, she thought, lined face suntanned even in winter, the white beard and long white hair round his bald crown, the same sinewy, if slightly stooped stance. His deep blue eyes lit up with pleasure at the sight of them all.

'Well now, lass – what've we got here?' Though he knew Maryann had been expecting, this was the first time they had been to Oxford since the girls arrived.

'Look at these two!' Alice Simons exclaimed. 'Here, your arms must be pulled out of their sockets. Put them down on my chair!' Maryann laid the girls down and they kicked and gazed round, stimulated by the faces looking down at them. Esther smiled and blew bubbles. Ada kicked and moved her head, trying to see everything.

'This one is Esther,' Maryann said softly. The old man's wife, Joel's mother, his 'best mate' for years on the cut, had been called Esther Jane. When she died, he had renamed the boat in her honour. 'And this is Ada.'

A wistful smile appeared on the old man's face. He watched the babies, fascinated.

'Two of them,' he said eventually. He shook his head in wonder. 'With the best names.'

Tears came into Maryann's eyes. She could tell how moved this reserved old man was at the sight of his granddaughters and she loved him for it. He stood for a long time, eyes fixed on them.

'Bonny,' he said eventually. 'Very bonny, the pair of 'em.' As he passed Maryann, for a second she felt his hand pressed warmly on her shoulder. He went to the front and they heard him putting on his jacket and old trilby. The front door opened and closed. Darius didn't want to be away from the *Esther Jane* a moment longer.

'Well now,' Mrs Simons said, 'we'll have a nice cup of tea. Let those men do the stroving – you stay here and have yourself a rest, moy dear.' She filled the kettle and set it on the range, where it whispered as it heated up. 'Now – I want a nice long hold of these lovely babies.'

They passed a happy hour together. Joley and Sally always enjoyed the novelty of being in a house, which seemed like a palace to them in comparison with the *Theodore*. Mrs Simons found them some bits and pieces to play with and they went out the back to see the chickens. Maryann settled contentedly with the old lady, who had always been kindness itself to her. Whenever they came to Oxford, Maryann felt she was truly coming to see family. Alice had been heartbroken for them when they'd lost Harry.

Alice Simons cuddled Ada and Esther in turn, talking to them, making them smile. When they started squalling she handed them back to be fed.

'Our Nancy's expecting again,' Maryann told her. 'Pleased as punch about it she is.' Nancy and Darius had been working the Grand Union a lot recently and hadn't been down to Oxford.

She had Alice Simons's immediate attention. 'Oh well, isn't that nice! Marvellous. You girls've been such a blessing to Esther's boys. She keeping all right, is she? And how're you managing, Maryann dear?'

'Oh – I'm all right,' Maryann said. There was a silence. The clocked ticked. She so longed to pour out her worries to someone. She'd met boatwomen who'd brought up fifteen children, more even, on the boats. Was that what Joel wanted? Children and more children in a never-ending line? She had some better days now, but come the hard winter, the times of heavy rain, of ice, she knew she'd start to feel herself sliding under it all again.

Hesitantly she said, 'I don't know how I'll manage if we have any more, though.'

'Oh no, dear.' Alice Simons snapped to attention, sitting forward to perch on the edge of her chair. 'Dear me, no. Thin as a railing you are already. No – child-bearing's all very well in its place, but you have to call a halt somewhere. My mother died after she'd had her eleventh. I saw her slip away – worn out she was, with it all. Now you know I was the eldest daughter, so of course I was landed with it all.' She shook her head.

Maryann thought bitterly for a second of her mother. Even if Flo had been prepared to see her, she'd never've been able to talk about anything like this. There'd be no sympathy there. Flo's attitude was always, 'I've had to suffer, so why shouldn't you?' Since she'd met Alice Simons, though, the old woman had always been on her side.

'I wasn't having that – not for me,' Alice went on. 'When I met moy William down here and we was wed I told him straight: "William, I said, "I'm not marrying you to be a brood mare like my mother." Well – as you know, we had the three, and they was enough for me. Quite enough. You want to look after yourself, dear.'

31

Maryann looked down at the colourful peg rug by the range, longing to ask the unspoken question which now hung between them. *But how did you keep from having any more?*

'Joel's a good boy – I've always said so,' Alice Simons was saying. 'I know the men in my family and we've never had a bad 'un. Not really. But they're men – you know what I'm saying, dear.' Maryann could feel a blush rising up her neck to her ears. What was Mrs Simons going to say next?

Just then Sally ran in from the back, her coat flying open, and clearly full of excitement.

'Them hens want some food!' she said. 'Can Joley and me give them some corn?'

Maryann clenched her hands, desperation rising in her. The moment was lost. She couldn't ask now.

'You go out to the privy,' Alice Simons said. 'And you and Joley take a couple of handfuls from the bag out there. Let Ezzy have a go too, there's a good girl. Shut the back door now!'

Sally's boots clattered out again in a great hurry.

Alice Simons leaned forward. 'I wouldn't normally say such a thing –' she touched Maryann's arm – 'because I know people don't go for talking about it. P'raps they *should*,' she added fiercely. 'Only I don't want to see you waning away in front of my eyes.' She lowered her voice. 'You'll have to have a word with Joel and get him to change his habits. You have to get them to pull back before they goes the whole way. That way you don't catch, see?'

The blush had taken over what felt like Maryann's entire body by now, but she looked back at Alice Simons with gratitude.

'Are you sure? Oh – I don't know if Joel . . .'

32

'Well, tell him it's that or nothing,' Alice said with a sniff. 'That'll make him think.'

Maryann looked down again, trying to imagine. *Is that really how you do it?* she wondered. *Joel gets so carried away. How am I going to ask him to stop?*

But she heard the urgency in Alice Simons's voice as she spoke again. 'Sometimes what it comes down to is it's them or you. And you don't want these children growing up without their mother, do you?'

Four

Old Darius Bartholomew was up to watch them pull away from Juxon Street Wharf early the next morning. Maryann saw him fade into the mist of an Oxford dawn, his face lined by time, just standing still in his coat and hat, eyes fixed on the boat as it moved away, putt-putting gently past the other moored craft. The sight of him wrung Maryann's heart, as she knew it did Joel's.

'He goes down to the wharf every day,' Mrs Simons told Maryann each time they visited. 'Every day without fail. Stands there watching. Poor Darius – he'd give anything to be young again.'

Maryann feared that the same fate – being left behind on the bank – would befall her husband and perhaps at a much earlier age. Joel's chest was weak from a dose of gas in the last war so his health was fragile. She had come to dread winter and the first cough. The crackling wheeze in his chest, which was always there, even in summer, was made far worse by the wet and cold which crept up on them through the autumn. She always hoped for Indian summers and mild winters, dreading his racking coughing fits, the risk of him falling so sick he could no longer work his boats. It was too painful to imagine Joel stranded on the bank with that deep, longing look she saw in his father's eyes. Darius, at least, was old. He had known it would come to him one day and he still had the comfort of knowing that his two sons and their families were working the cut.

They loaded a cargo of stone for Birmingham. The following days were wet, and in parts where the locks were widely spaced Maryann sat in the *Theodore* with the children, while Bobby took the helm. In between her chores she tried to teach Joley his letters.

'Oh, Mom, do I have to?' he'd complain as she tried to get him to stay at the table with a scrap of paper and a pencil.

'Just sit still for a minute and have a go,' Maryann urged. 'You don't want to grow up and not be able to read, do you?'

Joley shrugged, resting his chin wearily on his hand as if to say, 'Oh well, if I *have* to.' Maryann was unusual in being a woman on the cut who was a 'scholar'. Having been brought up on the bank, she had been to school until she was fourteen. She couldn't imagine what it must be like not to understand any of the signs in the shops or to read a newspaper, and she wanted her children to be able to do the same as her. But, to Joley, what counted in his everyday life was being able to catch a rope, jump on and off a boat or have the strength to shaft the fore end off the mud. Why did he need to know letters? With a long-suffering air he wrote his name, JOEL BARTHOL-OMEW, laboriously with the stub of pencil, tongue curled back over his top lip. She taught him to write THEODORE and ESTHER JANE and the names of other boats they passed, which he did under sufferance, wriggling wrestlessly all the time he was made to sit on the bench. Sally was quite different. Her clear blue eyes took in everything and even at three she had been keen to copy everything, struggling to mark erratic lines on the paper. At five, now, she had overtaken her brother.

'Look – I'm *writing*!' she'd proclaim proudly. Joley would scowl at her eagerness, and Maryann often found it tempting not to bother with him and to concentrate on Sally. But Maryann was determined that all her children would at least be able to read and write. What if they didn't spend all their life on the cut?

Those first days of the trip the rain fell and fell. Joel was delighted. The cut was low, the 'bottom too near the top' as some of the boaters put it. At least they weren't pumping out water to put out fires as they had in Birmingham and Coventry during the bombing, but it was never good news when the water level fell and Joel was glad to see some water coming in. They pushed on through the wet. Once they were well into the Midlands, though, the rain stopped and the sky cleared. By the time they reached the bottom of the great flight of Hatton locks up to Warwick, the afternoon was bathed in mellow autumn sunshine, weeds and grass shining with water droplets and the air heavy with moisture.

Maryann was at the helm, with Bobby on the bank ahead, lock-wheeling. Another pair of boats had gone up ahead, which meant that the locks would all be set against them. Maryann sighed. For a few seconds she dashed down into the cabin, brewed tea and fetched Joel's soaked corduroy trousers to lay on the cabin roof in the sun. When she came out, she could see Joel signalling to her that he was going to tie up and wait for another pair to come down. Even when the locks were set for them it was a good two to three hours' work getting to the top of Hatton. The great flight of locks, the 'Stairway to Heaven', towered above them, the black and white beams of the gates and the paddle ratchets rising up the hill towards the sky, looking as if they were stacked on top of one another. The combined rise of the twenty-one locks would lift them almost a hundred and fifty feet to the fringes of Warwick.

They waited at a distance from the bottom lock, drinking tea and eating bread and lard in the sunshine. Joley and Sally got off and scampered about on the bank and Maryann sat holding Ada. Bobby stood ahead by the lock, watching for boats. Something would be along soon.

'Once we get up here, we'll tie up before Warwick,' Joel said. 'That'll do us for the day.'

Quite soon Bobby called to them, 'Pair coming down!'

The two boats from the Grand Union Canal Carrying Company appeared eventually out of the bottom lock, side by side, loaded and sheeted up. As they emerged from the last lock, the butty was released skilfully so that the snubber extended gradually to its full length and the motor boat went on ahead. As they passed, the man at the helm of the motor started waving and shouting about jossers coming up, and turning to look, Joel and Maryann suddenly realized that there was another pair of boats from the Fellows, Moreton and Clayton company steaming up behind them. They hadn't heard the engine over the sound of the Grand Union carrier.

Eyes fixed on the approaching green-and-orange painted boats, Joel slammed his tea mug down furiously on the *Theodore*'s cabin roof. There was no sign of the pair slowing down.

'I don't believe it. Them buggers ent going to stop!' It went against the etiquette of the cut not to wait if another boat was lined up for a lock. 'Right.' Joel's voice was grimly determined. 'Bobby!' he roared. 'We're coming in.' He ran along the bank to the *Esther Jane*, whose motor was still gently turning. Maryann looked round for the children.

37

'Joley – Sally! Come back on – we're going. Quick!'

They children hopped aboard in seconds. Maryann speedily deposited Ada in the cabin and pushed the butty off as Joel pulled away.

If this other pair were determined to push their way in without waiting for them to come up, they'd be back to square one, with all the locks set against them. And besides, there was a principle at stake – how dare they try and steal the flight of locks!

The jossers (nicknamed after Joshua Clayton, a founder of the company) were almost upon them. Their fore end was almost touching the back of the *Theodore*.

'What the hell d'you think you're playing at, you silly sods?' Maryann yelled, furious, and frightened that the boat was going to ram them.

Seeing Joel had managed to cut in front just in time to take his rightful place in the lock, the man steering the josser motor flung it into reverse, which was the only way to stop a boat apart from driving it into the bank. Joel and Maryann, their skill honed by anger and determination to prove their point, breasted up the boats in quick time and edged side by side into Hatton's bottom lock. Over the engine they could just hear a trail of filthy oaths and abuse being flung their way from behind. As Bobby swung the gates closed, Joel turned to Maryann, lifted his cap and saluted her for an excellent job of work. Maryann grinned back and put one thumb up and Joley stood on the counter with her laughing and cheering.

'We beat those sodding jossers!' he piped.

'*Joley!*' Maryann ticked him off, but she was laughing. It was such a good feeling to beat someone who was trying to put one over on you. She had felt better and more energetic in those moments than she had in weeks.

After that, they were full of energy for the Hatton flight, and always a few locks ahead of the jossers, who had to empty every lock they entered since they were in too much of a lather to get on to wait for anyone else to come down. Every time the crews caught sight of each other there was yelling and sparring, triumphant on the Bartholomews' part, but with genuine resentment on the part of the jossers. Joel grumbled about them thinking they owned the Grand Union. Thought themselves above an S. E. Barlow boat.

The afternoon stayed warm and sunny, and halfway up the locks they received unexpected help. As Bobby was leaning on a gate to open it and let the boats through, he was joined at the other side by a man in shapeless, ill-fitting clothes, who pushed against the beam with solemn concentration. Bobby called out his thanks in his usual good-natured way.

As they waited for the next lock to fill, Maryann watched the man. It was difficult to guess his age. He could have been in his thirties, perhaps older. The sleeves of his jacket were far too short, barely reaching down below his elbows, yet his trousers were loose and too long. He walked with a strange, lumbering gait. He was a large man with heavy features and a slow, childlike look to him.

He'll have come from the asylum, Maryann realized. The Warwick asylum loomed to the left of them, a little further up. On fine days some of the more capable inmates did come out at times and help boaters work the locks.

A couple of locks later she took her turn on the bank, moving from lock to lock with the windlass tucked in her belt. The man kept pace with her, carefully watching her movements to see what he needed to do next. As she crossed over a pair of gates to raise the paddles on the other side, she said, 'Ta – I could do with some help.'

The man nodded and gave a sudden laugh. He had narrow, dark eyes and his hair was receding at the front, two smooth inlets curving back into his hair line as if water had washed the hair from his scalp. 'I can help,' he said in a wooden voice, but she could see the eagerness behind it. 'I can help.'

'You from the asylum?'

He nodded, pointed at the high, forbidding building.

'What's your name?'

He thought for a moment. 'Thomas.' And snickered again.

'Well, ta, Thomas. You're doing a good job for us.'

All the way up the remaining locks, Maryann chose to stay on the bank, as Bobby signalled to her that the twins were asleep. Although the lock-wheeling was tiring, it was good to be off the boat, walking the bank. But she was filled with a sense of unease, which increased as the afternoon went on. Her feeling of buoyant well-being earlier on seeped away and she felt strange and tight inside, brushed by memory. She knew what it was: the asylum. Seeing the buildings, meeting Thomas, brought to the surface another thing she preferred not to think about. Little Margaret Lambert, the child whom Maryann's stepfather, Norman Griffin, had brutally degraded. As her sister Amy was helpless to protect her, Margaret had tried to end her tormentor's life in order to save her own. Margaret had been nine then. Now she'd be fifteen, a young woman. Instead of being sent for trial she was consigned to the asylum in Winson Green. One prison instead of another.

Maryann fastened her windlass onto the ratchet of one of the final set of paddles and pulled it round with all her strength, feeling the muscles work in her arms, stomach and back. She tried to let out the fury and grief which rose in her when she was assaulted by thoughts like these. Margaret in there, locked away all these years of her young life – because of him. Beginning to sob, she crossed the gates and flung herself at the second paddle. Once the gates were open, Thomas peeled off and vanished down the hill again without waiting for thanks. As the pair emerged from the lock, Maryann called to Joel, 'I'll walk on.' She saw he had noticed her tears. But she knew he wouldn't ask. Joel was cowed by emotion.

Maryann walked slowly behind the boats, glad of time to be alone. Just a few minutes away from the children, from the non-stop demands, the cabin being in a mess and the washing not done – the feeling that she just couldn't keep up. Now thoughts of the past welled up, raw and bitter, as she walked, pushing weeds and tussocks of grass away with her feet, trying to force the past back to where it belonged: behind her. Hadn't she come to this life to get away from all of that? To be with Joel and begin again? It was all years ago: there was nothing she could do about any of it now, so why couldn't the memories leave her alone? But this evening her mind wouldn't obey her, wouldn't fold its old emotions away, and dark thoughts followed her all the way to the spot where they tied up for the night.

She had been quiet all evening. The lamp was lit and Joel sat on the side of the bed as Maryann stood undressing, legs straddling the twins, who were bedded down on the floor because she worried about them rolling off the side bed.

She could feel Joel's eyes on her as she unbuttoned

her blouse, loving him watching her, yet dreading what it might mean. She felt desperate. She loved Joel so much, but every time he touched her now she felt worried, angry that he couldn't see how terrified she was of catching with another baby. *Why does it have to be like this?* she thought.

She had her back to him, and his warm hands reached for her, pulling her back onto his lap. He sighed with pleasure, kissing her neck, watching, over her shoulder, as his hands parted her blouse, lifting and stroking her pale breasts.

Maryann's mind flailed from side to side like someone locked in a cupboard.

She wanted to ... to ... She scarcely had a name for their lovemaking. To give in to him, to give him pleasure, give him everything he wanted. But all that went with having babies crowded into her memory. Even him touching her filled her with dread and she felt panicky. She'd never felt like this before with Joel. *It's just because I don't want to catch for another one*, she told herself.

As Joel laid her back on the bed, Mrs Simons's advice rang in her head. 'Get him to pull away ...' Last time she hadn't found the courage to say it. But she had to do something or she'd be expecting again, sick and worn out – no, she couldn't stand it.

Hands under his shirt she stroked his wide, strong back, felt the muscles in it working as he moved in her, his excitement gathering. She struggled for words. Quick, she had to say something or it'd be too late!

'Joel,' she burst out desperately, 'don't go all the way in me – pull out before you finish.'

But her words seemed to have the opposite effect and it was too late. With a low groan her husband completed the act which gave him seconds of pleasure and her weeks of fear. He stayed on top of her, face pressed close to hers.

'What did you say to me?' he asked, contentedly.

Maryann's cheeks burned. She managed to make herself say, 'I asked you to pull away – before you finished.'

There was a silence. Joel lifted his head at last, frowning. 'What? You mean – when I'm going strong?'

'So's I don't have a babby every time,' she whispered.

She saw genuine puzzlement, hurt almost, in his eyes. She was learning about her husband, that while he was the most kind and tender of men there were certain things you couldn't get past him on: boats and babies.

'But we'll get by. We always do, don't we, eh? And think of little Harry. What if summat happens to them, eh? Then where'd we be?'

'But I can't do it again – not yet,' Maryann said, stroking his face, her eyes pleading. 'I can hardly drag myself about some days and I never get everything done.'

'Course you do. You're a good 'un.' Joel kissed her. 'Best wife and best mate a man could ask for. I've no complaints, my little bird.'

Tears in her eyes, she looked up at him.

'Please. Just see if you can!'

Doubtfully he said, 'Well – I'll try it. But that don't sound natural at all to me.'

Five

'Ah – Mrs Bartholomew, how nice to see you. I'll be with you in just a moment!'

The woman in front of Maryann in the queue at Osborne's turned and gave her a nasty look.

Maryann, her shopping bag in one hand, Sally's hand in the other, gave a faint smile, feeling a blush rise in her cheeks. It was embarrassing to be singled out like that, but at the same time she couldn't help being pleased. It was nice to find such a welcome. It almost gave her a sense of family.

'Come on, let the ladies off the cut through first, they've got work to do!'

'Well, so've the rest of us,' someone grumbled from by the door.

Maryann and another boatwoman in the queue gratefully produced their ration books and the butcher served them straight away. As he put together Maryann's rations, he was full of questions. Tied up at Tyseley Wharf again, were they? Loading up this morning? Pity the weather wasn't nicer for them, wasn't it? Wouldn't be staying tonight then?

Handing her the bag of meat, he said, 'And how are those two fine babbies of yours?' As Maryann answered, he winked at Sally and beckoned her closer, slipping something into her palm.

'One each for your brothers as well – and mind you hand them over!' he whispered.

'Oh – say thank you!' Maryann instructed her daughter, and blushing even more deeply. 'Mr Osborne's ever so good to you.'

By the time they stepped out into the cold and rain clutching the meat rations, Sally's cheek was already bulging with the lump of toffee Mr Osborne had given her.

'Well – wasn't that nice?' Maryann said to Sally, stopping to retie her scarf round her head to keep out the wet. 'Though I don't know what those other people must've thought.'

The child wasn't taking in anything she was saying, but was gazing dreamily round her at the street, the shops and houses. She was a sturdy, solemn little girl. Her coat, which Maryann had made herself out of a piece of wool tweed, was too big and trailed almost to the ground.

I never was much good at sewing, Maryann thought gloomily. *At least I remembered to wipe her face before we came out.*

You could only just see her little boots below the coat. Sally's thick blonde hair looked as if it had long been stranger to a comb and her hands were grimy with coal dust, but her face was round and glowing pink in the cold. Maryann suddenly bent over and pressed her lips against the chill, peachy skin of Sally's cheek.

'You're my little bab, aren't you?' she said fondly.

'Why don't we live in a house?' Wide eyes looked up at her, topped by a slight frown.

Maryann took her hand. 'Oh – because we're a boater family. We don't live in houses. But when I was a little girl I lived in a house. Over there – a few miles away. In

45

a place called Ladywood.' Your grandmother lives there even now, she could have said, but kept the words to herself. Her children had never met her mother.

'Can we go there? See your house?'

'One day. D'you remember your uncle Tony? We'll go and see him one day soon.'

Sally and Joley were intrigued by life on the bank. She could see Sally excitedly drinking in the sights around her, even though they were in the drabbest back end of Tyseley. On Maryann the streets of Birmingham had quite the opposite effect: they filled her with a profound sense of anxiety. The later years of her childhood here had been so unhappy, tainted by experiences which robbed her of her innocence. When she went to live on the cut, hard as the life was, it gave her back something of herself. She found love, a sense of safety, enchantment even, out in the open air, with nature all round them once they were away from the cities with their soot and grime. The routine of the cut and the birth of her children had given her back something of her own childhood sense of life again, before it was spoilt and corrupted. But back here in these grey streets shadows of the past seemed to lurk, waiting to pull her down again, breaking through the peace that she'd struggled for. She liked to come back to Birmingham, but there was always a sense of relief, too, when they slid out again from between its black, confining walls. Instinctively, she took Sally's grubby hand as they turned back round the corner into the wharf.

'Mrs Bartholomew!' The voice cut through her thoughts, and the clattering of chains on the hoists, the heavy thud and rattle of cargoes being loaded and unloaded around the wharf. Maryann smiled in recognition as one of the men from the toll office came over to speak to her. He was a friendly fellow, a few years her senior, with arched eyebrows which gave him a perpetually humorous look and a grin from which every other tooth seemed to be missing.

'All right, Charlie?'

'All right,' he panted, adding, 'hello, little 'un,' to Sally and patting the top of her head. 'Just thought I'd tell you – there was this bloke come looking for you a couple of days back.'

'That'd be my brother . . .' Maryann frowned. She'd written to Tony not long ago and had a message via the toll office saying he'd be glad to see her whenever she got round to it. He was married now, Tony was, with a baby daughter. Could there be something wrong? 'Thin fella, dark?'

'Oh no,' Charlie said. 'No – it weren't him. This were an older man, in a big coat, like . . . That's what I came to tell you. Bit of an odd bloke, I thought. Kept his hat pulled right down, wouldn't look at you. When he turned to go, I saw he had this scar all down his neck – like a burn or summat.' Charlie frowned. 'Hey – you all right?'

Maryann felt him catch her arm and guide her backwards, letting her sink down onto a pile of wet sacking as her knees gave way and the wharf seemed to swim round her. She saw lights at the corners of her eyes, a wave of heat rose up in her and, knowing she was about to faint, she pushed her head down between her knees. Sally was pulling at her, saying something, and from somewhere in the hazy air above her she could hear the man asking her questions. After a few moments the sick dizziness passed and things round her became clear again.

'Sorry.' She gathered her wits, brushing down her

coat as she tried muzzily to stand up. Charlie took her hand.

'You awright, bab?' While concerned for her, he couldn't help noticing what a sweet, handsome wench she was. Bit of awright, he thought, feeling her rough little hand in his as he helped her to her feet. She made him feel soft and protective.

Maryann nodded. 'But that bloke you said came looking – he asked for me by name?'

'Must've done.' He was taken aback by the intense way she questioned him. 'D'you know who he is?'

'Oh yes,' she almost spat the words. 'I know who he is all right.' Her limbs still felt weak and shaky with shock. Who else could he be, a man with a burned face, a man who had decided to come looking for her? She looked round, suddenly overtaken by fear, everything out of proportion. The very wharf seemed sinister now. 'Sally?' she cried. 'My little girl – Sal? Where are you?'

'She's here – just behind you.' Charlie spoke gently, as if soothing an infant, for the young woman seemed like a terrified child in those moments, as she grasped her daughter's hand and pulled her close. He resisted an impulse to put his arm round her, as if she were one of his own. 'Look, are you sure you'll be all right?'

'Promise me' – she clutched his arm – 'that if he ever comes here again you won't tell him anything. You've never seen me – we never come here. I don't want him knowing anything – I never want to see him again. Tell the others in the office – for God's sake don't let him near us, *please*, Charlie.'

'Course,' he said, frowning. 'I'll tell them. Who is he, anyroad?'

'No one,' she snapped, her voice full of loathing.

'He's *no one*. And I don't want him anywhere near me or my family.'

She walked away fiercely, holding tight to Sally's hand, then she turned.

'I don't want him knowing anything – not about us, not the names of our boats . . .'

'Oh, he knows them, I'm afraid,' Charlie said. 'When he come in, as far as I remember he said he was looking for the Bartholomews on the *Esther Jane*.'

Disturbed by the look of despair which crossed Maryann's face, he said hastily, 'But I won't tell him anything if he comes again.'

She nodded, whispered, 'Thank you,' then turned away. He saw her draw her coat more closely round her as if a deadly chill had infected the November air.

'What's the matter, Mom?'

Sally's eyes were wide with alarm as her mother sank down on the bed beside the twins in the *Theodore*, deathly pale and shaking.

'Nothing.' She struggled to compose herself. 'I just come over a bit funny, that's all. I'll be all right when I've had a cup of tea, bab. You sit and do a bit of your drawing.'

Sally retreated into her favourite activity and Maryann sipped her tea, trying to steady herself. She was raw with shock. She was certain that the man who had come to the wharf was her stepfather, Norman Griffin, and the layers of security she had built round her during the years of her marriage seemed to peel back all at once, leaving her trembling under the gaze of the past. That time she thought she saw him before – it *must* have been him, though she'd tried to make herself believe she'd been mistaken, or at least, if he had been there, that it was a coincidence. He was after her. He had asked for their boats by name . . . But why was he looking for her? What could he possibly want from her now? Whatever his reasons, they would be warped and cruel. After these years of peace and safety his disfigured features were raising themselves to look at her again and the thought chilled her to the core. But to tell Joel meant bringing the loathsome creature into the centre of her family again. Even the sound of his name repelled her. She didn't want to say it, not on the cut, her refuge. He had no place here.

She put her cup down and held her hands out in front of her, angry at their tremor, at the thought that he could still do this to her.

We'll be out of here in the morning, she thought, *and we shan't be back in a while. I shan't say anything to Joel. Not unless we're given another load to come back up to Brum. Then I'll tell him.*

Six

'Christmas at Sutton then,' Joel said.

He had hauled the *Theodore* in alongside the *Esther Jane* and was tying them both up. It was Christmas Eve and they weren't going to make it to Oxford after all. But their disappointment was soon dispelled.

'Look!' Maryann called, jumping with excitement on the counter of the *Theodore*. As Joel and Bobby were securing the boats, her eyes were searching the narrowboats already in at Sutton Stop, and immediately she spotted the *Isla*, with its butty the *Neptune* breasted up neatly beside it. Nancy and Darius were only two boats away from them, Darrie and Sean scampering towards them on the bank. 'Joel – they're here – look – the *Isla*! Nance! Hull-oo! You there?'

Nancy's dark curls appeared immediately out of the *Neptune*'s cabin and she waved back madly, cleaning cloth still in her hand. She had a bright red jumper on and her cheerful grin lit up the day, despite the cold and leaden sky. Maryann beamed, full of happiness. Joel waved as well. The moment he could reach the bank, Joley was throwing himself off to join his cousins before his mom could say anything about letters and book learning. That was the last thing on Maryann's mind, though – her best pal was tied up nearby!

Nance was across in seconds, politely calling out that she was coming across and averting her eyes in the customary way as she moved over the counters of the two boats which lay between them. She stepped nimbly onto the *Theodore*.

'Look at you!' Maryann laughed, laying a hand on Nance's round stomach. 'Well out at the front, aren't you? You look ever so well, though – don't know how you do it, that I don't.' Nance's abundant energy never ceased to amaze her.

'I went in to see Sister Mary on the way back up,' Nance said. Sister Mary was the nurse who lived by the Grand Union at Stoke Bruerne. She was much loved among the boat families for all the care she gave them. 'She says everything's going perfect. I should be coming to town with him March time.'

They saw Joel's brother Darius coming back along the towpath and both waved. His arm came up in greeting. Joel favoured his mother's looks, with the auburn hair and more rounded face. Darius was the image of how his father, old Darius, must have looked as a young man, with his peaty hair and sharp, chiselled features. He wore a cap and a colourful scarf knotted in the neck of his shirt. With Nance beside him, with her dark looks, bright clothes and gold earrings, they looked an exotic pair. Their children were as striking as they were, Darry and Sean both dark-haired and agile as monkeys, and Rose already sultry-eyed under her own mop of curls.

The two brothers greeted one another on the bank. Maryann and Nance watched them fondly.

'Our two old chaps.' Nance laughed. When they were all together they often teased their men about their age and the 'young wenches' they'd managed to persuade to run off with them. Joel was sixteen years older than

Maryann and the gap between Nance and Darius was even greater – almost twenty-two years.

'His age don't mean anything,' Maryann often said. 'He's just Joel – he's always looked the same to me.' They liked to make a joke of it, though. The two of them chattered nineteen to the dozen, before they managed to tear themselves away to get on with their mountain of chores. Maryann spent the afternoon racing to the shops, washing on the bank beside Nance and some of the other boatwomen, pounding heavy clothes in dippers and galvanized tubs, sharing a mangle and exchanging news, all the while surrounded by their children. Maryann fitted in as much cleaning as she could, getting Sally and Rose polishing the brass strips round the chimneys. She sang to herself that evening as she went about her work, full of a burst of Nance's infectious energy. The children looked quite startled, coming upon her humming 'The Sheikh of Araby' and 'I'm always chasing rainbows'. *I feel better*, she thought at last. *More myself.*

'We're going to have a nice Christmas,' she told Joley and Sally as she tucked them into bed on the *Esther Jane* and kissed them both. 'Sleep tight.'

One of the best things about Christmas was that it was a rest and a change, a chance to celebrate and socialize in what was otherwise a life of almost non-stop work. The family of Ernie Higgins, who worked with Nancy and Darius, were tied up at Sutton too and he and Bobby went to them for the day, leaving all the Bartholomews together. They congregated instinctively in the family's old boat, the *Esther Jane*, somehow squeezing everyone in out of the cold. Maryann cleared the bedding off the back bed and stowed it in the *Theodore* so that the younger children could perch on the bed while they all ate chicken and plenty of spuds and cabbage, with a good jug of ale to wash it down and Tizer for the children. It got so hot inside that they slid the hatch open, until an icy rain began to fall and they had to close it again. And all the while they talked, about recent journeys, of bad bends and hold-ups and engine trouble, wharves and lock keepers and news gathered in passing from acquaintances met on their journeys. They reminisced about how things had once been on the cut and about the time when they had all met. Their favourite story, one they never tired of retelling, was of the morning Nance had finally escaped from her old life and her miserable marriage to Mick Mallone to join them on the cut, dashing after the boat at dawn as they pulled away from the basin at Gas Street.

'Happiest day of my life, that was,' Darius said. He sat back, content to be on his old boat, well fed, a cup of ale in his hand. Maryann watched him fondly, the dark, wavy hair round his face, his powerful, almost eagle-like features. He was, like his father, a man of few words, but his eyes, when he looked at Nance, conveyed everything that needed to be said in the way of affection and regard.

Maryann felt Joel take her hand under the table and their eyes met for a moment. Seeing the way he looked at her, she was startled by a rush of desire for him, an inner throb as if their bodies were connected by something even more powerful than touch, and she was filled with relief. She could still feel for him – it was not lost! In the early days of their marriage, trusting and loving him as she did, she had let him caress and wake her body to the discovery of shared pleasure, of excitement, to lovemaking instead of the forced pain and revulsion which was all she had experienced before. It took time. Often she could not enjoy it; sometimes, when she could feel very little, and could not seem to concentrate, she knew it was his pleasure she was enjoying, not her own. But that was all right. It was not *bad*, not terrible as it had been before and she was grateful for that. She still liked the closeness, the comforting warmth of him. She longed for children then and they had soon arrived. She had no idea how quickly lovemaking would become fraught with fear of its consequences, a bittersweet intimacy of desire and dread. How she would find herself doing anything to avoid it – pretending to be asleep, saying she was too tired ... And now, though her gaze as she looked back at him held love and gratitude, her mind raced ahead ... *Oh Lord, he's going to want it tonight. Will he remember what I asked? Oh, please let him just fall asleep straight away!*

'Maryann?'

Even in her heavily pregnant condition, Nance seemed to land in the hatches of the *Theodore* as if she'd flown there. Her laughing features appeared between the doors.

'Still feeding them gutsy little so-and-sos are you?'

Maryann was pinned to the bed by the twins.

'You can laugh,' Maryann retorted. 'It'll be your turn soon. What makes you think you haven't got two in there, eh?'

'Oh Jaysus, no!' Nance rolled her eyes. 'Listen – Mr Barlow's sending us down London again, but he's asked Joel if you'll do a long haul and come down with us?'

'What – the Grand Union?'

'Yep – he's even giving you the choice, you having

55

your hands full and that. Anyroad, as I was coming back, I told Joel I'd check with his missis! If we got ourselves sorted out right we could all go down there together.'

Maryann brightened. Today was Boxing Day and after yesterday's celebrations it felt very flat. Now all that faced them was work and more work. The thought of being able to do it alongside Nance cheered her no end. Though they had good relations with most of the other boatwomen, they were always a bit conscious of being 'the Brummies from off the bank' and they shared the same sense of humour. Maryann sometimes found she would crack a joke to another of the boatwomen, only to be met by a solemn, slightly mystifed stare. On the other hand a gaggle of them might be splitting their sides about something which she couldn't see the funny side of. With Nance she could really share a joke. And the children, who enjoyed switching families and travelling on another boat for a change, would be delighted with the idea.

The journey down was reckoned to take a week or so, depending on delays and calamities. They loaded up at the coalfields, spending a freezing morning sheeting up to keep the cargo dry. The side sheets, which when not in use lay folded along the gunwales, had to be pulled up, hard and crackly as they were, and knotted over the top of the planks which ran the length of the boat over the cargo. Then, their hands cracked and chaffed from the cold and from pulling and knotting the rough strings, they had to work the main tarpaulin along the boat, making their way backwards, tying it at the sides. By the end of helping to sheet the *Theodore*, Maryann's hands were so stiff and sore she could barely move them. Joley had disappeared somewhere when she wasn't looking and Ada and Esther were screaming to be fed. She wanted to weep, but just then Nance appeared with cups of cocoa.

'I don't know where Joley's got to – have you seen him?' Maryann was looking round anxiously.

'Oh – 'e's in the *Isla* with Darrie and Sean. Don't worry, kid – he's not run away to sea. Not yet, anyhow!'

As they chugged south, the weather grew colder. Frosts turned the ground to stone and the morning trees to sparkling works of art. For most of the time the boats managed to keep together. In the long pound from Hawkesbury to Rugby they moved smoothly on as a convoy. Once they reached flights of locks they would see each other only intermittently, Joel and Maryann, who were the second pair, having to wait for other pairs to come through and set the lock for them, or reset them in their favour before they could continue. But they would catch up later and tie up together for the night.

The burden of work was no less than usual and the temperatures harsh and cold, but for those days Maryann's heart was lighter. She felt almost carefree. Having Nance around lifted life more into a pleasurable realm, a game almost. They bow-hauled the buttys through the double locks at Rugby, Maryann scolding all the way, telling Nance she shouldn't be pulling at all in her condition, Nance arguing that Ernie was really doing all the work, she was only helping. At other locks they raced to canalside shops for supplies, moving bulkily in their layers of winter woollens and coats, bright scarves tied over their hair, arriving back just as the last butty was being pulled out of the lock, both of them panting and giggling, cautious on the frosty stones, their breath furling white on the air. They climbed into their respective homes with armfuls of bread, eggs and vegetables. In the mornings they waved blearily to each other, stepping out of their cabins as the dawn light reflected off the perfect mirror of water, their movements the first disturbance in the deep stillness of morning.

'It's nice travelling like this,' Maryann said to Joel the first evening. 'With Darius and Nance, I mean. Can we do it again, d'you think?'

He looked up, surprised at the enthusiasm in her voice.

'It'll depend on the loads,' he said, 'but I'm happy with it. It seems to suit you, so that's all the better.'

At Stoke Bruerne the two of them went to see Sister Mary in her surgery by the cut. She wore a white coat and her kindly face, looking out from under a long white nurse's veil, broke into a delighted smile at the sight of Maryann with her twin daughters, wrapped up plump as sausages, in her arms.

'Well I never!' Sister Mary helped Maryann lie them down so that she could examine them. 'Goodness me, you have got your hands full now, haven't you? But what lovely healthy babies!' She made a fuss of Joley, Sally and Ezra as well, before turning to their cousins.

'And you, Nancy – are you still keeping all right?' Sister Mary had delivered Nance's last two babies.

'Yes, ta,' Nancy said cheerfully.

'You do look the picture of health,' Sister Mary chuckled. 'You were obviously made for this life. I don't think there's anything I need to do for you – except remind you not to go pulling those boats about. D'you hear?'

'I hope she'll listen to you better than she does to me!' Maryann said.

'Yes, Sister.' Nancy grinned at her. They were all very fond of Sister Mary. She did such a lot to support the women of the cut and keep them and their children in good health.

58

Seven

It was a long haul down to London.

'Blooming long journey – started in 1942 and ended in 1943!' Nance quipped. After the New Year arrived they eventually slid between the green sides of Cassiobury Park, then past Regent's Park to the docks, or 'Limehouse' as it was known to the boaters.

Maryann and Joel had seldom worked the Grand Union route. As they travelled the last leg east, Maryann stood on the gunwales in the cold wind, looking round as Bobby steered. The cut was so wide down here that it felt quite intimidating. Along the Regent's Canal, boats were tied up on each side, sometimes two deep, but this still left plenty of room in the middle of the channel. Travelling along this wider cut came huge river barges, which would loom in front of them suddenly, making Maryann's pulse race with panic at the thought of a collision. The further south they had travelled, the more barges they seemed to meet.

And London itself came as a shock. She had seen some of the effects of the bombing in Birmingham, and the skyline of Coventry was drastically changed. At one period it had seemed diminished every time they came back to it. But, as Nance told them, London had 'taken it' for weeks on end and she and Darius had been down a couple of nights after the great fire storm raged almost up to St Paul's cathedral. The further east they went the more devastation they saw, whole neighbourhoods lying smashed apart.

When they got to the last lock, the lock keeper examined their loading orders and told them which wharf to go to. The gates swung open and Maryann looked round, awed at the great vista unfolding in front of them. Their boats seemed dwarfed and humble in this vast steely-coloured pool, flanked by wharves where lighters, barges and narrowboats were loading and unloading, cranes spiking up into the sky.

The boat was emptied that night and they were due to be loaded with a new cargo in the morning. After their tea of stew, the Bartholomew brothers and Bobby went to find the pubs outside the dock gates while Maryann and Nancy settled the children for the night. Then Nance came over to the *Theodore*.

They brewed tea and Maryann sat on the back bed with Esther and Ada, and Nance lay along the side bed with her feet up. Occasionally they heard voices as people passed outside.

'I shouldn't want to live down here,' Maryann said.

'No – me neither.' Nance reached over and poured from the old brown teapot. 'Dunno why, but I've always been glad to head home again. Specially when the bombs were coming down. Weeks of it, they had – how their nerves stood it I'll never know. A couple of nights of that almost finished me off, I can tell you. We went into one of them shelters one night. Never again. It was like a bleeding madhouse in there – and the pong! You'd rather die in your own bed, honest you would. Here—' She handed Maryann her tea.

'Ta. I could get used to being waited on!'

'Best not – not if you're staying on in this life!'

They sipped the hot tea, laughing and joking. *Why do*

I get so down in myself? Maryann wondered. When Nance was there she cheered up and everything seemed all right.

'This is nice,' Nance said, settling back. Her earrings shone in the lamplight. 'Won't last long, though – I can't get comfy anywhere when I'm this far on.' She soon had to shift her position again, giving a comical grunt and laying a hand on her swollen belly. 'This one's on the go like mad tonight – kicking and thumping about. Must be another lad.'

Maryann smiled. 'I'm pleased for you, Nance. Can't say I'm envious though.'

But Nance looked contented. Comfortable in mind, if not body.

'Ah – nothing like it. New life – kiddies. I know it's all hard work, like, but I wouldn't change it, not for nothing.' She looked across at Maryann's pale face in the shadows of the bed hole. 'I mean, what if I'd stayed with Mick? If I hadn't run down to the cut that morning? If I'd done the right thing and stayed with the man I married? 'Cept it *wasn't* the right thing, staying with him. I know our mom says I could go to their new priest, Father Ryan – get an annulment. But I don't even know where Mick is. They think he went up Liverpool, but no one knows for sure. And the Church takes no end of time over it. We'd all be dead by the time they got round to it. None of that seems to matter out here, anyway. We're a family, Darius and me. That's the important thing.'

A blush rising in her cheeks, Maryann asked, 'But Nance – are you just going to go on and on having babbies?'

Nance sat forward, easing her back. 'I've not really thought. I s'pose so. Darius always wanted a big family and he's not a young man any more. Who knows what might happen. And I like giving him babbies, Maryann. His face when he sees a new life. As many as God gives. Seems what's natural to me.'

Maryann fell silent. Natural. The natural thing. That was what she kept hearing. Was she not natural then, feeling that she couldn't just go on bearing more and more children until it killed her?

'You been over Ladywood recently?' Nance was saying. 'Seen Tony – or your mom?'

Esther was beginning to wake, snuffling, and Maryann took her on her lap.

'I saw Tony a few weeks back. The babby Joanie's a nice little thing. I don't know as they're getting on all that well, though. Dolly gets mithered about the smallest thing – goes on at Tony no end. Don't know how he stands it. And no – I've not seen our mom. To tell you the truth I don't even know if her house is still standing. I'm not going to see her, Nance. I've been bitten that way before and I'm not going back for more. She's made it very clear where she stands. As a matter of fact . . .' She gasped. 'God, Nance – I've just thought . . .' She stopped, a new suspicion forcing into her mind.

'What?'

'The other week when we was tied up at Tyseley, one of the wharf men come to me and said someone was asking for me.' She related to Nance Charlie Dean's report of the visitor to the wharf.

Nance sat up straighter, her face turning deadly serious.

'He was asking for me by name, knew the name of our boats and everything . . .'

'You don't think it's – not *him*?'

'Well, who on earth else could it be, looking like that?

62

But how would he know where I was? Someone must've told him and now – I've just thought – what if he went back to see our mom?'

'She *wouldn't*?' Nance's eyes were wide with horror at the thought.

'Oh, I wouldn't put it past her,' Maryann said bitterly. 'She blames everything that's happened on me.'

'But after all this time? What would he want?'

'I don't know.' With a shudder, Maryann cuddled Esther more tightly to her. The tiny lighted cabin of the boat now felt like an island of safety surrounded by threatening, icy darkness.

'Well, he won't be looking you up to take you dancing, will he? Have you told Joel?'

Maryann shook her head. 'Joel doesn't know the half of it. I don't want him to know – I don't want him near us, even the thought of him!' She was getting worked up now, panic rising in her. 'He's like poison – he eats away at you until there's nothing left. Oh, Nance – what d'you think he wants?'

They left before midday next day, after craneloads of long, rusty steel billets for Tyseley were swung from the wharf and came crashing down into the boats. Even that late in the day a freezing mist hung over the cut like a ghostly grey blanket. Maryann made sure she kept the kettle constantly on the hob. Bobby was feeling the worse for wear from the night before.

'How much did you let him drink?' she scolded Joel teasingly. 'Look at the state of him – he'll have to go in and sleep it off, looking like that! Never mind, Bobby – only a hundred and sixty-six locks to go!'

Bobby, groaning, was allowed to recover until the

flight at Marsworth, when he was turned out onto the bank to recover by doing some vigorous lock-wheeling.

Maryann was very uneasy when she heard that they'd been detailed to go to Birmingham again. But they couldn't turn a load down because of her fears, could they? Fears of a grim phantom from her past life? How would they explain that to Essy Barlow? She said nothing to Joel.

The journey back was going well until they got to the lovely green stretch at Tring summit. It was a brighter day than the one on which they'd started off, one of sunlit, dazzling cold. The *Isla* and *Neptune* had steamed on ahead of them after their descent down the locks the other side of the summit. When they were breasted up to go down, Joel called across.

'There's summat not right with her!' He pointed to the engine hole and the chimney, which was issuing blacker, angrier looking smoke than usual. There was a sinister knocking sound.

'She sounds bad!' Maryann yelled back.

'We'll try and make it to the bottom and then I'll see to her,' Joel shouted.

As Bobby shoved the last lock open, the *Esther Jane*'s motor was making ever more bronchial sounds and Joel pulled over and tied up. Darius and Nancy's boats were already well out of sight, and by the time Joel had spent two frustrating hours leaning and squatting in the engine hole over the ailing Bolinder engine, the other pair were irretrievably lost to them. The cats, Spots and Jenny, strolled along the gunwales of the *Theodore* as if bemused by the delay. Bobby kept the children entertained on the bank, letting Ezra jump and climb all over him. Maryann was thankful for the umpteenth time for his kindly nature. Ezra was a real handful to keep an eye on and Bobby often helped out. Eventually Joel said, '*Ah!*' Hands black, oil on his face he started up the engine again and after a couple of coughs, it shuddered into life.

Maryann kissed his oil-smeared beard. 'Clever clogs.'

Joel grinned. 'Not letting that blooming moty beat me.'

A mile further along the sound of the motor became clogged and dragging. Joel signalled back to her. He pulled in again and spent a further hour in the bilges, patiently removing thick shreds of rope and what looked like the remains of a wool sweater which were caught in tortuous twists round the propeller. By the time he had done all this they couldn't go much further before the cold and darkness descended and they had to tie up for the night. Maryann was despondent. They were so far behind now that they'd never catch up, and she missed having the *Isla* and *Neptune* tied along the bank just ahead of them. Instead, they were alone in the freezing country silence, under the stars. But as they was falling asleep Maryann heard an engine puttering past outside.

'There go the beer boats,' she murmured to Joel. The Guinness boats worked fly – they had a larger crew, which meant they could keep going day and night chugging on along the black cut. 'Glad we're not working them.'

Joel, almost lost to sleep, just managed to grunt in agreement.

The morning was bitterly cold, the grass crackling with frost, and a thin film of ice covered the cut. The bright blue sky of the day before had been replaced by an unyielding grey, which seemed to fit like a lid over the fields. Climbing out through the hatches at dawn, they felt the air sting their noses and their breath left them in clouds of white.

Joel drank from his steaming teacup and looked round.

'If this keeps up, they'll have to get the icebreakers out.'

But the ice was thin enough for the boats to nose through quite easily, cracking it into thin, glasslike sheets. The cold and stillness did not lift all day and the ducks, which usually appeared round the boats looking for food, stayed tucked in the undergrowth and reeds. Only a solitary heron braved the cold and flapped languidly ahead of them, landing at intervals on the bank until the motor grew nearer and drove it onwards again.

Soon they were approaching the junction at Braunston, where they would turn onto the Oxford Canal. As they came through the tunnel at Braunston, enveloped in damp darkness, Maryann thought, *Nancy and Darius'll be about at Warwick or Leamington by now*. Would they see them on the way back? She was disappointed and uneasy. She had wanted the reassurance of Darius and Nance tied up near them when they reached Tyseley Wharf.

She only became gradually aware of the shouting ahead because she was in the cabin. They'd made the turn and Bobby was at the helm. She could hear something, but then Bobby's voice came to her: 'Maryann – you'd best come out!'

He pointed as she came and stood outside. They'd tied the butty on a shorter strap to go through Braunston, so she was not far behind Joel on the *Esther Jane*. The first thing she saw was a small crowd ahead on the bank, who were waving and shouting at them, while a tan and white dog ran back and forth about their legs, barking in agitation. It took only seconds to see that something was seriously wrong. Maryann took in the scene in small glimpses of understanding, as if the corner of a large picture was being gradually revealed to her. A space had been reserved for them along the bank and several of the women were beckoning them urgently to pull in. As they drew close, she made out that the boats the gaggle of people had gathered by were the *Isla* and the *Neptune*. Her mind struggled with this: why were they here instead of much further ahead? Then Joel turned and signalled to them that they were pulling in and Bobby was saying, 'Oh my – what's amiss here?' and at that moment, from the cabin of the *Neptune*, Maryann saw Darius appear and step off the boat. There was a stiffness in the way he moved and his face was like that of a statue carved from the hardest granite.

'Oh, Bobby.' Maryann went cold all over at the sight of him. 'Summat terrible's happened, I can tell. Where's Nance?'

Helping hands seized the straps and secured them as they jumped onto the bank, Maryann taking Sally's hand. Everyone stood back and became quiet as Joel went to his brother. Maryann walked behind, suddenly acutely conscious of following Joel's footsteps, the brown corduroy of his trousers above his boots, of turning to reach out to Sally again as she ran up beside her, of stopping as Joel put his hand on Darius's shoulder. The older brother crumpled, lowering his head, a hand going up to cover his face.

No! Maryann was screaming inside herself. *Not one of the children, not Nance, not any of them, O God, please, no!*

Darius looked up again, face twisted with grief. 'Her's

67

drownded.' His voice cracked. 'My little mate. My Nancy.'

Maryann heard the sound of a woman weeping behind her. Darius, sobbing openly now, led them into the cabin away from the watching eyes. He went and sat on the edge of the back bed. The first thing Maryann was aware of was the three children, squashed like peas in a pod along the side bench, all crying heartbrokenly. It was the most miserable sight she could imagine. She and Joel squeezed inside the cabin. Nancy lay on the back bed, covered with a blanket, its curving line tracing the shape of her heavy pregnancy. As Darius leaned back to allow them closer, Maryann saw that her friend's face was a bluish white, the features lifeless, somehow impersonal. Nancy, yet not Nancy: the power, the spark of life extinguished in her. Maryann stared, unable fully to take in the sight. The children continued to cry behind her.

'Oh, Nance,' she whispered. Leaning over, she reached under the blanket for her old friend's hand and grasped the cold fingers. 'Come on, Nance,' she said, squeezing them. 'Oh, Nance, what've you done? What's happened to you?' She recoiled, a howl of horror and protest trapped in her chest. 'What's happened?' she demanded of Darius. How could he have let this happen to her friend, to Nancy, who was brimming with energy, with joy, her body leaping with the life of another child? She felt Joel's hand on her shoulder and turned to him, his arms clasping her tight. All of them were weeping. Maryann pulled away and put her arms briefly round Darius, then went and knelt in front of Darrie, Sean and little Rose, trying to draw them all to her at once.

Eight

It was some time before they were calm enough to hear from Darius what had happened. They climbed out and stood in a gaggle, the crowd on the bank tactfully retreating.

The previous evening Darius and Nancy had gone on, getting ahead right into the dusk, aiming to get to Braunston for the night. Darkness seemed to fall even more quickly than usual and they were still on the move, persevering on through the gloom with their blacked-out headlamp. They'd get through the last few locks on the Grand Union, they agreed, tie up at Braunston and get a good start in the morning. It was already punishingly cold, ice forming on the ground, making the towpath and lock sides treacherously slippery. Nancy had been inside the *Neptune*, bedding the children down, and Ernie was at the tiller. At the bridge-hole before the locks, though, Nancy had completed her chores and picked up the windlass.

'I'll go out for a bit. I could do with stretching my legs,' she said to Ernie. 'You stay here.'

Before he could argue she'd stepped off. Darius hadn't known that she'd got off instead of Ernie until he looked back, wondering why Ernie hadn't already passed the motor boat, running ahead to make sure the lock was ready. Instead, he saw Nancy puffing and panting along.

'I was a bit put out with her,' Darius said. 'We was

trying to get on and she couldn't move as fast as she can – could – normal like, her being so big. I thought, what did Nance want to go getting off for? But it were too late by then.

'We got through two and Nance was managing all right, she were strong, you know. And nippy, even when she was expecting . . . We was breasted up and Nance'd shut the gates behind us.' He shook his head, still disbelieving of what had happened. 'She'd gone and got the first paddle up. I dunno how she came to fall. She knew she always had to hold on. It was second nature. She was crossing the gate to get the other one and . . . I wasn't even looking. I'd gone into the cabin for summat. She come off the gates, fell right down.' His distress mounted as he talked. 'I don't know if she hit her head on the gate or on the *Isla* . . . But I looked up – the water was only coming in from one side so it was pushing us about and I thought why ent she got the other paddle open? And she weren't there.' His face crumpled again. 'She just weren't there any more.'

It was a silent, grief-stricken cortège which made its desolate way back to Sutton Stop, outside Coventry. Other boaters who called greetings, ignorant of the tragedy, were met by the frozen, unresponsive faces of people lost in their own thoughts and emotions and the one-sided 'How d'you do's?' faded unanswered on the air. Darius stood straight and still at the tiller of the *Isla* as the boats bore the love of his life back to be buried among the people and villages they knew so well.

For Maryann, every chug of the engine seemed to hammer home the pain inside her. Even here, at the heart of her family, she felt very alone without Nancy. Nance

70

had been her oldest friend, and each had linked the other with the past, with their childhood. Now Nance was gone. It was so difficult to believe and hard not to wait expectantly for Nance to pop up through the *Neptune*'s hatches in her bright clothes and shine the brass bands on her chimney with her usual vigour, or wave and make daft faces at them as they followed behind. All the times she would not see Nance now, all the chats and shared chores and confidences poured into her mind, bombarding her with a future of sad loneliness.

She had managed to find a quiet moment before they left. She asked Darius if she could go aboard the *Neptune* alone to say goodbye and had taken with her a few sprigs of winter jasmine and some pretty red berries which, in their colourful flamboyance, reminded her of Nance. She sat beside her old friend's body. Nance's face was very bruised on the left side, her clothes were still damp and her coldness made Maryann recoil – it seemed so foreign to the warm, vibrant friend she had known. But she took Nance's hand and held it. If she didn't hold her now, soon it would be too late.

'I don't know what I'm going to do without you, old pal.' Her throat ached and the sobs began to rise in her. She pressed Nance's cold hand against her cheek and its strange stiffness made her cry even more. 'Oh, Nance – why did you go and get out of the boat? Couldn't you've sat still, just for once? Why did you have to go and leave us all?'

She drew the blanket back a little, and through her tears looked at Nance's distended body. The poor little baby! Did he die when Nance died or after, living on inside his dead mother, not realizing she was not able to care for him any more and keep him safe? It was a terrible thought. Grief tore at her, for herself and for

Darius and his motherless children. However would he manage now?

'I'll do all I can for them, Nance, you know I will. For Darrie and Sean and Rose. But oh, Nance, it's going to be bitter hard for us all without you.'

Nancy lay so peacefully, so uncharacteristically silent. If it were not for the bruising she looked as if she were sleeping, enjoying a sweet dream in her cosy little home. Here she lay on this bed, Maryann thought, which was hardly a bed at all, more a board with a few bits of bedding, but which had served as a happy marriage bed for what was not even a real marriage either in the eyes of respectable people. But Nance had been real all right. And what she and Darius had had made a pale shadow of a lot of other people's marriages. The cut and its people had truly lit the fire of life in Nancy, and the cut had also taken it away.

At last she leaned down and kissed the unbruised side of her old friend's face, her tears falling on Nance's pallid skin.

'You rest now, my love,' she said. 'Sweet dreams.' And, before covering her again, she laid the yellow jasmine and the bright berries on her breast.

Maryann sent a telegram to Cathleen Black, Nance's mom.

They were to finish the journey to Birmingham later. All that week the family clung together. Maryann did everything she could for Nancy's children. Darrie preferred to stay with his father and Rose was very young. Of all of them it was little curly-haired Sean who most wrung her heart, asking and asking where his mom had

72

gone. He and Rose seemed to take some comfort from the presence of their auntie Maryann.

Cathleen Black came from Birmingham for the funeral, with four of Nancy's brothers and her two younger sisters, Lizzie and Mary. Cathleen and Nance had been close, as for many years Nancy had been the only girl among a gaggle of brothers. Cathleen's curly hair had long turned from salt and pepper grey to a silvery white. She had on a squashed black felt hat pushed down over it and a brown tweed coat belted tightly at the waist. She wore spectacles now and her eyes, one of which had been crossed from birth, peered out rather rakishly from behind the thick lenses. Her children were all in their Sunday best, Lizzie and Mary in frocks that were too big for them. All of them were pale and strained with loss.

They knew Nance would have wanted to be buried from the cut rather than back in Birmingham, so the funeral was to be at the church in Longford, where so many narrowboat women had been churched and their babies christened. Maryann put on her one and only best dress which she had kept from her wedding, in soft, blue wool. It felt very peculiar wearing it again.

It was a cold day, but dry. Nancy's coffin was lifted with great care onto the roof of the *Isla* and decorated with flowers. Darius took the tiller, Darrie and Sean beside him. Sean looked bewildered and sad, but Darrie, togged up in his best clothes, dark eyed and solemn, seemed older and more dignified than his seven years. Maryann travelled on the *Neptune* with Cathleen and Nance's sisters, Rose and the twins. Joel brought up the rear on the *Esther Jane* with all the other youngsters squeezed aboard, the lads thinking it great sport to cling along the gunwales which were very low in the water as the boats were still loaded with their Birmingham steel. And behind came Ernie's family, the Higginses, on their boat *Dragonfly* and a number of other families who all wanted to support the Bartholomews.

'At least on the way I can talk to Cathleen and explain properly,' Maryann said to Joel before they untied. 'Poor thing – you can just see what this's done to her, can't you?'

Cathleen seemed dazed and not at all herself. Once they'd started, Maryann handed the tiller to Lizzie, who was twelve and thrilled by the responsibility.

'Just hold it steady in the middle. Shout if you're worried.' She went in to make more tea and see Cathleen, who was sitting in the cabin, looking round her in bewilderment.

'God, Maryann, how d'you manage to live on here? I thought our house was cramped! I can't see Nance keeping one of these spick and span! My poor girl . . .' Her eyes filled again. Maryann handed her a cup of tea with a sizable portion of their sugar ration in it.

'She did, though. Loved it. She was always full of beans, Nance was. Better at keeping up with it all than me.'

Cathleen almost managed a smile. 'Well, she didn't get that from me.'

Nancy's little Rose who was now three, came and pawed shyly at Maryann's arm.

'Hello, bab.' Maryann put her arm round her, cut by the lost look in the child's eyes.

'God love her.' Cathleen looked round for somewhere to put her tea down. 'Come here, darlin' – come and see your nanna.'

Rose looked fearfully at the strange lady peering at her from behind thick spectacles, then back at Maryann.

'It's all right, pet – that's your nanna – your mom's mom. Don't you remember Nanny Cathleen? Go to her for a love.'

Eventually Rose consented to be cuddled. Tears came into Cathleen's eyes. 'She's the image of our Nancy, she is. What'll become of the children, Maryann? Whatever's he going to do?'

'I don't know,' Maryann said wanly. She had been so numb, this week of grieving, that just getting through each day had been hard enough. 'I don't know how Darius is going to get along, Cathleen. I've never seen a man look more lost.'

'I know.' Cathleen paused, then looked across at Maryann. 'Our Nancy really loved him – she did, didn't she? I know it really – it's just that if she'd stayed with her husband, with Mick Mallone, none of this would have happened . . .'

Maryann leaned across to her. 'Cathleen, Nancy had more happiness with Darius these few years than she could have had in a lifetime with Mick.'

Cathleen gave a heavy, sorrow-laden sigh. 'I know.' She kissed the top of Rose's curls, holding the child close. 'I know that really. You only had to look at her.'

Nancy's coffin was carried into church with great ceremony, borne on the shoulders of Darius, Joel, Ernie Higgins and three of her brothers, Charlie, Jim and Percy. The rest of them processed behind with the other mourners. Nance had won a great deal of respect and liking among the boating people, for her skill and cheerfulness and her well-scrubbed family; now they had come to support the Bartholomew brothers and see Nancy off in style. Maryann had been surprised and grateful at their reaction to Nance. This community of people were, in the main, sticklers for convention. Because they were different, not readily understood by outsiders, they fought off the insults that they were dirty 'water gypsies' by strict adherence to social codes. Boaters were married and buried in style, and woe betide a boatwoman who associated too much with another woman's husband unless his wife was within earshot as well! But though Darius and Nance had never married, their situation was understood and accepted. Darius was respected and his 'best mate' was respected too.

Maryann walked with Cathleen, whose nose was pink with cold.

'I've never set foot in a Protestant church before,' she whispered, holding Rose's plump hand and gazing fearfully up at the benign facade of Longford parish church.

'It'll be all right.' Maryann squeezed her arm. 'It's nice. Nance liked it.'

'Did she?' Cathleen sounded surprised, then determined. 'Anyway – Father Ryan's not here to see me, is he?'

In their pews in the musty old church, the boaters and Nance's family sang and prayed Nancy to rest. Out of habit, Cathleen took her string of white rosary beads from her pocket and told them throughout. As they sang 'Abide with Me', Maryann felt the desolate, unjust sorrow of it all overwhelm her and she wept with her arms round Rose and Sally, who cried too at the sight of her. After, while the vicar was reciting the service, other words came back to her, spoken to her during her time in service in Banbury by Roland Musson, one of the sons of the family. Roland had survived the Great War in body, if not entirely in mind, and lived as a recluse at home. That morning he had told her about a young lad in his unit who had completed a successful raid in No Man's Land one night, but was killed first thing the next day. For a moment Maryann was back standing in the sun-filled room at Charnwood House, with Roland Musson saying, '. . . chap stood up for a few seconds and bang – killed by a sniper. So what was it all about? Man grows up, becomes himself overnight, then –' He snapped his fingers. 'Like a bloody butterfly.'

And what was it all about? Maryann thought bitterly, when they watched Nance's coffin being lowered into the ground. God takes the best young, some people said. This enraged her. Why bother with God if he was like that? Why tangle with God at all of he wasn't the sort who'd be there crying beside her because Nance's life had been cut short?

The sun broke through and shone bravely against the cold as they stood there, Joel beside his grief-stricken brother, who broke down over the grave.

'My Nancy,' he groaned, 'my lovely Nancy . . .'

'Oh, the poor man,' murmured Cathleen Black. 'Holy Jesus, why did this have to happen?'

Before the family left again for Birmingham, Cathleen asked Darius whether he wanted her to take any of the children to look after.

'They'll all be too much for you on your own, won't they, God love them?'

Darius, already distraught, could not contemplate the idea of losing any more of his family that day, even as a temporary measure. He thanked her a little brusquely, but said he wanted to keep his family together. Cathleen suddenly put her arms round him and pulled him close with affection.

'We've all lost a jewel in our Nancy,' she said, 'but I want to thank you for giving her these few truly happy years. I've never seen her bonnier or more full of life than when she was with you, Darius.'

Finding it hard to speak, Darius managed to thank her for her daughter and shyly embrace her.

'Come and see us whenever you can,' Cathleen said, trying to be brave. 'I don't want to miss my grandchildren growing up.'

After they had waved the Blacks off to catch their evening train, Maryann helped Darius to settle the children, all together in the big bed for comfort. They were tearful and exhausted and soon fell asleep, while Maryann and Darius sat on the side bench. Sean was still snuffling pitifully even after sleep overtook him. Darius looked across at his sleeping children, an anguish beyond words in his eyes.

'Well,' he sighed. 'We'll just have to keep on, somehow.'

Maryann nodded, tearful again, and touched his arm. She loved Darius like a brother. 'I know,' she said, and for them these simple words were enough to acknowledge the chasm of emptiness left by Nance's passing.

'I want you to have these now.' Darius slid a hand into his jacket pocket and laid on Maryann's hand two gold hoops: Nance's earrings, which had belonged to Esther, Darius and Joel's mother. She knew this was an honour, as if to say, you're the only one left in line now.

She nodded again, understanding. 'I'll always wear them.'

*

It had been a gruelling day and her own children were asleep when she got back to the *Theodore*. Joel poured each of them a generous tot of whisky, which they drank gratefully, along with their tea, and sat on at the table, somehow reluctant to go to bed.

Once lying side by side, they seemed unable to sleep, as if loss of consciousness was a denial of life, and after this day of death and heavy sorrow they needed to seize life and hold on to it. Maryann lay with her head on Joel's chest, his arm round her, hearing the whisper of his lungs.

'You sound chesty tonight.'

'I can feel it coming on a bit.' He wheezed, and gave a cough to clear it. 'Bitter today, wasn't it?'

There was a pause, then Maryann raised her head to look at him. 'How's Darius going to manage? He won't be able to, will he? Not with the three of them and no Nance?'

Joel shook his head. 'I don't know what's going to be best. Can't think. But we couldn't say much about it today could us? I reckon we'll need to help him out.'

'Take the children you mean?'

Joel's nod meant 'maybe', Maryann saw with some dismay. But she knew she had to do anything she could to see Nance's children were taken care of. She peeped over at their twins' sleeping faces.

'I couldn't bear it if it was you.' She looked down at Joel. 'I don't think I could go on. Not without you.'

Smiling, his vivid eyes looking deep into hers, Joel reached up and stroked her cheek. 'My lovely,' he said, 'my little mate. We're here now though, ent we? Now is what we've got.'

'Oh, Joel—' A shudder went through her. 'Nancy was so cold! I don't want to die.'

He stroked her back, making loving, soothing noises, and in a moment they were kissing, pressing close together, fierce with desire for each other, for life. As they loved one another it did not even cross Maryann's mind to stop him, to ask him to pull away at the last minute. The heat of their bodies, the joy and healing comfort of it was all, life and its celebration was what mattered. She pulled him close, her arms clenched to hold him tight, and after their lovemaking they slept, curled tightly together in the freezing night.

Nine

'You poorly again, Mom?'

Maryann just managed to grab the dipper in time and leant over it, retching. Though she was secluded in the privacy of the cabin, she was being watched by a row of curious children, Ezra, Sally and Rose, as her morning tea gushed out into the bottom of the wide container.

Maryann wiped her lips and watering eyes, grimacing at the acid taste in her mouth. She nodded absent-mindedly at Sally's question, not having the strength to reply. She knew this sickness all too well. After drinking down a cup of water she went out, amid the shouts and rattling of chains of the wharf, to empty the dipper. The contents met the surface with a glutinous 'plop' and the milk curled in the dark water for a moment before disappearing. They were at Tyseley again, their cargo being unloaded. Exhausted before the day had even begun, she rested for a moment against the cabin, looking out across the piles of deep orange steel, the scrappy wharf refuse of wire, nails, bits of wood and greasy rags scattered over the cindery ground. She'd been too caught up in her present woes to be afraid of coming back here. All she'd been able to think of on the wet trip up from Limehouse was keeping going, trying to get through the day and not show that she felt sick or weak or faint.

It was two months since Nancy's death and the harsh freeze of that winter had given way to March winds and rain. Starting work again after the funeral, they'd all had to make decisions about how things were going to be managed. Should Darius give up his Barlow boats and come back aboard the *Esther Jane*? But Mr Barlow was desperate to keep all his boats and crews working. The war created an almost bottomless demand for coal, steel and other materials. Let Darius keep the *Isla* and *Neptune*, he said. He could work them with Ernie and he'd find him an extra crewman. The man who filled Nance's place – in no other respect except that he was a lifelong boater – was a middle-aged man called Joe Toms. Joe had also been a Number One and had kept on with his own horse until recently, when his wife had died 'of the bronchitus'. Darius already knew Joe quite well and thought they'd be able to work together. He also said that he could manage aboard with Darrie and Sean, but was grateful when Joel said he and Maryann would look after Rose. Sally was delighted with this arrangement as she was two years older than Rose; it provided both another female playmate and a subject to be bossed about. She immediately started teaching Rose her letters. For Maryann she was another child to be fed and protected from all the dangers of the cut, but she was also a link with Nancy and she did her best for the little girl. But during those months of freezing wind and rain Maryann's spirits had been very low, and when she started to be sick she was filled with despair.

They were mostly working the old routes, the Coventry and Oxford cuts, with occasional trips to London and Birmingham. Maryann had said nothing to Joel about her fears that her stepfather, Norman Griffin, was looking for her. This was only their second trip to Tyseley in the past two months and nothing had happened so far that was out of the ordinary. She was beginning to relax again. After all, why on earth should Norman Griffin want to have anything to do with her after all these years? If anyone was capable of leaving one life and starting off again in another, with a new name and identity, it was him. Why would he want to come back, disturbing old memories?

Leaning over the side, she rinsed the dipper out. A dead bird floated, stiff-legged, close to the bank, rotating slowly on a twisting current. Jenny, the tortoiseshell cat, watched it mesmerized, head twitching back and forth.

'Can't we get off yet?' Ezra demanded behind her.

'No!' Maryann snapped, standing up. 'How many times've I told you, you can't be out there running about when we're unloading. See them chains swinging about? They could have your head off.' She softened a little, looking into his eager, if filthy face. 'They've nearly finished, pet. Just stay on a bit more. A wash wouldn't hurt you, would it?'

Back in the cabin she managed to force a slice of dry bread down her throat and feed the children. It would be a relief when the unloading was completed and the cooped-up children could escape onto the bank, scampering over to find Joel and Joley in the offices.

Maryann sank down on the side bed, still feeling weak and sick. Lord, if only she could lie down and sleep again! Everywhere she looked there was muck and mess – jobs staring her in the face, crocks to be washed, a pan gluey with porridge, crumbs and dirt everywhere, the stove all rust and a pail of dirty napkins outside, beckoning with their smell. Ada and Esther had had a feed and gone back to sleep behind the curtains of the back bed. She shut them in to keep it dark, hoping they'd sleep as long as possible. They'd wake soon, though, and while they were tied up here she ought to be cleaning and washing like mad to get caught up with herself! But her head felt muzzy in the hot cabin and her limbs just wouldn't seem to move, however much her head ordered them to. Her ribs and stomach felt tender from retching. She sat, staring dully at the stains down her skirt, her innards still turning uneasily.

Ada and Esther were seven months old now. Really bonny, everyone said. Esther's hair had grown into dark curls, her eyes big and blue, cheeks rosy and plump. And Ada was still the live wire, smaller featured, red haired and with a nose-wrinkling smile. But only seven months since they were born! How could she have caught again so soon? Her despair sat in her, cold as stone. She felt pushed down too low even for tears. So far she had managed to hide the fact that she was expecting from Joel. She was ashamed of not telling him. She would have liked his happiness, his sympathy, when she felt so ill, but she hid her exhaustion and poorliness as well as she could. Because Joel would never forgive her if he knew what was in her mind. To Joel his children were the fruits of his manhood, his success, his pledge for the future. She couldn't confide in him, not this time. Though she was now certain she was expecting, she didn't allow herself to think of the infant as 'he' or 'she'. She pushed away any imaginings of it as grown up, running among her other children, hand in hand along the flowery towpaths of the Oxford cut. Because having another child was unimaginable. It was impossible. There were already six infants on board. Her whole over-whelmed being cried no! It could not be. In that cold, hard place inside her, she knew she could not do it. Not now. She'd give Joel more children later, but not so soon. She needed more of a gap or she would go under, and then, as Alice Simons had said, where would the rest of the family be?

Moving carefully so as not to lurch her insides about, she eased herself to her feet, rinsed the dipper out again with clean water and piled the family's few crocks in it. All the time, shouts and clangs came from outside. Her ears were cocked for sounds of the twins waking. She must get some things done before they woke! She was so slow, fighting sickness and faintness when she stood up too quickly. All the time, as she poured hot water and soap over the dishes, while she hurriedly rinsed out the napkins and strung them along the empty hold of the *Theodore*, her mind worried frantically at her problems. Bobby usually went and filled the water cans for them when they tied up. But maybe if she went to fill them, lugged those arm-breaking eight-gallon cans back and forth, would that do it? Would that be a way of starting things off? Doing away with ... it?

Scraping porridge from the sides of the pan, she tried to recall fragments of conversations overheard in her childhood, the things women whispered over the grimy walls of Ladywood backyards. These were the scraps of wisdom and hearsay she called upon when the children fell ill: tea-leaf water for sore eyes, goose fat for bad chests, the middle of a boiled onion in the ear when they had earache. But it was more adult, whispered remedies she tried to remember. Drinking water which had had pennies boiled in it, pennyroyal syrup, gin? Wasn't there something about gin? And, whispered more quietly, more shamefully still, 'putting something up inside'. Once she'd followed her mother into a house where she was helping another woman who'd 'had a miss', and before Flo shooed her out again she'd glimpsed at the foot of the bed the po' half full of blood. The image made her innards contract with fear. Round and round spun her thoughts. What could she do? Oh, if there were just someone she could ask, could confide in! If only Nancy were still here! She couldn't have told Nance, though, not about this. Not life-loving, Catholic Nance – she would've been horrified. But at least she would've been here, the comfort of her, not gone for ever. She ached with loneliness, the tears running down her cheeks and dripping into the washing-up water, but when she tried to stop, wiping her face with her sleeve, the sight of a fraying tear in her old brown cardi made her cry even harder. *If only I had someone to talk to*, she wept. *God, the way I nearly blurted everything out to that preacher last night. That would've given him something to pray about, all right.*

They'd reached Tyseley in the late afternoon and Maryann had hurried out without the children, to get to the shops for their rations before everything closed. Even a brief chat with Mr Osborne hadn't lifted her spirits. As she came back across the wharf with her bread, meat, spuds and tinned milk, she saw the pale young man whom she had caught sight of with his bible on the wharf a few months back. He was speaking to one of the other boatwomen as she stood on the counter of her butty boat, lifting out the tiller to upend it for the night. The man was dressed shabbily in black and wore a trilby hat. His one flash of colour was a red tartan scarf, the ends of which were blowing back over his shoulder in the breeze. Maryann saw the woman nod politely, say something which was evidently dismissive, and disappear into her cabin.

And as Maryann moved across to the *Theodore*, he was suddenly beside her.

'Good evening, madam,' he said, touching the brim of his hat.

'Evening,' Maryann said brusquely. She knew nothing about the man except that he must be one of those 'holy Joes' and they were people she had long found disquieting. She remembered the odd figure of Jimmy Jesus, who used to stand shouting out his message in the Bull Ring. And as children they were frightened of running into the Mormons because people said they would steal away young girls and force them to be brides in Salt Lake City.

'May I presume upon a moment of your time, madam?' he persisted. From his accent, Maryann could tell he was not from Birmingham but from somewhere further north. He held out to her a pale, thin hand and when she felt forced to stop and glance into his eyes, she saw they were large and dark grey and somehow melancholy in a way which made her soften a little towards him. He had well-pronounced brows and lips so full that she found them off-putting, they looked so plump and moist. But she felt obliged to push her packages into the clasp of her left arm and shake hands, conscious of her rough, callused palms.

'I'm Pastor Owen,' he told her. 'James Owen.' Instead of releasing her hand, he turned it over and examined it.

'A hand that knows a hard-working life,' he said, giving her another of his deep, mournful looks. To her consternation, Maryann felt tears pricking her eyes. She pulled her hand away, making out that she was about to drop her shopping.

'What d'you want?' It came out sharper than she had intended.

'Only a moment of your time to share with you the good news of the risen Christ. I'm quite new to the Lord's work in this area.' He spoke so humbly and sincerely that she felt guilty, but had no idea what to say in reply. In her head, her mother's voice admonished, 'Tell him to bugger off!'

Instead, she said, 'Oh, I see.'

From the pocket of his coat he drew a small, plump bible. Without opening it, but holding it out on the flat of his hand as if proffering a plate of sandwiches, he said, '"Come to me, all ye that labour and are heavy laden, and I will give you rest." The words of our Lord Jesus – and I am very certain that upon Him alone you can lay all your burdens, Mrs . . .?'

'Bartholomew.'

'Mrs Bartholomew.' He went on to tell her how Jesus was the only gate to eternal salvation and to ask whether she had any pressing burdens upon her soul.

Maryann almost quipped that if he had a couple of hours to spare she could tell him a few, but she was prevented by the genuine sense of sympathy coming from the young man, along with his gangly, rather pathetic look. He could only have been in his early twenties and looked as if, had she laid the burdens of her soul upon him as he suggested, his knees might have buckled under the strain.

'I don't think so, not today, thank you,' she said, as if refusing wares from a fish salesman.

'Well, just remember – Jesus is the way,' he said earnestly. 'And I will pray for you, Mrs Bartholomew. I trust you will do the same for me.'

As she nodded, he touched the brim of his hat again and turned away, and she watched his long, skinny form move along the wharf, looking out for other boaters who would stop and listen to his message. Boaters whom he no doubt saw as the unschooled and unsaved souls of the cut whom he must rescue.

Thinking of him now as she struggled through her chores, Maryann knew how close she had come to blurting out her woes to him – a young man, wet behind the ears and a complete stranger! But in her fear and loneliness he was the one person who had asked about her concerns, and who might listen. But then, on hearing, how sharply he would have condemned her! She was contemplating nothing less than the murder of a child in her womb! She was a terrible mother, a terrible woman. But, she thought defiantly, what did that young lad know about being a mother? How could he judge her?

More tears ran down her cheeks.

'Oh, Nance, come back! O God, forgive me for feeling like this!'

She pushed her hands down into the bottom of the dipper and straightened her arms, leaning over the warm water. She was so lost in misery that she didn't move until she heard Joel's voice talking to the children as they all came across the wharf.

Ten

Joel Bartholomew stood at the tiller of the *Esther Jane* later that morning as they made their way, empty for the moment, through Birmingham and out to the coalfields. It was grey and overcast, the warehouses and factories black as shadows as they closed in on each side, and the air darkened by a pall of smoke. Joel breathed in the fume-filled air, then coughed. The Birmingham sky was cluttered with chimneys, the tallest and blackest being those of the fires of industry, belching aggressively into the clouds and creating further clouds themselves. Many more belonged to the endless rows of houses, which seemed to Joel so gloomy and confining. But he only caught glimpses of them: the cut showed him little of Birmingham's life, and it saw little of theirs.

Joel took in less than usual of his surroundings that morning, beyond an automatic watchfulness for the care of his boats, because his mind was restless. Men steering the horse-drawn corporation refuse boats out from the centre of Birmingham to Small Heath tip or to the incinerator at Hay Mills would have seen the *Esther Jane* and her butty heading towards them, washing flapping over the hold of the *Theodore*, and Joel at the tiller, burly, bearded, cap pushed down over his thick hair, his wide-sleeved brown jacket buttoned against the cold. They might have heard his racking cough as he drew nearer, from the damp getting into his lungs. But as they drew alongside and shouted, 'Mornin'!' or 'How d'you do?' as was customary among the politer boaters, they received only the vaguest, most half-hearted response.

When they were approaching Camp Hill locks, Joel signalled back to Bobby. The boats were on a short strap as they were empty, so they were not far apart. Bobby jumped off the butty at one bridge-hole in Sparkbrook and ran forwards to jump aboard the *Esther Jane* at the next.

'You come and steer her through,' Joel ordered, pushing his windlass through his belt. 'I'm going off for a bit.'

'But . . .' Bobby tried to protest. Maryann said the exertions of lock-wheeling made Joel's cough worse and that Bobby should stay off and do it, but Joel was not in the mood to be argued with.

'Can I come, Dad?' Joley called, but too late as another bridge passed and Joel was on the bank.

'You stay on,' he called tersely.

All the way along the flight at Camp Hill he worked with fierce energy, turning the paddles, cursing when his cough doubled him up and made him stop, fighting for breath. He felt taut and explosive inside, his blood hammering in his veins, and he wanted a way to release the tension inside himself. As they worked along the fast-filling locks, he kept his eyes on the immediate task, only casting his glance over the boats in a general, instinctive way, to make sure all was going smoothly. His muscles pulled and strained on the windlass as he turned the paddles.

Every step of the way, though he did not allow his eyes to meet hers, her presence, the white-faced figure of his wife seemed to burn itself into him. His Maryann, his little bird, at the tiller of the *Theodore*, Sally and Rose perched in their coats in front of her on the cabin roof. Once or twice he heard her speak sharply to them. He could hardly avoid catching glimpses of her, in her black skirt and boots, a scarf tied over her hair and her old tweed jacket over her woollens, upright and stony-faced at the helm. Round her had grown up an aura of such misery and loneliness that, however much Joel loved her, he couldn't seem to break through it and now could hardly bear to see it. He knew it was over the loss of Nancy, and he was full of pain and grief too, for Maryann, for his brother, for himself. And Nancy was the one person who knew Maryann from deep in the past, knew her in a way in which no one else did, and Joel knew Maryann's grief cut sharp and raw. But he sensed it was more than that. Over the past few days he felt that something else was troubling her, something he couldn't understand, and he couldn't seem to reach her.

Last night, when they'd lain together in the warm, stuffy air of the *Theodore*, the bitter smell of coal mingling with their breath, he soon realized that though she was silent she was lying awake beside him. The bed was very narrow and no small movement or catch of breath could pass unnoticed if you were awake. Out of the darkness he heard a long, only half-suppressed sigh. For days her face had worn a strained, unhappy look, a frown constantly on her face, sometimes a look of pain. He knew that pale, sick look from when there was a child on the way, but she had said nothing. He knew she was worried about that. Once or twice she had, very shyly, said something about could he pull away – before the last moment. He wasn't sure if she really meant this. It seemed to him such an unnatural, perverse request to ask him to withdraw at the moment when he was giving himself to her and was least able to control himself. He had managed it a couple of times, the second when she cried out, begging him to move away, and with a huge effort he had wrenched himself from her, almost too late. He found it so hard, such a denial of what he needed, that it hadn't always worked. But when he asked if there was a child she shook her head.

'No.' She looked away. 'I've just got a bit of an upset tummy.'

He knew she found the life hard, especially since the children had come along, but in the past she had always reassured him about how much she loved him and how she would not exchange this way of life for any other. But something was eating away at her, he knew, and her quiet suffering made him feel tense and helpless. What should he say? How was he to understand her?

Hearing her sigh in bed, sensing the burdened spirit behind that small outrush of breath, he had reached for her, hoping to achieve with his touch what he could not seem to with words. He felt the comfort of her slight, strong body, his hand sliding over her breast, its soft rounded shape, utter pleasure to him. With his lips he found her neck, moving closer to her, wanting to love her, to give affection and comfort. He stroked her back, her breasts, his hand working downwards over her belly. As he eased his fingers between her legs, her voice burst into the darkness in a wail.

'Oh, Joel, *please* don't!'

She was shaking beside him, sobs breaking out of her like waves taking their time to reach the shore. Weeping brokenly, she turned her back on him.

Having no idea what to do or say, he pulled away, keeping only his hand on her back as she wept in an attempt at comfort, swelling inside with feelings of help-lessness and rejection. When her crying abated, she fell

93

into an exhausted sleep, leaving him restless and frustrated.

He stayed on the bank for a long time that afternoon as they set off along the Bottom Road. He bow-hauled the butty in and out of the locks, through Aston, amid the black, enclosing walls of that part of the cut, the towpaths clogged with oily filth and cinders and its narrow, slime-choked locks. Despite Bobby's repeated offers to exchange places with him, and Joley hopping off to walk warily at his side, he worked on like a dynamo, coughing, working the paddles, tugging on the line to haul the butty, his spirit in turmoil.

Never before in their marriage had he felt this distance from his Maryann. There had been times when the poor, troubled child he knew, before she came back to him as a woman, had closed off from them all and sat sunk in misery. And on many occasions, amid the stress and physical struggles of the boating life, their tempers had crackled and exploded at each other. But that was temporary, was about something he could grasp the meaning of and was over in moments as the annoyance or danger passed. He had never before felt her to be so wholly distant, so completely wretched, and, as if she were his lodestar, he felt thrown off course and afraid.

Is it because she's from off the bank? he wondered. She *was* baffling at times. He often could not work out what was going on in her head. If he'd married a boatwoman born and bred, would it have been easier? Were they more straightforward, the women of the cut, having been known no other life? Was Maryann finally discovering that she couldn't endure it any longer and secretly longing for a house and unmoving days on the bank?

Joel stood at Garrison locks as the water roared

through the paddles. This was the filthiest, most demoralizing part of the whole journey. Overhead, railways criss-crossed over black, clattering bridges; warehouse walls hemmed them in on each side so that the rodent-coloured sky was almost out of sight altogether, but, like a grim reflection, several dead rats were bobbing in the cut amid the scum and oil of the water. A crewman from one of the joey boats waiting to come through the other way bawled along the path, waving his arm.

'Get bloody moving will you?' and Joel realized the water had levelled and he was still standing, staring.

Passing onwards, he tried to imagine any other life than the one he had known. His only time on the bank had been two years in the army, most of it away in France. He had volunteered the year after his mother's death in 1916 in childbirth, when Ada was born. Joel's twin brothers Ezra and Sam had already gone and he left his father and Darius to man the boat, and his sister Sarah to keep house and tend to Ada. Joel was nineteen when he left for France. By the time he returned with his injured lungs, both Ezra and Sam had met their deaths on the Somme without him ever seeing them again, and soon afterwards Sarah had died of the influenza.

Before France, Joel had a part-time sweetheart. Part-time in the sense that boating courtships were capricious affairs, meetings dependent on the movements of cargoes and criss-crossing of boats which might or might not meet. By the time he came wheezing home to what was left of his family, Clara had married one of the 'joshers' and gone to work the Grand Union. Very occasionally, he caught sight of her now, looking across from one of the orange and green Fellows, Moreton & Clayton boats, face hardened by work and weather. A stiff, restrained salute was their only acknowledgement that they had exchanged youthful kisses and – Joel had believed – promises in the Warwickshire meadows all those years ago.

The years after the Great War had been a time of survival for the Bartholomews. By then the family consisted of three men, all numb with grief, and one infant girl, Ada. Ada grew up to be an adept boatwoman. She had been ten years old when a dark-haired girl just a couple of years her senior, skinny as a foal and fiery with mutinous emotions, wandered up to the *Esther Jane* one white, frozen day and announced fiercely to Joel that her name was Maryann Nelson and always would be. Only years later, as a grown woman, had Maryann consented to change her name to Bartholomew, and Joel knew what a store of trust she had invested in him.

He knew it wasn't easy marrying into his way of life, which, before the war began, had been under threat. The boaters kept moving their cargoes, pushing onwards, knowing that if they didn't shift a load they wouldn't get paid, whatever the season, whatever the weather. For Joel, boating was the life he knew in every cell of his body. Any length of time walking in city streets, caught between high buildings and away from the veins of the cut, made him feel fidgety and lost. Family history was a matter of word of mouth, with nothing written down, nor, until his marriage to Maryann, had any photographs ever been taken of his family. Now a framed photograph of that day, him smiling joyfully beside his young bride, hung in the cabin of the *Theodore* amid the ribbon-threaded plates. What he did know, though, was that for at least three generations, back into the haze of those days when Queen Victoria was a young bride herself, Bartholomews had worked the cut and, in particular, the

Oxford cut. Joel's landscape, inner and outer, was marked by winding contours, the black and white beams of locks, the graceful tilt of road bridges which leaned aside to let them past, by those soft, green hills. On that cut, for as long as anyone could remember, they had been Number Ones, working their own family boats, and Joel longed deeply to be a Number One again, for his sons and daughters to work the cut and to feel the dignity and self-respect which had been owned by the previous generations. And he could feel it slipping away from him.

Maryann, too, was so much a part of him now that her deep unhappiness weighed him down. What was troubling her? What could he do to lighten her, to make her smile again?

That night they found a place to stop at Minworth, out beyond the aerodrome. When he went to the *Theodore* after tying up, the three older children were out on the bank. From inside he could hear what sounded like both the twins crying. Timidly, he looked down through the hatches. Maryann was sitting opposite the stove, where bacon was frying in a pan, the fat spitting loudly. In a bowl nearby rested five eggs. She leaned forward to jerk the pan by the handle, her face white and impassive. His heart went out to her. He knew it was hard, that she had so much to do. But that was the life, wasn't it? That was how it was.

He climbed down and squatted on the coalbox and the screams battered his ears. Maryann didn't even look at him.

'Pass us one of them over,' he suggested.

Maryann leaned over and lifted an irate Ada into his arms while she latched Esther onto her breast, still jiggling the pan with one hand.

'We've got out through there, anyway,' Joel said. It was always a relief to get past that bit of the cut, even though soon they would reach the coalfields, where everything, landscape and people, was blackened by its dust. He spoke feeling nervous of her, though. He could tell there was something coiled up inside her.

Maryann nodded, still not looking at him. She leaned forward and flipped the rashers over with a knife.

'You all right, little mate?' he asked eventually.

She turned to him then, and in her eyes, for a second he saw a look of utter desperation. But then, by a miracle of will, a smile appeared on her face.

'Yes,' she assured him. 'Course. Tea's nearly ready. Tell Bobby, and the others, will you?'

Eleven

Maryann found herself jerking into consciousness now before dawn, sweating from her dreams. There was a recurring one in which the boats were tied up at Limehouse dock. Maryann was standing on the bank, her boots poised at the edge of the wharf, watching the tide go out, the sea sucking the water back rapidly, boats sinking deeper and deeper down until they seemed much further away than they would be in reality, tiny specks of colour at the foot of the grey wall with its clinging weed and slime. Round them stretched a sea of thick, oozing mud. She felt herself launch forwards over the edge, down, down, knowing that she was going to land smack across the empty hold of a boat and that her belly would pop open like a seed. Except it was the sickening feeling of falling which woke her every time so she never reached the bottom but woke, gasping.

God forgive me, she thought, lying trembling beside Joel's hot, oblivious body. *Just let me be free of it this one time. I'll be able to manage another babby later on, but they're all so close together. I can't. I just can't.*

As the days passed, Maryann knew she had to act. Fear held her back. What was she going to do? If only there was someone she could go to, someone kind like Sister Mary to whom she could pour out all her troubles. But they weren't going down through Stoke Bruerne, and in any case, how could she ever go to Sister Mary and admit what was on her mind? That she had reached such a pitch that she wanted to do away with her baby?

But if I'm going to do it, I've got to get on with it, she kept saying to herself. She could think of nothing else. The thought of it, the dread of childbirth, of another child to cope with possessed her. And supposing it was twins again! In front of Joel and Bobby she tried to act normally, to be cheerful and hide her sickness, though she was constantly pale and strained and she knew Joel had noticed. When she denied that anything was wrong, though, he didn't press her.

Her thoughts wouldn't leave her alone. The cold, closed-off feeling returned, which had come over her when she had run away from home as a young girl and come to Joel and his father on the cut. It had been like that later, for a time, after baby Harry died. If only she could tell Joel how she felt. But that was completely out of the question. If he knew what was in her mind . . . Well, she couldn't bear to think how he would react. She felt more desolate and alone than she had for years.

The easiest way, she thought, would be water with pennies boiled in it. And she slipped into a chemist in Birmingham for pennyroyal syrup. Both tasted vile and made her even more sick, but neither had any result at all. She couldn't bring herself to jump, or pretend to fall, not like in the dream. She knew she'd never have the courage. There was only one way left now that she could think of, and a cold shudder of fear passed through her every time she thought about it.

They were on their way south now with coal for Oxford. It was a while since they'd been down there and Joel was pleased, as it meant meeting up with family. By the time they left the coalfields, the grit catching in their nostrils, clothes and hair, the family were all as black and begrimed as ever, especially the children. Maryann felt another deep wave of despair. They looked like a load of chimney sweeps! The old taunt of 'dirty families' haunted her. But how was anyone supposed to keep clean in these conditions, especially feeling the way she did?

Joel and Bobby had sheeted up and put the top planks up over the hold. As well as keeping the rain off, the tarpaulins stopped so much gritty dust from blowing back in their faces.

On the way south they found themselves followed closely by another pair of Barlow boats occupied by the Higgins family, whose son Ernie crewed for Darius. Mrs Higgins was an older woman – it was impossible, Maryann thought, to guess exactly how old – with a wizened, leathery face and a terse but not unpleasant manner. She had a scarf dotted with brightly coloured flowers tied over her hair and her forearms were as knotted and muscly as branches.

'You going down the paper mills then?' she asked as they were untying. When Maryann said they were, Mrs Higgins shook her head.

'Ah well, watch that there river. Can be a booger down there.'

They knew she was right. To reach Wolvercote paper mills they had to go through the lock at Duke's cut and onto the Thames. There was nowhere to turn the boats at the mill, so they had to wind them on the wide Thames and take them down backwards on the rushing current. Maryann never did that part of the trip without her innards turning with fear, and most other boat-women were prepared to admit that they felt the same.

'Least I'll get a good wash done, though,' Maryann said. There was plenty of hot water on offer at Wolvercote Mill and most of them tried to get their wash tubs out.

Mrs Higgins gave her a sudden, gappy smile. 'That you will,' she agreed. 'We're off to the aloominum works, down Banbury.'

With the Higginses on their tail so much of the way south, Maryann felt somehow on display, even though they were as respectful of the privacy of others as anyone could be. But for the first two nights they were all tied up nose to tail along the bank and Joel went out for a drink with Mr Higgins the first night, while Mrs Higgins stayed aboard with the two youngest children, who still worked the boats with them.

Mrs Higgins was one of those women beside whom Maryann felt weak and inadequate. She couldn't forget that Ernie had been the ninth of her thirteen surviving children, who'd all grown up on the cut. It made Maryann dizzy just thinking about it. Where had they all slept? They must have been stuffed under the cratches, she thought. The cratch was replaced on some boats by a very small forecabin in which a couple of young children could be tucked out of the rain for the night. But Maryann felt that women like Mrs Higgins were somehow a different and hardier breed from her altogether. Whatever would Mrs Higgins think if she could see into her mind now?

The days were grey and dull, though the clouds let out nothing more than drizzle. As they wound along between pastures and ploughed fields, Maryann saw that spring was coming in the buds pushing out on the trees, the fuzz of green shoots along the furrows, all the spring promise of new life. But she felt so ill, so unequal to giving life herself, that the sight made her feel even more lonely and desperate than before.

On the second afternoon she sat in the cabin as Bobby steered the butty; Joel was way ahead of them with the motor. Maryann was positioned opposite the stove, cooking and feeding the twins in turn. She could balance a baby on her lap and let her feed, keeping her hands free to chop onion, carrot and beef, though it made her back ache. Suddenly the smell of onions filled her with nausea and she had to snatch Ada from her breast and lean over the waste bucket as Ada lay back roaring on the bed.

Spent, she sat with her head down, too tired to move, even after the retching had stopped, the smell of old potato peelings unpleasant in her nostrils. A sob escaped from her.

'I can't go on . . .' she whispered. 'I just can't. Not like this . . .'

They left the Higgins family behind at last and headed south. When they reached Thrupp, Joel found a spot to pull in for the night.

'Don't want to be starting down the Thames in the dark,' he said. 'Best start fresh for that in the morning.' He lifted the water cans off the roof and went off to fill them.

The family ate their stew and potatoes without speaking. Meals were often silent at the end of the day when they had all been up since before dawn and sometimes worked on until after dark. Joel scraped his plate clean and made a satisfied sound.

'Ready for a quick one, Bobby?'

So the men went out to the pub, which nestled among the pretty stone cottages of Thrupp.

Maryann cleared the crocks away, her hands trembling as she stacked the plates. There was no Higgins boat tied up behind them tonight and the place wasn't busy. She knew the time had come.

'Joley, Ezra, Sally, Rose. Come on.' The four of them bedded down on the big bed on the *Esther Jane* still, while Bobby squeezed onto the side bed. Still in their clothes, they snuggled down together, Joley and Ezra at one end, heads in the cupboard into which the bed could be folded up when necessary and the two girls at the other end.

'Night, night.' Maryann kissed them all. She tried to be as affectionate to Rose as to her own children, which wasn't difficult as she was very fond of the little girl. Poor little mite – no mom and now separated from her real brothers as well.

'Night, Mom,' they said. Even Rose called her Mom already.

'Oh, Nance.' Maryann found her lips moving as she closed the hatch and went, shivering, back to the cosy cabin of the *Theodore*. 'I know you'd never understand what I'm about to do, but if you're watching, don't be too hard on me. I won't be able to carry on being a mom to any of them if I have another one now. It'd just finish me off, Nance, heaven forgive me.'

Inside the cabin she continued muttering to herself. The twins slept on on the side bench, and she tried to keep herself calm.

'Now or never. I've got to do it – it's got to be now or they'll be back. Oh, please don't let it hurt too much. Let it just be over!'

She knelt down and reached into the monkey hole under the bed, where Joel kept a few of his tools. The screwdriver felt heavy in her hand. It had a sturdy wooden handle and a long metal shaft leading up to its flattened end, which was about a quarter of an inch wide.

Maryann knelt there, turning it round in her hands, which she noticed were trembling. The metal was tarnished, dotted with rust. She knew she could have sat there for hours putting off the moment, but then it would be too late. It had to be done.

Feeling something was necessary in preparation, some ritual, she poured a cup of hot water over the metal part of the tool and wiped it on her skirt. As she went about these humble preparations, tremors began to move through her body, as if she was running a fever; her teeth started chattering. With difficulty she adjusted the wick of the lamp and the shadows shifted round her.

'It'll be all right,' she whispered, trying to steady herself. 'Calm down . . . Steady . . . Tomorrow it'll all be over. I've just got to do it . . .'

For a moment she stood by the bed, holding the screwdriver, at a loss. She realized suddenly that in order to begin she would have to remove her bloomers. She wore the full, old-fashioned kind still, for warmth. To do that she'd have to take her boots off. Perched on the edge of the bed, she struggled with the laces. Her hands were shaking so much that this seemed to take for ever, but at last she pulled off her boots, placing them silently on the floor, then rucked up her skirt and pulled down her bloomers, feeling vulnerable, embarrassed even, at finding herself standing there with no drawers on and no shoes either. It was a relief to let her skirt fall down again over her thighs.

'Come on, come on,' she urged herself through chattering teeth. It had to be done quickly or she would lose her nerve.

Again, she sat down on the edge of the back bed, the implement with its sharp, square end in her hand. Everything felt unreal, as if she was dreaming. Her legs twitched convulsively and she couldn't control them. She opened them shakily, closed them again. How was she going to manage this? She had to prod hard enough to make sure she started bleeding. The only way, she saw, shuddering, was to lie back, to get in the right position. Shifting her weight, she lay diagonally across the bed so that her head was pressed right into the darkest corner. She could smell coal strongly. It got into every crevice of the boats. The hard wall pushed against the top of her head, the blanket was scratchy against the back of her neck.

Her skirt fell back as she lifted her legs and at once lying in this position filled her with horror. It was unbearable. The air felt somehow indecent about her private parts and she felt helpless and full of shame. She was a child, lying pressed to her mom's front-room floor by Norman Griffin, when he had forced her dress up. She began to sob, but she made herself remember what she was doing. She couldn't stop now: it had to be done to free her of the child. Just this one, she promised. She'd never, ever do anything like this again.

Quick. It had to be quick. The steely end of the screwdriver felt cold as she eased it into herself, guiding the handle. Her breath was coming in loud, juddering gasps. In a couple of seconds she felt it reach in as far as it would go. What now? Push in further, slowly? No, quickly . . . Do it, do it, the blood throbbed in her ears.

She pulled the handle out a little, trying to take aim. Without giving herself any more time to consider she jerked her hands back towards her with all her strength, driving it into her.

The pain was instant. Her eyes stretched wide at the shock of it and she heard herself giving off screams and moans. She thought she knew pain, but this was not the coming, going waves of labour pains but an appalling sharp agony which was getting worse, tearing at her. Waves of heat and nausea swept over her. Unable to control her cries of agony, she tried to sit up, to pull the thing out, but she could hardly keep her hand still enough to get a grip on it she was shaking so much. God in heaven, what had she done? It wasn't supposed to be like this!

Sweat soaked her chest and back. Grinding her teeth, she grabbed at the handle and tried to pull on it, but it wouldn't come. She tried to get to her feet, easing forwards, the thing still in her, but her legs wouldn't stand the weight and she nearly collapsed onto the stove. Sounds came from her mouth, whimpers, groans.

Crouching half upright, she felt a hot surge over her hands, running down to drip from her wrists, over the handle of the screwdriver to the floor. It took her a moment to understand why her hands were red. From somewhere she could hear a baby screaming, and she knew it was the baby inside her crying out in pain, the tiny life to whom she'd done this terrible thing.

'I'm sorry, little one . . . sorry . . .' she managed to say. She slumped back across the bed and in seconds a thick, rubbery darkness had covered her face.

Twelve

Something was pressing on her eyelids. It was not painful, but warm, and seemed to have weight. Next she felt her left ear, that it was pressed down into a pillow. Maryann became aware of herself piece by piece, as if a thaw had set in throughout her body, each part of it warming slowly back to life. She could feel the air passing in and out through her nostrils. There were unfamiliar smells. Her head, the central core uniting her eyelids, ears and nostrils, was throbbing with pain.

She moved her fingers and, somewhere far away, her toes. Pressure mounted inside her which it took a moment to recognize, its urgency increasing so rapidly that her eyes snapped open and seeing a bowl on the chair beside her bed, she grabbed it and leaned up on her elbow, suddenly aware as she moved, that there was a tube attached to her arm. Her innards contracted until a miserable spurt of liquid was wrung from her and she lay back, unable to control her moans. There was a sick banging in her head and in the lower part of her body raw, tearing pain.

She squeezed her eyes shut, waiting for it to subside and struggling frantically to make sense of things. Where, from this white glimpse of her surroundings, was she? A hospital, that much was clear, but where? What had happened to her to cause this agony? Had she fallen in and been hit by the butty? She forced her eyes open, squinting, the bar of sunlight from the long window opposite still falling across her face. She saw the tube running into her arm, and then another bed next to hers. Panic flooded her. How did she get here from the cut? And where were Joel and the children?

Gradually her life poured back to her. She'd been in the cabin, that much she knew. She remembered kneeling there in the lamplight, that she'd been alone. Then blackness. Lord above, what had happened?

A face leaned across from the neighbouring bed, a skinny brown plait draped over the shoulder. Narrow grey eyes stared at her, unashamedly curious.

'You've come round then?' the young woman observed. 'Took your time. You've been out for ages.' She sounded neither friendly nor unfriendly. 'Only had my appendix out, me. What're you in for?'

Maryann wondered if she could make her voice work. 'Wh...' she attempted. Her mouth was dry and sour. 'Where am I?'

'Where *are* you? Don't you even know that! The Radcliffe, of course.' Seeing Maryann's blank look undispelled, she added, 'In Oxford. D'you want the nurse?' Self-importantly she called out to one who was not far off, sitting at a table in the middle of the ward. When the woman came she was tall and very thin, with porcelain skin and pale eyes.

'Ah –' she stood over Maryann – 'you're back with us. How're you feeling?'

'My head.' Maryann pressed her hand against her forehead. 'I've been sick,' she added wretchedly.

'I don't suppose it'll be the last time either.' The nurse had picked up Maryann's other hand and was taking her pulse. After a short silence she nodded and released her hand. 'Good. Yes – it's the after-effects of the anaesthetic. Makes everyone feel ropy.'

She removed the bowl and Maryann watched her willowy figure go along the ward, before coming back with it empty and rinsed.

'She's not so bad, that one,' her neighbour said during the nurse's absence.

'The doctors will be in to see you soon,' the nurse told her. 'Drink plenty of water.'

Evidently it was morning. There was a flurry of bed-making and bed baths, although Maryann was left alone. Then the doctors came. The nurse drew screens around her bed and a middle-aged man, with a clipped voice and a moustache, and two very young men came and stood in a row at the bottom of her bed. Maryann lay looking up at them. The older man had papers tucked under his left arm. The two younger ones looked uncomfortable and their glance kept flickering towards her and away again.

'Well,' the older doctor said, 'I hope you're ashamed of yourself. You've managed to do yourself a great deal of damage.'

Maryann tried to fight the tears which welled up in her eyes. Why was this man accusing her in this cold, cruel voice? What had happened? And where were her family, all the people she cared about and most wanted to see?

He flicked through the notes, while the two students stared at the wall above Maryann's head.

'I'll tell you, I take a very dim view of this sort of thing,' the doctor went on. 'You damaged your uterus beyond repair and we've had to carry out a complete hysterectomy. You've lost a good deal of blood in the meantime and we've had to transfuse you.' He spoke as if these medical necessities had been a huge personal inconvenience.

'Of course, there was no possibility of saving the child.' Abruptly he pushed the notes back under his arm. 'But then I don't imagine that was what was required, was it? Anyway – ' for the first time he looked directly at her – 'there won't be any more babies for you, that you can be sure of.'

To his two underlings, he said, 'Ten-inch screwdriver – still in place when they brought her in. These women are beyond belief.' Shaking his head, he pushed the screen out of his way and moved on without a further word to Maryann.

Tears streamed down her cheeks. The way he had spoken made her feel lower than nothing. She hadn't understood a lot of the words he used but he had made her remember what had happened. Of course. She was expecting . . . she remembered the light in the cabin, her legs bare to the air, the screwdriver . . . and then those dying cries of the child, which seemed to ring in her head. Oh, God above, what had she done? She covered her face with her hands. The screens had been taken away and there was no privacy now. She felt so exposed in the long ward with eyes all around her, when she was used to her tiny cabin. And she hadn't meant any of this to happen! Not like this. No one was supposed to know. How would Joel ever forgive her if he knew she'd murdered their little babby?

She pulled the thin covers over her head and lay weeping bitterly, her body hurting with each wrenching sob, but it was the thoughts which filled her mind that caused her the greatest agony of all.

*

That day was punctuated by sickness and misery and sleep. Maryann didn't take in anything around her or notice time passing. All day her head throbbed. But when she woke the following morning, still very battered and sore but at least free of the thumping headache, she was more alert and able to take in her surroundings and she saw that the tube had gone from her arm. It was then she began to realize that, when the nurse had drawn screens round the bed for the doctor's round the previous morning, the tiny enclosure of privacy had done nothing to contain the doctor's booming voice. It soon became clear that the words 'baby' and 'damaged' and 'ten-inch screwdriver' had bounced the full length of the ward and into the ears of those occupying the lines of beds. Anyone who had missed the sordid details was soon informed, and there was a lot of whispering and looking. Maryann felt eyes staring at her with fascinated disgust.

The tall nurse who had been on duty the day before treated Maryann with a professional detachment which was neither warm nor disdainful, but this was a good deal better than she received from a few of the others. That morning she raised one hand to attract the attention of a young nurse, who bustled over to her, looking irritated.

'Can I go to the toilet?' Maryann whispered. She hadn't been aware of wanting to go the day before, but now it was urgent.

'No, of course you can't!' the nurse snapped. 'You know perfectly well you can't get out of bed. I *suppose* I'll have to bring you a bedpan.' Every line of her bearing implied that she resented having to do anything for *that* sort of person.

When she brought the bedpan and drew the screens

round, Maryann found the courage to ask, 'I was wearing hoops in my ears before. Gold hoops. Please – ' she appealed. 'I don't know what's happened to them.' She'd missed them suddenly when she sat up that morning, their familiar feel.

'Well, *I* don't know about that sort of thing,' the nurse said haughtily, removing the bedpan. 'I expect they've been put away for safekeeping. Why don't you look in your cupboard?'

Painfully, Maryann leaned round and opened the little cupboard by the bed. Inside she saw her clothes bundled up at the bottom and, on the shelf above, the gold hoops Nancy had given her. She reached in for them, her eyes filling with tears, and lay down again, holding them close to her.

All day she had to endure the knowledge that everyone was talking about her. She felt bathed in shame, as if her very skin was raw with it. She was glad she wasn't allowed to move about the ward because she couldn't bear the thought of people looking at her. No one said a friendly word, apart from the woman with the plait in the next bed, whose nosiness outdid any scruples she might have had. Every so often she leaned over and hissed questions in Maryann's direction. These questions pierced her misery like wasp stings.

'Where're you from then? Not from Oxford, are you?' She had a country accent and a village gossip's manner. Maryann tried to ignore her, but she kept on.

'Not a secret, is it? I'm only trying to be friendly, not like the rest of them in here. You come in from one of the villages?'

Maryann shook her head, keeping her eyes closed. She definitely wasn't telling this tittle-tattler that she was off the cut.

'Sounds as if you've had a bad time of it. A screwdriver didn't the doctor say? Dear, oh dear, there's a thing. You must've been in a fine old state.'

Gritting her teeth against the pain, hand pressed over the scar low on her belly Maryann eased herself over in the bed, presenting her back to her nosy-parker interrogator and pulled the covers over her head. In their darkness, trying to shut out the disgruntled complaint that she was 'only trying to be friendly', Maryann lay picturing her home, the boats with their woven ropework and Turk's heads when they were scrubbed white, the shiny brasses. She longed to be in her cosy bed on the *Theodore* with the cats curled up on her feet, to see her children's faces as they played on the bank or in the hold. Her whole being ached with the need to be at home instead of in this harsh, stark place among strangers who condemned her. Where were her family? Had they all abandoned her?

But the thought of home only increased her pain and shame. If strangers condemned her, however was she going to be able to face Joel? *You've killed his child*, she repeated over and over again. *You're a murderer*. And the thought of Joel's face, of having to see him again after what she'd done, made her long for darkness, for the relief of not being able to feel, to be blotted out.

Later on in the afternoon she sensed there was someone near the bed and opened her eyes. In front of her was the rough blue weave of a coat. A body bent over and a face appeared close to hers, which she recognized: blue eyes, features deeply lined by the years and squirrel-grey plaits coiled round her head. At the sight of her, Maryann burst into tears.

'Oh, Auntie!' She tried to hide her face in shame, but found her hand grasped between two tiny cold ones.

'Now, moy dear, don't you go taking on so!' Alice Simons sat down and stroked Maryann's hand. 'Oh dear, oh dear, I don't like seeing you in this state, I don't at all.'

'I've done such a terrible thing,' Maryann sobbed. She tried to speak quietly, conscious of all the other people around them, but she was becoming hysterical. 'I never meant it to be like this, Auntie, I promise I didn't. Only I couldn't manage. I felt so sick and worn out and now I've done the worst thing I could ever do . . .'

'Shh, dear, ssh now,' Alice said, clutching at her hand. 'You don't want all this lot in on your business do you?'

'They are already,' Maryann said despairingly. 'Where's Joel, Auntie – and all our little ones?'

'They're all safe and sound,' the old lady assured her. 'All the girls are at our house with Darius. I said that'd keep him on his toes when I came out to visit you! At his age he could do with a bit of young life around him. We've given Esther and Ada a bit of that form'la milk and they're happy enough, dear. Joley's gone down the mill with Joel and Bobby, but they'll come up Juxon Street tonight, so he'll be in to see you as soon as *they* let him.' She grimaced over at the sister's desk.

'Oh, Auntie . . .' Maryann couldn't stop weeping. She felt wretched and ashamed, yet it was such a relief to see someone she knew, her family. 'Is Joel very angry with me?'

'I've never seen the boy in such a state,' Mrs Simons said, kneading at Maryann's hand in affectionate

115

agitation. '"My little mate," he kept saying. "My Mary-ann." Sat down in my house and cried like a child, he did, over you. "Why daint she say nothing to me?" he kept saying. Up and down, he was. Couldn't settle. "I knew there was summat on her mind," he said, "but she'd never say. And now look what she's gone and done."

'"Well," I says to him, "the girl'd had enough. That were a desperate act she done, if ever I saw one. She weren't put on this earth to be a brood mare, anyone could see that by the look of her. There's more to life than wearing yourself out with one child after another, Joel," I said. "Look at your mother – and mine. You don't want to lose her, do you, lad?"'

Hearing this, Maryann wept even more. After the doctor's condemnation of her she had expected the whole world to turn against her.

'I heard it crying.' She couldn't control her sobbing, however much she didn't want to attract attention to herself. 'It was crying when I . . . when I killed it.'

'Oh *no*, dear.' Alice squeezed her hand tightly and Maryann was more distraught to realize that the old lady was trying not to cry herself. Her voice was thick with tears. 'That can't be right. You can't hear a tiny babe crying in the womb. I s'pect it was the twins you heard.' She sniffed, then pulled a handkerchief from somewhere about her and briskly wiped her nose. 'That'll be it. Don't think like that any more. What's done's done and you have to go on.'

'He said I shan't have any more babies. I've damaged myself.'

'You've had everything taken away, dear.' Alice Simons was whispering now. 'I had a word with the matron. I'm not frightened of her. You've been foolish

116

hurting yourself so badly, I won't say you haven't. But you mustn't keep dwelling on it. You've plenty of children to care for – a good-sized family, and that poor young Rose. We must all make sure we take good care of them now, mustn't we?'

Thirteen

Joel walked along the shiny floor of the ward, amid the sickly smell of human illness, overlain by onions and gravy. He held his cap clasped tightly in both hands. When he found his wife, he lowered himself onto the chair by her bed, oblivious to the eyes fastened on him all round the ward. For a time he sat leaning forwards, his sorrowful gaze fixed on Maryann's sleeping face, mauve cresents of exhaustion beneath her eyes.

She seemed like a stranger lying there, as if she had gone somewhere far away from him. Where was it she'd gone, his sweet little bird? What had possessed her to do this brutal act, which had nearly finished her as well as their child? Emotions he could not have named swelled up in him until he had to clench his hands into fists, then hold onto his cap to prevent himself from lashing out. He lowered his head and looked helplessly down between his legs at his boots. Their worn leather, shaped by years of wear into the exact contours of his feet, was pale from the repeated rubbing of mud and rain and cinders. They gave out a whiff of the earth compacted in the soles. It calmed him a fraction: the smell of the cut, of what was real and wholesome. And she was part of that, his little wife lying here in front of him.

He took her hand, which lay outside the covers, and looked at it. The lack of privacy didn't enter his

118

thoughts: these strangers in the ward were nothing to him. He was too deep in his own concerns even to see them. He held Maryann's hand between his own, feeling its hard-worked roughness, warming it, then pressed it cautiously to his lips.

Maryann's eyes opened. She looked bewildered until she turned her head slowly and, seeing him, gasped, trying to sit up. Her face creased with pain and she was forced to lie back again, whimpering.

'Steady,' he said, alarmed. 'Don't move. You just stay still, where you are.'

'O-oh,' she moaned, a hand covering her face, tears of remorse flowing at the sight of him. She was in too much distress to speak. Joel couldn't say anything either. His throat was choked and the tears ran down into his beard. He leaned in close, pressing the back of her hand against his cheek. Feeling his tears on her hand, she gradually pulled herself over onto her side to face him, curling herself up tightly, needing his comfort but unable to look into his eyes.

'How could you've done it?' he managed to say. 'I thought you was dead.' He shook his head, shuddering at the memory. 'When I came back and found you . . . You nearly bled to death – you was that close. How *could* you've . . .?' He saw her hide her face again and he had to lean forward to hear her muffled voice. As he did so, he caught the smell of her body, of his woman. A pang of longing went through him. This was all wrong, her lying here among strangers. He wanted to lift her out of this cold white bed and carry her home.

'I wasn't myself,' she said. 'I felt so bad. Couldn't seem to see a way out. It's too much – the twins, all the kiddies, keeping up with the loads and everything . . . I just couldn't seem to go on.' Her shoulders shook with more sobs. 'I daint want to do it – only I couldn't think of another way . . .'

There was a long silence as Joel fought to control his feelings, all the hurt and fear. Their children were his hope of security in a future which, he knew, looked more and more threatened for the boaters. They were a forgotten people, only useful again for a bit now there was a war on. The cut grew more neglected every year. What would happen when peace was declared? All those road hauliers, who barely knew of the existence of the cut, would they be the new Number Ones? How could they keep the life of the boatpeople going, the only life Joel knew, if there was no one to carry it on? If there were no children to put to the tiller and teach boating instincts, the knack of loading and handling, of splicing ropes and working locks? And children died on the cut: sickness and accidents scythed through them. You needed plenty to make sure enough survived to carry on. He tried to tell himself this was only one child lost, that there would be others.

Yet he looked at the frail figure on the bed in front of him, lying with her face hidden for shame and sorrow, and he saw the young woman he loved with all his heart, who had married him, fresh-faced and full of hope, who had made him happier than he had ever been in his life, and now here she was, felled and exhausted, on a hospital bed.

Slowly he moved his hand and laid it on top of her head.

'Don't cry like that, little mate,' he implored her. 'Please don't.'

The sorrow and kindness in his voice made her cry all the more, but she reached out for him and pulled his hand against her breast, holding him tight, her face pressed to his arm.

'I've done such a wicked thing. I never thought I could do anything so bad . . . Our little babby . . .'

He stroked her hair, trying to find words, wanting to climb onto the bed and love and caress her, but of course he couldn't. Above all, he wanted her home. Wanted things back as they were before.

'We'll have others,' he tried to soothe her. 'Lots more little ones.'

She grew very still suddenly and looked up at him. He could see the fear in her eyes. 'Joel – they say I'll never have another babby. They've had to take it all away.'

He stared, not understanding at first, then closed his eyes as her words cut through him. No more children. No more sons to grow up strong and work the boats.

'Oh. Oh my . . .' He stood up, half-staggering, recoiling from her. 'No more? Never?' He was reeling. 'What've you gone and done?' He heard his own voice, very loud. 'What in God's name've you done?'

'Joel – wait . . .' She sounded faint and far away.

He didn't mean to leave her so abruptly, but he had to get out of the ward, to breathe the fresh air, to steady himself. He strode along the polished floor and out through the heavy doors.

Maryann spent a month in the hospital in Oxford and it was one of the loneliest times she'd ever passed. Her body, as well as recovering from the operation, had lost a lot of blood and needed time to recuperate.

When Joel had come to see her on the ward, looking

so out of place in his boots and his working clothes all blackened with coal dust, yet so strong and manly with his broad shoulders and thick beard, he had attracted a lot of stares and also a lot of conjecture about his working life.

'D'you work on the canal then?' Nosy next door asked the following day, after the gossip had spread. Not feeling she could lie, and in any case fiercely proud, Maryann nodded.

'Ooh, well – my word!' The woman stared at her as if looking at a weird new creature in a zoo. 'Well, I've never come across any of you lot before . . . I wondered why your arms look so weathered and brown.'

When one of the nurses had given Maraynn her first bed bath, she looked down sneeringly at the grime of coal dust trapped in the creases of her skin.

'Well, I've never washed anyone *quite* this filthy before.'

Maryann looked away, trying to pretend she hadn't heard.

You try it! her mind screamed in retort. *You try living on top of a heap of coal in all weathers with your kiddies to keep fed and washed. I'd like to see how long you'd last, you starchy little bitch!*

But she couldn't stand up for herself. Not now and not in here. She felt too beaten down. And she wasn't going to say anything about where she came from. The nurse also asked if she always wore 'those gold gypsy hoops' in her ears. All Maryann said was, 'Yes, I do.'

She was glad of the wash, though, and the clean nightdress to replace the bloodstained one she had been wearing. The new one was from the hospital store and was pale pink. But even this small amount of effort exhausted her. She seemed to have an endless capacity to sleep. They woke her to give her meagre platefuls of stew and dumplings or potato pie, and as soon as she'd eaten them and the watery junkets that followed, she would sleep again. As well as relieving her huge weariness, these long, dreamless sleeps were a welcome release from the stark, alien ward and from the hostile stares and prying questions of the woman next door. '*Is it true, what you did . . .?*' And, worst of all, the memory of Joel's back moving away from her, as if he never wanted to see her again.

As much as she could, she kept herself to herself. Within a week the nosy body in the next bed was replaced by a reserved, middle-aged woman, who told Maryann that her husband worked for the university but was now in some army education department for the war effort. She was polite, didn't go poking her nose in and read a great many books.

As Maryann's body gradually recovered from the injuries it had suffered, she began to be able to move about the ward. She could go to the bathrooms by herself and along to the day room at the end. From the newspapers left in there, and from the talk among the other patients, she caught up with news about the war, more than she normally heard on the cut. A great many ships were being sunk in the Atlantic, and she picked up snippets about tighter food rations and how crimes were going unreported amid the chaos of blackout and bombing. She found she enjoyed having time to read newspapers and the few storybooks left in the room. They helped her escape. She tried not to let herself think about Joel and how much she had hurt him.

Easter came and went and spring blossomed outside. As her body healed, Maryann grew more and more restless. When the weather was fine, all she could think of was how it felt to be on the cut on days like these, with the trees all coming out and the sun on her face. She was so used to being able to step straight outside from her cabin, into the fresh air, when they were in the country that she found the stuffy, shut-in atmosphere of the ward stifling. When it rained and the drops blew against the long windows, she imagined the feel of them falling on her skin. Sometimes she would stand at the washroom window, arms folded, glad to be away from everyone and look out, wondering where, beyond those trees and buildings, the cut ran, narrow and barely acknowledged. She missed her home terribly. The fields and trees, the colourful sides of the boats and the familiar faces.

Above all, with an ache that seldom left her, she missed her children. Knowing she had taken away her chance of having any more made them all desperately precious. She trembled sometimes with the need to hold them in her arms, grieving for the children she would now never have. She had wanted to slow things down, to give herself a chance. She'd never meant it to turn out like this. At night she lay picturing them in her mind: Joley and Sally with their blond heads and Ezra's dark one, playing on the bank near Fenny Compton or Aynho, the feel of their urgent little bodies, their grubby faces and hands, eyes full of expectant life and laughter. Did they miss her? Were they unhappy? Alice Simons assured her that they were doing very well. Maryann trusted her completely, but everything felt wrong. The family was scattered and broken up. They should all be together on the cut again. Thoughts of Ada and Esther were the most difficult to cope with. In the early days her breasts ached when they let down milk that no one could drink. As the days passed, she knew the milk was drying up. And the girls would have changed by the time she came out! Sometimes she cried in sheer frustration, which was made worse by the fact that she knew she had only herself to blame. Although a few of the other women on the ward were kind, she knew how most of them saw her. She was a wicked woman who'd done away with her baby. When they looked at her it increased her sense of shame, of being dirty in a way which water could not touch. Shame seemed to pulse like through the blood in her veins.

The days passed slowly and miserably. She did not see Joel again in all that time. Mr Barlow had sent Joel and Bobby back up to Hawkesbury Junction to do runs to the power station.

'He's taken it hard,' Alice told her after his visit. 'He said, "I ent going in there again – I can't do it."' Seeing Maryann's distraught expression she said, 'Give him time. He's a good boy, Joel is. He just needs to go on in his own way for a bit.'

But could Joel ever forgive her, Maryann wondered, for what she had done to herself and to his family?

Joley and Ezra had gone with their father, but the girls were still in Oxford. Children were not allowed to visit the wards, but fortunately the hospital was only a couple of roads away from Adelaide Street and Alice Simons came to see her as often as she could. Maryann was overjoyed to see her as she brought news of them. She would try to press Alice for details, but scarcely ever got more than, 'They're quite happy but they miss you.' She returned to them with the simplest little notes written by Maryann for Sally: HELLO SALLY. BE A GOOD GIRL. LOVE FROM MOM XXX Sometimes Sally and

Rose scribbled little pictures to send back and Maryann treasures these small masterpieces. Her favourite was Sally's attempt at Alice's fat black cat. She'd given it a gigantic tail, curved up over its back like a crescent moon.

Every time Alice stood up to go home, Maryann said, 'Tell them I'll be home as soon as I can!'

In the first week of May, Maryann finally stepped out through the hospital gates onto the Woodstock Road. Too excited to stop and take stock of her surroundings, she hurried towards Adelaide Street.

It felt strange to be wearing normal clothes again. Alice had brought her a pretty frock which she had bought secondhand, in bold blue and white checks which fitted nicely at the waist, or would have done had she not lost so much weight. It hung loosely on her for now, but she put her cardigan and coat over the top. She had no stockings, but enjoyed the feel of the air on her legs. Her hair had grown and she coiled it up at the back and pinned it. She only had a small bundle of belongings to carry.

The row of snug terraced houses in Adelaide Street looked very inviting, the patches of brick which still showed through the soot glowing a warm colour in the slanting sun. Almost running in her impatience, though her long unused legs felt wobbly, she finally arrived at Alice Simons's front door.

'Home at last!' Alice greeted her. 'Well, you've come just in time – I've got the kettle on, and potatoes baking in the oven...' Their delicious smell was drifting through the house. But Maryann was hungry for something else.

'Where are they, Auntie? I can't wait to see them!'

She ran through to the back. 'Sally and Rose are in the yard feeding the hens.' Alice called after her. 'But there're the twins – good as gold, they are, bless them. Told you they was crawling, didn't I?'

In the pretty cabin of a back room, Maryann found the two little girls busy with an assortment of objects to keep them amused: a handful of clothes' pegs, a wooden spoon, an enamel bowl and a couple of cotton reels. Esther was sitting chewing determinedly at the end of the wooden spoon and Ada was crawling across the floor aiming for the open door.

'Oh!' Maryann cried, full of joy at the sight of them and flung herself down on her knees, scooping up Ada. But the child gave a squeal of alarm and her face crumpled. She squirmed so much that Maryann had to put her down.

'Esther?' Maryann pleaded. The other twin stared at her with mild curiosity and continued to chew on the spoon.

'They don't know me!' Tears filled Maryann's eyes. She felt cut to the heart. 'They don't know I'm their mom!'

'Don't you worry,' Alice Simons reassured her. She carried in the tea tray and set it on the folding table with quick, birdlike movements. 'You sit with them a while and they'll soon come round. They're just not used to you, dear. Why don't you come and see Sally and Rose?'

They stepped out into the tiny garden. At the end of it the two girls were leaning over the chicken run, scattering seed through the wire.

'That'll do now – come and see who's here!' Alice called.

The children turned, and Maryann saw an expression

in Sally's eyes that she would never forget. There was a tiny pause as she registered who was there, then a breaking in of relief, of absolute happiness, like a light going on.

'Mom?' she faltered. 'MOM!' And her little legs couldn't seem to carry her fast enough, her wheat-coloured hair flying, face stretched with eagerness. Rose, less sure, toddled behind, dark curls bobbing, and Mary-ann squatted and gathered first one then the other into her arms.

'Thank God,' she heard herself saying as her tears wet their firm cheeks. 'Oh my lovelies, my lovely little girls!'

Fourteen

'It's our dad!'

Sally's shriek of excitement rang through the house seconds after they heard the knock at the door.

'Let's let him in then,' Alice Simons said, hurrying along the hall as fast as her stiff hips would allow. 'No good keeping him on the doorstep.'

Maryann tensed. She was feeding Esther in the back room – to her great relief she had been able to get back to breastfeeding – and heard the giggles of excitement as Joel gathered Sally and Rose into his arms. She heard Joel's father come downstairs and his voice; then light footsteps hurried towards her and halted hesitantly at the door.

'Joley!' She was overjoyed at the sight of him. He looked bigger to her, and older, and his fair hair had grown down to his collar, thick and curly. His clothes were filthy, but he looked healthy and strong, standing there in the doorway, and she saw with a pang just how much he was trying to be a little man.

'Come 'ere, bab.' She held out her spare arm and Joley's solemn face broke into a grin in spite of himself. He ran to her and she pulled him close, kissing him. At that moment, Ezra's swarthy face appeared round the door and he launched himself at her.

'Mom!'

'Hey!' she laughed, trying to cuddle them both, kissing Ezra's black curls. 'Mind our Esther!'

'You awright, Mom?' Joley's blue eyes looked deeply into hers.

'Yes – ' she squeezed him round the waist – 'and seeing you has made me properly perfect! You been helping your dad?'

Joley nodded proudly, the soft, little-boy moment over as he tugged away from her. 'Been steering the *Theodore* with Bobby. I done all sorts!'

'I been steering an' all!' Ezra piped up. 'And sheeting up and making tea!'

'*Have* you?' Maryann said admiringly.

'Can we go and see the hens?' Joley ran to the back door and Ezra followed. The children loved coming to Adelaide Street.

A moment later Joel was the one standing at the door, his eyes uncertain. Maryann felt herself twist inside. She felt acutely shy of him, as if the time of separation meant them starting all over again, like young lovers. Except that they were not young lovers, there was a history between them, so much to be ashamed of. She looked up timidly, moved by the sight of him back here, steadfast, in his worn old working clothes.

'Ready to come home? he asked gently, and she saw the need for reassurance in his eyes.

Silently she nodded. There was nothing she could say now to make things better. It would have to wait.

However much she longed to be back home with the family, it was hard saying goodbye to Alice Simons and old Darius, who had been so kind to her during that week she stayed after leaving the hospital. Both of them came down to the cut. They made quite a family party that warm afternoon, Joel and Maryann each carrying a twin and everyone else bringing their modest bits of luggage.

When they got to the wharf, they saw Bobby, bucket in hand, just finishing off giving the boats a swill down. A line of washing hung along the *Esther Jane*.

'Hello, Mrs Bartholomew.' In his shyness he turned formal with her. Usually he called her Maryann.

'You've got them looking nice,' she told him, a smile breaking across her face. It was so lovely to be back, to see the boats and smell the cut again! And in the cabin she exclaimed, 'Oh, Joel – you've got it so clean! It looks ever so nice!'

She had been bracing herself a little, knowing the men had had to work hard and two-handed and wouldn't have had time to keep house. But everything was tidy and clean, the stove was blacked and the brasses shining.

'Bobby and I had a bit of a set-to,' Joel admitted bashfully. 'Couldn't have my wife coming home to a pigsty, could us?'

There were more surprises. From the empty hold of the *Esther Jane* Joel lifted out two little dolls' prams. Maryann gasped.

'Look Sally, Rose! Look what your dad's got you!'

'Well, look at them,' Alice Simons said. 'Their eyes're nearly popping out of their heads!'

'Put your dolly in, Rose,' Sally ordered, and the two were immediately busy. Joley and Ezra showed Maryann the fishing rods Joel had found for them. He'd been round secondhand shops in Banbury and found the prams, and one of the lock keepers had given him the old rods.

'It's like Christmas,' Maryann laughed. She felt like a queen coming home to her palace.

'And we'll have fish and chips,' Joel said. 'Don't you go stroving tonight.'

They said their goodbyes to Darius and to Alice Simons.

131

'You've been so good to us,' Maryann said, kissing Alice's soft cheek. She felt a great rush of fondness and gratitude towards her.

Alice kissed her back and took her hands. 'You look after yourself now, dear.' Very quietly she added, 'You'll be all right now, you'll see.' Their eyes met. Maryann knew what she meant. Even amid the shame, there was the relief of no more worry about having baby after baby.

Maryann also went and kissed Darius and thanked him. He blushed, coughed and looked at his boots. 'G'bye now, girl,' he said, pushing his hat down more firmly onto his head.

Joel put his arm round Maryann's shoulders as his father and aunt walked away, Darius with his slow, loping gait, like an old crow in his black clothes, and Alice, limping slightly, but neat and spry in her hat and coat. They didn't look back.

Alone in the cabin of the *Theodore*, Joel drew Maryann into his arms. She leaned against him, breathing in his familiar smells of old wool and engine oil and his own Joel smell. She began to feel the hard twist of dread which had burdened her for weeks, begin to unwind itself.

'I'm sorry, love,' she said into his chest. 'So sorry for what I've done.'

When he spoke, she felt the vibration of it against her cheek.

'If we had any more, I might not have a wife, might I? And she's worth all the little 'uns in the world to me.'

His arms wrapped round, holding her close and she felt him draw in a great breath, his chest expanding. Releasing it, she heard him say, 'Home, my lovely,' on the long exhalation of breath which spoke to her, without further words, of all his longing, his relief.

For the next few weeks after Maryann was back, Mr Barlow kept them on short runs out of Hawkesbury Junction, up and down the Coventry cut to Griff and Baddesley collieries and back to the Electric Light, its maw ever open for coal, its chimneys like huge nostrils snorting out smoke.

The boat families who worked round Sutton Stop greeted Maryann warmly and seemed glad to see her back, asking if she was well recovered. Their kindness lifted her a little, making her feel accepted, as if they were all part of one big family. Joel had reassured her that no one except him knew exactly what had happened that night. He was the one who had found her when he and Bobby came back from the pub, and he had shouted to Bobby to go back and get them to call an ambulance. So far as everyone knew, Maryann had suffered a miscarriage followed by an operation.

They wouldn't be so sympathetic if they knew, Maryann thought. But she tried to bury her feelings of loss and shame and revel in being back with the family, close to her children. The time away recuperating had given her an opportunity to appreciate how much happiness she had with them. The early summer was beautiful. The hedgerows were full of birds, the mayflower and elder blooming at their most exuberant, surrounded by the vibrant green of grass and trees. She steered the *Theodore*, drinking in the feel of sunlight on her skin, the breeze ruffling the leaves, animals in meadows along the cut, and the ducks clamouring for food alongside the boats. Ada and Esther were old enough to be getting into mischief now so she sat them on the roof, harnessed to the chimney, to play and watch the world go by. It was a treat to see the children tucked up cosily in bed or playing out on the bank with hoops and rods, with the prams and on makeshift swings. And, as the warm days passed, her energy returned and she felt better than she had in a good while.

But still somewhere deep inside her was a chilled, sad place that she did not like to visit. One afternoon at Sutton she was out on the bank with some of the other women. They had their wash tubs going, with dollies for pounding the clothes and a couple of mangles on the bank. It was a good chance for catching up on chat as well as getting the washing done. Two of the others were heavily pregnant and a lot of of the talk revolved round family and these new lives. Maryann did her best to smile and join in, but she felt sad and lonely. She missed Nancy so badly. Of course, Nance would have found it hard to understand what she'd done, but she would have listened and tried to comfort her. They'd seen Darius a couple of times while they were working round Sutton Stop. He was so silent, so obviously bereft and miserable without her. The pain of the fact that there would never be Nancy to confide in and share jokes with came back raw and fresh now she was back on the cut.

She kept her sadness to herself. She and Joel did not talk about what had happened. It was done. Over. What was there to say? But although the two of them would be able to love one another freely now and without worry once she was fully healed, something had changed. There was a difference in knowing that no child would ever result from their lovemaking. Not now or ever. And in a hidden place deep in her heart Maryann was weeping for all these things.

Fifteen

The summer passed quite peacefully. It was not until the autumn that Mr Barlow found them a longer trip, up to Birmingham. They drew into Tyseley well on into a smoky September afternoon. The wharf was very busy, and the Bartholomews were told they would have to join the queue for unloading and would probably have to wait until morning.

'I'll get down the shops before they close,' Maryann said.

Sally and Rose insisted on coming too and bringing their dollies' prams. As they didn't have much chance to push them about when the boats were on the move, Maryann relented.

'So long as you carry summat home in them,' she told them.

Moving round the edge of the wharf and keeping well out of the way of the roaring trucks, swinging chains and busy wharfmen, she led the girls, both solemn with the importance of the occasion, out onto the Birmingham streets. The bomb-damaged buildings looked a little less raw now, the rubble softened by grass and weeds.

Maryann pressed on quickly from shop to shop. There was no bread – come back in the morning, they said. She bought onions and carrots, stashing them in the little prams, and a bag of potatoes. When they reached the butcher's, the door opened with its usual 'ting' but the shop was quiet. Then Mr Osborne came through from out the back and Maryann saw his expression change to one of pleasure. He seemed quite delighted to see her.

'Well he*llo*, stranger!' he said gushingly. 'What a long time since we've had the pleasure . . .' He peered over at Sally and Rose with a mischievous grin. 'And I'm sure I can find something nice for you two young princesses.'

'I want some mince, please,' Maryann said, taking her ration books out of the basket, 'if I'm not too late.'

'I've just the thing.' He held up his index finger and disappeared out the back again for a moment. 'I've been telling them that stocks are finished but, of course, I've got a little put away for *special* customers.'

Maryann frowned, truly baffled. 'What's so special about me?' Surely he couldn't be making advances to her. Look at the state of her – scruffy and covered in coal dust!

'Oh, I like to keep our boatladies happy.' He eyed the needle on the scale. 'There we are. Just over.' Wrapping the meat with a flourish, he kept his conversational patter going. A nip in the air now, wasn't there? Autumn on its way. At Tyseley Wharf again, were they?

'Yes,' Maryann said absently, wondering whether there was anything alse she should be buying.

'I can throw in a pair of pig's trotters as well. That suit you?'

'Oh – ta very much!' The food was welcome, of course, but for some reason she couldn't identify Maryann felt suddenly uneasy. He's just being kind again, she told herself. Mr Osborne had never given her the heeby-jeebies before, as men did when they seemed to be after something, but today she sensed something forced in his kindness to her.

136

'There we are.' He handed her the package and dipped his hands into his overall pocket. 'And – for you. Butterscotch!'

Sally and Rose took the sweets with eager hands.

'Say thank you to Mr Osborne,' Maryann told them.

Just as they arrived back at the boats, Charlie Dean from the toll office came over to her in the dusky light, smiling, his cap clinging to the back of his head. Maryann put the potatoes onto the counter of the *Theodore* and waved in greeting.

'All right? Long time no see!' He called a greeting to Joel, who was splicing ropes with the boys on the *Esther Jane*. Charlie stood leaning against the cabin, smoking as they chatted. Maryann was pleased to see him, but she also felt fraught and distracted. One of the twins was crying in the cabin and she hadn't even begun on the tea yet.

'Where've you been then?'

'Essy kept us on short trips,' she told him. He didn't need to know more than that. She kept up a conversation while lifting the groceries down into the cabin, kettle on.

'Shall I fetch your water for you?' Charlie asked, seeing how busy she was. He ground his cigarette butt into the ground with the ball of his foot.

'Would you?' Maryann rewarded him with a brief smile. 'That'd be a godsend.'

He was just turning, the empty water cans in each hand when she heard him say, 'Ey-up – old Weary Willie's back again.'

Standing in the hatches, Maryann narrowed her eyes and saw, coming across the wharf, the slight, tense figure of Pastor Owen.

*

137

'Good evening, Mrs Bartholomew!'

Pastor Owen approached them raising his hat.

'I'm off – tara,' Charlie muttered, slinking away. 'Don't want to get stuck with him.'

'Evening,' Maryann replied, struck afresh by the foreignness of the young churchman's northern accent. But she was surprised and unexpectedly affected by the fact that he had remembered her name. And he spoke with disarming simplicity, looking hard at her. It made her feel she mattered.

'And how are you today?' he asked.

'All right – not so bad.' She wasn't sure what else to say. She saw Joel look round from where he and the boys were perched on the cabin roof and counter of the *Esther Jane*.

'Family all all right?'

She nodded. 'Yes, thanks.'

'I'm very glad to hear that.' Pastor Owen pushed his hands down into the pockets of his threadbare black coat, and for a moment Maryann thought he was about to bring out his bible again, but instead he kept his hands in there and hunched his shoulders. She saw that he was cold.

'There's tea in the pot,' she said, feeling sorry for him. He looked so thin and underfed. 'Would you like a cup?'

'Oh – ' his lips turned up in a nervous smile – 'that'd be right grand. I've been out and about. I can't say it wouldn't be welcome.'

Maryann poured a cup, sugared it and gave it to the young man, who curved his hands round it gratefully and drank it down at high speed. She found herself wondering in a maternal sort of way when he'd last eaten and why he was so quiet. He hadn't mentioned Jesus once yet. Wasn't he supposed to? Standing in the hatches of the *Theodore* as he drained his cup, she tried to decide whether he was ill.

'Thanks very much.' Wiping his mouth with one hand, he handed the cup back with the other and she saw how long and bony his fingers were. The sight of them made her shiver, but when he looked at her with those large grey eyes, again she saw in them a kind, straightforward sympathy.

'Last time we met you seemed burdened, Mrs Bartholomew. I have a feel for a troubled soul. You know that you can find ease for your mind by laying your cares at the feet of our Saviour? He makes no exceptions in forgiveness.'

'I – yes, I know.' Maryann stumbled over her words. His eyes seemed to look right in her, to the cold, heavy shame which was curled deep inside her.

'There will be a service tonight – of prayer for healing,' Pastor Owen was saying, 'where repentant sinners can lay their cares upon the Lord and listen to the blessed assurance of His Word proclaimed. It's only a few minutes' walk from here. Would you care to join us?'

'I don't—' she began. Out of the corner of her eye she saw Joel step off the *Esther Jane* and walk towards them, as Pastor Owen was telling her the address.

'Come and be with us.' Again, his eyes seemed to penetrate right through her. 'Please.'

'How d'you do?' Joel said. Maryann heard the curtness in his voice. He wasn't keen on outsiders who came to give advice, whether they were welfare people coming poking their noses in and trying to make the children go to school, or holy Joes with their missions to the boat-people. He came from a tradition of self-reliance and preferred to stick to his own people.

Pastor Owen returned the greeting and held out his hand, which Joel shook reluctantly.

'I was speaking to your wife about the redeeming love of the Lord.'

'Were you?' Joel said, sounding neither approving or disapproving.

'If you should decide to come it'll be eight o'clock.' The young man backed away, raising his hat. 'God bless you.'

And he walked away along the wharf looking, Maryann thought, as if the cares of the world had been laid not at the feet of his Saviour but on his own thin shoulders.

'I've got a pain in my belly.'

Joley sat beside Maryann on the side bench as she stirred the mince and gravy on the stove; every so often he screwed up his face in pain. 'Don't want any tea tonight.'

'You must be sickening for summat.' Maryann felt his forehead, but it wasn't hot. 'Best get you to bed soon.'

When the food was ready, Joel and Bobby brought the other children in, Joel lifting Ada and Esther over onto the boat. They could toddle about outside now, holding his hands or on reins. Bobby said he'd take his plateful back to the *Esther Jane*, while the family squeezed into the *Theodore*.

'S'coming down thick now,' Joel told her, rinsing his hands in the dipper of warm water Maryann had put out for them all on the counter. She peered out. Fog was curling round the wharf, rising over the dark water so that the outlines of everything were blurred and uncertain.

'Should be ready to unload us first thing, any rate.' He climbed down and sat on the back bed next to Joley, while the others squeezed round the table, telling her bits of news he'd picked up from the boats round about. A new baby in one of the families, a Mr Baines had had his leg crushed. Maryann responded with as much interest as she could, but her thoughts were preoccupied with Joley, who was now dozing uneasily on the back bed, and in another, distracting side alley of her mind with the idea of walking the streets until she reached the address Pastor Owen had given her. She tried to dismiss the thought. Of course she wasn't going to go! Joley was poorly, there was a pea-souper gathering out there and the man was most likely barmy anyhow. But all the time the thought kept coming back, refusing to be chased away. A feeling of need kept rising up in her. It was connected somehow with the way the young man had looked at her, had seemed to see into her. The argument went on in her head as Joel lit the lamp and she spooned out mince and potatoes onto plates. She *couldn't* go! What would Joel say? And what did she want to go for anyway? *For relief* . . . the answer floated up from inside. *From how I feel.*

'Best have this one sleeping in with us tonight,' Joel was saying, eyeing his son beside him on the bed.

She nodded, settling to her tea. 'Joel?'

'Ummm?' He reached over and his hand pressed warm and heavy on her thigh.

'I want to go. To that place Pastor Owen was talking about. Just for a bit.'

He looked across at her, baffled. 'Do you? What for?'

'I can't explain, love.' She looked at her plate. 'It's just – for Nance . . . And everything else that's happened . . .'

'Well –' he shrugged – 'if you want. But it's come

141

down bad out there. D'you want me or Bobby to come with you?'

'No, ta.' She managed a wan smile. 'I'll be all right. It's not far.'

She would be a bit late, she thought. She could just hear a clock from somewhere distant striking eight as she set off along Wharf Road. Almost immediately she stepped out through the hatches she had regretted saying she would go alone. The fog was very thick, making her cough, and was tinged with yellow where it met the light escaping from the cabin.

'Tara-abit.' She parted from Joel and hurriedly closed the hatch, tying her bright scarf with the red flowers on over her hair to keep her ears warm, pulling her coat close round her and hurrying as fast as the murk would allow. The road was dark and deserted, hemmed in by warehouses. *Left, left and left again*, he'd said. *Can't go wrong – it's no distance.* It felt a long way, though, groping her way through the noxious fog, thick with chemicals and smoke. The only sound she could hear was her own footsteps until she reached a pub and was grateful for the sound of voices and laughter and the whiff of ale on the air. She could still hardly explain to herself what it was that drove her on, shivering in the cold, the need that forced her along these dismal streets.

The chapel was in a side road. Between a toolmaker's and the end of the houses, he'd said, and from what she could make out of the buildings on either side he seemed to have described it faithfully. From the front window, high up, a tiny thread of light was escaping round the blackout, and once more she was relieved to hear the sound of voices, only this time they were singing. The meeting had obviously begun and Maryann was glad. She could slip in during the hymn and she wouldn't feel so self-conscious in her old coat and dirty boots if she sat at the back. If she didn't like it, she'd slip out again and no one'd be the wiser.

To her relief the door opened silently, but when she pushed inside she was dismayed to see how small the chapel was. On each side was a row of pews, only eight or so deep, pressed up against the walls on each side with a narrow aisle in the middle. They looked outsize in the place, as if they had been passed on from a bigger church, and she saw that they were only occupied by a small scattering of people. The singing, of a tune with which she was not familiar, was thin and strained.

The back row of the pews on the left was empty so she slipped into it, moving half way along so she could see round the heads in front and loosening her scarf. Standing with the others while the singing carried on, she looked round. At the front was a raised dais with a plain wooden lectern on it. On the back wall, which was pale green, hung dark blue curtains drawn apart. Between them a wooden cross was fixed to the wall and to the right of it was a door.

Maryann saw that one of the two men standing at the front – dressed in just their own sombre suits – was Pastor James Owen. She was surprised at the sudden sense of relief she felt in seeing him in this strange place. She wasn't used to public buildings or meetings now. She was used to the cabins of boats. Pastor Owen was not wearing his hat and she saw that his hair was a sludgy brown and obviously not recently aquainted with the barber's, as it hung in a bedraggled fashion down to his collar. His eyes moved soulfully over the pitiful little congregation as they sang, though his own voice was

143

drowned out by that of the other minister beside him, who seemed to think he had to compensate for the feebleness of everyone else and was booming out the words. 'Blood ... ransom ... die ...' came floating to Maryann. She took in the all-over roundness of the man. He had no need of a barber as his head was completely bald and his cranium, cheeks, nose and stomach all had a cheerful, doughnut-like rotundity. She was just taking in another realization, that all the congregation were women, bar one pale, intense-looking man whom she guessed to be in his thirties, when Pastor Owen caught her eye. To her consternation she saw him leave his place and walk down the aisle towards her.

God Almighty! she thought, her hands going all clammy with nerves. *What's he doing?* Her heart was pounding. *What's he coming over here for? He's not going to show me up in front of all these people is he?* But Pastor Owen simply gave her a faint smile of acknowledgment and stood in at the end of the pew. When the singing stopped he stayed there.

Maryann sat down on the hard seat, which seemed to have been designed to deny any possibility of comfort and forced her to sit bolt upright. She couldn't get away now, could she? He was blocking one end of the pew and the other was hard up against the wall! Again, she had an unnerving sense that he could see into her mind. There were prayers. Maryann put her hands in her lap and closed her eyes, but didn't take in a word of what was being said. Her mind was fluttering between the worry that she was sniffing all the time and had nothing to wipe her nose on and noticing that the room smelt of a rank mixture of camphor, urine and frowsty clothes. All the time she was acutely aware of the long shape of Pastor Owen to her right and wondered why had he sat there. What did he want? It had not, before, occurred to her that he wanted something from her.

Next, the minister stood up and loudly, with dramatic sweeps of his arms, preached about the paralysed man whose friends let him down through the roof to be cured by Jesus. Every time he said the Lord's name, in his Black Country accent, he emphasized it: *JESUS*. On and on he went, about being paralysed by our sins, but the only time Maryann took in anything was when he hammered home the word *JESUS* . . . *JESUS* . . . She felt her mind seize up with boredom. What the hell had she come here for? *JESUS*. She should be back at home with her lad, who was poorly, not sitting here on this flaming hard seat with her backside . . . *JESUS* . . . turning numb!

At last, after endless prayers and another dismal hymn, the service ended. She found herself feeling angry and cheated. Where was the sense of forgiveness, of release she had come to find? She rearranged her scarf over her hair and tied the ends, but as she did so, Pastor Owen slid along the pew towards her and looked into her eyes in that way which always made her feel stripped naked.

'I'm glad you came.'

As Maryann couldn't truthfully claim the same, she said, 'So this is your church, is it?'

'I work with Pastor Joyce, yes. Though, as I'm not in charge of the mission here, I have a little more freedom to go out to the needy instead of waiting for them to come to me.'

Was that what she was then? One of the needy?

There was a pause as she looked down into her lap and Pastor Owen sat forward with his lanky arms resting on his thighs. Maryann just wanted to go, to be at home, but she wasn't going to be able to get past him yet.

Other people were leaving, gathering up their hats, walking sticks and torches, nodding and smiling at him as they went.

'There's someone here I'd like you to see,' he said, staring ahead of him at the cross on the wall. 'Someone whose soul is also in need of succour and healing – as I believe yours is.' He looked deep into her eyes again and Maryann felt herself tremble inside at this close attention. 'That's why I especially hoped you'd come.'

'To see? Who?' She felt panicky now. What was she letting herself in for? She felt suddenly as if Pastor Owen, young and unlikely a prophet as he seemed, knew every single thing about her, that she was dirty and wicked, that she was a woman who had taken the life of her unborn child. And who on earth was he going to present to her? Some ill-used woman whom he'd picked up on the streets, bulging out at the front with some bully's spawn? A lady of the night that he wanted her to reform? Was he out of his mind? She had come to him for help but he was the one making demands on her.

'I don't think . . .' she tried to protest.

'There's nothing to be afraid of. It's just a member of our congregation who carries a weight of sorrow in their heart.'

Maryann thought of the ladies who'd been sitting around her. She couldn't imagine what possible help she might give any of them, but they hadn't looked all that fearsome had they? She hoped it wasn't the intense young man he'd got lined up for her with some odd request, but she was pretty sure she'd seen him leave.

Pastor Owen stood up and turned to her. 'Assist me – just for a few moments – please, Mrs Bartholomew. It would make a great different to someone, and I believe it would give you rest in your own soul.'

146

She was drawn in. How could she refuse him? If he had held out his hand to her then, she would have taken it. Instead, he indicated with a movement of his head that they should move along to the front of the chapel. Aflutter with nerves, she followed him.

Sixteen

Pastor Owen led her to the front of the chapel, towards the door which opened off to the right of the cross. Just as they reached it, it opened and Pastor Joyce came out. His big mixing-bowl face took on an expression that was grave about the eyes but smiling at the mouth, the sort of smile he might give to someone bereaved.

'Ah!' he cried. 'Good evening to you! You've come to see our poor friend then?'

'The healing grace of the Lord may well be seen in this place tonight,' Pastor Owen said. The combination of this pronouncement and the other man's coffin-side expression made Maryann want to run down the aisle and escape through the back doors. Bewildered, she followed Pastor Owen into a small, dimly lit room. It was bare: a wooden floor, small table in the middle, over which hung a dimly burning light bulb with no shade. There were a couple of hard chairs. The only other thing she noticed was the jaundiced colour of the light, for the walls were yellow. She took in all of this in a couple of seconds because what snatched her attention from anything else, was the figure kneeling sideways on in the far corner. The sight stole the breath from her. She stood quite still, unable to move.

'Our friend is a spirit deep in remorse,' Pastor Owen was saying. 'He has come regularly to our congregation, pouring out to me his misdeeds, his sorrows, which weigh him down and blacken his soul in the eyes of the Lord. All he needs to free him now is to feel the forgiveness of the people he has transgressed against. Without that forgiveness . . .' But Maryann wasn't listening. For her the only thing in the room was the broad-shouldered figure in the black coat, trilby hat pulled well down, raising itself to its feet with a heavy, lumbering movement and beginning to move towards her.

Everything seemed slow, dreamlike. Closer he came, his shape, the gait so utterly familiar, the figure that had haunted her days and polluted her dreams for so many years. He reached the table and loomed over her, his body like a box, filling the room with his square shoulders. The bulb dangled over his head, and with the unhurried relish of one who enjoys inflicting pain, her stepfather raised his head slowly, turning his face out of the shadow to the light and looked into her eyes.

The features were more disfigured than she had even imagined. She began breathing again, with a gasp of revulsion. That night when little Margaret Lambert, driven by his cruelty, had smashed a lamp over his head, the oil had poured out and burned fiercely on him. The left side of his face was completely altered, a mass of puckered flesh reaching right down his neck, where raised ridges alternated with flat areas which had an unnatural shininess. His left eye was completely hidden in the contorted skin. The right side had been burned, though less severely, and it was into Norman Griffin's lashless right eye that Maryann found herself looking back. She gripped the edge of the table, afraid her legs might give way.

'Maryann – you came then.' His voice hadn't changed. Oh, heavens no, it hadn't! Now it contained a humble, wheedling tone, but it was still the voice that had whispered to her through her bedroom door, had spat such vile words into her ear as he laid his weight on her, forcing, fouling her. In those seconds a flare of rage lit in her that had lain dormant all these years. She was suddenly possessed by it, shaking all over as if she was running a fever. Turning to Pastor Owen she lashed him with it.

'What the hell d'you think you're playing at bringing *him* here? How *dare* you deceive me into coming here to meet . . . *this*?' She could only finish the sentence with a gesture of revolt, slapping her hands down on the table. 'What d'you want from me? You're mad! You've no idea what he's like – what he's done . . .'

Pastor James held his hands out as if he thought he was Jesus calming the storm.

'Mrs Bartholomew – please. I beg you. Don't reject this man. He knows he has done terrible things. He's full of remorse for his past sins. He has told me of them and he needs to express his sorrow. To repent and begin afresh.'

'Maryann – please.' Norman Griffin's voice came out brokenly, hoarse with contrition. 'You've no idea what it's been like all these years living with this.' He pointed at himself, at his scarred face. 'Like a leper – the sign of my guilt. I need to know forgiveness. To be able to live at peace with myself.'

Maryann looked from one to the other, having to grope for words. 'To live at peace?' In order to speak normally at all, instead of raging or screaming which her whole being felt tuned to do, she had to lower her voice to a snarl. 'You don't deserve to live at all. Yes, you're guilty all right.' Again she turned on Pastor Owen. 'I suppose you think you know about him. I s'pose he's told you some soft soap about a few little pinches and smacks, about his wicked, ungrateful stepchildren? You think a few smacks would drive a child to do *that*?' She pointed at Norman's face. 'D'you want to hear what he did? What he really did? You poor, stupid, little man – you really think you're doing something grand, saving his soul, don't you? Well, let me tell you – you've picked on the one person on this earth who doesn't have one.'

'Please – let me say I'm sorry. I want to make amends for what I've done.' Norman Griffin started to move round the table and Maryann backed away from him.

'Don't come near me!' she shrieked, losing control of herself. 'You make my flesh creep. You're vile and disgusting. Keep him away from me!'

To her surprise, Norman stopped, standing still, lowering his head. For a moment she was at a loss.

'No deed is beyond our Saviour's forgiveness,' Pastor Owen pleaded, holding his hands out towards her. He seemed really distressed, his eyes like huge pebbles under the light. 'Forgive for your own sake, Maryann. If you can't forgive, your soul is trapped in darkness. Forgiveness is new life.'

A sound broke through the room, something so foreign and unknown that Maryann at first could not recognize it. It came to her that it was a sob, that it had come from Norman Griffin, from beneath the lowered brim of his hat.

'He lives day by day in hell.' Pastor Owen declared emotionally. 'And you too will live in hell if you don't forgive him.' He went to Maryann and attempted to take her hand.

'Don't you touch me, you bloody nutcase!' She backed away, tightly folding her arms. She'd had quite enough of Pastor James with his earnest Mancunian

151

pleading. 'What's it to you? You don't care about how I feel – you just want to be able to show off about how many souls you've "saved".'

But she was deflated. The room felt very cold and she was suddenly full of doubt, seeing the scarred, broken figure with his head bowed, across the room. For those seconds, she was the one here who was made to seem cruel. But other pictures flashed into her mind, rescuing her: of Sal, her older sister, on the bed that day she'd found her lying in the dark, the blood still dripping from her wrists; of Margaret, dead-eyed in the asylum.

'Can you find it in your heart to forgive him?' Pastor James pressed her. 'To free this troubled soul?'

Maryann looked across at the young man in his poor, sagging clothes and pitied him his naive ardour.

'You've no idea, have you?' She managed to speak more quietly now. 'He can't just change in one night. Not someone like him. It won't just drop off him. If he lives in hell, it's where he belongs. He put himself there – no one else did it.'

To Norman she said, 'I don't know what you want with me now. But whatever it is, you're not getting it. I was the one who was never fooled by you, remember? I know you, and I know you don't have a remorseful bone in your body.'

She moved towards the door. 'I wouldn't tangle with the likes of him,' she told the young man. 'He's beyond redemption.'

As she turned to leave there came a sudden movement and she found the door pushed shut by Norman Griffin's hand. He was upon her suddenly, and so close to her that she could feel his breath on her cheek and she recoiled, but he moved closer, forcing the door shut.

'Don't go – not yet,' he entreated. The voice was soft,

caressing. She couldn't look at him. She kept her eyes down, fixed on his black boots, her own brown ones. 'It's all right, Maryann. Don't worry. I can wait.' And then he let her open the door.

She fled out through the chapel, to the dark street. It was difficult to hurry outside, even though her whole being cried run, run! The night fog swirled round her, seemingly full of threat, of unknown presences.

'Turn right, and right!' She was muttering feverishly to herself. It was hard to see where she was going, to hurry. 'It's not far. Keep going . . .'

Every so often she stopped, but there was silence as soon as her own footsteps were stilled. She knew really that Norman Griffin would not come after her. If he had run out of the chapel behind her, Pastor Owen would surely have followed as well. And knowing Norman Griffin as she did, she knew he was a man who would bide his time. After all, if all he'd wanted was to jump out on her, why go through all this rigmarole of repentance in order to see her? But even so every nerve in her body seem to jangle, her breath sobbing in her lungs as she scurried through the dark streets. Oh God, she knew she had seen him on the wharf all those months ago – and then someone else had said he was asking for her? She knew she had not imagined it – he was after her. What did he want with her?

Most of all, what she could not get out of her head were his final words, speaking in that remorseful, patient tone for the benefit of the young missionary: *Don't worry. I can wait.*

Seventeen

By the time she arrived back at the boats, Maryann was in such a state she could hardly get the hatches of the *Theodore* open. Once she had managed to, she almost fell inside and slammed the doors shut again, panting so hard that she was sobbing.

Joel's face appeared round the bed curtain. He'd been lying down but was not asleep and the light was still burning.

'What's got into you?' It took him a moment to realize she was seriously frightened.

'*He* was there!' She spoke in a hoarse whisper, trying not to wake Joley and the twins. 'Norman Griffin! That preacher's a right stupid bugger.'

Joel gave her a look which said, 'Well, I could have told you that.' With trembling legs, Maryann climbed over the sleeping toddlers in their nest on the floor, where Jenny the tortoiseshell cat was curled beside them, and went to sit by Joel, shivering. She turned to look at Joley on the bed behind them.

'He's been sick a little while back,' Joel told her.

'Poor lamb.' Frowning, her own preoccupations calmed for a moment she stroked his head. Beside it lay his precious tobacco tin of cigarette cards. 'He doesn't feel feverish. Maybe that'll be all for tonight.' She snuggled close to Joel and he put his arm round her.

'What's up with you then?' He squeezed her tight, trying to still her shaking.

She felt jarred with shock and anger. Now she could let it out and tell him what happened, tears came as well.

'Seeing him again was *horrible*,' she wept. 'His face is such a mess and there he was, pretending to be all sorry, as if he's changed and I know he hasn't. He's got that Pastor Owen wrapped round his little finger – I bet he told him to come and find me. Oh, Joel, what does he want? When I was leaving he told me he could wait – as if he's going to keep coming after us.'

'Eh, there.' Joel wrapped his arms round her, rocking her, her head pressed against his chest.

'What can he do to us? He's an old 'un, must be nigh on seventy, ent he? And we're hardly ever up here in Birnigum. Don't you worry about him – we'll be loaded up and gone in the morning and he won't know where to find us then, will he?'

'I know.' She looked up at him, tearful like a child. 'But I thought we were safe after all this time.'

Maryann could see Joel was right about the facts of the situation, at least. They'd be gone. What could Norman Griffin do to hurt them? All Joel said to comfort her was right and reasonable. But Joel did not know about Norman Griffin. Not really. She had never told him, fully, what her stepfather had done to Sal and to her. She felt she couldn't speak of it to anyone, had never wanted Joel to know, and Joel had never asked. He didn't truly understand the horror that Norman Griffin could arouse in her, the thoughts of him like tentacles forcing her back into the shame and fear of her childhood. He might travel with her every mile of the way, even though he was not physically present. Though externally calmer, she was left feeling completely churned up inside and knew she'd have trouble getting any sleep.

There was no room to move round the cabin, so she and Joel took it in turns to undress, standing in the tiny space, which was enough to put two feet down at the edge of the bed.

'I'll move Joley over now,' Joel whispered.

Joley stirred as Joel set him down on the side bench, a coat bundled under his head. Maryann passed over the tin of cigarette cards. Spots, the other cat, had been asleep at the end and got up, rather disgruntled, then settled back at Joley's feet.

'Mom?'

'I'm here, pet.' Maryann peered round the curtain at him. 'You awright Joley?'

'I been sick,' he murmured sleepily.

'I know. Your dad said. How d'you feel now?'

'Bit sick . . .' But he was almost asleep again.

Maryann got out to let Joel settle on the far side of the bed, and kissed Joley's cheek. She put the bucket in the corner by his head and made sure the torch was handy.

'Sleep well, son.' She blew out the light and climbed in beside Joel. 'Maybe he'll be all right by the morning.'

'Hope so.' Joel was almost asleep. It had been a long day. He kept himself awake long enough to wrap his arm round her, and his beard prickled her face with a kiss.

'It'll be all right,' she just heard him say, before he was lost to sleep.

Maryann lay curled under Joel's arm, her body bent to his shape. Usually, tucked in this warm proximity she fell asleep almost instantly, but tonight her mind was jangled, darting from one harsh thought to another. For once she didn't mind if the children woke up, since she didn't seem likely to get to sleep anyway. The scene in the chapel ran vividly in her mind's eye. Pastor Owen's pleading, rock-pool eyes. What a silly fool the man was! How he'd been taken in, thinking he could deal in forgiveness as easily as that. His naive ignorance, the glibness of his thinking, made her feel violently angry. But worst of all was the thought of that voice, Norman Griffin's terrible face, his ruckled skin, the cold gaze of that one eye boring into her. *I can wait.* The words came whispering through her mind, over and over.

All she managed, for a short time, was a restless doze. She jerked awake later at the sound of a high, seagull wail and realized it was Ada. She didn't need the light on to see the child, knowing her cry and where to find her, and she leaned over and brought her up into bed to suckle her. She still fed them herself from time to time, more for comfort than anything as they had long since eaten other food. She sat up, holding Ada's slight form until she was sleeping again, then tucked her back in bed.

She had no idea how much later it was when Joley woke. Once again she was washing back and forth along the shoreline of sleep when his voice, a frantic 'Mom!' came out of the darkness.

'You getting sick, Joley?' With a pang she heard herself say 'getting sick' the way Nancy used to. Nance was always popping up, never far from her thoughts.

'Yes!' Joley wailed.

She was just in time with torch and bucket and Joley heaved until no more would come. Maryann perched on the bench beside him, wiping his forehead.

'Don't like it,' he said miserably.

'No – I know. Here – have a drink of water.'

She climbed to the door and let herself out quickly to empty the bucket. Joley lay limply down again.

'Will I be sick more?'

'Don't know, bab. You might. Look, I'll turn this light off and sit here with you for a bit, awright? Till you're settled.'

Shivering, she reached for her cardigan at the end of the bed and pulled it round her. She already had socks on. The nights were very cold on the cut now once the heat from the range had died out. She sat in the dark, fiddling with the ends of her hair, enjoying the peace and quiet. She could hear Spots purring at Joley's feet, Joel's breathing, the light snuffles of the twins. Every so often she caught the lapping sound of the water against the wharf outside. Her hand gently stroked her son's thick curly hair. *He's such a little boy still, really*, she thought. As the oldest, and a boy, he spent a lot of time with Joel and was given the most responsibility. Joel was determined he was going to be an expert boatman. After all, there was Ezra coming up too, but now they knew there would be no more sons . . . She knew Joel tried to hide his grief over this. Touching Joley's cheek, she thought about the hospital, how much she had ached for this cosiness – warm bodies to kiss and stroke, the breathing of loved ones around her at night. She must make the best of all they had now, she thought. She had six children to bring up, after all.

She was gathering herself to get back into bed when something jolted her fully awake again. There was another sound, something that didn't belong, not at this time of night. Yes, there it was, outside. Footsteps along the wharf. A chill went through her and she held her breath, fear swelling. Who was out there? She tried to calm herself, reminding herself to breathe. There was a watchman on the wharf gate at night, so surely no one could get in? It was probably him wandering about, checking that everything was all right.

There it was again. Movement, a slight crunch underfoot. The footsteps came closer, treading quietly, obviously cautious. Had she been asleep she would never have heard them. The side of the wharf was just behind her head, beyond the thin cabin wall. The footsteps moved along a little, then stopped. At last she heard them moving away.

Impulsively she pulled herself up and over the twins onto the coal box. Clenching her teeth, praying to make as little sound as possible, she slid back the hatch far enough to poke her head out.

'Sod it!' she cursed under her breath. Of course it was very dark and still foggy and she couldn't even see the front end of the *Theodore*, let alone anyone moving further away. The only thing she could see clearly was the tiller beside her, upended for the night. But standing very still, yes, surely she could just hear footsteps dying in the distance along the path? Shuddering, she pulled the hatch closed and climbed into bed beside Joel. The darkness outside felt full of threat. It was a long time before she slept.

Joley was sick twice more in the night, and the final time Maryann got up rain was drumming on the cabin roof. It was still raining in the morning, the sky low and burdened. She was feeling quite energetic despite the poor night, though she knew it was a nervous, jumpy sort of energy. Joley was pale and floppy but past the worst and she left him on the back bed to continue recovering.

The unloading began early, as promised. Joel and Bobby were outside with steaming cups of tea soon after seven when it was barely light, untying and stowing away the top cloths. All the supports that held the planks and tarpaulins over the load were thrown onto the bank, the cranes were swung into position and the unloading began.

Maryann fed the rest of the children aboard the *Theodore*.

'Sally – just keep an eye on them for me will you? I'll be back in a couple of ticks.'

Pulling her coat and scarf on, arms folded, head down against the rain, she set off across the wharf, which was fast turning into a quagmire. The place was full of activity: the wharf men shouting and horse-pulled wagons and trucks all arriving to pick up loads, with muted headlights still on to see through the dark and rain. She passed Charlie Dean, who called, 'Morning!' to her chirpily. 'All right are you? Manage to get shot of that holy Joe, did you?'

She turned as they passed each other, rain running down her cheeks. 'Oh, I don't think I'll be seeing him again!' She raised a grin. The sight of Charlie always cheered her. She hurried over to the nightwatchman's hut, wondering if he was still there, but he was in the doorway, talking to two other men. They moved back, seeing her approaching.

'There's a lovely lady here to see you, pal!'

'I thought you might've gone by now,' she panted.

'I should've done, bab, but I got held up canting to these two!' He was a big, cheerful bloke, the backs of his hands hairy like an ape.

'Only – I wanted to ask, like – was anyone else in here last night?'

160

'What – in my hut?' The three men laughed. 'No, love – I didn't get that lucky!'

Maryann smiled patiently. 'No – up and down the wharf, I mean. Did you go out and walk about?'

He frowned, seeing she was serious. 'Me? No, I can't say I did.'

'I heard someone. They were walking round our boats.'

She could see he was struggling to believe her. 'Well, I s'pose it's possible. But I don't know how anyone could've got in or out past me.'

Maryann knew what she'd heard, that she wasn't imagining it, but obviously they weren't going to get to the bottom of it. 'Oh well,' she said. 'Ta anyway.'

'Tara-abit,' he said easily. 'Don't worry. No one can get in here.'

She hurried back, boots sloshing through puddles. There was water to fetch, kids to see to. She raised her head, letting the rain fall cold on her face as she watched the crane swing high over her head from the hold of the *Esther Jane*.

Yes, she urged the machine, *lift it all out, quick, and let us get out, away from here.*

PART TWO

1944

Eighteen

The days were diamond hard, sparkling with frost. They were travelling south down the Oxford cut, and in the mornings they had to wrench the hatches open, stepping out into a world of white, the trees rimed, twigs gnarled and pale like witches' fingers.

They had to take great care along the icy lock sides. Straps froze stiff as iron and the sheets over the coal were as solid as planks.

The icebreakers were at work, freeing up the channels to allow them to set out, and once they did, often very late, the boats nosed through chunks of floating ice. They stood working the tillers, bundled up in all the clothes they could squeeze into, sleeves pulled down over their hands against the gnawing cold. Maryann kept the kettle on the hob all day, making cup after cup of cocoa or tea to stave off the deep, brittle cold of February.

One day, while she was at the tiller of the *Theodore*, she saw a pair of boats tied up beyond the bridge at Nethercote. It was the section of the cut shared by the Oxford and the Grand Union, and this pair were from the Grand Union Carrying Company. This was nothing unusual and Maryann hardly gave them a glance, until her eye was caught by the figure moving along the bank towards the butty, shouting to an unseen companion in the cabin. The person was very slight in build, and was dressed in slacks and a loose jacket, and wore a strange cap with a peak and earflaps. Maryann sheltered her eyes from the glaring winter sun and stared with blatant curiosity, still turning her head to look after the person had passed behind them. To her amazement, she realized that the lithe, energetic-looking figure was that of a woman – in trousers! And striding about like a man! She'd never seen a woman on the cut looking anything like that before.

Later, when she mentioned it to Joel, he said, 'I saw them. They'll be them volunteers.'

They'd heard mention of them lately in the pubs along the cut. Because of the shortage of crews and the need to keep loads moving for the war effort, there were all sorts coming off the bank to work the cut.

'There's women working in teams by themselves now, so they say,' Joel said. 'Still, they don't mix with the likes of us. They're working the Grand Union, most of them, anyway.' The way he said it made Maryann feel rather superior. Of course, she was 'off the bank' too, but she belonged now, didn't she? She was part of a proper boating family.

It never crossed her mind, then, that she'd ever have anything to do with these strange creatures. These girls in trousers. But later it felt as if that glimpse of them had been a premonition, a warning that she would need to prepare herself for what was to come.

She had asked Joel to try and get loads from Essy Barlow that didn't involve going to Birmingham, and especially Tyseley, to avoid any possibility of meeting Norman Griffin.

Joel tried to reassure her. 'What can *he* do, when you

come down to it? He's only trying to frighten you, lass. The man's a bully, born and bred. But he can't hardly go creeping about with a face like that on him, can he? He'd scare the horses all right! Everyone'd see him coming for miles.'

Joel didn't understand how the very thought of Norman Griffin could upset Maryann, could throw her right off balance, but he didn't much like Birmingham and was quite content not to go there. Mr Barlow was a reasonable man, who tried to give them what they asked, so they were working round Sutton again and up and down the Oxford. They'd had a good winter so far, the children were thriving and mostly well, and they'd spent Christmas in Oxford. Their own situation was good. Maryann felt better in herself than she had in a long time. It was Darius's silent sadness and the gap left by Nancy that gnawed at them.

That day was a little warmer. A slight thaw had set in, the trees were beginning to drip and a sheen of moisture lay over the ice on the stones, gleaming in the sun. They'd left Banbury behind, heading south. Joel gave Bobby the tiller of the *Esther Jane* and climbed out to lock-wheel with Joley and Ezra.

The boys waved at Maryann from the bank, and she could hear Joel urging them to hurry. They had to run ahead and prepare the next lock at King's Sutton. She smiled at the sight of Joel's burly figure moving past them. His run, taken in long, unhurried strides, was surprisingly graceful. He had his windlass in his hand and the two boys were pursuing him, relishing their release from the boat's confining space. Soon they were at the lock, Joel and Ezra forcing the windlass round together. Bobby skilfully slowed the *Esther Jane* right down and released the butty, and Maryann steered the

Theodore into the bank and jumped off with a line to pull her in and wait while the *Esther Jane* passed through the lock.

They had filled the lock and Joel was opening the gate to let Bobby in when Maryann was distracted by a loud wail from inside the *Theodore*.

'Sally?' She knocked on the side of the cabin. 'Is that Esther? What's up with her?'

Sally's flustered face appeared. 'She's banged her head and her nose won't stop bleeding!'

'What the hell was she doing?' Maryann tutted, exasperated. Why did things like this always happen when she'd just stepped off the boat? 'Get one of them rags – wet it in the dipper and bathe her face with it.' She was shouting, pulling on the rope to brace it and keep the boat in by the bank. The current moving into the filling lock kept trying to tug it forwards.

The bawling inside the cabin continued. 'It won't stop bleeding,' she heard Sally wail. 'Oh, Esther, just sit still!'

'Just keep the rag on her nose – dab at it till I get back in,' Maryann yelled.

Joel was closing the gate behind the *Esther Jane*.

'Come on, come *on*,' Maryann urged, still leaning back on the rope.

It seemed to take for ever to empty the lock again and for a second she nipped back on board. Sally seemed to be managing.

'I'll come and see to her when we get in the lock,' Maryann said, disappearing out again.

The *Esther Jane* vanished down, down, as water poured out through the bottom paddles. The drop here was considerable as they travelled downhill – about fifteen feet.

She saw it happen as she stood there, eyes fixed on

the lock, willing it to finish emptying quickly, ears pricked to make sure Esther's screams were finally subsiding. Joel was moving away from her, going back to close the paddles on the bottom gates, when she saw him trip. He struggled to right himself, but the foot he put down slipped from under him, taking him over the edge of the lock. He twisted, flailing in the air, then disappeared.

'Oh my God . . . *Bobby*!' Maryann screamed.

Joley and Ezra moved to the side of the lock, looking down. Maryann waited for Joel to appear again, climb up the ladder at the side of the lock, but there was nothing, only the little boys, both watching, not moving.

'Sally – get out here, quick!' Maryann yelled at the top of her voice. 'Your dad's had a fall!' She flung the rope into her daughter's hands and tore along the path. Water was trickling in through the top gates. Apart from that it seemed so quiet. She dashed round the arm of the lock gate and looked down into the emptied lock. Bobby had scrambled along to Joel, who was in a precarious position, having slid down the side of the cloths covering the load, and lay crumpled at the side of the boat close to the lock wall.

'Joel? Bobby? Is he all right?' She ran to the ladder and climbed down, then struggled along the gunwale to reach Joel. His eyes were open, but there was a pained, stunned expression on his face. Bobby's normally cheerful expression was very sombre. Squatting close by, he looked helplessly at Joel.

'He fell on his back – hell of a crack – right across the beams, and then he rolled down . . .'

'Joel?' She got as near to him as she could, horrified by the way he was just lying, not moving. 'Love, what's up? What've you done?'

'I can't . . .' he raised his head to speak to her, but then lay back with a groan. 'It's no good. I can't move.'

Two days later they pulled into Oxford. Helped by the crew of the boats following behind them, they'd managed to shift Joel onto his bed in the *Theodore*. He cried out in pain as they moved him so that Maryann could hardly bear to hear it, but he refused to let them call any medical help for him there.

'Let me call the doctor,' Maryann begged, beside herself with worry as she saw his face contort with pain every time he tried the smallest movement. 'I can't stand seeing you like this. I don't know what to do.' What if he'd broken his back and could never walk again?

'Just get us to Oxford,' Joel insisted. 'I ent getting left in Banbury or Lord knows where. I'll be all right here for a bit. I'm not that bad. Just leave me be.'

He slept a great deal, groaning with pain whenever he tried to move. Lying beside him at night, Maryann tried to soothe and comfort him. The family had to see to his every need and as Maryann and Bobby took the boats down to Oxford she was willing away every mile of the journey.

At last they arrived, and this time it was Joel's turn to be taken away in an ambulance. Though she tried to control herself in front of the children, Maryann wept as it drove away from the wharf.

'What's he done to himself?' she sobbed. It unnerved her completely to see Joel, who was always so rock-like, in this broken state. 'Supposing he's done summat really bad to himself and he can't work again?'

'He'll be all right.' Bobby tried awkwardly to comfort

her, though he was very shaken by what had happened as well. 'He's a tough 'un, he is. You'll see.'

Bobby was a godsend to Maryann in those days. She was surprised because she still thought of him as a young lad, but he had a steady kindness which helped to keep her calm. When she went back into the Radcliffe to see Joel's doctor, he said a whole lot of things she couldn't really understand, but what she did come away knowing was that Joel's back was not broken, but that there had been 'severe damage' to it and that he needed to lie flat and rest it completely.

Timidly, she asked, 'Well, how long for?'

'Quite a long time,' the doctor told her. 'Months, certainly.'

'Months!' she reported, anguished, to Bobby. 'How on earth are we going to manage?'

As ever, Alice Simons came to the rescue. If Joel needed complete rest and care, where else was he to find it other than with his father and aunt? There was no need for him to stay in hospital, so soon he was lying upstairs in the little house in Adelaide Street.

The children were very happy to spend a few days in and out of their auntie's house, but they all knew that if they didn't get moving again soon there'd be no money. Joel lay on his aunt's clean white sheets, fuming with frustration.

'We'll manage for a bit,' Maryann told him. 'Bobby and me. We'll just have to. Joley's a big help now.'

'I know – but I feel a right useless article lying here!' He thumped the mattress beside him with his fist, then winced. 'It's like being a baby again – having to have someone help me, you know – do my business and that every time. Not doing right by my family. I feel a right fool, I do.'

Maryann took his callused hand and kissed it. 'Should Bobby and me look for a load?'

'You'll have to. Get Bobby to go round all the usual and get back up to Sutton and see Essy. Tell him how it is. He can keep you on short trips for a bit.'

Later, over a cup of tea, Alice Simons said to Maryann, 'Look, dear, if you'd like you could leave some of the children behind for a bit while you're short-handed. The twins maybe? We could manage here and they'd be with their father.'

Despondently, Maryann swirled the dregs around in her cup. It was tempting, and was the practical thing to do, but her response was immediate.

'No – ta very much, all the same. It's kind of you, but I don't want them split up if we can help it.' She wasn't coming back to find that Esther and Ada didn't know her again! She wanted to keep her flesh and blood close by, even if they made life harder. It was bad enough leaving Joel behind.

Heavy hearted, she set off north again with Bobby the next day, after a loving farewell to Joel. His words still sounded in her ears.

'Look after them, won't you, little mate?' She knew he meant the family, all the children. But he also meant his beloved boats.

Nineteen

Mr Barlow was not about when they reached Sutton Stop.

'He's up Glascote,' Maryann reported back to Bobby. The main S.E. Barlow offices were at Glascote, near Tamworth. 'I told Mr Veater what's happened and he said he'd have a word with Essy and see if there might be a spare-wheeler going for us.'

She had hoped they might just find the *Isla* and *Neptune* tied up there so that Rose could spend a bit of time with Darius and she could chew the situation over with him too, but there was no sign of them. They were off on a long haul somewhere.

The next morning she and Bobby had begun washing out the boats when she saw Mr Veater's trilby bobbing along the path towards them.

'Morning!' he called, and bent down to stroke Spots, who was standing on the bank with his back arched in a disgruntled fashion, keeping out of the way of the sloshing water.

'I've got a proposal for you,' Mr Veater said, straightening up.

Maryann jumped down onto the bank, straightening the scarf she had tied on to keep her hair back out of the way.

'Proposal?' The only proposal he usually came along with was their clearance papers.

'There's a new crew for you. Two girls. Got a couple of 'em from down London spare-wheeling at the moment. You can have 'em till Joel's on his feet again.'

'*Girls?*' Maryann protested. 'Two of them? But I don't need two – I've got Bobby! Are they them volunteers?'

A smile tugged at Mr Veater's lips at her indignation. 'They've got them trained up, or so they say. What I reckon is, it's best if the two of them stick together, them being birds of a feather, sort of thing. Bobby can go and work for someone else for a bit. That way it won't upset the er . . . sleeping arrangements. And it'll keep you three-handed. You've got your hands full as it is.'

Maryann was aghast. She couldn't even begin to put her objections into words. She just gaped at Mr Veater. The volunteers were all very well in their place, but they didn't work with real boatpeople, did they? Not as a rule. And here she was, about to be landed with two complete strangers who hardly knew one end of a boat from another. What in God's name was the use of that?

'But . . .' she began, as Mr Veater started to turn away.

'Apparently they're already on their way from London,' he said. 'Don't fret – it won't be for long. And you'll be able to teach them a thing or two.'

Bobby said his goodbyes and removed his small bundle of possessions to another boat.

'Soon be back.' He winked at Maryann, who was trying, dolefully, to smile. 'Go easy on 'em now!'

Right, she thought, as soon as he'd gone. She was still reeling with shock. *I'd better get to work. I'm not having some posh London misses coming down looking down their noses at my cabins!* While the children played on the bank and made dens in the boats' empty holds, Maryann set to, washing clothes and hanging them in the crisp air and scrubbing every nook and cranny of both boats. She washed the plates and crochetwork and polished the brasses.

Sleeping's going to be a squeeze, she thought, as she polished the stove in the *Theodore*. She planned to move herself and all the children into the *Esther Jane*. It was the smaller of the two cabins, as the *Theodore* had no engine, but it was the family boat, after all, and she'd be in charge of it. Her children couldn't sleep in with strangers: they'd all be in together now. Oh, why had she let herself be pushed into this? She missed Bobby already, with his relaxed, capable ways.

She was on edge all morning, snappish with the children, dreading the arrival of the two women. They were bound to be snooty and look down on her and how was she going to work with them when they barely knew the cut? As the day wore on, her mood darkened to the point where she had to ask herself why she was feeling quite so low and afraid, so angry at what was happening.

'I don't want strangers on our boats,' she fumed, slamming her mattress down on the bed in the *Esther Jane*. 'I don't want them coming here, prying into my life!' She threw the pillow to the end of the bed. She felt raw and exposed. 'I just want things to stay the same. I don't want them here!'

She hurried the children along with her to buy some groceries, then rushed back to begin cooking. By the late afternoon she had the stewpot bubbling away, the kettle on and the boat was well stocked and spick and span. It was only then that she took in the state of herself and the rest of the family.

The twins were smeared with everything they'd had their hands in all afternoon, Ezra looked as if he'd been down a coalpit and all their clothes were dark with grime. Maryann's own frock was filthy and the front of her brown cardigan was coming unravelled. As Nance would have said, *Jesus, Mary and Joseph, will you look at the state of you!* They really did all look like gypsies!

'Come over here and wash your hands and faces!' she shouted to them. 'We've got visitors coming. They'll be here any minute!'

She drew up some cold water from the cut in the dipper and was about to add more hot from the kettle, but it was too late.

'Look Mom – ' Sally pointed – 'they're coming.'

Maryann froze in the hatches, the rag with which she had been about to begin on the children's faces in her hands. Through the smoky dusk she saw two figures moving closer along the towpath, both heavily laden with bags and bedrolls, the taller of the two staggering slightly under the weight. Maryann narrowed her eyes. The taller one had pale, shoulder-length hair. The other one's head was almost hidden behind the bundle in her arms. And they were both wearing trousers.

The family waited, mesmerized by the sight. Maryann had sat Ada and Esther side by side on the cabin roof, their little legs dangling above the counter, knees pink from the cold above their socks. Joley stood balanced on the gunwale close to them and Sally, Ezra and Rose stood on the bank. No one said a word as the two figures drew closer.

Peering at the front of the *Esther Jane*, the taller one said, 'Ah – here we are. At last!'

Maryann felt herself tighten inside hearing that voice. It sounded like high little bells ringing. The way that small utterence was pronounced seemed to open up a vast gulf between her experiences and the kind of life the other woman had come from. It had been different at Charnwood House, when she'd worked in service. Everyone had their place there – family or servants. But now she was expected to live and work with these women!

Then she heard the other one say, in a deeper, booming voice, 'It looks as if we've got a reception committee.'

They came on down to the *Theodore* and now they were visible: one slim with wavy blonde hair, the other round-faced and very plump, dark hair tied tightly back, but with a severe, very straight fringe.

'Well, hello!' the blonde said. 'You must be Mrs Bartholomew.'

Maryann nodded, throwing the rag in through the cabin door. 'That's me.' She couldn't think of a single thing else she might say.

'I say,' the blonde said to her companion. 'Let's put this bally lot down and introduce ourselves properly.'

They were about to dump everything, bedrolls and all on the towpath, but Maryann, appalled at the thought of the mud being transferred into her spotless cabin, protested.

'No – don't do that! It's mucky down there – put them inside. Here – I'll show you.'

She stood outside the *Theodore*, arms folded, as they deposited their things.

'I say, what a *superb* cabin,' she heard the dark one say, and the other woman made some reply. When they came out again, the blonde one climbed down carefully from the counter. Maryann didn't offer to help. The dark one bounced down, landing with surprising agility for her weight.

The blonde held her hand out. Close up, Maryann saw that her hair was rolled back from her forehead and pinned stylishly. She had a wide-eyed, rather birdlike face, not quite pretty, but sympathetic. In the half light Maryann thought, but was not certain, that she was wearing lipstick.

'I'm Sylvia Cresswell. Mrs – normally, anyhow!' Her laugh tinkled into the air. 'I'm awfully glad to meet you, and I'm so sorry to hear about your husband's frightful accident.'

Maryann shook the thin, cold hand and said awkwardly, 'Thanks – how d'you do?'

'And I'm Dorothy Higgs-Deveraux,' the other girl boomed. Her handshake was a lot more forceful. She had a broad, large-boned face and dark eyes. 'Most people call me Dot.'

'I'm Maryann Bartholomew,' she said, as they both seemed to be waiting for her to add something more. She felt so rough beside them: her voice, her manners.

'And these are your children?' Sylvia asked, moving closer to them. 'Goodness me – are they all yours? Who are these little lovelies then?'

'Tell the ladies your names,' Maryann commanded them sharply.

Joley and Sally managed to get theirs out, but the others were too overwhelmed by all the attention from these strangers.

'That's Ezra – he's five,' Maryann finished for them. 'Rose here's four – and the twins, Ada and Esther, are eighteen months now. Anyroad –' she lifted the little ones briskly off the roof – 'you'll be wanting a cup of tea and summat to eat?'

'That'd be *marvellous*,' Dot said. 'I'm parched and I could eat a horse!'

They made as if to move into the *Esther Jane* with the family, but Maryann stood looking down at them from the counter.

'We'll bring you a plateful in your cabin. There's no room in here with all of us.'

'Ah –' Sylvia faltered. 'Yes, of course. So sorry.'

Maryann could see Sylvia had heard the chill in her voice and she felt rather triumphant. She wasn't having them just moving in here and taking over the place!

She got Joley and Sally to carry the plates of stew and cups of tea along to the other cabin. When Sally came back, wide-eyed, she said, 'That lady with the white hair's got some pretty things.'

'Has she?' Maryann said sourly. Whatever fripperies she'd brought with her wouldn't stay pretty long on here, she thought. Not once they got covered in smuts and muck.

'They want to know what time to get up,' Joley said.

Maryann spooned out their stew – a little ration of meat padded out with carrots and turnip. 'Go and tell her, early – by six. We've got a load of coal to fetch.'

From now on she would have to bunk up with Joley and Sally, end to end beside her, and the two younger ones top to tail on the side bench, twins on the floor. Maryann lay in the darkness, hearing the occasional, mournful squawk of a water bird. She ached to be able to reach out and touch Joel beside her. Everything felt so peculiar and sad and she didn't feel safe without him, so solid and true, beside her. She pictured him in his bed in Oxford and sent him a goodnight wish. Then the loathsome thought of the two unknown women lying in the *Theodore* came to her. Even the thought of them filled her with unease. Why had she agreed to let strangers come barging into her life, her family? She and

Bobby could've struggled on together. As it was, that Sylvia looked as if she'd break if you dropped her and as for Dot, she was going to be a right bossy one, Maryann could see. What use were they going to be, coming onto the cut from their mollycoddled lives?

She turned on her side and tried to sleep, dreading the next morning.

Twenty

'I say – hello? Anyone up in there? Only we thought you might like a cup of tea.'

The voice came to Maryann in the depths of sleep and she forced her eyes open. Memory flooded in. That voice – of course – those blasted women! The clock by her head said twenty-past six – she was the one who'd overslept! Cursing ripely, she scrambled over the twins to the door, which opened onto a cold, overcast morning.

Sylvia was outside, looking neat and fresh with her hair pinned back, and she held out a steaming cup.

'*So* sorry to wake you.' Sylvia seemed almost to cringe with apology as she spoke. 'I've put a spoonful of sugar in – I do hope that's all right?'

Cheeks burning with embarrassment Maryann leaned over to take the tea, trying to hold the torn neck of her nightdress together: it had a rip in the hem too. Her hair was all over the place, she hadn't lit the stove on the *Esther Jane* yet – and these two clowns had to be up with the lark, sod them!

'Ta. Good of you,' she said, barely able to hide her fury. 'We're nearly ready.'

'Good-oh. Well – I must let you get on. You must have an awful lot to do.' Sylvia moved away, folding her arms, shoulders hunched, as if trying to minimize her presence. Maryann was taken aback at how cowed the woman seemed by her curt response. She got halfway along the *Theodore*, but then, to Maryann's further irritation, turned and came back.

'Er, Maryann, Dot and I brought our rations with us – and Dot's got some extra as well. Of course it makes most sense to combine everything – so how about us doing breakfast for everyone this morning? Dot's already made a start . . .'

'I can manage, you know,' Maryann snapped. She could feel herself frowning and knew she must seem very hostile. But she felt very nervous and under pressure – it was unbearable having these strangers coming and taking over her life! But then Joley pushed passed her and poked his nose out through the door, saying, 'Umm! I can smell bacon – is that for us?'

Forced to swallow her pride Maryann said more politely, 'All right, then – you do it for today. Thanks.'

When the breakfast was ready, Sylvia started carrying plates of it along to them until Maryann ordered the children out to go and collect it.

'We don't need you waiting on us,' she said.

'Oh, it's quite all right!' Sylvia laughed. 'You know how it is. One gets used to it.'

Maryann didn't know how it was, but was puzzled by how cringingly eager Sylvia was to please her.

They all felt well set up after a share of crispy bacon, with wedges of bread and cups of sweet tea. Sylvia and Dot stood outside to finish drinking their tea, and Maryann peered uneasily at them out through the doorway, taking a good look at her new companions in the unsparing morning light, wishing she could examine them even more closely without them seeing. The children kept looking and whispering as well and she had to shush them. She had taken in, this morning, that Sylvia was older than she had supposed the night before. Her thin, oval face looked surprisingly tired and worn, even though she was already made up, with scarlet lipstick to match the wool scarf she was wearing. She had on a pair of workmanlike blue slacks and a loose-sleeved brown jacket. In the neck of this Maryann could just see the neck of a green woolly with the scarf tied round it. She held her tea cupped in both hands to warm them, her long neck bent forwards to sip. She looked to Maryann like a slender, timid deer.

Dot, however, was far more sturdily built – more of an ox, with her plump face, thick arms and chunky thighs encased in brown corduroy trousers. Over these she had on a tweed jacket, and a navy beret perched sidelong on her head. Maryann guessed that Sylvia must be in her late twenties, but with Dot it was very hard to tell. The two women were talking in low voices; every so often Maryann saw them look over towards the open doors of the *Esther Jane* and she tried to pretend she wasn't watching them. What were they talking about? she wondered, full of dread. What *did* women like that talk about?

Then she heard Dot's hockey captain voice cry, 'I say – look at those simply marvellous cats! Do they live aboard, d'you suppose?'

Jenny and Spots were climbing along the cabin of the *Theodore*. The Bartholomew children listened wide-eyed as Dot made cooing, cajoling noises to the cats.

'Oh, aren't you a *darling*!' they heard. Joley and Ezra started giggling and set Ada and Esther off as well.

'Are those ladies living with us now?' Sally asked, bemused.

'Only for a bit,' Maryann said irritably, piling their few crocks in the dipper for washing, with more force than was necessary. She was very anxious about the day ahead. She was skipper of both the boats now, with those two green beginners. She'd only worked with Joel and Bobby and was full of worry that she'd make a mess of it all. What she dreaded most was the thought of all the other boaters watching what was happening to the *Esther Jane* – one of the old, well-known Number One boats. She knew what to do, really, but she was afraid her nervousness would make her do something wrong – and who knew if those two painted birds out there really knew anything about working boats? She was damned if she'd let them make a fool of her and let Joel down. That was how she saw it – she had to do this for him.

'I thought we'd start you off gentle like,' Mr Veater told her when she went to the office. 'Then I'll see about a trip to Oxford.' Seeing Maryann's furrowed brow, the agitated way she was rubbing her hands together, he added, 'They'll soon cotton on – don't you worry.'

Outside, her breath streamed white from her and the smoke from the boats' chimneys hung in long, slowly dispersing banners in the still air. One of the other boatwomen accosted her.

'Who're those two you've got on board with you then, Maryann?' She eyed the Bartholomews' pair, beside which Sylvia and Dot were waiting for her with the eagerness of newly trained dogs.

'Volunteers,' Maryann told her.

'Blimey.' The woman peered at them. 'My eyes aren't so strong now, but if it weren't for that one's hair I'd've said they were chaps.'

Maryann knew the news would spread round the boaters of Sutton Stop at a fast pace. In the seconds it took her to get back to her own pair again, she decided that the only thing was just to get through this period.

After all, she thought, *they'll be on their boat and we'll be on ours. I shan't have to have too much to do with them, shall I? But, Joel, you'd better get right soon and come back. I can't stand the thought of working with these two!*

She knew the women were watching her as she walked towards them and folded her arms to protect herself, as if their eyes were scraping her skin. She wondered how she looked in her frayed cardi, with scuffed old boots. They were waiting for her, all eager like new Girl Guides.

'Morning!' they both chimed, although Sylvia had already seen her once.

'Are we nearly ready for the off?' Dot asked.

'Right.' Once again, Maryann heard her voice come out brusquely. 'Let's get going. We're going up Bedworth for a load for the Light.'

Sylvia and Dot looked at each other in bafflement.

Maryann nodded over towards Longford Power Station, only a quarter of a mile behind them, covered, as usual in a pall of cloud. 'Fuel for that.' She went to climb aboard the *Esther Jane* ready to start the engine. 'It's a day's trip. You steered a butty before?'

'Oh *yes*, of course,' Sylvia said eagerly. 'We've done all our training trips you know. Kit taught us ever such a lot – really threw us in at the deep end.'

Maryann looked up. 'Who's Kit?'

'Oh, *sorry*. Kit Gayford – our trainer. We thought everyone knew Kit by now! She trains most of the female volunteers on the Grand Union. She's absolutely marvellous. Don't worry, Maryann. We shan't let you down. We'll do our very best.'

As the engine of the *Esther Jane* began to turn over, breaking into the morning peace, Maryann thought grumpily that this was yet another instance in the past twenty-fours of someone telling her not to worry.

The first part of the trip passed without a hitch. There were no locks on this stretch and once Maryann was at the tiller she felt better. Of course she could manage! She'd been a boatwoman long enough now, hadn't she? Joley took the tiller, while she ducked inside to do odd jobs and deal with Ada and Esther, and her son's quiet confidence steadied her and made her proud. The day was overcast and they passed through a ghostly land-scape along that part of the cut, a wasteground of former coal tips and abandoned mine shafts. In one spot a group of gypsies had set up camp with their sturdy ponies and coloured caravans, scrawny dogs barking at the boats as they chugged past. The cut was busy with joeys coming and going, and pairs of 'Joshers' and Barlow boats. A family from another S. E. Barlow boat greeted her with waves and the usual 'How do's?' She saw their amazed expressions when they caught sight of the butty with Sylvia at the tiller, now wearing a red and white head-scarf, and Dot perched on the gunwale sporting her navy beret.

'Look at their faces!' Maryann laughed to Joley. 'They weren't expecting that, were they?'

They reached the Bedworth arm and queued for loading. The day had become even more heavily overcast.

During the wait, Maryann fed the children, and she was outside emptying wash water over the side when she saw Sylvia coming towards her and she tensed. Now what did they want? She kept trying to put those two back there out of her mind – pretend they weren't there! Even if she had to suffer working with them, it didn't mean she wanted anything else to do with them. Bucket in hand, she waited.

'We wondered how long we're likely to be here?' Sylvia looked up at her, giving a tight smile. Maryann saw that she had pale blue eyes. She had a naturally vulnerable expression, which softened Maryann's feelings a fraction.

'Shouldn't be long.' Maryann nodded at the pair ahead of them. 'There's only them in front of us.'

'Only, Dot and I have made some cocoa and we wondered if you'd like some?'

'No, ta. We've just had our dinner.'

The smile faded in Sylvia's eyes. She hugged herself as if cold and stood, uncertain, by the boat. For a moment Maryann thought she was going to say something else, but she turned away. The odd thing was, Maryann thought, she looked almost nervous. Surely not about speaking to her? After all, they were the ones with lah-di-dah accents and their clothes weren't running to holes like hers. What had they got to be flaming nervous about?

The afternoon did not go well. They were heavily laden and low in the water, though they hadn't stopped to sheet up the boats: even though the sky was heavy, no rain had fallen yet. Maryann decided to risk it, since they'd deliver at the Coventry Light that afternoon.

By the time they'd reached Sutton Stop again, it had grown colder and a bitter wind was blowing. Ada and Esther had been perched up on the cabin roof, and Maryann moved them inside for warmth.

I hope it's not going to go and rain now, she thought, glowering at the sky. She couldn't remember the last time she'd felt in such a thoroughly out-of-sorts bad temper with everything. All afternoon she'd been acutely aware of the butty behind. She had to glance back every so often to make sure they were following without any hitches. Otherwise she faced ahead, glad of the long snubber between the boats, but still prickling with awareness of the two women at the tiller which for so long had been hers. All the time she felt this inner tension, and that the two of them were watching her from behind.

Sutton Stop was the meeting place of the Coventry and Oxford cuts and the power station was south of the junction on the Oxford. The two waterways met at an angle, which meant taking the boats round two right-angled bends to reach the stop lock dividing the two.

As they approached the bridge before the junction, Maryann slowed to a crawl, allowing the *Theodore* to catch up a bit. She released the snubber and handed it to Joley.

'Get off at the bridge and tell them to pull in and wait while we get round. Then get back and help me. Sally, go forward and get ready to throw him the line!'

Joley leapt off under the bridge-hole and ran back to the *Theodore*. Maryann heard him calling out instructions to the two women.

He knows more than the pair of you put together, she thought. She saw the *Theodore* begin to veer into the bank and Joley running back to join her.

She faced the busy junction nervously, even though she and Joel had been back and forth through it endless times. Sally threw the cotton line attached to the small mast over to her brother and he looped it round the bollard by the iron bridge, playing it round as Maryann brought the boat under. As she kept the engine ticking steadily ahead, the stern swung round nicely, just as required. She smiled grimly for a second. Thank God for that. When they were safely round both bends, she tied up and told Sally to mind the younger ones.

She ran round and over the bridge with Joley, expecting to find the women waiting with the *Theodore* tied up as instructed. Instead of which, by the time she got down to the bank, she found Dot bow-hauling the butty along, almost at the bridge. Dot, who was leaning into the job like a dray horse, had got the butty moving at quite a pace.

'What the hell's she playing at!' Maryann cried. 'She's never going to make the turn like that – how does she think she's going to stop!'

Waving her arms she shouted, 'Stop pulling, you bloody fool! What're you doing? *Slow down!*'

It was already too late. On a monkey boat with an engine, the only way to brake it was to throw the engine into reverse. On a butty with no engine, Sylvia, holding the *Theodore*'s tiller, could only watch helplessly, hauling on it to try and turn the boat in time to make the turn.

'She's going to crash,' Joley said matter-of-factly. 'Good job Dad ent here.'

'If he was we wouldn't be in this bloody mess, would we?' Maryann said furiously.

In those seconds she became aware of several other things. One was that the women had pulled the boat out in the path of a horse-drawn joey, which was bearing down close behind them, the man at its tiller yelling at them, outraged. The other was confirmation of Joley's observation that nothing now was going to stop the

Theodore except a collision. All she could do was watch, hands pressed to her cheeks.

'You cowing, stupid *idiots*,' she breathed.

Instead of managing the left bend, the *Theodore* shot across the turn and rammed, shuddering into the corner of the bank on the other side, leaving Dot with rope scorching through her hands. Sylvia, who had been leaning back, pulling desperately on the tiller, lost her balance on the jolt and fell in over the back into the water, in the company of the *Theodore*'s water carrier, which clunked and sploshed into the cut after her.

Sylvia surfaced, gasping, in the freezing water to see the front of the joey boat coming straight at her. With the speed born of survival instinct she flung herself round to the right of the *Theodore* as the two joeymen shafted and pulled, tweaking the fore end round to the left of the *Theodore* and made the bend.

Dot, standing shaken by the bridge, called to the men in her ringing voice, 'That was a close one. We're most terribly sorry!'

The joeymen eyed her with a contempt more corrosive than even Maryann could have managed and loud expletives trailed in the air behind them. A small but interested audience was gathering on the bank.

Maryann ran to help Sylvia out of the water. Her teeth were chattering convulsively and the black, slimy water poured off her. Her hair had turned an interesting shade of gritty grey. Otherwise she was perfectly all right.

'Come on,' Maryann ordered, holding on tightly to her rage. She led her back over the bridge to help Dot haul the *Theodore* round out of everyone's way. As they joined the *Esther Jane*, Maryann saw all her children perched at various points on the cabin and gunwales, watching the events with fascination.

The three of them went into the cabin of the *Theodore*, Sylvia smelling abominable and dripping all over the floor, and Maryann let rip. She found she was trembling with fury at them making such a spectacle of her and of Joel's boats. She hadn't been deaf to the ribald comments levelled at them from some of the boatmen who'd been watching. After years of trying to prove herself as a boatwoman, a Bartholomew, of trying to belong, these two idiots had humiliated her completely in one afternoon. She let them have it with both barrels.

'When I tell you to wait, you bloody well *wait*!' she bawled at them. 'What in God's name did you think you were playing at, barging out in front of that other boat and bringing her in at that speed? If there'd been anyone else tied up at that corner you could've rammed them and sunk them, d'you know that? And you've gone and lost our water carrier, so unless someone fishes it out we're going to have to get another one. D'you know how long that carrier's been on this boat?' She paused, glowering at them. Dot opened her mouth, then closed it.

'I s'pose you think you know better than people who've been on the cut all their lives, coming along with your airs and graces, 'cause you fancy a little rest from painting your nails? Well, if you're coming to work with me, you can sodding well do it properly or go back to wherever it is you come from!'

'Look,' Dot managed to say. 'It was my fault, not Sylvia's. I admit, I made a mess of it . . .'

'Yes – not half you did!' Maryann yelled. 'I thought you said you knew what you were doing!'

They were silent. Maryann was surprised they didn't argue. Sylvia was too busy dripping and shivering, but even Dot, whose face was puce with embarrassment, stood in silence, nursing her rope-burned hands under her armpits.

'Get changed,' Maryann ordered Sylvia contemptuously, finally running out of steam. 'And then we've got the lock to get through. D'you think you can manage that without sinking us?'

Twenty-One

Maryann's foul temper lasted long into the evening. She banged about in the cabin, slamming the pan down as she cooked bubble and squeak, snapping at the children. Her head was thumping and all she wanted was to lie down and forget today had ever happened.

'You gave those ladies a talking to, daint you, Mom?' Sally said as she waited for her food. Maryann knew the child was trying to break the tense silence around her.

'Yes, I flaming well did!' she retorted. 'Coming here with their airs and graces, thinking they know better than anyone.'

'Are they leaving tomorrow?' Rose asked hopefully. Like Maryann, she wasn't very good at coping with change in her life. She liked things to feel unchanging and secure.

'No, bab – no such luck.' Maryann sighed. 'If only Bobby was about I'd have him back like a shot and manage two-handed. I wish to God I'd never let him go, only Mr Veater never gave me much choice.' She turned and started dishing out the food. 'We're going down Oxford tomorrow, so we've got to put up with them.'

Ezra's dark brows were pulled into a frown. 'Ent you allowed no slip-ups when you're grown big?'

'What d'you mean?' Maryann asked, perching wearily on the back bed.

'Our dad says to me when I do summat wrong: when you're starting out you're allowed some slip-ups.'

Maryann sighed into a silence in which the children waited for her answer. She could see they were really puzzled by the intensity of her reaction to the two women. Even with the justification of the afternoon's troubles, she could barely explain it even to herself, how having them there made her feel unsafe and exposed. The tight feeling inside her increased and her temples throbbed.

All afternoon she'd held onto her self-righteous anger. The power station was only a quarter of a mile south, looming huge over the landscape, creating its own pall of cloud from the chimneys and cooling towers which poured out smoke and steam. The afternoon had darkened and, although it was only about four o'clock, already dusk was falling as they slid through the black, refuse-strewn water, in the shadows of the cranes and gantries, to the wharf. Here the coal was lifted from the boat by grabbers onto conveyor belts, to be carried into the insatiable power station. Sylvia and Dot kept out of her way, only exchanging the tersest of remarks about what needed to happen next. By the time they were heading back, gunwales higher in the water, Maryann had calmed down, but her headache was setting in, and a sour, shameful feeling had come over her which she found hard to admit.

Ezra's question made her feel even worse.

'Yes, bab, we all make mistakes,' she said, adding defiantly, 'and there are some people need to learn from them more than others.'

It was a relief to get the children to sleep. Ada and Esther were all but weaned now, just having a drink from her sometimes at night to settle them. Once the children were down, there wasn't much for her to do but go to bed herself, since there was no room to move about in the cabin. They were squeezed in tight as a pea pod. She was about to make herself a drop of hot milk to ease her head, when she felt the boat rock slightly, and there came a soft knocking on the door.

Sylvia was outside, looking solemn and upset.

So you damn well should, Maryann thought, looking up at her. The sky had cleared and it felt very chill outside.

'Look,' Sylvia whispered, 'if your children are settled for the night, Dot and I would really like to have a talk with you. Mend some fences, sort of thing. Will you come and join us for a cup of tea?'

'I was just going to bed.' It came out abruptly again. More so than she meant it to. How was she supposed to talk to these people? She couldn't speak the way they did, could she?

'*Please*,' Sylvia said. To Maryann's astonishment she heard tears in Sylvia's voice. 'We both feel ghastly about what happened today. And we can't go on like this, can we? We've got to learn to work together somehow. We need to try and make friends.'

Maryann knew that what had happened had not been Sylvia's fault. Why wasn't Dot the one here eating humble pie, she wondered. She desperately didn't want to go and sit with them, but she felt sorry for Sylvia and there was something sweet, almost pathetic, in the way she had asked. Grudgingly, she nodded. 'I'll be over in a minute.'

It was an uncomfortable feeling, being invited into what for years had been her own home. She stood out in the cold, starry darkness for a moment, knotted up inside with nerves. Why didn't she just go back to her own cabin and go to bed? She knew suddenly that part of the reason she wanted to hold onto her self-righteous anger was that she was afraid. She realized that it was the word 'friends' that really frightened her. It had been different with Nance, who had known her for years. Of course Nance accepted her. But to try and be close to anyone else felt terrifying. How could she ever show them who she was, what she had come from?

She took a deep breath. They didn't have to know anything about her, she reasoned with herself. Only what she wanted to tell them. All she had to do was try and patch things up so they could manage the work properly. For the sake of the boats. That was all that mattered. She tapped on the *Theodore*'s hatch.

'Here she is . . . Come on in and sit with us for a bit.'

Sylvia welcomed her so kindly that, to her irritation, Maryann found tears in her eyes and tried fiercely to blink them away, though she knew Sylvia had seen them. She sat on the side bench near Dot, who was perched on the edge of the back bed, knitting something with big needles out of thick orange wool. Sylvia came and sat on Maryann's left and poured the tea. She'd obviously managed to wash her hair, as it was pale and silky looking again. She was such a fragile-looking thing, she didn't look strong enough for this life, Maryann thought, sipping the tea. Sylvia could make a good cup of tea, though, she'd give her that. The oil lamp was burning and it was as cosy as ever inside. It felt very strange, though, being here with these strangers with their possessions about: a bar of Pears soap, a pretty mirror edged with shells and a little pink washbag. Sylvia's trousers were hanging over the range, still steaming, and there was a copy of *Woman's Own* on the table, a woman with glossy chestnut hair smiling from the cover. Maryann eyed it curiously. She wanted to reach out and turn the pages, and was surprised by her sudden hunger to see what was inside.

'Look,' Sylvia said carefully, 'we seem to have started off on completely the wrong foot with you. What happened today was our fault entirely . . .'

'No – it was my fault,' Dot said robustly. She looked different with her hair loose over her shoulders, making her look voluptuous and much more feminine. Somehow it looked wrong, as if the hair belonged to someone else. Maryann wondered how old she was. 'I misunderstood your boy when he shouted over to us – I thought you wanted us to follow on. And I must say' – she began to sound rather heated – 'that it wasn't exactly my fault if I could barely understand a blasted word the child was saying. I think it's a bit thin if you won't accept an apology that's genuinely meant. I mean, dammit, I've said sorry. Haven't you ever made a mistake?'

Maryann thought of some of the terrible mistakes she made when she started out on the cut and the shameful feeling nudged harder inside her. How would she have felt if no one had forgiven her? But she felt so lost without Joel, and worried and tense about taking charge of the boats with strangers on board whose background she didn't understand, that it was easiest to take it all out on them! And there was something about Dot especially which made her hackles rise. The way she strode about on her buxom legs and that *voice*. Sylvia was well spoken all right, with her tinkly voice, but she didn't have the posh, overpowering blare that Dot had. She stared back at her, feeling her expression harden, about to make a curt reply.

But Sylvia was saying, 'The thing is, Maryann, we've never worked together before either, and we haven't got used to each other yet – or your family . . .'

Maryann turned to her, frowning. 'I thought Mr Veater said you were a team?'

'Well, if he did, he got it wrong. We only met on the train coming up here. We've done our training trips, but not together. Quite a lot of the girls dropped out and we were leftovers for the moment – spare-wheelers, as Kit would say.'

'We are new girls, it's true,' Dot said, 'but we aren't as bad as . . . well, as we were today. That was me getting the wrong end of the stick and then putting too much oomph into it altogether. But we've both come through quite a few sticky situations on the Grand Union. We'll do our best not to let you down again.'

'The thing is – ' Sylvia cut in again rather intensely before Maryann had a chance to speak – 'we so love the life here, and we think you're *marvellous*, how you manage and everything. I just don't know how you do it with six children. I struggle with only two even when I'm living in a house.'

'*What?*' Maryann was nonplussed. 'You've got children?'

'Oh yes – a girl and a boy. Kay's twelve and Dickie's ten.'

'Twelve!' Maryann blurted. The woman's children were older than her own!

Sylvia gabbled on nervously. 'As a matter of fact I was going to ask you if I might put up some pictures on the walls. Dot, dear, pass my bag over, will you?' She showed Maryann a picture of two smiling faces, a girl and boy side by side. The girl's hair was shoulder length, waving prettily round her cheeks and darker than her mother's, though she had a look of Sylvia.

'Her face is the same shape as yours,' Maryann said, peering in fascination at the picture. 'You can see the likeness. She's pretty.'

'Thank you.' Sylvia smiled. 'Of course, Dickie's the image of his father.' The boy had a squarer face, a rather thin mouth and narrow eyes, but was handsome in his way. Maryann took another look before handing it back.

'And this is my darling Roy.'

The second picture showed a thickset man with cropped, fair hair who looked out of the picture with the sort of half smile which shows no teeth. He was wearing a suit and tie.

'Oh – I see what you mean,' Maryann said. 'Your son *does* look just like his father.'

'Yes.' Sylvia put the pictures back in her bag. 'Though they're not alike in temperament. Oh, I forgot!' She reached over to the cupboard. 'I brought a cake from home. Would you like a piece? It's cherry madeira.'

Maryann wasn't hungry, but she thought she'd better accept a piece out of politeness. And she was beginning to warm to Sylvia, even if she couldn't take to Dot.

'But where are your . . . Kay and Dickie then? You left them with your mom?'

'Oh no,' Sylvia said. 'My mother's been dead for a number of years. No, they're at boarding school. I sent them some time ago, to avoid the bombing, of course. They're not far from each other, fortunately – outside Worcester. I've dropped them a line to tell them to send their letters here. Is that the best thing? I so miss hearing from them. I've been told I'll be able to have leave to go home for the Easter holidays.'

Maryann was still struggling with the idea of Sylvia being a mother and of sending your children away to the other side of the country.

'How old are you, then?' she blurted out.

Sylvia chuckled at her frankness. 'I'm just thirty-two as a matter of fact.' Maryann was even more astonished. The woman was older than her! 'Dot here's a mere pup – only twenty-one.'

'I think you'll find I'm old for my years.' Dot looked up for a second, somehow challenging them. Maryann wondered why she had to be so aggressive, as if she felt permanently under attack. 'What happened today won't happen again. I can promise you that.'

'And you?' Sylvia asked.

'Me? Oh – I'll turn thirty in the autumn.' Surely she looked older, didn't she? she wondered. Some days she felt as old as Methuselah.

'Were you born and bred on the cut?' Sylvia asked, in rather awed tones.

'No,' Maryann admitted. 'I married into it.'

'Told you, didn't I?' Dot said triumphantly. 'I knew she had a Birmingham accent!'

Maryann stiffened in annoyance. She didn't like Dot's tone, or the fact that they'd been making guesses about her life. She felt prickly about any of her life being exposed beyond her control.

'Yes,' she said, 'I'm from Brum. That's where I met Joel – my husband.' She said it in a way that did not invite more questions and looked down into her lap.

Gently, Sylvia asked about Joel's accident. She said her own husband, Roy, was an RAF officer in Coastal Command.

'Will he get leave at Easter as well?' Maryann asked, trying to get off the subject of herself.

'Oh, perhaps,' Sylvia said lightly. 'I imagine he might. But the poor darling never seems quite sure when he'll be home.'

By the time she went back to the *Esther Jane* that night, Maryann had a picture of Sylvia's life in a nice family home in Wimbledon. She saw a pretty garden edged with roses (this was far more than Sylvia had told her, but she enjoyed embroidering this charmed picture), the two children playing out on the greenest of lawns and her husband coming home, broad-shouldered and handsome in his air-force blue. Of Dot's background she had learned almost nothing, except that she came from Buckinghamshire.

I just don't take to that one, she thought, squeezing into bed beside Joley and Sally. Dot seldom met her gaze, except with a challenging stare. Maryann just couldn't imagine what her real life was like. *I'll just have to try and rub along with her somehow*, she thought. *It'll only be for a trip or two.*

But Sylvia ... course, she was from another life altogether, but there was a nervous sweetness, a sympathy, about her which Maryann had warmed to. And at least Sylvia was a mother: that was something they had in common. It felt new and strange, the company of these women not from the boating life. As if a door had opened, giving her a glimpse into something new.

As she slipped into sleep, she realized her headache had gone.

Twenty-Two

It was true, as Maryann found out on the trip to Oxford, that Sylvia and Dot were not bad boaters, especially for beginners. But they were still early on in their learning and some things took a frustratingly long time.

The first day they travelled back to the coalfields. This time, though, after loading they stopped to cloth up before departing for the long journey south, as the weather looked uncertain. In the past Maryann had usually left most of this to Joel and Bobby, who were quick at it after a lifetime of practice. Now, with Joley's help, it was she who had to cloth up the *Esther Jane*, leaving the others to deal with the *Theodore*.

'Are you sure you know what to do?' she asked them.

'Of course,' Dot said, already climbing along the hold to the cratch at the fore end where they stowed the cloths and tarpaulin. Dot's tone was prickly with resentment at having her competence questioned again.

'I've done it a few times,' Sylvia said. Maryann could tell she was trying to soften the effect of Dot's brusqueness.

'I'll let you get on with it then. Come on, Joley.'

Joley had helped do the job many times. Balanced on the top planks, Maryann shuffled along on her knees, knotting the tough, hairy strings of the side-cloths over the planks, while Joley stood in the hold threading them through in the right places and passing them to her.

'This one needs splicing,' she told him, holding out one that was frayed and in danger of snapping. They had to take constant care of all the ropes on the boat, and these strings had to be pulled very tight and knotted taut; their rough fibre blistered her hands.

She had tied the final string and she and Joley were opening out the top cloth to lay it over when they heard a shriek from behind on the *Theodore*. Maryann swivelled round in time to see Dot hurtling down from the top planks. Her hands reached out, trying to clutch anything to save herself, but she failed and rolled at a very undignified angle over the gunwale and into the cut, her large backside the last thing to disappear under the water. The splash was impressive. A moment later she surfaced like a flustered hippo, spluttering and enraged. Maryann caught Sylvia's gaze as she stood in the hold, a hand clasped horrified over her mouth. As well as consternation, Maryann was sure she saw a flicker of laughter in Sylvia's expression. The Bartholomew children were in fits of giggles, and the man who was clothing up his own boat behind them called out, 'Taking a good look in there, were you?'

Not entirely succeeding in straightening her own twitching lips, Maryann climbed down to help Dot out. Her bun had come loose, her heavy plait uncoiling down her back.

'What happened? D'you have a string snap?'

'Yes, I damn well did.' She took Maryann's hand resentfully and was hauled, gushing water, onto the bank. 'And I don't think it's very nice of you all to laugh!'

'I'm not.' She managed to look sober. 'Sorry, Dot. You awright?'

'Yes, of *course* I'm all right!' She shook herself, almost

203

like a dog, looking ready to explode with anger. 'Don't be so bloody ridiculous.'

'There's no need to get upset.'

'I'm *not* damn well upset!'

For the second time in twenty-four hours, one of the trainees went dripping into the *Theodore*'s cabin to change an entire set of clothing. Maryann frowned, watching Dot's furiously hunched shoulders disappear through the hatches. There was no need to get that mithered about it, was there? Everyone fell in sometimes. Again, she and Sylvia exchanged glances and Sylvia shrugged, rolling her eyes. For the first time Maryann wondered just how well Sylvia and Dot got on when they were on their own. Just because they were different from her didn't mean they had anything in common themselves.

Maryann had hoped to get past the first set of locks at Rugby that day, but the clothing up took at least twice as long as usual – she helped Sylvia finish on the *Theodore* – and they still had to get past the junction at Hawkesbury again. Dot was silent and morose all day, but with brooding determination completed the manoeuvres round the bends almost perfectly this time. She was still barely speaking to any of them until the evening, though, which added an extra strain, but then she just seemed to snap out her mood.

In a quiet moment that evening Sylvia said to Maryann, 'Kit did mention to me that Dot can be rather touchy, so don't take it personally, will you?'

The next morning, when they reached the double locks at Hillmorton, Maryann gave Dot the mildest of reminders to go back and close a paddle that she'd left open. She got a furious reaction,

'I'm going to!' Dot's fleshy cheeks flushed angrily.

She stomped off with the windlass, calling over her shoulder, 'I do know what I'm doing, you know.'

'Well, if you know what you're doing, why don't you do it then?' Maryann retorted to her back, fed up with her. She'd asked politely enough, hadn't she? Who did she flaming well think she was? She had to admit, though, that Dot was strong. She bow-hauled the butty into the locks at Hillmorton with the force of a man.

Most of the journey went better. There was a hint of spring in the air and the biting cold had softened to mildness. They woke in the mornings to the first, tentative sounds of birdsong. Maryann found that, despite her own burden of being in charge of loaded boats, children and everything, Dot and Sylvia were very efficient at getting shopping in whenever there was a chance to. Sylvia also insisted that she and Dot cook for everyone most of the time.

'How can you possibly do everything – all your washing and looking after the family and cooking? No – you let us do that,' Sylvia said. Maryann had more of a sense that the work was being shared by them all than when she worked with the men.

As the days passed along the winding Oxford cut, Maryann gradually became more used to the women and they to her. She found Sylvia immediately easier – they were closer in age, and Sylvia was always nervously anxious to please. Dot, in spite of her prickliness and determination always to be right, was extremely hard-working. It seemed that her way would have been to push on and on, never stopping for a rest.

'You'll have to go and work the beer boats,' Maryann told her. 'Then you'd never have to stop at all!'

Sylvia was kind and motherly to the children, especially to Rose when once Maryann confided, though without going into too much detail, how the child came to be in her care. She always chose very carefully what she did and did not tell.

'Oh, the poor little lamb!' Sylvia exclaimed. She made a special pet of Rose, always cuddling and spending time with her when she had the chance, and Rose loved the extra attention. Maryann realized that Sylvia needed this. Once she came into the cabin and found Sylvia cuddling Rose, tears running down her face.

'I do miss my own children,' she said wretchedly. 'I love this life here, but some days I just wish it didn't have to be like this.'

To Maryann's great surprise, it was Dot who formed a special bond with the boys. As the children gradually relaxed with 'them ladies', Joley and Ezra shyly showed Dot their fishing rods and she seized on them with great enthusiasm.

'Marvellous. I say, look at those!' She squatted down to talk to them. 'Well – we must give these an airing.'

In spare moments when they were tied up, she encouraged the boys to take up their fishing again, and went to fetch bait for them when they were at Napton, queuing for the locks.

'Nothing like a tinful of squirming beasties to delight a couple of lads,' she said gruffly.

'That's nice of you,' Maryann said, astonished and touched by the trouble she'd taken and the smiles it had brought to the boys' faces. She handed Dot a mug of tea as they stood waiting. The small gesture felt like a friendship offering. The children were clustered round the fishing rods in great excitement, Ezra scolding the twins for nearly tipping the tin of maggots over. 'Joel – their dad – usually gets them doing it. You done much fishing then?'

'Oh, *hours* of it.'

Maryann was still trying to get used to Dot's way of talking. 'Hours' came out as 'ars'.

'We grew up on the Thames, you see. My brother Steven and I practically lived on the river. Steven's a couple of years younger than me. He's in the Navy now – somewhere in the Med. But we were always out and about, he and I. There're just the two of us, you see.'

Maryann saw the softest expression she'd yet seen come over Dot's face as she spoke.

'My two've never been fishing, or anything like that,' Sylvia said, staring out over the water. 'I s'pose I always hoped Roy would take them out and do these sorts of things. But he's always so frightfully busy, of course, poor darling.'

'Well – you'll be able to take them yourself now, won't you?' Dot said.

'Yes.' Sylvia looked pleased. 'I shall, shan't I?'

Sylvia's Roy had been high up in an insurance firm in the City of London in peacetime. Dot, who had been working in London as a secretary in a legal firm, told them her father was a Judge. In other circumstances Maryann would have felt intimidated by this, but now she was getting to know the women a bit better and they were on her territory, making all their beginners' mistakes, she felt better and even risked joking about it when she heard about their backgrounds.

'Aren't I mixing with the nobs these days?'

Sylvia laughed at this. 'Hardly, dear!'

It dawned on Maryann then that, though Sylvia's voice sounded like a tinkling chandelier, she didn't see herself as anything special, and this came as a surprise. And she knew now that they really *had* been nervous of her when they arrived.

'Completely terrified, actually,' Sylvia admitted. 'You've no idea how we all look up to you real boatwomen.'

As the trip progressed, they worked more and more as a team, taking turns lock-wheeling, sharing the cooking and other chores, and Sylvia, especially, helped Maryann with the children.

'I don't mind giving a hand in the least,' she told her. 'It's a treat to be with your kiddies – I miss Kay and Dickie so much. I do hope there'll be some letters waiting when we get back!'

It wasn't so bad, Maryann thought, relaxing more with them as the days passed. It wouldn't be for too long, having them aboard, would it? And when they got to Oxford they could see Joel. Despite what the doctor had said, she couldn't believe it would take him long to recover. He'd always fought back so hard against any kind of pain or illness. As they pushed south to Oxford, she started to feel more optimistic. There were leaf buds on the trees and you could feel the land coming to life all around, the air full of the hopeful scents of spring. Surely Joel would be better soon and they could all get back to normal?

He held out his arms to them as they crowded into the room.

Maryann was holding Esther, the heavier of the twins. Sally had managed to half lead, half carry Ada up from the wharf, cajoling her impatiently.

'Come on, Ada – we're going to see our dad!'

Joel was lying propped up on pillows on the bed upstairs. His normally weatherbeaten face looked pale and, Maryann thought, a little thinner, though he was beaming with delight at seeing them. A strange sensation passed through her at the familiar sight of his body, a kind of inner leap of recognition, as if, having been temporarily stripped of a part of herself, she had found it again.

Apart from a quick hello kiss, she let the children go first, the older ones chattering nineteen to the dozen and Ada and Esther wanting to climb up onto the bed. Joel cuddled each of them in turn on his chest, and the little ones snuggled close, trying hard to be careful and keep still once they'd been told.

'Hello, my little beauties!' Joel kissed and stroked each of them. 'Oh, it's such a treat to see you. And how's our Joley, eh? And Ezra? You keeping your mother in order for me?'

The boys grinned. 'We've got ladies working the butty,' Joley said. 'And Dot likes fishing.'

'Fishing again, eh? You caught anything for me?'

After a time, Alice Simons appeared in the doorway. 'Well, I don't suppose any of you want some ginger cordial and my fresh buns, now do you?'

Left alone with Joel, Maryann knelt by the bed and rested her head on his chest as they held each other. Feeling his arms round her always made her feel safe and loved. She felt herself relax and she reached up for a kiss. Joel's eyes looked searchingly into hers.

'How're you going along, my mate?'

'Oh, I'm all right.' She kissed him again. 'Missing "moy chap", though.' Most of the boatwomen referred to their husbands as 'moy chap'. Maryann grinned. 'My old man.'

'I feel like an old man. I ent half fed up lying here day

after day, I can tell you,' Joel said, wincing as he tried to shift up the bed a bit. 'It's enough to drive you half mad.'

She stroked his face, knowing how frustrated he was and longing to have him back with them, to lie in his arms at night, for things to be normal.

'Isn't it getting better?'

'Well it is, yes. Slowly. I can just about get up now and move about a bit. But I ent fit for the cut. Nowhere near. This ent me – lying about like this. It's boring, hour after hour. Alice's brought this up for me –' he nodded at the wireless set perched on the chest of drawers by the bed – 'so I can listen to all the world's woes. But my head just goes round and round, thinking about where you are and all I should be doing.'

Maryann tried to reassure him and hide her disappointment that he was not more improved. It was so good to be with him again, but she'd hoped he might be closer to coming back with them again than this.

'We're doing all right,' she soothed him. She was proud to be able to tell him how she was managing. 'Bobby's gone off with the Bevans for a bit. Mr Veater got us two of these women trainees off the Grand Union. Sylvia and Dorothy they're called. Well, Dot. You should hear the pair of them talk – it'd make you curl up. Talk about lah-di-dah. They're all right, though. I can't work Dot out, but Sylvia's nice. Seems a bit scared of her own shadow – always apologizing. But she's come on just in this week, and she says she loves living on the cut. She's ever such a good cook too! We'll be awright – I just wish I could take you with us.'

'Not half as much as I do,' Joel said gloomily. His warm hand stroked along her thigh. 'Oh, I do miss you, my little bird.'

Twenty-Three

Over the next few weeks the Bartholomew boats made several trips up and down the Oxford cut to and from the coalfields, and every time Maryann saw Joel he was a little improved, but his recovery seemed long and slow. Then, for a return journey, Maryann was offered a trip to Birmingham. She almost turned it down. If she went to Birmingham she felt, somehow, Norman Griffin would know they were there. But she agreed to it, telling herself not to be so stupid. The load was a consignment of timber for a private wharf in Saltley and they wouldn't be tied up at Tyseley. On a cool morning in March they set off north again.

Things were becoming easier between the women as they worked so closely together day after day, though Maryann still tried to keep her distance, especially with Dot. Sylvia was forever asking Maryann to come and join them in their cabin in the evening and she did go increasingly often, though at first she'd been convinced that they were only being polite and didn't really want her there. Dot and Sylvia seemed to rub along all right, even though they were very different: Sylvia timid and so eager to please and Dot prickly and stubborn. Dot was bullish and determinedly careless of her appearance, while Sylvia never appeared in the morning without carefully applying make-up – her powder, mascara and bright red lipstick, no matter how early it was.

'I feel undressed without it on!' she told them. 'I can't face the world like that.'

One evening, once they'd tied up and finished their evening meal, Sylvia appeared at the door.

'Sorry,' she said uncertainly.

Maryann smiled up at her. 'You'll wear that word out.'

'Oh! Yes – sorry. I mean . . . !'

Both of them laughed and Sylvia climbed down and sat on the coalbox for a few minutes. The older children were all outside except for the twins, who Maryann was washing in turn in front of the range, and Rose, to whom Sylvia held her arms out. Rose gladly climbed onto her lap for a cuddle. Sylvia rested her forehead against Rose's and Maryann heard her give a long sigh.

'What's up?' she asked.

'Oh,' Sylvia raised her head, 'nothing much. Just a bit weary, I suppose.' She smiled at the sight of Ada's little body, standing shiny and wet in the dipper. 'Dot's got the kettle on for a bit more than a lick and a promise too. I've come out to let her have the cabin to herself. Are you coming over later?'

Maryann looked across at her. 'That all right?'

'Of *course*. You're always welcome, you know that. We'll have a bit of a shindig. There's that last nip of whisky to jolly us along. Well, for you and me, anyway!'

Dot seemed to have a deep, almost puritanical aversion to spirits and turned her nose up every time she was offered any.

When Maryann did go to the *Theodore* in the evenings it was after she'd settled the children for the night. The three women were learning to relax together. At first they had been stiff and wary, talking mostly about the events of the day, about the cut. Of course, there was

212

always plenty to chew over there and often a lot to laugh about as well. But now, gradually, they were beginning to learn about each other's lives. Maryann was guarded about what she told them about her early years, only mentioning the bare bones – that her father had died when she was young and she wasn't close to her mother. She never even hinted at the darker, more shameful aspects of her childhood. She didn't have enough trust in them: how could they understand how it had been to grow up in Ladywood, let alone in her family? Sylvia, with her thick blonde hair and English rose face, looked so sheltered and innocent – how could she have any idea of someone like Norman Griffin? And Dot, coming from her boarding school life and going home every holiday to that big house in the country. They were from another world, like the Mussons, who she'd worked for in Banbury. She just told them pleasant little things she could remember – about her brothers and her dad coming home with a bicycle for Tony, and Granny Firkin and her cats. After all, she could pretend she'd had a happy childhood, couldn't she? She couldn't bring herself to talk about Nance either. The pain was still too close.

Sylvia had been a housewife before the war and always maintained that her life was settled and dull.

'Nothing much to say, I'm afraid,' she'd told them. 'You know – house, husband, children. Getting his supper on the table in time and his shirt studs ready in the morning. I have a lady who comes to wash and clean, but I always do all my own cooking. Roy wouldn't have it any other way. He likes me to change before we eat and to make my face up. Our lives are fearfully staid – not like yours, Maryann, coming away to live on the cut!'

'But you have now, haven't you?' Maryann said.

'Well, yes – for the moment. I really thought I ought to do something for the war effort with the children away, but it's so tricky with having to work around their holidays. Then I saw a piece in the paper about the training scheme and how they were prepared to be flexible, and I thought, perhaps that's a little chance for me to do my bit. I couldn't really believe I was doing it, even when I turned up at Southall with all my bags!'

'I met one of them,' Dot said. 'One of the first trainees, actually, and she told me about it. Thing was – the work appealed. I've always liked being out of doors – that's what I wanted really. But it was more than that. It was something about the way she talked about the work and the life. She was just full of it and I thought, that's what I need. I was desperate to get out of the job I was in.'

That evening they sat together with cups of cocoa, Maryann's and Sylvia's laced with 'hooch' as Sylvia called it. The chocolatey, whisky-laced steam filled Maryann's nostrils comfortingly. Jenny the tortoiseshell cat was curled on Sylvia's lap and she stroked her, looking at Dot over the rim of her cup. 'I can't imagine you being a secretary at all. Were you really?'

Maryann was taken aback too every time she remembered this. She could much more easily picture Dot doing something with horses, or being a games teacher, running round freezing hockey pitches and bellowing at girls in short skirts.

'Yes.' Dot frowned, fingers still knitting away without her having to look. The orange jumper was long finished and she was making something in soft cornflower blue. 'Detested every moment of it.' Maryann and Sylvia stared at her, taken aback by the anger in her voice.

Maryann thought her cheeks had blushed redder, but it was hard to tell in the dim light.

'It was Daddy, he set it all up through his contacts. Didn't leave me any choice. He said the only thing for a girl was being a teacher or a nurse and he wasn't having me doing either of those "demeaning jobs" as he called them – or a secretary, so I'd best do that. I wanted to get away from home, you see. Once Steven joined the Navy it was ... well, I was the only one left at home and Daddy and I ... let's just say we don't get on. He had marginally more time for Steven, being the boy, though not much. I wanted to go and that was what was on offer.'

'What about your mother?' Maryann asked. It was the first time they had heard Dot open up at all about her family. Apart from her brother Steven, who she was obviously close to, she normally dismissed the others as, 'oh, the normal, sort of thing'.

'Mummy died when I was thirteen.' She turned her cup round and round on the table without looking up.

'Oh, poor you!' Sylvia cried.

Dot talked on rapidly, as if suddenly resolved to let some of it out. 'After that there were housekeepers. Steven and I called them the housemice. Misfits, of course. They always are, people like that. Why else would they take on someone else's family? Same thing with the matrons at school – a succession of the crossed in love, the unmarriageable, the widowed and the barmy – we had them all.' There was a satirical, almost harsh edge to her voice now. 'There was a Miss Gateley, who came to look after Steven and me one summer. She was about fifty and had been working somewhere in Africa. Well, she went down with a frightful dose of malaria and was no use to anyone for days on end! Daddy was furious. He doesn't believe in people being ill. And Mrs Longford – her husband had hanged himself and left her with no money, and she kept taking some sort of medicine all the time and barely ever seemed to be awake. Once I went into her room and she was injecting something into her arm . . . Oh, and there was a Miss Peters. She was tremendously odd – obsessed with birds. She kept the windows open and fed them crusts – she'd have pigeons flying in and out messing on everything . . .'

Maryann listened, astonished. This was not how she had pictured Dot's life in the country at all. And how strange she was, speaking about sad things in that offhand, almost contemptuous way. She really couldn't understand Dot at all.

'Dear oh dear,' Sylvia gave a horrified laugh. 'I do hope they're not all like that where Kay and Dickie are! Didn't you have any other relatives who could have come and helped?'

Dot gave her a scornful look from under her dark brows. 'Help? God no – we're not that sort of family.'

There was a silence, as if suddenly the conversation could go no further and they sipped their cocoa. Then Sylvia said hesitantly,

'Maryann – I wondered . . . I hesitate to mention it and I hope you won't think this rude . . .?'

'What?' Maryann frowned.

'It's just that – you are able to read and write, aren't you? I mean I've seen you reading the clearance papers . . .'

'Course I can read and write!' Maryann said indignantly. 'I went to school, you know! I'm not stupid.'

'Of *course* you're not. But it's your children I'm thinking of. Have they never had any schooling?'

Maryann looked down, ashamed. 'No. Only what I

can teach them – and that's not much when there's no time to catch your breath.' She was ashamed, somewhere in her mind, of her children's lack of education, but there was so little time to give it any attention. And here on the cut, where no one's children went to school for more than the odd day at a time or learned more than the very basics, it didn't seem to matter all that much. Being a 'scholar' who could read and add up numbers was unusual. To get by in this life there were other, more important things to learn.

'Sally's the one who likes to try and read. Joley'll only learn summat for as long as he can sit still – and that's not long.' She sighed, looking into Sylvia's face. 'I've done my best but I'm always so pushed and mithered, and with him it's a battle.'

'Well, we could help, couldn't we, Dot?' Sylvia said enthusiastically. 'I mean here you are with all these children – let us help them with their letters. I bet Dot could get Joley and Ezra more interested in reading. They've taken to her. And I'd be very happy to help Sally and perhaps even little Rose, if she'd like to join in.'

'All right – if you want,' Maryann said. She was grateful, but didn't really think the offer would come to anything. Had they forgotten that most days on the cut didn't just go according to plan?

As Maryann got up to go to her cabin that night, Sylvia said, 'Would you like to borrow one of my magazines?' She reached over into the space at the head of the bed, in the cupboard. 'I've got a little stash here – some are a bit out of date, but take your pick.'

Maryann hesitated. She wanted to look at the magazines, but something held her back, some reluctance to be drawn in. She was almost afraid to take too close a look at how things were outside the cut, as if she might discover what she was missing. She didn't want her life disturbed. But seeing Sylvia's eager expression, she picked out a copy of *Woman & Home*, and one of *Home Chat*. A young woman posed on the cover of the second magazine in front of an aircraft propeller, a pair of goggles perched on her head.

'Thanks,' Maryann said.

'Go on – treat yourself to a good read,' Sylvia said. 'It helps chase the blues away.'

Back in her own cabin, beside her sleeping children, Maryann turned the pages of the magazines, surprised by how excited she felt at reading about young women who flew planes, and about fashions and a short story in which she lost herself, oblivious to everything around her. She lay down to sleep with the lives and voices of the story characters still turning in her head.

Whenever they had a spare half hour, which wasn't every day by any means, the trainees took Maryann's older children aboard the *Theodore* and tried to advance their education. Dot took on the boys, schooling them in their letters by trying to make sure that if they were to read and write, it was about something they were interested in, while Sylvia worked with the girls. The lessons were short, but Sally was often still there begging for more when time had run out and there were other things to be done.

What with the extra help cooking and the attention being paid to the children, Maryann could relax a little; her grudging gratitude towards Sylvia and Dot was increasing day by day as they worked closely together. She saw their hard work on the boat and their consideration towards her. Sylvia was less jumpy and seemed to have blossomed over the past few weeks, and Dot, though still prickly, was less liable to fly off the handle at the slightest hint of criticism. Maryann realized they had been rather in awe of her and the physical struggle her life demanded, and needed to prove themselves to be capable and of use. Maryann found herself touched by this.

A few days later they nosed through Birmingham and pulled into the wharf at Saltley to deliver their load.

'Where'll we pick the next load up from?' Dot asked as they snatched a cup of tea while the timber was being unloaded.

'We'll get a load of coal on the way back.'

'I s'pose that means the dreaded Bottom Road?' Sylvia said. Even though they were heading in the Coventry direction they were obliged to return south along the Birmingham–Fazeley Canal, with all its filth and its single locks, and not go back along the Grand Union. The official reason was that this helped to keep the water supplies up on the Grand Union.

'How ridiculous,' Dot muttered. 'We could save hours going back on the Grand Union.'

By the time they had completed the trip along the Bottom Road again, where a group of boys jeered and spat and another hurled stones at them from a bridge, one of which hit Sylvia on the side of the head, they were all confirmed in their view that it was the most dreary and depressing place of any along the cut. But as they moved further away from Birmingham, Maryann felt lighter with relief. It seemed sad, though, that the city of her birth had become such a place of dread.

✳

Sylvia was in a state of high excitement. She could hardly wait to get back to Sutton Stop to see if there were any letters waiting for her.

'Kay and Dickie must have written a couple of times by now,' she said. She had posted them letters all along the route, but hadn't heard back.

'Will your husband write as well?' Maryann asked. She'd formed very little impression of Roy Cresswell so far, except that Sylvia had said he was 'marvellous'. He sounded a bit of a stickler for routine, but apart from that she was surprised how little Sylvia mentioned him.

'Oh yes,' she said. 'I expect I shall hear. He's very *good* like that, but he's an adult, isn't he? He has to be able to take care of himself. It's different for Kay and Dickie – those poor darlings are the ones who've been sent away.'

Maryann knew there wouldn't be any letters for her. She had almost lost contact with her brother Tony now, and her little brother Billy barely knew she existed. Joel certainly couldn't write to her. She watched wistfully as Sylvia and Dot went off to the post office to ask after their mail, the four older children trotting along with them, interested in the novel idea of there being letters for anyone. Maryann had to stop Ada and Esther from following as well.

'No – you stay here.' Bad-temperedly, she lifted them into the *Esther Jane*, whereupon they set up a furious, cheated shrieking.

'Stop that racket, the pair of you!' Maryann said fiercely. 'They'll be back in a minute.'

Sylvia came running along the path a few moments later, her baggy jumper billowing round her slender figure.

'Five letters!' she panted, waving them happily. 'Just

what I was hoping for. Oh, look – Dickie's drawn a little face on the back of this one!' She raced back to her cabin.

Soon the children came back.

'Where's Dot, then?' Maryann asked.

'I dunno,' Joley said, kicking a stone along the path. He looked very put out as Dot was normally his friend. 'She said to come back – she'd be along in a while.'

'I wanted her to do some writing with me,' Sally complained, looking wistfully along the path.

Half an hour passed before Dot returned. Maryann was just walking along the path with the empty water holders when she met Dot coming the other way, an envelope in her hand. Her fleshy face was pale and set and she seemed lost in thought. There was no reply when Maryann said, 'Got some letters then?'

She'd staggered back with the full water carriers when Sylvia came over, looking worried.

'Maryann – it's Dot. She's come back and she won't say a word. She just came in and lay on the bed. I don't know if she's ill or if she's had a letter or what it is. Maybe she'd say something to you? I don't know what to do.'

Not knowing what she was supposed to do either, but feeling somehow responsible for the young woman, Maryann climbed down into the *Theodore*. In the gloom, she saw Dot lying on the bed, the curved shape of her back covered in a moss green sweater. She was very quiet.

Stepping closer, Maryann leaned over, about to touch her shoulder, but at the sight of Dot's face she withdrew her hand. Dot was lying on her side, curled tightly, eyes closed and her face contorted in a terrible grimace of pain.

Twenty-Four

Maryann sat herself timidly on the bed.

'Dot? It's Maryann. Is . . . are you in pain?'

There was no reply. Maryann could not even hear her breathing. It was as if Dot was paralysed. Maryann's eyes met Sylvia's in a troubled gaze. She felt intimidated by the young woman lying there, and by the power of her silence, out of which something overwhelming seemed to be crying out to them. But she also felt very sorry and maternal, and she found the courage to touch Dot's shoulder.

'Look, love – can you tell us what's the matter?'

But she'd barely got to the end of her sentence when her hand was flung off convulsively by Dot, who then curled herself even tighter, hands over her face. A strangled sound came from her, half whimper, half snarl. Maryann stood up again, stunned and helpless.

Sylvia came over, her face full of pity. 'Dot – Dorothy, sweetheart, don't suffer in silence like this. We just want to help. Can't you tell us what's wrong?'

Abruptly, Dot jerked herself upright. Her face looked altered, tightened. Pushing them out of the way, she sat on the edge of the bed, suddenly gulping, so that for a moment Maryann thought she was going to be sick. Barking the words out savagely, she said, 'My brother's dead. That's all. Daddy wrote to tell me. So now you know.'

Pushing past them, she left the boat and Maryann looked out to see her stride off along the path.

'Oh God, how awful.' Sylvia sat down, unsteadily. 'And there was I rattling on to her about the children and it was an age before I noticed she was so quiet . . .'

'You weren't to know.' Maryann felt sick. Dot's pain seemed to siphon off into her. It all came back in that moment, how she'd felt on losing her sister, Sal, all the rage and helplessness compounding the grief. She stood looking out through the door.

'He's everything to her.' She heard the tears in Sylvia's voice. 'She's such a funny, crusty girl in some ways – her upbringing, I suppose. She doesn't say much about it. But whenever she's talked about Steven, that's the one time you can see how soft she really is.'

Maryann swallowed hard, trying to force down the ache in her throat. It was no good. If she let herself go down into thinking about Dot and Steven, or started opening up the wounds from her own losses, she would drown in sorrow. *Stop it!* she screamed inwardly, clenching her fists, forcing the feelings away. Taking a deep, shaky breath she said, 'We'd better leave her be. I'll go and see to the tea.' When Sylvia started to protest she insisted abruptly. 'It's all right – I'll do it today.'

Arms folded, head down, she marched back to the *Esther Jane*, cursing in her head. Damn and blast these women, these trainees! Why did they have to be here, bringing all their foreign lives, their troubles and grief to her door when she'd had enough already? She'd found peace, hadn't she, hard-fought-for and won. Now everything was getting stirred up with Norman Griffin smashing back into her life, and now this. If only Joel was back and they could forget anyone else existed: go back to the quiet, secluded life they'd shared all these years!

Her hands shook as she peeled potatoes and she felt cold and brittle inside, as if she might easily break. The light was dying now and the air smoky grey outside. There was no sign of Dot. Where could she have gone? Where *would* someone like her go? Should they be looking for her? As the darkness fell, her unease grew.

Sylvia ate with them in the *Esther Jane*. Maryann could see she had been crying. For a second she felt angry. She couldn't afford to let herself cry. If she did, there'd be no end to it.

'D'you think we should be looking out for her?' Sylvia whispered to Maryann. 'I thought she'd just go off for a few minutes by herself, but she's been gone hours!'

'I don't know where we'd start,' Maryann said. 'Not now, any rate.'

'Where's Dot?' Joley demanded as Maryann spooned out mashed potato and baked beans. She hesitated, glancing at Sylvia.

'We're not sure where she is – she's gone for a little walk.' She paused in her serving, holding the spoon. 'Dot's had some bad news.' Gently she told them about Steven.

'Is he her little brother?' Sally asked.

Maryann nodded. 'A couple of years younger, I think.'

'Like Harry?' Joley turned his eyes on her with such solemn intelligence that once more Maryann had to fight off her tears. She could see Sylvia watching, puzzled.

'Harry?' she asked gently.

'I had another son.' Maryann finished serving the

food and sat down on the step to eat. 'Before Ezzy. We lost him before he was a year.'

'Oh, Maryann, how dreadful,' Sylvia said, shocked. 'I'm so sorry. I had no idea.'

Maryann acknowledged the sympathy with an abrupt nod.

'Anyroad – ' she forced herself to stay in control – 'I s'pect Dot'll be back soon. She's just gone off to take in the news by herself.'

All evening she tried to keep her mind from straying to the worst that could have become of Dot. Sylvia went back to her cabin. Maryann busied herself with children and chores.

It was after ten when Sylvia tapped on the door. Her face looked pale and tense in the moonlight. 'She's back,' she said softly.

'Where's she been?' Maryann began to feel some of the tension unknot inside her.

'Round the fields was all she'd say. Then all I could get out of her was, "Leave me alone." I've left her to get to bed. A good night's sleep should help – if she can manage it.'

Over the following days they could get nothing out of Dot. She just wouldn't talk about anything.

Soon after they heard the news, Maryann asked her, 'Don't you want to go home and be with your dad?'

Dot was pulling fiercely on the rope to untie the *Theodore*.

'Oh, don't be so ridiculous!' she snapped. 'Of course I don't.'

She worked with a crazed energy. They were sent

225

north along the Ashby cut, a long, lockless stretch to Measham colliery. The stretch was gradually silting up, neglected like all the cut these days, and some of the bridge-holes were a very tight fit with empty boats, not weighed down in the water. They had to take everything off the cabin roof and lay the chimney flat to get through, but otherwise it was easy going. Maryann could see that Dot, the state she was in, would rather have had steep flights of locks to toil through, such was her need to burn up and down, expending her energy. But it was uncomfortable to be with her. Her silence was far from serene: it was full of unspent emotion. Maryann and Sylvia kept exchanging worried glances when they were within sight of each other. Sylvia told Maryann that she'd found Dot one evening hacking furiously at her fringe with the blunt scissors. Her fringe had grown and looked softer on her face, but she insisted, 'It's too *long*. It's got to go.' Now it was severe and uneven and Maryann warned the children not to say anything about it.

Next, they set off down the Oxford. After the first day on the move, Sylvia came to Maryann and said,

'I don't think I can stand much more of this – it's awful!'

More and more tension built up between them all. Dot insisted on lock-wheeling, storming along the towpath and throwing herself at the paddle mechanisms. They could see she was explosive and both Maryann and Sylvia became almost afraid to speak to her. When they did, she answered abruptly, angrily. Sylvia looked pale and strained. She had told Maryann she was finding it hard to sleep with Dot lying close to her and so knotted up in herself. She was at her wits' end to know what to do. They reached Fenny Compton late one afternoon when the sky was heavy with cloud. They had tied up at a reasonable hour and fetched in supplies. Sylvia suggested that they go over to the pub for a drink.

'It might help her to have a break – make her feel a bit better. If I can persuade her to come out.' Dot was usually game for a trip to the pub even if she never drank alcohol.

'You go,' Maryann said. 'I'll stay in. I've got umpteen things to do.'

'Well,' Sylvia said doubtfully. 'I'll see if she will. But it'll be hard going!'

She must have eventually persuaded Dot that a change would do her good because the two women stopped at the *Esther Jane* to say they were leaving.

'It's getting pretty awful out here!' Sylvia said from under her sou'wester. The wind was getting up and the drumming of rain on the roof accompanied Maryann as she worked through her evening chores. Maryann was relieved not to be with Sylvia and Dot. She found it hard to bear the weight of Dot's silent agony and had no idea how to break through it. The strain was telling on all of them and tonight she didn't want to think about anything. She undressed, got into bed and picked up one of Sylvia's magazines. It had become her nightly treat to cuddle up on the tiny bed with her family all round her, hair loose, hugging her old cardi to her, reading and re-reading the articles and stories. The magazines presented her with a world of feminine things she had barely been aware of over the years. Even though fashions and clothing were very limited now by shortages and rationing, to her it seemed exciting reading about patterns and sewing tricks and make-do-and-mend.

She gradually grew sleepy, but struggled to keep awake to finish a story. As she sat with the magazine propped against her knees, a strange sound came from outside in the dark. Maryann raised her head. For a second she thought it was an owl, but that could hardly be in this pouring rain. It was followed by more noises and her heart began to beat fast.

Pulling on her coat and boots, she let herself out, jumping down onto the squelching bank, the sound of the rain all round her, the plop and gurgle of it in the cut. A little way ahead she could make out the bobbing light of a torch, and as she moved closer against the wind, she could make out Sylvia leaning over the figure on the ground. In gusts there came to her the wrenching, almost retching sound of weeping.

Dot was kneeling on the ground, one moment curled forward, the next throwing herself up onto her knees, swaying and moaning, as if trying to work the pain out of her body.

'Dot, sweetie – oh, do get up! Let's go inside . . .' Sylvia sounded distraught, as she begged Dot not to kneel out here in the rain. But Dot couldn't seem to hear her, or anything. She was lost in her crying, and the sound of it cut through Maryann. She felt herself swell with pity at the little figure, wrestling in the darkness.

When Sylvia saw her she cried, 'Oh, Maryann! She just – I don't know what happened. I can't get her to hear me, she's in such a state and she's getting caked in mud . . .'

Maryann didn't need to think what to do. She flung herself onto her knees beside Dot, rain running down her face, the wet soaking through her nightdress, melting inside with pity for the girl's distress.

'Come here . . .' She embraced Dot's lunging, weeping form in her arms and held her, managing to still her a little, tender, motherly words falling from her lips.

'It's all right, Dot, you're all right, have a good cry, that's it – you let some of it out, my love.' She rocked Dot back and forth like a child, feeling her shaking and sobbing.

Broken words and groans of pain were snatched from Dot's lips by the wind. 'My Stevie ... my lovely Stevie...' There was a long moan of pain, before she cried, 'Oh God, he was all I had!' Then her sobs would empty her of breath and she quivered, gulping until she managed a great, gasping breath.

Maryann's own tears came then and Sylvia came up and hugged Dot from behind. 'Poor darling,' she kept saying. 'Oh, poor love.'

Holding each other, crying, the three of them were soon soaked. Maryann lost track of how much time they crouched there. Then Dot's crying quietened to shaking and gulping and she seemed to come to, as if from a trance.

'Sorry.' She struggled to her feet, regaining some of her gruff self-control. 'We must all go in. This is ridiculous of me ... only I ...' She lowered her head and began to weep helplessly, but more softly than before.

'Come on.' Sylvia took her hand and, sodden and shivering, the three of them all went to the *Theodore*.

For a moment, in the light of the cabin, they were at a loss what to do. Water ran from them, forming puddles at their feet.

'We'd better take these wet clothes off,' Sylvia said, suddenly brisk, as if the emotions released just now should be swept away now that they were back in the light again. Dot perched numbly on the side bench, as if exhausted. Maryann sat beside her and unbuttoned her coat for her. Dot didn't resist. She suddenly looked very young and beaten, her chopped fringe slicked to her forehead, her cheeks wet and eyes red.

'Let's have a cup of cocoa,' Sylvia said. 'Dot – you going to have some?'

Dot looked up slowly and nodded, her eyes filling. 'I'm sorry – I can't seem to stop now I've started,' she said. 'Oh, Steven . . .'

Maryann put her arms round Dot's shoulders and held her close.

'What're you saying sorry for, you silly so-and-so?'

Twenty-Five

Easter was drawing near. Daffodils rippled bright in the spring breezes in gardens backing onto the cut. Soon it would be time for Sylvia to join her children for their school holidays.

During that time Dot allowed herself to begin to grieve. In fact grief took hold of her and would not let her hold it at bay any more.

'I don't know what's come over me,' she would say, finding tears running down her cheeks at unexpected moments. 'This just isn't like me at all.'

'Dot,' Sylvia would say, 'you've lost your brother, who you loved more than anyone in the world and you don't know what's come over you!' Their sympathy made Dot cry all the more. Maryann and Sylvia, both so much older, had developed a big-sisterly affection and protectiveness towards Dot in her unhappiness. It had changed everything.

On those chill, lamplit evenings they sat in the *Theodore*, and Dot began to talk about herself and her family in a way that she never had before. Things just seemed to come pouring out. One evening, to Maryann's astonishment, she told them that her mother had died in her forties of a diseased liver and alcohol poisoning. When she came out with this in her strange, abruptly matter-of-fact, Dotish way, Maryann saw shock register on Sylvia's face too and their eyes met for a horrified second.

'It took Stevie and me years to work out what was the matter with her. That she was a tippler.' Dot kept her eyes on her knitting. Her hair was loose over her plump shoulders and Maryann suddenly thought how young she looked. She could imagine her as a little girl of seven or eight, with her big eyes, rosy cheeks and sudden vulnerability.

'How terrible!' Sylvia murmured. Dot glanced up and Maryann could see she found sympathy hard to accept, even now. She had been so accustomed to burying her feelings.

'When you're young you accept things the way they are, don't you? Stevie and I just knew that at times – in fact much of the time – our mother had to be left alone, or that she seemed to spend such a lot of time asleep. Passed out was nearer the truth. Then, other days she'd turn on us like a hyena. Poor Stevie – it was far worse for him. He was such a shy little boy. Clingy. Cowed, really. He needed a nice, soft, attentive mother.' Dot gave a harsh laugh. 'I suppose I got by by being his protector, poor little chap.

'Of course, as we got older, we began to put two and two together. There was that smell our mother had about her: Scotch was her poison. Other things would do if there was none going, but that's the smell I remember.' Dot grimaced. 'When she smelt like that, you left her alone. She gave up trying to hide it long before she died. We had housekeepers and *they* didn't smell like that ... And, of course, we'd hear them talking. One of them, I heard her say to one of the maids, "Mrs Higgs-Deveraux – proper dipsomaniac she is, if you ask me." I went and looked it up.' Dot sighed and stopped knitting, hands in her lap. 'D'you know, I can still see the dictionary. It was a big, heavy thing, the edges of the pages all brown. I sat

232

with it in my lap, in the parlour. I was about eleven. And I just sat there reading the word over and over again. Dipsomaniac. It was almost like discovering you've got a brother or sister you've never been told about, but somehow you always knew was there – things suddenly making sense. Stevie and I had always kept out of her way – if we weren't at school we were out somewhere. And soon after that, I remember, was one of the times we hid for *hours* under the big bed in the spare room when Mummy was in one of her states. We both lay there on the floorboards, on our backs, looking up at the springs, and the sheets tucked under the mattress and it was all dusty and smelt of mothballs, and we could hear our mother and father. He was so cold and cruel to her. Stevie and I started singing little songs, very quietly. "Here we go gathering nuts in May – " Things like that. We didn't want to hear what they were saying. Or what Daddy was doing to her . . .' Dot's voice faltered.

'Is that why she drank – to get away from him?' Sylvia asked gently.

'I don't know. Partly.' Dot was silent for a moment. 'No – I think she was frustrated. She married young when she really had wanted to have a life of her own, and there was just nothing for her in the country, where we lived. And she was married to a man who was as cold as the grave. A narcissist. Couldn't see anything from anyone else's point of view. He never gave her an inch. He always, always had to be centre stage. If we had visitors, everything revolved around him. He's a completely self-obsessed man. D'you know . . . ?'

Maryann tensed inside, almost panicky, as if she wanted to shout, *Stop! Stop – don't tell me any more! Let me believe that you had a happy, charmed childhood, not one like mine, full of cruelty. Please let something, somewhere, be innocent and loving!* Sylvia was silent as well. They could hear her little alarm clock ticking in the background.

'When Stevie was fifteen, he—' Again she ground to a halt, taking deep, distressed breaths.

'Don't.' Sylvia had tears in her eyes. 'Not if it's too much for you, darling.'

But Dot couldn't seem to stop now. The words poured out.

'He took a rope into the stables. Tied it over the beam. And a chair. Only the chair wasn't really high enough – he left the rope too long. Norris – the man who worked in the garden – found him hanging, just off the ground. It'd only been a matter of seconds, I think. But he'd meant it – to take his own life. Stevie would never do something like that without meaning it. Afterwards he couldn't speak properly for days, he'd bruised his throat so badly. It was a Saturday and my father was in his study, preparing papers for some case or other. My mother ran to him to tell him what had happened, and he refused to come down before he'd finished the piece of work he was doing. It was nearly an hour before he came and my mother and I had put Steven to bed and called the doctor. He was in shock, of course: his neck was red and burnt from the rope. And my father came, finally. He stood in the doorway – he's very tall and thin – and stared at Stevie with such *contempt* and anger. He said, "You bloody little fool."'

Dot stared at the table with the empty cocoa cups on it. She was quivering slightly. Then she looked up.

'So – that's my family. A right jolly old crew. Stevie joined the Navy as soon as they'd have him. I know he felt frightful about leaving me, but I was about to go to London anyway. I was delighted for him. It was far worse at home for him than me. Daddy expected so much more of him.'

Maryann was surprised at how much she was beginning to dread the three of them being separated. Of course Sylvia would be back, and in the meantime Dot would stay and they'd have to rearrange things so that Bobby could come back and crew with them. She wasn't worried about shifting the loads, but they'd got into a routine of hard work and support for each other, of sharing laughter and beginning to share some of their lives during their cosy evenings together, although Maryann knew she couldn't share much of her past. Even the thought of talking about it was too big, too frightening. She felt much easier with Dot, now she had shown her softer, more vulnerable side. Of Sylvia, Maryann felt she knew less, but she thought perhaps there was less to know. She was a sweet girl, settled in marriage, and she was a helpful presence and a good worker. When they reached Coventry, Sylvia would get on her train back to London, to her cosy, suburban life, to her house with a bath, her children and her lawn and roses. Maryann liked to think of that – that somewhere people had lives like that in which there was no squalor and unhappiness, no one like Norman Griffin to cast a foul shadow over them.

She began to wish she could slow down their journey to Oxford, that it might not end yet, so that she didn't have to face any more changes. But time seemed to gallop past.

In Oxford she found Joel still slowly and painfully on the mend. He was able to sit downstairs now and move about just a little. Maryann and the children stayed with him for as long as they could manage, sitting in Alice's little parlour. Maryann sat on a stool beside him, holding his hand (which she teased him was getting soft) and telling him about all the ups and downs of their journeys and snippets of news from other boatpeople.

'You sound as if you're getting along perfectly all right without me,' Joel said, as Maryann laughingly told him stories of Dot's and Sylvia's antics.

Hearing his wistful tone, Maryann reached up and kissed him. 'Not perfectly, no – nothing like! But we're getting by, keeping ahead all right. You've made a boat-woman of me, see? And you'll be back soon, won't you?'

'Doctor says two to three months yet,' Alice Simons said, eyeing Joel sternly. 'Don't you go getting any ideas about taking off, spoiling all that resting up you've done.'

Sylvia was lock-wheeling that morning as they headed north away from Banbury. She ran ahead along the towpath, full of frisky energy, and waited on the bridge beyond, her slim, feminine figure silhouetted against the pale sky. She signalled them to slow down: the lock was busy. Maryann slowed the engine.

'We're out of bread – and milk!' she shouted up to Sylvia over the throaty chug of the engine and saw her nod in reply.

Once they were through Cropredy lock, they tied up for a few moments beyond the bridge while Dot hared off with Joley and Sally for supplies. Once she'd seen them climbing back onto the *Theodore*, Maryann and Ezra cast off the *Esther Jane*.

That evening, after tea, Dot said to her, 'Oh – I picked this up as well when we stopped. Course they were going to use it for wrapping, but I pleaded the cause of us poor, deprived souls.' She held out a copy of the *Birmingham Post*. 'I thought you might like a look.'

Maryann thanked her and put the paper aside until she was in bed that night. Sleepily, she reached for it, only half wanting to bother. Sally was pressed up against her in bed, and she feared the crackly paper might wake her. But otherwise there'd be no chance until the next night.

I'll just look at the first couple of pages, she thought, yawning, and glancing over the first page. Gingerly she opened the paper, watching Sally as she did so. A moment later she read something which banished her drowsiness completely. She jerked upright, pulse galloping.

MURDERED WOMAN IDENTIFIED the headline said. The details were bad enough: the young woman, now known to be aged twenty-two, with auburn hair and a pale complexion, had been found beaten and strangled on a piece of waste ground. She had been reported missing by her mother two days previously. But it was the names of the woman and her mother, who had identified her, which almost seemed to shudder on the page in front of Maryann's eyes. The dead woman's name was Amy Lambert. Her mother was a Mrs Janet Lambert.

In her guts she knew immediately. It couldn't be anyone else. In those terrible seconds she knew that this Amy Lambert was the same Amy, the sister of Margaret, who had been locked away all those years in the asylum. Amy, the strong one, the older girl, who had tried to protect her sister, who had looked to Maryann for help and friendship as a frightened twelve-year-old.

Maryann's hand went to her throat, rereading the

report. Amy was dead. And she knew with sudden, terrifying instinct who had brought about her end. Her stepfather, Norman Griffin, had also been Amy and Margaret's stepfather; he had conned his way into Janet Lambert's family and wreaked his brutal havoc on them. After little Margaret attacked him he had been so badly disfigured that he was barely decent to be seen in the light of day. He'd gone to ground then, festering in obscurity like some foul disease. But now he had crawled out of his hiding place, more twisted than ever before. His was the face she had looked into that night in Pastor James's church. What he had done in the meantime, why he was pursuing them now, she had no idea. But she knew it was him. And that he was waiting.

Twenty-Six

'Dot, I need to go to Birmingham.'

Maryann had not said a word to Sylvia and Dot of the turmoil and horror she was feeling. She had been barely able to eat or sleep since seeing the newspaper, but she had held all her feelings inside her during the last leg of the journey. How could she even begin to explain to anyone?

Dot looked nonplussed for a moment. They were back at Sutton Stop and were expecting to spend the day cleaning the boats.

'Family business,' Maryann said. She could see Dot thinking, *How on earth has this come about suddenly, with no letters, and barely any contact with anyone else?* But Maryann couldn't and wouldn't explain.

'Just for the day. I'll go when Sylv goes tomorrow and be back by the night. Sorry, but I've got to. We'll rest up tomorrow and Mr Veater says Bobby should be back in here tomorrow or the next day.'

'Right-oh,' Dot said cheerfully, and Maryann was immediately comforted by the sense that she would cope with everything. 'I'll get cleaned up tomorrow then. Are you leaving me the children?'

'If you can manage. I'll take one of the twins – Ada. She's the fidget.'

'We'll get along famously,' Dot said. 'It'll be a challenge.'

That night, as Sylvia was about to leave, they had a little party. They were tied up at 'home' at Sutton Stop again. It helped take Maryann's mind off things a fraction. Sylvia baked a cake and they fetched the children's sweet rations and made a nice little high tea, Ada and Esther drooling as they sucked on their highly coloured jelly babies. When Maryann explained to the family that Sylvia had to go away for a while, they were full of questions. Maryann managed a smile, as she listened to them trying to understand that Sylvia's children lived in a big school with a lot of other children. But little Rose, who was tucked in beside Sylvia as usual, started crying.

'Oh, darling!' Sylvia put her arm round her and kissed the top of her head. Maryann was surprised at the pain she saw in her eyes as she did so. 'I'm not going away for long – just a few weeks and then I'll be back with you. I'll bring you a present back, sweetheart, all right? And the rest of you!' With an effort to look cheerful she smiled round the table.

Later they spent their last night together chatting in the *Theodore*. Sylvia had bought a bottle of whisky.

'Sorry, Dot – I like my little tipple – I know you don't go for it.'

'For rather obvious reasons,' Dot said, screwing her face up in disgust at the smell. She unlaced her boots and tugged them off, wiggling her toes in their woolly socks and sighing with relief.

'Well, I like a drink,' Sylvia said defiantly, giving some to Maryann and pouring herself a generous tot. Maryann watched surprised. She saw an edge of tension, of aggression in Sylvia that was not evident in her normally placid personality. 'Sometimes it's the only way to get through, isn't it?'

'*No*,' Dot insisted. 'It's the one thing to avoid getting stuck on, I'd say.'

'Here – you're going back to a nice comfy house and a bath!' Maryann laughed. 'What've *you* got to get through?'

Sipping her drink, Sylvia stared at her over the rim of her cup, as if considering something. She put the cup down. 'Oh – nothing,' she said brightly. 'Don't be silly, it was just a figure of speech.'

But as the evening wore on and they sat reminiscing about their trips together so far, Sylvia went quiet suddenly and they saw she was fighting back tears. Maryann and Dot immediately tried to comfort her.

'I know I'm being a soppy old thing,' Sylvia wept into her hanky. Through all the rush and chaos and often grimy squalor of life on the boat, Sylvia always seemed to have a cotton hanky on her somewhere at the ready. Nasally, she said, 'I just can't tell you how much I've *loved* being here – this time on the cut has been the best time of my life! I'm longing to see Kay and Dickie, of course, but it's so hard to leave you all. I wish I could just bring them back here.'

Dot and Maryann exchanged puzzled glances, but they jollied Sylvia along.

'Oh, you'll be glad enough when you're lying in a nice hot bath, thinking about us having a lick and a promise out of the dipper!'

The next morning Maryann set off, with Ada balanced on one hip, to catch the bus to Coventry station with Sylvia and her bundle of clothes. Before they set off, Sylvia hugged Dot and all the children emotionally.

On the bus, Maryann saw her looking out at the wreckage of Coventry, a bleak expression on her face.

'Don't you want to go home?' Maryann couldn't help asking, perplexed by the gloom that seemed to have overcome Sylvia.

'Umm?' Sylvia looked round and gave a smile that didn't quite reach her eyes. 'Home? Yes – of course I do.'

They parted at the station and once more Maryann saw tears welling in Sylvia's eyes. She embraced Maryann and Ada tightly and kissed them both. 'See you soon, darlings.' Maryann watched her walk away, her blonde hair bouncing on her shoulders as she went off to find her platform. What a stranger she seemed suddenly, from quite another world. After all, what did she really know about Sylvia?

Her own train drew into New Street before midday.

'Here we go,' she said to Ada as they climbed down from the carriage. 'Back in Brum.' It was the first time in a long while that she'd been into the middle of Birmingham, and walking along New Street from the station she was shocked by the smashed gaps in long-familiar facades of buildings. It took time for her to orientate herself and find the right bus stop.

Janet Lambert had lived in Handsworth during her marriage to Norman Griffin, who by then was calling himself Albert Lambert. She had long since moved to Erdington, for a fresh start.

I suppose she was trying to get away from the memory of him, Maryann thought grimly, sitting on the Erdington bus with Ada in her lap. The little girl was looking round, fascinated by all the new sights and people's faces. But Maryann felt hemmed in by the city, by its greyness, the lines of low, grime-covered houses and by the shreds of memory which it stirred up for her. Was there no end to this? she thought despairingly. To the pain and damage caused by this man, whose presence seemed to echo like an evil chorus in her life?

The closer she came to seeing Janet, the more the emotions she had been trying to suppress came seething to the surface: the rage and sorrow and horror of reading Amy's name in the *Post*. *Murdered*. Getting off the bus, she felt crazed, as if she might rage and scream in the street, and by the time she reached Janet's black front door she was shaking with the effort of holding herself together. It was a help having Ada chattering in her arms. It steadied her. And she had to remain strong, she commanded herself. For Janet. It was she who had lost her daughters – both of them.

It always took Janet Lambert some time to reach her door. She had a tubercular hip and walked awkwardly with a stick. At last the door opened. Maryann barely recognized the woman who appeared. She had faded hair which showed only traces of the fiery rust colour it had been the last time they met, and her face, which had once been that of a serene beauty, was now battered by life, marked with the scars of grief. She looked out with a dazed expression.

'Janet,' Maryann said gently, 'it's Maryann.'

Janet sagged. Prepared to see a stranger outside, her grief surfaced immediately at the sight of a friend. 'Oh.' It was almost a whimper. 'I didn't know you for a minute ... I'm in that much of a ...' For a moment she seemed quite at a loss, then collected herself. 'Come in, dear.'

Maryann followed Janet's painful progress into the parlour at the front. As in her last house, it was a tastefully decorated room in greens and browns and she had trimmed her own curtains. Maryann set Ada down and she immediately headed for the fireplace, where there were brightly polished brass fire tools in the grate. The two women could not contain their emotion any longer.

'I saw it in the paper,' Maryann said. She went to Janet and the woman crumpled into her arms. 'Oh my God, poor Amy – our poor little Amy!'

They clung to one another, pouring out their anguish, both of them trembling and weeping.

'Why? . . . why?' Janet kept crying. 'Oh, my little girl . . . my baby girl . . . my lovely Amy.' Maryann could feel the force of her sobbing, and she too cried, at last, feeling the pain deep inside herself as if it was being wrung out of her. For a long time neither of them could calm down, but at last, a small portion of emotion spent, they drew back from each other.

'Let me make you a cup of tea.' Janet said dully.

'No – don't bother with that,' Maryann tried to protest.

'It's no bother, love. It'll help.'

And Maryann, too, was relieved to go through the ritual of kettle filling and helping to fetch cups and saucers. Janet had always been ladylike in her ways, and even now, out of habit, she laid the cups out nicely on a tray.

'The funeral's next Wednesday,' she said while they waited for the water. 'They say they should have finished with her by then.'

While they drank their tea in the neat parlour and Ada pottered about exploring, Maryann sat listening as Janet poured out the events of the past days. She kept hold of the handle of one of her walking sticks in her left hand, as if it steadied her.

Amy had gone to work as usual. She had a job in a

dress shop in town and went in on the bus. But that Thursday night she hadn't come home.

'I didn't know what to do.' Janet's agitated fingers bent and straightened round the handle of the walking stick. With her other hand she worried at the material of her skirt. 'I suppose I should have gone to the police straight away, but I thought she'd been held up, or she'd gone out with Geoff, her young man, and forgotten to mention it to me. I wasn't terribly worried to begin with. And then it got late and, well, I waited and waited ... I was frightened to go out. It was very dark and it's a long walk to the telephone box.' She sobbed again, then spoke through her tears. 'I thought it'd be all right. I never dreamt ... I should have gone! I was up all night and by the morning – then I was afraid something had happened. Amy was always such a good girl – didn't stop out of a night, nothing like that. But I was frightened to go and tell anyone because then I'd have to find out there'd been an accident. If I just stayed here, I could go on thinking she was all right. But of course I did go, eventually. I never thought of .. ... not that she was dead.' Her face creased and she began to weep again.

Maryann cried with her, unable to stop. Poor, lovely Amy! She kept seeing her in her mind's eye as she had the first time she set eyes on the girls that day in Handsworth Park, those two silent children full of pain and fear, always beautifully turned out by Janet in their matching frocks and hair ribbons. And though she had only seen Amy occasionally since then, she knew she had grown into a kind-hearted and beautiful young woman.

'They found her up near the hospital two days later. Course I'd reported her missing. I had to go and see her, to identify her as my girl, my baby.' She was silent for a moment, shaking her head. 'He'd made such a mess of her.' Arms folded, she began to rock back and forth in the chair in distress. Unable to bear it, Maryann went to her and put her arms round Janet's shoulders, rocking her gently. She waited until Janet was a little calmer, then went and refilled the teapot and topped up their cups.

Kneeling beside Janet she looked up into her eyes. 'It was him, wasn't it?'

'No!' Janet reacted immediately. '*No*. What're you *talking* about?'

She looked down into her lap, shaking her head. There was a long silence. Once more, she began to rock, unable to contain her agitation.

'I've been trying not to – to think it. To think about *him*.' Her gentle face twisted with loathing. 'It could have been anyone who did it. But then it goes round and round in my head. Why would anyone do that to my lovely Amy? They'd have to be insane. An animal.'

'Have you seen him since he left?'

Janet shook her head. 'He just vanished. Never came back. That was what we wanted, of course. Amy and I moved – we needed a fresh start, but not too far from Margaret. I did hear the odd thing about him. One of my old neighbours reckoned she'd seen him, said he was a mess to look at. He closed that business down in Handsworth. I suppose he must have gone and set up somewhere else – done something to make a living for himself. But I haven't set eyes on him.'

'I've seen him.' Maryann said. She told Janet how he had come looking for her, about the episode with Pastor James, how he'd tricked that foolish man into believing him, about what happened in the back room of the church.

'God in heaven!' Janet laid a hand over her heart. 'I remember that first day I ever saw him, all upstanding and smart. And I was so desperate I just took to him, just like that. Let him into my life, my family. My God!' It came out as a howl. 'Look what I've done. What I've made happen!'

'Stop it!!' Maryann's voice came out loud and sharp. Rage flamed in her at hearing Janet say the thing she still had to fight against perpetually in herself. *It's my fault. All my fault. What happened to Sal, to our mom, to Amy and Margaret – all of it. I'm dirty and shameful and always have been. That's why he did it. I asked for it. It's all my fault.* Why could she see so clearly that this was not true for someone else when she still, deep down, felt she was not like other people, that she must hide from them? When she still blamed herself?

Leaning down, she looked urgently into Janet's face. 'Don't do that! He's the one that did all of this – *all* of it! Nothing's your fault – *only* his. As soon as you start thinking it's your fault he's got you!'

'But what should we do? Whatever can we do?'

'Tell the police about him.' Even as she said it, Maryann felt a sense of despair. How could the police ever find him, let alone prove it was him who murdered Amy, however sure she was that he and only he could be responsible? He was so sly, so slippery. None of them knew where he was or even by what name he went these days. She could see that Janet was thinking the same.

'But his face,' Maryann said. She stood up, her expression hard and determined. 'No one else has a face like that. We've got to tell them.'

*

The grey-haired police officer looked at her wearily over the counter as she walked into the dingy light of the police station, carrying Ada in her arms.

'Can I help you?'

Maryann put Ada down and the child instinctively stayed close to her.

'It's about...' Maryann felt shaky, and somehow foolish. It was as if none of this was quite real. 'That murder. The one in the papers – the girl with the red hair, Amy Lambert. I know who killed her.'

She had his attention now. He stood straighter and his eyes widened, but his expression and the way he rubbed his hand over his chin made her see he was wary of her. Did people come in claiming things like that every day, she wondered?

Trying to steady herself, she gripped the counter. There was a gouged wound in the wood under her right index finger.

'It was a man called Norman Griffin – least, that's what he used to call himself.'

She poured out her story, gabbling, desperate for him to believe her. He nodded a lot as she spoke and after a time he pulled his notebook from his pocket and wrote something down, frowning as he did so. When she stopped at last, waiting for something – what? – for him to jump into action, he said, 'Well thank you, Mrs er ...?'

'Bartholomew.'

'We'll follow this up.'

'Well, I should hope so!' She burst out, her voice loud and shrill now with frustration. 'He murdered her, I know he did! And what're you going to do about it?'

She immediately regretted losing herself as she could see the policeman was thinking she was some silly woman, no doubt funny in the head. Backing away from him, towards the door, she cried, 'You'll see. You go and find him! I know it was him!'

Outside she leaned against the wall, taking deep, distraught breaths, holding tightly to Ada's hand. It was a few moments before she managed to begin walking along the street, trying to tell herself she'd done the best she could. Who else was there to turn to but the police? Surely he had to believe what she'd told him! At least they'd be looking for Norman Griffin, wouldn't they? He would get what he more than deserved at last.

Standing at the tram stop, her mind raced on. What if they couldn't find him? What if – the thought sent a spasm of fear through her – what if he went after Janet next? As the tram swayed into view, the thought chilled through her. Was he coming back after all of them now? Was that it?

Twenty-Seven

A shadow fell on Dot as she knelt in the spring sunshine the next morning, splicing a rope in the empty hold of the *Theodore*. She looked up and saw a young man with dark eyes, a swarthy face and thick dark hair falling over his forehead. He had with him a rusty bicycle, poised with its front wheel at the edge of the cut.

'How do? So you're one of the new 'uns are you?'

Dot stared back. Something about the way the young man was looking at her, the frank appraisal and twinkle of amusement in his eyes made her feel immediately prickly and self-conscious. She clambered to her feet, feeling plump and ungainly.

'I suppose I am, if you insist on putting it like that.'

He laughed, not seeming to take offence, laid the bike down with a clatter, climbed in over the gunwales and held out his hand.

'I'm Bobby. I'll be crewing with you for a bit.'

Dot shook his hand, stiffly. 'How d'you do? I'm Dorothy – Dot. And I've heard a lot about you.'

'Ah – it's the bits you ent heard that are the best!' he laughed.

Dot glowered at him. Why did young men with good looks and easy charm like Bobby make her feel so grumpy? As if her skin was being rubbed over with sandpaper. It was made even worse by the fact that he was a boater born and bred. She knew what they tended to make of trainees like herself. Here she was, just beginning to feel she fitted in, and she was going to have to prove herself all over again. And to make it worse, she knew he'd see her as posh and clownishly plump.

She was saved from further chat by hearing shouts along the bank. 'It's Bobby – he's back!'

The Bartholomew children were charging wildly towards them, raggle-taggle brigade that they were, in their motley collection of clothes. Rose had on an old frock of Sally's that was almost down to her ankles and she had to hold it up to run along. All of them were grubby from top to toe. It was a losing battle for Maryann, trying to keep them clean. Bobby laughed at the sight. Maryann was at the back, being pulled along by the twins, one tugging on each hand, and smiling at the sight of Bobby. Dot suddenly saw for a second a sweet young woman beneath the careworn wife, mother and boat skipper whose face was always lined with tiredness and worry.

Bobby leapt back onto the bank and the older children ran at him, all talking at once.

'Bobby's got a *bike*!'

'Whose is it? Is it yours?'

'Where d'you get it?'

'Can we have a ride?'

'Hello, Bobby – got here at last! All right, are you?' Maryann called out over the children's din. She felt like flinging her arms round him, she was so pleased to see him, but she knew he would just be embarrassed. Her inner heaviness lightened a fraction. Bobby was like part of the family. Having him here for a while gave a feel of things returning to normal. She was puzzled, though, to see Dot looking aloof and rather bad-tempered. *Back to how she used to be*, Maryann thought. *What's got into her?*

'A feller gave me that, down London,' Bobby said, nodding at the bike. 'Thought it'd speed us up a bit.'

Maryann nodded. She and Joel had never used a bike, though the trainees had expressed their surprise at not finding one on the boat when they arrived.

'I s'pose so,' she said doubtfully.

Once they'd swapped their news, Maryann said, 'I'll get the kettle on for a brew and we'd better get cracking.' Bobby had said he could stay with them for as long as was needed, and certainly until Sylvia was due back at the end of the school holidays. They started on re-arranging the boats. It was to be boys in one, girls in the other. Maryann would be in the *Esther Jane* with Dot, Sal, Rose and the twins, and Bobby would have Joley and Ezra bunked up with him in the *Theodore*.

Dot silently carried her belongings onto the *Esther Jane*. The children were all very excited, both with Bobby being back and by the changes, and ran back and forth shouting shrilly to each other, begging Bobby for rides on the bike.

'It's going to be more crowded in here than you're used to,' Maryann apologized to Dot as she carried her belongings in.

'That's all right,' Dot said and smiled. Maryann was reassured. She wanted to ask if there was something wrong but didn't quite dare. Dot had only just begun getting over Steven's death, hadn't she? That was surely what was wrong. Overwhelmed by her own worries, she sometimes forgot.

Dot was quiet all afternoon, but for most of it Maryann was too lost in her own thoughts to notice very much. As well as sorting out and cleaning both boats and keeping an eye on the twins, her thoughts swam round and round all that had happened when she visited Janet, the horror of Amy's death and the visit to the police station. Her nerves were so jangled she jumped at the slightest sound. Bobby stuck his head through the hatches of the *Esther Jane* while she was polishing the stove, lost in thought, and she shrieked, laying a hand over her pounding heart.

'Flippin' eck Bobby! You nearly made me jump out of my skin!'

'I've finished taking my things in. All settled. Good little cabin you got there.'

'You only just noticed?' Maryann forced a grin onto her face.

'Now I've worked a few others I can see how nice you've got it. You should be proud.'

'Yes,' Maryann sighed. 'But – you know Joel. Only thing'd make him proud is if it's his own, with "Joel Bartholomew, Number One" on the cabin.'

Bobby moved a bit further in. 'That Dot's a bit of a rum 'un, ent she?'

'She's all right.' Maryann looked up from her polishing again for a minute. 'Good sort. Don't know what's up with her today. She'll come round.'

'Well, I flaming hope so,' he said. 'I ent said nothing amiss that I can think of and all I get from her's looks – and not very nice ones.'

Maryann laughed at his indignant expression. 'Well, there's a challenge for you, eh, Bobby? Time you found yourself a nice girl anyway.'

'Ooh – not like that 'un! He rolled his eyes, as if to imply that Dot was like someone from outer space.

'You got your eye on anyone yet?' Maryann often felt like Bobby's mother.

He grinned mischievously. 'Might have. Might not. We'll have to see, won't we?'

Mr Veater put them on short trips shifting coal again to begin with, to Baddesley colliery, then Griff. The spring days increased in warmth and the cooling towers of the power station puffed out their clouds of vapour towards a fresh, blue sky.

Bobby took charge of the *Theodore* and Dot chose to do whatever lock-wheeling was called for, often with some of the kids scrambling along beside her. Sometimes now they used the bike.

Maryann found her mind scattered and forgetful. She would find herself standing, forgetting what the task was she was supposed to be carrying out, and she couldn't seem to keep her thoughts together. As she stood at the helm the past kept welling up, however much she tried not to think of it. She could not stop thinking about Amy, especially as the day of her funeral passed. Janet understood that Maryann wouldn't be able to be there, but it was a hard, bitter day for her and, as she worked, her mind was with Janet. Every time she thought about it she was overwhelmed by rage. Round and round it all went in her head. She didn't want to be here, she needed to be in Birmingham, tracking Norman Griffin down, bringing justice upon him. How could they find him? Of course – she could ask Pastor Owen. Why hadn't she remembered to tell the policeman about him? Norman might have let slip to him something about where he lived and worked. *Someone* must know. After all, it wasn't as if you could miss him with looks like that. You couldn't forget him.

She became aware gradually, though, that all was not

well with her crew. A sparring match had begun between Dot and Bobby. They seemed to have started off on the wrong foot with each other and it wasn't getting any better. When Bobby heard Dot's full name of Dorothy Higgs-Deveraux, he'd chortled with great amusement and sent Dot off into a huff by nicknaming her 'her ladyship'. Dot was not showing much sense of humour about this and was now, to Maryann's exasperation, back to being as abrasive as when she'd first arrived. With Bobby behind her on the *Theodore* Maryann didn't notice what was going on a lot of the time, but once when she turned to look as he was bringing the boat through a lock, she saw him making an exaggerated bow towards Dot, who was on the bank, and doffing his cap. Dot completely ignored him on this occasion, sailing past without turning her head. Bobby always seemed to be trying to get a rise out of her and often succeeded. He couldn't seem to find any other way of dealing with Dot or she with him.

At the end of their first trip, when they were back at Sutton Stop, he invited her out to the pub with him. 'Would your ladyship fancy a drink at the Greyhound?' he asked teasingly.

Dot was thumbing through a newspaper and didn't even look up. 'No thank you,' she said coldly.

'There's not much joy for Dot going to the pub – she don't drink,' Maryann excused her.

'Oh.' Bobby frowned, as if finding all this very peculiar. 'Suit yourself. What about you then?'

'No, ta – I'll stay in tonight. You go and find your pals.'

When he'd gone, she said, 'It was nice of him to ask, Dot. He didn't have to. He's all right you, know, Bobby is. He's just a lad. He's got a good heart.'

'I'm sure he has,' Dot said breezily, folding up the newspaper.

'He's just not sure how to talk to you, that's all. He's never met anyone like you before.'

'Come on, Joley, Sal – and the rest of you!' Dot said, as if Maryann hadn't spoken. 'How about a bit of writing practice before bed?'

'You want your heads knocking together, the pair of you,' Maryann grumbled. 'I hope you're not going to carry on like this for a month!'

Twenty-Eight

This is going to be one of those trips, Maryann thought as she climbed out of the cabin again into the driving rain. Dot was at the helm, collar up, huddled under a sou'wester, trousers soaked dark with water. Her boots were over-flowing as she stepped squelchily from foot to foot.

They were on the route down to Oxford and every-thing had gone badly from the beginning. The rain had barely let up for days, slowing, even stopping to allow brief, overcast intervals before starting again and falling hard and steadily. Loading up had gone badly, the coal getting wet as soon as it rattled down into the hold, and trying to sheet up in the wet and in a hurry was always an ordeal, with the slippery boards, the ropes chafing rough and wet against their hands and having to be spliced when they snapped. Maryann kept barking at the children to stay indoors and not get all their clothes wet because, before they'd even started out, the adults' clothes were soaked through. The bedding was damp as they hadn't been able to air it outside for days, the cabin floors were thick with mud and filth and, worst of all, the bedbugs were back and everyone was scratching bites. The snubber snapped on the long, lockless route down to Rugby and then they'd just missed getting through Banbury before the gates were locked up and had to tie up earlier than they wanted. Everyone was wet, cold and bad-tempered.

'You go in and warm up – there's tea in the pot,' Maryann said, climbing out to relieve Dot.

'Ooh, marvellous.' Dot climbed down stiffly into the cabin, trying not to bend her legs because of the discomfort of cold, wet trousers.

Things on board had improved only a bit over the past fortnight.

'Don't keep on at her,' Maryann had said to Bobby several times during their trips, when the only way he could seem to talk to Dot was to rile her. 'You're upsetting her. She's only like you and me, Bobby. She's got feelings, you know.'

'I'm not keeping on!' he protested sulkily. 'I'm just having a laugh and a joke!'

Maryann was surprised by the strength of Dot's reaction to Bobby. It was only teasing, Maryann could see that herself, and it was the way his own kind of shyness came out. But Dot seemed hurt and enraged and to take it all terribly personally.

'He treats me as if I'm a complete idiot!' she fumed.

Maryann was bewildered by the pair of them and weary of it all, but they managed gradually to work together with a little more civility. Bobby stopped trying to get a rise out of her and Dot mostly ignored him. The result wasn't the most harmonious crew ever, but at least they'd stopped their constant jibing. Last night, though, sitting in the *Esther Jane*, they'd had a spat about the business of the Bottom Road. Dot said contemptuously that it was quite ridiculous having to trek all round the north of Birmingham to get back when they could turn round and go via Warwick. Bobby, whom Maryann knew perfectly well loathed the Bottom Road as much as any other boater, got on his high horse and said it

258

wasn't ridiculous, if she really wanted to know, it was to save water. Dot said she knew perfectly well it was to save water, thank you very much, but it was still ridiculous and they ought to be able to wind the boats and go back. The two of them got really heated and glowered at each other across the table.

'Oh, for goodness *sake*, you two, pack it in!' Maryann snapped at them at last. 'I feel as if I've got two extra kiddies on board with the pair of you. Bobby, if you don't stop going on you can just get out. Go on! Go back there on your own.' She pointed back towards the *Theodore*.

Bobby got up, wearing a surly expression. 'All right, I'll go. I know when I'm not wanted.'

'But it *is* ridiculous,' Dot murmured to his departing back. 'Whatever you say!'

Never mind, Maryann told herself, feeling the rain plopping endlessly onto the scarf she'd tied over her hair and soaking through it. Water ran down her face. All around was the rank smell of slimy mud. She'd see Joel again in a few days and it wouldn't be many more trips before he was back and she didn't have to worry about all these other people. She did feel a pang at the thought, though. She'd miss them now. They'd had a postcard from Sylvia, sent to Sutton Stop on what Dot worked out must have been her first or second day home!

'I *miss* you both ever such a lot. Children well and happy, but can't wait to get back! Keep 'em ahead! All my love, Sylvia.'

Maryann found it very strange that she had thought to write to them so soon when she must have so much to occupy her, seeing her children and her husband again.

Dot had to leave her half-drunk tea to see them

259

through the locks at Upper Heyford. But not long after they'd got under way again the engine started to take on a sluggish, complaining tone.

Oh, here we go, Maryann thought. *Something's in there.* Instead of anger and impatience she just felt resigned. *I might've known something like this would happen today.* She slowed the engine, turning to signal to Bobby that she was pulling in.

Dot appeared. 'I say, what's up? Problems down below?'

'We've caught a bundle down here,' Maryann said. 'Joley, stay in – you'll get soaked, else.'

Her son scowled up at her from the cabin. 'But I want to come out and help. S'boring in here.' In the background one of the twins wailed and started crying.

'Well, help by keeping yourself dry!' was all Joley got back from his mother.

'Right –' Dot shoved her wet sleeves up her arms once Maryann had brought the boat in – 'let's have a look in there, then.'

Maryann gave a brief nod and stood back out of the way to let Dot at the bilges. Dot had quite a way with the mechanics of the boat and was willing to get stuck in. Maryann was grateful to her. She didn't seem to have the energy for anything herself.

Now the engine was off, all they could hear was the sound of the rain falling into the water. Dot knelt in the wet, leaning forward and reaching down into the sludge-green water, bottom in the air, tugging at the snarled-up mess round the propeller.

'What the hell've we got down here?' she grunted.

Bobby appeared, splashing through the puddles along the path, water dripping off his cap.

'Let's have a look-see then.'

He climbed up on the gunwales, expecting Dot to move, but she completely ignored him.

'What we got in there?' Bobby was all eager, ready to spring into action. Again he received no reply.

'Whole load of stuff,' Maryann said.

Dot got hold of something and and began to pull, but after a moment the piece of what turned out to be rag tore, leaving only a small fragment in her hand. Dot cursed under her breath and went back to her reaching and grunting, hands in the cold, filthy water.

Bobby couldn't contain himself. 'Come on – move over and let us have a look. I'll soon have her freed up.'

Dot pulled herself upright and stood up, muddy water running down her arms. She was breathing heavily and Maryann saw, to her consternation, that she was brimming with emotion.

'All right.' The words exploded out of her like bullets. 'You do it. You're the expert.'

She pushed past Bobby, jumping down onto the bank, and strode off furiously along the towpath, head bowed against the rain. Bobby swivelled round to watch Dot's receding figure.

'I only said . . . What the hell's the matter with her?'

'Oh, Bobby – you could've given her a chance,' Maryann said, exasperated with all this carry-on. 'She's quite good if you let her get on with it. Can't you just keep your mouth shut for five minutes? Look, you get on with it now. I'll go after her.'

Slipping and jumping around the puddles, Maryann followed Dot. Another pair of boats was passing and she saw the man at the tiller turn to look curiously at her.

'Dot – wait!'

She put her hand on Dot's shoulder and Dot stopped and turned grudgingly round. To her surprise, Maryann saw she was in tears.

'Bobby didn't mean anything. He was just trying to help.'

'I *know*.' Dot didn't meet Maryann's eyes, but looked down at her muddy boots. For a moment she seemed like a child.

'Well, what's up then?' She couldn't help her impatience. Here they were, soaked and getting behind on the trip and now there was all this upset.

Dot shrugged angrily. 'He just ... He always has to do that, doesn't he? Push you around, show he knows best because he's a man and they always have to be in charge. I *hate* it. And I hate *him*.' She let out a deep, shuddering breath, as if suddenly running out of steam. 'No, I don't,' she said more quietly. 'I didn't mean that.' There was a silence as the rain fell. 'I just – he makes me feel ... peculiar. That's all.' She shook her head, as if ashamed. 'I can't explain. I feel so stupid.'

Maryann could barely begin to understand and she was shivering with cold. 'Come on. Let's get back. We can't go on like this.'

Dot looked up, shamefaced. 'Sorry, Maryann.'

'It's all right. Come on.'

As they walked back, Bobby stood up and they saw him yanking at something, then he stood upright, a grin on his face, waving a tattered length of some filthy object that had been wrapped round the propeller.

'That was quick,' Maryann said. Her teeth were chattering. 'Let's get the kettle on before we go.'

Bobby looked down at Dot, her round face pink from tears and the weather, hair soaked and flattened to her head. 'I just thought you wouldn't want to be in there, in all that muck and mess, that's all.'

He spoke with such straightforward friendliness that no one could have taken offence.

'It's all right,' Dot said stiffly. 'I was being silly.'

'Not *you*?' Bobby said. Hearing the teasing note in his voice, Maryann tensed. Surely he wasn't going to start the whole flaming fight off again?

But Dot gave a cautious smile. 'Yes, me, I'm afraid.'

Dreaming that night, Maryann was back in the old house in Ladywood, the one they had moved to when Norman Griffin came into their lives. The house was the same as then, except that it had no roof. Flo, her mother, was downstairs and she kept sending Maryann upstairs to fetch things. When she went into her old room, it was open to the grey sky and the rain fell onto the bed, gathering in its sunken dip like a small pond, onto the chest of drawers and her few possessions, her hairbrush and comb. Water washed over the floor and poured down the stairs as she climbed up them. She twisted and turned in her bed, trying to escape, to leave the dream, the place. It was nothing she could see, not anything frightening in itself. But the smell of the house came to her, overpowering in the dream, and the way her mother sat, always with her back to her down in the front room, snapping orders, the way the light fell on the stairs and she knew he was there, somewhere, waiting for her, and she couldn't see him . . . All these things filled her with horror and a panic that forced up suffocatingly at the back of her throat. She felt a weight on her chest and woke, moaning, fighting for breath.

'Maryann? What's the matter? Aren't you feeling well?'

She'd sat up, moaning, clasping her arms round herself and rocking, still half inside the dream, although she was half awake and could hear Dot's voice from the other end of the bed. She ached for Joel to be there, to hold her.

'Hey – whatever is it? Goodness, you're shaking.' Dot moved closer, putting her hands on Maryann's shoulders. Her tone was soft and full of sympathy. Maryann could only whimper a reply.

'Bad dream, eh?' Dot's arms came round her now. 'I know. It's lousy, isn't it?'

Dot didn't ask any more questions, as if she knew already that they could not be answered. She just held Maryann until she was calmer, the atmosphere of the dream fading a little. She would have liked to put a light on, to get up and do everyday things to push away the feelings, the oppressive mood of the night, but she didn't want to wake the girls.

After a time she whispered, 'I'll be all right now.'

'Righty ho,' Dot said doubtfully, releasing her. 'But don't be afraid to wake me.'

Maryann lay on her back, looking up into the dark, the sound of the rain insistent on the roof.

It was only when they reached Oxford that she was able to let out some of her feelings. She laid her head on Joel's shoulder and wept until she could weep no more, and he held her close, comforting her as he had always done.

'It's him, I know it is,' Maryann sobbed.

Joel's eyes had shown his horror and reluctance to believe it when she told him about Amy. He was so kind, Maryann thought, looking at his big, gentle form in Alice Simons's little room. She knew it had been hard at first for him to take it in, to believe what effect Norman Griffin had had on herself and Sal as children, and she had only ever told him a little. He knew of Norman Griffin's cruelty. He'd seen the effects of it on Amy and Margaret. But she had never talked, even to him, about what else their stepfather had done to them all, robbing them of their bodies, their sexual innocence. She knew that Joel found even the part he did know hard to believe. He had once told her he found it harder to take in than what he'd seen in the trenches.

'I was there though, then, see,' she remembered him saying. 'You have to believe your own eyes, don't you? And that was war. But what he did – to children – well, that was something else altogether.'

As he held her now, she knew he would be having the same struggle to believe in the further wickedness of what had happened.

'What makes you so sure?' he asked, eventually.

Maryann pulled back and looked into his eyes. He had to believe her. She knew it was the truth. 'Because he's on the warpath. He is – I remember the way he looked at me in the church that night. I don't know what he wants, but he won't stop until he's got it.'

Twenty-Nine

'Maryann?'

Dot leapt up onto the *Esther Jane*, making Maryann almost jump out of her skin. She was sitting on the bench facing the stove, dazed, as if unable to move. She had been about to do something. What was it? She couldn't seem to hold a thought in her head for long and Rose and the twins would keep on, 'Mom ... Mom ...' and she'd get as far as saying absently, 'What?' and then not hear the rest of what they said to her.

'You all right?' Dot asked. She came down and squeezed herself onto the coalbox, looking at Maryann with embarrassed concern. Dot wasn't comfortable with emotions and Maryann felt herself stiffen and go red with embarrassment.

'I will be,' she said tersely. 'Just getting cleared up.'

Dot, seeing she wasn't going to get anywhere, stood up and went again.

But Maryann had seen it in Dot's eyes, the thought, *I know you're not all right, but I don't know what to say* ... Her nights were full of dreams now, fragments of childhood which she forced away from her memory when she was awake, but which made her cry out or wake up sobbing and shaking. It had not been as bad as this for years, not since she first ran away and started working at the big house, Charnwood, near Banbury. A number of times Dot had had to comfort her, and in the darkness

266

she had held Maryann, speaking to her with a sweet gentleness that Maryann was learning to accept instead of pushing her away, but which she found hard to reconcile with Dot's awkward gruffness in the daytime. And in daylight she could not seem to keep her mind on anything, could not remember from moment to moment what she was supposed to be doing. It didn't help that she knew why it was happening to her. Through all the shocks and loss of the past months she had managed to hold onto herself, to keep the past at bay, even when Norman Griffin came back into her life. If any memories had forced themselves at her she had pushed her mind elsewhere, made herself go numb as she had when he was with her, forcing himself on her. But the horror of Amy's death seemed to have stripped her, left her bare and there was no Joel, her support and mainstay, to rescue her and keep her safe. She was frightened, overwhelmed by her feelings. It seemed to take an effort almost beyond her strength for her to stand up and get on with all her chores that morning. The kettle was boiling furiously on the stove. How long had it been like that? she wondered, yanking it off the heat. She must get on – they had to get moving . . .

It had been Bobby's idea that they make the trip down to London. Mr Veater had no trouble finding loads needed for Limehouse. The war effort's hunger for coal was bottomless. Bobby would find a boat to crew his way back on and they could pick up Sylvia for the return trip now that the Easter holidays were over.

Spring had truly arrived over the past fortnight and suddenly the worst of the cold had passed. Standing at the helm, Maryann felt her limbs relax a little in the warmer breeze, after the months of cold. The boats were heavily weighed down with a full load of coal and tidily sheeted up by Dot and Bobby. She tried to keep her concentration together. Once they got onto the Grand Union, you could turn a bend and find yourself nose to nose with the huge river barges, which loomed above tiny narrowboats. To her surprise, Dot had suddenly said she'd take the older girls and stay awhile on the *Theodore*, to give them a lesson with the boys, while they were on a stretch with none too many locks. But Maryann read the worst into this. Normally Dot would have done anything to avoid being too near Bobby. *She wants to get away from me*, she thought. *Can't blame her, I suppose.* But she suddenly felt sad and lonely with just Ada and Esther on the roof. Rejected, almost. As they drew closer to Sutton Stop, she turned to signal that she was slowing down. Bobby was standing in his usual easy fashion, cap perched on the back of his head, tiller behind him, and to Maryann's surprise Dot was standing out there beside him and they were talking, apparently quite amiably. It took her a moment to get their attention.

I should be glad, she thought. It's about time they stopped being so silly and got on with each other. But that day the sight of them together made her feel even more bleak and alone.

The journey south went smoothly. Maryann was astonished at how smoothly, considering she felt as if the days were passing in a dream. She was exhausted. It seemed so long since she had had a really good night's sleep. She felt as if the flashes of memory – sometimes not even memory, discomfort rather – were sapping all her energy. They came south towards Stoke Bruerne and once more she was steering the boat alone. When Dot had said earlier that she'd go aboard the *Theodore* again, Maryann teased her.

'You're getting mighty friendly with Bobby all of a sudden!'

'Oh, don't be so *silly*,' Dot said huffily. 'Joley and Ezra want to fish off the side and I said I'd help.'

'I don't think you'll catch much like that, will you?' Maryann said.

'You never know – and it'll keep them happy for a bit. You don't mind, do you?'

'No.' She wanted to ask, why can't you stay on here with me and do it, but she felt childish and bit back the words. Of course Bobby was the main attraction for Joley and Ezra – he'd always been Joley's hero.

So she steered the *Esther Jane* with no one else on board except Ada and Esther. They were napping in the cabin as the boats came towards Blisworth Tunnel at Stoke Bruerne. The black mouth of the tunnel grew bigger as they drew closer, swallowing the front of the boat. Its cold shadow fell over her and abruptly Maryann found herself in the darkness. She had put her scarf and coat on in preparation, collar up, as the place was permanently dank and dripping, cold water splashing down on you.

She forced herself to concentrate on the steering. It was hard at first, disorientating to be plunged into darkness; it was easy to lose any sense of direction and steer the boat into the opposite bank and end up veering back and forth, crashing into the walls. There was only the boat's dim lamp ahead, with no light from an oncoming boat. She peered ahead, sometimes standing on tiptoe to try and see better, glancing back every so often to make sure the *Theodore*'s light was following behind. In here, if the snubber snapped, there'd be no chance of hearing a cry over the echo of the engine, which roared off the curved brick roof of the tunnel, filling her ears so it was impossible to hear anything but the loudest of sounds over it.

Every so often ventilation shafts in the roof let in a ghostly cylinder of light from above, from the world outside, convincing you for a few seconds that real daylight still existed. Otherwise, for over a mile and a half, all was darkness and engine throb, and the dim yellow beam of light casting forward only a few yards onto the ripples to show the way. A freezing splash of water dropped down the back of her neck.

After a time she saw the far end of the tunnel, a tiny dot of light at first, growing very slowly bigger. *Thank heaven for the motor*, she thought, shuddering at how they would have had to get through here the old way, when the horses would be walked over the top and the men lay out on planks half over the black water, feet pressed to the wall to leg the boat through step by step.

It came over her with no warning, about halfway through. She could not have said exactly what set it off: some half thought or memory, or simply the darkness, the way the white light so far away never seemed to get any bigger, however much they moved towards it. The blackness became suffocating, as if it had weight and was pressing itself on top of her. Her lungs felt crushed, incapable of pumping air in and out. Heat rose in her, her own body seeming to suffocate her and she was sweating and overtaken by panic. She tore her coat off, flung it down into the cabin and bent over the tiller gasping for breath. Her lungs were sobbing as if she had run to the summit of a cold mountain. Her neck and forehead were wet with sweat.

Maryann was jerked back to her surroundings when

the *Esther Jane* hit the opposite wall with an awful crack and scrape and she was almost flung over backwards. She just managed to clutch onto the cabin roof, and immediately fought to straighten out the boat and get her running on the right side of the channel.

It was a few moments before she gained proper control again, the tiller was throbbing in her hand and she was trembling with shock. She leaned on the cabin and, knowing no one would hear, let out a great howl of pain which echoed round her amid the throb of the engine.

When the boat finally moved out into the sunshine it was like emerging from a nightmare. She breathed in hard, still shaky but longing for the light, for the sense of release it brought. Stoke Bruerne was busy, and Maryann knew they should press on through, but the moment she saw the familiar buildings along the canal she was filled with longing. It made her think of Nance and the time they'd brought their children in together to see Sister Mary Ward. She wanted desperately, suddenly, to see Sister Mary. Just the thought of the woman's comforting face would make her feel better. She turned and signalled that they were going to stop.

Holding Ada's and Esther's hands, Maryann walked to Sister Mary's little front-room surgery. Another boat-woman, heavily pregnant, came out and then it was their turn.

The sight of Sister Mary in her white overall and long white veil, even the smell of iodine steadied her. Sister Mary was busy over on one side of the room. Maryann heard the clink of glass as she arranged a jar on the shelf. After a moment Sister Mary looked round and gave her warm smile.

'Ah – now I know you, don't I?'

Maryann found herself smiling back. 'I haven't been to see you in a while, Sister. Last time, I came with my friend Nance – Nancy Bartholomew.'

'Of course, the Bartholomews.' Sister Mary came across and gestured for Maryann to sit down. 'You take a rest when you can, dear.' She looked solemn. 'I remember. Poor, poor Nancy. That was a real tragedy. I was so very sorry to hear about it. That must have been a couple of winters ago now?'

Maryann nodded, looking down into her lap as her eyes filled. She spoke more roughly than she meant to.

'Can you look these two over for me?'

'Ah now –' Sister Mary bent over, putting her hands together almost as if praying and smiled at Ada and Esther – 'I remember these two as babies, don't I? Let's have a look at the pair of you then, shall we?'

As she examined the girls, their heads, necks, ears and throats, she asked after the rest of the family. Maryann told her about Joel's accident, about the trainees.

'Oh – we have quite a few of them up and down here.' Sister Mary laughed. 'You've got a couple of them working on the Oxford as well now, have you? Most of them are marvellous, of course – there's just the odd one or two can get a bit uppity.' She glanced at Maryann as she worked, and after observing that Ada might need her tonsils out one day she pronounced the twins to be fit and bonny.

'And what about their mother? Are you keeping well?'

Maryann nodded, feeling herself crumple, hearing the kindness in her tone. Her throat hurt with the effort of not breaking down. 'Mostly. You know how it is.'

Sister Mary knew all too well. After years of working with the boatwomen she was awed by their stamina and capacity for endurance. Her eyes twinkled down at Maryann.

'No problems, then?'

Problems? Maryann longed just to lay her head on the woman's shoulder and sob out all her need and confusion. She shook her head, but the tears welled up again unbidden. She was getting up out of her chair to leave, afraid of embarrassing herself, but Sister Mary gently took her arm and encouraged her to stay sitting.

'What is it, dear?'

Shaking her head, Maryann felt sobs rising up again. She was so mortified, she wished she could become invisible. How could she even begin to tell Sister Mary what she felt, however kind the woman was?

'I can't say ... it's nothing.' She wiped her eyes on her sleeve and stood up. She couldn't begin crying: if she did she might never stop. 'I'm just being silly. I just feel a bit anyhow today, that's all.'

Sister Mary watched her with concern, but she could see that Maryann was determined not to say more.

'Well, you make sure you look after yourself properly, dear. Don't put yourself last all the time, will you?' She opened the door to let Maryann out. 'Goodbye, dear – I'm always here, you know.'

Thirty

Limehouse Dock was very busy. Once again they moved across the great expanse of water, dwarfed by many of the vessels around them. They joined the queue for unloading and got busy on all the chores and the shopping. By the time they had finished those it was dinnertime, but their two heavily laden boats were still waiting.

'When's this Sylvia coming, then?' Bobby asked through a mouthful of bread and cheese. He was seated casually on the back of the *Esther Jane*, feet on the bank.

'Oh, she's not coming here,' Maryann said. 'She's s'posed to be getting a train up to join us in a day or two. She doesn't know we're down here.'

'Seems silly, doesn't it?' Dot said, perched up beside Ezra on the cabin roof, tea mug in hand. 'Why don't we telephone her? Have you the number?'

'No. Got the address, though.'

'Well –' Dot tipped her dregs into the water and jumped down with a thud onto the platform – 'we'll just have to scout out a telephone directory.'

'Don't you know where she lives?' Bobby asked. 'Dunno why you don't just go and see her.'

'I say –' Dot turned to Maryann, excited – 'how about it? We could surprise her! What if we took the kiddies along? It'd be a little outing for them as well.'

Maryann looked at Bobby, who gave his easy smile. 'I'll see to the unloading. Don't you fret.'

As they began on their journey, having speedily gathered up the children, Dot looked back at the pair of boats and said, 'I never cease to be amazed by Bobby's relaxed attitude to life.'

'Oh, he's a good'un,' Maryann said. 'Nice family, the Jenkses.'

They made their way through the shabby Limehouse streets and got onto a crowded bus, standing all the way, packed in. Maryann saw Dot wrinkle her nose as she registered the strong smell of unwashed bodies pressed close to them. Peering out between people's heads, Maryann caught glimpses of the damage the Blitz had inflicted on the East End. She was glad Dot knew London so well as she guided them onto the Underground. Rose looked really frightened at being led down into a dark, squalid hole in the ground. Dot took her hand and reminded her that they would soon be seeing Auntie Sylvia, and the little girl's face relaxed, her eyes lighting up. Soon all the children were peering out, watching excitedly for each stop. There were a few moments of peace, and Maryann felt she might easily fall asleep here in the warm, stuffy carriage, rocking back and forth, her coat on to cover her grubby frock. She gave a wide yawn, feeling muzzy in the head. She felt Dot looking at her.

'I'm not very good at talking about things and so forth,' Dot said abruptly. 'Thing is, Maryann, you've obviously got something on your mind. Don't want to pry. But – I can't help but notice – bad nights and so forth.' Dot was blushing, looking down at her plump thighs, clad in black corduroy. 'If I can be of any help, you would say . . .?'

Maryann was touched, but at the same time the old panic rose in her. *Don't ask me! Don't let anyone find out!* How could she possibly explain to Dot – how could she name the strange feelings she had? It was true Dot had family problems, but nothing like this. Sometimes she longed to pour it all out to someone. But she couldn't even tell Joel! She sensed he didn't really want to hear it. So far as he was concerned, past was past and they had their own family now. Did anyone, ever, really want to hear the truth? She didn't believe they did. Naked truth was too horrible. She swallowed hard.

'It's all right, Dot. I just have the odd nightmare sometimes. Don't know why.'

It seemed a long walk from the tube station to Sylvia's, but the afternoon was warm and pleasant.

'Is this her house?' the girls kept asking, but then there were so many houses on the way that they gave up and became weary and just stared round them.

'Aren't we *ever* going to get there?' Sally complained wearily, her old boots scuffing along the pavement.

Looking at her children, Maryann was suddenly full of misgivings. Now they were away from the cut and in this neat neighbourhood with its little front gardens with trimmed hedges, they did all look a scruffy bunch with their old clothes and grimy skin!

'D'you think she'll mind?' she said as they looked over the gate. 'I mean us turning up, showing her up?'

Dot snorted. 'Oh, I can't imagine so! Sylvia's not like that, is she?'

Isn't she? Maryann thought. How could they really know what she'd be like away from the cut and in her nice home? The neighbourhood was such a world away from the jerry-built Ladywood houses she'd grown up in that she felt nervous and out of place.

Sylvia's house was painted white, but Maryann was at once disappointed and relieved to see that the roses and shrubs in the front garden looked straggly and there was plenty of groundsel and dandelions. It spoiled her pretty picture of Sylvia's perfect house! But, of course, Sylvia had not been at home to see to any of it, and the fact that everything was not perfectly neat made her feel reassured. The house had a pea-green front door, with a window set into it edged with coloured-glass fruits. A cinder path ran alongside the grass.

'I wonder if her husband's here,' Maryann found herself whispering. 'What's his name again?'

'Roy.' Even Dot was whispering. '*Darling* Roy.'

'Oh yes – how could I forget!' This set them both off into giggles and for a few moments they were both helpless with nervous laughter in the road.

'What's so funny?' Sally frowned at them. 'Aren't we going to knock on the door?'

Ezra ran ahead and started banging his fist on the lower part of the door and Maryann went and dragged him back, saying, '*Sssh!* Don't!'

'One way to find out.' Dot's hand was poised over the knocker. 'Ready?'

Its brass clatter sounded very loud in the silent street. The houses looked down on them from all round, with their anti-blast tape on the windows. Where was everyone? Maryann wondered. The only life about was the lady next door, who stepped out through her front door carrying a cloth bag and peered at them over the wall.

All of them jumped, startled, when the door opened and they found themselves faced with a well-built man with fair hair shorn into a very short serviceman's haircut and a wide, strong face. The man from the photograph.

'Yes?' His voice was clipped and conveyed no expression, either of disapproval or welcome. Maryann could not meet his eyes and kept her gaze on the sharp creases in his trousers, his well-polished black shoes. She saw that the floor was a pale wood parquet. Dot could do the talking. She wasn't going to open her mouth with her Brummie accent and have him sneer at her. She felt instinctively that he might be the sneering type.

'Dorothy Higgs-Deveraux,' Dot announced briskly, though she too appeared uncomfortable as Roy Cresswell looked appraisingly at her generous figure, dressed in her worn black trousers and the brown baggy sweater. The one touch of colour she wore today was a red and green scarf tied as an Alice band to keep her hair back. She pointed at her 'IW' badge. 'I'm a colleague of your wife's – Inland Waterways – National Service. This is Mrs Maryann Bartholomew, whose boat we're crewing. Sylvia's due to join us again tomorrow, of course.'

'I see.' He stood looking at them, holding the door open with one arm, which protruded hairily from his white, short-sleeved shirt.

Well, he's not very pleased to see us, Maryann thought. Though his face betrayed no emotion, she sensed that he was angry.

'Is Sylvia in?' Dot persevered. 'We'd like a word with her.'

'Just a moment.' He swung the door almost closed and they heard him calling, 'Sylvia. Sylv! Someone to see you.'

Dot turned and grimaced at Maryann. 'Not exactly a gushing welcome,' she whispered.

Rose was pulling on Maryann's hand, her face anxious. 'When's Sylvia coming out?'

A moment later the door opened again. Sylvia was wearing a very pretty floral dress with a floating skirt, a white cardigan over the top and leather navy pumps. As ever, she was well made up, with her favourite scarlet lipstick. She looked delicate and feminine. Maryann was quite taken aback. They'd only ever seen Sylvia in her boat clothes and the children looked especially abashed, as if they could barely recognize her. Maryann felt Rose's hand clutching at her skirt for reassurance.

'Oh, my goodness!' Sylvia hissed. She sounded horrified and immediately it all felt a terrible mistake that they'd come here. She glanced behind her and pulled the front door closed and squatted down so that her skirt fell in soft swathes over her knees. 'Oh, Rose, it's all right – come here, darling!'

Rose, whose face had crumpled ready for tears, let go of Maryann and went shyly to Sylvia, who immediately cuddled her, despite Rose's grubby frock. Sylvia greeted all the other children and then stood up, still holding Rose's hand. She looked back anxiously towards the door again and gestured them to move further away along the path.

'Is everything all right?' Maryann asked. There was a tight fearfulness in Sylvia's face that she had never seen before.

'I'm *so* sorry.' Sylvia spoke quickly, in short bursts. 'I'd love to invite you in – only I can't. The children could have played in the garden if . . . but not with Roy here, you see. He's very . . . particular about everything, you see. You do understand, don't you?'

'Where're your children?' Maryann asked. She was filled with unease at the sight of Sylvia. She looked lovely, fresh and well groomed, and she was the same, sweet-natured Sylvia, yet somehow quite different.

'Oh, Kay and Dickie have gone back to school. I put them on the train yesterday. It was a couple of days early, but I thought it was for the best. I wasn't expecting Roy home, you see – not now – and he likes to have me to himself. He had a couple of extra days' leave, you see.' She gave a valiant smile.

'So you don't want to come back with us today?' Dot tried to joke. 'You don't look dressed for the part, I must say.'

'No – it'll be a couple of days. I'll find you – don't you worry. If it all goes wrong, I'll get to Sutton and pick you up there. Oh look – ' she glanced behind her – 'it's so sweet of you to come and I'm longing to see you all properly, but I'd better not stay now.' She began to back down the path. 'Roy goes back tomorrow. I just need to stay and see him off.'

'It's all right – you make the most of it.' Maryann felt herself twist up inside, though she didn't really know why. Sylvia seemed so anxious and unlike her normal self. 'We'll get back and help Bobby with the unloading. You enjoy the rest of your time. Have a bath for us both, won't you?'

'Oh,' Sylvia said yearningly, 'I *wish* I could ask you in, I really do! It's a bit difficult to explain.'

'You're all right – I was only joking,' Maryann called lightly, shepherding the children in front of her. 'TTFN!'

'Cheerio, Sylvia!' Dot called.

Sylvia waved and, as she pushed the front door open, they caught a glimpse of Roy Cresswell standing in the hall, arms hanging at his sides. Then the door closed.

As they went out of the gate, the woman from next door was coming towards them along the pavement. Her bag was still empty and Maryann sensed she had been waiting for them. She was in her thirties, hair scraped into a bun, and wearing a faded flowery frock.

'Could I have a word?' She spoke in a quiet, guarded voice, looking back at Sylvia's house.

'Of course,' Dot said.

'You'll probably think I'm ever such a nosy-parker,' the woman said, fiddling with the frayed handles of the bag. 'My name's Lois, by the way. Lois Parmenter. Are you friends of the lady in that house?'

'Yes,' Dot said. 'What's the trouble?'

'Well, I don't know, that's the thing. Dear, oh dear, you are going to think I'm an interfering busybody.' Her eyes darted anxiously back and forth between Dot's and Maryann's faces. 'You see, I've been wondering because I haven't been living here all that long and there hasn't been anyone in next door for some weeks.'

Dot explained briefly that Sylvia had been away working with them.

'Oh, I see – well yes. But then they came home and the kiddies were playing outside and that was all perfectly all right. And Mrs – Cresswell, isn't it? Yes, we exchanged a few words. But then her husband's been about once or twice, and he's there now. It's just that, well, he seems a bit of a queer fish. Oh dear, I do feel funny about asking, but I just wondered if everything's all right.'

Maryann immediately sensed that the woman was not just being nosy, that something had caused her to feel real concern.

'We don't know, really,' she said. 'We don't know him either. But Sylvia's coming back to work with us tomorrow.'

'Oh – oh good. Well, that's probably all right then.'

The woman started to back away. 'Sorry to bother you.' She retreated inside her gate. 'Sorry,' she said again. 'Goodbye.'

They retreated down the road, pacifying the disappointed children, who had all hoped to see Sylvia's nice house and be able to run in her garden.

'Look, I tell you what,' Maryann said, fishing in her pocket. There was a corner shop at the end of the road. 'I've got this week's coupons – we'll go and get you some rocks, eh?'

The children cheered up immediately at the thought of sweets.

'Take them in, will you, Dot?' Maryann handed her the ration coupons. 'Get them sorted out. I don't like this. I'm going to go back.'

'What the hell're you talking about?' Dot said. 'Go back? What, knock on the door and ask Roy Cresswell why he's such a "queer fish"? You can't do that!'

'I *know*,' Maryann snapped. 'What d'you take me for?'

'Well, what can you possibly do?'

'I don't know.' Maryann couldn't explain the tight feeling of dread in her chest that Roy Cresswell had given her. 'I've just got to . . . to see. Hang on for me a few minutes, will you?'

Full of nerves and afraid she was being stupid, she hurried back along the crescent towards Sylvia's house. To her relief, Lois Parmenter had gone indoors. An elderly man scuttled along the pavement with a hairy terrier, which seemed to be pulling him along at the full stretch of its lead. The man touched the brim of his hat with two fingers and was propelled off round the corner.

Maryann felt very foolish. The house was quiet, just as when they had left. Supposing Sylvia saw her out of the window? What on earth would she say to her? She opened the front gate very quietly and closed it behind her, gritting her teeth. Her heart was banging wildly. What the hell did she think she was doing? She should just turn back now and go: stop being so downright ridiculous. But she felt driven on, partly through curiosity, but also by a sense of recognition. That fear she had seen in Sylvia's face, the instinct that she was hiding something, that there was a dimension to her life that she could never admit to anyone. These were things Maryann knew herself as if they travelled in her blood. She recognized them when she saw them in someone else. And she doubted if Sylvia would ever tell them. She would just suffer on in respectable silence.

There was no sound at the front of the house and all the windows were closed. The front windows were swathed in net curtains. The houses were built in twos, semi-detached. Maryann eyed the little path running round to the back garden. She pushed past a hydrangea bush and stepped into the shadow of the house, its wall to one side, a fence on the other.

This is daft, she thought, heart pounding. *I'll just have a peep at the garden and then I'll go. What am I going to see doing this?*

She heard something then, though. Faintly, from somewhere at the back, she could hear a man's voice. Sliding along the side of the building, Maryann saw there was a window open further along and she moved until she was standing close to it. It must be the kitchen's side window, she realized: she could hear water running, then the clatter of cutlery being put into a drawer. There was a long silence, though Maryann could hear movements from inside, and her curiosity got the better of her. She leaned round and peered through the window, quickly moving back again so that no one should see her. But in that moment she saw that Sylvia was on the other side of the room at the sink, with her back to her, and she just caught a glimpse of Roy Cresswell sitting at the table, bent over something.

Maryann leaned round again. Roy Cresswell had one hand on the table and was holding a cigarette, above which the smoke hovered in an upward swirl. With the other he was holding a box, or biscuit tin, and shaking it, examining the contents. Maryann squinted. She couldn't make out what was in the tin, but there was a shape on the table beside him, and she realized he must be building a model ship out of matches, or small slivers of wood. She could see three masts sticking up from the main hull.

Sylvia was wringing a cloth out at the sink. She hung it over the tap, dried her hands and placed the towel over the back of the chair with slow, deliberate neatness. As Sylvia turned, undoing her apron, Maryann shrank back until she was still just able to peer round the window-frame. Sylvia tugged at the apron strings and there was sharp anger in her movements. For a moment she stood with it crumpled in her hand, then flung it decisively down onto the table.

'D'you know, Roy—'

He looked up, evidently startled by her tone.

'I really don't care what you think. You're going tomorrow, anyway, so what possible difference can it make to you? I'm going back and that's that. And it doesn't matter a fig to me any more what you think about it. Think what you like.'

And she strode out of Maryann's line of vision and left the kitchen.

Roy Cresswell sat for a moment staring ahead of him with the same blank expression. Maryann saw his jaw tighten. With a sudden movement, which made her jump, he brought his fist down on top of the matchstick model, smashing through it. He picked up the tin and hurled it with great force across the kitchen. Matches flew out and spilled all over the floor.

Thirty-One

They were up early the next morning. Dot handed Maryann a cup of tea in through the hatches, and she and Bobby stayed outside on the towpath, hands cupped round the hot mugs, shivering in the early morning chill although the sun was already beginning to break through. Around them they could hear the clanking of cranes beginning to work, the splash of water as men pumped out the holds of their boats and the distant, mournful sound of a ship's siren. Soon the tannoy would start crackling and blaring over the wharves, calling crews to be assigned their loads.

They'd talked it over and over the night before – Roy Cresswell and the burst of temper Maryann had seen through the window.

'I just don't like the look of him at all,' Maryann said on the way home, while the children were quietened by mouthfuls of sweets. 'The way he threw that box across the room – and the way his face was. There's something about him makes my flesh creep.'

'He certainly struck me as *odd*,' Dot said, 'but in the end you didn't really see anything much, and you can't just go barging in on other people's marriages, can you? Sylvia'll be back with us in a day or two, anyway.'

'Darling Roy,' Maryann mused. 'She's ever so loyal to him.'

'Or the lady doth protest too much.'

'What d'you mean?'

'I'd guess she's been covering up for him a bit. She's certainly succeeded up until now, I'll give her that. But she is nervy, isn't she? Maybe that husband of hers accounts for it.'

They busied themselves with the morning chores, Maryann sorting out the children and shooing them outside, then starting on breakfast, and Dot and Bobby readying the boats for loading. Maryann had just begun on the food when she heard a cry of excitement from Rose, who was jumping excitedly on the counter.

'Look – Sylvia's coming!'

'No –' Maryann called up to her. 'Not today, bab. She'll be along soon, though. Couple of days.'

But Rose was off along the path and then Dot poked her head into the *Esther Jane*, looking bemused.

'Sylvia's already here, it seems.'

Maryann climbed out, shading her eyes in the morning glare. Sylvia's neat figure was moving towards them along the path, carrying her bundle of belongings. As soon as she was close enough she threw it down on the path. She looked pale and exhausted. After a second Maryann realized this was almost the first time she had seen Sylvia without her make-up. It made her feel uneasy.

'Hello, stranger!' Dot exclaimed. 'What're you doing here?'

'You're early!' Maryann said. 'How the heck did you get here by this time?'

Sylvia gave a tight smile. 'Oh, Roy decided he ought to get back to his squadron a day early. So I thought, rather than miss you, I'd high-tail it over here as soon as I could. I woke very early, so I walked some of the way until the buses started running. Anyway, here I am. Sorry about yesterday, by the way.'

'Not at all,' Dot said. 'Did your husband get off all right?'

'Oh yes,' Sylvia said brightly, leaning down slowly to pick up her things. As she bent over she gave a little grunt, as if it was a huge effort. Maryann saw Dot glance at her.

'Here, let me take that.' Dot swooped down for the bundle. 'I expect you're worn out already – you must have been up well before the lark! Oh, this is Bobby by the way.'

'I'll get you some tea,' Bobby said.

'Thanks awfully.' Sylvia straightened up, and they all pretended not to see the tears in her eyes, which she quickly brushed away. 'I could certainly do with it. And, Bobby, I'm sorry if this inconveniences you dreadfully. Are you going to be able to get another trip?'

'Oh, I s'pect so,' he said easily. 'Don't you worry.'

'Thanks awfully.' Sylvia's eyes filled again. 'You're so kind, Bobby.'

She held out her arms to Rose, who was waiting expectantly.

'Are you coming with us now, Sylvia?' Rose asked.

'Oh, *yes*,' Sylvia said. Suddenly she held the little girl close and the tears she had been holding back spilled down her face. She put Rose down. 'It's all right, darling,' Sylvia reassured her, wiping her eyes again, but still unable to stem her tears. 'It's so lovely to see you, but I do miss my Kay and Dickie as well. Oh, I'm sorry – I didn't mean to do this!'

'You're all right,' Maryann comforted her. 'Why don't you just go and settle in? I'll get us some breakfast.'

'Why's Sylvia crying?' Sally asked as Dot helped Sylvia take her things to the *Theodore*. With Bobby gone, Dot would be able to move back in there herself.

'Oh – I think it's just saying goodbye to her children and her house,' Maryann said. But she felt uneasy. Seeing Sylvia's house yesterday and her husband, she had suddenly begun to view her in a new light. She had so much wanted to believe in a perfect marriage and family, a perfect life, but it wasn't like that. Somehow she felt cheated and worried for Sylvia. But she couldn't just ask, could she? Not about things that were private like that. She knew she didn't like it when people asked her questions.

Bobby was taking the last of his things from the cabin of the *Theodore* when she carried food over to them. Maryann felt a rush of fondness for him.

'Here, get that down you before you go.' She handed him a couple of sausages with hunks of bread. 'Thanks, Bobby – you've been marvellous. And we'll be back to normal soon – Joel back and that.'

Bobby nodded shyly. 'S'all right. I shouldn't have no problem finding a trip. We'll all be back right as rain in a few weeks. Sorry to go, though.' He glanced at the cabin of the *Theodore* and just as he did so Dot climbed out.

'Breakfast,' Maryann said. 'Pass the other one to Sylvia, will you?'

'I'll be off then, soon.' Bobby said.

'So you will.' Dot stood, somehow at a loss. She looked down at her boots then back at Bobby. 'It won't be the same – not without you to squabble with!'

A grin spread over Bobby's handsome face. 'You're all right,' he said, then added with a chuckle, 'Dorothy Higgs-Deveraux!'

Dot blushed. 'All right – I can't help it!'

There was a crackle and a hiss and a voice called out harshly over the tannoy, 'Mrs Bartholomew, Bartholomew, of S. E. Barlow carriers – to the office, please!'

Putting her half-finished breakfast down, Maryann hurried over to be assigned the next load.

The office was already humming with activity and the red-faced man at the desk handed her her clearance papers, hardly even looking up at her.

'Steel billets – up to Tyseley.'

Maryann froze. She couldn't seem to force her hand out to take the papers. She could hear the blood banging in her ears.

'Come on – here y'are.'

'But—'

'What's the matter?' He spoke impatiently. 'You're unloaded and ready, aren't you?'

'Yes.' How could she begin to explain why the thought of going to Birmingham filled her with such fear? There was a huge quantity of steel to be shipped to the Midlands and it was one of the main cargoes and a good load. Why on earth would she object? The silence went on and her cheeks burned. She felt more and more stupid, as if everyone in the office was watching her. Forcing her hand out, she took the papers and walked shakily out into the fresh morning. She pulled her old cardigan round her and stood for a moment, looking out across the low tide of the dock. She took in a deep breath, smelling the rank mud.

I won't be afraid, she told herself. *I won't let him make me be afraid.* And she turned and marched back to the boats, where the others were waiting.

'Right, let's get going,' she said. 'We're carrying steel to Tyseley.'

'Can you come?'

Dot was standing out in the darkness. They'd tied up

quite late after the first long day of work, of getting used to crewing together again. 'It's Sylvia. In a state. I need you. You know me. Can't think what to say.'

Maryann glanced round her cabin. The children were only just settling for the night.

'I've got to go and see Sylvia for a minute. Go to sleep,' she commanded, fairly certain they would. It had been a hard day and it was late. She felt fluttery with nerves, wondering what was wrong. It was only at times like this that the age gap between Dot and the other two of them became so obvious. Dot hadn't the experience of men and marriage.

It had started to drizzle and Maryann could feel the droplets brushing her face as they stumbled back to the butty in the dark. From inside the *Theodore* came the low sound of Sylvia sobbing. Maryann felt Dot's hand on her arm.

'Thing is,' she whispered, 'she's been all right all day. At least I thought she was. We were just getting ready for bed and I knocked her with my elbow by mistake, when I was taking off my woolly. And she just *crumpled*. I don't know . . . I'm so bad at all this.'

So am I, Maryann thought. She already felt over-wrought because of her own worries, but she was full of unease about what she had seen at Sylvia's house. Not that she'd seen much, but there was just something about the atmosphere, about Roy Cresswell that had disturbed her.

'Let's go in to her,' she whispered to Dot.

Sylvia was sitting on the side bench opposite the stove, on which the dipper stood which she had been using to have a wash. Rose was flat out, asleep on the bigger bed. Sylvia had her blouse unbuttoned down the front and was holding the sides of it together across her chest, arms wrapped round herself, head down and shivering. Maryann cautiously sat beside her.

'Sylv?' she spoke softly, but instinct told her not to touch the woman.

There was a silence before Sylvia said, 'I just can't stop crying.' She sniffed and loosed one arm to search for her hanky. It was the first time Maryann could remember her not having one to hand. She wiped her eyes, but more tears ran down her cheeks, shining in the lamplight. She stared ahead of her. Her shivering seemed to increase in intensity.

Dot picked up the kettle and indicated that she was going outside to fill it from the water can. 'I think we need some tea,' she said.

Into the silence, Maryann whispered, 'What happened?'

Sylvia turned to her, looking into Maryann's eyes as if seaching for something and her own filled with tears again.

'Oh, Maryann, I've tried so hard, for so long.'

'I know,' Maryann said soothingly, sensing it was the right thing to say. 'I know you have.'

Abruptly, Sylvia pulled open her blouse and let it slide down over her shoulders so she was naked but for her brassiere.

'*This* is what happened.'

Even in the poor light Maryann could see the welts, sharp and angry across Sylvia's back and shoulders. Just then Dot climbed back in and stared, wide-eyed, at the sight of Sylvia's back.

'Dear God!' she breathed.

'Oh, Sylvia.' Maryann couldn't hide how appalled she felt either. 'That looks terrible. Why didn't you say before? Those must have hurt so much all day while you were working. Dot, get the kettle on and we'll bathe them for her! Put your blouse on and keep warm a minute, Sylv.' She tried to sound calm, but she felt shaky, horrified at the violence inflicted on Sylvia's back. The marks were big and deep and angry.

'He did most of it with his belt.' Sylvia was sobbing, shaking. She looked up, with frightened eyes. 'The thing is, I think I've just left my marriage.'

The words sunk into the quiet of the room.

'He did that to me last night after we'd got ready for bed. I'd told him I was coming back here, to the boats. He doesn't like me working or doing anything outside the house at all. It's got worse since the children have been away. I suppose he thought they kept me inside, in his control. I never went to bed afterwards, last night. I sat up until he'd fallen asleep and then I got all my things ready bundled up and I left before it was light. Walked for miles. Didn't care. I've . . . I think I've left him,' she said again.

'But – your children?' Dot jiggled the kettle as if hoping this would encourage it to boil faster.

'Well, fortunately they've just gone back for another term.' She drifted off, still hugging herself, rocking slightly back and forth.

'Has he done this to you a lot?' Maryann asked gently.

'No – oh no. Hardly ever. Just once or twice, but never as bad as this. This isn't the worst thing. Not really. At least when he did this he was full of – something that I could see. Something like feeling, anyway.' She glanced at Maryann for a second. 'I'm afraid there's something terribly wrong with my husband. It's taken me years to see exactly. I always thought it was me, you see. That I was doing something wrong.'

Dot poured some warm water into a basin.

'Let us see to those sores, Sylvia, eh?'

'There's a clean hanky of mine under my pillow,' Sylvia said. 'And I've got a bottle of witch hazel – over there.' She pointed. 'There's iodine somewhere.'

Between them, with gentle hands, Maryann and Dot bathed all the welts and cuts and dabbed iodine and witch hazel on the cuts and bruises. Sylvia hissed with pain when they dabbed on the iodine, but she didn't complain. When they'd finished, they helped her ease her nightdress very gingerly over her head and shoulders. Dot made and poured the tea.

'Perhaps you could do with some of this?' Dot held out the whisky bottle.

'Yes,' Maryann and Sylvia said together and Sylvia laughed suddenly.

'Look at us!' she spluttered, voice rising hysterically. 'Dot's even handing it out like medicine!'

'Each one to their poison,' Dot said dryly, pouring a tot into each teacup.

'What did you mean, you thought you were the one in the wrong?' Maryann asked.

For a second Sylvia sagged, leaning her blonde head on Maryann's shoulder. Moved by this, Maryann put her arm gently round Sylvia's waist. After a moment Sylvia braced herself, sitting straight again.

'Roy and I were introduced through a friend of my mother and father. We're both about the same age. He was nice looking – handsome really – and polite. A bit stiff – I noticed it even then, but I thought it was shyness. He liked me, I thought. Oh, I was such a silly thing. I was young and I just thought it was astonishing that any man would like me. Hadn't really had any experience, you see – sheltered life, girls' school. He asked me to marry him quite early on and we got engaged, nice ring, the lot. I mean, it took me quite a time into the marriage to see, *really* see that there was something not right. Roy had been to one of those public schools which can make men a bit sort of stiff and humourless. He was never nasty, exactly, not then. It wasn't anything really that you could put your finger on. He was trying to be pleasant and a few months after the wedding I conceived Kay.' She paused for a moment. 'It took me years to work out that it wasn't me. You couldn't exactly fault Roy. He got a good job in town, he worked hard and we had our children. He was quite considerate, but I always found him very cold, in his feelings. As if he was going through the motions but wasn't really there. That's what I mean about thinking it was me. I thought maybe I couldn't make him feel the right things, make him laugh more or be sort of spontaneous. He's very wooden. I barely knew any other men – not well, and I've no brothers, just Ruth, my sister – so I thought maybe they were all a bit like this and if you were a proper wife you could get round it. I tried so hard. He's always liked me to look the part – you know, nicely dressed and made up. D'you know, I've got to the point where I can't stand my face without make-up now! Silly, isn't it? Anyway, he was all right with the children – not demonstrative, but *proper*. A good provider. But he can't stand change. Not without warning, anyway. I moved the furniture round in the sitting room once while he was at the office and when he came home he was absolutely *furious.*'

She took a drink of tea, then stared bleakly into her mug. 'I've been so lonely. I didn't know how much until I came on here with you two. Actually, just a few months before I came I had to go to my doctor about something. He's a nice man, not one of the sort who talks down to you. Roy had been home on leave then as well and I was feeling very low. Really in the doldrums. He'd been worse than usual – perhaps he found the adjustment to coming home again difficult – but he was cold and silent and wouldn't talk to me or the children. It's like living with a machine, really it is!' She stopped for a moment, fighting back tears.

'He just kept on making these wretched models he's forever building. He's obsessed with them. He gets obsessed with all sorts of odd things ... Anyway, I was so miserable and I didn't have anyone to turn to, and I ended up blurting it all out to the doctor. He was rather wonderful, I must say. He listened and asked me some questions. Then he said, "You really shouldn't be blaming yourself, Mrs Cresswell. I do believe it's not your fault." He told me he thought Roy might have some sort of mental condition. He said there were doctors who'd done new research and that some people were born like Roy, and they can't understand emotions like other people. You see, I felt sometimes, if I looked at Roy and smiled, perhaps, that he was sort of reading my face and waiting to find out what to do before he could smile back. As if he didn't know how without watching me. Anyway – I did feel better thinking he really had something the matter. But then he's still my husband and all these years of living with him have made me feel dead inside. And when the war ends I'd still have to live with it, whether it's my fault or not, and I can't.' She wept again for a moment before going on.

'Yesterday he was very edgy. As bad as I've ever seen him. He was having to go back and he can't stand the fact that I'm on here. He more or less ordered me to give it up and stay at home. He was hateful about it. And I just told him I wasn't going to take any notice of him ... I rather lost my temper. That *stupid* matchstick ship he keeps fiddling about with and never any proper company or conversation. Not ever, really. That was when he came after me.'

She sat silently, shaking her head, before saying, 'What have I done? I can't take in what I've done.'

'But,' Dot said, 'does your husband know you've left? Really left? I mean you could go back – if you wanted.'

'Oh no. No.' Sylvia sat up straight. 'I'm not going back to that. Never. Whatever I have to do – even if I have to live in a potting shed with Kay and Dickie, I'm not living like that any longer. Being here with you two has shown me how much better things can be. I can't go back.'

Maryann watched Sylvia's face, the determined tilt of her chin as she spoke, feeling for her. *But*, she thought, *you can't just stay here! Joel will be back, and Bobby, and we shan't need you.* But she touched Sylvia's hand, and at this sympathy Sylvia's face crumpled again. 'Whatever have I done?' she said. 'What am I going to do?'

Thirty-Two

'Hello there – you're a sight for sore eyes!'

Maryann walked into the toll office at Tyseley, to be greeted by a familiar gap-toothed smile.

'Awright, Charlie?' She felt a grin spread across her own weary features, which immediately froze again as Charlie said, 'Funny you should roll up today. Had a bloke in with a message for you yesterday. Come in special like. Here – what's up with you? Don't you want to hear it?'

'No!' she was already on her way out of the office. They had to leave straight away. How did he know? The very day she was coming back to Birmingham – only hours before and he was here, looking for her! Her chest tightened until she could scarcely breathe and every hair seeming to stand up on her body. *How did he know?* Once more she had the feeling that he knew every move she made, as if he was forever watching.

'Maryann . . .' Charlie ran after her, grasping her arm to stop her. He looked into her eyes and she saw his face change at the fear and desperation he saw there. 'Look – he said he was your brother.' He held her for a moment by her upper arms, then his hands dropped to his sides. He saw her panicky breathing subside a little.

'You all right?' he asked gently.

'My brother? What did he look like?'

'Young. Dark.' Charlie shrugged. 'Thin, like.'

It sounded like Tony. Certainly not like Norman Griffin.

'He said your mom's been took bad – thought she wouldn't last the night. Said if your boats was to come in in the next day or two, you're wanted at home.'

'*Home?*' Maryann laughed bitterly. 'That's a good 'un. Anyroad – ta, Charlie. Sorry for snapping at you.'

He watched for a moment as she set off back along the wharf, arms folded across her wiry form as if holding herself in. She was a smasher, that one, he thought. Worked like a little Trojan.

Maryann slowed her pace and stopped, looking along the wharf towards where their boats were tied up. She stood still, the life of the wharf going on around her, and felt cold and suddenly exhausted. All the way up from Limehouse she'd forced away her dread of coming back here. There was enough else to think about. As well as the everyday busyness of the boats and the family, Sylvia was in pain and Dot was still quietly grieving. She felt for them both and it was easier to think about their problems than face her own. They sat together at night and talked about Roy Cresswell and what on earth Sylvia was going to do, and allowed her to cry and let out some of the anguish over her marriage.

'I never felt loved,' she sobbed one evening. 'Not properly. Not once in twelve years.'

Though they were so fixed on comforting Sylvia, Maryann sometimes noticed Dot looking at her, wondering, and she was sure Dot and Sylvia talked about her, about the nightmares, trying to work her out. But how could she talk to them, bring all the past out into the open? It was dirty and shameful. No one else would ever understand except Janet Lambert. And Amy . . . oh God,

Amy! How could she tell them any of the nightmare that went on in her head day after day?

And now Tony had come. *For what?* she thought angrily. As their mom's messenger? *And what the hell does she want? Me there at her deathbed telling her what a wonderful mother she's been and how she'll go straight to heaven?*

She felt her face twist with hurt and bitterness. If there was anyone she needed to be with while she was here it was Janet Lambert. Janet had been kinder to her than her own mom had ever been. And they were in it together – the hell that was ever having anything to do with Norman Griffin.

But she thought about Tony coming all the way over to Tyseley to find her. He needed her. And she owed him, her little brother, little Tony whom she'd left behind when she ran away from home to join Joel on the cut. She couldn't just ignore him. She'd tell Sylvia and Dot that they would have to delay leaving.

'We're going to visit your grandmother's house.'

She couldn't call her mother any of those pet names – Nana, Nanny, like she'd called her dad's mother, Nanny Firkin. Just the cold truth. Your grandmother. My mother.

'Have we seen her before?' Joley asked, puzzled, as they set out the next day. She took all the children except Rose, who begged to stay with Sylvia. There was enough for Dot and Sylvia to do on the wharf without minding all her kids again, and she wanted them to see Tony. It was a Sunday, but as they waited for the bus into Birmingham, Maryann thought for a moment that the atmosphere of the morning was missing something. It was too quiet. Of course, it was missing the sound she remembered from childhood – church bells. The war meant that they were still not allowed to ring out and the street felt eerily deserted.

It was only a short distance from the middle of town to Ladywood. As they walked through the familiar streets, Maryann experienced the mixture of feelings that returning to the neighbourhood always aroused in her: of recognition, of a deep sense of belonging, but also of anxiety and vulnerability. She was back in the home of her young years and it made her feel like a child again. She didn't want to do the things which might have recalled a happier childhood – to take her own children to the house in Garrett Street and say, 'Look – that's the house I grew up in. That's where me and Auntie Sal played.' Their Auntie Sal was long dead and the house a place of grim memory. Her mother had moved out of it after Norman Griffin left her; forced deeper into poverty, she had gone to a house in a yard on Sheepcote Lane.

Court Two, it said over the narrow entrance to the yard.

'Does she live up here?' Sally said, puzzled.

'Yes, she does – oi, stop that, you'll end up black as the ace of spades!' Maryann snapped at the boys as they rubbed their hands along the slimy walls of the entry.

The children had never been anywhere quite like it before. These houses made even Alice Simons's little terrace in Oxford look spacious and the brickwork was crumbling and caked in soot and dirt.

Maryann saw Tony immediately. He was standing at the door of the house, blowing a blue stream of cigarette smoke from his lips. The other side of the yard, beyond the washing line, from which hung a single pair of limp, yellowed long johns, was a tap, fixed to the high wall and constantly dripping. A rotten smell drifted along the yard from the rubbish heap down the end.

Maryann led her children across the dirty blue bricks, her brother watching them approach, though he didn't move. He looked so much older, she thought. What was he now – twenty-three? A father with a small child, aged and pinched in the face. She felt a pang of pity for him, trapped here in this static life.

'You got my message then,' he stated.

'This is your uncle Tony – remember?' Maryann said as the children stood looking. Ada and Esther loosed her hands and wandered off across the yard.

'Don't go messing with anything,' she called after them, without much hope of being obeyed. 'What's happened?' she asked Tony. 'How is she?'

'She went. Last night.'

Maryann nodded. She felt a lurch of emotion inside her, but that was all. And she knew that it consisted as much of relief as of sorrow that she would not see her mother alive again. 'What took her then?'

Tony shrugged. 'She were bad with her chest.'

The older children waited, taking everything in.

'Are we going to see our grandmother?' Sally asked solemnly.

'No, bab. She's passed on. Last night.'

There was a silence.

'How's your Dolly – and the babby?'

'All right.' Tony crushed the remains of the cigarette under his heel. 'Joanie's getting big. Dolly's got another on the way.'

'Oh – that's nice.' How quickly time passed, she thought, their lives moving on.

'I'd better see her then,' she said, as Tony didn't

volunteer anything else, and he stood back to let her in. 'Joley, you all stay out here and keep an eye on the twins for now. You can come in a bit later.'

Inside, she asked, 'Who was looking after her – anyone?'

'Couple of neighbours. Mrs Biggs.' He nodded towards number four. 'Lives over there. It went quick in the end. Someone came over to fetch me Friday night. The undertaker's coming later.'

Undertaker, Maryann thought grimly, clattering up the bare staircase. That had been the start of it all: her father's death. The undertaker – Norman Griffin. She'd never been deceived by him, even then, she thought. Perhaps that was what had saved her sanity – not like Sal, who'd tried to believe in him, let herself be beguiled by the sweet talking, the outings to the cinema and his offer of a job working for him. Maryann had loathed him from the very first time he had set foot in their house.

Stepping into her mother's room, even now, when there had been so little feeling between them, tears of pity came to her eyes at the state to which Flo had been reduced. The bare room with its crumbling walls, without so much as a peg rug to relieve the splintered grime of the floorboards, was bigger than Maryann's whole living space in the *Esther Jane*'s cabin, but without one iota of its intimate cosiness. This room was bleak, its only furniture the single iron bedstead, a rickety chair by the bed and an old chest of drawers.

Maryann sank down on the chair. She barely recognized her mother. In her prime Flo had been a voluptuous, stately woman with thick hair of a natural blonde which had kept its fine colour until she was well on in years. It was a sickly grey now. She was thinner, yet her face seemed to have lengthened, making her look different, and the flesh of her cheeks had become slightly bloated and puffy. Had it not been for her familiar profile, her large nose, Maryann would have had difficulty in recognizing her.

She sat struggling to think how old her mother would have been. When was she born? 1890, she thought she remembered. Fifty-four then. She stared at the yellowish face there beside her. Flo looked twenty years older.

She hadn't expected her tears. Her heart had been hardened against her mother for so long. When she had left this house it was with Flo's screams of condemnation in her ears, words spat out with loathing – that she had been the ruin of them all, that everything that had happened in the family had been her fault because she was a liar who'd turned their stepfather against them. It was her fault that her mother was reduced to live in utter poverty. Maryann had barely wept over it then, but the tears came now. They came when she remembered other things she had long shut out of her thoughts: how Flo had been when they were all small, during the Great War and after. She'd been harassed and often beside herself with worry, it was true. And when Maryann's father, Harry, came home a shell of the man he'd been, her worry and anxiety increased. But Maryann's father had been a good, kind man and Flo, then, a strong woman. She was never a tender mother, more tough and matter of fact. But Maryann could remember being held in her lap, the rich sound of laughter that could rise up from her. She recalled being sent out with halfpennies for sweets. And, above all, she remembered that once the days had felt normal and untroubled. Back then, such a long time ago, she had felt safe. With her hands over her face, she felt tears run out through her fingers. Sobs were wrung out of her from somewhere deep inside and she knew she was crying not just for her mom, but for her lovely dad as well, for both her parents with all the hardships they'd had to face. And for herself too, for all they'd once been before the war, before that motor car knocked her father down one afternoon and he never came home again.

She didn't know how long she had been sitting there, but after a time she heard feet on the stairs and Tony appeared with a cup of tea, stirring in the sugar as he came into the room.

'Here y'are, sis.'

'Ta, Tony.' She wiped her eyes, dazed. 'Are the kids all right?'

He went and stood looking out through the dirty window, hands in his pockets. 'They're in the yard.' She thought how deep his voice was now, how his skinny body already sagged, as if worn down.

'What's next?' she asked, feeling somehow that he was older now and knew what to do.

'She'll be buried, Tuesday.'

'I don't think I can stay.'

'No.' There was a pause.

'Sorry, Tony.'

He turned. 'S'all right.'

She sipped the tea. It tasted funny now, with stera. She was used to fresh milk.

'It's a shame,' she said.

His eyes followed her gaze round the room.

'She wasn't always like this. Did you come and see her much?'

'She daint like Dolly. I come of a Sunday sometimes – just to see she was all right, like. Billy never come. He hasn't been near for years.'

After a moment she asked, 'D'you remember our dad?'

Tony turned to the window again, his head dark against the light. 'A bit. Not much. I remember the day he passed away.'

'You were hardly more than a babby. And then Nanny Firkin passed on. And *he* was there by then.'

Tony didn't say anything. Maryann knew he understood what Norman Griffin had done to his sisters, that he believed her, had seen and heard things he knew should not have been done. But he didn't want to talk about it. Not again.

'Did she . . .' She trailed off, hardly able to put into words what she wanted to ask. 'Did she ever say anything about him – you know, regrets – that she knew . . . about him? What he did?'

Tony hesitated, then shook his head.

Pain roused itself in her again. 'Nothing – ever?'

'Look, Sis – ' he came over to see if her tea was finished – 'just leave it. It were years ago. She's passed on now.'

Maryann looked up into her brother's dark eyes. 'I know, Tony – but he hasn't.'

'We'd best get cracking then,' she said when they were downstairs. 'The landlord'll want the house after Tuesday.'

She was looking round the tiny downstairs room when the sound of yells and shouts of pain came from the yard. Tony ran out.

'Oi!' she heard him shouting. 'Pack that in! Get off of him!'

'You didn't hear what he called me!' Maryann went

to the door to find Joley, fists clenched and puce with fury, being pulled off another, bigger lad by Tony, who had to clamp both arms round him to restrain him. Ezra, though, was busy landing a punch on another boy who'd appeared in the yard.

'Ezzy – stop it!' Maryann ran to him and hoiked him away. 'What's going on?'

'Fuckin' water rats!' the older boy shouted. He had a thin, unhealthy look and was wearing long shorts that looked too tight and no shoes on his blackened feet. Maryann saw his nose was bleeding and he was wiping it on the sleeve of his shirt. He backed away, shouting, 'Water rats, water rats! Gyppos!'

'You shut up!' Sally yelled, defending her brothers. 'You're dirtier than us – what're you calling us names for, eh?'

Joley suddenly managed to twist free of Tony and launched himself on the other boy, who although bigger had not expected a water rat to have the strength acquired by working narrowboats from a young age. Joley ran at him and punched him hard in the belly and he sank with a groan.

'What's all this fucking racket about?' An elderly man with a furious, drinker's face appeared out of another house along the yard. 'Who're you lot? Clear off and stop making all this fucking carry-on!' He waved his arms and there were suddenly two large women there as well, carrying on about gyppos and rough, nasty brats and how the likes of them oughtn't to be allowed near the place, mixing with ordinary people. Maryann managed to get all the children into the house, her temper raging.

'My family's worth ten of you cowing slum roaches! Go on – you can all bugger off back indoors now, you nosy bastards!' She slammed the front door so hard it shuddered.

'I remember why I wanted to get away from this bloody place now!' She was still shouting inside the house. Seeing the children all grinning with apparent approval at this outburst, she lowered her voice. 'Fighting's no way to carry on,' she scolded. 'Don't do it again. Come on, Tony – let's get this house cleared and get out. There can't be much to get through. And you kids'll have to find something to do in here – I don't want you going out in the yard again, d'you hear?'

She found a dog-eared pack of cards in the one little cupboard in the downstairs room and told the children to make do with them.

'It won't take all that long,' she said. 'There's hardly anything in the house.'

'I don't like it here,' Sally said miserably.

'It looks as if most of this is only fit for burning,' Maryann said to Tony, her face creasing with disgust. 'That old chair looks riddled with vermin. How long's she been living like this?'

Tony shrugged. 'I dunno. I s'pose she just let it all go.'

When they had finished, Maryann carried Flo's small collection of clothes down to the pawn shop. She walked back along the road looking around her, curious to see the old houses and entries and hucksters shops, yet still uneasy. She could never be free in this neighbourhood. It was too full of ghosts.

She sorted out the scullery, going through her mother's few pots and pans. Anything useful she and Tony divided between them.

'There's some papers and stuff in here,' Tony said, opening a drawer at the bottom of the small cupboard.

308

'Don't look like anyfing much. Will you have a look, sis? You were always better at reading, like.'

Maryann sat at the table with the thin sheaf of papers, most of them yellowed with age. The birth certificates of the four Nelson children were there. She stared sorrowfully at Sal's for a moment, then put them aside. *Don't think about it*, she told herself. *Don't start wallowing.* To her surprise, the next sheet of paper was a receipt for payment from her father's funeral all those years ago. Whyever hadn't Flo thrown it out? Perhaps she had felt it was one of the few things she had left of Harry. She stared grimly at the fragile sheet of paper with *N. Griffin & Son, Undertakers* in faded black ink at the top. *Had* Norman Griffin ever really had a son? she wondered, frowning. If so, she'd certainly never met him. She tore up the paper into tiny pieces. As she was looking through the rest of her mother's old, pathetic paperwork, a card fell out from between the sheets into her lap. It was whiter, newer than the rest. In blue ink it read, *Albert Griffin, Toolmakers & Machinists.*

'Tony – come and have a look at this.'

Tony glanced at the card over her shoulder. 'What about it?' he said, moving away.

Maryann frowned at it, the horrible realization only fully dawning on her now.

'It's him, isn't it?'

'Who?'

'Oh, don't be bloody dense, Tony!' She stood up, scattering the rest of the papers. 'You know who! Is this who he is now? Has he been here? Has she been seeing him?'

'No!' Tony raised his voice so that the children all turned to look. 'I mean – I dunno! I dunno anyfing about him or who he is and I don't want to!'

Maryann felt as if she'd been punched.

'God in heaven,' she gasped, 'it *is*. I know it's him. After all this – all that happened and she'd *see* him . . .' She looked up wildly at Tony. 'She didn't take him back, did she?'

'No! Of course not. Why the hell would she do that?'

'I don't know . . .' Maryann's hand went to her head, as if rubbing it might make things clearer. Why should she be surprised that Flo would have her stepfather back in her house? After all, she had never wanted him to leave. She had blamed Maryann for driving him away, her source of financial security. She'd never believed anything Maryann said, anyway.

She dragged her eyes back to the card again. The address of the works was in Highgate. Face set grimly, she slipped the card into her pocket.

Thirty-Three

When they got back to Tyseley that evening, Maryann found Dot and Sylvia sitting out on the *Theodore*. Both boats had been unloaded and were riding high in the water. Sylvia stood up on the counter and waved when she saw them coming along the wharf.

'We've got a potful of tea here!' she beckoned. 'Come and sit down for a bit. You must have had a lousy day.' When they'd all clambered aboard, Sylvia put her arm round Maryann's shoulder. 'Poor old you. I remember when my mother died – I felt as if the stuffing had been knocked out of me for weeks.'

'We weren't close,' Maryann said. She spoke so tersely that she was immediately ashamed. 'I mean – I've hardly seen her in years.' She knew Sylvia's sympathy was well intended but she felt like a fraud. What grief and loss did she really feel for Flo? Nothing, but for that glimpse of the young woman she had once been, too long ago for Maryann to remember clearly. 'Me and Tony've cleared the house. There's only the funeral now.'

'Well, I think you're being very brave,' Sylvia said, handing Maryann her tea.

Maryann smiled absently. She didn't feel grief or sorrow at this moment. In her mind all evening, as she sat with Dot and Sylvia and they told her how the unloading had gone and that they'd managed to stove both boats in her absence to get rid of the bugs, was the thought of the card pushed into the pocket of her cardigan with its blue lettering.

Longing to be alone, she told them she wanted an early night.

'We were thinking of popping out for a bit – see if we can find a pub that's not too soul-destroying,' Dot said.

'But we won't if you'd rather we didn't,' Sylvia said hastily.

'No – that's all right. You go,' Maryann said.

Even when she was by herself on the *Esther Jane* later on, the children bedded down for the night, she still didn't give any thought to the fact that she and the children were alone. Her head was too full of other things. She took out the card and propped it against the alarm clock near her head. She lay on her stomach in bed, staring at it in the candlelight. The words seemed to ripple and flicker as the flame moved gently. *Albert Griffin, Albert Griffin . . .*

'Should've been a bit cleverer than that, shouldn't you?' she whispered. 'Calling yourself Griffin again.'

Thinking of him, of all he'd done, she felt herself clench up inside with anger and her own sense of defilement. And Flo had, at some time, seen him again, perhaps had him visit her house . . . However much she told herself she had no feeling left for her mother, that she didn't care what she'd done, now she knew pain and outrage flooded through her until she could scarcely breathe. Once more she made herself force the thoughts aside. If she let them take her over, they would destroy her. She had protected herself from him so far as well as she could – she wasn't going to let it happen now.

Turning onto her side, she looked at Sally's sleeping face beside her, the pale hair in disarray on the pillow, and smiled at the thought of her yelling at those boys in

Flo's yard. She was glad to know her daughter had more mettle in her than she would seem to have from her angelic looks. Very lightly, Maryann stroked her head.

Tomorrow, Albert Griffin, *I'm going to the police*, she thought. *And then they'll have you*. Settling herself, she blew out the candle and the smell of its waxy smoke was the last thing in the darkness before she slept.

She was in a tunnel. It wasn't Blisworth Tunnel or Braunston. She knew that. It wasn't the same: it was much, much longer and there was no reassuring keyhole of light at the end, the tiny beacon to which the front of the boats could be directed. There was a path to one side. As it was completely dark, she could feel rather than see how narrow it was. It was barely more than a ledge and certainly not wide enough to lead a horse. She was making her way along it, moving sideways, her right arm scrabbling forward along the slimy bricks for finger-holds, her left arm stretched out on the other side to help her remain close to the wall and not topple off into the water. She seemed to move so, so slowly, her progress impossible to measure in the dark, and there was no light drawing closer, bringing hope of release. Although the sound of a boat came from somewhere in the distance, she didn't know whose boat it was or which way it was moving. The echoes in the tunnel mixed directions into confusion. All she could hear were the muffled sounds of the motor and the drip of water, close and loud from the roof of the tunnel. She cried out for the boat to come and help her, to get her out, but it was too far away, its engine throbbing and she couldn't make herself heard over its noise. She couldn't make out its headlamp in either direction. As she struggled along agonizingly slowly, she began to hear the other sound: the breathing. She knew it was his breathing and it was becoming louder than anything else in the tunnel, the echo swelling, bloating the sound until it seemed to be all round her. He was there – behind her? In front of her? Seemingly everywhere, not speaking, only breathing, the sound moving closer all the time. Somewhere in the wall she knew there was a door, a niche cut into the tunnel that only he knew the position of. That was where he wanted to take her, to lock her away! Behind the door of the hidden cupboard he kept an upright wooden chair. A chair, the same one he'd had in the cupboard of his undertaker's business. The chair he tied Sal to . . . She tried to hurry, nails scrabbling at the wall. Yet she didn't know where he was coming from, her left or her right, and his breathing was moving closer, its secure, unhurried rhythm gaining on her until she was sure she felt his breath on her neck . . .

The dream seemed to last for an eternity, as she clung, suspended in darkness, and at last started to fall backwards, throwing herself into the black water, anything to get away from him. She woke with an anguished cry, her body soaked in sweat. For a moment, in her confused state, the rain on the cabin roof seemed oppressive and terrifying. She knew she couldn't just lie there: the darkness wouldn't release her from the world of the dream. She groped for the box of matches and lit the candle, sitting up, tightly hugging her knees, weeping and shivering, rocking herself to try and find comfort. She looked round at the familar lines of the cabin, the range, the coalbox and dipper, Ada and Esther sprawled together on the floor, her clothes, bolts of colour at the foot of her bed. It was a long time before she stopped shaking and could begin to see things more normally, though the dream still lurked close to the surface. When would this ever end? she thought, like a howl inside herself.

It was getting on for five in the morning. It would be light soon. She hadn't heard Dot and Sylvia come back from the pub, she realized. And it was only then she remembered that she had allowed herself to be left alone with the boats at Tyseley! Thank goodness she hadn't thought of it while they were away! She'd been so tired the night before.

As they were staying, not loading up, today, there was no need to rise early. She bedded down again for more sleep, blowing out the candle, dreading another onset of the dream. Its images crowded in the moment she closed her eyes and for a time she fought with them. At last she slept.

'Here we are, my love!'

The hatches opened and Sylvia's face appeared, smiling against the sunlight. Spots the black and white cat tore in past her legs and jumped up onto Maryann's feet.

'Goodness – what's got into him?' Sylvia climbed in, carrying a cup of tea. 'He nearly knocked me down the steps. Here – drink it while it's hot.'

Maryann sat up blearily and looked round at the clock. 'Half-past eight! Ta, Sylv. Where are the twins?'

'We came and fetched them out a good hour ago. And Ezra. Dot and I thought it'd be good if you got all the sleep under your belt that you could. She's taken them off to get more bread. Have a good night?'

Maryann nodded a lie. She didn't want to mention her nightmare. To her discomfort she felt tears come into her eyes at this kindness and managed to mumble,

'Thanks,' feeling frustrated that she couldn't find more words to express her gratitude to them both. When Nance had died she'd thought she'd never have a good friend again, but now she'd been through so many things with these two women that she felt closer to them than she'd ever imagined possible and that was also part of her tearfulness.

'Cheer up.' Sylvia looked tired and strained herself, but she smiled sympathetically into Maryann's face. 'Look – you must go to the funeral tomorrow. It's not right to miss your own mother's funeral, whatever you feel about her. Dot and I were wondering whether we should try and work a day trip today and come back. Only we've left it a bit late now ... Of course, we could come to the funeral with you – help with the children.'

'Don't go,' Maryann heard herself say. She suddenly couldn't bear the thought of being left alone here. 'You have left it a bit late to get going – and I *would* like you to come.' She felt her cheeks go red. 'If you don't mind. It's not much of a treat for you.'

'Oh, don't be silly. Of course we will.'

'I've got a few things to get done today ...'

'Right – well, let's all take it easy for once. And I tell you what – I'm going to treat us all to fish and chips tonight, as well!'

'Mom! Mom – come and look!' Ezra appeared on the steps, his dark eyes wide.

'What's up?' His voice told her immediately that something was really wrong.

'Quick—' He beckoned, and was gone again.

She wasn't yet dressed, but pulled on her winter coat over her nightdress. It felt too hot in the warm May morning, but she followed Sylvia up out of the *Esther Jane*, and on the towpath they looked along and saw

Ezra with Rose and the twins at the front of the boat, standing silently, their eyes fixed on something.

'What's going on?' Sylvia said.

Joining the children, their eyes followed the others' to the little mast. Hanging from a short length of rope was Jenny the tortoiseshell cat. The rope was twisted tightly round her neck and her body dangled from it, stiff and bedraggled from the night's rain. The neck was at an odd angle. There was no movement, no life left in her.

'Oh, Jennykins!' Sylvia's hand went to her mouth. 'Oh, that's horrible! How did that...? Someone must've ... mustn't they? Who on earth would have done that?'

Maryann turned away, beginning to tremble. She could feel herself going to pieces. She'd seen enough to know immediately: could not bear to take in the sight any longer. Even while she'd been dreaming of his hot breath on her skin he'd been out here. He liked to inflict pain. He took relish in exactly this kind of cruelty. She had seen it all before, her own childhood kitten Tiger dead at his hand. She remembered leaving her cold, dead body under a pile of leaves on the bank by the cut. And once again he had known their boats were here. This more than anything chilled her blood. *How did he know?* And what was the message of this? It was all too clear: *I'm here. I'm waiting.*

Sylvia was trying to comfort the children, and as she hurried back to the cabin to dress, Dot had just come back with the twins.

'What's all the kerfuffle about?' she asked cheerfully.

But Maryann was already heading past her, back to her cabin.

'I've got things to do,' she announced. 'I'm going out. Now.'

317

Thirty-Four

'Maryann –' Sylvia's voice was terse with tension and anxiety – 'you really must stop shutting us all out. You know who did that to Jennykins, don't you?'

They were all gathered in the *Theodore* that evening and the air smelt tantalizingly of the fish and chips and tangy vinegar that Dot had fetched on Bobby's bicycle, which he had kindly left for them to use. The children were wolfing down the food.

'Sorry,' Maryann said, 'for taking off and leaving you with it all today. The kids and that. I'm ever so grateful.'

'But where've you *been*?' Sylvia burst out. 'We've been beside ourselves wondering what's going on. You do know who did it, don't you?'

Maryann saw all the children's eyes swivel towards her. 'Oh, some nasty man I expect. I don't s'pose he'll ever do it again.' She gave Dot and Sylvia a look which said, *later*. She could only pick at the fish and chips with difficulty, even though they were a treat. She felt sick and full of inner turmoil.

'You can come and have a drink with us later,' Sylvia said.

'No!' Maryann almost shouted. 'I mean – no, sorry. I don't want to leave the kids on their own. Not tonight.'

It had been agonizing enough leaving them in the day. She had spent hours moving round the city.

'I've got to go out again,' she'd told Sylvia in the

morning. 'I wish I could take everyone with me, but I can't. Just keep them close – don't let them out of your sight, *please*.'

'I won't,' Sylvia said. 'I promise.' She was obviously deeply unnerved by what had happened. 'Maryann – where're you going?'

'Tell you later.'

First she went to the police.

'This is the man you're looking for,' she announced, handing over the card. She grasped folds of her skirt, pleating them with her fingers to hold herself steady, to stop her screaming and making an exhibition of herself.

'I see.' It was the same policeman she'd seen the last time. He thought she was bonkers, she was certain.

'I grew up with him.' She was almost begging, trying not to weep. *Believe me, for God's sake, someone please believe me.* 'I *know* it was him. He's cruel and violent and . . .' She couldn't go on, couldn't speak, could only squeeze on the folds of her cotton skirt until she thought the bones in her hands would crack.

'We'll look into it,' the policeman said calmly. Why was he so calm? she thought, infuriated.

'He's got a scarred face. A terrible, hideous face . . .' Oh, this sounded ridiculous, like something she'd made up. For a split second she doubted herself. Had Norman Griffin simply been the stuff of her nightmares? Then she thought of her sister, of what he had reduced her to. 'He's dangerous,' she gulped. 'You mustn't let him get away. He killed Amy Lambert – I know he did.'

Afterwards she went to see Janet, Amy's mother, to tell her the news, to try and bring her some comfort, even though she felt so agitated herself. Janet seemed to have turned into an old woman just in the past weeks. With Amy's funeral now over she was calmer, but the pain of loss was written in every line of her face. When Maryann told her she was sure she had found Norman Griffin's new premises, Janet stared back at her fearfully.

'I just wish – ' her already watery blue eyes filled with tears – 'I wish he'd just disappear . . . that it was all over . . . I just want my Amy back.' She sobbed brokenly and Maryann tried to give comfort, knowing that really there was none.

Late in the afternoon she walked through Highgate. The address on the card was Cheapside, almost at the bottom of the hill. Maryann walked down the long slope of Cheapside, factories on either side all the way down, the clang and clatter, the drone of machines, the shouts above the noise, coming at her from everywhere. Her eyes darted from side to side. She felt as if everyone must be staring at her, at her clothes, her dirty boots, as if her every thread shouted 'boatwoman', and here she was, born in Ladywood, but feeling like a foreigner in her own town! What really frightened her was that she might meet him, that he would appear from somewhere, out of a factory or one of the side alleys, with his box-like body, those wide, square shoulders, hat pulled down to hide his face. That she would have to look into his eyes again.

She saw the sign from a short distance away: *Albert Griffin, Toolmakers & Machinists.* For a moment she doubted herself. Could he really have anything to do with this place? It was certainly a new line of business for him. He'd been an undertaker for years – would he go into toolmaking instead?

The factory had quite a narrow frontage, but the buildings reached back some way from the street. For a moment she stopped, almost paralysed with nerves, as if the factory had an invisible electric fence round it that she did not dare to pass.

For goodness sake, she urged herself, *I'm only walking past down the road. It'll look even odder if I stop.* Her hands were so sweaty she had to wipe them on her skirt.

There was nothing to see. The doors were shut and no one came in or out. She hurried past and turned, relieved, back onto Bradford Street, where the trams went rattling past and things felt safer again.

But I know *it's him*, she told herself, hurrying away. Her heart was still pounding. Why else would Mom have had that card in her house?

She thought again of Jenny the cat, hanging by the neck from that scrap of rope. A chill went through her which grew into panic. All she wanted was to get home.

She wouldn't go back to the *Theodore* with Dot and Sylvia once the children were in bed. The three of them stood outside, coats on against the chilly evening.

'Maryann, we're your friends. At least, we want to be, don't we, Dot?'

Maryann stood with her arms folded, closed in on herself as the others tried to get her to talk.

'You've seen us both through a lot. You've been a real brick – and so kind.' Sylvia stepped closer, as if to embrace her, but Maryann stepped back. She didn't want to be touched.

'It'd make you feel better,' Dot said gruffly. 'To talk, I mean. Goodness knows, I'm bad enough at opening up. But after Steven died – well, you did a lot for me.'

But that's different! Maryann wailed in her head. *You loved your brother and he died. That's natural. It's clean*

– not like this, not like him *and all he's done! How can I tell you? Things like this don't happen to people like you – you're different. Or I'm different: that's what it is.*

She stared out at the water beyond, at the broken light reflected in the ripples. There was a smell of frying onions coming from another boat. Inside her the worst thought of all swelled, unspoken. *If I told you, you'd never believe me. You'd think I was a liar and you'd find me disgusting.*

'What is it, Maryann?' Sylvia said softly. 'Can't you trust us? I saw your face this morning and you were really frightened, I could tell.'

'You're even frightened in your sleep.' Dot spoke with such sympathy suddenly that Maryann felt an unbearable tightening in her throat. A pool of unshed tears seemed to press behind her eyes.

'You know who killed little Jenny, don't you?' Sylvia persisted.

Maryann turned to them. She had to tell them something. It was such an odd, horrible thing to have happened.

'I think it was a man called Norman Griffin. He was my stepfather.'

There was a silence. She saw Sylvia and Dot glance at each other.

'But *why?*' Dot said. 'He must be quite mad.'

'He's not very nice, no,' she said flatly. All energy went out of her suddenly. The tears subsided. She couldn't say more, couldn't begin on it. After the funeral they'd get away from here again and she could feel safe, keep away from Birmingham, leave it up to the police to catch him. She could put it all away again.

'I just don't want him anywhere near my family, that's all. It makes me a bit jumpy sometimes. That's

why I asked you to keep an eye on them, Sylv. Anyroad
– it's been a long day. I'm going to bed now.'

She could feel them watching her as she opened the
hatches of the *Esther Jane*

''Night, 'night,' she said.

She knew they were perfectly aware that she wasn't
telling them all of the truth. *They're not stupid*, she
thought, climbing over the twins to her bed. *But I can't
– I just can't. What would they think of me?*

Lying in bed, she felt wide awake. It was a relief
because she dreaded the dreams. She lay in the dark for
ages, listening for any sound outside.

Thirty-Five

They woke early the next morning and a light mist hung over the water, the sky colourless and hazy. It seemed to Maryann that she hadn't slept at all, but she did not feel tired. She was in too wound up a state for that. Even before her morning cup of tea – once more made by Sylvia – she was full of agitated energy.

The night before they had decided that, instead of leaving the boats and resorting to buses and trams, they would take the *Esther Jane* across town to where they could walk to the cemetery. Maryann had sent a message to Tony to say that they were not going to join the modest funeral procession across from Ladywood. Dot got the engine going, while Maryann and Sylvia finished getting everyone dressed.

'Neither Dot nor I have anything really suitable to wear for a funeral!' Sylvia said, slipping a frock over Ada's head. Her wiry little arms thrust up through the sleeves.

'Can't say I have either,' Maryann said. 'Never mind. We'll just have to make the best of it. There'll be hardly anyone there except Tony and Billy.'

She found, almost to her shame, that she was quite looking forward to the day. It was a change, after all – another day off before all the hard work began again, and a chance to see her brothers. Tony had said Billy was coming home on leave for the funeral. Perhaps she might get to know him a bit better, to feel he really was her brother.

They had breakfast moving along. After they'd crossed town they moved onto the Worcester Canal, chugging along past Davenport's Brewery, its bitter, hop smell filling the air. The sun began to break through and melt away the mist, and the air started to feel warm and muggy, so they laid some of the bedding out to air. They passed carriers whom they didn't normally see, clothed-up pairs of boats from the Severn Canal Carrying Company, which transported goods out to the West Country, out through the long tunnel at Tardebigge and down to the Severn.

'I haven't been down here in a good while,' Maryann said to Dot, as she stood out with her eating breakfast. Familiar landmarks moved past them, Sturges's Chemical Works, the tunnel at Edgbaston, the copper works at Selly Oak. It was a stretch full of poignancy for Maryann. It was one of the greenest parts of the cut in Birmingham and today the trees were covered in fresh spring leaves. She remembered coming along here on another lovely day with Nancy and Darius when they were first falling in love and how she, seeing what was between them, had fretted and tried to prevent it: Nancy was married then to Mick Mallone. How ridiculous her worries seemed now, when Nancy had only had such a brief time of happiness with Darius. This sadness added itself to all the rest. For a moment, as they brushed through the green light of overhanging branches, she was filled with a hard, hungry ache for Joel. For him to be at her side, to feel him holding her. She felt surprised, ashamed even, at how little she had missed him in the last few weeks, how she had grown used to his absence. But it couldn't be long now before he would be strong enough to come back. And then, she realized with another pang, she would have to say goodbye to Sylvia and Dot, and she knew how much she didn't want to lose them either.

They tied up at Selly Oak and walked to the gates of Lodge Hill Cemetery in time to meet the carriage bringing Flo's body.

'Well, we look a motley crew, don't we?' Dot said as they set off. It was the first time Maryann had ever seen Dot in a skirt, straight, tightly fitting and navy blue, and she had complained like anything when she tried to squeeze into it.

'I've put on pounds doing this job! Good heavens, I can hardly do it up at the waist!'

'Never mind – you look as healthy as a hunter,' Sylvia told her.

'Well, it's not fair,' Dot protested, going red in the face as she breathed in, trying to do up the zip. 'You and Maryann stay as thin as twigs and I rush about far more than either of you!' She had to resort to leaving the top button undone. They had all put their coats on, even though it was quite warm, in order to look a bit smarter.

The funeral cortège was as basic as it could be because there was no money in the family. In the event, the only mourner apart from the family was a neighbour of Flo's, a middle-aged, corpulent lady called Mrs Biggs, who waddled towards them in front of Maryann's brothers, in her hat and coat. She had dark, thick brows and prominent cheeks, above which her deepset eyes appeared only just able to see out. She nodded with sharp disapproval at Maryann.

'I were a friend of your mother's,' she said, adding tartly, 'somebody had to be,' before turning away.

Walking beside Tony was a tall young man with fair

hair, dressed smartly in Air Force blue. He was the taller of the two and, although Maryann knew it had to be Billy, it still took her a moment to recognize him.

Her hand went to her mouth, 'Oh, my word, look at him!'

As he came closer, she saw that he was handsome and big-boned like their mother had been. *He looks like our mom and Sal*, she thought, *and he must be all of twenty now*. His eyes were vivid blue and he had a cropped RAF haircut.

'Here's Uncle Tony,' she said to the children. 'And this is Uncle Billy.'

Billy looked round at them all and nodded, though he didn't smile. 'Maryann. All right?' was all he said, and that quite abruptly. The cold expression in his eyes made Maryann sink inside and she turned away, hurt. *Well, I suppose I never was much of a sister to him*, she thought. *Or not so's he remembers, anyroad.*

Even though Dot and Sylvia were there, she felt terribly alone as they walked behind the carriage taking her mother's body into the cemetery. Mrs Biggs's hostility and the coldness of Billy's greeting sunk deep into her. *Oh, Sal, you ought to be here with me now*, she thought, *not lying six foot under already, with our mom coming to join you. We should be doing this together.*

They reached the plot that had been reserved beside Sal's and their father's graves. Maryann saw Sylvia and Dot discreetly reading the words on the headstones. Sylvia's eyes lingered on SALLY ANNE GRIFFIN, 1913–28, and Maryann saw her wondering how Sal had died when she was only fifteen. How could she begin to explain?

She barely noticed the undertakers bringing her mother's coffin to the graveside. Standing by Sal's grave again she felt desperate to see her, to be able to pour out all her troubles. Sal was the one person who would have understood.

He's back, Sal, she told her in her head. *And I'm so scared. He's worse than before. He's killed Amy, murdered her, and he's always there. He always seems to know where we are. I can't sleep, I can't think properly ... I wish there was someone could help me.* Had she been alone she might have broken down and wept then, but Sylvia was nudging her. The burial was about to begin.

'D'you think we'd better pick these two up?' Sylvia nodded down at the twins.

Maryann lifted Esther up and Sylvia took Ada. No good having them running off in the middle of it. The other four children stood solemnly in a line in front of them.

'I am the resurrection and the life,' the vicar was saying. Maryann felt some comfort from the old, formal words and from her daughter's warm, plump body in her arms.

As the body of her mother was lowered into the grave, she glanced across at her brothers, who stood on the other side. Tony had his head lowered, cap in his hand. She saw him wipe his eyes as the earth rattled onto the coffin and felt sorry for him. Poor Tony – he was always the soft lad. He was also the only one who'd been really close to Mom. Billy, however, stood very upright, in a military stance, hands behind his back. His cool blue eyes gazed beyond them all at the trees behind. Little Billy, the round toddler she used to bath and sit on her knee, while he chuckled and bounced. She wanted him to know that, to reach out to him.

When it was over, they walked slowly away from the

family graves through the peaceful cemetery. The children, released at last, began to run and jump ahead of them, loving the open space and the trees to dodge round to let off steam.

Dot and Sylvia walked together, each leading a twin by the hand, discreetly allowing the family to be together. Mrs Biggs collared Tony and Maryann went to walk beside Billy. He seemed even taller than she'd realized, with a long, muscular stride.

'How you keeping?' she asked nervously.

'All right. Going back tomorrow.' She knew he was in Coastal Command. She asked questions, but he wouldn't be drawn about it and they lapsed into silence. Maryann looked down, watching her old boots with their scuffed toecaps moving over the dry ground. She heard Joley and Ezra shouting to each other in the distance, knew she ought to tell them to quieten down, but she didn't want to move away.

'Billy –' she looked up at him, but he didn't turn his head – 'I know I haven't been much of a sister to you – not being here and that. Only it seems a shame not to try and see more of each other like, now Mom's gone . . . You know, family – keeping in touch.'

Billy shrugged, and in that movement of his shoulders was complete indifference. But what cut her to the heart was the look in his eyes when he turned to face her. She saw that her blond, handsome brother was like a hard-faced stranger beside her, staring down at her with contempt.

'You're not really from round here any more, though, are you?'

And she saw her clothes, her ragamuffin children, her life, through his eyes and how he despised her – for not being there as he grew up, for what she had become.

'No,' she conceded miserably. 'I s'pose I'm not.'

He turned away and went to join Tony and Mrs Biggs. Maryann waited for Dot and Sylvia, forcing a smile to her lips to hide how much Billy's words had cut her. She wrenched her hurt round into a tough, defiant anger. Yes, she'd moved on from here and this was who she was. She was Maryann Bartholomew, a skilled boatwoman, and her family were boater's children and proud! *So sod you, Billy Nelson – you may be my brother, but you're a cold bastard and stuck up with it!*

'You all right?' Sylvia put her arm round Maryann's shoulders.

'Yes. Ta.' Maryann shrugged her off. She couldn't manage sympathy or closeness. Not at the moment.

'The vicar handled it all all right, didn't he?' Dot said.

'I thought he was rather nice,' Sylvia agreed, and Maryann could tell they were just talking for something to say and she was grateful to them.

'Do you want to go back with your brothers – spend the evening with them?' Sylvia asked.

'No.' Maryann just managed to keep the bitterness from her voice. 'All I want is to get back home. Get going again.' *Away from here*, she thought.

They reached the cemetery gates. Billy and Mrs Biggs had already gone. Tony waited, though.

'Bye, sis,' he said. 'Come and look us up, won't you?'

'Course I will,' Maryann said. She knew she would, every so often. But she also realized that probably, she'd never see Billy again, and with a pang, she knew that it no longer mattered.

The twins ran to catch up, skipping along the path. Joley and Ezra were chasing each other in and out of the gate, while Rose was picking up bits and pieces off the ground. Seeing Sylvia coming, she ran to her and took her hand.

'Right – all shipshape everyone?' Dot said.

'Where's Sally?' Sylvia said, headcounting the children.

'Good job someone's looking after them,' Maryann said. 'Shows what a daze I'm in! Where's she got to?'

They called back along the path, but it seemed wrong to be shouting in a cemetery.

'Knowing her, she'll've gone off in a dream somewhere,' Maryann said. She frowned. 'I thought she was in front of us.'

'Well, she was at one stage,' Sylvia said. 'But they were all dodging about so much. She's probably got herself lost in there.'

They spent the next half-hour searching the big cemetery, calling and looking, walking right down to the far side.

'It's not like her to hide and be naughty, is it?' Dot said.

Maryann was bewildered. Sally could be dreamy at times, it was true, but she'd never done anything like this before. And she wouldn't run off into the unknown streets of Birmingham without the rest of them. None of the other children knew where she'd gone and Maryann could see from their faces that they weren't having her on. She became more and more uneasy.

'It feels as if she's fallen down a hole or something,' she said. 'What the hell's happened to her?'

On the far side of the cemetery, in a newer part where there were few graves, they saw a middle-aged man kneeling, mending the fence.

'I say!' Dot called to him. He turned, startled.

'We're looking for a little girl – she seems to have lost

her way in here. Have you seen her? She's – how old is she, Maryann? Seven?'

Maryann nodded miserably. A coldness was beginning to creep over her. Sally had been missing for too long now to be playing up or have just wandered off. Realization was just beginning to dawn in her.

The man frowned. 'I've only seen one girl this afternoon. About half an hour ago. Blonde. Pretty little thing.'

'Long blonde hair?' Sylvia asked, excitedly. 'What – wandering about here?'

'Well, no. She was with someone – walking along the path over there – a bloke.'

'How odd,' Dot said. 'What did he look like?'

The man shrugged. 'Not young. Quite a big feller. Sort of wide-chested. Trilby pulled well down – couldn't say what his face looked like.'

The sound which came from Maryann made them all look round: a sharp exhalation as if she had been punched. She couldn't hide the fact that was trembling all over, everything round her was reeling. For a moment she thought was she going to pass out.

'Maryann?' Sylvia and Dot hurried over to her at once, asking questions, but she managed to stay upright and ran to the gardener.

'Where did they go? Which way?'

She tore off in the direction in which he pointed because it was all she could do, knowing that it was too late, too long ago, that when she reached the gate the road would be empty, but she could only run with desperate prayers streaming from her lips that he hadn't got her, hadn't really got away with her little girl . . .

There was no one on the road. A lone car passed in the quiet afternoon.

Dot, Sylvia and the others caught up with her and it was Dot who ran to Maryann and seized her by the shoulders.

'Who is he? Who's got her? For God's sake, Maryann, you've got to tell us what's going on.'

Thirty-Six

She couldn't be still.

'I've got to go – got to find them.' She pulled away from Dot and started running blindly along the road, unable to do anything else but move in the direction her child had gone. But of course she didn't know the direction. They were gone, they could be anywhere by now. When Dot reached her again and caught her arm, dragging her to a standstill. She felt herself cave in. Everything seemed to whirl round her, overwhelming her as if she was drowning. Her nightmares had merged into the reality of day and there was screaming and crying somewhere in the distance and she could not catch her breath . . .

'Maryann – MARYANN!' Sylvia was there now, shouting in her face. Why was she yelling like that? 'Maryann – I don't want to slap you, but I'm going to have to if you don't calm down!'

She felt herself being shaken hard by the shoulders and at last the world steadied a little.

'That's better.' Sylvia gripped her arms. 'Now tell us – who is Sally with?'

'With . . . with my stepfather – he used to be. I know it's him – I know he's taken her and we've got to get her. You don't know what he might do . . .' Her hands went convulsively to her cheeks and she was sobbing, shaking so hard that she could barely stand.

Supporting her on each side, they asked her over and over if she was sure, if it could be a mistake. *No, no* – all she could do was shake her head.

'Look,' Dot said, 'we must go and tell the police.'

'No!' Maryann cried. 'I know where we need to go. He's got a factory in Cheapside. We'll go there – I bet he's taken her there!'

Sylvia's eyes were full of doubt at how they were going to manage this when she barely knew the geography of Birmingham's great sprawl, didn't understand anything of what was going on.

'Look,' she decided, 'I'll go home with the children. You and Dot go.'

On the tram, the two of them sat side by side in silence, Maryann filled by a numb sense of inevitability that now they could only do small things, one at a time to get Sally back, when her nerves were screaming that she had to find her now, *now*, and have her back safely in her arms. She tried to close her mind to everything but the next step. The tram crawled along the Bristol Road. There was too much to say for them to begin talking now so they reserved speech only for practical things.

They went to the police station in town, where Maryann talked to them with a sense of hopelessness. Yes, her daughter had been taken away and it was by the same man, she impressed upon them, who had murdered the red-headed woman Amy Lambert. She told them the name of 'Albert Griffin's' factory. And they had to look for Sally *now* because otherwise he would harm her. He was evil, capable of the most terrible things. And Maryann wept helplessly in front of the policeman as she described her pale-haired little Sally.

When they left, Maryann stormed at Dot, 'It's no

good. They keep saying they're doing their best, but they're no ruddy good to us. They never *do* anything.' So many of the police had gone away to war that only a skeleton service was operating. 'We'll have to do it ourselves.'

'Maryann,' Dot panted, trotting to keep up as Maryann tore along the street, 'what were you saying to him? About that woman, a red-haired woman, you said. You said *murdered* . . . ? What in heaven's name were you talking about?'

'He murdered her, I know he did.' Maryann didn't stop for a second, firing out disjointed scraps of thoughts. 'Amy – and Sal. And Margaret might just as well be dead. It's all him, all of it. And they won't believe me – and we'll have to do it. No one else has ever – no one believes me except Janet because she knows. She's seen . . . she's the only one who knows.'

Maryann couldn't see the expression of appalled sorrow in Dot's eyes, couldn't see her own distraught, pitiful state. Dot knew that this had not come out of the blue. She had lain beside Maryann, known the terrors that haunted her sleep. What on earth did this poor, sweet-natured woman have in her past to cause all this? What had she suffered? Dot was filled with sorrow and tenderness, but she was out of her depth, inhibited by her own youth and lack of experience. Maryann's life was another world to her. All she could do was follow, look for Sally, and try to gather what was happening.

Maryann led her to Highgate, half running along Bradford Street and across to Cheapside, until they stood outside *Albert Griffin, Toolmakers & Machinists*, both of them panting hard. Maryann went straight to the open door. Inside, the long, dark factory extended back from the road. Dot saw a row of women seated at lathes, and a long table surrounded by a mess of packing cases. There was a subdued roaring from the far end of the workshop, over which they could hear the sound of music from a wireless on a smaller table to their left. A man was singing somewhere. The women nearest the door turned and stared at them but didn't stop work. After a moment the singing stopped and a man appeared, wearing a dirty overall.

'You looking for someone?'

'Yes, Mr Griffin.'

Dot was surprised at how collected Maryann seemed suddenly.

'He don't come in much, afternoons. He's not here. In fact he said he was going to a family funeral, now I think of it.'

'Yes,' Maryann said, 'that's it – he's my uncle, see. We've just come from there. We don't see much of Uncle Albert, but I left my daughter with him and he said he'd meet us here. You sure you haven't seen him – with a little fair-haired girl?'

The man shook his head. 'No. Like I said, I've not seen him all day.'

Maryann managed to look bemused. 'I must've mis-understood him. P'raps he's taken her back to his house. What was the address again?' She turned to Dot, who managed to shrug as if she'd momentarily forgotten it.

'Oh dear. I'm sorry to trouble you – would you be able to tell me his home address so's we can catch up with him? Only, we was hoping to have tea with Uncle Albert – get to know him a bit better like.'

'Just a minute,' the man said noncommittally. 'I'll have to ask Doris.' He went to the back of the workshop and vanished through a door. When he came back, he gave them an address: 33 Cameron Road, Acocks Green.

This time they caught a tram along the Warwick Road. When they alighted in Acocks Green, Dot saw to her surprise that they were not far from Tyseley Wharf. She wished, not for the first time that afternoon, that she wasn't dressed in this damnable skirt and court shoes, but in her usual slacks and boots so she could move freely. Maryann, in her full black skirt, was able to stride along unimpeded. She was running, still possessed by an insane energy. All Dot could do was follow, feeling her feet blister as they rushed along the row of terraced houses.

'Here!' Maryann cried.

Dot felt her heart lurch. Whatever was she going to do?

Maryann didn't miss a step. She marched straight up and hammered the knocker with such force Dot thought the door must split. Maryann couldn't stand still for a second. She was moving back and forth, one hand resting on her waist, elbow out. She chewed fiercely at her other thumb. But suddenly she snatched her hand away from her lips and started screaming.

'Come out! Come on – get out here! I know you've got her, you evil bastard! Get out here!'

Her cried sounded frail in the open air and the house felt silent and unoccupied. The windows reflected back the sky's late afternoon light, but inside it was dark and there was no sign of movement.

Maryann hammered again desperately. Again, no response.

'He's in there – I know he is!' Her hands went to her

face and she wept, distraught. Feeling helpless, Dot went to try and comfort her. But Maryann fought her off to begin her pacing again.

'I'm not going till we've been in there! We've got to get in – I'm going to get in if I have to break the door down. He's got to be here – where else can he be?'

Dot knew that Maryann felt it was their last chance of finding Sally today. She went to the door herself and pushed on it, banging once more on the knocker. It felt like a firm, strong door. Then she heard the sound of smashing glass and turned to see Maryann bashing at the front window with a lump of wood she'd found. Having smashed the window, she was clearing away the splinters of glass to climb in.

'Oi – what the bleedin' 'ell d'you think you're doing?' A gaunt woman in an apron had appeared from the next-door house. 'I'll have the coppers on you . . .'

Before Dot could turn and give a reasonable explanation for their conduct, Maryann had stormed over to the low wall and let out the loudest and most colourful string of invective Dot had ever heard. It brought the blood to her cheeks. She'd never heard Maryann so fluent and there were certain words she didn't even recognize. It looked for a moment as if Maryann was going to punch the woman, who eventually retreated back indoors, mouthing oaths. A moment later she was peering out of her front window. Dot didn't dare say a word. She wondered whether the woman would go for the police but, after all, what did it matter? Maryann turned on her, her face pale and taut.

'You coming in with me?' she demanded.

'Yes, of course.'

They hauled themselves in over the sill, Dot wrestling with her tight skirt. She cursed, scraping the back of her leg on the way down. They climbed into the front parlour, and as their eyes adjusted to the light they saw that the room was set out in a stiff, formal fashion, the walls, floor and furniture all varying shades of brown. But there was nothing else to see and they moved quickly through the lower part of the house – back room, kitchen, all very neat and tidy. There was no sound.

Without speaking, they ran up the dark stairs with their runner of brown carpet. Although there was no point in trying to be quiet, Dot found herself wanting to tiptoe. She didn't like the musty smell of the place, its drabness, and most of all her growing dread of who might be here, what they might find.

There were three bedrooms off the landing. The smallest back room was completely empty, without even a covering on the floorboards. Having poked their heads inside they moved on to the middle one. A single bed-stead was pushed up against the wall, with no bedclothes on it, only an old mattress, the ticking cover unpleasantly stained.

They exchanged glances and moved to the main bed-room at the front. Again the colouring of the room was brown, and it looked dark and uninviting in the strained light filtering through the nets. In silence they stood looking at the single bed with its coppery brown eider-down, the bedside chair, chest of drawers and wardrobe, the long mirror on its door reflecting light from the window. The wallpaper was a deep coffee colour, marked with a thin, swirling pattern in black. There was no other decoration except for long moss-green curtains and, on the wall by the bed, a photograph in a frame.

Dot moved over to look and Maryann followed. A woman in her middle years looked out from the picture. Her hair was caught up and piled on her head, topped by a white bonnet with a flower at the side. She had a wide, handsome face with dark, emphatic brows. At the bottom edge of the picture could just be seen the frill of a white, high-necked blouse. She stared steadily out at them, rather solemn, neither smiling nor severe. Dot peered closely, leaning across the bed. The eyes, close up, seemed penetrating, hard, and she stepped back, somehow disconcerted.

'His mother,' Maryann said. The picture had wrung a distant memory from her. He had had it in the room he shared with her mother in Ladywood, but propped somewhere in the room, not on the wall. She only dimly remembered, having hardly been in there after her father died.

With loathing, she added. 'Oh, he'd've done anything for Mother, all right. She was the only person who ever mattered.'

She went to the wardrobe and opened it. Two suits of clothes hung there, smelling of camphor. Maryann was about to shut it again when Dot saw her reach down and pick something up from the floor of it. She turned, her face set grim.

It was a square of cloth, pale blue with a pattern of tiny diamonds in a darker blue. It was clearly torn from a small blouse because one side was part of the fastening edge with two buttonholes.

Dot couldn't make sense of this. A piece of rag?

'This'll be something,' she heard Maryann say, almost to herself. She looked at Dot. 'He always has a reason for everything. He's like a machine.'

She pushed the clothes out of the way and bent over once more. The only other thing, lying coiled in the corner of the cupboard, was a length of rope. Dot felt her stomach turn with dread as Maryann brought it out.

Before she could say anything, Maryann ran back out of the room, taking both the rag and rope with her. 'Cellar – there'll be a cellar.'

Dot followed the sound of her rushing boots down the stairs. Maryann was searching frantically, in the understairs cupboard, along the hall, anywhere where there might be a door to an underground room, and Dot helped, increasingly bewildered but filled with a sense of horrified misgiving. But they could find nothing and no one. The house was empty.

Eventually, once the possibilities all seemed exhausted, Maryann sank to her knees in the hall, gripping the skein of rope in her hands. She slumped forward, letting out a helpless, anguished howl.

'Where are you, you evil bastard? For God's sake, where's my baby? Give her back to me – just let me have her back!'

Thirty-Seven

Sylvia and Dot did everything for Maryann that night. She was in no state to manage. Dot had to lead her back to catch the tram from Acocks Green. All the energy, the fight, seemed to go out of her and she stumbled along helplessly on Dot's arm like someone barely alive.

Between them, Dot and Sylvia took the *Esther Jane* back to Tyseley Wharf. All evening Maryann was in shock, unable to eat, to move or do anything, and the other two women saw to the boats, the food, the children, as she sat, numb, unable to concentrate on anything that was happening. Dot and Sylvia had to try and explain to the children what had happened, to give comfort. Time swam past and when Sylvia came to Maryann, offering a generous tot of whisky in a cup, she found she was sitting on the edge of her bed in the cabin, the family already bedded down.

'Look, darling, get this inside you,' Sylvia instructed. 'You can't go on like this. Dot's going to sleep in here tonight. You come over and bunk up with me.'

Maryann put the cup to her lips, and sipped the pungent liquor. It trickled hot down inside her and within seconds she could feel its effects. Her head went swimmy and she felt as if she was swaying from side to side. Things became even more muddled and unreal. She allowed herself to be led, head reeling.

'I'll never sleep,' she said to Sylvia when they were

aboard the *Theodore*. She began to weep again. 'What can I do? I can't stand it.' She tore at her hair, trying to find an outlet for her pain. 'I want my Sally back, my baby – I can't stand to think of what he'll do to her!'

'We'll find her, we *will*! You've just got to hold on till tomorrow.' Sylvia pulled her into her arms. She was crying too and the two of them wept together, Sylvia rocking Maryann as if she were the baby. Maryann closed her eyes, wanting to surrender to this comfort, but instead, her guard weakened by the alcohol, she found that she was suddenly unable to stop herself sliding, sinking into dark, deeply remembered places inside herself, haunts of pain and revulsion so acute that suddenly she was gagging. She had to pull herself up shakily, hand over her mouth and struggle out of the cabin to retch into the cut again and again until she felt wrung out and exhausted. She couldn't move, couldn't think. Head spinning, she rested wretchedly against the cabin, wanting to bang her head against the roof so hard that she lost consciousness, escaped from the pain filling her every pore.

'Come on – I've brewed the tea.' Sylvia's pale head appeared beside her in the darkness. She spoke as if to a child. 'Come back in, lovey.'

The tea steadied the reeling in Maryann's head a little. Eyes swollen from weeping, she looked round at Sylvia.

'How can I sit here drinking tea? I should be walking the streets. I ought to know where to go and find her.'

'We'll do everything we can when morning comes,' Sylvia said. 'What can we do tonight? We've told the police.'

'I can't . . . I can't . . .' Maryann started to lose herself again.

Sylvia grasped her hand. 'Tell me,' she said gently. 'You've never said – about your stepfather.'

Maryann stared blearily across the cabin, seeming so distant that Sylvia thought for a moment she hadn't heard. But then she said, 'He killed my sister. D'you know that? And he's killed Amy. And now he's got our Sally . . . and I've got to find her – I can't sit here like this.'

She stood up and struggled to get out, stumbling up the steps.

'No, Maryann – ' Sylvia caught her by the waist and held on, speaking softly, but firmly – 'you can't, not like this. Where're you going to go? Look, the police'll be looking for her – they *will*.' She steered her back to her seat and Maryann sank down.

'Come on – let's get you to bed.' Sylvia carefully shifted Rose from the main bed onto the side and helped Maryann to lie down. Neither of them undressed for the night. In her muzzy state Maryann was just aware of Sylvia easing herself onto the bed beside her. She didn't top and tail as was more normal on the narrow bed, but came in beside her.

'Come here, you poor love,' Sylvia whispered.

Maryann felt the comfort of arms round her, pulling her close, trying to console her.

'What's the address where your husband's staying in Oxford?' Dot asked the next morning.

Without question, Maryann trotted out the Adelaide Street address and a moment later Dot was off across the wharf in the morning sun.

The night had been terrible, almost sleepless, but the

345

brief periods when she lost consciousness were full of fractured, terrifying dreams. Daylight arrived like a reproach. How could she have slept? She was in a fever to be off again, searching, pursuing.

She shrugged off Sylvia's offer of breakfast. Still in her black skirt, an old blue cardigan pulled round her, she hurried over to the toll office. Before she reached it, amid the morning hubbub a voice reached her.

'Maryann – here, Maryann!'

It was Charlie Dean, grinning all over his face.

'Well, you're miles away this morning, aren't you? Must be in love or summat!'

Her expression as she turned to him wiped the smile off his face.

'Oh, have I gone and put my foot in it?' Contritely he took his cap off. 'What's the trouble?'

'It's my daughter.' As she spoke it felt as if words could not begin to convey the horror of the situation. 'She's been taken – by a man. A bad man...' She couldn't go on and ended by shaking her head.

'Oh.' Charlie looked nonplussed.

Urgently she moved closer to him. 'Charlie – there was a man before. You said you'd seen him on the wharf, looking for me – ages back. D'you remember? With a scarred face?'

Charlie nodded. 'You wouldn't forget his mug in a hurry I can tell you. Terrible. I've seen him about a couple of times. Not often.'

'When?' Maryann was so urgent to know that for a moment Charlie thought she was going to grab him by the throat. She looked a little deranged. 'Where? Where've you seen him?'

'Well, you know – about the place. In the road, like. I haven't seen him on the wharf again. Just walking about.

346

Oh – except once. The last time I saw the bloke he was up the shops – in the butcher's, I think. But other than that . . .'

'The butcher's? What – Osborne's?'

'That'd be it, yes. Can't think of anywhere else. Don't s'pose that's much help.'

Once Maryann had hurried on she realized it probably wasn't much help. He went to the butcher's once – well, so what? Mr Osborne would have been his polite, jolly self and have pretended he hadn't noticed the dreadful state of Norman Griffin's face and that would have been all there was to it. She asked a couple of other people round the toll office, but although they thought they'd seen him once they didn't have any more to say. But she couldn't keep still. Someone had to be able to help. That preacher was the one to go to. He might know something.

She found Pastor Owen saying goodbye to a small knot of people dispersing after a prayer meeting and launched herself at him.

'Well, I hope you're pleased with yourself!' she burst out, sending the remnant of the congregation scattering. She was too overwrought to care who heard her.

'Mrs Bartholomew!' He looked very startled. And just as malnourished and dishevelled as ever in his black clothes. She had wondered if he would remember her. Oh, he remembered all right.

'He's got my daughter now. Snatched her away while we were burying my mother in the cemetery and God alone knows what he's doing to her!' To her immense frustration she found herself weeping again. She wanted to hurt him, to make someone else feel the agony she was in, but something in her still responded to his innate sympathy and her anger melted into distress.

'What's this?' Pastor Owen's large eyes widened in consternation. He hovered before her, hands dithering in the air. 'What are you telling me? Can you say it more calmly?'

But she couldn't, could only sob, distraught. Pastor Owen stood before her looking agonized, as if he simply did not know what to do.

'I haven't seen our Mr Griffin in months,' he told her. 'Not since soon after you came that time. I'm very sorry. I've always meant to see you – down at the wharf, but the Lord has had other pastures for me lately.'

Gulping and trying to control herself, Maryann didn't reply.

'You must believe me.' The young man wrung his hands as he talked. 'When he first came to me, he did show genuine signs of contrition. He had a burdened soul. Yes, a burdened soul. He laid his troubles over his mother before me, and—'

'Burdened soul!' Maryann found she was screaming, hysterical. 'He's got a burdened soul all right! He's a murderer, he's filthy . . . oh, I can't even tell you.'

Sobbing, she ran from the church. Pastor Owen was no help to her. She had to go, to run and find Sally before it was too late. Why did she think anyone could ever be any help?

All day they searched. Another boater family looked after the children and Maryann, Dot and Sylvia moved between the police, the factory in Highgate and Norman Griffin's house in Acocks Green. He did not, as they had been assured he would, turn up at the factory that day. The house was empty and did not look as if he had returned to it. The window was still smashed and nothing had been moved inside. Round and round they went, as if on an awful circuit which yielded nothing.

The three of them stood outside the house, burning to keep moving, keep looking, but unsure what to do next.

'His mom!' Maryann said suddenly. 'She had a house in Handsworth.'

'Is she still alive?' Dot asked.

'Don't know – but let's go and find out.'

Across the city they went again.

'You must eat something, Maryann,' Sylvia said anxiously as they moved along on the tram. 'You've barely had a thing. You'll drop with exhaustion if you don't. Here – have this.'

Maryann ate the biscuit Dot offered, scarcely seeming to notice. She had to keep going, had to keep on, not keep still for a moment.

At the house in Handsworth they were told that old Mrs Griffin had died a few years back, having been well into her nineties by then.

'It's no good,' Dot said, when they had been back to the works in Highgate yet again. 'We're not going to find him like this. I vote we head back to Tyseley and get ourselves a meal before we drop.'

On the way back, Maryann left the others and called in at Mr Osborne's shop.

'Hello, m'dear!' he greeted her, beaming. 'Well, I haven't seen you for a month of Sundays. How're you keeping?'

'All right,' Maryann said. 'Look, I haven't stopped by for meat – I wanted to ask you if you've seen a man who's been into your shop lately.' She explained, described. Mr Osborne stood leaning forwards on the counter, considering, beside a plate of pigs' trotters.

'I think I do remember the man you mean,' he said, 'because, as you say, his face was so badly disfigured. You couldn't help but notice him. But he hasn't been in for a while now. No – not that I remember. What's your reason for asking, m'dear?'

'Oh, I just need to see him,' was all she was going to say, but Mr Osborne's kind, twinkly face made it all come spilling out, about Sally and how she knew it was this man who'd got her and *please* to keep an eye out.

'Well – ' Mr Osborne stood up straight, looking shocked – 'what a terrible thing for you. Are you sure? I expect you've told the police, haven't you?'

'Oh yes,' she said desperately. 'They're s'posed to be looking too. But you know how it is these days.'

'Don't I just. Goodness me – I'll certainly keep my eyes peeled.'

She walked back to the wharf, exhausted, in despair. All day she had forced herself to think of anything except the reality of her child in the hands of Norman Griffin and what he might be doing to her because if she let herself imagine, she knew she'd go mad. All they could do was to keep searching, keep looking and hope and pray that it was not too late.

Dot and Sylvia were trying to cook tea when she reached the boats, but there was a knot of people round the *Theodore*, talking, asking questions, all deeply shocked by what had happened. Everyone wanted to help. Maryann saw that Charlie was among them, leaning against the cabin. She quailed, feeling she couldn't face any of it, the questions and especially the sympathy. Needing to avoid them all, she went to the *Esther Jane* and picked up the water cans.

'I'll fill up,' she called to Sylvia, who began to protest,

but she waved this away. ''I've got to keep on. It's the only way.'

She stood watching the silver thread of water filling the cans and imagined taking her kitchen knife and dragging it through the flesh of her arm or leg. She almost ached for it. Wouldn't that kind of agony be easier to bear than this? Once the cans were full she lugged them back towards the boats, glad of the harsh strain on her arms and back. The others kept a respectful distance, seeming to sense her need, for the moment, to be alone.

But as she made her way across the wharf she caught sight of a figure moving over towards the boats with a slow but sure stride. For a moment she just stared. It couldn't be! He wasn't supposed to be here! In a second she was almost running with the water carriers hauling on her arm sockets and reached him before he got to the boats, dropping the cans to the floor.

'Oh – you're here, you're here!' Tears streaming down her face, she was taken into Joel's arms, clasped to the familiar smell and shape of him, sobbing her anguish into his chest as he held and stroked her.

Thirty-Eight

Everyone was looking at them. Clinging to Joel, Mary-ann poured out all that had happened in incoherent snatches.

'He's got our Sally – I know it's him and I've been looking and looking and ... we've got to find her ... I can't stand it ...' After holding onto her feelings all day they poured out now, running out of control. It didn't matter who was watching – she didn't even see them. For a few moments she could only dimly hear Joel's rumbling voice trying to comfort her, to make sense of what had happened. He took her face between his leathery hands and made her stop and look up at him.

'It's all amiss,' he said. 'Everything's amiss about this. But I'm here now. We won't stop till we get our Sally back.'

Dot and Sylvia had climbed onto the bank and were standing discreetly nearby, obviously full of sympathy but feeling awkward at the distraught state that both Maryann and Joel were in. Joel released Maryann and turned to them. They had never met him before and came and shook hands formally. Everyone was shy with one another. It was not a good time for Joel to be dealing with new people.

'Pleased to meet you,' Dot said, holding her hand out. 'Except for the circumstances. You received the telegram, then?'

Joel nodded, seeming a little overwhelmed by Dot's powerful presence.

'Came straight away. First train I could.' He looked down at Maryann with pained eyes. Then the others were crowding round, those who knew Joel greeting him, asking if he was better.

'Not quite myself, but nearly,' he said. 'Near enough so's I couldn't sit still there for a moment hearing this news.'

'What're we going to do?' Charlie asked. He seemed full of agitation. 'You can't just have some bloke run off with your daughter . . .'

Others called out their agreement. 'Come on, Joel – we'll come and help you find him.'

'We're ready – let's go now!'

As Maryann and Dot filled Joel in about all that had happened, Sylvia brought them cups of tea. Maryann couldn't seem to stop crying, the tears running down her cheeks as she talked.

'I've been back and forth all day – every place I can think of, his house, his factory and I can't find him. The police're s'posed to be looking but I don't know what they're doing. I don't know where they can! I don't know what else to do—'

'Let's go again.' Charlie seemed on fire with the need to do something. His tender feelings for Maryann were inflamed by seeing her in such distress. Some of the others called out in agreement.

'Let's go and track the bastard down – we'll find him! Come on – where do we start?'

'I'll come!' Maryann cried. 'I've got to – I can't sit still here till we've found her!'

Sylvia came over to Maryann and gently took her arm, speaking both to her and Joel.

353

'You must have some food first. Maryann, you've been on the go all day with nothing – and your husband must be hungry as well.' She ignored Maryann's protests that they didn't need food, that they should go right away. 'Come on, love, there's some stew ready.'

'We'll have ourselves a bite to eat –' Joel steered Maryann by the arm – 'and then we'll go and get him.'

It was already getting dark by the time they set off. Three of the men said they would go to Norman Griffin's house and see if there was any sign of him. Charlie wanted to come to the Highgate factory with Joel. Maryann refused absolutely to be left behind. Sylvia said she and Dot would stay and put the children to bed. Sylvia stood on the back of the *Theodore*, a neat figure holding Rose's hand, watching as they left. The men had instinctively armed themselves with some of the few things they possessed: screwdrivers, hammers and windlasses.

Maryann walked through Highgate with a sense of hopelessness. She'd been back and back to these places. What could they possibly hope to find? But what else could they do except go round and round, watching, waiting for Norman Griffin to appear, to slip up and give himself away? If he was not at his house or his business, where could he be, and how would they ever be able to find him? A sick, unbearable feeling rose in her at the thought of Sally with him. But she pushed it violently away. If she opened the door to it she would end up tearing her clothes like a madwoman. She must think of nothing but *finding* Sally. At least Joel had come now, and with Charlie's reassuring presence too she felt much less alone.

The evening had clouded over after a warm day and a light drizzle began to fall, which brushed her face like cloud. Charlie tactfully walked a few paces ahead of them. Maryann looked at Joel beside her, noticing with anxiety how stiffly he was walking. She put her hand on his arm.

'Is it still hurting?'

'Not much – not enough to fuss about.' A few seconds later his voice burst out in the darkness. 'Why's he done this? *Why*? What does he want with us, to do this?'

Maryann heard all the grief and anger in his question and in anguish she squeezed his arm tightly.

'That's what he's like ... what he's always been like.' But Joel had never really wanted to hear it.

Charlie stopped and waited for them. 'How far along is it?' he whispered in the quiet street.

'Down on the right,' Maryann said. She walked ahead. A car was parked ahead of them on the road, but there was no sign of anyone about. A few moments later they were standing in front of the works – *Albert Griffin, Toolmakers & Machinists*.

In Acocks Green, the three boatmen who'd walked from Tyseley Wharf found their way to the house in Cameron Road. Maryann had told them they should be able to climb in through the front window, but they found that a board had been nailed over it. He'd been back then, or someone had. Between them, with their few tools, they quietly prised the board off and climbed inside.

They had no fear of switching the lights on. If they were caught, what did that matter? They were only doing what the police should have done – they had right on their side. Walking round the house, they could see nothing amiss. They looked round downstairs and then went up to the bedrooms. Had they been there before, with Maryann, they might have noticed that certain things were different: the wardrobe door was swinging open and there was nothing inside. Some items had disappeared from the chest of drawers and the walls were now completely bare, where before a portrait had hung above the bed. But these details were lost on the men.

Downstairs they looked, as Maryann had done, for signs of other hiding places in the house. They went out to the back and opened the door of the privy. The flush toilet looked innocently back at them in the gloom. They shook their heads. Nothing doing there.

As they were passing back through the kitchen, one of them noticed something that made him stop. The floor was covered with grey lino, and he stood puzzling, noticing that it had been strangely laid. Instead of being arranged to cover the largest amount of floor with the least number of cuts, there seemed to be a panel of linoleum covering the middle section of the small square room. At one end it met the wall, at the other it was held down by a small cupboard with a meat safe on top.

'Let's have a look here,' he murmured, and shifted the cupboard across onto the other strip. The linoleum easily rolled back, and underneath they saw the square shape of a trapdoor. For a moment they all looked at each other.

It took them seconds only to lift the trapdoor. On a beam just below they found a switch for the cellar's light, and climbed down the brick stairs, each waiting at the bottom until all three of them were down. The cellar was not large, nor did it feel damp; it was very clean and obviously recently swept, though there was a stink in there which they did not recognize as the source of their unease. All they could see were a couple of shelves to their left on which rested bottles and jars and, in the far corner, what looked like a heap of old linoleum.

One of the men went over and, almost idly, lifted up the corner of it. He dropped it again instantly and recoiled, cursing.

'Lord God Almighty . . . oh my word . . .'

The other two went to see for themselves. They looked at each other pale-faced. One clamped a hand over his mouth.

'For God's sake, let's get out of here,' the other said.

They ran, stumbling up the stairs and out into the dark street.

'This his place then?' Joel looked up at the frontage of the Cheapside works.

'There's no night shift, anyroad,' Charlie commented.

'So – you reckon we need to go in?'

Maryann could hear the doubt in Joel's voice. His innocence both touched and enraged her. Joel's life had not contained the darkness of Norman Griffin and in some way he still could scarcely believe that such cruel wickedness as Griffin was capable of could truly exist. It was in the cellar beneath his premises in Ladywood that Sal, her sister, had suffered at Norman Griffin's hands.

'We've *got* to go and look,' she hissed at him, enraged by the doubt in his voice.

Charlie tried to peer down the grating at the front of the factory.

'Can't see a thing – but there's sure to be a cellar. It's just how we get down there . . .'

Maryann was burning with impatience. 'Can't we get the grating up? Climb down there?'

'It's not as easy as all that,' Charlie said. 'Let's have a look round first – see if there's any other way.'

Narrow alleys led down each side of the works. The three of them moved cautiously along the one to the right, Maryann between Joel and Charlie, who was in the lead. He tripped and almost fell over a piece of wire.

'Bugger it! – 'Scuse us,' he said, catching his balance against the wall. 'It's so bleeding dark down here.' They could just make out that there were windows in the side of the building, which must have let in precious little light in the daytime, as they were so close to the wall of the premises next door. Gradually, struggling over the uneven ground, which seemed to be strewn with rubble, they reached the end of the works. There was a thin yard at the back, fenced off from the one belonging to another factory in the street behind. The three of them stood, straining their eyes in the darkness.

'Why didn't we bring a torch?' Maryann said desperately. 'This is hopeless! How're we s'posed to get anywhere like this?'

'Hark – what's that?' Charlie held up a hand and Maryann's heart began to hammer, almost unbearably.

From the street they heard the sound of an engine starting up.

'That's a moty car,' Joel said.

They breathed more easily again.

'Come on – let's move on round,' Joel said.

He led the way round the back of the building, sliding his hand along in the darkness. Maryann was now immediately behind, and when they had almost reached the far end, Joel suddenly gave a gasp and almost toppled forward. He had been unable to see that the ground suddenly fell away and had almost tumbled down a deep cleft in front of him.

Charlie struck a match, and in the couple of seconds' flash of illumination they saw that there were steps down from the corner of the works.

'Why the hell didn't we bring a proper lamp?' Charlie grumbled.

Another match, held lower, showed them that at the bottom was a rusty iron door. When they climbed down they found it was held shut with a chain and a hefty padlock. Charlie shook his head.

'We'll have a hell of a job getting in here.'

Joel tried his strength against the door. It gave slightly, tugging on the chain, which seemed to rattle far too loudly in the quiet.

'If we can't smash the padlock, I reckon we'd be able to break that down,' Joel said. 'If I was up to full strength, I could.'

With their hammer and the windlasses they smashed at the padlock, an erratic process in the pitch dark. Striking another match showed them that they had only succeeded in denting it, and the chain wouldn't break or give. Maryann stood watching, her whole body tensed to breaking point, wanting to smash at the door herself.

'It's no good!' she cried after a few moments. 'We'll never do it like this!'

Joel stood up straight, considering. 'Look, pal – let's go at the hinges. I don't reckon they're up to much.'

They leaned and shoved and kicked. Joel aimed a blow low on the door with his leg and reeled back in the narrow space with a grunt.

'Confound this back of mine!'

'Here – let me.'

With a few kicks from Charlie's powerful leg, the lower hinge came away.

'I can get in through there!' Maryann cried.

'Just hang on.' Charlie kicked at the door again and Joel joined in. Soon the top hinge gave as well and the door fell in with a crash and fell, hanging at an angle from the chain.

They walked into even more profound darkness, straining their eyes to see anything of the space around them.

'This is hopeless,' Charlie said. In the flare of light from another match, they saw they were in a narrow room. Maryann had a brief impression of a large, dark shape to her right.

'Here – there's a light!'

She turned on the switch by the door. The dim bulb in the middle of the ceiling gave off light that strained to reach the walls. The big object by the wall turned out to be a rusting old lathe. Ahead of them was a partition wall with a door in it. Otherwise the space was clear: brick walls, earth floor. Nothing else.

'Oh, where is she!' Maryann wailed. 'What's he done with her? Could she be in there?'

She went to the door in the partition and hammered her fist on it, beginning to sob. 'Sally – Sally, it's your mom. Are you in there?'

Nothing. They stood listening.

'Let's get in there and see,' Charlie said grimly. 'Why's he got so many locked doors in this place? What's there to nick?'

'Sally!' Maryann banged again. 'It's all right, bab – it's your mom and dad.' She turned to Joel. 'Oh, this is no good. She'd call out if she was there wouldn't she?'

Joel nodded miserably. 'Unless . . .' They neither of them wanted to put into words unless what.

'Right,' Charlie said, positioning himself to kick the door.

'What's that?' Joel held him back. From low down somewhere came a tapping sound, getting louder, insistent, frantic.

Maryann went to the door, throwing herself against it. 'Get it open, for God's sake!'

'Mind out!' Joel caught hold of her, shifting her away and he and Charlie set to at once, kicking at the door with all their strength. Unlike the outer door it was made only of wood and one of Charlie's kicks splintered it. In a few moments they'd kicked it down.

Maryann ran in ahead of the men, looking round frantically in the poor light coming through the door. It was a continuation of the long cellar, only twelve feet or so across, partitioned off and empty and completely bare except, except for . . . A cry escaped from her. There in the corner was all she needed to see: lying on sacking, Sally's blonde head, the torn cloth tied round her mouth, the ropes round her ankles and wrists, head straining up, her pleading eyes burning into them.

Thirty-Nine

Joel carried Sally back all the way, cradling her in his arms. Only the deep sound of his breathing betrayed to Maryann the depth of his distress and anger. He sat on the tram back to Tyseley with Sally's head pressed to him like a tiny infant's and every so often Maryann heard him make a low, comforting sound, which seemed to rumble up from deep within him.

For a moment Maryann let her head rest on his shoulder in the tram's gloomy light. It seemed to have been the longest day of her life! All she could feel now was overwhelming relief at having Sally back, alive and safe in their arms. What had happened to her, what state she was in, only time would tell. They would have to go to the police again, to deal with everything, but that could wait until the morning. They had her back – her baby would be home and safe. Tears ran down her face again. She leaned round and laid her hand on Sally's head.

'Mom's here,' she murmured. 'It's all right. It's all going to be all right.' Joel freed one of his hands and pulled her close, stroking her cheek.

After thanking Charlie, they walked home across the wharf. It felt later than it was – barely ten o'clock – and Sylvia and Dot were still up and waiting. Both jumped off the *Theodore* and came running towards them. At the sight of Sally in Joel's arms, Sylvia burst into tears.

'Oh, thank God! I can't believe it! Oh, the little love – is she all right?'

'Where was she?' Dot asked.

Briefly they explained.

'Look, we've got the rest of the children in with us,' Sylvia said, wiping her eyes. 'We thought it was for the best – not knowing what time you'd be back. They were unsettled.'

Maryann knew that in normal circumstances Joel might have bridled at the idea of someone like Sylvia taking charge of his children. Bad enough having them on the boats at all. But tonight everyone felt close, united in relief, even though Joel and the two women barely knew each other.

'Good of you,' he said gruffly, beginning to move to the *Esther Jane*. 'We'd best get this 'un tucked up.'

'Our kettle's just boiled,' Dot said. 'I'll bring you over a drink in a minute.'

Maryann looked at them. 'I don't know how to thank you. You've both been so kind.'

'Don't be silly,' Dot said briskly. 'Absolutely the least we could do in the circumstances.'

Sylvia reached out and squeezed Maryann's arm. 'Is she all right?'

'I don't know. God, Sylv – you should've seen where we found her.' Her voice began to crack. 'But we've got her back – that's the main thing.'

They'd tucked Sally up in their bed and she lay on her back, staring up at the ceiling.

Joel and Maryann looked at each other, eyes very troubled. Ever since they had rescued her she had lain limp and silent.

363

'Sally?' Maryann perched on the bed beside her and took her hand. It was ice cold. 'Would you like a nice cup of hot milk? Or some cocoa? Warm you up?'

There was no response, except a flicker of her eyes.

'I'll put a bit on to warm anyway,' Joel whispered behind her. Both of them knew they had to have something they could do: they both felt so helpless.

Maryann waited, stroking Sally's hand, her hair, making soft, reassuring noises. She was appalled, wrung out by the sight of her child. Sally looked like a shell of the pretty, lively little girl she had been.

'Here.' Joel handed her a cup of warm, sweet milk.

'Can you sit up and drink a bit of this, pet?' Maryann supported Sally into a sitting position and she managed to take a couple of mouthfuls of the milk before turning her head away.

'All right – you sleep now, my lovely. I'll sit with you. You're safe here. No one's going to hurt you ever again.'

She sat on the edge of the bed, tears running endlessly down her cheeks as the fear and tension gradually drained out of her. Her little girl was here, she was safe! But she was so sad and frightened by the state Sally was in. She held her hand and tried to hum to her, until at last Sally began to drift off to sleep. Maryann sat on for some time, unable to let go.

When Sally had slipped off at last, Maryann and Joel squeezed onto the side bench, their eyes turning every few seconds to the tormented little figure on the bed.

Joel put his arm round Maryann's shoulders and leaned down to kiss her hair. She heard the soft whisper of his lungs close to her and the rhythm of his heart.

'Back home,' Joel said softly, stroking her back. 'With my little bird at last.'

She nodded into his chest, feeling warm and cared for. She kept her head down, knowing that if she looked up he would kiss her, knew he was longing to kiss her, but she couldn't face that. Not now. She only wanted to feel the comfort of him near her.

'I don't know what we're going to do. She looks so bad,' she said desperately.

There was a silence, filled only with the tinny tick of their alarm clock, then she heard Joel's voice, filled with a bitterness she had never heard in him before. 'We've got to get that bugger. That we have.'

It was a few minutes later that they heard the tapping at the door. When Joel opened up, they saw the three boatmen waiting with pale, solemn faces. Beside them was a policeman.

'It's all right.' Joel spoke quietly, standing in the hatches. 'We got her – found her at the works – Griffin's. She's in here with us, fast asleep.'

The solemnity on their faces turned to bewilderment. They looked at each other, seemingly unable to take in what Joel was telling them.

'Are you sure?' one of them said, eventually. They seemed totally confused. Joel climbed out onto the bank into the damp air and Maryann followed.

'Course we're sure!' Joel told them. 'Not going to mistake our own daughter, are we?'

'What's up?' Maryann asked them, a sense of dread coming over her once more.

The policeman, a chubby-faced man, seemed to think he'd better take over.

'While these men were searching certain premises in Acocks Green – according to your instructions, I understand – they found a body in the cellar. A child's body.'

Maryann couldn't move. She clamped her jaws together.

'Thing is,' one of the boatmen said, 'we thought it must be your wench. Only she were...' He stopped, face creasing in distress.

'The way the body was,' the policeman said flatly, 'anyone'd have been hard pushed to say who she is.'

'My God,' Joel said.

Now do you believe me? Maryann thought. 'I've been telling them for weeks he's a murderer!' she blurted out. 'So now you know for certain, don't you?'

'Thank Christ it's not your little 'un, Joel,' one of the men said. They all looked extremely shocked.

'But it would've been if we'd left it any longer,' Joel said grimly. 'What're you going to do about it?' he demanded of the policeman.

'We'll find him and arrest him, of course,' he said with dignity. 'As soon as we possibly can. We'll put all the men we can onto it.'

''Bout bloody time too!' Maryann lost control of herself. Her voice was edged with hysteria. 'None of you've ever taken any notice of what I said, have you?'

When they went back into the cabin after thanking the boatmen for their help, she could no longer contain herself but shook uncontrollably, as if she was having one of her nightmares while she was still awake. Even Joel holding her close didn't dispel the terror and despair which filled her.

'We've got to get away from here,' she said between chattering teeth. 'Away from Birmingham – away from *him*. While he's still on the loose, none of us are safe.'

Joel gave a long sigh into her hair, stroking her back.

'I don't s'pose we can just go like that. We need to talk to the police – make sure they get him before he does anything else.'

The whole Bartholomew family moved into the *Theodore* for those days. They towed the butty to a quieter part of the wharf, and Sylvia and Dot took the *Esther Jane* back to Coventry to work short trips out of Sutton Stop and bring in some money. The children enjoyed the enforced break and being able to play on the bank, though Maryann knew the boys were aware of the unease and trouble around them, and she insisted that they never move out of sight of the boat.

All she could think about was Sally. She knew that she might be able to tell them things which would help catch Norman Griffin, but she could not stand the thought of forcing anything more on the little girl. For the first couple of days Sally seemed to be in a trance, sitting or lying staring ahead of her, not speaking, barely eating, her pale face wearing a vacant expression, as if she couldn't bear to inhabit her body. Maryann sat with her whenever she could, holding her hand, stroking her hair, making gentle noises to try and reassure her that she was safe now, that everything would be all right.

Joel was finding it hard to bear. His eyes, when they rested on his daughter, were full of pain and anger at what had been done to her. He was tender with her but also full of frustration that she could not, or would not, tell them what would lead them to Norman Griffin. The weather was fine and to relieve his feelings he took refuge in working on the *Theodore*, scrubbing her out, splicing ropes, doing repairs. Maryann could see that his back was still hurting. She went to him outside on the first afternoon with a mug of tea. Joel was squatting in the hold, looking at the tarpaulin sheets, and she climbed along to him.

'Cuppa for you.'

Joel looked up, letting go of the coarse ropes to take the mug.

'Ta.' He drank some of the sweet tea, then stared out to his left across the cut. At last he said, 'Can't stand seeing her like that.' She saw tears in his eyes, which he wiped away quickly with a rub of his sleeve.

'I know.' She swallowed, unable to comfort him. All the time, inside herself, she was terrified of identifying too much with her daughter. She had to prevent herself revisiting places of pain and horror which she had shut away in herself so long now, or she would fall to pieces. She had to stay calm, to hold herself together for all of them.

The other children couldn't understand why Sally was like she was and kept asking why she didn't come out and play. 'She's poorly,' Maryann told them. 'Just leave her be for a day or two, eh? I s'pect she'll be better soon.'

She felt torn, as if on a rack, between all her family's emotions. And, stretched across the middle of it, she forced herself to remain numb in order to be strong.

The police came several times. They had visited Janet Lambert and now believed that the two murders had been committed by the same man. They had no idea of the identity of the other young girl found in Norman Griffin's cellar. The only clue was her long blonde hair. On Maryann's advice they visited Mrs Biggs, her mother's neighbour, who had been to the funeral. She admitted that Norman Griffin had been to visit Flo a number of times before she died. But they had no idea where he had disappeared to now. Neighbours had been asked to watch his house. So far, he had not returned.

'Where can he be?' Joel kept saying, with more and more pent-up frustration as the days passed. His ignorance of the city, of anything but the cut, only added to his sense of angry helplessness. It was against all his habits to sit still like this, on these calm days in early summer which were ideal for trips, while strangers were working his boat and he couldn't get a load on and get ahead. How much longer would they have to wait?

After a few days Sally seemed a little improved. She had slept a lot and began to eat a bit more. On a sunny morning Rose came to her and asked timidly if she wanted to come and play out and Sally nodded. Maryann felt a leap of hope inside her. Tears came to her eyes as she saw Nance's little girl take Sal's hand and lead her into the bright light, along the towpath to where the others were waiting. Maryann got on with her chores, and about an hour later Sally came back, slipping down the steps into the cabin.

Maryann followed her in and found her sitting on the side bench, her face pale and drawn.

'What's up, bab? Don't you feel very well?'

Sally shook her head. 'I wanted to be inside for a bit.'

Seeing the fear in her eyes, Maryann gently put her arms round her. She knew those feelings; the sense of fear, of panic suddenly taking her over.

'That's a good idea,' she said, kissing the top of Sally's head. 'It's nice and cosy in here, isn't it?'

She felt Sally nod. They sat in silence for a few minutes while Maryann rocked her frightened little girl back and forth.

'Sally,' she said very gently, 'you know when we found you? Had you been in that place for long?'

The child shook her head. Into Maryann's chest, she said, 'He'd just put me there – just before. I was somewhere else before. He left me there, then you came – straight after. He took me there in his moty car . . . I had to lie down in the back . . .'

As she spoke Maryann felt the hairs stand on end all over her body. She pulled back and looked into Sally's face.

'You mean – when we found you he'd only just left you there?' She heard again in her mind the sound of the car engine starting up in the street as they stood at the back of the factory. Seeing Sally nod, she whispered, 'Oh, my God!' A shudder passed through her. He had been there behind the factory as they arrived at the front! As they felt their way down one side of the works he must have been creeping along the other. How was it he always seemed to be invisible, to move like a shadow that no one could find or catch?

Holding Sally close again, she whispered, 'It's all right, my lovely. We'll never let him near you again.'

Days passed and still the police were making no progress. Sylvia and Dot brought the *Esther Jane* back, as arranged. Joel was feverish with the need to get going again, however overwhelmingly he wanted to see Norman Griffin caught.

Maryann had hoped to see Sylvia and Dot off in style when they left the cut – at least to have a little goodbye celebration. As it was, there was too much grimness and worry to occupy everyone and the two women didn't want to intrude any further on the family's problems.

'We're going back down to the Grand Union to be allocated new boats,' Dot said. The children were all very sad to see them go. Rose cried heartbrokenly when she heard that Sylvia was leaving.

'Never mind, darling.' Sylvia hugged her tightly. 'I'll see you whenever I can. And one day I'll have a home where you can come and see me.' Maryann was touched by Sylvia's bravery. Her future was very uncertain. Who knew how she was going to make a life when she had to leave the cut?

Both of them hugged Maryann and even Dot was tearful when the time came to depart.

'This is certainly a time I'll never forget,' she said.

'You've been so good to me,' Maryann told them. 'I shall miss you both – all our chats and that.'

Sylvia put her arms round both of them and they stood together in a tearful huddle, until Dot broke away. 'We'll miss our train if we carry on like this,' she said.

'We'll see you whenever we can!' both of them promised.

The family waved them off as they disappeared across the wharf, bundles of belongings in their arms; they turned at the last moment, each managing to free an arm to wave. Maryann thought of the night they'd first arrived, how strange, how alien they'd seemed. She could see especially how Dot had changed. Even the way she wore her hair was softer, her fringe had grown again and was no longer a hard line across her forehead. She knew them both so well now, knew that whatever their upbringing, their class, and however seldom they might be able to meet, they were friends for life. She blew them a kiss to answer their last wave, then looked up at Joel beside her. It was just the two of them now. Bobby was working the Grand Union and they wouldn't get him back for a while. She was so happy to have Joel back, yet she felt very distant from him, as if shut in on herself,

371

frozen inside. She felt a sudden pang of dread at being alone with him again.

The next day they untied their pair of boats from Tyseley and slipped quietly away from the wharf, heading south in the cool, quiet morning with a load for Banbury.

Later that day, in a Birmingham street, a blackout curtain moved at an upper window. Had anyone been looking they might have caught sight of a face peering cautiously out. It was a face which did not dare venture out into the light of day. The face of someone whose features were so distinctive, so disfigured, that for the moment hiding in an upper room was the only way left to live. The face turned a little from side to side, looking up and down the street, as if waiting for someone. Then the curtain fell back and it disappeared into the darkness.

Forty

The *Esther Jane*'s engine coughed, then jumped into throbbing life in the dawn, scattering alarmed moorhens towards sanctuary in the reeds. The Bartholomews had tied up the boats for the night on a remote stretch of the Oxford cut, and woke to find themselves still alone, no other boats nearby. The water was a deep, muddy green, lightly veiled by shreds of mist.

From the back of the *Theodore* Maryann watched Joel, ahead of her on the *Esther Jane*, catch the rope flung to him by Ezra, who then scampered expertly back aboard before Joel poled the boat off the mud close to the bank. Maryann fixed the helm in place while Rose untied the *Theodore* from its mooring pins. They were in a good position to move off, she noticed with the small part of her mind that was paying attention. The routine of morning departure was so familiar as to be automatic. She steered out behind the *Esther Jane*, smelling the churned-up mud. Ahead of her, Joel stood at the tiller, cap on his head, looking resolutely in front of him.

When we were first married, he kept turning round, waving at me, she thought. *As if he couldn't stop looking, couldn't believe I was really here. And I was the same. Not now, though.* She gave a sigh out of her deep sadness, watching Joel's implacable back, which was turned firmly towards her. *God help us*, she thought. *What's happened to us? How did everything get like this?* Here they were again, Joel with the boys on one boat, her and the girls on the other. That was how it was now – separated by night as well. And, in the daytime, barely speaking. Nothing had been right since Joel came back. The initial shock of events had brought them close for a while, but ever since they had seemed to grow further and further apart.

Distracted by a sound from the cabin, she peered through the hatches to see if the kettle was boiling yet. Sally was trying to wipe over Ada's and Esther's faces and Ada was squawking and fighting her. The twins were a handful, but Sally was managing.

It was her fault, Maryann knew, but she couldn't help it. She wanted Joel close to her, to feel the comfort of him, yet she couldn't bear it when he came near her. At first they'd had Sally with them in their bed, keeping her safe, trying to comfort her. After two nights they had moved her onto the side bench so they could reclaim their marriage bed, and Joel was so hungry for her, so insistent. He was her husband, of course he was – what was wrong with that?

She lay frozen in the roseate light, hearing his sighs of pleasure as his hands moved over her, caressing, pulling her close against him so she could feel how urgently he wanted her.

'Oh, that's better.' She felt his breath against her ear. 'Oh, my bird, I've missed you. I know I'm home now.'

She tried to respond, to lie close to him, her hands stroking his wide back, his hair, trying to desire him, to want what had to happen. Eyes closed, she tried to force her body to cooperate with the sensations of Joel's lovemaking. His breathing became fast, excited. Maryann felt a frightening tightness growing deep within her. She

She broke out in a sweat, not just from the heat of his body close to hers but from utter panic, and she found herself struggling for breath. Forcing her eyes open, she looked into Joel's face. Why did she feel so cold and detached from him? Why couldn't she just love him back? *This is Joel, your husband! Joel, who loves you.* His eyes were shut, his lashes rusty-coloured arcs, closed against her, mouth feeling for her with the blind instinct of a baby, wanting her, kissing, nuzzling ... The tightness in her swelled and a whimper escaped from her which Joel heard as an indication of pleasure and he rolled over onto her, weighing her down with what felt an inescapable weight. And all at once, in the shadowy light, the lips reaching for hers were not his, the face breathing hotly on her in the gloom not Joel's, but scarred and pitted, horribly distorted and the eyes boring into her with what seemed sadistic lust were Norman Griffin's when he forced her down in the front room in their Ladywood house, heavy as a fallen statue on top of her, trapping her under him so she could not move. Revulsion and panic exploded in her and she tore at Joel's back with her nails, kicking, struggling, letting out desperate, muffled cries under him.

'Get off me – get off, let me out!'

She sank her teeth into his shoulder and bit hard, panting and crying and Joel reeled back from her, clutching at the deep welts she had made with her teeth.

'Darn it! What the—? What the hell d'you do that for?'

Through the blood pounding in her ears, she could barely hear the frustrated anger in his voice. She had curled into a tight ball on her side to protect herself and for some moments couldn't be sure if she was inhabiting her younger self or her daughter. Sally's suffering possessed her, wrapped itself round her tightly with her own memories. She was a child again, trapped in a dark place, terrified of what would be done to her. The horror began to choke out of her. She moaned and sobbed.

'Maryann? Love?' Joel sounded frightened. Cautiously he touched her shoulder, but she fought him off. She was still horror struck and could not see him as he was. He was someone else, someone dangerous. She was so far down in her pain and fear that she barely knew he was there. Joel knelt, watching her, bewildered. Nothing had happened like this before. Not even in the early days, when she was afraid to give herself to him. He had known she was fragile, had suffered something, but he had been confident then that with enough patience, his gentleness and the pleasure of love would thaw her and bring her through. He knew no other way – this was what was natural to him. And it had done, he thought. He had touched her with care and respect and loved her into pleasure. He had never before seen her as she was now.

After a time her crying stopped and she lay quiet. They were both silent behind the little curtains veiling the bed. Maryann looked out from between her lashes, as if emerging from the darkness to see little chinks of soft light, and sensed Joel still close to her, heard his breathing. Her cheeks were wet with tears and she felt exhausted, wrung out. She could not look at him.

'You don't want me,' she heard him say flatly.

She couldn't bring any words to her lips to reassure him.

Eventually Joel pulled up the bedclothes with a heavy sigh, turned away from her and was soon asleep.

It had not got any better. It was a month now. In those early days when Sally was back with them, Maryann had been very gentle with her. At first the little girl wouldn't speak at all and seemed in a trance. Day by day, though, she became more herself as the impact of the shock receded, and she began to get up and play with the others. Maryann had warned them not to ask her questions, and in any case they soon forgot their curiosity about where Sally had disappeared to and she, though quiet and seeming older suddenly, fitted in with them as before. Alone, though, sometimes Maryann tried to get her to talk.

'Did he touch you?' she asked her, one day in the cabin.

Sally stared back at her, wide-eyed. It took Maryann back to the day she had asked the same question of Amy and Margaret Lambert and seen the fear and shame flicker in their eyes.

'That man – Mr Griffin. Did he do things you didn't like? Touch you where he shouldn't?' She wanted to speak calmly but somehow the words came out sounding harsh. 'It's all right,' she added more gently. 'If he did, he shouldn't've done. It's not you that's wrong – it's him.'

She saw her daughter's blue eyes fill with tears. 'I shouldn't've gone with him. He said he'd get us all some nice things – sweeties and that . . .'

'Course he did!' Maryann said fiercely, sitting down beside Sally and putting her arm round her. 'That's because he's a bad man and a liar. Weren't you frightened – of his face and the way he was?'

'A bit. But he spoke to me ever so nice. And he had a little dolly with him in a pretty dress, said he'd give it me in a minute, when we got to where we was going. He never did, though.'

'And where did you go?' Maryann asked, heart beating faster.

'He took me in his moty car, said I could have a ride if I was good and quiet. We went to a shop and bought some mints and he said I could have them when we got home. He never gave them me. Then he took me to a house. Later, when it was dark. I kept saying I wanted to go home.'

'Where was it?' Maryann couldn't help asking, even though she knew that Sally could really have no idea.

'He wouldn't have me sitting in the car. Said it was a game and I had to lie down on the floor and he put a rug over me so I never saw nothing. When we got to the house –' her voice stalled, became halting – 'he said I wasn't to make a noise, wasn't to cry. I don't know where it was. It was all brown inside. And he took me upstairs and there was a bed and a woman's face and he made me . . . he made me . . . she kept looking at me all the time . . .'

'A woman?' Maryann frowned.

'On the wall. I went into the picture with the lady. She was pretty. She had a hat on with a feather in.'

The picture. It came to her. The picture of Norman Griffin's mother with her proud, stern face.

Maryann gently pulled her into her arms. 'Oh, my baby. My poor baby.'

Thoughts of what he had done to Sally wouldn't leave her. Maryann felt scraped raw. She knew now that the fringes of these feelings had begun to surface again when she was in the hospital in Oxford, and she had pushed them away. But now memories kept coming to her at odd times, unbidden except by a chance fall of the light, certain smells: sweat, a whiff of smoke from someone's cigarette, an odd sound or feeling of cold on her skin. Her own wounds tore open, memories she had long hoped to bury seeping out again and, with them, the terrible knowledge of what he had done to her daughter when she had been unable to protect her. Once again he seemed to be everywhere, creeping, oozing into every situation. Life became like a bad dream, in which he was the dark shadow at the end of each corridor, the face at every window.

Yet she couldn't speak of it, or explain it to Joel. Standing at the helm of the *Theodore* that morning, she felt utterly hopeless. Even to Sally she could not bring herself to say that this man had been her stepfather and had committed the very same foul acts with her. It was too shameful, too hard to bring the words out or explain. She found herself longing for Dot and Sylvia. Though she had never brought herself to talk to them about it, now she felt as if that might just be possible. They would try to comfort her, would not demand anything from her. It would be so much easier than trying to speak to Joel, who wanted her love and her body so badly, yet each time he tried to get close to her she suddenly became like a frightened child again, crying out and sobbing with panic. And, she thought, rage flaming in her, he never asked, never tried to understand why she felt as she did. He had just cut himself off from her, hurt and rejected, unable to find any words of comfort for her. She felt utterly abandoned and lonely, even though Joel was here with her only yards away along the cut.

Forty-One

As spring slid into a warm summer, the Bartholomews' boats worked the Oxford cut. As they travelled north this time, on the stretch where the Oxford shared a section of cut with the Grand Union, Maryann kept an eye out to see if she would spot Sylvia and Dot. Last time they came along here, they had spotted each other close to Nethercote and there had been much excited waving and calling out, exchanging scraps of news while on the move. Sylvia, steering the monkey boat, actually jumped with excitement on catching sight of them.

'Maryann, we miss you! Is everyone all right? Coo-eee – Rose! Hello, darling – see you soon!' And she blew kisses as they passed and her voice faded.

And then Maryann spotted that their third crew member, all smiles beside Dot on the butty, was Bobby! The children waved and shouted.

'We need you!' Maryann teased. 'What're you doing on there with them?'

'Keeping these two in order!' Bobby shouted.

'That's what he thinks!' Dot called.

Bobby's grin and Dot's tanned, radiant face came to her and her spirits lifted. If only they could all be together, she thought as they moved apart, calling, 'See you soon – somewhere!'

It was a month since they'd been to Birmingham. They made their way through the city on a muggy afternoon, the air heavy with smoke and fumes. The noise of the place seemed overwhelming to Maryann: the roar of buses and shriek of brakes on the bridges running over the cut, the clatter of trains and racket from the factories along the banks. She felt wound up to the hilt, her nerves assaulted by the noise, and she wanted to ask Joel to turn round, for them not to have to be here. But of course they couldn't turn round when they had a full load of coal to deliver, the laden boats riding low in the water. Even if she called to Joel, who was ahead of her, he couldn't hear her. After all, she thought sadly, when did they ever really speak to each other these days in any case?

While they were unloading at Tyseley, Maryann went to find Charlie Dean. Looking up and down the wharf, she soon spotted his jaunty figure by the cab of a truck, squinting as he looked up at the driver, cap tilted to the back of his head. She waited, arms folded, until he turned and saw her. She forgot for a moment all her grim troubles, when his face broke into a grin at the sight of her in her blue frock and boots, dark hair curling round her face. She was one who didn't half make him wish he was young and free and that she wasn't already wedded to another man!

'Hello there!' He strode over. ''Bout time you got yourselves back here – haven't seen you in weeks!'

Maryann managed a smile at the sight of Charlie's cheerful, coal-smeared face. The sensation of the corners of her mouth lifting felt unfamiliar. God knew, there'd been precious little to smile about recently. But Charlie's features grew solemn again.

'No news for you, I'm afraid. Nothing, even now. The fuzz aren't getting nowhere and no one's set eyes on that Griffin bloke. Not a peep. Sorry, Maryann.'

He saw her face tighten and, as on other occasions, had to fight a desire to put his arms round her to try and give comfort.

'What're they playing at?' she demanded furiously. 'They must've done summat by now! How many more people's he going to do in before they get to him?'

'They just can't seem to find where he's gone to earth. His car turned up, miles out somewhere. But no one's seen hide nor hair of him. D'you think he might've gone away from Brum?'

Maryann shrugged. 'Someone must've seen him.' Her mind seemed to drift. 'Ta anyway, Charlie,' she said and began to walk off, her thoughts miles away. Charlie watched wistfully. Maryann always touched a soft spot in him. And her suffering wrung his heart.

Being in Birmingham tore the wounds back open. Unable to think of anything else, Maryann did the rounds again. One of them must know something: Pastor Owen, Janet Lambert. There wasn't time to go and see Mrs Biggs, her mom's old neighbour. And she didn't see any reason why Norman Griffin would want to go back there now. Nor did she bother visiting the works. If he'd turned up at his factory, they'd have had the police onto him straight away.

She found Janet Lambert even more pale and worn.

'I can't rest until I know they've got him and put him away,' she said, leading Maryann into the back kitchen. In the gloomy light of the little room, her skin seemed to have a yellow tinge and her eyes were sunken. Her hair was a dull mousy-grey now, thinner and scraped carelessly back into a bun. Maryann was alarmed by her appearance. She looked really ill. As she made tea her hands shook, clattering the spoon convulsively against the side of the cups as she put the sugar in.

'Janet.' Maryann moved closer to her and looked into her eyes. Gently she said, 'Janet, love, I know you're going through hell, but you must look after yourself. Don't let him do this to you.'

Janet turned to her and Maryann saw the utter despair in her eyes.

'What more *can* he do to me, Maryann? He's already taken away everything I ever had. He might as well just come and kill me now. It doesn't matter any more.'

They sat in the parlour, the cups on a small occasional table on a cloth embroidered with butterflies. Janet had always kept a genteel home. They talked for a while and Maryann steeled herself to ask about Margaret, Janet's other daughter.

'I want to go and see our Margaret.' Janet looked across with begging eyes. 'I don't go often. Can't stand it. And I can hardly manage the tram and all that now. But it's a visiting day tomorrow. Will you come over there with me so's I don't have to go on my own?'

Maryann felt a plunge of dread inside her. Oh God, not this on top of everything else! The asylum! The very word filled her with horror, let alone the thought of the huge, grim building with its dark gates. She had only seen Margaret there once before and the images she carried in her head of the child were terrible. How could she stand to go and face Margaret now? But how could she refuse Janet, the state she was in? Her mind raced. If she was to go with her tomorrow, they'd have to put off leaving Birmingham after they were loaded up. She'd already left Joel to do everything this evening and he'd be cross at the delay. Joel became angry so easily these days. She knew the pain in his back and his sense of helplessness in the face of her suffering made him frustrated, but it didn't make anything easier.

'Course I will, Janet,' she heard herself saying. She felt melted with pity inside and reached over to take Janet's hand. How could she not meet this desperate request? 'Course I'll come with you.'

Janet accepted the comfort, fingers exploring Maryann's palm, and the feel of the callused skin distracted her for a moment.

'You lead a rough life, don't you, dear? Hard-working, I mean. It must be tough on you.'

'It doesn't let up much,' Maryann agreed. 'Best never to think about how tired you are.'

'You've a good husband, though.' Janet's eyes searched her face. 'Counts for everything, that does. Look what happened to me. Don't you forget it.'

Maryann looked down to hide her emotion. 'Yes – he is.'

There was a silence while Janet still held her hand.

'You'll come with me?'

'I said I would.'

'Bolt the door tonight, won't you?' she said to Joel. He nodded. Joel had been surprisingly patient about her request to go and see Margaret the next day. For a while that evening she thought things might be getting better, that they could be easier together. But at bedtime he had almost ordered her and the girls out of the *Esther Jane*'s cabin. It felt as if he was afraid to be near her.

She settled the girls in the *Theodore*. Before locking up, she pushed the hatch open and stood on the step, breathing in the night air and gazing round the wharf. With an ache she looked back at the *Esther Jane* and pictured Joel inside with the boys. If only he could just hold her, give her comfort instead of always wanting more when he touched her . . .

The shadows round the wharf seemed to mock her and her flesh came up in goose pimples. Fear grew in her. Was someone standing in those deep pools of darkness? He was out there somewhere. The sense of being constantly watched overtook her and she hurried back into the cabin, feverishly pulling the hatch closed and fastening the bolt.

It was never going to get better, she thought, lying down on her bed. Not while he was still out there. The great darkness outside seemed to be pressing in on the boat and she curled up, frightened, her arm round Sally, trying with her body to protect her from all harm.

Forty-Two

They stood at the asylum gates on a grey, rainy afternoon. Maryann had helped Janet on and off the tram, and the physical exertions of the journey, of struggling with walking sticks on her bad leg, had only added to Janet's emotional distress.

Maryann walked beside her on her painfully slow progress up the drive. Their coats were silvered with rain. As they reached the entrance, Janet faltered. For a moment she stared at the wet ground, then turned to look at Maryann. She didn't speak, but her anguished expression said, *I can't bear it*. Maryann took her arm.

'You're still her mom. She's your daughter. It's not your fault she's here, Janet.'

Janet shook her head, a desolate expression on her face. 'I think that I've come to terms with it until I come back here. She'll never be my Margaret again. Not after all this time.' She squeezed her eyes tightly closed. Maryann saw tiny, convulsive movements in her jaw muscles as she fought to remain in control of herself. 'It *is* my fault. For bringing him into the family . . .'

'No!' Maryann gripped Janet's arm fiercely. 'It's his fault. *All* his fault! Don't ever say it's your fault.'

Janet took a deep breath and looked up again. 'Oh Lord.' She sighed desperately. And after fighting for composure, she said, 'It's all right. Let's get in out of the wet.'

Immediately inside the entrance they were in another world. The sound of the big doors closing behind them made Maryann shudder. Outside they had left the wet air, full of factory smells and smoke, wind-shaken trees and buses and trams passing on the distant road. Now there were other smells, alien and institutional: whiffs of floor polish and disinfectant, stale cooking and another sweet, sickening smell which Maryann couldn't identify. Here they were in a world of high ceilings, of grey, distempered walls, of footsteps echoing in long, gloomy corridors, of locked doors, odd sounds. It felt sealed off and utterly separate from life outside.

The orderly who met them was a bald, middle-aged man who walked with a limp. As he led them to the visitor's room, Maryann saw the silhouette of a male figure moving away along the corridor in the distance, sliding close to the wall, with an odd, slouching walk. It was impossible to guess his age, but the brief glimpse made her feel profoundly unsettled. She shivered, cold even though she had her coat on still. She had a horror of places like this and if it hadn't been for Janet she would have obeyed the impulse to turn and run, to escape from the oppressive atmosphere.

There were three other people waiting in the visitors' room, who sat in silence looking subdued and anxious. A plump lady in a brown pork-pie hat stared at them as they came in, but the others looked away.

'She'll be brought to you at half-past two,' the orderly said, before backing out as if they might all turn on him and shutting the door. Perhaps it was just habit, working here, Maryann thought. There were only a few minutes to go, according to a clock on the wall, but the minute hand seemed to take an eternity to creep round from the five to the six. Everyone waited, not speaking. Maryann and Janet both sat in their coats: although it was June, the room held no warmth. The windows were long but high, letting in cobweb-coloured light. Other than the wooden chairs round the walls the only furniture was a table, pushed up against the wall in one corner, with an empty vase standing on it.

Just after half-past two they heard footsteps in the corridor and three women were brought in: the first a suety, middle-aged woman, her frizzy black hair caught up in a bun, followed by a scrawny girl whose age was hard to guess. There was a pause, and then they heard a man's voice in the corridor saying impatiently, 'No, it's not – it's two women. You going in or not?'

Margaret appeared then, but she clung to the door handle, peering fearfully across at them until she was sure who it was before she came towards them. She was a slight figure, her bright auburn hair tied back into a greasy-looking bunch, grey eyes squinting as she peered across the room, looking, Maryann thought, like a frightened hound. She was wearing a brown pinafore dress several sizes too big which hung on her, the waistband too low and the skirt falling well below her knees. Under it was a fawn blouse. Her face was still freckled, and very pale, not pretty – the eyes were too narrow, her expression dull and vacant. For a moment she stood in front of them staring at her feet on the wooden floor.

'Won't you sit down, Margaret?' Janet suggested. She hadn't got up to greet her. When Margaret was perched, ill at ease, on a chair, Janet went on, 'I haven't been in a while, love. Sorry. I haven't been all that well.'

Margaret accepted this without comment. Her hands, in her lap, were never still, and Maryann's eyes kept being drawn back to their restless movements. Her fingers were thin and red raw, as if she had them constantly in and out of water. Her nails were bitten down to the quicks and there were sores where she chewed and picked compulsively at them, as she was doing now.

And neither was Janet at ease. Her walking sticks were resting at an angle against her legs, and she held the handle of one, her fingers twitching nervously. Janet's discomfort, her remorse, was something you could almost smell in the room, over the whiff of floor polish. Maryann saw, with pity, that she was afraid of her daughter and barely knew what to say to her. From her own instincts as a mother she knew Janet ought to be able to say, I want you with me, child. Let me take you away, take you home. But they both knew Margaret was not going home. She had come here when she was exceptionally young, ten years ago, because of the seriousness of what she had done. Looking at her, Maryann could see she was not fit for life in the normal world out there. She was docile enough, but her mind had been badly scarred as a child, and now she had been here too long. No one was going to plead for her release. The rest of her life would be behind the asylum walls.

'You all right, love?' Janet asked, a tremor in her voice. Margaret was not looking at them, but staring distractedly round the room as if only half aware they were there. 'You remember Maryann, don't you?'

Margaret's gaze returned to them and she looked at Maryann blankly then gave a faint nod. Maryann wasn't sure if she really remembered. It was impossible to tell. She found herself hoping that Margaret *didn't* remember her.

'Hello, Margaret,' she attempted gently. 'You keeping all right?'

Margaret nodded tersely, then looked accusingly at her mother.

'They're giving us that stuff to eat again – gruel like. It's horrible. I don't like it,' she said petulantly. Her voice was thick, clumsy, as if her tongue was unpractised in speech, and her gaze didn't fix for long on the person she was talking to, but shifted about.

'Well,' Janet said, 'I suppose with the shortages and everything—'

'It's nasty.' Margaret cut in across her. 'We had porridge before. I like porridge. I don't like gruel.' She spoke loudly like a sulky child, almost shouting, so that the woman in the pork-pie hat glanced round at them. Margaret couldn't seem to fit her talking properly round the rhythm of anyone else speaking. Conversation with her felt like a jigsaw puzzle in which none of the pieces slotted together properly.

'When's our Amy coming? She hasn't been in ages. Tell her to come.'

Maryann saw Janet's jaw tighten. 'Oh, she'll be along in a few days I expect. She's been very busy. Started a new job, and she—'

'But she hasn't been! She always comes and she hasn't been!'

Maryann sat horrified, watching the two of them. All this time and Margaret didn't know Amy was dead? Whenever was Janet planning to tell her? Janet carefully avoided her gaze. Margaret was chewing her left thumb like a starved person.

'She's my sister!' she cried.

Maryann was disturbed by the look in her eyes at that moment: something fixed and cold, animal, not quite human, or that was how it seemed to her. Margaret pulled her hair forward over her shoulder and tugged at the ends of it, moving her body agitatedly.

'He came. He came to see me.' She was rocking back and forwards now.

Janet cast Maryann a worried, sceptical look.

'Who came?' she asked with exaggerated patience.

'*Him*. My *stepfather*.' This last was said in a mocking, sing-song tone.

'What d'you mean?' Janet's voice rose with panic. 'You haven't got a stepfather! What on earth're you talking about?'

'I have! *Him*. Your husband – you haven't forgot him, have you? He came in here visiting – with that face. Trying to hide – under his hat.' She giggled suddenly, a harsh snicker. 'I did that to him all by myself!'

Janet was on the edge of her chair, grabbing at Margaret's hands.

'What d'you mean?' Janet implored her. 'What're you saying – he came here? Margaret, is this true or are you making up a story?'

'He told them he was my stepfather – well, he was once, wasn't he?' Margaret sneered.

'*When*? When was he here?'

'I dunno.' Margaret looked sullenly down at the floor. 'Since Amy came. Long time ago. Dunno now.'

'Well, what did he want? What did he say?'

Margaret shrugged. Maryann felt a sudden urge to shake the words out of her.

'Talked about his mother. Said he was sorry. I wasn't listening.'

The two of them sat in stunned silence at the preposterousness of this. Rain blew against the window behind them. It was coming down more heavily now, the sky even darker.

'Margaret, did this really happen?' Maryann asked,

though she already sensed that Margaret was telling the truth. She wouldn't have the ability to invent such a story.

'He came. I told you. You could ask that lady.' She jerked her head towards the woman in the pork-pie hat. 'She was here then, an' all. Kept staring at him.'

'But what did he *want*?' Maryann could hear a note of hysteria in Janet's voice and felt something similar rising in herself.

'Dunno. He asked me about the family – where everyone is. I dunno where they are. Asked me about Auntie Maureen and if she was still in Alvechurch. She was the only one I could remember. We went out there, daint we? She had them kittens.'

'What else?' Janet demanded.

Margaret shrugged. 'Dunno.' Her mind seemed to slide away and she looked about the room again, chewing savagely at the end of her finger.

For the rest of the visit, however hard they tried to press her, she would say no more. Conversation flagged. After all, what life did Margaret have to tell them about? Only that she was still apparently doing sewing. Mending clothes.

At last they had to say goodbye. As Janet kissed her, Margaret stood passively and asked if she could bring some sweets next time. She didn't seem to understand about rationing, even now.

The two of them were ushered out and the doors slammed behind them, leaving them to face the rain.

'It's easing off a bit, I think,' Maryann said, trying to sound cheerful. In fact it was still raining just as hard, but it was a relief to get out of the dim, enclosed world of the hospital. She longed to get back to the cut, to get untied and away from Birmingham.

Janet closed her eyes for a second and let out a long,

shuddering sigh. 'I find it hard to believe she's mine any more.' She opened her eyes and looked at Maryann. 'My little Margaret.'

Maryann couldn't stand any more emotion. She took Janet's arm.

'Come on. Let's get home.'

But Janet was staring ahead of her at the steady fall of rain. In a despairing voice, he said, 'What does he want? What more *can* he want from us?'

Maryann was in the fringes between waking and sleep that night when the knocking forced her awake again, knuckles wrapping insistently on the door. Her body tensed in a rigor which left her for several seconds incapable of movement.

'Maryann?' she heard. 'Don't worry, it's only me – Charlie.'

Whatever did he want? She liked Charlie, but felt apprehensive, remembering what she had seen in his eyes sometimes when he looked at her. His attraction to her was not something she found comfortable. And why would he be coming to see her at this time of night?

She opened up the back, pulling her coat tightly round her. The rain had stopped and the night was clear. Charlie must have retreated when he heard her unbolting the door, as he was now standing on the bank. With him was a woman. In the poor light Maryann made out a sweet face and curly hair falling round her cheeks. Was that his wife? she wondered, bewildered.

'Sorry—' Charlie began. Though he was speaking in a low voice, it communicated urgency. 'Only, Liza and me – this is Liza, by the way –' Maryann gave the young woman a faint smile – 'we was out near Osborne's – by

Mulligan's ironmonger's. That's Liza's dad's shop, see – and we was up the entry –' Maryann saw Liza look at the ground and sensed rather than being able to see her blushes. No, not his wife then. Her estimation of Charlie sank a little.

'Anyroad – this motor car came and stopped in the road and these blokes got out. We just heard voices and that. We wouldn't've taken any notice, would we, Lize? Only then there was this noise, like – how would you describe it?'

'It was a kiddie crying out,' Liza said.

'Not just crying – howling,' Charlie said sombrely. 'As if it was in pain. Like a little rabbit. And I said, ey-up, summat amiss here. Didn't I, Lize?'

Liza nodded shyly.

'I looked out the end of the entry, Maryann, and I didn't hear anything else. But I got the shock of my life, 'cause that's when I saw him, just going up the entry to Osborne's!'

'Him?' Maryann's throat tightened. 'Mr Griffin?' Charlie had seen him before, of course, but could he be so sure in the dark street?

'Oh, it was him all right. Hat pulled down like he wears it to hide that fizz-hog of his. There was three of them – another big bloke went in behind him and the other one drove off again after.'

'*Osborne's?*' Maryann was completely bewildered. Charlie must be mistaken. Whatever could Norman Griffin want with kind Mr Osborne? 'Maybe it was the place on the other side he was going to?'

'Nope. It's Osborne's all right. Heard the door go. And Liza's room's across the road from them and she says she reckons there's someone else living above the shop in the attic.'

'They suddenly put blackouts up a few weeks back,' Liza said. 'There was nothing before. It was all empty. And I've seen someone moving about once or twice in the day. I've never seen anyone come in or out, though.'

The hatch of the *Esther Jane* slid open and Joel came out, pulling on his jacket. Maryann explained what had happened.

'You think they're still up there, then?' Joel said.

Charlie nodded. 'We came straight here.'

'Come on, then.' Joel was all set to go and roust them out himself. 'Let's go and see.'

'But the coppers,' Charlie protested, 'they're s'posed to be looking for him. Shouldn't we get them?'

This was an idea foreign to Joel's self-sufficient ways. He hesitated.

'Well, all right then. But if they don't get on with it we might just as well do it ourselves.'

Forty-Three

Joel and Charlie waited for the police to arrive, standing along the street from Mr Osborne's shop. Maryann had stayed with the boats, the children. She wasn't leaving them alone, for Sally to wake and find her gone.

'Take their flaming time, don't they?' Charlie ground the stub of a cigarette against the cobbles with his heel, then immediately reached into his pocket for his packet of Woodbines and offered it to Joel.

'No ta.' Joel knocked his fist against his chest. 'Can't.'

'Sorry, pal – forgot.' Charlie lit one up for himself. He was too young to have fought in the Great War. 'Gas, was it?'

Joel nodded. His back was giving him a lot of pain too – it hurt far more than he would admit to Maryann. Beside Charlie he felt old, done in.

Charlie peered along the dark street. 'Better watch in case they sneak out again without us seeing,' he said through his cigarette. He took it from his mouth and spat on the ground. 'Filthy bastards.'

Joel said nothing. He was not much of a one for words in any case, and he could not have expressed what he felt towards Norman Griffin. Since his return to the boats from Oxford, his daughter had been taken away, his wife had withdrawn from him, and he knew that the mute misery he could see in Maryann was somehow rooted in what she too had experienced at the hands of her stepfather. Joel had never known exactly what went on while Norman Griffin was with Maryann's family. She'd never said and he couldn't bear to ask, had no idea what to do to make it better. He longed to take her to him in bed, to love and caress her sorrow away, but he knew he couldn't. Since he had been back she had been closed off to him. If he touched her she fought him off or turned away, rigid, weeping. Better in some ways that they sleep on different boats. Then at least the warm shape of her beside him was not a temptation. But it was a sad, lonely state of affairs which he found hard to bear. His fists clenched with fury at the thought of Norman Griffin. He wanted to storm into the house and do him violence, never mind waiting for these duffers, the police.

'Why the hell don't they hurry up?' he burst out eventually. 'Bloody useless idiots.'

A few moments later they saw the shaded lights of a car approaching from the far end of the street. Charlie flagged it down a little way along from Osborne's shop. Three policemen climbed out carrying truncheons and stood looking around them.

'In here,' Charlie said.

The most senior policeman must have been nearly sixty and had a neat little moustache.

'You sure it's him?'

'It's him,' Charlie said. 'You couldn't mistake that face. I only caught a glimpse, but he's the one.'

'All right, lads.' The three of them stood apart by a lamp post and conferred for a moment. Joel saw the two younger ones listen, leaning in for instructions.

'I reckon he's only a sergeant, that one,' Charlie murmured. 'You'd think they'd manage to send a bigger fish along for this, wouldn't you?'

'Right,' the sergeant said as they came over again.

'Only thing we can do is take them by surprise. You think they're up at the top of the house do you?'

'The attic,' Charlie said.

'And how many're in there?'

'Three, I'd say.'

'Right,' he said again. 'Come on then.'

The three men stepped into the pitch black of the entry. Joel and Charlie glanced at one another, then followed. One of the policemen switched a torch on, creating a picture show of jumping shadows. They all crept silently round to the back door.

'Ready, lads?'

The door broke open on the second try and banged back hard. The policemen raced through it and upstairs, making the most terrific racket on the bare boards. Charlie raced after them and Joel followed, up through the dark house, frustrated by his slowness. There was a particular, cloying smell, and he realized after a few seconds that it was of meat. Of course – this was a butcher's shop. Fancy living with that horrible stink all the time!

He heard the other men reach the top of the attic stairs and the door crash open. He paused at the last bend in the stairs, expecting instant sounds of mayhem, of shouts, even fighting. But there was a moment of stunned confusion and during it he followed them into the room, panting from the stairs.

He was in a dingy attic room, with a sloping roof at one side. Three men were round the little table in the middle; a bottle lay on its side dribbling its contents over the table and onto the floor, evidently knocked over as the round-faced fellow facing Joel had leapt to his feet. On one side of him was grey-haired Mr Osborne; on the other Norman Griffin sat hunched, looking impassively in front of him. Under the high, dormer window was an old iron bedstead with a filthy mattress on which crouched a little girl, her distraught face smeared with dirt and tears.

'What d'you think you're—?' Mr Osborne got to his feet then. He sounded frightened.

'Stay where you are,' the sergeant said. 'No monkeying about. You're all under arrest.'

At his nod the other two policemen jumped into action. The round-faced man struggled, panicking.

'No – you can't do this to me! This is ridiculous – a mistake! I shouldn't be here –'

'No – quite right, you shouldn't, sir,' the policeman said, forcing the man's hands behind his back as he tried to struggle. In a moment the handcuffs were fastened on. The other officer had handcuffed Mr Osborne, who stood in shocked, sullen silence.

Norman Griffin hadn't attempted to move from the table so they left him until last. There was something about his brooding stillness and the grotesque distortion of his face that made them hesitate, reluctant to move closer or lay hands on him, almost as if he were an unearthly creature, not fully human. Joel saw him look round and fasten his one good eye on him, and held Griffin's gaze, revolted at what he saw. That puckered, shiny skin – what a horrible sight he was! For a second Joel even pitied him.

Norman Griffin pushed the chair back and stood up slowly. Out of the corner of his eye, Joel saw the sergeant take a step forward.

'So – Mr Bartholomew,' Norman Griffin said. His tone was mocking. 'Little Maryann's husband.'

Anger flared in Joel. 'How do *you* know who I am?'

'Oh, I get about, don't forget. Quite a regular visitor

to the wharves. I keep an eye on things – I like to look out for my old family members.' He made a sound which could have been a laugh or a clearing of the chest. 'Make sure they're not coming to any harm. I've never been sure at all about you, for Maryann. Far too young, she was, when she first took up with you.'

Joel drew his fist back, but in that split second Norman Griffin launched his weight at him, catching him off balance and thrusting him back against the open door. Joel cried out with pain and fury as the hard door crashed into his back. Norman Griffin took off down the stairs.

'Well, get after him, you gormless clods!' the sergeant yelled, furious at himself for hesitating. 'How could you let that happen?' The other two let go of the scowling Mr Osborne and the third man and took off in pursuit.

'They'll soon catch him up – he's twice their age,' the sergeant said.

'Yes, but they've only half his intelligence,' Mr Osborne muttered sourly.

'Downstairs!' the sergeant barked at the two prisoners.

'I'll give you a hand with them,' Charlie Dean said, roughly catching hold of the plump man. 'It'll be a pleasure.'

Joel was going to follow when he realized everyone seemed to have forgotten about the little girl. She was pressed against the wall, squatting on her haunches, arms clasped round her knees. Joel saw that she was wearing a skimpy yellow frock, heavily soiled and with one sleeve badly torn. His heart went out to her. Although she had dark brown hair, unbrushed and messy, in every other way she reminded him of their little Sally. They must have been much of an age.

'Hello there, little 'un.' He spoke very gently.

Her eyes widened further and she tried to press herself back harder against the wall.

'I'm going to come over and sit by you.' Joel felt uncomfortably conscious of his enormous size in comparison with her. He seemed like a giant and felt a discomfort that recently, for the first time in his life, his wife had also made him feel: a sense of contamination as a man. What had been forced on this poor waif of a girl? What must he seem like to her? Just another heartless monster come to harm her?

'Don't run away.' He tried to make himself smaller, bending his knees, shrinking down as he walked until he sat himself gingerly on the edge of the grubby mattress. He could see a damp patch on it and there was a pungent smell of urine. The girl flinched, but didn't get up to move away. Close up to her, Joel could see why. Her ankles were tied together with a piece of cord, so tightly that he could see the mauve bite of it where it met her flesh.

'Poor little thing.' He felt close to weeping at the state of her. 'Can you tell me your name?'

'Carol,' she whispered.

'I'm Joel. I won't hurt you, I promise. I've come to help you. Now – let's get these off, shall we?'

Taking his knife from his pocket, he cut the cords away from her ankles and she whimpered at the pain as he did so. She rubbed at the angry welts on her ankles when he'd finished, tears running down her cheeks.

'Now then,' Joel told her gently, 'we're going to get you home safely to your mom and dad, aren't we?'

When Charlie Dean came back up he found Joel sitting on the bed, his arm round the little girl, who was sobbing her heart out beside him.

*

When the two policemen ran out in search of Norman Griffin, they got out of the entry only to find that he had already disappeared. For a moment they stood at a loss in the street.

'We're going to get it in the neck for this,' one said gloomily.

'He can't've got far, old geezer like him. You go that way and I'll go this. We'll soon find him.'

They ran off in opposite directions.

Just a few yards away, pressed into the shadows at the back of the house, only feet from the back door, Norman Griffin smiled grimly into the darkness.

Maryann sat at the table in the *Theodore*. In the quiet night she heard the chucking sound of a water bird, which must have strayed out unusually late.

Should be safe on a nest somewhere by now, she thought protectively. *Perhaps it's a young one.* She sipped her tea, feeling very tense, wondering what was going on and where Joel and Charlie had got to. At moments she wished she'd gone with them so she wouldn't have to wait in an agony of wondering. Had they found him? Were the police there? Or had it been the wrong place, wrong person? Had Charlie Dean made a mistake?

She'd put all the girls down to sleep, top to toe, on the main bed. There was no point in her trying to sleep. Filling up her cup from the old brown and white teapot, she sat holding it with both hands, her thoughts spinning round. She thought of Amy Lambert, of what Margaret had said to them, such as it was. Why was Norman Griffin asking about their relatives in Alvechurch? Janet had said that her sister had young daughters. Surely he wasn't planning to track down every member of every family he'd ever been involved with? It was a terrible thought. Her mind moved on to the night the boatmen had found the girl's body in the cellar in Acocks Green and at that she could stand her thoughts no more. She picked up one of Sylvia's old magazines, dog-eared by now, desperate to distract herself. The sight of it brought a faint smile to her lips, remembering Sylvia exclaiming over some of the pictures, but she couldn't concentrate.

Oh, I wish Dot and Sylvia were here still! Maryann thought, giving up and closing the magazine. She missed them more than she could ever have imagined. Thinking back to their arrival on the boats, she remembered how resentful and irritable she'd felt, how all she'd wanted was to have Joel back and for nothing to change. But now he was back and things had changed more than she could ever have imagined. It all felt impossible. She couldn't be close to him or give him what a husband wanted and needed. And it was her that was at fault. There was something deeply, horribly wrong with her to make her like this. Unable to bear the pain of her thoughts, she pushed them away. Tonight, maybe they'd get *him* once and for all. Get him put away, and then maybe her nightmares would come to an end.

Sighing, she picked up the magazine again. Another small sound came from outside and she tensed, listening. But nothing else followed. It must have been one of the other families further along the bank. Maybe she'd even imagined it, the state she was in. Then, a moment later she heard sounds she knew were real: hurrying footsteps and then they were back, knocking on the cabin. At last!

'Coming!' she called.

She undid the bolt and the hatch was abruptly pushed back.

'Did you get him . . .?'

But the questions died in her throat. His form filled the doorway and he was climbing down into the cabin, his ravaged face caught in the lamplight as he leaned in towards her, lips curved into a triumphant smile.

'Hello, Maryann,' he said.

Forty-Four

She could hear his laboured breathing as he slid the hatch closed and shut the door. He'd obviously been hurrying over some distance.

'Sit down,' he ordered.

In that instant it was as if all her will had been stolen from her. Maryann sank onto the side bench as she was bidden, with a wild glance at the back bed. To her relief she saw that the curtains were drawn right across, hiding the girls as they lay sleeping. She prayed that none of them would stir and cry out.

Norman Griffin struggled down the steps. He was a bulky man and unused to moving in this confined space.

'Move up, so I can sit by you, then,' he ordered, and she slid along the bench as if she was programmed to obey him. She couldn't seem to think properly, as if he had scrambled her thoughts. How could she ever get out? She noted that he had not fastened the bolt at the bottom of the door, but even if she managed to get past him, she couldn't leave him with the children. She was trapped in here with him again, and now he was not just her stepfather with his vile, dirty ways. He'd done worse things, terrible things! She despaired, then, paralysed with fear. *Oh, please*, her mind begged, *let someone, come! Joel, where are you?* She pressed herself as far along the bench as she could, trying to get away from him.

'Don't know how you manage in here.' He lumbered round, stooped to avoid banging his head and squeezed himself, grunting, into the space beside her. 'Like living in a matchbox.'

It was such close quarters that avoiding her cramped proximity to him was impossible, though she tried to shrink away, every cell of her body in revolt.

Norman Griffin laid his hat on the table, and the sight of his face, horribly visible now in the light, the smell of him, of sweat and damp clothing, the press of him against her, turned her into a child again: petrified and at his mercy.

He turned and looked at her, having to swivel his body to fix her with his good eye. Up close she could see with horrible clarity the damaged skin, the way the flames had shrivelled and distorted it. She became aware of her own blood pounding through her veins.

'You always were a nice-looking girl, Maryann. I know the passing of the years takes it out of us. None more so than me—' He made a harsh, self-mocking sound which made her jump and he noticed. 'No need to be nervous ... Yes – you've still got your looks, wench – a freshness about you. Must be living in the open air that does it.'

His voice was soft, wheedling and seductive in the way that she remembered, how he would be before he touched her. The sound filled her with sick dread.

'We go back a long way don't we, you and me?'

You and me. As if there had ever been a 'you and me'!

'What d'you want?' she managed to whisper. She knew she shouldn't show him how frightened she was, but she couldn't control it. She knew her eyes were stretched wide with fear.

'What do I want? Don't be like that!' To her horror he reached for her left hand and pulled it to him, holding it tightly, stroking it. 'You were my daughter once – remember?'

'Stepdaughter,' she corrected, screaming in her head, *You were never my father, never!* All the time he was talking she kept looking round the cabin. How could she get away?

'I used to bath you when you was just a tiny, skinny little thing. And look at you now – a grown-up woman with, how many kiddies is it?'

She didn't answer. *Keep him from thinking about the girls.* She stared back at him as he went on and on stroking her hand.

'I miss having family,' he said plaintively. 'It's a lonely life with no one.'

He paused and she heard his rasping breaths. She felt the dreadful thud of her heart.

'I was sorry to hear about your mother going like that. I went to see her a few times before she died, you know. I've missed her over the years. She were a good woman, Flo was. Good to me. That's why I've come to see you – chew over old times for a bit.'

Maryann almost laughed at the grotesqueness of this. *He's mad.* Her mind was racing. *Stark staring bonkers.* She might have expected all sorts of horrors from him, but not this – not a reminiscence session! Perhaps she should keep him talking, keep his mind off her, off the children, and, pray God, Joel would soon be back . . .

'You used to take us to the pictures.' She managed to make her voice sound almost even and normal. 'Best seats and a nice bag of bulls' eyes. D'you remember? Me and Sal and the boys – all with Mom? Family outing.'

He was listening to her attentively, seemed to be

smiling. She watched his face, appalled. Didn't he remember what had happened to Sal? That she'd lain alone with the life blood dripping from her wrist because of all he'd done to her? Didn't he know that? Or was it stored away in some forgotten part of his mind, like a locked trunk?

'We had some nice times, didn't we?' he was saying, suddenly sounding so plaintive that for a second she felt as if there was a child speaking beside her.

'Yes, we did,' she lied.

'We were a family. Amy and Margaret were family too – we used to sit round the table of a night, cosy as anything. I was a dad to you, wasn't I, Maryann?'

This grotesque travesty pierced her so that again she could not speak, but she nodded. What would he do if she told the truth about what he had caused? What if she shattered the shining wall of illusion he was building round them both? She barely managed to hide her shudders at him touching her hand.

'You're trembling,' he said, closing his other hand over hers. 'There's no need to be frightened of your old dad.'

She said nothing.

'I've had a lonely life since ... since Janet and the girls. Walking the streets looking like this. You might as well be a leper. No one'll come near you. I've got my business, of course. I couldn't go on being an undertaker with this face on me – had to move into something else. The business is doing well, thanks to Herr Hitler. And they have to treat me all right. All they want is to feed their families, their kiddies.' There was a savage tone in his voice. 'I'm the boss. I hold the purse strings, see. But other than that, I've taken to going out at night so's I don't get noticed. I'm a wreck of a man, aren't I? I'm loathsome, inside and out.' He looked up at her and all she could do was to stare back, mute. 'Who'd ever look at me now?'

After staring at her for a moment he said, 'I've come to apologize.'

She waited, hardly breathing, deeply suspicious. What was this now? A trick? It would be easier if she knew what he really wanted. But he sounded sincere and abject with self-pity.

'I was never a good enough father to you girls. Never had a father of my own, see. He took off when I was a babe in arms. He was a soldier. And Mother...' he stalled. 'No one ever understood Mother, understood *about* her, should I say. No one knew, you see.'

Maryann thought of the portrait, the sole decoration on the drab walls of his room. Mother's eyes looking out at him from that sternly beautiful face.

Norman was staring down at her hand, stroking it again. Maryann struggled to remember what age he must be. Getting on for seventy by now and sitting here bleating about his mother. It seemed peculiar and deeply pathetic. She was startled by a tiny sound from the back bed, one of the children shifting in their sleep and she held her breath, managing to stop her eyes from moving in the direction of the sound. Norman didn't seem to notice.

'You're a kind mother to your kiddies, aren't you, Maryann? My mother wasn't kind. She was .. unnatural.' He seemed to lose his thread again, then said, 'I've done some terrible things. I tried to tell that young man – that Pastor Owen. Not that other fool, of course – Joyce. Owen's an innocent. He's a real believer. Terrible for someone like me to come face to face with it – with someone who thinks there's goodness. I tried to tell him

– never got far. I wouldn't've got him to believe all I've done. D'you know, I abandoned my own son? Never saw him again from when he was seven years old. I don't know where he is to this day.' To her horror she heard his rasping voice begin to crack.

'You're the only one left, Maryann! You know me, don't you?' He was wrestling with his emotions, beginning to sob and she watched, horrified. 'I can talk to you. You know who I am. But even you don't know. You thought your mother was a cruel woman, but Flo was a saint compared with my beloved mother. She was the beloved, you see. My beloved. And I was hers.'

His shoulders heaved and in the second that he loosed her to reach for his handkerchief, Maryann pulled her hand free, nursing it to her as if she'd been stung. The sight of Norman Griffin weeping was horrifying. She shrank back, fascinated yet repelled, her loathing unmixed with any shred of pity. Her body tingled all over with the instinct to run away, but she was trapped.

'She was so beautiful,' he was sobbing. 'The smell of her. She was so soft. Her bed always smelt of her – her soap, her body.'

Maryann sat very still, caught by what he was saying, by the tone of it. His voice had turned into a high, infant whine, and she saw a tear fall from his good eye and drop, glistening, onto the lapel of his coat.

Norman Griffin squeezed his eyes closed and shook his head violently as if to dislodge a picture from his mind. 'Her body – she was always there, with that body.' Looking round at her, he said, 'You're a mother, Maryann: you wouldn't have your own son in your bed, would you? Standing in for your husband?'

Maryann looked back at him, almost unable to believe what she was hearing.

'She was such a cruel woman – so cruel in the daytime when she didn't want me, you know, like that.' He halted again abruptly. 'I've never said this to a living soul before . . .' He tried to swallow, struggling as if there was something stuck in his throat.

'Night-times, most nights – it never ended, the feel of her, making me touch her, and I wanted to in the end, couldn't stop . . . All soft, damp . . .' He closed his eyes, face contorting even further. 'She wanting me to touch her, kiss her. It was all different in the daytime. When she wasn't pleased with me her mouth went straight and hard, eyes drilling into me. She looked as if – as if she couldn't stand the sight of me. And she kept her cat-o'-nine-tails tied to her belt.' There was a silence, then words flooded out.

'She always beat me on my backside. Made me take my trousers down – short trousers when I was younger, of course. Always in the parlour, behind the nets. The things she used to say while she was doing it. She'd reach her arm right up as far as it would go and bring it down, nothing held back in the sting of it. I was red raw when she'd finished. The school chairs were so hard, I could barely sit. She made me bend over the sideboard. There was a china dish on there with a blue glaze on it and I'd always stand by it. I could see my face in it. I'd look at it while she was beating me. If I made a noise she did it even harder, told me I was weak, no good. So I thought, I'll keep my face straight so that boy in the dish will look back at me and he doesn't look bad and he's not having a thrashing off his mom and he can't hear the things she's saying about me being dirty and wicked . . . I'll be like him. It got so's I was always that other boy, hiding with him till she'd finished.' He let out a shuddering sigh.

'I never knew what was coming then. Sometimes she'd just go out and leave me with my backside all welts, and she'd close the door very quietly as if there was someone poorly asleep in there and she didn't want to disturb them. As if I was sick. Then sometimes –' he shuddered – 'she'd pull on my shoulders while I was still bent over and make me stand up. I was half naked and she'd make me put my arms round her and kiss her and she'd press herself against me.

'"It's for your own good, Normie – it'll make you a proper man, like your father was."'

He had his eyes closed, as if trapped in the memories. Maryann eyed the door desperately, sickened by what she was hearing, by him expecting her pity, playing on her sympathy, perhaps even inventing all this for some warped reason of his own. But, worst of all, she knew in her heart by the way he talked that he hadn't invented it.

'Course he was always a proper man, a soldier. She made me feel like . . . nothing. A weak, spineless reed.'

She could hold her silence no longer.

'So why did you do it to us? To my sister – and to Amy and Margaret?' Unbidden, tears came, the surge of grief stronger even than fear in that moment, like a deep crack opening in her onto the pain of it all, the awfulness of being here with this man who had caused it and his monstrous, pathetic story.

When he answered her, his tone had changed as if her speaking had brought him to a different plane in himself. There was a hard coldness which brought her up abruptly and stemmed her tears.

'I have to. It's the only thing that makes me feel better. Feel nothing. For a while. I had to tell someone. It got so's I had to. I tried to tell that Pastor Owen, but he's a man and he's too . . . clean. I had to tell a woman.

Only I couldn't have her spreading it. I started with Amy. She grew up into a right pretty thing. I thought she'd be kind. But she wouldn't listen. I tried to make her hold still, but she kept struggling and she wouldn't let me finish. I had to do it. Couldn't have her telling anyone else.'

Maryann froze again. He'd told all of it to her now, his sad, dirty secrets, the perverted bullying of his mother. She'd been the one to hear it whether she chose to or not, and now ... She had to keep him talking, to keep him calm. She saw him staring at her and his expression was cold and terrible.

'Good at asking questions, aren't you? Wheedling things out of me? You always were a devious little thing – always the one I could never quite get to grips with.' He caught hold of her wrist abruptly, so hard that she gave a yelp of pain.

'Don't,' she panted. 'Don't hurt me. Why hurt someone else? Where does it get you? I've got a family. Just leave us, leave us alone instead of making everything worse. It doesn't make anything better for you – it just goes on and on.'

'But it *does* make me better – for a little while. It makes me happy and light, better than a tumbler of Scotch. As if there's nothing in the world to feel, to worry about.' He was pulling her gradually closer to him and she could smell stale drink on his breath now, see his scarred face looming before her eyes, blocking out everything else. She heard herself whimpering.

'Make me feel better now. You can do it – you know you always could . . .' Gripping her hard with one hand, he started to fondle painfully at her breasts.

'Like old times, eh, Maryann?' He breathed into her face. 'You were always the fighter, the little wildcat,

413

weren't you? That's what made you the best one, the exciting one – and you haven't changed, have you? I knew you'd come back to me in the end – that I'd have you in the end.'

'No-o—!' Maryann moaned. He was hurting her, squeezing, pinching, tearing at the front of her blouse.

'Confound it – there's no room to move in this damn place!' He struggled, trying to sit round, but finding his legs caught under the table. He shoved at it. 'Can't you get shot of it? Hold still,' he roared, as she struggled. 'You little bitch, I'm going to have you!'

A sound grated in the air, the broken mewl of a child. Norman Griffin sat up straight.

'What's that? You got one of your kiddies in there?'

No! she wanted to say. No, no! It was one of the twins, she could tell.

'She'll sleep again,' she said hurriedly. 'She's only a babby.'

'Aha – let's have a look then, shall we?'

He flung the table back and lumbered, stooping, to the back bed.

'Well, well. All bagged up together, just like little rabbits. Oh – there's our Sally again. What a lovely child she is!'

As he stood with his back to her, Maryann saw one desperate chance. Eyes fixed on the lamp burning on the little shelf across the cabin, she began to slide herself along the bench. If only she could get there without him noticing! It seemed to take an endless time to inch herself along, holding her breath as she watched Norman Griffin's back. In a moment she launched herself to her feet and swooped towards the lamp. He caught her movement and lurched in front of her, pushing her backwards as he got between her and the lamp. She fell against the stove, banging her head on the wall behind. Ada was still crying.

'Oh no you don't!' He snatched the lamp and held it up. As she stumbled groggily to her feet, Maryann saw his face lit up by the glow of the lamp.

'Thinking of coming that one again, were you? Oh, I don't think that one would work a second time. I saw Margaret the other week, by the way. Fine girl – not that she'll ever breathe the air outside the asylum again. Now – what shall we do with this?' He eyed the lamp, half turned, dangling it over the sleeping children.

'Very fitting, wouldn't you say? Do as you would be done by?'

'No!' She pulled at him with all her strength, trying to get at the lamp. 'For God's sake, have some pity. They're babbies, all of them – my babbies! I never burned you – it was Margaret, not me!'

'But you'd have liked to, wouldn't you? You find me every bit as disgusting as she did.' With his left arm he caught her round the neck and wrenched her in close to him, looking down into her frantic face.

'I could always tell with you. You had too much spirit, too much defiance, my girl. No doubt these little lovelies have your spirit – so let's snuff that out, shall we? Stop it spreading any further. Women with spirit – with their pretty faces and their cruel mouths.'

Maryann threw herself on him, trying to pull his arm back, to get the lamp from him.

'Sally, Rose – wake up!' she screamed. 'Get out – get the twins out of bed!'

Sally and Rose had begun to stir.

'Quickly – *get out*!' She was screaming at them hysterically, but he shoved her off and once more she crashed into the stove. As she fought to get back towards the children she could see what he was about to do, jerking the lamp outwards, swinging it by its handle. She saw it arc to the furthest point, then begin the path back towards the ceiling over the bed.

'Sally!' In that second all she could seize hold of was her daughter's hand to pull on as the lamp hit the ceiling. The glass shattered and burning oil burst from it and scattered flaming over the bedspace where Rose lay with the twins.

Forty-Five

The cabin was full of smoke. No sound but that of screaming. The darkness was broken by the glow of flames licking round the bedding of the terrified children.

Immediately Maryann felt the normal passing of time alter. In those first elongated seconds she was shrieking at Sally, 'Get the doors open – get yourself out! Rose! Get up out of bed! Quick!' Sally tumbled from the bed onto her feet in the small space.

They were hampered by the obstructing bulk of Norman Griffin. Whichever way Maryann tried to move, he was in the way, though she could tell he too was trying to get out, away from the fire. Iron-limbed with fear and determination she turned her body and shoved at him, and in the darkness he seemed to give way, to disappear with a crash towards the door. She heard a yelp of pain, a muffled curse. She didn't care what happened to him as long as he was out of the way. The smoke was thickening, the small space filling with it fast. Coughing, she seized Rose's shoulders and steered her towards the cabin door. Norman Griffin seemed to have gone.

'Get on the bank with Sally – I'm getting the twins . . .'

Her eyes were streaming. The smoke was fast filling the tiny space and she was racked by coughing. All she could hear was the terrified screaming of the two little ones in the burning bed. The edge of the curtains had caught light, but Maryann shoved them aside and climbed onto the edge of the bed, seeing both of the babies' faces, each end of the bed, mouths open in the murky orange light. Most of the oil had fallen in the middle of the bed and flames were shooting up to the low ceiling. The heat was intense, but she leaned inside, regardless.

'Come here!' she shouted, reaching for Esther, trying to hold her head to one side while the flames leapt hungrily at her. She could feel the bite of them on her cheek and neck. She snatched Esther out, plonked her on the floor and immediately went back for Ada. As she reached for her, she heard her crying, in between choking coughs, with a distressed shrillness that she'd never heard before. She picked her up, and Ada racked up her screaming even higher.

Maryann balanced her on one hip and reached down for Esther, dragging her to the door by one arm. Within a second she was aware of a strange glow accompanying her, then a burning pain in her right ear and realized her hair was on fire. Loosing Esther she swiped at it, panicking, coughing, her hand smarting, until the flames seemed to have died out. All she could do now was get the three of them up the step into the night air. The twins were gagging on the smoke.

She managed to lift the girls off the boat and onto the bank, setting them down to bend over and cough and cough, her lungs straining for air. She gradually became aware of people moving round her, of voices amid the children's crying. The fire had brought others out from their boats who were shouting to each other to fetch buckets and dippers. But as she straightened up she heard Joel's voice, and Charlie's and Sally and Rose shrieking to them, that there was *fire*, fire on the *Theodore*.

'Our boat – and our lassies!' Joel was distraught, couldn't seem to see the girls in front of him.

'I'll get them off!' Charlie shouted. He was fully primed to help, to do something. They'd let Norman Griffin slip through their fingers, and now this! 'Where're the lads?'

'On the motor,' Maryann said, and realized with amazement that Joley and Ezra inside the *Esther Jane* must be sleeping through, oblivious to all this. 'The girls are all out – look, here,' Maryann managed to say. Sally and Rose came to her and clung round her, beginning to cry now the immediate danger to them was over and she stood stroking them, beginning to tremble all over herself. Joel had run to the boat, seized the dipper from inside and joined the others who were trying to douse the fire.

'It was *him*! He did it – set the fire – he's gone . . .'

'Griffin?' Charlie Dean demanded. 'What – he came here? Where is he? Where did he go?'

'That way – he ran off along the path,' Sally said, pointing.

Charlie was off. 'I'll get him this time,' floated back as he disappeared. 'I'll get that bugger and I won't let him go.'

Charlie tore along the dark towpath. He was a strong, fit man and fuelled by an almost insane, rage-filled energy, which stemmed from his soft feelings for Maryann and from the memory of that child on the bed in the room above the butcher's shop. He knew they'd been made proper fools of, letting Norman Griffin get away the first time. He ran tirelessly, almost as if he was flying, were it not for his feet crunching on the stones and cinders. There was a half moon tonight, which he could see reflected in the cut, and it seemed to bob about as he ran.

I'll get you this time. He'd given them the slip once, the slimy bastard, and he wasn't getting away again. That lumbering hulk of a bloke couldn't've got far in this time, surely? Charlie stumbled on something in the darkness and only just managed to stay upright. The jerking this gave his body only increased his anger. His lungs were pumping hard.

It can't be far, he thought. *There must be a place where he gets off the path – I've got to get to him before he gets there or he'll be gone and I'll've had it then.*

And a moment later he thought he heard something along the path ahead. Charlie stopped immediately. Now his feet were not pounding the ground, his own breathing sounded terribly loud. Yes, a cough from up ahead, and the sound of hurrying feet. He ran on, trying to be quiet, almost tiptoeing, gaining quickly until he could see a form moving, a deeper smudge of black in the darkness around them.

They hadn't got the fire on the *Theodore* under control yet. Smoke was pouring out of the door. Maryann watched hopelessly as she began to see flames burning their way through the roof, despite the efforts of Joel and the other boatmen. Maryann and the women tried to comfort the children, but while Sally, Rose and Esther were calmer now, Ada continued to give off agonized wails. Maryann was holding her and she'd screamed even more loudly on being picked up.

'What's up, Ada?' she said, despairingly. 'I can't see if she's got burnt or summat. She just won't stop blarting.'

'Bring her into our cabin,' a woman next to her offered. 'And the others. I'll find a drop of milk for them.'

She was a middle-aged woman with the prematurely aged, weather-worn face of so many of the boatwomen and large, kindly blue eyes. She ushered them all into her cabin. Most of her children had grown up and gone, she told Maryann. There was only one son left, working their pair with them. She signalled to Maryann to put Ada down on the table. It was immediately obvious what the problem was.

'Oh, Ada!' Maryann cried.

'Ooh – that's a nasty 'un,' the woman said as they both leaned over the long, angry burn on Ada's leg. 'My word, you're lucky it didn't set her clothes afire!'

'I don't know what to put on it,' Maryann said.

'Here – we'll put a shaking of flour over it,' the woman said. 'That'll help dry it up.' She produced a rusty tin and scooped out a couple of spoonfuls of flour, dusting it over Ada's leg, which made her scream even more. Maryann watched helplessly, though she was glad of the older woman's confidence in what she was doing.

'Let's give them all a nice drop of milk,' the woman said. 'I've just got some in, lucky for you.'

Charlie could hear Norman Griffin's rasping breaths along the path in front of him. *You're struggling, mate*, Charlie thought, triumphantly. *Not so young, are you? Bet you're not used to running.* Charlie felt like a superior, strong animal closing in on its prey. He was gaining on him fast, that inky, lumbering patch of movement. As he drew closer, he could just see Norman Griffin's coat tails flapping behind him like slipped wings.

Charlie felt a further surge of energy as he closed in. He stretched out his arm, straining to reach him, clawing at Norman Griffin's shoulder.

'I'll have you!' he roared and with a final effort threw himself forward onto the man, hurtling into his back and flinging him face down onto the ground. Norman Griffin went down with a loud grunt and Charlie fell sprawling on top of him.

'Got you!' Charlie roared, scrambling up, but remaining bent over the prone figure. 'You needn't think you're going anywhere now, you bastard.'

There was no immediate reaction. He saw Norman Griffin's head lift and jerk from side to side, then there came a long, groaning inhalation as he tried to fill his winded lungs. He pushed desperately to sit up, to be able to breathe after his severe winding.

'Get up,' Charlie said. He watched over him with a feeling of power mingled with revulsion. What a foul wretch he was!

Norman braced himself, panting hard, struggling to stand and slowly lurched to his feet, but remained bent over, crumpled.

'They'll put you away for a long time,' Charlie said contemptuously. 'You're disgusting.' The man was a mess, hanging over like that, limp at the waist as if he couldn't straighten. He'd have to get him back to the wharf. Get the police – see if they could manage to keep their hands on him this time.

The few seconds it took Norman Griffin to rally took Charlie completely by surprise. Righting himself in an instant, he ran at Charlie, who had no time to brace himself. Propelled by a great shove from Norman Griffin, he skittered backwards and over the bank, hitting the black, moonstruck water, which closed over him, cold and filthy, filling his ears, eyes, mouth. For a second all was darkness and confusion in the muffled underwater world, but the cut was shallow. Charlie pushed himself furiously to his feet, above the water, spitting out the oily brew. He coughed, and cursed with rage. Norman Griffin was once again in flight along the path.

'I'll get you – you needn't think you'll get away!'

Clothes streaming, he hauled himself up onto the path, weighed down by his sodden garments. He could hear Norman Griffin's footsteps receding in the distance and, boots squelching, Charlie hurled himself along the path after him.

He soon caught up again, just as Norman Griffin turned off the path and began to scramble up through the nettles on the bank. No wonder they'd never seen him come and go on the wharf: he had this other way down!

'No you don't!' All he could do was throw himself on the man's legs, gripping on to his left ankle with all his strength. Norman Griffin kicked viciously, trying to shake him off, but Charlie gripped on, trying to pull himself up the man's body as if climbing a pole.

'Get off me – don't touch me!' Norman Griffin's shrill words came to Charlie, the voice almost a squeal. He was struggling like a pig at the slaughterhouse, and Charlie was astonished by his strength. As he got a grip further up the man's legs. Norman Griffin began to punch him, blows cracking into his cheek, smashing open his lip. Enraged by the pain, Charlie hauled himself up and lay on top of the older man, pinning him down.

'You fucking bastard!' he screamed into Norman Griffin's face. He could feel blood running down his chin. 'I'm going to make sure they lock you up and throw away the key!'

He barely got the words out as the hands locked around his throat. Charlie didn't even manage to inhale first and within seconds he was in trouble, chest straining, body crying out for air. His throat was held in an agonizing vice and he knew that if he didn't save himself that instant he was going to die.

Drawing on all his strength, he managed to fling his weight forward and clamp his hands on each side of Norman Griffin's head, which he lifted, then smashed down again onto the ground as hard as he could. For a second there was no reaction. He couldn't see the expression on the man's face in the gloom, but the grip on his throat slackened and Norman Griffin's arms, as if controlled by a separate life of their own, flopped to the ground. Charlie sobbed in gulps of air, gagging from the injury to his throat. He staggered to his feet, hands at his neck to try and ease the pain and landed a vicious kick at Norman Griffin's ribs. '*You fucker, you nearly bloody killed me!*' he rasped.

As his first crisis of needing to breathe calmed, he began to sense the silence in the other man. Kneeling down in sudden panic, he peered at him. He found he was starting to get the shakes.

'Here, come on – wake up!' he croaked. He'd only wanted to get him off – had to, didn't he? To save himself. Close up, he could see that Norman Griffin's one good eye was closed. He was out cold.

'Oh Jesus – God Almighty.' It was an agony to speak. He was in a real panic now though. 'Come on.' He slapped at Norman's face. 'Get yourself up, will you!'

424

Stopping, he listened for the man's breathing, but could make out nothing. His heart? He groped for what he thought was the right spot under the man's heavy coat. Again, he couldn't feel anything. Wasn't there supposed to be a spot where you could feel a pulse? Fumbling around Norman's wrist, he had no more success. He stood up, filled with panic.

'Don't let him be dead!' he breathed. He knew suddenly how cold he was in his soaking clothes. His teeth were chattering.

Backing away from Norman Griffin, he turned, his triumph shrivelled now to fear, and ran stumblingly back towards the wharf.

Ada had drifted into a light, whimpering sleep. The woman settled all the drowsy children on her bed.

'I must go and see what's happening,' Maryann said. 'The boat – my husband.'

The shock seemed to have snipped her mind into tiny fragments so she couldn't hold a thought together. She was beginning to feel smarting pain from the burns on her hand and neck, but she tried to ignore it. In the cabin she could hear the muffled voices of the men along the bank.

When she stepped outside, a terrible sight met her. Though there were no longer flames pouring out of the *Theodore*, the cabin and all their meagre possessions had virtually disappeared; the fire had only been stopped when it had burned some way along the hold. Smoke was still rising into the darkness.

The men were still working hard, filling bucket after bucket of water from the cut. But she saw Joel, no longer even attempting to carry on, a little distance away, bent over with his hands clenched to his knees as if in defeat, overtaken by bouts of coughing, the smoke too much for his already damaged lungs.

Thank heaven above it's not the Esther Jane, Maryann thought, though this was bad enough. The sight of her husband suffering, his defeated stance, filled her with a tenderness she had not been able to feel for a long while. Cautiously, shyly, she walked along to him.

'Joel – love?'

He straightened up and stood looking at her.

For the first time in weeks, she moved towards him and put her arms round him.

Moments later, while they were standing, numbly looking at the smoking wreck of the *Theodore*, they heard running footsteps.

'Maryann!' They heard him before they could see him and Maryann peered into the murk. Was that strained, gravelly voice Charlie's?

'I'm over here!' she called, and a moment later he was in front of her, panting, obviously in a state.

'He's along there – Griffin. On the towpath. I think I've … I don't know …' He gulped, struggling for breath. 'There was a fight. I think I might've done him in.'

Forty-Six

Everyone followed: it would have been no good telling them not to. The helpers from the surrounding boats had been drawn into the Bartholomews' drama and could not be expected to miss the next stage of it.

Charlie was already out of sight ahead of them, tearing along. They hurried after him down the narrow path, their only light the half moon. The other boaters followed and she could hear their boots on the path, their voices muffled yet excited. Maryann and Joel were together at first, but Joel was soon overcome by a fit of coughing and had to drop back.

Maryann ran under the bridge, felt for a second its deeper, echoing darkness, and came out the other side, straining to see Charlie ahead of her.

What's happened? What's he done? The questions hammered in her mind. He hadn't stopped long enough to explain. Something terrible had taken place and he thought Norman Griffin was dead. Her mind could not take this in, or the thought of what might happen to Charlie if this were true. Could he be dead? Over and over, tolling like a bell. Could he? Norman Griffin dead, after all this time?

'Charlie!' she shouted, sensing him ahead of her.

'Up here – come on!' she heard and ran on nimbly ahead of everyone else, soon catching Charlie up as he stopped abruptly, looking round.

'This was where ... It was, I'm sure!' Charlie ran back and forth, frantic, stamping at the nettles as if they might yield an answer. 'He was lain down there, I'd swear he was! He's moved himself ... that means he can't be dead. I haven't killed him!' Charlie was almost sobbing with relief. 'I thought I was going to prison!' he croaked. 'Thought I'd finished him off!'

'Charlie – ' Maryann gripped his arm, trying to bring him back to his senses – 'if he's not here, we've got to find him.'

'You sure this was it?' Joel and the others came up from behind.

'He was trying to get up there when I pulled him down.' Charlie pointed up the low bank. At the top was the end of a wall enclosing a line of factories and a tree next to it, then a fence. Between the wall and the tree was a gap. Joel and the other four men immediately sprang up the bank and started pushing their way through.

'There's a path here! We can get along,' one of them called. One by one they disappeared. Maryann watched, without hope. It was so dark and Norman Griffin had had so much time to get away. He knew the lie of the land and they'd lost him once again. He was like the strongman they used to see in the Bull Ring, she thought. He'd be tied with chains in a sack, so it looked impossible even to move, but he'd always manage to escape.

Charlie couldn't seem to stop talking, even though he was clearly in pain, his voice rasping. He was explaining what had happened that evening at the house, seeing the young girl and how Norman Griffin had escaped them there and now again here.

'*Twice* we had him, Maryann, and he still got away. I feel such a blithering idiot.'

428

'It's not your fault,' she said flatly. 'You did your best for us.' In the distance she could hear the others moving away between the factory walls to the road. They'd never find him now, she knew. He'd be long gone, a malignant shadow slipping through the streets to some new hiding place. It seemed he was always destined to be out there somewhere beyond their reach, untouchable. Victorious.

Once Charlie's torrent of speech had rasped to a halt they stood listening. They could not hear Joel and the other men any more and the night was quiet. Something moved on the water close to them, a little flurry and a splash. Maryann became aware of other sounds, a mechanical throbbing from a factory somewhere, a train, its chugging passage building then receding, and, as the quiet descended again, a low, odd noise which didn't fit the usual sounds of night. She listened, alert. Seconds later it came again.

'Charlie – what's that?'

'What? I can't hear anything.'

They strained to hear, but no sound came.

'Come with me.' They began to walk along the path, further away from the wharf. Only a short distance away they found him, his prone figure like a dark stain on the path. Maryann gasped.

'Oh Lor' – ' She felt Charlie put his arm protectively round her shoulders. She was terrified. Unable to see Norman Griffin's face, she felt he was staring up at her through the darkness, waiting to seize hold of her if she leaned over him.

'It's all right.' Charlie released her and very cautiously they bent down. Norman Griffin did not stir. He was lying face down, as if he had crawled here, and as Charlie touched him a groan came from him. Maryann saw

Charlie feel round the back of the man's head. He stood up, wiping his hand on his trousers.

'He's bleeding. Banged his head. He won't be going nowhere. I'm going for the coppers.'

'No!' Maryann panicked. 'We can't leave him here! He might still get up and run off. You can't trust him an inch. And I'm not staying here on my own with him. Wait till the others get back, Charlie.'

'All right. Don't s'pose there's any hurry now,' he said, adding tremulously, 'oh, thank Christ for that.'

Hands shaking, Maryann slowly knelt down, her body tensed, heart hammering, ready to jump away at any sign of movement.

'Can you hear me?' Her mouth was so dry, the words would barely come out and she had to try again. 'Mr Griffin. I hope you can hear me. It's Maryann.'

She stopped, unable for a moment to think what to say. But there were things she wanted to say. He had to know she was here, present at the moment when they finally had him, helpless in front of her, wiped out. Defeated. Breathing deeply, she looked up for a moment at the white glow of the moon. What words could ever encompass all the years of fear and shame and pain? But she had to say something. Just something. For herself and Sal, for Janet Lambert and Amy and Margaret.

'It's Maryann,' she said again. 'I hate you for what you did to me and to everyone else. You're an evil, twisted man and you're never going to hurt anyone again. You've destroyed people. You've wrecked and broken them. But you're finished now.' She took a long, shuddering breath and stood up. 'And you haven't got me.'

*

Pastor Owen sat on the front pew in the little church, his eyes red from weeping. He was slumped in his large clothes, like a crumpled bird. The pews looked even more outsized in the room than Maryann remembered. The place was empty except for the two of them. Sunlight slanted in through the windows onto the cross and a bird was singing out on the roof. A place of peace, it should have been. But there was no peace. Maryann had been standing, but she sank down beside him on the pew.

'You had no idea, did you?'

Pastor Owen hung his head. He shook it, utterly desolate. Maryann almost put her arm round him, but she held back. She kept her hands in her lap, the right one bandaged and sore.

It was the afternoon after Norman Griffin had been driven away by the police. When Joel and the other men returned to the cut the night before, they had all helped carry Norman Griffin back to Tyseley Wharf, as he gave off faint, semi-conscious groans.

'He's not going to die, is he?' Charlie asked.

'Don't sound like it,' Joel said. 'Take more than a bang on the head to finish that 'un off.'

The police came. This time it was Joel who had his arm round Maryann's shoulders as they carried Norman Griffin into the back of the vehicle.

'That's him gone,' was all Joel said.

Maryann nodded numbly. She could find no words.

More shock was to follow. The police had taken the two men from the house and had them in the cells. One was the butcher, Mr Osborne, something Maryann was still almost unable to take in. The third, round-faced man was Pastor Joyce.

'He's been like a father to me.' Pastor Owen's

shoulders began to shake. 'We've lived in the same house, done the Lord's work together. And all this time – what have I been living with?'

His bony hands clutched to his face, he began to weep. 'They say he took a young girl's life.'

Maryann could think of no words of comfort. She truly felt for him in his shock, for this terrible shame upon his friend, his church. She knew now his genuine goodness. He was an innocent, caught up in a horror he could barely understand. After a moment she laid her bandaged hand gently on his back.

'You couldn't have known,' she tried to reassure him. 'The other one, Mr Osborne, he was always nice as pie to me. Reminded me of my dad. I bought all my meat off him. How could anyone ever guess something like that?'

Pastor Owen lifted his head, cheeks running with tears, face twisting with emotion. He looked so young! So pinched and battered.

'I don't know what to do.' More tears welled in his large eyes. 'I can't stay here. I thought this'd be my life's work, in this place. I'm lost, Mrs Bartholomew. How can I go on?'

Maryann stared back at him. She sighed, a long, deep sigh which seemed to have been waiting there for years to be expelled.

'I don't know. But you will. You'll find the strength, same as we all do.'

Forty-Seven

August 1944

'Mom – Mom!' Joley and Ezra came tearing along the bank where they were tied up near Napton. 'Look – it's Dot and Sylvia, and Bobby's got his arm round Dot!'

Maryann pulled the panful of sausages off the heat and hurried outside, where the faces of her sons, swarthy with a combination of grime and suntan, were lit up with excitement. A pair of boats was chugging steadily towards them and she narrowed her eyes. Sure enough, it was a pair of Grand Union Canal Carrying Company boats heading south towards them, and yes, there was Bobby at the helm, tiller held easily in his left hand, the other apparently draped in a relaxed way round Dot's shoulders. The children were already shrieking and waving and she saw Dot and Bobby recognize them and start waving back. Sylvia was waving from the butty boat as well.

'Sylvia – Auntie Sylvia!' Rose leapt up and down on the path with excitement.

'We're tying up – just up here!' Bobby called. Within a few moments they'd found a place to pull in and all the Bartholomews were hurrying along for a grand reunion on the bank in the late afternoon sun. Rose ran straight to Sylvia, who picked her up, and Maryann smiled at the sight of Rose's dark, curling hair against the paleness of Sylvia's.

'Ooh, you're getting a heavy girl now!' Sylvia said, kissing Rose's pink cheeks.

Joel and Bobby greeted one another warmly and stood slightly apart, talking boats and gauges and cargoes, while Maryann and the children all crowded round Sylvia and Dot. At first no one could get a word in edgeways. The children were all asking questions at once. Maryann saw Sylvia making a special effort to draw Sally out. She was still quiet and withdrawn, although she was much better than she had been straight after her terrifying time with Norman Griffin.

'It looks *awful* just seeing you with the *Esther Jane* and no *Theodore*!' Dot's powerful voice rang out above the children's chatter.

'You *poor* things – whatever has been happening to you?' Sylvia planted a kiss on Rose's cheek. 'Let me put you down now, darling – my back won't stand it. Of course we heard through the grapevine that there'd been a fire, a couple of months ago now, wasn't it? And that there was all sorts of to-do at Tyseley, but no one's told us properly. You must have had a terrible time!'

Maryann nodded. A lump came up in her throat at the thought of the last few months, the raw, fearful wretchedness of it all. But she didn't want to let go of her emotion, not now. She swallowed hard.

'We're managing,' she said matter-of-factly. 'Essy Barlow's got us another butty for when we get back this time. Joley and Ezzy are sleeping out in the hold most nights as it's warm. You lot tied up for the night now?'

'Yes,' Dot said. 'Bobby says we'll not get much further than here tonight in any case with them all locking up so early. The water's so low they're rationing who goes through. It's a gamble to try and get over the top at Tring these days – they only let so many through, then close all the locks!'

Maryann watched her in wonder as she spoke. She was so suntanned and strong looking and, yes, happy, in a way she'd never been before. Maryann grinned.

'So – I see Bobby's steering with his arm around his first mate these days!'

Dot gave her hooting laugh, and blushed. Sylvia was looking fondly at her.

'Oh, we've got *lots* to tell you. But let's get the tea brewed first, eh? I'm absolutely parched – and famished, as usual!'

'Bobby and me'll be off then,' Joel said. The meal was over, chores finished for the night and the children getting ready for bed.

'All right.' Maryann smiled at him gratefully. Bobby and Joel would enjoy getting a few pints inside them at the inn along the bank, and she knew Joel was giving her the chance to catch up with Dot and Sylvia. It would be a night like old times, even though in a strange cabin, not the *Theodore*, but she was full of a welling sense of pleasure at the thought of female company, a sensation which even now took her by surprise.

On these light, sultry nights it would be hard for the boys to get to sleep outside, so she settled them inside on Joel's and her bed, parting from them all with dire warnings that they must go to sleep and not monkey about. Even now, climbing out of the cabin, she felt a reflex of fear at the thought of leaving the children alone.

Don't start that again, she told herself. *He can't hurt us any more. Never.*

But how long would it be, she thought, weeds brushing her bare ankles as she walked the towpath, before she could say she had recovered from it, from him, and close the door on it all as she longed to do? Would that ever happen?

'Look what I've got!' Sylvia greeted her jubilantly from the back of *Magpie*, their monkey boat, waving a bottle of Johnnie Walker. 'At last I've got someone to share it with! Bobby's an ale man.' Her hair was up in a pale blue scarf and she'd put on her favourite geranium red lipstick.

Maryann grinned. 'Got yourself a sweetheart in a distillery?'

'No – still working on that one!' Sylvia said.

Dot appeared, all in black still, her short shirtsleeves pressing tight into her plump arms. She looked like a nice, wholesome cottage loaf, Maryann thought.

'Let's not sit inside.' Sylvia jumped up onto the cabin roof, using it as a table to pour Scotch into white cups. 'Not until those blasted beasties nibble us too unbearably.'

Dot and Maryann perched comfortably on the gunwales at the back. Another pair of boats was tied up behind, but not too close, a line of washing flapping along the hold and their children out on the bank. The evening was bathed in rich light, and a warm breeze came over the fields. Maryann drank in the moment, this precious evening to enjoy with her friends. A year ago who would have thought it could feel like this?

'Cheers!' Sylvia raised her chipped cup. 'Down the hatch!'

They found they were all laughing just at the sight of one another, out of happiness.

'Too much to catch up on by far,' Sylvia said. 'Where do we begin? Let's take turns. You first, Maryann?'

'Ooh no.' She felt herself tense up immediately. If she

told them what had happened she knew it would lead to questions. How much could she say, even now? She was so used to not telling things that it felt terrifying to be asked. She looked at Dot. 'I want to hear all about what's been going on here. Come on – you can't keep me in suspense any longer.'

Dot looked sideways at her with an irrepressibly jubilant grin.

'Oh!' Sylvia rolled her eyes in mock exasperation. 'I've been living with a proper Romeo and Juliet. Makes me feel quite old and washed up sometimes!'

'There was me thinking you and Bobby didn't exactly hit it off,' Maryann teased. 'I wonder what gave me that idea?'

'Well, we didn't,' Dot said brusquely. 'But we do now. That's all.'

'For "we do now –"' Sylvia leaned confidentially towards Maryann and almost toppled her precious bottle into the cut in the process – 'you have to substitute the words, "We're completely half-soaked and besotted with one another." So that certain people on lock-wheeling duty are standing there in a complete soppy fug and forgetting to close paddles or get back on the boat at the right moment – or getting off it with no windlass and getting a proper mouthful from other boaters.'

Dot was laughing now. 'I only did that once!'

'And in fact, "we do now" actually, I'm almost sure, means the sound of wedding bells will be in the offing soon.'

Maryann was laughing, astonished. 'But how the hell did this all happen, Dot?'

'Bobby's not like I thought at the beginning,' Dot said with dignity. 'I didn't know him, that's all. And now I do, I know him to be kind and he makes me laugh and, well, I just think we'll be able to rub along together, that's all.'

Maryann and Sylvia were both laughing.

'Here speaks one of the great romantics of our time!' Sylvia giggled.

'All hearts and flowers, aren't you, Dot!' Maryann said. 'But are you really getting wed?'

Dot took a sip of tea and her face grew more solemn.

'Next month. Goes without saying we want you all there with your boots blacked. All Bartholomews in a line! Actually – ' she looked shy suddenly – 'I wondered if Joel would agree to give me away. There won't be any of my family there, you see.'

Maryann saw Sylvia looking at Dot with a concerned, sympathetic expression.

'Not your dad?' Maryann asked hesitantly. 'Isn't he going to give you away?'

Dot cradled her cup between her hands and spoke, looking down at the floor.

'Appears not. Course, apart from a couple of stray cousins who I barely know, Daddy's the only real family I've got left now. I took a couple of days' leave and went up there a month ago. Mainly to tell him about Bobby. I mean I thought I should at least *tell* him, although I wasn't too surprised at the upshot.' She drew in a deep breath.

'Odd, being back there. Seeing the house. Garden was a mess. Daddy saying he's doing some sort of war work, hush, hush, but I'm not sure it's true. He's just trying to sound terribly important as usual. I'd gone to stay the night, but I just couldn't. I missed the last train back, so I slept on the platform . . .'

'Oh, Dot!' Maryann was horrified. That great big

house, her home, and poor Dot didn't even feel she could take up a little corner of it!

'Daddy and I had a conversation which lasted about a quarter of an hour.' Again she paused. A bee lumbered past. 'He made himself abundantly clear. If I lowered myself by marrying like this, I could forget that I was his daughter – you know, inheritance and so forth. Apart from these inescapable financial factors – ' she looked up now, with her ironic grin – 'forgetting I'm Daddy's daughter won't feel all that new or troublesome.'

'That's terrible.' Maryann watched Dot's face.

'Yes – she's had a rough time,' Sylvia said.

'You must really think a lot of Bobby.'

'Yes.' Dot smiled. 'I suppose that's how it was for you and Joel?'

Again the plunge of misgiving. How much could she say? Yes, she'd loved Joel, but how much more there had been to her running away, her quest for safety. 'Yes,' was all she said.

'Bobby's done wonders for me.'

Maryann could see that he had.

'Of course we'll be at your wedding.' She reached across and squeezed the top of Dot's arm. 'We wouldn't miss it for anything.'

'Thanks.' Dot said briskly. Maryann saw her eyes fill with tears, but she soon had them under control again. 'That means a lot. More than you might imagine.'

'So – you're going to be a boatwoman! Sure you know what you're letting yourself in for?'

'I think I've a fair idea,' Dot said dryly.

'And you still want to do it!'

'Well – would you swap it?'

'No.' Maryann sighed. 'Not most days, anyroad.'

'It's Bobby's life. He doesn't know any other. We just want to carry on working, and Sylvia can crew for us, for as long as they need her – Inland Waterways, I mean. Once the war ends, who knows?'

'Yes,' Sylvia sighed, sliding down from the cabin roof. 'I'm going to have to face up to the mess my life's in. It sounds *awful*, but I almost don't want the war to end. When it does, I'm going to have to decide all sorts of things I'd rather not think about. Come on, girls – let's go in. I'm starting to get nibbled more than I can stand.'

The evening was cooling and they sat in the *Magpie*'s warm cabin, light and a breeze coming in through the door.

'I can't go back to Roy – not after all this,' Sylvia said, pouring more water into the kettle. 'I've thought and thought. I feel I should for the children's sake. After all, what can I offer them on my own? But I just can't. They weren't happy with us at home. That's why I sent them away in the first place. And it'd be like climbing back into a cage!'

'Lion's den, more like,' Dot commented.

Sylvia gave a wan smile, putting the kettle back on the heat. 'You know, I never thought this would happen to me. I used to look down terribly on women who couldn't make their marriages work. As if it was always their fault, for a start! And the truth is – ' she sank down on the side bench next to Maryann – 'mine barely even worked right from the beginning. There's something terribly wrong with Roy, I've known that really. But it's amazing how long you can kid yourself something is working, that it's normal.'

'What will you do?' Maryann asked.

'Don't know. I'll stay here as long as I can. My sister's

been having the children, but she can't manage all the holidays. I'll have to bring them on here for the last two weeks.' She looked solemn, but determined. 'In the long run, I don't know. I'll have to find a job and somewhere to live ... Roy'll carry on paying the school fees. He's dead set on that. But I know now that I can do it. I'd never have been able even to begin thinking that before I came away.' Her face cleared and she chuckled. 'What a year, eh? And goodness me, Maryann, for you more than any of us the last few months, by the sound of things. *Do tell* – what on earth's been happening to you all?'

The question roused the usual mixture of panic and longing in Maryann. The hunger both to tell and to conceal, each equally pressing. It was like a scouring of inner wounds. But they'd shared so much of themselves with her now. She could tell them some of it quite easily of course, about the fire, and Charlie Dean's chase along the towpath. And she did so while they brewed up again and drank tea round the table, Dot and Sylvia listening avidly.

'Charlie was scared stiff he'd finished him off. It was just a bang on the head, though, and he came round all right. Course, there was no doubt about what they'd all done, him and that Pastor Joyce and Mr Osborne.'

'Mr Osborne was always such a sweetie, though,' Sylvia said, bewildered. 'Least, I thought so.'

'So did I.' Maryann knew she sounded abrupt. This was another betrayal which was only now beginning to hit home. 'Anyroad, the girl in the cellar in Acocks Green – turned out Pastor Joyce was the one responsible for her. He was blarting in the witness box, saying it'd all been an accident, that he never meant to.'

Despite the horror of what she was telling them, Sylvia and Dot were taken back by the bitter loathing in Maryann's voice.

'The girl was called Ellen. She was eight years old and she was Janet's sister's grandchild. They live out at Alvechurch and he – Griffin – had gone all the way out there to track her down. God alone knows what they did to her . . .' She couldn't speak for a moment, almost choked by rage and pain. 'It was anyone connected with any of us – my family, Janet's. If we'd've had more relatives . . .' She shuddered. She couldn't look Sylvia and Dot in the eye. The others were silent. Maryann sensed that they just didn't know what to say, were out of their depth.

'But,' Dot stumbled into speech, eventually, 'why, Maryann?' She spoke very gently. 'He must be completely insane. They all must be!'

'There was a girl that night in the room above the butcher's. She was one of Pastor Joyce's congregation, from the church. They were just the same, the three of them.'

'So – ' Sylvia was struggling to make any sense out of the horror of it all – 'Norman Griffin was the man who killed Jennykins that night and who . . . who took Sally, and all these other terrible things. And you said he was your stepfather? But none of it makes any sense. Why would he do these things to you of all people?'

'Oh – that's his way of being family,' Maryann said with harsh flippancy. She felt as if there were hands around her throat as she looked guardedly up into Sylvia's kind eyes. Her longing was overwhelming, the need to be able to tell someone who had never known Norman Griffin or been touched by him, to lay it all out before them and have them witness and believe her and not condemn. To know that someone understood all the hurt and shame inside her and could accept her. The shame which never seemed to die, and which, roused again by all the events of the last months, still left her sickened and weeping every time her husband tried to touch her, and breaking down at other unpredictable moments. These last two months had been awash with tears. They gave her some release, but still she had not been able to break through Joel's own pain and bewilderment and tell him the truth. She still felt as if she was living behind a mask and no one ever saw the real her underneath, the lonely, trembling her. If she could just lift the mask, even just a corner of it ... But it was so frightening.

Feeling Sylvia looking at her, Dot's eyes on her across the table, she felt herself go weak, her palms sweating. How could she say it? Put the gross truth into words: her childhood, her sister Sal's, Amy's, Margaret's. She clasped her hands in her lap to control her trembling. If she never spoke, didn't he, Norman Griffin, in his cell in Winson Green prison, where he would stay until they hanged him – didn't he still have sway over her? Even when he was dead, how could she ever be free? She remembered her last sight of him in the courtroom before they took him away, hatless for once, sitting hunched forward, trying to hide his face. Even in the packed court she had felt her skin crawl at being so close to him. How could she banish him, and the everlasting sense of dirtiness he had given her, and begin to live properly again?

She knew Sylvia and Dot had sensed her inner struggle. Folding her arms, almost hugging herself, she spoke, staring down at the table top with its rings of stains.

'Yes, he was my stepfather.' She could barely raise her voice above a whisper. It felt impossible, crushing, as if the whole world was listening. 'He came to live with us after our dad died. And ... and ...' She was weeping then, unable to speak.

'Oh, darling.' Sylvia's arm came round her shoulders. Eventually it gave her the courage to go on.

'He wasn't a father to us. He interfered with us. Both of us. But my sister, Sal, most of all.'

The sobbing took over, wrung out of her. Sylvia cradled her in her arms and Maryann was conscious of her head being pressed against Sylvia's shoulder, of motherly, comforting noises, of feeling warm and safe. All she could do was to cry and cry. She couldn't go on speaking, telling it all. Not tonight. But she had lifted the edge of the mask, allowed a chink of light into her darkness. She knew she could go on now. Tell them more, and at last be able to take what seemed the hardest step of all: telling Joel.

She had spoken.

Forty-Eight

'Time to come and get scrubbed up!'

Maryann was ready with the dipper on the table, full of steaming water. They were at Sutton Stop and all six children were out on the bank, among a gaggle of others having conker fights. They were so engrossed in bashing each other's conkers they didn't hear her, and Joel went to hurry them along.

'Boys first!'

Joley and Ezra groaned. 'Do we *have* to?'

Maryann set about washing and dressing them, tutting as the pockets in the boys' trousers and girls' frocks yielded up stashes of the horse chestnuts, polished shiny as leather, and a couple still encased in their prickly shells.

'D'you have to pick up all these? It's not as if they're on the ration.'

'But the others'll get 'em if we don't,' Ezzy yelled urgently. 'And then there won't be none left.'

'Don't *shout* – I'm not deaf.' Maryann scrubbed at Ezra's soot-begrimed cheeks. 'And I don't want any of them conkers in the church, d'you hear?' She attempted to get a comb through his dark curls as he squirmed and moaned. The girls were waiting on the back bed.

'Are we wearing our new frocks now?' Sally asked.

'That you are – and once you've got them on, don't flaming *move* in them until the wedding's over!'

'Oh, Mom!'

'Is Sylvia putting hers on now?' Rose wanted to know.

'Yes – and she's helping Dot. Oh keep still, Ezzy – it's like trying to comb a hedgehog.'

For the past month, every spare moment had been spent sewing. Sylvia, who was very good at it, had taken over the problem of dressing everyone for the wedding. In the last two weeks of the school holidays she had introduced Kay and Dickie to life on the cut, and they had evidently taken to it with enthusiasm. Fetching them had also given her an opportunity to go home and collect some of her belongings. She was a keen seamstress and had found a generous length of pretty blue cotton with trailing daisies on, and devised a simple pattern to make dresses for the Bartholomew girls.

'Oh, I wish I could've brought my sewing machine!' she said. 'It's at home, but it's so heavy. I'll have to get hold of it later. But never mind – we can handsew.' She showed a nervous Maryann how to make the little girls' frocks up, while she concentrated on the other dresses, as well as making outfits for the boys. She had a marvellous collection of material at home, accumulated over years, including a yellow flowery fabric for outfits for herself and Maryann.

'I was going to make this up just before the war,' she mused, lifting the corner of the bright, sunny cloth. 'Somehow I didn't have the heart. I think the colour was too happy for me!'

For Dot's wedding dress she managed to acquire something highly prized from her favourite draper's. Parachute silk!

'This is going to be a fancy wedding,' Maryann laughed, seeing it all. 'We aren't used to all this.'

446

Everyone was gathered at Hawkesbury now: the Bartholomews with the *Esther Jane* and a new Barlow butty boat called *Jonquil*. Sylvia and Dot were tied up behind them and Bobby's family, the Jenkses, were there too. Word had passed also to Joel's brother Darius that there was a celebration in the offing and they were hoping he might arrive in time.

Sylvia appeared in the doorway of the *Esther Jane*, still in her old slacks, hair turbaned up in a scarf. Maryann had managed to finish off the boys and made them sit down with 'Don't move and don't get dirty!' ringing in their ears.

'Aah!' Sylvia exclaimed, seeing Maryann put Sally's dress on over the child's head. Her long blonde hair was newly washed and brushed and she looked very pretty. 'I knew it would match your eyes, Sally. You're a picture! You and Rose will make perfect bridesmaids.' Seated on the coalbox, she reached out and squeezed Sally's hand. 'It fits very nicely, Maryann – you've done so well.'

'It's a blooming miracle.' Maryann laughed. 'I've never been any good at sewing. How's Dot? She dressed yet?'

'No – I'm going to go and help her in a few minutes. Just thought I'd see how you were getting on. Dot's having a wash. Poor darling – you might not think it, but she's really very worked up and nervy this morning. It's good that we got shot of Bobby to the Jenkses' last night – just gives us all a bit of breathing space. And I suspect he'd have been in even more of a flap than her!'

'There.' Maryann finished combing out Sally's hair. She was pleased to see a smile on her daughter's face. The life was gradually coming back to her over these months. 'Rose, you next!' She nodded towards Ada and

447

Esther, on the bed, who were watching with rapt expressions. 'Goodness knows how I'm going to keep those two out of the muck once they've got their finery on!'

The boats set out in convoy along the cut to Longford. Summer was waning, but the leaves were only just beginning to turn, and Maryann caught a whiff of smoke from a garden fire as they chugged along. In the hedgerows were sprays of ripe blackberries and Maryann grimaced, standing at the tiller of the *Jonquil*, imagining all that magenta juice down the front of her offspring's new clothes if they were to catch sight of them later on the bank. She had on her own yellow frock, and, as ever, wore Nancy's gold hoops in her ears. The outfit made her feel very smart and happy, but for the moment she had put her coat over the top to try and keep the coal dust at bay. Dot and the children were all safely inside their respective cabins, keeping well protected.

Maryann glanced at the line of boats behind her and smiled. The sun was coming out and the boats were decked out with as many pots and jars of flowers as they had been able to find on the cabin roofs beside the bright roses and castles on the water cans and dippers. All the boats had been washed and their rope work and Turks' heads were a miracle of whiteness in the sunshine, after a good scrubbing with cut water. At the back of the line they had been joined in the nick of time by Darius's pair, with his crew and the boys, Darrie and Sean.

They tied up at Longford in a colourful, celebratory line. Maryann swiftly went indoors to take off her coat and tidy her hair. Sylvia had given it a trim for her and it felt clean and bouncy, curling at the ends and pinned stylishly back.

'Now you lot—' She managed to drag the comb once more through the children's hair and smiled proudly at them. It was a long time since she'd seen her boys so smart. Joley with his thick blond mop and Ezra very dark.

'You look like princes,' she told them.

'Oh, *Mom*,' Joley groaned, disgusted, 'can us *go* now?'

Rose and Sally, equally contrasting in looks, and being self-consciously careful with their clothes, were next out, tiptoeing along the plank, and then Maryann led the twins out. Ada's leg had healed from her burning, but she would be scarred for life, and the look of the ruckled patch of skin was a bitter one for Maryann every time she saw it.

Joel was waiting on the bank, as proud and upright as his sore back would allow, his beard trimmed and wearing his ancient 'Sunday best', which included an old jacket of his father's. He came to help the twins out and Maryann looked across at him as he took their hands, seeing him afresh for a moment. She knew he was still struggling with the terrible things she had at last told him about her past. Part of his hurt was that she had kept it all from him for so long. But she also knew that he was solid and true, that she knew him so well and trusted him, and that they would endure.

'When's Dot coming out?' Rose demanded.

'In her own time,' Joel told her. 'Come on, little 'un – your dad's tied up back here. Come and see him.'

Rose greeted her father shyly, and when he went to lift her up she said, 'Don't get me dirty!' in a panicky voice. So Darius knelt down and talked to her instead.

She was shy with her brothers too, but Joley and Ezra were soon tearing up and down with Darrie and Sean and Maryann knew Rose would come round eventually.

'You all right, Darius?' she asked, tender towards him. She missed Nancy so much – how much worse it must be for him!

He nodded, pushing his hat back from over his eyes. His striking, chiselled face was beginning to look more like old Darius's, with its deep clefts and lines wrought by weather and by the grief of losing Nancy. And he looked dirty and exhausted from a rushed trip, trying to get here on time.

They exchanged bits of news: Joel and Maryann had not long been to Oxford and they told Darius that his father and Aunt Alice were both in good health.

'Better get in and clean myself up,' Darius said, after a time. 'The bride'll've left without us, else.'

Bobby and the rest of the Jenks family went ahead to the church. The others waited on the bank for Dot to make her appearance. Rose kept peering round at the back of the *Magpie*, trying to see what was going on.

'Can I go in?' she asked repeatedly.

'No, you stay out here,' Maryann said, wondering how much longer she could restrain Ada and Esther. She and Joel were each holding one of them to keep them from dabbling in every bit of muck and mess around. As they stood there, the sunshine grew brighter and it became quite warm.

The *Magpie*'s hatch slid back and Sylvia came out first in her sunny yellow dress, lovely as a flower herself. Then everyone 'oohed' as Dot followed her and stood before them, blushing more bashfully than Maryann had ever seen her, sheathed in her silk dress, which emphasized her considerable curves, her nut-brown arms protruding from the short sleeves. Her black hair was pinned in a knot at the back and topped by a little cream skull cap which Sylvia had somehow managed to fashion as well. The children all stood suddenly silent, in awe.

'Oh, Dot!' Maryann exclaimed. 'You look lovely! Sylvia, how did you manage to make all these things, just in there?'

'Well – we managed.' Sylvia laughed. 'By hook or by crook.'

'You all look like three pretty flowers together,' Joel said, and Maryann was touched by this rare romantic outburst from her husband.

'Well,' Dot said, 'this might be the last chance I ever get to dress up properly, so it's jolly nice to be able to do it in style! Now – what about my little bridesmaids? You both coming along with me?'

Sally and Rose came timidly forward.

'Aren't you both beautiful?' Dot said, making them smile, pleased with themselves. 'Now, don't be scared. We've all got to manage this together.' She took their hands, and everyone set off for the church.

Maryann walked with Sylvia, holding Ada's hand.

'Who's that then?' Sylvia nodded towards Darius and his sons.

'Oh – you've not met, have you? That's Darius – Joel's brother.'

They caught up and Maryann introduced them.

'Sylvia's been ever so good to your Rose,' she told him.

Darius shook her hand, shyly touching his cap and clearing his throat. He wasn't used to the volunteers yet, not having worked with any.

'I'm ever so fond of little Rose,' Sylvia told him. 'She's a real poppet. You must miss her terribly.'

Darius nodded. 'We do. It's been a while now and the lads miss her. But our Rose's better off with a woman to see to her.'

They all filed into the cool darkness of the church. Bobby was waiting at the altar, his thick hair slicked as far down as it would stay, looking smart and solemnly nervous. As soon as he caught sight of Dot moving along the aisle towards him on Joel's arm, though, an unstoppable grin spread across his face.

Sally and Rose both looked round at Maryann, needing reassurace as they followed on, and Maryann smiled at them, full of pride. What a picture they made! She filled up with mixed emotions. Most of the time she tried never to think about what might have happened to Sally had they not rescued her when they did, but sometimes she was overwhelmed by still having her with them and safe.

Joel slipped into the pew beside her with Ada and Esther. As Dot and Bobby began to say their vows, she felt him glance at her. She knew they were both remembering their wedding day, which seemed so long ago now. How much had happened! Her heart was scarred by some of the worst times; losing their little Harry, the awful thing she had done to their last child when she just couldn't stand any more, almost losing Sally, and her own pain and confusion. That was not over, even now: it would take time to emerge from, like a dark, confusing forest, because the hurt in her went so deep.

As the vows were pronounced in the shadowy church, Maryann felt Joel gently take her hand and squeeze it. She didn't look round at him, but with her own hand answered his gentle pressure. *We're still here, whatever,* that loving squeeze seemed to say. *Aren't we?*

Forty-Nine

A bird was singing, so that lying in the dark cabin Maryann could tell it was dawn.

She lay wide awake beside Joel's sleeping body, listening to the day coming to life.

Back to work, she thought, with a sense of deflation. These times of rest and celebration were always over so quickly, and then it was back to the grind. Dot wouldn't be wearing a silk dress today or any day from now on. She knew that her yellow frock and the girls' daisy ones would soon be pressed into everyday service and become as worn and grubby as the rest, and it seemed sad how quickly their day of finery had passed.

But she smiled at the thought of Dot and Bobby. At how they used to squabble. But they did go well together, she could see now, like bread and cheese. And the Jenks family, though at first bewildered by their son's choice of wife, had seen Dot's good nature and enormous capacity for hard work, and had taken to her in a shy sort of way.

'Least she's got a proper name now,' Bobby joked, when they came out of the church into hot sunshine and the children showering them with their collection of flower petals. Dorothy Higgs-Deveraux had become plain Dot Jenks and she seemed quite content with the transaction.

Maryann ran over the day in her mind: her children

looking so clean and smart for once, the solemnity of the service, and after – eating and drinking together at the boats, having gathered all the food and drink they could muster, the enjoyment of being able to sit and relax, merry with ale, celebrating outside. She ran her eyes over the faces in her memory. Dot full of happiness and laughter, Bobby grinning as if he still could not believe his luck, Sylvia ... She ground to a halt on Sylvia. Something had caught her attention, but she hadn't identified it at the time. The expression in Sylvia's eyes when she sat out on the grass, talking to Darius. It was something familiar ... With a jolt she matched up what she had seen. Nancy, the first time she had met Darius. That irresistible drawing of the eyes to Darius, in fascination, attraction ... Was that really what she'd seen, or was she mistaken?

And last night, when it was all over and they were dropping with fatigue, she bedded down the older children in the *Jonquil*, as was her habit now, keeping only Ada and Esther with them on the *Esther Jane*, end to end on the side bed.

Joel turned to her in the cosy light of the cabin as they prepared for bed, his eyes solemn, appealing to her. Maryann tensed immediately. *Is this what he expects now?* she thought. *For everything suddenly to be all right again?*

'I don't know.' To her frustration she began to tremble. 'I don't know if I can yet. I'm trying, but ...'

'I know you are.' He stroked her cheek with his thumb. 'Never mind that. Just come here.'

She felt herself enfolded in his arms, held close to that warm, fleshy, comforting body, which she knew like her own, and felt him stroke her back, his lips brushing the top of her head.

'It's all right,' he murmured. 'There's time aplenty.'

They lay down together and once more he drew her into his arms, demanding nothing more than to hold her. She lay with her cheek pressed to his shoulder as he stroked her hair, both of them growing drowsy.

'It's all right, my lovely,' was the last thing she heard him say. 'It'll be all right.'

And sheltering in his warmth she felt herself drift into sleep, safe, comforted. Home.

Glossary

bow-hauling – pulling a boat, usually a butty, into a lock by hand

breast-up – tie boats side by side, at night, or in some cases when going into locks empty

butty, butty boat – a narrowboat which is not powered, but towed as one of a pair

cratch – a small timber and tarpaulin covering at the fore end of the hold

the cut – any canal

dipper – large metal vessel with a handle, used for washing, cooking and laundry

joey – unmotorized narrowboat without living accommodation or covering for cargo. Pulled by horse or tug and usually used for short trips around Birmingham

joshers – slang name for boats belonging to the company of Fellows, Moreton & Clayton, after Mr Joshua Fellows

lengthsman – employee of the Waterways, whose job is to maintain the 'length' of the canals, e.g. keeping clear of trees etc

lock-wheeling – to go ahead on foot or bicycle and prepare the locks for passage by boats

monkey, monkey boat – a power-driven narrowboat which can tow a butty

monkey hole – storage space inside the boat

pinner – apron

to shaft – to manipulate the position of a boat by using the shaft (boathook), a long pole

snubber – towing rope made of coconut fibre and used between the fore end of the butty and the stern of the motor – at full stretch, usually seventy feet long

spare-wheeling – filling in for a crew member when a boat was short-handed

to stove – to fumigate with sulphur to rid the boat of bugs

strap – ropes used for tying up or short-length towing

stroving – working hard

Turk's head – decorative rope fender found in numerous places on all narrowboats

winding hole – wider spot in canal, where boats can turn round

windlass – L-shaped cranking handle used for winding the lock paddles up and down

to work fly – work on one of the fly boats with larger crews, which did the London to Birmingham round trip non-stop in something under sixty hours